Praise for *Brink of Chaos*

When one adds up the total number of all the books in circulation that have been authored by Tim LaHaye, you quickly see that he is one of the most read authors in the entire world! Few can compare. There is a reason for that. What he writes, matters. Once again, he has written a compelling novel on the end times. Fast-paced, filled with action and adventure, and an accurate biblical portrayal, you won't be able to put it down.

Jim Garlow, pastor, Skyline Church, San Diego
and chairman of ReAL, Washington, DC

Praise for Other Books in The End Series

Dr. Tim LaHaye writes about the future with the kind of gripping detail that others would use to describe the past. I've been reading Tim LaHaye's books for over thirty years, but *Thunder of Heaven* may be his best yet!

Mike Huckabee, former Arkansas governor

Tim LaHaye's books always entertain, educate, and thrill, but *Thunder of Heaven* takes it to a new level. I never thought the End of Days would cost me so much sleep!

Glenn Beck, number one *New York Times* bestselling author

Tim LaHaye writes about the prophetic future with such accuracy and passion that once you get started reading what he has written, you do not put the book away until it is finished! In our generation, he has led the way back to a proper appreciation of the prophetic writings of Scripture. Everywhere I go, I meet someone who has read one of Tim's books and been blessed by it. This book will continue that tradition!

Dr. David Jeremiah, senior pastor of Shadow Mountain
Community Church, founder and CEO of Turning Point

Other Books by Tim LaHaye

The End Series

Edge of Apocalypse

Thunder of Heaven

Brink of Chaos

Revelation Unveiled

Finding the Will of God in a Crazy, Mixed-Up World

How to Win Over Depression

Anger Is a Choice (Tim LaHaye and Bob Phillips)

The Act of Marriage: The Beauty of Sexual Love
(Tim and Beverly LaHaye)

The Act of Marriage after 40: Making Love for Life
(Tim and Beverly LaHaye with Mike Yorkey)

#1 *NEW YORK TIMES* BESTSELLING AUTHOR

TIM LaHAYE
& CRAIG PARSHALL

A JOSHUA JORDAN NOVEL

BRINK OF
CHAOS

THE END SERIES

ZONDERVAN®

ZONDERVAN.com/
AUTHORTRACKER
follow your favorite authors

ZONDERVAN

Brink of Chaos
Copyright © 2012 by Tim LaHaye

This title is also available as a Zondervan ebook. Visit www.zondervan.com/ebooks.

This title is also available in a Zondervan audio edition. Visit www.zondervan.fm.

Requests for information should be addressed to:

Zondervan, *Grand Rapids, Michigan 49530*

Library of Congress Cataloging-in-Publication Data

LaHaye, Tim F.
    Brink of chaos / Tim LaHaye and Craig Parshall.
        p. cm. — (The end series ; 3)
        ISBN 978-0-310-32646-5 (hardcover, jacketed)
        1. End of the world — Fiction. I. Parshall, Craig, 1950 - II. Title.
    PS3562.A315B75 2012
    813'.54 — dc3   2011019479

Published in association with the literary agency of WordServe Literary Group, Ltd., 10152 S. Knoll Circle, Highlands Ranch, CO 80130.

Cover design: James Hall
Cover photography: 123RF®
Interior design: Christine Orejuela-Winkelman
Editorial team: Sue Brower, Nicci Jordan Hubert, Bob Hudson, and Samantha Vanderberg

Printed in the United States of America

12 13 14 15 16 17 18 /DCI/ 22 21 20 19 18 17 16 15 14 13 12 11 10 9 8 7 6 5 4 3 2 1

*To all those who see
the chaotic events in the Middle East
as a fulfillment of End Times Bible Prophecy
and want to be ready when it happens*

BRINK OF
CHAOS

PROLOGUE

In the Near Future

"Joshua."

The voice called to him so powerfully that it reverberated in his chest as if he were standing on the thundering edge of Niagara Falls.

"Joshua Jordan."

For a split second he couldn't feel his heart beating. When he sensed it thumping again, he tried to speak, fumbling for the words. When he was finally able to reply, the words caught in his throat. "Here. Yes. I'm here."

The darkness began to part, first at the edges. Then there was the flood of illumination, an ocean of light like nothing he had ever seen. He had seen the northern lights a few times, years before, when he was stationed in Alaska. The night sky had lit up with a shimmering, iridescent band. Sweeping waves of color had rippled across the night sky like translucent ribbons.

But that was nothing compared to this. What he saw now was ... indescribable. He tried to catch his breath.

Am I in the air?

Yes, there was the sensation of flying.

Airborne.

But flying had been his life, hadn't it? Piloting test planes for the Air Force. Flying a series of combat missions in Iraq and advanced U-2 spy-plane flights over Iran. Shaking hands with a president.

Finishing his MIT degree and his defense-contracting work on fighter jets at his own tech company, Jordan Technologies, and his spectacular business success and impressive financial fortune that quickly followed. And later his creation of the ultimate missile defense system, Return to Sender — RTS. And the incredible turn of events that led to another meeting with yet another president, and his reluctant defiance of Congress and his having to face down a court order from a federal judge to protect his country. And then those political, legal, and personal hurricanes that resulted from all of that. But all the time, at the center of it all, flying machines. Those designs and schematics of his for devices that utilized the rules of engineering, physics, thrust, and avionics to blast through the air. Inventions of speed and deadly accuracy. Made of steel, electrical wire, computer chips, and lasers. The genius of man.

But this was different. What Joshua was experiencing now, his journey upward as he defied gravity, this was beyond the ability of man. Beyond all physics. Beyond nature. Somewhere a golden note sounded like the chorus of a thousand trumpets, and it filled the sky with sound. Thrilling, thrilling. His heart beat faster. Then he looked down at the ground disappearing under his feet, and he saw the houses and cars and fields and highways grow smaller. He recognized a farmhouse down there. Was it his boyhood home in Colorado? It all grew dimmer. But there was no sadness in that for him.

No looking back.

Now he was aware that there were others. Flying. An army of human beings rocketing upward. A voice was calling. The voice of a woman. His mother? It was her voice as she led his Sunday school class when he was a boy. What verse from Scripture was that from? The voice was saying ...

Caught up ... Caught up ...

Joshua looked around in utter amazement. A sea of faces. He called out to find one in particular. He had to find her. The woman he loved. He was searching frantically for his wife.

Abby! Abby! Where are you?

But the lights suddenly went out. Darkness. He was falling. Hurtling downward.

Tumbling back to earth.

Mayday! Mayday!

Joshua found himself grabbing frantically for the controls. He realized he was in the cockpit of a jet and it was going down. Warning bells were ringing from the flight deck. He tried to bring the jet out of its death spiral, but it plunged toward earth in a sickening, dizzying spin.

Hit the Eject button. Now.

He fumbled for the control that would blow the canopy open, flinging him into the sky with the line of parachute in a thin trail above him, catching the air and expanding over his head with a billowing curtain of safety.

More frantic grabbing. He couldn't find it.

The earth in all its permanence was racing up to meet him at supersonic speed. *No time … the end … I'm going to …* Silence. And darkness.

Joshua bolted upright.

He tried to clear his head, wondering whether his eyes were open or still shut.

Where am I?

He was in bed, sweat beading on his forehead. The realization now hit him.

A dream. It was only a dream. All of it.

Joshua ran his hand over his face and swung his legs over the side of the bed. He grabbed the clock on the nightstand next to him. Five in the morning. What time zone was this? Then he remembered. He was in a hotel in Asia, and in a few hours he would be speaking to a large church group. *Might as well get up,* he thought.

He made his way to the bathroom, turned on the light, and splashed water on his face. He looked in the mirror. The face still had a square jaw framed against the athletic neck and shoulders. But his dark, short hair was thinning into a widow's peak, with signs of grey at the temple. There were bags under his eyes.

Getting older.

He had the unmistakable feeling that time was running out ... the two-minute warning for the world. The powerful impression left from his dream still hung in the air, like a thin white contrail in the sky. He had always been a rock-solid guy, not one to put much stock in dreams. But this one was different. He felt immersed in the sensation of urgency, as if he had just taken a bath in it and was still dripping wet. But there was something else. An undeniable sense of impending danger.

He tried to shake it all off and threw more cold water on his face. But it was still there, almost palpable. He toweled off and walked back to the hotel bedroom, which was blandly decorated with grass paper and paintings of thin, wispy trees. Joshua picked up the small framed photo from the nightstand. A picture of his wife, Abigail, taken shortly before they were separated by circumstances beyond their control. She was still beautiful, ageless it seemed. Dark hair, dark eyes, and a deep dimple that appeared in her slender face when she smiled.

Abby, are you alright?

The room felt gloomy. The darkness was breaking into dawn outside. A few moments later he could see slivers of sunlight framing the window shades. Joshua dropped to his knees next to the bed with the simplicity of a boy.

Time to talk to God.

ONE

Seoul, South Korea

Early morning in Seoul. The sunlight was starting to flash across the windows of the high-rise towers of the city, causing the panes of glass to look as if they were mirrors of fire.

In his hotel room on the city's outskirts, a few blocks from the huge Junggye Gospel Church, a North Korean national, Han Suk Yong, was getting dressed. Soon he would climb into his rented car and drive to a service at the church. He was breathing faster. His heartbeat had quickened, he could tell. He would have to control it. He had to look and act natural, collected, if he was going to accomplish the single passionate plan that burned within like a flame. By the time the church service ended, he hoped to have fired several bullets into the man he hated.

Han knew his target would be heavily protected. He had cased the church the night before and noticed the security staff setting up metal detectors in the lobby, at each entrance to the ten-thousand-seat sanctuary. The main speaker was controversial, and the church was not taking any chances. But Han anticipated that. During his time with the North Korean military, he had worked with a team that specialized in advanced small-arms weaponry. When he had slipped covertly across the border the week before, he had brought a sample with him.

The newly developed .45-caliber lignostone handgun was perfect for the job. A super-compressed wood product, lignostone was as strong as steel but much lighter. More important, it could pass through metal detectors. Russia and their Arab allies had used the material for many of its weapons in the recent ill-fated invasion against Israel. The lightweight material had avoided radar detection, and the newly designed Russian trucks, Jeeps, and tanks constructed from it would have been effective had it not been for the frightful forces of nature that seemed to revolt against the military assault.

But Han told himself that his plan was different. He was a skilled assassin against a single high-profile target. And no one, he told himself, had a more powerful reason to kill.

After straightening his tie, Han assembled his lignostone gun and inserted the clip full of bullets made of the same material. He put it in his suit-coat pocket, packed his suitcase, and carried it to his car in the parking lot. Before turning the ignition, he sat behind the wheel for a moment. He pulled out a photograph and stared at it. He saluted the North Korean officer in the picture, gave a quick bow, and put it back in his pocket. Then he reached over to the passenger seat where he had a printout of a Seoul online city newspaper. He lifted the front page to his eyes, reviewing the photograph, just under the headline, which showed the man who was scheduled to be the main speaker at the Junggye Gospel Church. The target of his rage. Han studied the smiling face of the man who would soon be dead.

The gunman glanced once more at the headline —

"Joshua Jordan to Speak at Seoul Church."

□□□

Every seat was filled as the thunderous applause echoed through the mammoth sanctuary. On the dais behind the pulpit the church's pastor, Lee Ko-po, was smiling broadly and nodding. Next to him was Jin Ho Kim, one of South Korea's hottest professional pitchers. Earlier that day he had pitched a no-hitter with his blazing fastball and led his Nexen Heroes in a 5-0 victory over the Han Wha Eagles. The baseball player seated behind the podium had his eyes glued on the speaker in front of him.

At the lectern, against the backdrop of a fifty-foot stained-glass cross on the wall behind him, Joshua Jordan was trying to finish his message, but the crowd kept interrupting him with wild applause. This was not just because he was the man whose engineering genius had saved New York City from a North Korean missile attack three years earlier — or because in so doing he handed South Korea's communist enemy to the north its most humiliating defeat to date. It had more to do with the fact that Joshua was connecting powerfully with the audience by articulating a timeless message that went beyond geopolitics or national security or even their most basic hopes about good or their fears about evil.

What Joshua was speaking about was God's master plan and the future of every member of the human race.

When the crowd quieted down, Joshua continued. "Long before I started my defense-contracting business, I had been in the United States Air Force. And I chose that life for a specific reason — because I wanted to protect my country. I was honored to achieve the rank of colonel and to fly some of the most exciting missions a pilot could ever hope for. When I retired from the service, I started my defense company so I could work with the Pentagon and continue that mission — once again to protect America. While it turned out that my anti-missile invention was the right answer to the greatest airborne risks that faced America — it proved to be popular with the wrong kind of people ... Some bad folks wanted their hands on my design, and the next thing I knew they had me in their clutches and I was taken by force to Iran. I was locked in a jail cell as a hostage, and as you know, they did some rough things to me there. But frankly, it made me appreciate the courage of other brave men who have endured much, much worse. On the other hand, there's nothing like being tortured, totally alone, in a totalitarian state, thousands of miles from home to make you feel utterly helpless. Yet all of that taught me something. Yes, I believe in a nation's right to defend itself. But in the final analysis, it is the living God who is our ultimate protection. We can trust in Him. In Psalm 125 we read this:

> Those who trust in the LORD are like Mount Zion,
>   which cannot be shaken but endures forever.

As the mountains surround Jerusalem,
    so the LORD surrounds his people
Both now and forevermore.

Joshua closed his Bible, which his wife, Abigail, had given to him two years before, the last time they had actually been together face-to-face. It was during their clandestine reunion on board a ship off the coast of New York, anchored on the very edge of American borders and the beginning point of international waters. Given the legal spider web that had ensnared the couple, and the outrageous and unfounded criminal charges lodged against Joshua, it was the only way they could meet. Now, on the platform of the church in South Korea, he reached out and touched the brown leather cover. Joshua longed to put his arms around the woman who had given it to him. For a moment he felt a tightening in his throat. But he steadied himself. He couldn't afford to think of that right now. So he looked over the sea of faces and moved to his final comment.

"When Israel was attacked two years ago by an advancing wave of Russian and Arab League armies of overwhelming strength, military leaders gave Israel little chance of victory. But the miraculous rescue of that nation was the fulfillment of a promise God had made thousands of years ago. You can read it for yourself in chapters 38 and 39 of the book of Ezekiel. So, what is the message? First, we see over and over in those verses from Ezekiel, God is telling us through His chosen prophet exactly why He could rescue Israel in such a stunning display. He says: 'So that the nations may know me ...' to prove that He is truly the Lord.

"But there is something else, and we must not miss this ... the message is that human history will shortly be wrapped up. All signs are pointing to that. The news of the day seems to be shouting it to us. The Son of God is on His way. Christ is coming — to establish His Kingdom, to reign and to rule. Jesus Christ, the King, is returning ... get ready, ladies and gentlemen, boys and girls. The King is coming ..."

As Joshua moved away from the podium the crowd leaped to its feet, clapping and cheering in a roar of praise and amens and hallelujahs. Then Pastor Lee, waving his hands to the sky, led the congregation in a hymn, followed by a closing prayer of benediction.

At the other end of the mammoth church, Ethan March, Joshua's tall, muscular young personal assistant, had been watching from a side entrance. Ethan's job, ever-changing it seemed, was to coordinate security that day and keep the media under control. There had been a request for a formal press conference, but at the last minute Ethan had nixed the idea, and Joshua reluctantly deferred to his assistant. But Ethan knew that some in the media would still try to grab a comment or two from Joshua as he exited the church. Ethan scanned the thousands of attendees who were starting to disperse. He eyed the two security guards stationed in each aisle, each with a wireless radio. One by one they delivered their messages to Ethan, and he bent his head slightly to the side and covered his other ear with his finger, so he could listen in his earpiece to their security check.

"All clear." "All clear."

Ethan felt himself unwind. The service was over. No incident. No threats to disarm. He knew Joshua was still the target of several hostile nation-states — some, like North Korea, partly out of a desire for payback against Joshua for engineering their missile failure and the destruction of one of their naval military vessels with all hands on deck. Other nations simply wanted to get inside Joshua's head and learn what he knew about his own RTS weapon design. Any one of them could have slipped their agents into a crowd like this. But now it looked like the risk to Joshua was over.

Being a part-time bodyguard, part-time scheduler, and full-time personal manager for Joshua Jordan was a job that Ethan, a former Air Force pilot like his boss, had never trained for. How could he? His job was just as improbable as the way that their lives had intersected. As Ethan watched the crowd slowly wind its way to the exits he thought about how, having once served under Joshua's command at an air base, they had been brought together again years later. This time through a chance meeting on a plane with Joshua's daughter, Deborah. Sure, there was some heartbreak, the way things ended between Ethan and Deborah. But it did bring Ethan face-to-face again with a man he had admired like few others. Joshua had his own take on that, saying that the two pilots had been brought together "by divine providence."

But that was what made them different too. Ethan just couldn't buy into Joshua's newfound faith. The "God thing" wasn't Ethan's thing. Not that it diminished Joshua in his eyes. After all, any guy who had been strung up from hooks by Iranian tormentors until his shoulders were dislocated, then beaten with rods and electrocuted — an experience like that could radically change anyone who survived. The way that Ethan saw it, religion was simply what got Joshua through the experience.

Ethan now strode up to the dais and shook hands with the pastor. Joshua was chatting with the pitching marvel, Jin Ho Kim, who had just presented him with the winning baseball from the game he had pitched that day.

Joshua spotted Ethan and flagged him over. He introduced him to the pitcher. Motioning to Ethan, Joshua couldn't help mentioning his background to Jin, "This is my assistant, Ethan March, who knows something about pitching, by the way. Before joining the Air Force, he tried his hand on the mound in a triple-A ball club in America."

"Oh, you pitcher?" Jin Ho Kim exclaimed with a bright smile. "Have a good fastball?"

Ethan blushed. "Yeah, well, Mr. Jin, I had a pretty good fastball. Except for one thing — "

Jin jumped in. "Problem with control?"

Ethan laughed loudly. "Exactly! Problem with control." Ethan was the only one who got the joke. His desire for control was the one thing that drove him onward more than anything else. But the reckless abandon that typified much of his life, the risk-taking, the broken rules at one Air Force base after another — didn't that seem to undermine his obsession in trying to control his own future? It was pretty funny that the one thing that dashed his dream for a big-league career was that very thing — a problem with control. On the other hand, maybe it wasn't so funny.

"I know one thing," Joshua said, pointing to Ethan, "he turned into an excellent pilot." Then with a smile Joshua added, "And I ought to know. He was one of my rookies at an airbase in Florida. He set a few flying records."

Ethan silently thanked his lucky stars that Joshua had too much class to mention his several trips to the brig for bar fights with a couple of Marines and his failure to get clearance before taking out a few new test planes.

Joshua looked at the baseball he had received from Jin Ho Kim and tossed it over to Ethan. "Let's see if you still know how to handle one of these."

Ethan caught the baseball with ease.

"Okay," Joshua said, "you'd better show me the way out."

"The side door," Ethan told him quietly. "Less likely to be ambushed by the press." The two men moved toward the exit.

In the rear of the sanctuary, still hanging back as the crowds trailed out, stood two men. One was an Australian newsman. The other was a stone-faced Han Suk Yong, with forged media credentials hanging from his neck. He stared at Joshua and Ethan as they passed through a side door into an adjacent hallway. The Australian reporter was watching him. "You're a newbie, right?"

Han gave him a funny look but kept eyeing the doorway.

"A rookie reporter, I mean."

Han nodded a little nervously. The Aussie grabbed Han's fake press credentials badge hanging around his neck and studied it. "*South Korean Weekly Journal?*"

Han nodded again.

"Never heard of it. Must be small."

Han said, "Very small. Just started."

"Well, you're not exactly competition for me, I guess, so I'll do you a favor. I've got a hunch where we can get up close, get in Joshua

Jordan's face for a quick Q&A. I've scouted out the church. I think I know which route he's taking. Follow me."

Han brightened. "Great idea." He slipped his hand into his coat pocket until he touched the smooth lignostone surface of his handgun. "I would like to get up close. You know … get right in Joshua Jordan's face."

TWO

Joshua and Ethan walked down a corridor that led to the back parking lot of the church. Ethan walked a step ahead, checking corners and intersecting hallways as they went. He told his mentor, "The back exit's coming up."

From behind a voice called out. A security guard trotted up. "Colonel Jordan, let me escort you."

Ethan turned and cut in. "Not necessary, thanks. I got it covered."

The security guard stopped, still looking at Joshua, who had a cautious look on his face.

Ethan lowered his voice and flashed a grin. "Josh, really, I got this. I know we're in South Korea," he said with the mock cadence of a school teacher, "which is right below North Korea, and I know you've got some nasty history with the North Koreans. But I'm your security guy on this trip. I've checked the route. Let me earn my salary here, okay?"

Joshua studied his assistant for a moment. Then he nodded to the security guard. "Thanks so much for your help. We'll take it from here. God bless."

The security guard smiled, waved, turned, and headed out of sight.

As the two men continued down the hallway, Ethan thought of something. It had been on his mind for a while, but it was touchy. Now seemed like a good time.

"So, Josh, I was going to mention something. I've got this friend back in the States. He knew pretty much everything that had gone on, you know, how I'd been interested in your daughter, and about the fact that Debbie eventually gave me the heave-ho, telling me that she didn't think it would work out between us. Well, when I told him I'd been hired as your personal assistant, he thought I was crazy. He told me this kind of arrangement would never work. He said, 'How can you ever hope to impress your boss, when your boss knows his daughter told you to buzz off?' Which got me thinking …"

"About what?"

"My working for you. You have to admit we have a pretty unusual working relationship."

Joshua stopped in the hallway and studied Ethan's face. Then he said, "Actually I think you're missing something."

"Oh, yeah?"

"After Debbie told you that it wouldn't work out between the two of you, I wondered why in the world you would still want to work for her dad."

"That's easy," Ethan responded. "Despite everything, you're still one of my heroes. I always wanted to work for the best. You're it."

"You're giving me a big head," Joshua said, giving Ethan a pat on the shoulder. "Let's get moving."

Ethan picked up the pace and trotted ahead. He came to an exit door, pushed down the bar handle, and swung it open. Ethan was now out in a private parking area that was blocked off from the public lot by a toll gate at the other end. He had the plastic pass key to swipe at the gate, and he craned his neck to survey the area, first looking to his left. The parking lot that was empty except for their rental car. Then he turned to the right but jumped a little to see two men standing against the church building, next to the open exit door.

Han Suk Yong was standing off to the side, a little behind the Australian.

"Sorry," Ethan barked, "this area's restricted. You both have to leave."

The Australian journalist lifted up his press badge, which was hanging around his neck. "Aw, now, that's not friendly. I'm a reporter. International press corps. I always thought you Americans believed in freedom of the press."

"In case you didn't notice," Ethan snapped back, "we're not in America. Maybe you ought to find an Outback somewhere and have them grill you some shrimp on the barbie —"

But a voice stopped him. "Ethan," Joshua said as he put his hand on his assistant's shoulder. "It's okay. I'll give them a few minutes. Then we'll be on our way."

"Thanks much, Mr. Jordan," the Aussie said. "You're a true gentleman." Then he snatched his tiny notepad from his pocket. "Just wondering, sir, whether you have any regrets —"

"About what?"

"About designing the Return-to-Sender anti-missile system, which ended up dropping two nuclear warheads onto a North Korean navy vessel and incinerating it, evaporating every sailor on board."

Joshua had heard that one before. Different approach, but with the same sharp point at the end of the stick. He said, "I don't regret the fact that my RTS stopped those nukes from detonating in New York City where they were heading at the time, no. And yes, I know that my RTS system — my missile-defense shield — took the trajectory of those nukes and reversed them, sending them back to the vessel that launched them. I'd always hoped that my RTS laser defense would be a deterrent to war. Saving lives. And protecting nonaggressors, my country in this case, from the hasty actions of despots who fire missiles first and think later."

From where Joshua stood, the Aussie was blocking Han Suk Yong from view. So Joshua could not see the eyes of the North Korean, which were so intense they looked like they had been lit on fire.

"And then," the Australian continued, "there is the matter of the criminal charges pending against you in the American court. Charges of treason. Your group, the so-called Roundtable, was blamed for botching a vigilante attempt to stop some unidentified individuals with a portable nuke. As the leader of that group, of course, you must take some responsibility. So how do you feel knowing that as a result, thousands died in New Jersey when the bomb went off?"

"There isn't a day that goes by that I don't think about that — the loss of life," Joshua replied. "But one clarification. In point of fact, the allegations technically refer to my supposed conspiracy to interfere with the operations of the United States government. False charges, I might add."

"If that's true, rather than avoiding extradition, which you've been doing, why not return to America and fight the case like the hero that some folks think you are?"

Ethan intervened. "Okay. Interview's over ..."

"No, Ethan, I want to answer," Joshua snapped back. Then he stared the reporter down and threw him a cocked eyebrow. "You see, sir, I've been given advice from Abigail Jordan to remain out of the jurisdiction of the U.S. until I can get a fair trial for those wrongful, politically motivated criminal charges brought against me by the current administration in Washington. Now, the thing about Abigail is this — she's not only my lawyer, she's also my wife. So right there," he said, breaking into a grin, "I've given you two good reasons I ought to listen to her. Now, if you'll excuse us, we have to be on our way."

The Australian scratched a few notes on his pad, nodded and then trotted off.

Han Suk Yong approached Joshua.

"Sorry, no more interviews," Ethan said.

"But Colonel Jordan," Han said, "I am great admirer."

"Thanks," Joshua said.

"I am with, uh ... a very small news office." Han lifted his phony press badge. "But I have something very, very personal. Need to ask you. Just take a minute. Please sir, could we just walk to quiet place. Here in parking lot?"

"It's okay," Joshua said to Ethan. "It'll just be a minute."

The two men walked across the parking lot to a point about thirty feet away and stopped.

Han's back was to Ethan, who was at the exit door, studying him and nervously rolling the baseball that he still had in his hand. Ethan glanced down at his watch and muttered to himself, "Come on, Josh, don't do this to me. Let's get out of here."

Han Suk Yong was struggling to keep a tight-lipped smile, as if his face had been fashioned out of metal. "You don't know me, do you?"

Joshua noticed that Han's right hand had now been slipped into his right coat pocket.

"No, I'm afraid I don't," Joshua replied.

"I am the man who will be the hero of my country."

"South Korea?" Joshua asked.

The metallic smile vanished from Han's face. "No, not this nation of dogs." Then he spit on the ground in disgust. "No, I speak of the Democratic People's Republic of Korea. North Korea, Mr. Jordan. The honorable nation whose ship you blasted into a ball of fire with your RTS device."

Joshua glanced down at the man's press badge. It read "Han Suk Yong." As he thought about the name, he flashed back to the Pentagon briefing after the unsuccessful missile attempt by North Korea. Though it was three years ago, he still remembered. How could he forget?

Afterward, he had been given the classified details of the ship that had launched the nukes at New York City. That vessel, *The Daedong*, and its entire crew were vaporized when the guidance systems of the missiles it launched were reversed by Joshua's RTS system and the nukes were looped back to the ship. Joshua recalled the name of the captain of that ill-fated vessel. *Han Suk.*

"You are related to the captain," Joshua began to ask, "who was — "

That is when Han pulled out his handgun and pointed it at Joshua's chest. "You will not speak the name of my father. You are not worthy to have my honorable, departed father's name on your filthy American lips."

From his position at the exit door, thirty feet away, Ethan could see the look on Joshua's face. Ethan could see he was in trouble. Ethan moved quickly to one side to get a better look. He saw something in Han's hand. Joshua tried to shake his head no, warning Ethan not to get closer, but Han caught that. He whispered to Joshua in a guttural voice, "Tell him not to come any closer."

"Stay there," Joshua shouted to Ethan who could now see something shaped like a clip-loaded revolver in Han's hand. His mind was whirling. He had to figure out a plan. In milliseconds. *If I rush this guy, he'll get off a shot, point-blank. Right into Josh.*

Thirty feet away, Han grunted to Joshua, "You're going to die like the coward you are." Han lifted his gun to the left quadrant of Joshua's chest, directly at Joshua's heart.

Ethan muttered a single, desperate hope.

Strike zone.

He gripped the seams of the baseball in his right hand, all one-hundred and eight red, double stitches. Ethan did a pitcher's wind-up, kicked his leg up, and let fly with a ninety-four-mile-per-hour fastball. Han's eyes darted to the side momentarily, as if he had noticed something. But it was too late. Ethan's fastball buried itself with burning speed into the assassin's left shoulder.

Han screamed out in pain, his body went limp, and he began to crumple to the pavement. Joshua grabbed the gun out of Han's hand and moved away from Han, who was now kneeling on the asphalt. In two seconds Ethan sprinted to the scene and jumped on the gunman, pinning him to the ground. He put him in a wrestler's full nelson. "Josh!" he yelled. "Get security and have them call the cops. I'll keep this guy quiet here."

Joshua glanced at the gun in his hand, then began to run back to the church building. As he did, he called back, "Nice pitching. You just earned your salary."

Ethan, still pinning Han down, shouted, "Actually, high and outside. And I was aiming for his right shoulder, not his left."

Joshua slowed down just slightly. "I'm the umpire here ... a solid strike!"

It took the officers from the Seoul Metro Police Agency only six minutes to arrive and take Han into custody. The SMPA investigators took statements from Joshua and Ethan and headed back to the station with the assailant. Back in the church, Joshua said his good-byes to the pastor and his staff, assuring them that he would be safe, and receiving their extended, heartfelt apologies for the attack.

"You must let us make this right," Pastor Lee Ko-po said, bowing with tears in his eyes.

Joshua grabbed the pastor by the shoulders and smiled. "By your kindness to me, you already have." Then Joshua climbed into the rental car with Ethan at the wheel.

When they were within three blocks of the hotel, Joshua checked the Allfone watch on his wrist. He then pointed to a side street that ran alongside a large park. "Ethan, turn off the boulevard right here."

"That's not the route we took from the hotel earlier today."

"I know. Just take it."

Ethan turned off the boulevard and down the quiet tree-lined street. A black limousine was parked along the curb.

"Pull behind the limo," Joshua said.

Ethan followed orders but shook his head as he did. "Josh, what's going on?"

Joshua gave only a cryptic reply. "Now for the second reason we came to South Korea."

Ethan wasn't going to wait for an explanation. "Whatever this is, why didn't you let me in? Why am I always on the outside?" But before he could continue, he noticed a military star on the license plate of the limo in front. He lowered his voice. "Okay. I'm starting to get the drift ... sort of."

"You'll find out shortly," Joshua said and nodded toward the South Korean military attaché who had just climbed out of the limo and was coming their way.

Ethan kept talking, and there was anticipation in his voice. "Looks like things are beginning to get interesting."

"And dangerous," Joshua added.

"You mean an attempt to assassinate you doesn't qualify?" Ethan shot back.

Joshua smiled but didn't respond. At the side of the car, the South Korean officer saluted Joshua and then reached through the open passenger window to shake his hand. "Colonel Jordan, it is a great honor to meet you."

"Likewise, Lieutenant Colonel Quan." Then Joshua introduced Ethan to the officer.

"Well, gentlemen," Quan said with a placid expression that belied his next comment. "Are you ready to make history?"

THREE

Ethan glanced around the room, which was occupied by several special-ops professionals. The place was windowless with thick sound-deadening walls, located deep within the tactical operations sector of the South Korean Army headquarters. It was impervious to outside surveillance. The participants around the conference table included a Middle Eastern – looking couple with International Red Cross ID tags hanging from their necks. The man, known as Gavi, was affable and had an easy smile, shaved head, and a muscular neck and torso. His partner, Rivka, was a slender woman with dark, intense eyes, who wore a short-sleeved shirt that revealed tight biceps. Ethan figured out they were more than humanitarian-aid workers.

The head honcho, the implacable Brigadier General Liu, sat at the head of the table and welcomed the attendees, identifying them by name, and called the meeting to order. Next to him was Lieutenant Colonel Quan, who had met them at the car earlier, and to his right was Major Chung, who would lead the briefing. The only other person was a young Asian man in blue jeans named Yung Tao.

Chung began with an intriguing question. "How many people, outside this bunker, even remember Captain Jimmy Louder of the United States Air Force?"

In an instant, the pieces fell into place for Ethan. As a former pilot, he knew the story well. Three years earlier, Louder had been flying a Navy Prowler along the DMZ between South and North Korea. Louder's jet was shot down in a skirmish with a sortie from the North. It rapidly escalated into a military crisis with the United States. No one could have foreseen the cyclone of geopolitical events that followed. A misinterpreted message was bulleted from Pyongyang to a North Korean nuke-armed ship on maneuvers in the Atlantic. That scrambled digital telex to the nuclear destroyer caused it to launch a retaliatory strike against America. The two nukes launched from that ship were aimed at New York City but were diverted when the Pentagon chain-of-command ordered the use of Joshua's brilliantly designed RTS anti-missile system. The warheads turned back like twin boomerangs and returned to the North Korean ship that had launched them, liquidating the ship and its captain, the father of the gun-toting Han Suk Yong.

Ethan had always wondered why President Tulrude had never publicly addressed the outrage of North Korea's keeping Captain Louder hostage — she had seemingly forgotten about his plight — but clearly the South Koreans hadn't. Nor had Joshua. Ethan had even heard rumors from his flier buddies that the Department of Defense was, under the radar of course, supporting some kind of effort to get Louder out. It now looked like it was coming together.

Chung continued, "Those of us in the South Korean military remember Captain Louder, who provided courageous service by monitoring the border with our enemies to the north. We do not forget his bravery. And neither do you, Colonel Jordan. Thank you for playing your part."

Joshua nodded and said, "Captain Louder's a good man. I'm glad we're going to get him a 'furlough' from that North Korean prison."

A glimmer of a smile broke over the face of Brigadier General Liu.

Ethan's heart rate jumped. *Whatever this is, I want in*, he thought.

"We have a double agent inside the North Korean prison," Chung continued, "and he has processed the request by the International Red Cross to inspect the conditions of Captain Louder's confinement. And at the same time our source in the prison slipped a message to Louder, suggesting that he ask for a personal visit from Colonel Jordan. It was thought that the North Koreans would jump at the chance to get Joshua Jordan, their public enemy number one, within their reach and would do anything to accomplish that, including allowing the

International Red Cross to gain access to their prison. And of course, we were right. But our intelligence also indicates that they won't arrest Colonel Jordan until he has made face-to-face contact with Captain Louder. The North Koreans plan to have guards posted in the meeting room at first, but then a short time later they will be called out of the room. The North Koreans have bugged the room and are hoping that Colonel Jordan or Captain Louder might get sloppy when they think they're alone and reveal some useful information before Jordan is taken into custody. But our plan should short-circuit all of that. Literally. It will happen quickly, within just a few minutes of Colonel Jordan and our 'Red Cross' workers entering the room."

Everything was clear to Ethan now. The mission needed an entry to the communist north and then into the prison where Louder was being held — and Joshua was their ticket in. It didn't take much imagination for Ethan to guess what the North Koreans had planned for Joshua once they had him within their borders. He began to raise his finger to ask a couple of pointed questions about Joshua's safety, but Joshua gave him a disapproving shake of the head. Ethan didn't like it, but he knew how to take orders — mostly. And Joshua was the boss. So Ethan complied and put his hand back down as Chung explained the plan.

"Gavi and Rivka will play the part of International Red Cross workers and will escort Colonel Jordan to the security facility where they are holding Captain Louder. There, the prisoner meeting will take place. Afterward, the three of them — Gavi, Rivka, and Colonel Jordan — will exit the building."

Ethan wasn't going to stay quiet. He didn't know why Joshua had volunteered for this mission, though knowing his boss the way he did, he wasn't surprised. Ethan whispered his concerns to Joshua. "You're a hated guy up in the north. Case in point — they tried to kill you today at the church. Once you're inside North Korea, they'll never let you go."

Joshua quietly replied, "They won't need to." Then he motioned for Ethan to pay attention to the rest of the briefing. Chung described the operation. He finished by saying, "If the operation is successful, then

Captain Louder will be walking out with our two friends posing as Red Cross workers and Colonel Jordan."

Gavi had a question. "What about the timing of the shut-down of the security grid?"

"Satellite telemetry will direct the overcharging of the system. The timing will be accurate within a tenth of a second — occurring when you are five minutes into the meeting with Captain Louder. We should be able to override their software and shut down their security codes, their door lock-downs, and their information systems, and then insert our own command codes."

"And the backup software?" Rivka asked.

"That's where Yung Tao comes in," Major Chung said and nodded to the young man in blue jeans, who picked up the explanation from there.

"The North Koreans have a secondary software backup, of course, which is engaged instantly when there is a power loss. We will input our data and codes, which I can manipulate at will. I know all their algorithms and the codes for changing the data in that backup program." Yung Tao flashed a grin. "My software company in North Korea installed their systems." Then he added, "Obviously, by this time tomorrow, my company's small staff will have relocated to new offices outside North Korea."

When the briefing was over, Ethan and Joshua were the only ones who remained in the room. Ethan cornered his boss. "I'm not questioning your judgment, but why didn't you bring me into the loop earlier?"

"I wasn't sure this was a definite go until we arrived in Seoul."

"And those two Red Cross workers — are they for real?"

"If you mean, are they really members of the International Red Cross ... the answer is yes. If you mean, does the Red Cross know that Gavi and Rivka are also highly trained agents of an intelligence agency, the answer is no. This time the North is letting them inside — but only because I'm accompanying them."

"Who else do Gavi and Rivka work for?" Ethan asked. Then he answered his own question. "I'm betting the Israeli Mossad." *Yes*, Ethan thought, *that fits.* Israel's commandos handled most of the difficult foreign intelligence and national security work in protecting Israel. Then he wondered out loud to Joshua, "And my role?"

Joshua patted him on the shoulder. "To stay here in Seoul. You need to monitor this from headquarters."

"You just pulled the rug out from under me," Ethan complained. "Come on, I was Air Force too, Josh. Trained in combat. Survival skills. The whole nine yards. I've got a top-secret security clearance with the United States government. I can be useful somehow ..."

"You will be," Joshua said. "Back here in Seoul. This is my deal, my risk. For a long time I've felt a personal connection to Jimmy Louder. He and I were swept into the same tidal wave together — at opposite ends maybe — Louder being shot down over North Korea, the event that sparked the launching of those North Korean nukes in the first place — and my being back in New York as a defense contractor, working with the Pentagon to stop those missiles. As a pilot I came close to crashing behind enemy lines myself. I would have liked to know there were guys out there willing to come after me. Anyway, I made up my mind if I ever got the chance to help Louder, I would do it. Then, several months after he was shot down, I happened to be at an Air Force reception in Washington, and Louder's wife was there. I told her the same thing — to her face, Ethan. I never really thought I'd have the chance to make good on that promise. So there it is."

Then Ethan caught a look on Joshua's face — but not one that expressed bravery or loyalty or even the keeping of a sacred promise. It had to do with something else. After a moment Joshua explained. "And then there's Abigail. She doesn't know about this, and obviously neither do Cal or Deb. To my knowledge no one back in the U.S. is aware of the plan, except for a few people in the Pentagon. If things go down bad, you have to be the one — "

"The one?"

"To explain it to Abby. You're the only one who could. She's the love of my life. I've always felt she got the short end of the stick when she married me. The least I can do is to make sure she's told the truth. And considering my history with the current president, you can bet that Jessica Tulrude and those in her administration wouldn't care if Abigail ever found out. After all, this whole mission is off the Pentagon's official ledger. The Defense Department's support is strictly backdoor. It's a matter of principle with the Pentagon that we get one of their fliers out of a North Korean prison camp."

"Let me make sure I understand," Ethan said bitterly. "I'm staying here in case I have to be one of those messengers that no wife wants to meet ... knocking on her front door one day. So I can tell her how you died ... and why? That's why I'm staying behind?"

"Not a happy thought. But yes, that's the tough duty you have. And I wouldn't trust it to anyone else." Joshua broke into a grin that reflected an air of confidence, but still with a weighty look in his eyes. "On the other hand, I'm trusting God in this, Ethan. Let's leave the outcome to Him."

There it was again — the familiar angle that Ethan couldn't argue with. Ethan had chosen a different path from his mentor when it came to religion, and he was okay with that. Still, Ethan had to admit to himself privately that he was curious about the change in Joshua. When Ethan fell quickly for Deborah, Joshua's daughter — too quickly, as it turned out — he soon learned that the "God-stuff" was huge in her life as well. And the same with her mother and her brother. Of the whole family, Joshua had been the last holdout — until the hostage situation in Iran nearly cost him his life. Since then he seemed preoccupied with idea of the second coming of Christ, even more, it seemed, than with his anti-missile defense system.

As Ethan broke out of his thoughts, he eyed Joshua and noticed that his boss had tapped his wrist Allfone and pulled up a small image of Abigail on the screen. After gazing at it, he waved his finger over the screen and the image disappeared.

Ethan was struck by two thoughts, both of which hit him like a punch to the chest. He knew, once again, how Joshua was willfully exposing himself to high-stakes danger for the sake of another person. But there was something else. When Ethan saw Joshua looking at the image of his wife, that impressed him even more — how much Joshua was about to lose, what he would be leaving behind — if the mission failed.

FOUR

Manhattan

Abigail Jordan strolled into the den of the high-rise penthouse. Several of her bar-association certificates hung on the wall, including her admission to practice before the Supreme Court and her black-framed law degree. She walked up to Cal, her twenty-year-old son, seated at the desk with his laptop, and she looked over his shoulder. He was tapping furiously on the keyboard. Then he stopped. And waited.

Abigail knew Cal had been trying to contact Joshua.

"Okay," Cal said with his fingers still on the keyboard. "It'll take a couple more minutes to finish the encryption to get an email contact with Dad."

Using the complicated security-enabled email procedure to communicate with Joshua while he was exiled overseas had become a regular routine for the Jordan household. Ever since Joshua had found himself facing trumped-up charges brought by the Department of Justice, Abigail had been counseling her husband to take advantage of the asylum that had been provided to him by Israel — at least until Abigail could prove his innocence and guarantee him a fair trial. But given the energy put into the case by the administration of President Tulrude, and the political corruption that Abigail believed was at the bottom of it all, she knew that would be a Herculean task.

The charges accused Joshua of treason, painting him as a domestic terrorist who had used his own defense-contracting firm and the

Roundtable group to infiltrate the Department of Defense and manipulate America's national-security apparatus so it would conform to his
own political agenda. Abigail considered the allegations an absurd insult. Her husband was a decorated hero — yet the Tulrude administration and its attorney general had concocted a wild theory that through
Josh's leadership of the Roundtable, he was attempting to create his
own "shadow government," using his influence and connections to
subvert American domestic and foreign policy. There was no greater
patriot than her husband. Painting him as a revolutionary willing to
use violence to oppose the White House policies was an atrocity. It was
the lowest kind of "dirty tricks" that the Tulrude administration and
Attorney General Cory Hamburg could have used. Abigail believed
that the criminal case against Joshua was the only way to shut him up,
to stop his work in exposing the dangerous direction that President
Tulrude had taken the country.

For the last two years, the case had been hanging in limbo in the
U.S. District Court for the District of Columbia while Joshua remained
in Israel, beyond the court's jurisdiction. Meanwhile, Abigail and her
husband's lawyers reviewed the evidence that the Department of Justice had been ordered to disclose during discovery. It all boiled down
to one witness: the government's case hinged on the testimony of a
lawyer by the name of Allen Fulsin. The attorney had told the federal
authorities that he had been interviewed by a member of the Roundtable, Fort Rice, a retired judge, about joining the Roundtable. That
much was true, as far as it went.

But it didn't end there. Fulsin, who was later rejected for entrance
to the group, went on to tell the DOJ that according to Rice, Joshua
had repeatedly declared his Roundtable group existed for the purpose
of "revolution." That also was true, though only technically. Fulsin had
cleverly parsed Joshua's actual words, which in the full context were
much different: Joshua had stated to the members of the Roundtable
that they were in the "business of revolution — a moral and political
revolution in America — from the top down, starting with the federal
government and the White House." Clearly, Joshua had been talking

about lawful means to turn around the wretched direction that Washington had taken over the years.

But Fulsin's other statements to the feds were pure fantasy. He recited a raft of supposed quotes from Joshua, calling for an armed militia to take down the government, allegedly declaring that the Pentagon and the national security apparatus needed to be "interdicted." When Abigail read Fulsin's bogus story the first time, she screamed — right in the middle of the conference room at the Department of Justice — "This is a pack of lies straight from the pit of hell!"

But Fulsin's story, and the DOJ's willingness to use it, wasn't the only problem. While Josh's attorneys were convinced of Joshua's innocence, they had repeatedly voiced doubts about their chances of proving it at trial. Sensing a near-certain verdict of guilt based on Fulsin's sworn statements, they had badgered Abigail to pressure her husband into accepting a plea bargain, pleading guilty to a lesser charge in return for a recommended sentence of two years in prison. In response, Abigail fired them all and took over her husband's case herself. It was time to brush the cobwebs off her former career as a trial lawyer. Still, she knew she was on thin ice. She herself would almost certainly be called as a witness if the case ever came to trial, and ethics rules made it difficult, if not impossible, for her to wear both hats at once.

But then, she never planned to allow Joshua's case to get to trial anyway. The optimal strategy was to expose Fulsin's lies and get the case dismissed. Until she could do that, she pleaded with Joshua to stay in Israel, his temporary home, where the government had given him asylum and refused the U.S. government's extradition requests. It tortured her to be separated from him. Her lawyer's brain told her that if Joshua were to rush into a courtroom now, it would be disastrous — the machinery of the entire government would be mounted against him, and he would end up spending the rest of his life in prison for a crime that didn't exist.

Because of the legal restrictions placed on her by a court order naming her as a "material witness" in her husband's case, and prohibiting her from leaving the United States, she and Joshua had to live at opposite ends of the world. Their lengthy separation, limited to chatting by videofone or email, was killing her. She was tired of it, right down to her soul. And so was Josh. He would always say that he missed her like crazy and kept threatening to ignore her professional advice and return to America and, in his words, just fly right into the flak. But she would talk sense to him and urge him to give her a little more time to figure things out.

This had been the hardest separation Abigail had ever had from Joshua. They had endured separation before. Many times. But there was always the promise of an ending point. Missions had beginnings and endings. Assignments would last for a finite amount of time. But not this one. She ached for him and prayed endlessly for their reunion. In the end, however, she was convinced that with God's help the only solution to their dilemma rested in her own hands. She had to find a way to crack open the phony case against her husband.

Suddenly she noticed Cal looking up from the computer screen.

"Okay," he said, "earlier I sent a message to Dad and asked him to update us. Now something just came through from him. But it looks like he embargoed it — sent it earlier but timed it for release now for some reason. I'm going through the ChangeCipherSpec sequence for encryption."

Cal held the palm of his hand close to the screen for five seconds.

Then the screen read — "Palmprint Authentication Complete."

Abigail grinned. "I can't wait to hear about his trip to South Korea. He must be back in Israel by now."

A few moments later Cal announced, "Here it comes."

Cal read it aloud: "'I will call you on the encrypted Allfone whenever I can. But currently caught up in paperwork. Love you all more than I can say. Buried in red tape. Be strong, Abby, and know I love you more than life itself. Love to you, Cal, and Debbie too. God is in control. Josh.'"

Abigail stood up straight, a stunned look on her face.

"Mom, what's up?"

"That business about 'buried in red tape' ..."

"What about it?"

"That's code."

"For what?"

"It's our private message. His way of letting me know he's on a dangerous assignment — again. He started using the phrase years ago, when he flew those missions."

"You sure?"

His mother threw him a look that left no doubt. She shook her head. "He hadn't hinted at anything to me. Just going to Seoul to speak at a church, then to return to Israel. His temporary home — the man without a country." Then she asked into the air, "So, what in the world is Josh involved in?"

"You know Dad," Cal said. "He takes risks, sure. But not foolish ones. I'm sure there's a good explanation."

Then a stern look swept over Cal's face, as if he were going to do a tricky U-turn in the conversation. "You know, Mom, I deliberately avoided talking about the deadline today ..."

Abigail's face tightened. She knew where he was going. "Cal, you know I've made my decision. I have to follow the leading of the Lord in this. Not that it's wrong for you and Deb. You had to make the decision yourselves. But for me ... I feel compelled to protest, knowing in my heart and from the prophecies in the Word of God where this BIDTag process is ultimately going to lead. I know what it says in Revelation ... how it all comes together in the end. And so do you, Cal. Total control. A mark that enables you to buy and sell, to function financially. No, I can't believe the BIDTag is the mark of the Antichrist ... but it's the first step, okay? Everything in my spirit tells me to fight this thing, to take a stand."

"You're going to catch heat by not getting tagged."

"Those are my reasons."

"So why did you let Deborah and me get them? Why didn't you tell us you were going to hold out?"

"Because Deborah would lose her job at the Pentagon ..."

"You mean that great assignment where all she does is file papers and sit on her hands? Every time I talk to her she complains."

"She ought to be glad she's there at all. You and your sister happen to be connected to one of the most controversial families in America. Sorry, but that's a fact. I'm shocked that some of our enemies on Capitol Hill didn't block her Pentagon assignment. As far as you're concerned, Cal, you needed to get tagged to get accepted to law school. A law degree is going to come in handy. You've told us you want to continue the work your Dad and I have started, right?"

"But they'll target you, Mom. You're already in their sights. With that material-witness order keeping you from leaving the United States while Dad's case is pending. And now if you refuse to comply with the BIDTag law, the government will come down on you like a ton of bricks."

Abigail had resolve in her eyes, but her voice was soft, confident, settled. "These are extraordinary days. We're called to take extraordinary risks."

Cal narrowed his eyes as he studied the back of his right hand, the site of the invisible laser "tag" that he had received like most Americans. "Well, anyway, I've been reading some stuff. There are some theories out there about possibly reversing the laser tag imprint by erasing the QR code imprinted in the tissues. Or possibly other ways to avoid complying with this tagging law."

Abigail turned to look out the big windows with a wistful expression, taking in the New York skyline. She and Joshua had felt that events in the United States and around the world were racing like a bullet train toward God's prophetic closure. How she and Joshua were going to face all of that as it unfolded — and the example they would set for their children — that was the challenge now.

"You know, Mom," Cal added, still not letting it go, "they will come after you. The White House. The president and her buddies. They won't rest. Just like they went after Dad when he stood up to them and exposed the rotten stuff that has been going on in this administration. They'll hunt you down, Mom. You know they will."

She smiled, but in her face was a faint shadow of fatigue, the signs of an embattled life. As usual, Abigail mustered an optimistic response. "I'm a good runner, remember?"

Iowa City, Iowa

A long line of people wrapped around the government office build-ing and wound down the street. Some were nervous, bouncing on their toes. Others looked around aimlessly, wrinkled their brows, or fidgeted.

A farmer and his wife stood with forty people still ahead of them in the line that stretched up to the glass door with black lettering on the glass: SECURITY AND IDENTIFICATION AGENCY — SIA.

In line immediately in front of them was a man in a suit with shoulder-length hair, who carried a briefcase. Behind them a truck driver was getting impatient.

The trucker patted his pockets for his cell phone, then realized that he had left it in his rig. "Who's got the time?" he called out.

"Almost noon," the farmer's wife replied.

"Oh, great," he groaned, "I've got a load to drop off in Traverse City, Michigan. No way I'm going to make it. This is crazy. Why am I here? Can somebody tell me that?"

"I'll tell you why," the guy in the suit said, whipping around. "Five years in jail and a maximum fine of $50,000 if you don't, that's why."

"You a lawyer?"

"Yeah. And don't blame me. I supported the legal groups that have been fighting this."

"Why didn't the courts stop it?"

"We tried. A few cases were won at the trial level, but even more lost. Then every single legal challenge got shot down on appeal. Very scary."

The farmer wasn't convinced. "I heard they caught some child mo-lester at a theme park yesterday using this tagging program."

His wife chimed in, "Because he had the tag marking on his hand, that's how they got him ... with this laser tattoo ..."

"Fine," the lawyer said, "so this one guy has a BIDTag — his Biolog-ical Identification Tag — and the police pick him up. So what? Mean-while the rest of us law-abiding citizens have the last vestiges of our right to privacy completely stripped away."

"But it doesn't hurt, they say. You can't even see it on your skin," the farmer's wife added.

"Which is beside the point," the lawyer countered. "It's the idea that creeps me out. Inside that glass door, you're going to have to stick your hand into a machine. Right? They put that invisible imprint on you. Bang, right there, keyed into that little digital imprint are all your medical records, court records, tax returns, every public record that ever had your name on it. And all that stuff, every bit of it is accessible because of that laser configuration ..."

"Yeah, I wondered how that works," the truck driver said.

"Look," the lawyer said, "you know those little UPC boxes with those lines inside that look like a maze — you've seen them in the corner of ads? They're called Quick Response, or QR, codes. For years we've been using them. Brilliant actually. Just scan the code box with your Allfone, and bingo, your cell is connected to some part of the Internet where the product is listed. You push a button, and just like that you've ordered something off the web, and in two days it shows up at your front door."

"I just ordered a part for my air brakes using that," the trucker said.

The lawyer bobbed his head. "There you go. Only one problem. The invisible QR code has all your personal data in it. Every time you enter a park, a shopping center, a post office, an airport, a restaurant, the federal scanning screens will be able to pick you up. So some civil-service creep in a government office somewhere can not only check out where you are at that very moment, he'll also know everything about you. With one stroke on a keypad. And they update your data constantly. Anytime you get a traffic ticket, go to court over something, or have a medical procedure, they update your QR code automatically. So now they've got your entire personal data file — everything — instantly accessible on the back of your hand, and at the same time they know where you are at any time. Time was that the government would need a warrant before they could get most of that information — but not anymore."

"All I know," the farmer said, "is that before we started this tag program, we had terrorist attacks all over this country. But not a single one since. I remember telling Mary here when the first one hit — when that ferry full of people got blown up — I said, look out, here it comes. Sure enough, after that we had the bombing at the Mall of America ..."

His wife added, "My sister-in-law knew someone on the plane that got shot down leaving O'Hare. I kept asking myself, how do these people get their hands on those little missile things ..."

"Shoulder-mounted missiles," the lawyer added.

The trucker leaned in closer. "I got a better one than that. So, those scumbag terrorists set off that portable nuke in New Jersey, and that was on a Tuesday. Well, I was scheduled to pick up a load. Guess where? About twenty miles from that exact spot, the very next morning. Can you believe that?"

"Well, actually," the lawyer said, "you're right, the nuke was set off by terrorists. And I know they were supposedly on their way to New York City, and that was their real target. But I think that the feds would have stopped them if that defense contractor, that Jordan guy and his right-wing Roundtable group of billionaire hyper-patriots, hadn't tried to use their private army to stop them."

The truck driver had a comeback. "Well, I thought that the feds, the FBI, and Homeland Security had messed up on that deal and weren't doing anything to stop it ... or that the White House blocked them or something ... so at the last minute that Jordan guy and his Roundtable had a bunch of former special-ops men try to stop them, and then the terrorists ended up pulling the trigger right then. I mean ... I don't want to sound like a jerk, but a few thousand dead in New Jersey's a lot better than a million dead in New York!"

The lawyer shook his head violently. "No way, no. We can't have a bunch of private Rambos trying to stop nukes, can we? They should've stayed out of it altogether. I'm glad they're prosecuting him. I hope he rots in jail."

"It's a crazy world," the farmer's wife said. "My brother keeps saying this is the beginning of the end —"

Her husband elbowed her and whispered, "Let's leave Bobbie out of this; the guy's got problems ..."

His wife shrugged but kept on talking. "I'm just saying that with what happened over in Israel, the way that war ended there, with earthquakes and volcanic eruptions — anyhow, Bobbie said that's what finally convinced him. Ever since then he's been going to church regular, talking about Jesus and the Bible all the time. And if you knew my brother before, my gosh, you'd never believe it was the same guy."

"Hey, look," the truck driver said pointing. "Finally. The line's moving."

The Security and Identification Agency, Washington, D.C.

Jeremy, the data clerk, stared at the list of names on his computer screen. As his supervisor, Mr. Porter, walked by, Jeremy flagged him over. "Mr. Porter, I have a question."

Porter carried his cup of coffee over to his clerk's desk. "What's the problem?"

"No problem. It's just I'm not sure of the directive."

"Which one?"

"The ETD — Enhanced Tracking Directive."

"You know the drill."

"Yeah, I understand the ETD. I've already synced everything onto the BIDTag tracking matrix, with the list of names with outstanding arrest warrants, the terror watch list, the dangerous deportees list, all criminal defendants ... I've got all that already loaded into the system."

"Then what's the issue?"

"This list, sir." He pointed to the screen. "Just got this today. It looks like the names of people who have failed to submit to the BID-Tag program, the ones who haven't been tagged. I assumed, based on your memo, they needed to be in-putted too."

"Right. The nontaggers. You need to put them into the same ETD system."

"Okay, I've been doing that. For some time. I'm up to the Js now. But two questions. First, if they haven't been tagged, how are we going to track them under the ETD system?"

"You forgot," Porter said, pointing to the computer screen, "to do this." He touched a small icon that read — FRS. When he did, a small box on the screen lit up with the words FACIAL RECOGNITION SYSTEM.

"You have to make sure you also load the nontaggers into the FRS program. So we can pick them up using facial-recognition coordinates off their drivers licenses rather than the BIDTag, which, of course, they won't have. Then we can pick them up through the video scanners and follow them wherever they are, just like the others on the list."

"Gotcha," the clerk said with a nod. "Second question. This is a list of people who never got their BIDTag. But today's the deadline. Some of them may have waited until the last minute to get their laser tag."

"No problem," Porter said. "We can simply purge their names from the list if they end up getting tagged today."

The supervisor gave a nod, indicating the end of the discussion, and he toted his coffee back to his office. The clerk returned to the list of names. He touched the screen to feed the next nontagger's name on the list into the tracking system.

The screen read: "JORDAN, ABIGAIL."

F1VE

The prisoner, Captain Jimmy Louder, was in his green jumpsuit, his face gaunt and eyes sunken. He was thinner now than in the pictures Joshua had seen in Seoul.

In the North Korean facility in Pyongyang, Louder was sitting at a metal table in a stark white conference room. Two military guards in drab olive uniforms and square caps were a few feet behind him, standing at attention, ramrod straight. Each held an automatic weapon.

Across the table, Gavi and Rivka, with their Red Cross ID badges hanging from their necks, sat on either side of Joshua. Gavi had a clipboard and was reading from it — a banal series of questions, inconsequential but perfunctory sounding. He asked about Louder's physical condition, sleeping habits, medical attention ...

Joshua stole a glance at his Allfone watch. They had been there three minutes. Two to go. Then it would begin. He felt the sweat trickling down his back, and his heart pounded. For an instant he wondered if the thumping in his chest was loud enough for the guards to hear. An impossibility, he knew, but he felt vulnerable. He was feeling his age. He could no longer run ten miles without getting winded or breeze through survival exercises. The years were catching up with him. He was not the special-ops pilot he used to be, but just a civilian defense contractor, currently barred from returning to his own country. And now he was in North Korea, trying to help a fellow pilot. As Joshua sat in the metal chair he wished he could encourage Louder somehow about the rescue that was about to take place, but he knew he couldn't. He had one simple hope, and he put it into a silent prayer. *God, I don't want to let this poor guy down. Help me.* And he added another unspoken request. *And let me see Abigail again.*

"Your eating habits," Gavi said to Louder without a flicker of tension, with an almost bored expression. "Are you eating regularly?"

Louder nodded. His eyes showed that he might be expecting something, but what, Joshua couldn't decipher. Did he know about the mission?

"Yes," Louder replied, "I'm eating."

Joshua had one job now, as he sat across from Louder. He simply had to keep his cool. That was it. But it was crucial. The plan to use these two Israeli Mossad agents, posing as Red Cross workers, to launch a rescue had been in the works for over a year. In the White House, President Tulrude had balked, undoubtedly because of her stated goal of melding the United States with the growing international movement toward a single global government. Then there was the pressure from Tulrude's close confidant — the secretary-general of the United Nations, Alexander Coliquin. He had urged the president against taking any unilateral action, even against tyrannical nations like North Korea, and presumably including even the rescue of a downed American pilot, for fear of another retaliatory nuclear strike. That concern had struck Joshua as far-fetched as long as the United States still had Joshua's RTS anti-missile-system technology. On the other hand, Joshua also knew how the Pentagon had decided to rescue one of its own, quietly, under the radar, encouraging and assisting the mission to get Louder out.

The only problem had been the North Koreans' repeated refusal to allow Red Cross inspections, until, that is, an idea was hatched: they would use Joshua as bait. When the idea was slipped to Louder through the inside double-agent, encouraging him to make a request for a visit by Joshua, and when he then voiced that demand to his captors, the North Korean military command reversed their decision. They said that the Red Cross could come — but only on the condition that Joshua Jordan joined them.

Ethan was right, of course, about one thing. And Joshua knew it.

By the end of the briefing, Major Chung made it clear that the North Koreans would have no intention of releasing Joshua once they had him. His knowledge of his own RTS system, and the revenge the North wanted for the nuking of its ship, were reasons enough. There was only one chance for a happy ending — not just for Louder's rescue — but also for Joshua to escape arrest by the North Koreans who wanted to subject him to a quick show-trial followed by torture and a painful execution: the mission would have to be executed flawlessly.

"And your diet, Captain Louder," Gavi continued, "the Red Cross would like to know about your meals. What kind of food have you been eating?"

Louder paused for a second.

One of the armed guards shifted slightly in place, narrowing his eyes and then staring directly at Joshua.

Joshua stared back. When he did, he gave a half-smile to the North Korean guard.

"Your diet, Captain?" Gavi asked nonchalantly.

But there would be no answer. In an instant the room was plunged into darkness. An alarm sounded, and a red light began flashing in the hallway, which cast a sliver of red light under the door.

At first, Joshua could only hear the attack, grunting and muffled groans, but then in the dim, red flashing light coming from under the door, he could see, in broken frames of light, like an old-fashioned movie, Gavi's arm striking out like the arm of a pitching machine. He was sending a series of blows to the throat of one of the guards. Rivka kicked the other guard in the groin, and then a high-wheeling kick to his face. His machine gun clattered to the ground as he collapsed.

Joshua tapped the "illumin" feature on his Allfone. A thin beam of light shot out like a miniature high-beam flashlight. He trained the light on the two disabled guards. They were out. Gavi and Rivka dragged the bodies behind the desk.

In the room lit only by his Allfone, Joshua made his way around the table to Louder, who had a startled look on his face, but he was already on his feet, instinctively ready for whatever was next. Grabbing Louder by the arm, Joshua said, "We're here to bring you home, son."

Louder gave a garbled gasp. He was fighting back tears. Then, just as suddenly as the lights had gone out, they blinked once and came back on. Everyone squinted in the stark illumination. Then a knock on the door. Gavi calmly went over to the door and opened it.

A tough-looking North Korean guard with sergeant's stripes stood in the doorway with an electronic com-pad in his hand. This next step was critical. Joshua knew that. He found himself holding his breath. It had to work perfectly. No room for error.

This sergeant, who was the inside source for this prison mission, spoke in fairly good English. "The guards?"

"Behind the desk," Gavi replied.

"Then follow me," the sergeant said. "And stay close."

SIX

The sergeant strode down the hallway with Louder in handcuffs, followed by Gavi and Rivka. Joshua, a step behind, brought up the rear. He was already wondering whether Louder, in his yellow prison garb, could get past the sentries who would be posted at each door. He knew the plan — from his distant location, Yung Tao, the IT genius, would hack into the prison's computer system and insert a new directive ordering the transfer of Captain Louder, under the custody of the sergeant, and to another facility for questioning. Once out of the prison, a local agent, posing as a police officer, would pick them up and take them to a rendezvous point by the river.

As the group walked, a few North Korean officers passed them in the hall. The sergeant held his electronic clipboard in his hand. He tapped it, swooped his hand over the screen, then touched the corner. "Got to check the daily orders for this facility." But as he did, his head bobbed down just a fraction to read what it said, and when he did, his jaw clenched. He slowed his pace and turned to look at the foursome behind him. Joshua could see the tight lips and the stress on his face. Something was wrong.

The hallway was momentarily clear. The sergeant touched his right ear where the tiny combination earbud/AllFone was located; then he tapped the External Line icon on the screen in his hand. He began to speak softly in Korean. "This is the sergeant."

Yung Tao, located somewhere in the North Korean capital, responded.

The sergeant got right to the point. "Got a problem."

The group could see the sergeant listening through his earbud to Yung, but the sergeant wasn't satisfied with the response. He shot back a hoarse whisper to his colleagues as they walked. "The MIS — master information system — hasn't been updated with our implanted information — doesn't say anything yet about allowing Captain Louder to be transferred out of the building ..."

The sergeant was at the point where the hall intersected with another corridor. Before turning right, he stopped. Louder followed his lead. Gavi, Rivka, and Joshua caught up to them from behind. The sergeant muttered something in Korean. To Joshua, it didn't sound pleasant.

The sergeant waited another few seconds, checked his digital clipboard again, but shook his head in disgust. Then, in English he addressed his group. "We can't wait any longer." Then another message in his earbud. The sergeant bent his head to listen, then said, "Yung Tao says he is rebooting, refreshing the system, says the new orders should appear on all the digital clipboards in a few minutes." Then he added. "He'd better be right — or we're all dead."

The sergeant motioned for the group to follow as he turned the corner into the intersecting hall. Now they could see a security desk with armed guards a hundred feet away. As he walked, the sergeant glanced down at his e-clipboard and gave a half shake of his head with a grimace. His jaw was still clenched. As he walked, the sergeant dropped his left hand to his side, close to his side-arm. Yung Tao's hacking job might not happen in time.

Four guards stood at the table ahead. Two of them, standing behind the desk, had patrol rifles, which to Joshua looked like the Chinese version of the AK-15. Though they were slower firing than a full automatic, they could still fire a full thirty-shot magazine with blazing speed. More than enough to take down their whole group.

The other two guards had clip-loaded pistols. One of the guards was already standing, while the other, even more mean-looking, remained seated at the desk in front of a laptop. Soon he too started to rise.

The sergeant slowed as he approached the security desk, still glancing down at his digital clipboard, still frowning.

Joshua had a single thought. *Oh man, this is getting close.*

The guard who had just stood up shouted something in Korean and gave a quick wave for them to hurry up.

As the sergeant stood at the table, he and the guard in charge began to talk. Another guard threw him a questioning look and a scowl. Then he motioned for the sergeant's digital clipboard. Then he snatched it up and stared at it. The angry guard bent down to his own laptop, tapped on the screen, and began comparing his data with the sergeant's e-clipboard. Then he straightened up. His face relaxed slightly as he picked up the sergeant's electronic clipboard, took out his digital pen, and quickly signed off on the bottom.

The sergeant bowed and then roughly pushed Louder ahead of him, playing the part of a military jailer, followed by the other three, as they all moved past the guards. Joshua could see the end of the corridor about thirty yards ahead. There was a doorway to the right. It looked like some kind of utility area. It had a red sign on it. To the left was another hallway. Now Joshua's group was about ten yards from the turn. The electronic pad was now flashing some kind of red warning message. The sergeant half-turned, picking up his pace as he did, and spoke in a tone that cut like razor wire. "We have been detected. MIS now reports our computer hacking. All orders suspended."

Behind them, an angry guard was shouting. The group was at the end of the hallway, and the hallway to the left led to one more security desk with armed guards, and beyond that, Joshua could see the streets of Pyongyang.

The sergeant turned to the utility door with the sign to his right. He pulled out an electronic card and swiped the card-box next to it. The heavy metal door clicked open. Once he swung the door open he reached around and swiped another card into the slot to jam the electronics. The door began buzzing and an alarm sounded. The group ran through the open entrance, and the sergeant slammed the door behind them with another loud click. They could hear the muffled sound of gunshots and the metallic ping as the bullets struck the other side of the heavy door.

They raced along a metal catwalk. "Hurry, hurry," the sergeant yelled. They sprinted along the walkway, down several flights of stairs, taking several steps at a time. When they got to the ground floor the sergeant led them to yet another heavy metal door that had large red and yellow warning signs. He swiped the door again with his card, and he swung it open.

Daylight and a blue sky above. A pathway led through a grassy yard outside, between two tall, windowless buildings with a concrete wall at the end, just a short distance away, perhaps forty feet. Inset in the wall was a single door. They could hear the car horns and street sounds of the capital just beyond the wall. It all looked too easy.

The sergeant unlocked Louder's handcuffs and swung around quickly to face the rest of them. But his face was now telling a frightful story. "This yard is a minefield," he said. "You must follow me — exactly."

He carefully inched out into the grassy pathway. The rest of them were close behind in a tight, snaking line, with Joshua at the end. The sergeant moved slowly to the right until he was three feet from the adjoining building and he reached out his arm until he could barely touch its bricks, as if to measure some invisible point. Then he stopped and half-turned his head but kept his torso and legs perfectly still.

"This way. Follow exactly."

Gavi, Louder, Rivka, and then Joshua followed the leader, walking with deliberate speed, with bodies hunched and tensed, careful not to let a foot stray to the side. When they were fifteen feet from the door in the wall, they heard it. A little snap, like a tiny twig breaking.

"Oh" was all that the sergeant said. He froze and looked down at his right foot, which was immobile on the spot where he had just depressed the trigger on a high-explosive land mine. There was silence for a second or two as the line halted behind him. The sergeant slowly waved them to pass him on his left.

Gavi led the way, stepping one foot in front of another, until he was even with the sergeant, who cautiously removed his handgun, which dangled gingerly from his fingers. "Take it," he said to Gavi.

"Go, straight-line now, to the door. Use gun to blow lock on the wall." Then he added, "Save the bullets. Use them if you get caught. Better that way ..."

When all of them had arrived at the locked door, Joshua turned to survey the sergeant's desperate situation. He was still frozen in place, halfway down the grassy path. Joshua said to Gavi, "We can't leave him."

"We have to, Colonel Jordan," Gavi snapped. "No choice. Besides, he's got a plan." Gavi then peeled off his shirt and pants, revealing another outfit underneath, and he gave the clothes to Captain Louder to cover up his prison garb.

Gavi fired a shot at the key lock, blowing it open, and stuffed the handgun in his pocket. After swinging the door open, they quick-stepped out onto the sidewalk along the busy boulevard. Gavi turned to the group. "We're looking for a police car."

They didn't have to wait long. A North Korean squad car, driven by a man dressed in a police uniform, stopped at the curb. Gavi jumped in the front, the rest in the back. As they pulled away, Joshua leaned over the front seat and said to Gavi with a voice full of pathos, "What kind of plan could he have had?" But before Gavi could answer, everyone in the squad car flinched as the sound of an explosion reverberated from the grassy yard on the other side of the wall.

For a long time they drove through the city traffic of Pyongyang without saying a word. Joshua was the first to speak. His voice broke.

"What was the sergeant's name?"

SEVEN

Gavi explained they were heading to the industrial harbor of the Tae-dong River, past the Nampho Cargo Terminal and the dry-dock shipping yard. The driver pulled up to an old loading dock on the river, and the group piled out. Gavi led them to a pier that stretched about thirty feet over the water. A half mile down the harbor, Joshua could see a few trucks unloading cargo from a ship. Other than that, the area was clear.

"Taedong's deep," Gavi said, leading them to the end of the pier. "Hopefully deep enough …"

Joshua asked, "For what?"

"You'll see." He motioned for them to follow him down a flight of rusty stairs to a wooden landing below, slimy with green algae, at the surface of the water. Gavi glanced at his watch. "A few minutes to spare."

Now they would wait. Joshua turned to Jimmy Louder, who had been quiet during the rescue mission.

"You okay, pilot?"

"Roger," Louder said with a struggling smile, and added, "Thank you, Colonel Jordan. For everything. Man alive, I can't believe you're really here … and I'm out of that hell-hole …" His voice started to quiver. His eyes filled with tears.

"We still have a few miles to go," Joshua said, patting his shoulder. "But things are looking good. God willing, we'll get you back to your family."

Louder smiled. "Oh, I can't wait to see Ginny ... my wife. And my two daughters. I've wondered what's been going on out there in the world. I've been so cut off. Haven't heard any news. What's happening in America? Who won the World Series? What are gas prices at? Let's see ... I guess Virgil Corland is still president ..."

"Not anymore," Joshua replied, his face tightening.

Jimmy Louder studied him. "What happened? Something bad?"

"President Corland had some serious health problems. Had to resign. His vice president, Jessica Tulrude, is in the White House now."

Louder looked down at the ground, like he was thinking back, searching his memory. "Oh," he groaned, "Tulrude. You're kidding?"

Joshua shook his head. "But that's just the beginning. So much has changed. A single, unified international power is growing. Spreading. Infiltrating like a cancer. God's clock seems to be speeding up. The light beginning to fade. Darkness coming. World events rushing up to the final climax. The return of Christ. Jimmy, I really believe we're getting close."

With a shake of the head, Jimmy Louder said, "Josh, I never took you to be a guy who's into that stuff."

"I wasn't. Not always," Joshua replied, "but one day God had me surrounded. He got my attention."

"You sound just like my grandfather, Eddie March," Louder said with a smile. "He was a pretty good guy. Backwoods sort of fella from West Virginia, who played guitar and sang in this little church. Always full of jokes. But serious about God. He used to talk to us about the Bible all the time when we were kids."

Gavi had stepped over to them and interrupted. "Excuse me, Captain Louder, but for this next phase, I'll have to calculate your weight."

Leaving Louder to be prepped by Gavi, Joshua walked over to Rivka. He asked, "How long till something happens?"

"Just a few minutes."

Looking out to the opposite bank of the river, Joshua noticed something. A line of willow trees gracefully swayed in the breeze. Suddenly he was somewhere else — recalling the willow tree in the backyard of his family home when he was a boy. Funny, he thought, how that house, a simple ranch-style with shutters painted an ugly neon green, had slipped out of memory for so long, tucked underneath everything else in his mental attic, long forgotten until a few days ago — when he had that powerful dream the night before delivering his message to the Junggye Gospel Church.

He was still studying the willows when Rivka stepped closer. "Why'd you do it ... the mission? You didn't know him, did you?" Rivka motioned toward Louder, who was talking with Gavi.

"Oh, I knew him," Joshua said. "Air Force pilots tend to be a pretty close-knit group. But there's something else too. A personal commitment that I made to somebody once." Rivka studied Joshua as he went on. "You see," he said, "I've been rescued myself. Once that happens, it's natural to try and rescue others ... because you know the feeling. Going from imprisonment to freedom."

"You mean the Iranian incident? The jailbreak?"

Joshua took a moment to reflect, then said, "Yeah, I was saved from an Iranian torture cell by some brave Americans, and your partners in the Mossad helped. But there's another part too, another kind of rescue I'm talking about. The kind that only God can orchestrate."

Rivka hesitated for a second. Joshua noticed that. It was as if her next question had a certain risk, a calculated danger to it — ironic for an iron-willed, take-no-prisoners member of Israel's famed spy service. But Joshua understood the look in Rivka's eyes. He had been there himself. Finally, Rivka asked, "So, what's the other part you're talking about, Colonel Jordan?"

Joshua thought back to that turning point in an ugly blood-stained cell in Iran. "I met a Christian pastor in that jail in Tehran who told me something I'll never forget ... he said there are different kinds of prisons, and they don't all have walls you can touch. At that point in my life, I was locked inside two kinds of prisons, but only one had bars on the door ..."

At that moment Joshua heard something — the sound of rippling water, like the rush of a wave hitting the pilings under the pier. He scanned the surface about ten yards away. The water seemed to be parting. The plan became clear. He now knew how they would escape the greater Pyongyang area — and North Korea.

Gavi strode up beside him. "Good thing the Taedong River is as deep … deep enough for a mini-sub to get in and exit to the Yellow Sea."

"What about North Korean sonar?" Joshua asked, but the answer visualized in front of him. As the mini-submarine surfaced quietly, Joshua recognized the gilt of metallic plates — almost like fish-scales — lining its exterior.

Gavi smiled at him. "You remember J-Tech 100, the anti-sonar, anti-wake program for submarines?"

Joshua smiled back. "Of course. The wave-cloaking sub skin …"

"Well your Pentagon was kind enough to lend us the prototype for this mission. It was designed jointly by a couple of defense companies, but the real genius behind it was a New York–based defense shop called Jordan Technologies … just one more nifty military design by your outfit, Colonel Jordan. Too bad the project was cancelled after the initial prototypes were built, like the one in front of you … on loan from the United States DOD."

Joshua nodded and gave a sly grin. "Let's hope my guys did their homework on this one."

Gavi addressed the group as the streamlined mini-sub continued to surface and a hatch opened on top. "Listen up, these will be tight quarters. I hope none of you are claustrophobic. I'll go in last and secure the hatch. No talking, no noise, the minute you enter the sub. I'll be communicating with our captain through my digital memo pad. Remember, absolute silence."

As Joshua followed Louder onto the metal topside of the sub, he passed Rivka. She looked as if she had something to say. Joshua wondered whether she was still thinking about his last comment to her and whether she was feeling caught in a prison of her own, the kind without bars.

After Gavi had watched everyone else disappear down the small round hatch, he slipped into the opening himself. No sooner had he pulled the heavy metal hatch over himself and spun the locking wheel than the slender sub submerged into the Taedong River and disappeared from sight, leaving no more of a wake behind than a fish might as it trolls under the surface.

Seoul, South Korea

Ethan March fixed his bleary eyes on the large, wall-sized screen in the headquarters of South Korea's National Intelligence Service, the NIS, in Seoul. On it was an illuminated map of North Korea, with the Taedong River snaking through it and leading out to the sea.

A U.S. Army major with a red-dragon arm patch on his shoulder was in the room with the rest of the rescue detail. He sauntered over to Ethan. "You've been up for forty hours, Ethan. Why don't you crash in the next room?"

Ethan shook his head. "No, thanks. I'm staying right here. I need to see that blip on the screen with my own eyes."

Major Chung joined them. "If they've managed to slip by the patrol boats and get through the waterway locks — that's the tricky part — then they should have passed by Ori-Som Island by now," and with that, he directed his laser pointer to a tiny misshapen circle in the Taedong River. Ethan caught something in Chung's explanation. "What's tricky about the locks?"

"The mini-sub had to tag a ride directly behind one of the big commercial vessels to clear the locks to avoid detection. Otherwise, the security system at the locks will close the water gate, and they'd be trapped."

"Tell me again," Ethan said, surveying the big screen, "where you think the blip for their mini-sub will first show up?"

Chung sent his red laser pointer to a point on the map beyond where the mouth of the Taedong River flowed into the Yellow Sea, directly under another small island. "Right here," Chung said. "Assuming everything goes well, they are supposed to leave the river estuary and enter the sea. As they pass by Sangchwira-do on their starboard side — " Chung pointed to another circle, this one in the open water — "the mini-sub captain will engage his Sat-locator, and we'll pick him up on our screen. Then we can get our aircraft to escort them out of there."

Ethan nodded as he eyed the area on the map where that lighted blip needed to appear. He stretched his shoulders and rotated his neck a little, trying to loosen up the stress. He turned to the major. "I get the impression that the Pentagon couldn't join this thing officially."

"Just like I'm not here now," the major said with a smile, "officially."

"Man alive, I can't figure that out," Ethan muttered.

"Politics and poker, Ethan. That's what we're dealing with. My unit — the 501st Military Intelligence Brigade — would have loved to have manned this rescue mission from top to bottom. A U.S. Air Force pilot captured by the North Koreans? We're stationed right here along the DMZ. We would have been the perfect group to spearhead this — would have been proud to do it. But the madam in the big White House on Pennsylvania Avenue wouldn't commit. That's what I heard from some of the Army brass."

A grin broke over the major's face. "On the other hand, we're glad to have lent our South Korean friends our mini-sub, our satellite service, our Defense Intelligence Agency data, and our clandestine service contacts inside Pyongyang — and outside too."

Ethan laughed. "Oh, is that all?" Then he realized that the Pentagon was pitching in some double agents inside the North Korean capital and had possibly helped to enlist the two Israeli Mossad agents as well. Things grew somber again as Ethan and the major stared at the screen. They looked at the spot where they hoped to see the lighted blip.

Just outside North Korea proper was a little circle, a tiny island in the field of blue on the illuminated map, and beyond the island, the open sea — and safety. Ethan looked at it, trying not to blink, but his eyes were heavy. He felt himself swaying where he stood. He caught himself. His eyes closed. Just for an instant. When he opened them, he blinked once. Then involuntarily closed them from fatigue. When he opened them again, he saw it. The blinking light. Right under the island of Sangchwira-do. In the open sea. And freedom.

Ethan leaped up, swung his fist in the air, almost striking the major, and yelled out, "Josh, you did it, man! You did it!"

EIGHT

Washington, D.C., the White House

Standing behind the podium with the seal of the United States of America on it in the press briefing room of the West Wing, President Jessica Tulrude was trying to put an end to the press conference, but one reporter's question seemed to go on forever. "Going back to the reason for this press conference in the first place," the reporter said, "and the successful rescue of Captain Louder in North Korea, there are reports the Pentagon backed this mission but that you vehemently opposed it ..."

"False rumors," Tulrude snapped. "I will never rest as long as I know one of our brave members of the military are in an enemy prison camp." Then, as she blinked a few times and nervously adjusted the collar on her suit jacket, she added, "I supported the rescue effort plain and simple."

"And as for Colonel Joshua Jordan, a highly decorated former Air Force pilot who is the subject of a criminal prosecution by your attorney general, is it correct that Colonel Jordan actually helped in this rescue effort?"

"What media group are you with?" Tulrude shot back.

"AmeriNews," she said.

The president snatched her prepared statement off the podium and smiled generously to the room full of press. She wasn't going to take any questions from AmeriNews, that newly formed media group spearheaded by Joshua Jordan, which seemed to relish every chance they got to expose what was going on in her administration, challenging her policies of bringing the United States under the blanket of international treaties. She knew what was good for America. She understood how a global society, a world system of government, was the future. Reactionaries like Joshua Jordan, his Roundtable extremists, and their AmeriNews project were practically ice-age creatures. She would be happy to help speed them into extinction.

"Thank you, all," the president announced without answering the last question. As she turned to exit out the side door, a reporter in the third row shouted out, "Any update on the condition of former president Corland?"

Tulrude whirled around and tossed out the answer, halting momentarily. "Still convalescing and permanently disabled — " she clasped her hands over her chest as if officiating at a funeral — "but while he can no longer serve America, I am sure you will remember him and reflect on what he meant to our great nation and place him in your warmest thoughts." She was about to turn toward the exit, but she stopped and added, "And your prayers, of course."

President Tulrude strode out the press room and walked down the private access corridor through the West Wing. Her chief of staff, Natali Traup, was waiting for her. "Well done, Madam President," she said brightly, though she had to jog to keep up with Tulrude who had just blown past her.

"Did you hear that?" Tulrude snapped.

"I caught it all on the monitor — "

"I want that AmeriNews reporter barred from all future White House press conferences. In fact, no one from AmeriNews is allowed within a hundred yards of me." Then she slowed down to issue the next directive to Natali. "And make sure AmeriNews doesn't get an invitation to the holiday media party ..."

"You mean the White House press Christmas party?"

Tulrude shook her head at her COS's miscue. "*Holiday* party, exactly as I said." As she swaggered down the hall the president added,

"This is an election year. I won't stand by while those AmeriNews morons launch torpedoes at me."

United Nations Headquarters, New York City

At the weekly policy meeting, two men sat in the secretary-general's office. They were the only two in his inner circle that he trusted. These two high-ranking United Nations staffers sat patiently in the overstuffed chairs as they waited for Secretary-General Alexander Coliquin to finish reviewing his agenda notes in his velvet wing-backed chair.

Bishop Dibold Kora, the balding special envoy on climate change and global wellness, had a placid smile on his face, hands folded gently in his lap.

The other executive, Ho Zhu, the deputy secretary-general, who managed Coliquin's administration, was customarily expressionless, but as the minutes ticked by he occasionally glanced over at the engraved black-walnut grandfather's clock in the corner to check the time.

Finally Coliquin looked up. "The Israeli situation," he said, "where are we on that?"

Ho Zhu said, "Our special reporter is broaching the subject with Israel. We thought it best to approach it as a human-rights issue, moving it up the ladder in Jerusalem."

"Meaning?"

"We believe Prime Minister Sol Bensky already knows we want to talk. We're waiting for a response."

"*Waiting*, you said?" Coliquin snapped. His rhetorical question was designed to show the self-evident stupidity of Ho Zhu's point. Coliquin, the handsome Romanian polymath, had little patience with his underlings — brilliant though they were — when they failed to keep up with his genius, particularly when it concerned his obsession with Israel. Of course, he was able to see things that they missed, but at least they should understand his priorities.

"I want no foot-dragging on this," Coliquin said, waving his hand in circles. "Timing is everything. Can you see that? Israel is in a unique position. On one hand, emboldened by the natural disasters that blocked the Russian-Arab incursion, yes, of course. Attributing their rescue to an act of God — and so, they have been basking in the sun ever since, like an overfed lizard. But at the same time, the people of Israel, deep down, fear further conflict. I know this to be true. They wish to avoid that kind of heart-wrenching drama again. There is a dread among the people at the prospect of further war. So very tired of conflict. Year after year, having to defend their homeland, yearning for some kind of permanent solution, which is exactly what I have for them — if they will only negotiate."

Coliquin raised a finger just then, as if he were playing the part of a history professor giving a lecture. "Never underestimate the effectiveness of human fatigue ... and national weariness. Remember Joseph Stalin's speech to the Politburo in 1939, outlining how Russia could advance into Germany and take it over after the defeat of the Third Reich. Stalin was counting on, even hoping for, a long and protracted war — so that England and France and the other allies — in his words — would grow *weary*, thus allowing the Soviet Union to seize Germany for herself. And in part it worked. It would ultimately become East Germany." He repeated, "Never discount the weariness of your opponent. It's a major strategic advantage."

Abruptly changing the subject, Coliquin asked Ho Zhu, "And the political situation in the United States, where are we on that? President Tulrude has been a strong supporter of our vision. We need her."

Deputy Ho bobbed his head, as if calculating the odds. "Our American sources tell us that President Tulrude is the favorite right now. She has the benefit of being the incumbent."

Bishop Kora chimed in, "But not elected — constitutional succession from her position as vice president when President Corland became disabled."

"Yes," Coliquin said, "that may reduce the benefit of her incumbency. Look what happened in a slightly different setting to Gerald Ford when Nixon was forced to resign." The secretary-general wasn't happy thinking about that. "How strong is her opponent?"

"Senator Hewbright is running an extremely aggressive campaign.

He'll get his party's nomination. The race will be close, by a very small margin."

Coliquin then asked a question that wasn't really a question. It had all the resonance of a mandate.

"Things could happen to change that margin?"

NINE

Arlington, Virginia, Pentagon

The little communications-center TV set hanging over the desk of Lieutenant Deborah Jordan was set to C-SPAN. Deborah's eyes were trained on the screen. President Tulrude had just hung the Medal of Honor around Captain Jimmy Louder's neck. Next to Louder, his wife, Ginny, a petite brunette, was beaming and dabbing her eyes with a handkerchief. Louder's head was held high, his back straight, and his face now fuller than it was since the first pictures on the web newspapers that broke the story of his rescue from North Korea.

Deborah made a private bet with herself as she watched. She knew that Medal of Honor winners were usually permitted to say a few words. *But not this time,* she mused. And she knew why. There was no way Tulrude was going to give Jimmy Louder the chance to publicly acknowledge Deborah's father's role in the rescue.

And she was right.

After President Tulrude shook Captain Louder's hand, she stepped back to the podium and talked about Captain Louder. "This humble, likeable guy, Captain Jimmy Louder, patrolled the dangerous DMZ to keep that region safe and was shot down by hostile forces. He exemplified the most extraordinary strength, resolve, and bravery during his captivity — some of the finest conduct America's military has ever seen."

Tulrude motioned to Captain Louder and applauded him,

wrangling the applause of the attendees in the Rose Garden like a maestro. Then she quickly escorted Jimmy Louder and his wife into a private White House reception, away from the reporters who were calling out questions.

Deborah shook her head silently, then turned the volume down on the TV. She returned to her work. Her office was located right next to the Press Operations Center in the titanic, five-sided fortress of the Department of Defense. The location of her desk was an anomaly because she hadn't been assigned to the press center. As it turned out, nothing, including her desk assignment, had matched her expectations since her graduation with honors from West Point.

As she resumed her review of a raft of bids for the new DOD computer software installations, she noticed someone standing, cap in hand, by her desk. He was a young red-headed fellow, a second lieutenant like herself. There was something familiar about him. Then Deborah pieced it together. She had seen him linger at her cubicle before as he had passed by.

Deborah gave him a glance.

"Lieutenant Jordan," the young man began, "just wantin' to congratulate you on your father's successful mission in North Korea. The folks around here all know about it and salute your father ... even if the politicians don't ... if you get my drift."

"Thanks, Lieutenant." She tossed him a half smile and eyed him more closely.

"And I'd say — *hooah*, Colonel Joshua Jordan, if I may."

Her smile got bigger. "Yes, you may." She glanced at his name tag — LT. BIRDOW. "Soldier, you have a first name?"

"Yes, ma'am.' Tom."

"I'm Deborah."

"Pleased to meet you."

Birdow cocked an eyebrow at her. "If I may ask, are you with the DOD press center?"

"No. People just think that because my desk is here."

"Then you're in the Defense Information Systems Agency unit like me?"

"Right. Except ..."

He filled it in, "You didn't get assigned to Fort Mead in Maryland where the rest of us in DISA are stationed."

"Nope." She didn't elaborate.

Tom Birdow looked like he was going to follow up but decided against it.

Deborah was enjoying the company—and the break from the tedium. "So what brings you to HQ?"

"Just dropped off some papers at the E Ring."

She wanted to ask him why he had just couriered something to the inner ring of the Pentagon where the senior Army officials had their offices, but she didn't pry. She didn't have to. He explained, "This information coordination between DOD and Homeland Security for BIDTagging citizens is one big complicated system."

Tom's last comment hit a sour note with Deborah, for intensely personal reasons. "I bet," she said, dropping her smile. Now she was thinking about her mother's defiance of the new government mandate and the risks she was taking. Her voice took on a formal tone. "Well, Lieutenant," she said, "back to business."

"I'll stop in again, next time I'm in the neighborhood."

"Please do."

After he left, Deborah felt the urge to call her mom. *Later,* she thought. *I'll call from my apartment.*

She looked around her cubicle and thought about Tom Birdow's unasked question, which she herself had asked repeatedly. Why *hadn't* she been transferred to Fort Mead with the rest of the DISA staff? Instead, she was tucked away in this obscure corner of the Pentagon. Deborah, of course, had her suspicions. And it had to do with the controversial nature of the "Jordan" legacy.

I'm being isolated because of my last name.

Colorado, Hawk's Nest Ranch

Abigail was on the video phone with Joshua, who was back in Israel. He had just finished briefing her on all of the details of the mission to rescue Captain Louder—the ones the White House would never admit and the American people would never learn — unless, of course, it was laid out in AmeriNews, the only remaining news source not controlled in some way by the current administration.

Abigail needed to know, so she asked once again, "So, you're really safe now? Really?"

"Yes."

She sighed. A shiver went down her back as she visualized the dangers and thought about what might have been. Then she collected herself. "Josh ... oh, Josh, you know I'm so terribly proud of you ..."

"That means the world to — "

But Abigail didn't let Joshua finish. "Please, listen. I'm also devastated by the risks you just took — once again — "

"Honey, let me explain — "

"And honestly, I'm a little angry — "

"I need to tell you something — "

"No," Abigail said. "Strike the record. Let me rephrase the question to the witness. Would it surprise you, Colonel Jordan, that I am not just a *little* angry. I am *very* angry — "

"I couldn't tell you about the mission."

"Top secret?"

"Absolutely."

"Clandestine?"

"You've got it, Abby."

"There's one thing you forget. I've been through all this before. Standing by you when you accepted every assignment during your Air Force days, the test-pilot days, the secret recon missions over deadly territories. When you took on every mission, I supported you and waited, praying and hoping you'd come back alive but always wondering if I'd hear the doorbell and see your commanding officer standing at the door with that painful look in his eyes. But you're out of the service now. You're a private citizen! If you'd at least told me something I could have prayed for you. But you shut me out!"

"Yes, I'm civilian now, but that doesn't change everything. It doesn't change my obligation to do the right thing."

"Let me suggest something, my darling husband."

Joshua was quiet. She could see on the screen that he was listening. Really listening. She continued, "Your obligations start with God — I'm with you on that. Your moral obligations to your country, your friends, your own conscience, you know how much I believe in that ..."

"I know you do."

"But somehow — " She could feel her chin starting to tremble and her voice quivering. She had to keep it together. "The next time you're up there in the wild blue yonder of what's right, noble, and courageous, remember your wife back here, down on the ground." Now her voice was breaking up. "And one of these days, let me know where I fit in as I sit here at Hawk's Nest waiting for you, not knowing when I'll ever feel your arms around me, looking you in the eyes, really seeing you when we talk. Not just having to settle for a video call. Don't you realize how difficult this has been? Josh, you're the love of my life, and I have no idea when we'll ever be back together again ..."

It all came pouring out — all the powerful feelings she had been holding in her heart for the last two years, during their forced separation. She had been trying to be brave about it all, managing Joshua's defense while the two of them were separated by an ocean, being the glue that kept the family together, and trying to be both parents to Deborah and Cal who were fully adults, of course, but still needed support and guidance. She felt guilty putting any of this on Joshua, but something had just snapped, and she had to let it out.

She could see Joshua nodding on the Allfone screen. There was that strong, square-jawed face she loved, which over the months seemed to look a little older, but his eyes, always keen and brilliant, now seemed to be watering.

"Abby, dear," he said, "oh, Abby, I'm sorry. I should have given you a hint — some kind of idea what was going on. I didn't mean to shut you out, baby ..."

Abigail fought to keep it together. She didn't want to make this harder on Joshua. "I miss you, darling."

After a moment of silence Joshua smiled and changed the subject. "You're at Hawk's Nest? I thought you were in New York."

"I was."

"Why'd you fly to Colorado?"

"So I could sit here in our big mountain lodge and feel sorry for myself." Abigail laughed at herself, and Joshua joined in.

Abigail looked at her husband's wide, handsome grin on the screen, as he gazed back at her. "You're still gorgeous, darling . . ."

She waved off the suggestion. "You can't trust these Allfone video images," she said, wiping a tear from her eye.

He laughed louder and tilted his head. "Wait a minute. I know why you're at Hawk's Nest. A Roundtable meeting's scheduled. I'm sure you've got more on the agenda than you can handle — as usual. "

She cocked an eyebrow. There was a twinkle in her eye. "I wondered how long it would take you to remember. Yes, the regular meeting. But I'm feeling like we're the Continental Congress meeting to fend off the Redcoats — except the enemy is our own government, a corrupt president who's acting like a queen, and who's trading our national sovereignty for a false promise of international peace and tranquility. And then there's my husband! Josh, you're John Adams and Thomas Jefferson all rolled into one. And, darling, you're absence is sorely missed."

"You're sweet, but *way* overexaggerating," Joshua shot back. "So, who's showing up?"

"John Gallagher's here. I think he comes for the home cooking!"

Joshua chuckled. The iconoclastic former FBI anti-terror agent, who had put on a lot of weight since leaving the Bureau, kept assuring everyone he was "thirty days from being in peak physical condition." That was something all of them were waiting to see.

Abigail ticked off the list of other members: "Our self-made billionaire-entrepreneur, Beverly Rose Cortez," she said. "I just love that gal. Tender but tough. She's coming in tomorrow morning. Along with Phil Rankowitz. The rest by videofone."

"About Phil," Joshua said, "I hope our resident media guru will address the issue of using AmeriNews to run the article about the U.N.'s new secretary-general, Alexander Coliquin."

"Already have it on the agenda. Didn't you get the email?"

"Sorry—I must have missed it." Then he added with a smirk, "I was busy sightseeing in North Korea ..."

Abigail tossed him a friendly barb. "See what you miss when you pull one of your super-hero-saves-the-day stunts?"

"Sure, but it goes to show you—ever since I've been a man without a country— you've been running the Roundtable just fine without me." Then Joshua dropped the grin. "Hey, I've been thinking."

"Uh oh, that's dangerous ..." Abigail gave a sly smile.

"How about I come home now? Face the legal music. Fly—"

"Right into the flak? Right. Heard all that before. Josh, I thought we had an agreement."

"We did. But I'm dying here without you."

"You know I feel the same. But we've filed our appeal. Maybe the court will decide that it's crazy to use that trial order to keep me from leaving the United States while your case is pending."

"You're the lawyer, Abby, but to me that seems like a one-in-a-million shot. Besides, it'll take another year for a ruling. I can't wait that long."

She thought for a moment. "I've got one more trick up my sleeve," she said. "I've got a lead into the federal prosecutor's office. I've been talking to some former law partners, and I heard that one of the assistant attorney generals in the AG's office, a guy who was on the team prosecuting you, just quit under strange circumstances. Very sudden. This lawyer—Harley Collingwood—had a reputation for being pretty tough on defendants, but also very ethical and eminently fair. So, you have to ask yourself, why did he up and leave the attorney general's office?"

"More money in the private sector?"

"Could be. But some rumors indicate otherwise. So, honey, I'm asking you to wait a little longer. I want to see if this Harley Collingwood thing might have something to do with your case. Who knows? What if he quit the DOJ because he discovered their case against you has an ugly, illegal underbelly? Until I get your defense set up, they've got a case against you based on seemingly invincible testimony. You and I both know the prosecution's case is built on a lie, but I have to find the proof of that lie first, to show that their chief witness is perjuring himself. I just need a little more time."

"Time? That's exactly what we don't have, Abby. I need to be with you if … or more likely, when …" There was silence on both ends of the line now. Abigail knew what he meant. He didn't have to lay it out for her. They were both keen observers of recent events, and they knew what the Bible said about the signs of His coming. It was too clear now for either of them to deny. They were convinced that the beginning of the end was rushing in like a bullet train. If there ever was a time for them to meet it together, in person, it was now.

"Just a little more time, Josh."

"Okay, just a little." Then he added, "I can't tell you how much I love you and miss you, Abby. And how I need to be near you."

Abigail couldn't dispute any of that. So she said the only thing she could: how passionately she ached for him and needed to be with him too. Before hanging up, Joshua returned to a final bit of business. He said that he would call in to the Roundtable meeting the next day via Allfone video. The discussion was too important for him to miss. Before ending the encrypted conversation, they prayed together. Then his final words to Abigail were, "Please find the loose thread in the government's case, will you, dear?"

Abigail sat down on the cowhide couch and began to weep quietly— until she had no more tears. She knew the kind of man Joshua was when she married him and was glad for it. He would risk his life to rescue a fellow pilot. And she wondered: had she been the wife of Captain Louder, wouldn't she want Josh to do everything and anything to save her husband? But it wasn't just about that. It was about this separation with no end in sight that was beginning to take a toll on her. She picked herself up from the couch and wandered into the kitchen to make herself some tea.

With her cup and saucer in her hand, Abigail moved into the study and sat down at the desk. Just above her on the wall were photos of Josh with members of the joint chiefs of staff and other photos of him shaking hands with presidents. Next to the photos were framed articles on some high-profile legal cases that she had won during her law career.

Abigail flipped open the file on her husband's case and once more dug into the thick paperwork. From all appearances, the prosecution's inflated case was huge and impressive and unreachable — like the Goodyear Blimp. What she needed was a needle to deflate it. Unfortunately, it was buried in a haystack somewhere — and she wasn't even sure which haystack.

But she did have an idea. As she flipped through the papers, she looked for something in particular — the news articles she had collected about the intriguing former federal prosecutor, Harley Collingwood, who had been assigned to prosecute Joshua's case. She was now trying to figure out why he abruptly left the Department of Justice and whether it had something to do with the high-level corruption that she knew lay at the bottom of the case against her husband.

TEN

Jerusalem, Israel

"Caught up."

"Say again?"

Pastor Peter Campbell seemed oblivious to the television cameras in the Middle East studios of the Global News Network. He leaned forward in his chair, looked his GNN interviewer in the eye, and repeated the phrase. "Caught up. That's the translation of the Greek term used in the original New Testament writings. The word *rapture* is also commonly used among Christians for this event. That word was taken from the later Latin translations. What we are talking about here is the supernatural event that happens right before the beginning of the most catastrophic period in human history."

Bart Kingston, the career newsman conducting the interview, struggled to produce a half-baked smile. He had read up on this New York City preacher who headed up the Eternity Church in Manhattan. Kingston knew all about Campbell making news with his band of "Bible prophecy" experts and their doomsday predictions. He always did his homework, even though this was not his kind of story. He considered himself a hard news guy. But Kingston happened to be in Jerusalem covering some political twists in the administration of Prime Minister Sol Bensky, so he was available; the religion reporter who should have handled the interview was already on assignment at a new United Nations center in Iraq, covering something called "One Planet — One Cause — One God" — the One Movement for short, a religious conclave fighting global warming through a collaboration of various religions around the world. Kingston, not a particularly religious man himself, thought the idea of a world unification of religions probably had some merit. Or at least the global conference promoting it could be a decent news story.

"You mentioned the Latin," Kingston said, "could you expand on that a little?"

"I'm talking about one of the epistles — New Testament letters — written by the apostle Paul to the early churches in the first century. In that particular letter he was talking about the fact that Jesus Christ will be coming again, back to earth — "

"The so-called second coming of Christ?"

"Exactly, but not the way most folks think."

"How so?"

"The New Testament lays out the order of events. The Lord Jesus will first be coming for his church, whisking Christians off the planet ... literally. Followed by a seven-year period, with the last half devolving into a time of incredible suffering on the earth. Then Christ appears on earth to establish His kingdom. That first part, though — the rapture — is just for Christ's 'church universal'; in other words, those who belong to Him, regardless of denomination, church attendance, or any other external factor — "

"Sounds exclusionary. Not very inclusive."

"Maybe it strikes you that way, but the standard has to be not what you or I think about it, but what God has said in His Word. And the Bible is clear that the true believers in Christ will be 'caught up,' literally snatched up to Christ. They are the ones who have trusted in Christ and in the sacrifice He made on the Cross right here in Jerusalem, a sacrifice for sins. That sacrifice, by the way, wasn't just for my sins; it was for yours as well."

Kingston tried not to react. He changed the subject. "Of course, right now, this week, religious leaders from around the world are attending a convention in Iraq to unify behind a plan to save the planet from a global-warming disaster — brilliant men and women, committed to their various religions. Yet many of them have denounced what you and your group are saying, calling it crackpot theology. And using words like *dangerously divisive* and *nonsensical*. How do you respond?"

Campbell took only a split second to reflect on Kingston's curveball. "During Jesus' earthly ministry He met with a member of the ruling religious group, a fellow named Nicodemus. Jesus explained to him that to know God and inherit eternal life, he would need to receive Christ and be born again. That came as a shock to this man, who was probably a brilliant teacher educated in the Old Testament Scriptures, the Tanakh, and who was undoubtedly a wealthy, influential man — a mover and shaker of his day. The point is this — I consider the opinions of the religious leaders of our day to be a moot issue — unless they're ready to follow the one path that God has laid out through His Son Jesus Christ and described in His Word, the Bible."

There was an edge to Kingston's voice as he dug in. "So then, all these other religions, all except Christianity, you condemn them?"

"I condemn no one. Judging the hearts of others is way above my pay grade."

Kingston offered a half smile as Campbell continued. "I'm just a sinner saved by grace. All I'm saying is that God calls us to an inner spiritual transformation, to be born again, the Bible says. That transformation must come from a personal faith in Christ, not from some outward show of religion. If we do that, then one day — very soon, I believe — we will be caught up with Him, in the blink of an eye. Those who don't, well, they will unfortunately face that short but horrifying phase called 'the tribulation' — unparalleled terror on the earth."

Kingston was more than a little dubious but remained objective; after all, he had a job to do. "How do you respond to your critics who say you're going way too far with this? You talk about the return of Christ as if it's practically on the doorstep of history, as if Christ was galloping down the lane right now, ready to start knocking on the door of Planet Earth. Your critics have called you Pastor Apocalypse … They suggest your brand of extremism whips people into fanatical, even violent, reactions. I've heard the Sol Bensky administration here in Jerusalem is concerned about what people might do as a result of your Armageddon religion —"

"The folks who have actually experienced the spiritual transformation that comes with knowing Christ won't be the ones doing the crazy things. They'll be the ones with the inner peace to know that their Redeemer is getting close. And they know that even the terrors of the end times will be used by the God-of-all-compassion to call the human race to Himself, giving them one last chance to receive Christ as Savior. Wouldn't you want God to give you one more chance, Bart?"

The reporter sized up Campbell's face before checking his clipboard, just to make sure he had covered all the bases. He turned to the cameraman. "We'll cut there. I'll do an intro and a wrap later."

As he stood and gave a perfunctory handshake to his guest, Kingston made small talk with Campbell. "So you're currently located in Israel?"

Campbell nodded. "I've set up an office in Jerusalem, just off the Old City."

"Close to the action, eh?"

He smiled. "In a way, yes. This is the only city in the world where geography, theology, and history are rapidly rushing together in one great climax. I'm keeping my eye on the Temple Mount, in particular. For me, that's where the starting gun of this race will go off. Or to use our national American pastime as an example, it's like being at the ballpark and hearing the National Anthem. That's when you know that the action — the human drama — is just about to begin."

That reminded Kingston of another question. He came at it obliquely. "Okay, pastor, you've raised the baseball metaphor ... I'm a Red Sox fan. You hail from New York — so, you're for the Yankees?"

"No, Mets."

"Ah, the underdogs ..."

Campbell chuckled.

Then Kingston made his point. "So these catastrophic events you're talking about, using your baseball analogy, what inning is the world in right now, would you say? Top of the ninth? Bottom of the ninth?"

"Neither," the pastor said. His face was flush with anticipation. "We're in extra innings."

National Headquarters of Hewbright for President Campaign, K Street, Washington, D.C.

In the middle of the crowded main room, Secret Service Agent Owens flagged down Katrena Amid, Senator Hewbright's harried and slightly mussed assistant campaign manager. As he tried to explain something to her, the noise of the dozen volunteers manning phones at desks made it difficult to hear.

"Let's go to my office," Amid said.

They entered and closed the door.

"Say again — something about a threat?" she began.

"Unconfirmed," Agent Owens said. "Nothing specific. We get these routinely during the political season. Just want you and the staff to be on the alert for unusual or suspicious people trying to get access to the senator."

"I'll be sure and pass it on to him. He's doing a press call right now." She motioned to the adjoining office separated by a glass wall where her boss was on the phone, smiling and gesturing as he answered a reporter's questions.

Just then, Zeta Milla, one of Senator Hewbright's junior advisors on foreign policy, swung open the door and stepped into the conversation. Milla sized up the man in the dark suit. "Secret Service?"

"Got it covered, Zeta," Amid snapped.

"And you are ...?" the agent asked the attractive Cuban refugee.

Zeta introduced herself and described her position on the staff. "Is there a problem?" she persisted.

"Just some information for the senator," the agent replied. "General threat, nothing specific. Just want everyone to be on the alert. Be vigilant."

"I told Agent Owens that Senator Hewbright is on a press call right now, but we'll be sure to advise him," Amid noted.

"This is your call, Katrena," Milla bulleted back. "But if it were me, I'd cut the senator's call short and advise him immediately. Safety first."

Katrena Amid threw Milla a withering look. Then she manufactured a smile for the agent, shook his hand, and thanked him as she walked him to the door. When he was gone, Amid confronted Zeta Milla. "From now on, you will remember that security issues are my department, not yours."

"Fine," Milla responded. Her tone was cool and unflustered. Then she added, "Just make sure you take care of our candidate. You're replaceable. He's not."

Inside the adjoining glass office, Hewbright was fielding the reporter's last question.

"As far as the differences in our vision for America," the senator said, "President Tulrude and I couldn't be farther apart. I see the need for America to regain its greatness as a world leader. To lead, not just join. To model true freedom, rather than trying to copy the emasculated version that Europe and the United Nations and the international community has adopted."

"You say emasculated —," the reporter started to say.

"Right. I use the word deliberately. The current administration has signed onto global treaties against hate speech that are now being used to throw people of faith into jail when they quote the Bible or speak their conscience on issues. Am I the only one who thinks that's just plain crazy? Those treaties have to be disavowed. If I become president I will urge the Senate to reverse all that. Tulrude has orchestrated the downfall of the American dollar and brought us into the CReDO. Sharing in that global currency is going to sound the death knell for any chance of a vibrant, independent U.S. economy. She's drawn down our military defenses, stopped defense weapons development necessary for the safety of our nation, and jeopardized our national security by trapping us in a spider web of international agreements that require us to share our weapons information with the rest of the world. Remember the old painting by Norman Rockwell? A Mom and Dad tucking their child into bed? Underneath it says "Freedom from Fear." Jessica Tulrude has given Americans a lot to be frightened about. I want to replace fear with freedom."

After the interview, Hewbright stepped out of the media office and trotted up to Katrena Amid in the big room. "Was that Secret Service?"

"Yes."

"I've got another press call in exactly sixty seconds. Anything important?"

Amid paused before answering. Then she flashed a smile. "No. Not really. Just a routine security reminder."

Hewbright nodded, then dashed back into the glass-walled office to take his next call.

ELEVEN

Jewish Quarter, Near the Western Wall, Jerusalem

The young bearded messenger, with prayer locks dangling along each side of his face, sprinted up the uneven stones of the street just off the Western Wall plaza. It was the section of the Old City where the massive Herodian Temple on the Temple Mount once dominated Jerusalem in ancient times.

But that was two millennia ago. Back then the smoke from the animal sacrifices of the Jewish faithful would rise up from the Temple and spiral into the sky during the days of Roman occupation, when political and religious strife made Jerusalem as tense as the strings on a lyre. Eventually the Temple would be leveled by Rome's legions in A.D. 70, after which, all Temple worship and animal sacrifices came to an abrupt halt. For nearly two thousand years, the Jews were without a Temple on that sacred plateau — with no immediate hope for its restoration.

Until now.

Breathless, the messenger stopped abruptly when he came to a weathered wooden door. He knocked three times. He waited ... and knocked two more times. He waited ... and knocked once.

The door opened.

A man in his thirties welcomed the messenger in. The messenger bowed to the rabbi seated on the couch at the far end of the room, an aged man with a pale, saggy face and a full grey beard. The rabbi's assistant pointed to a chair, and the messenger sat.

"Rabbi," the young man began. "Important news."

"Speak," the rabbi instructed him.

"About Prime Minister Bensky. Certain negotiations. Incredible ..."

"Catch your breath," the assistant chided. "Speak clearly."

"It's just that," the young messenger said, "as I watched our secret work in preparation ... the fashioning of the altar ... the water basins ... the great bronze basin ... all the sacred implements for sacrifice ... making ready for the day when the Temple will be restored to its rightful place on the Mount ..."

"Yes ...," the rabbi said, nodding slowly. The old man twisted his head slightly to look through the lace curtain of his apartment so he could catch a glimpse of the Western Wall's uppermost row of stones and the Temple Mount above, now occupied by Muslim mosques. He turned to the young messenger. "Please, tell us what you know."

"There are discussions within the Sol Bensky coalition government. I don't have the details yet. But hints. More than just rumors."

"What kind of discussions?" the rabbi's assistant asked.

"Between the United Nations envoy and the prime minister's office ..."

"About what?" the assistant demanded.

"Jerusalem. Some kind of international solution to control and supervise the city."

"That's old news," the assistant chided him.

"No, not this part ..."

"What part?"

The young messenger broke into an ecstatic grin.

"The part about the Temple Mount."

Hawk's Nest, Colorado

In the conference room at the Jordans' ranch, the members of the Roundtable were chatting around a long table of polished birch. The curtains had been pulled open, giving everyone a spectacular view of the Rockies. Even though they had all been there more times than they could count, they still found it awe inspiring.

The group had taken a five-minute break before launching into the last order of business. Some of them, including Cal Jordan, were helping themselves to the snacks on the split-log buffet. Cal grabbed a soda and a huge oatmeal cookie and wandered toward Phil Rankowitz, the Roundtable's head of media.

Rankowitz, standing in front of the floor-to-ceiling windows, stared off at the distant mountains. Abigail was next to him. Phil murmured, "I keep trying to remember that psalm ... about the heavens declaring the glory of God ..."

"That's one of my favorites," Abigail said. "How's your reading-through-the-Bible-in-a-year project coming?"

"Try to keep up with it. I miss a few days here and there. Funny though, thinking back to the old days. I was just like all the other TV exec's I worked around back then — reading the Bible, are you kidding?"

Cal laughed. "I remember not long ago when Dad would have had the same reaction. Funny how an encounter with God radically changes everything, doesn't it?"

"The ultimate paradigm shift," Phil replied. Cal took a bite of his cookie, and Phil reached out and patted him on the shoulder. "Cal, have I told you how glad I am to have you sitting with us on the Roundtable?"

Cal gave a smiling nod. "So, you don't think with my dad being the founder, my mom sitting as chair, and now with me here that it looks like the Jordan family show?"

"Naw," Phil replied. "Besides, even if it did — so what? You've got an extraordinary family. The more of you the merrier."

The rest of the group was now slowly migrating back toward the table. Cal got a back-slap from former FBI agent John Gallagher, a favorite of his, as they sauntered back to their chairs. Cal congratulated Gallagher on looking so fit.

"Dropped forty pounds, and now I'm a lean, mean fighting machine," the former special agent remarked. "Problem is, Cal, I still have the urge to be an eating machine. Got to work on that."

Cal looked around at the accomplished array — a dozen leaders in business, the military, the media, and the law. He had recently found himself yearning to be included. He wasn't sure exactly when it happened, but his plans to go to art school had given way to something else: an intense desire to follow the path forged by his parents — fighting to restore the most basic freedoms in the country they loved. It was almost laughable — how he used to shrug off his parents' commitment — he had silently considered it just a "political obsession." Now he had come to realize it wasn't about politics at all. This was a spiritual battle for the soul of a nation at a time in history when the world looked like it was about to head right into its darkest hour. Even some of Cal's Christian friends called him an "end-times freak" now. A few of them attributed his turnaround to the scary encounter he had had with a terrorist in a New York train station.

And, Cal thought, maybe it did have something to do with that.

Whatever the genesis, Cal had a powerful sense of calling to do what the Roundtable was doing. He would have wanted to be part of it even if his parents weren't involved.

For him, the timing seemed perfect. He had graduated early from Liberty University and had plenty of time before starting law school. Until then he would act as a paralegal for the Roundtable, something he had been pursuing like a dog on a bone. His parents had finally relented to his request. Joshua and Abigail told him, after everything he had been through, he had earned a seat at the table, even though they feared there could be political — and even legal — fallout against their son for his involvement. After all, they pointed out, under the Tulrude Administration, the Department of Justice had filed a vindictive criminal case two years before against every member of the Roundtable. True, for tactical reasons the DOJ had dropped the charges against everyone except Joshua, their prime target, but Cal's parents told him this might be the beginning of political retaliation.

Cal didn't care. It wasn't reckless abandon. Instead, it was a rock-solid conviction that this is where God wanted him, at least for the next few months. The Roundtable existed to counteract the ruthless, abject corruption that had been spawned in the corridors of power in Washington, and Cal now felt privileged to be part of the Roundtable, even in a small way, like today, when his primary task was to adjust the video feed on the big screen, as he was doing now.

The screen at the end of the room lit up. Ethan March's face appeared. The image was a little scrambled.

"Cal, is that you?" Ethan asked.

"Sure is," Cal replied and reached for the remote. "The feed's off. Let me reset the telemetry here."

"Fine. I'll sit tight," Ethan said. "I'm standing in for Josh, playing the part of a test dummy."

Cal chuckled. There had been a time, when Ethan first started working with Joshua, that Cal harbored some bad feelings about the arrangement. Envy? Maybe. Though Cal and his father had been through some tough, amazing things that had brought them closer together, still, there were occasional sparks between the two of them. He used to blame his dad for those. But lately Cal wondered whether he wasn't more like his dad than he had ever imagined. And now Cal felt comfortable with Ethan as a kind of adopted part of the family, even if he was on the other side of the globe, so much so that Cal wished Ethan was back in the States so the two of them could pal around. He didn't have a brother. Ethan was the closest thing.

Cal reset the feed, and Ethan's face was crystal clear. "Okay, you're coming in great. So, how are things in Israel?"

"Hot," Ethan said with a grin.

"And you're not just talking about the desert heat?"

Ethan nodded. "You got it. Yeah, there's talk over here about a major shakeup on the Temple Mount. Josh told me this morning there are plans to rebuild the Jewish Temple up there. Josh says, after two thousand years of waiting, there's a lot of excitement in Israel over this. I can't see the big deal, but then, that's just me ..."

"Wow," Cal shot back. "The Temple rebuilt? That's huge! Listen, bro, you got to get into your New Testament. It's all laid out in Matthew 24. Jesus predicted the destruction of the Herodian Temple on the Mount in Jerusalem when He was on earth. And it ended up happening — in AD 70 — just like He said. In that same place in Matthew, Jesus talks about the desecration of the Temple by the Antichrist at the end of days, which implies that the Temple has to be rebuilt first. Man, we're getting close ..."

"Thank you, Reverend Cal," Ethan cracked. "I'd start the hymn singing except I've got a lousy voice."

Cal chuckled and noticed Phil Rankowitz had finished gathering all the members around the big table. "Okay, Ethan, gotta go. Probably good too. I'm not sure how much of your off-key singing I could take." Ethan guffawed. "Can you do me a favor?" Cal asked. "Have my dad join us on the screen. Good talking to you. Stay safe over there, Ethan."

Cal touched the prompt for the multiple-screen option, and the video broke into quadrants, one for each remote participant. Once the meeting started, Phil Rankowitz took the lead. He described an article written by an eccentric investigative journalist named Curtis Belltether, whose research had revealed a seamy, even criminal, side to the brilliant and suave Alexander Coliquin, then a rising international diplomat with a global, rock-star kind of following. Belltether's explosive article had been mailed to AmeriNews on the same day that Belltether was found murdered in a hotel room. Since then Coliquin had been elevated to secretary-general of the United Nations, and the stakes over publishing the article had been raised exponentially.

"Here's the problem folks," Phil explained. "We paid Belltether for the article before his death. We own the rights. That's not the issue. The question is whether we can afford to release the article over our AmeriNews Internet/Allfone service at this time."

Retired Senator Alvin Leander spoke up. "Why not? Isn't that why we launched AmeriNews in the first place?"

Phil explained, "Well, as you know, we started the news service because the feds pushed all the TV and radio news over to the Internet so they could use over-the-air broadcast spectrum for other purposes. They said it was for emergencies. But it never worked out that way. You remember the story. A handful of networks and technology companies, mostly controlled by foreign money, became the gatekeepers for all the news and information on the web. And the White House willingly collaborated with them, allowing them to maintain a vise-grip monopoly over the Internet as long as they sang the administration's tune. Until we introduced AmeriNews, that is, and got it grandfathered onto the Internet through a technical loophole in the FCC regulations. The loophole was quickly closed for all other comers, so AmeriNews is the only show in town where Americans are going to get the other side of the story.

"By the way, an update for you. A few years ago we started delivering our news, free of charge at first, to the Allfones of every American who uses that device — about fifty percent of the population. Fifteen percent cancelled when it came time to pay for the service, leaving thirty percent on our news service. But we've added another twenty eight percent who use the cheaper Youfone device. So as of now, we've got fifty-eight percent of America reading some part of our news every day. We expect even more growth next quarter."

From his quadrant on the video screen, Rocky Bridger, a former Pentagon army general, brought the discussion back to the main point. "Phil, what's the problem? Just transmit the article."

"I'm not just a former TV exec," Phil replied, "I also consider myself a journalist. I have no way to corroborate the information in Belltether's article without going back to his sources to fact-check it."

From another quadrant on the screen, Joshua posed a question. "How long will it take to authenticate the information?"

"Weeks, likely. With Belltether dead, running down all his sources is going to take some time. This is pretty explosive stuff. Belltether makes Coliquin look like a sophisticated, brutal mobster back in his homeland before he gained international celebrity status. And let's not forget his close affiliation with President Tulrude. The shrapnel from our information bomb against Coliquin is going to hit the White House — and you know Tulrude's administration will pounce on any factual weaknesses in the article to tar and feather us."

Judge Fortis Rice, from his chair in the conference room, asked, "Is there a rush on getting this article out that I'm not seeing?"

"Here's the urgency, Fort," Joshua replied. "I think Coliquin is dangerous, and the U.N. he heads is no longer an international lame duck, a world-wide debating society with no teeth. We've all seen what he's turned it into: a coalition of nations that pass treaties and enforces them with large international armies in blue helmets. His global regulations against climate change have industries around the world being monitored by his environmental police. He's united major religions around this initiative, but I find it incredibly suspect. His international regulations on hate speech, for example, have sent ministers and pastors to jail right here in the United States. He's a man to be watched — and exposed. Until we can expose him, he will continue to hurt people ... good people."

Alvin Leander fidgeted in his chair. "Josh, no disrespect, but could this be about your religious beliefs? Ever since you became a born-again Christian you've been looking for bogeymen under the bed."

Beverly Rose Cortez, sitting across from Leander, cast him a teasing grin. "I don't know, Alvin. I've seen Congress in action and visited the White House. Let me tell you, those folks in power, including our president, really *are* bogeymen ..."

After the chuckles died down, John Gallagher raised his hand but didn't wait to be called on. "No disrespect to any of you folks, but there's only two guys in this room who've ever gotten close to a real bogeyman. One is me, when I worked in counterterrorism. The other is my buddy Cal here, who had his own face-to-face with terror. So Alvin, let's watch the trash-talking about Joshua and his family. As for the issue on the table, if Josh thinks this is a time-critical deal, then that's that. Phil, whatever you've got to do, you got to do it quickly."

Abigail put the motion on the floor for a vote. The ayes had it. Phil would use his editorial judgment in making sure that the Belltether story checked out before disseminating it over millions of Allfones and Youfones, but with the caveat that he needed to get the fact-checking done "with blinding speed."

"Speaking of Washington and the White House," Phil Rankowitz added, "at some point we need to consider whether we issue a formal endorsement in the current presidential campaign."

"No brainer," Rocky Bridger shouted from the screen. "Just think back to before President Corland's medical problems arose, when he was starting to come around. An amazing reversal. Just plain courageous, if you ask me. Then that stroke — or whatever that was — and what do we get? Vice President Jessica Tulrude ... Lady Macbeth in the flesh gets put into the Oval Office, sells out America to the European markets, dumps the dollar, practically gives away American sovereignty to the U.N., strips our national defense—"

"Been down this road before, Rocky," Leander said. "We all know that AmeriNews, if it endorses anybody, is going to support Senator Hewbright. So Phil, I hear you saying that the question is whether we should even make endorsements. Right?"

"That's it," Phil replied. "AmeriNews is a fledgling news organization, but growing fast. There's something to be said for not endorsing anyone this time around."

Ultimately, after much discussion, the issue was tabled. It was agreed the topic would be brought up again at the next meeting.

While Abigail wrapped up the meeting, Cal felt his Allfone buzz. There was an email, with a basic encryption system. He didn't recognize the sender's address, so he tapped the code into the permissions key. Then the message appeared.

Dear Cal—we have never met. I am writing for my husband, who, as you know, is in poor health. He needs to speak to you. Although he has never met you, he knows something about your story and, of course, has met your father. He has good days and bad days, so I am not sure how much he will be able to verbalize when you get here. But please come if you can. The address and telephone number of the convalescent center is at the bottom of this email. Please keep this in strictest confidence.

When Cal read who had sent it, he felt as if someone had sucked the air out of his lungs. But just as quickly he recalled the day his father received the Medal of Freedom in a Rose Garden ceremony, all because of an incident involving him. Cal hadn't attended that White House event. So he wondered why he was being swept into this strange rendezvous.

The email was signed,

Yours truly,
Winnie Corland—on behalf of President Virgil Corland.

TWELVE

Chicago, Illinois

Men with a strange-looking legal warrant were still downstairs in the lobby of D&H Smelting Co. They had just served process papers on Bob Dempsky, the sixty-six-year-old president and CEO of the industrial plant, who was now back in his office with no intentions of cooperating — and was telling his lawyer as much on the telephone.

"Look," his attorney advised him, "this international agency has the authority to seize your company, the plant, and all your assets. You have a right to appeal, of course — "

"But I've done everything the EPA ordered me to do, and we haven't had a single stain on our pollution record for five years — "

"Naw, Bob," the attorney said, "you don't get it. U.S. law is irrelevant here, except when it's time for enforcement; then the World Climate Enforcement Council — WCEC — rounds up federal marshals to make sure you obey the international orders. The United States is part of all of these world climate-change treaties and global-warming protocols. I've told you this before. If your company fails to convert to what they call 'green practices' — "

But Dempsky was in no mood to listen. He was now crumpling the papers that the foreign official with a French accent, flanked by U.S. marshals, had just delivered to him downstairs.

He shook the ball of documents in the air as he yelled into the phone, "These papers say we put smoke and carbon into the air. Of course we do! We're a smelting factory! But we've complied with every one of the American regulations. But you're telling me that doesn't matter. Okay, so get this ... on this form, under 'miscellaneous violations,' they're telling me we don't use the right kind of light bulbs, we don't use recycled paper towels in our bathrooms — paper towels, for crying out loud!"

"I told you, Bob," the lawyer said, trying to smooth things over, "to contact that firm specializing in international law on LaSalle Street. Did you do that?"

Dempsky just shook his head in disgust. "So where do I appeal this?"

"To the Hague."

"Where?"

"The World Court, in the Hague, the Netherlands."

"This company was founded by my grandfather. This is America. I'm not going all the way to Holland to protect my family's company —"

"You're going to have to —"

"Oh yeah?" Dempsky shouted as he slammed his Allfone down on his desk. Then he buzzed his secretary on the intercom. "Peggy, call security ..."

"Mr. Dempsky, the marshals and that French gentleman are walking outside to chain the gate to the factory shut —"

"Tell my security team to go out there and stop them!"

"I will sir, but what if the marshals and that French gentleman —"

"Tell my security guys they have my authority to start shooting ..." Then he added with some bitter sarcasm, "But only at the Frenchman ..."

"Mr. Dempsky, I know you're not serious —"

"Okay, fine. At least tell them to order them off my property ... tell them they're trespassing. Do something." Then Dempsky strode over to the big picture window on the third floor that overlooked the factory entrance. His security people in the parking lot were approaching the team of federal marshals and a man in a suit with a briefcase down by the main gatehouse. His guards were gesturing to them. Up in his office Bob Dempsky was alone and began shouting to no one in particular.

"What kind of a country is this anyway?"

Brussels, Belgium, Headquarters of the World Climate Enforcement Council

Faris D'Hoestra, a billionaire industrialist in his midfifties with a shiny bald head and steel-grey euro-glasses, sat in front of five small web-streaming screens. The monitors were keyed to markets around the world.

All but one. At the top of the menu, that one read: "WCEC Seizures — Service of Process Pending."

D'Hoestra had noticed a blue flag that had just appeared on that screen. He tapped on the site. His eyes followed the status list until he came to the most recent one. It read: "D&H Smelting — Chicago, IL — Seizure Complete."

He closed that site on his screen. He pushed his Allfone's video button and a small screen eased up from the surface of the desk. The face of Brian Forship, his executive director of international acquisitions, appeared.

The face spoke. "Good evening, Mr. D'Hoestra. Working late again, I see ..."

"When do I not?"

"Of course."

"I've noticed the Chicago seizure."

"I did too."

"How soon can we put this on the block for sale?"

"I have my American Midwest connections on this. They are making sure that that Mr. Dempsky will miss the deadline for appeal."

"Fine. Then we can put it up for auction. Which of our ghost-companies will you use to buy it?"

"Probably Union Consolidation, Ltd."

"How many other seizure buy-ups do we have in the works?"

"One hundred and seventy-two internationally. Those are the biggest companies — not including this Chicago company, which isn't big enough to make our list of prime acquisitions."

"Get me the timetable and net asset value of those companies on our prime list, will you?"

"Certainly. Two other things. First, we're still hearing some rumblings about your position as head of the WCEC, which, of course, is in the business of confiscating companies in violation of green standards, while you've also maintained control of your Global Industrial Acquisitions, Ltd. A small article appeared in a news service complaining of a conflict of interest."

"Who did the article?"

"An American news service — AmeriNews. It's available on Allfone and Youfone by subscription. It's only a few years old. They even have a picture showing how your United Nations WCEC headquarters is in the building right next to your private company. The photo in the web article is angled to display the WCEC building, and then off in the distance is the sign for GIA, Ltd."

"Don't we own enough stock in all the Internet news platforms to shut them down?"

"Not that easy. Somehow they managed to slip through some kind of grandfather clause in the Federal Communications Commission regulations. They apparently can't be blocked."

"There's no such thing," D'Hoestra shot back. He leaned back in his ostrich-skin executive chair and reflected. "On the other hand, I don't think this will be a problem. I can show that I kept my ownership in GIA in a blind trust during my U.N. tenure. And with my formal resignation from the WCEC this month, I think it will all blow over."

"I would hope so," his director said. "The second thing — did you see the article on you in *World Money* magazine?"

D'Hoestra swiveled in his chair slightly and grabbed the magazine with his face on the cover. "Haven't had a chance to read it yet."

"Excellent coverage, Mr. D'Hoestra."

After his assistant signed off, the financier took a closer look at the cover. Under his headshot it read: "Faris D'Hoestra — Ready to Rule the World?"

Under that, the subtitle read, "Acquisitions King Expands his Empire."

The Next Day, Babylon City, Iraq

On the platform, the speakers' table was draped with the blue and white logo of the United Nations — arched olive branches surrounding a globe. In the background was a banner that read: "The One Movement — One Planet, One Cause, One God." At the podium, Secretary of State Danburg, the American representative from President Tulrude's administration, was wrapping up his introduction.

Behind him on the dais were a few Muslim muftis, the twenty-three-year-old newly installed Dalai Lama from Tibet, several representatives from the Global Conference of Churches, and a Hindu priest. There were also several heads of state, including the crown prince of Saudi Arabia. Looming in the background was a monolithic office complex, the size of a small city, which was being commemorated that day. Palatial in its intricate stone-carved detail over the windows, doors, and facades, and with blooming gardens and flowering desert plants cascading down from the roof lines, the edifice magnificently captured both the architectural features of ancient Mesopotamia and the modern look of a headquarters of international power.

"We have many people to thank for this moment," Secretary Danburg addressed the audience from the microphone, "including, of course, our own President Tulrude, who has been a tireless advocate for global peace. But today we are here to recognize the vision of our celebrated guest of honor, Alexander Coliquin — not only the recently installed secretary-general of the United Nations, but a man of incredible vision and talents. Whether we're talking about his genius in successfully orchestrating the world's currency, the CReDO, to steady the money markets, or his work in bringing peace and stability right here in war-torn Iraq, so that this project would be possible, or his labors in fighting global warming, Alexander Coliquin — who I consider a friend as well as a colleague — is truly a treasure for our planet. Without further ado — I give you Secretary-General Alexander Coliquin."

Coliquin shook hands with Danburg and received the huge ceremonial scissors that he would use shortly to cut the blue ribbon stretched across the arched marble gate that lead to the front portico of the main building. The secretary-general held the scissors in one hand and paused to wave with his other to the crowd that was already on its feet.

"Thank you," he said, closing his eyes momentarily and nodding to their ovation. Then he began speaking. "These scissors will soon cut the tape to inaugurate the opening of the new Global Center for Peace and Prosperity — a personal dream of mine and, I know, of you good people as well. But there is something I would rather cut with these giant scissors — the chains of ignorance, oppression, poverty, and injustice that still plague our world. With the help of the international community and with the blessings of sacred and holy God, we will do exactly that."

As the audience thundered their response, Brian Forship, seated toward the back of the audience, texted a quick message on his Allfone back to Faris D'Hoestra, his boss in Belgium.

Coliquin has just started. Will livestream his comments to you via my Allfone.

A minute later the response came back from Belgium.

I know this man well. Keep your eyes open. Watch for vulnerabilities. Coliquin has them, I assure you. Advise ASAP.

THIRTEEN

Wichita, Kansas

Special Agent Ben Boling stood in the field, staring at the decomposed body in a shallow ditch. There, on the outskirts of Wichita, the FBI agent took one more look at the grisly scene, then made a puffing noise as he exhaled and stepped back. Not a fun day.

When Agent Boling had received the call from the local police, he drove straight through central Kansas, down I-135 to his destination. It was a dismal drive. With the multiple-year drought, the state had dissipated into drifting dust and sweeping winds. Miles of agriculture had been destroyed. The nation's "breadbasket" had become a near desert of wheat fields, turned a brittle brown by the sun and the un-ending drought. Their watering systems simply couldn't keep up.

Many farmers had simply walked away from their foreclosed farms. Several of them, in different parts of the state, had swung a rope over the rafters of their barns, tightened a noose, and hanged themselves. Since the banks couldn't sell the land, it lay in ruins. Agent Boling had noticed a lot of drifters on the road with backpacks. These were not college-aged hikers getting close to nature or going on a quest to find themselves. Several of them were middle-aged, with worn, sad faces. Some had their worldly possessions piled high on bicycles as they trudged down the highway.

Boling had two thoughts. The first was really a question — *even in bankruptcy, don't they let you keep one vehicle at least?* But he knew the answer: *Yeah, but you still need money for gas, insurance, repairs...*

The second thought was a flashback to the old black-and-white movie he saw as a kid. *This is* The Grapes of Wrath. *Only bigger.*

After Boling had finished examining the corpse, he stepped over to the deputy in charge of the investigation. "You're sure about the ID?"

"Yep. Perry Tedrich. Local guy. Thirty-five. Divorced. The culprit did a nice job of stripping the body of any identification. Even cut the skin out on the back of his hand where he had his BIDTag laser imprint. But they missed one thing …"

"What's that?"

"For some reason, the victim kept his gym membership card in his shoe."

"You sure about his political connections?"

"Absolutely," the deputy said, "he was the city campaign manager for Wichita's Hewbright for President Campaign."

"Coroner been here yet?"

"She showed up an hour before you got here. Doubted if we're going to get a definitive cause of death, considering the state of the corpse. They're sending someone to collect the remains so she can do an autopsy, though she might be able to get a fix on an approximate DOD, estimating the month of death at least. That's what she said anyway."

Boling flipped his daybook open and scribbled some notes.

"I thought you guys were high-tech and everything," the deputy said with a smirk. Then he pulled out his electronic Police Data Pad and displayed it. "Everybody in our department's using these."

"Sure," Boling shot back, "real neat way for headquarters to keep tabs on your investigation. I have one of those too. Routine issue for every agent at the Bureau. They log your notes as you write them into the master computer back at headquarters. I don't use it."

"How come? They sure work for us."

"That's the point. They work too well."

The deputy screwed up his face for a moment, then shrugged. "Well, we'll keep you informed."

"Better than that. If you really like being all digital, then why not email me a data file of everything you have on Perry Tedrich?"

"Sure — we can do that."

Boling thanked him and trotted back to his car.

As he put his finger to the imprint starter on the steering wheel and the engine started, he flipped his daybook open to what he had just written. He plucked the ballpoint pen from his top pocket and underlined the part that read: "Hewbright for President."

Denver, Colorado

Abigail Jordan watched as Senator Hank Hewbright shook hands with a group of supporters who had come to the Convention Center to hear his speech. He was standing right outside the door to the greenroom suite assigned to his campaign staff.

From her seat inside the suite, Abigail could see Hewbright through the glass door. She had driven down from Hawk's Nest to hear him, with the intention of just slipping in and slipping out. But Bob Tripley, a Colorado lawyer and a Hewbright volunteer, recognized her and urged her to meet the senator personally.

Abigail tried to beg off, but the attorney was insistent. Abigail was afraid she'd be too much of a political lightning rod. If the press started snapping photos of her with Hewbright, wouldn't it be used to smear the candidate?

The senator breezed into the greenroom, followed by Abigail's lawyer friend and the national campaign manager.

"Senator," Attorney Tripley said, "this is someone I want you to meet, one of the sharpest lawyers I know." He opened his arm toward Abigail, who rose to her feet with her visitor tag dangling around her neck. Then he added, "Mrs. Abigail ..."

"No need for introductions," Hewbright said briskly, reaching out his hand. "Mrs. Jordan, it's a pleasure and an honor. We've never met before, but I know about you ... your courageous fight for this nation, the risks you've taken, and the trouble you've been through." The Colorado lawyer slipped away to talk with some of the staff as Hewbright continued, "And I've met your husband, of course. Unfortunately, a pretty formal setting back then. And highly charged. He was testifying on the Hill at our intelligence committee hearing about his RTS system."

"Yes, I remember. Josh told how fair and evenhanded you were."

"Thanks. Though confidentially, it looked like Senator Straworth was trying to slice him and dice him."

"Josh couldn't tell me details because it was a closed hearing, but it sounded rough."

Hewbright tossed her a smile that told her more than he could share in words. "On the other hand, Senator Straworth's bullying backfired. Let me just say that in that hearing Joshua was a tough customer, a tower of strength."

"That's my husband!" Abigail said. Then she shared her concern. "Senator, I'm a great admirer of yours and a strong supporter, but I was reluctant to meet with you. I don't want to hurt your chances. You know, guilt by association. I know this election is going to be vicious."

"We're ready for it," he said with a square-shouldered look that made Abigail smile. It reminded her of Joshua.

Hewbright signaled for her to accompany him to a quieter corner of the greenroom, which was filling up with chattering staffers, volunteers, and high-value campaign donors.

"How is Josh doing?" he asked.

"Holding strong. But we both hate being separated by oceans and continents. So hard . . ."

"I've been briefed on this ridiculous case. It's an outrage."

"We still hope to get the whole thing dropped."

"And this rescue effort in North Korea. Really outstanding. I know the president is avoiding any mention of Josh, but my sources in the Pentagon said he was instrumental."

"He was in the thick of it. But he's safe now, thank God."

"When I'm president," Hewbright said. "Josh will be getting another medal for valor — from me this time."

Two women — Abigail assumed they were campaign workers — strode up to Hewbright, Styrofoam cups of coffee in hand. She knew the senator was scheduled to speak that morning at a technology convention in Las Vegas, which probably meant a redeye flight while the staff worked through the night on the plane. They were clearly pushing caffeine to keep up the pace.

The senator turned to introduce the women. "Mrs. Jordan, this is Zeta Milla, one of my foreign-affairs advisors. She may look young, but she's had lots of experience in the State Department," he said with a playful wink. "She recently left the State Department to come on board with my campaign. As a young girl she escaped from Cuba. Unfortunately, her parents didn't make it out alive, but she did — much to the benefit of my campaign. And America. I work closely with her."

The beautiful Cuban woman smiled warmly and grabbed Abigail's hand in both of hers and squeezed. "Like you," Zeta Milla said, "I am a lover of freedom."

Abigail, an admirer of fine jewelry, noticed the unique red sapphire ring in an unusual silver setting on Milla's index finger. "That's a beautiful ring," Abigail said.

Zeta glanced down at the huge diamond cluster on Abigail's own hand and nodded at it with a grin. "Thanks."

Then Hewbright turned to the other woman. "And here is my assistant campaign manager, Katrena Amid, a brilliant strategist and tough as nails."

Katrena gave Abigail a half nod and a tight-lipped smile. The woman seemed to size up Abigail. She looked uneasy. Then she handed a note to Hewbright. "Senator, here's that donor I mentioned to you. If you could give him a quick call, I think it would be beneficial."

"Well," Hewbright said, "duty calls."

He excused himself. With Hewbright out of the room, the donors and supporters started to drift out of the suite. Abigail followed.

As she made her way to her car in the parking ramp, Abigail was overcome by an oppressive feeling of dread. She struggled to describe it to herself. She should have been thinking about her flight to Washington, D.C., the following day with Cal or the new lead she would be pursuing in her husband's case. But she wasn't. Her mind was somewhere else.

Women's intuition? Or maybe spiritual discernment?

Whatever it was, Abigail found it hard to shake. She found herself seized by the fear that Senator Hank Hewbright was in danger. It was palpable. She had an inexplicable feeling of being trapped. As if she had been locked into an airless trunk.

When I get back to Hawk's Nest, she thought, *I need to check into something. Maybe it's nothing ... but I can't take the risk. I can't ignore this.*

FOURTEEN

Fair Haven Convalescent Center, Bethesda, Maryland

"So, Cal, your mother's doing well?"

Cal Jordan nodded politely. He was still coming to grips with the fact he was sitting across from the former first lady of the United States. A guy who looked like a Secret Service agent was posted just outside the lavish sunroom with its curved wall of glass and its view of the trees and gardens outside. This was all too surreal. Cal had racked his brain to sort out the reason behind this meeting but couldn't get to first base. He asked himself, *Why me?*

He did have one guess. A little more than two years earlier, before the president's health problems, Corland had made a dramatic turn in his policies, much to the chagrin of his vice president, Jessica Tulrude. As part of that reversal, President Corland had decided to honor Joshua at the White House for his bravery in foiling the terrorist-led hostage plot the year before at New York's Grand Central Terminal. Perhaps that was the point of connection — particularly because Cal himself had been the hostage, handpicked by the terrorist in an unsuccessful effort to pressure Joshua into giving up his RTS design plans.

But now that his dad had been exiled from the United States, Cal wondered whether Corland wanted him to be a messenger to his father — or to the Roundtable — or both.

Cal responded to Mrs. Corland. "My mother's in Washington on legal business today. I tagged along. I'm glad I was close so I could stop in to see you and the president."

He thought back to the warning in Mrs. Corland's email that he was to keep their meeting secret. He hadn't even told his mother. Abigail was meeting with a lawyer in downtown D.C. that day. Ordinarily, she would have included him, but since this meeting was particularly sensitive, Abigail had explained that she had to keep Cal out of it. Before they went their separate ways, Cal only told Abigail that he would be "nosing around town, checking the sites." Cal had formulated a lame justification in his mind — meeting with a former president and first lady — they were political monuments of sorts, weren't they?

Rising from her chair, Winnie Corland smoothed her dress. "Well, I will leave you two alone. Virgil is insistent that he speak with you privately."

Cal rose as well. As he shook her hand, she gave him some last words of instruction. "Virgil communicates better some days than others," she said. "But even if he can't tell you everything on his mind … his heart … I am sure he appreciates having the company."

She walked out of the brightly lit sunroom. Now it was just Cal and the former president, who was seated in a wheelchair. He was the same man who had once run the country, but he was pale now and thin, his eyes listless.

After a few moments of silence, Cal started the conversation. "I am honored to meet you, Mr. President."

Corland took at least half a minute before it looked like he registered. Then he nodded slowly.

"My father speaks highly of you," Cal added.

Only a blank stare from Virgil Corland.

Cal kept talking. "My dad is Joshua Jordan. He told me about meeting you at the White House, the day that you gave him the Medal of Honor."

Something in what Cal said, or maybe something else, a random memory perhaps, generated a look of urgency, almost desperation, on Corland's face. He spoke, hesitantly, with an athletic kind of effort to each word, "I was president once …"

"Yes, that's right."

But Corland shook his head, as if trying to move the conversation away from the cordial and superficial. "Vice President …," he strained to say.

"Yes, Mrs. Tulrude was vice president then, before she stepped into your shoes … into the Oval Office … when you had your health problems."

"No, no," he groaned.

Cal feared that he may have upset him.

Then Corland looked up at his young guest. "Never had … a son."

"You didn't?"

Corland shook his head slowly. "Your father. Got the medal. New York …"

"Yes, for saving me in New York. Right. The terrorist who had kidnapped me — "

"But you … too … you too," he said. There was a twisted, labored attempt at a smile on Corland's face. "You … brave too … like your father."

"I was just the victim …," Cal said.

"No. No. I read … the … reports … FBI." Then Corland added, "Brave," and when he said that word, he lifted his right hand and pointed a limp finger right at Cal's chest and gathered up an earnest expression. "Brave," he said again. Then Corland took a deep breath as if he were going to swim underwater. "Tulrude. What happened … no, oh no." But he ran out of breath. His head dropped to one side, as if a string had been cut.

The day nurse from the other side of the room quickly made her way over to Corland. "I think, young man, that the president has had enough for today. He's still quite fragile."

Cal reached over and rested his hand on the wrinkled hand of the former president and said good-bye. As he turned to leave, Cal heard three words, barely audible, from Corland's dry lips.

"Come … back … again."

Clyde's Restaurant, Georgetown, Washington, D.C.

Abigail stirred her Cobb salad with a fork. She wasn't hungry, but she had to go through the motions — the perfunctory professional lunch — to wrangle this meeting with Harley Collingwood, the lawyer now sitting across from her.

Since both had been trial attorneys in D.C., they swapped stories about arguing cases in the District. Collingwood said he knew about her work in Harry Smythe's prestigious law firm and had heard secondhand about her being a top-tier litigator. They exchanged law-school jokes, keeping everything light, amiable.

Eventually Collingwood pushed his plate away and said, "Okay, Abigail, I know you didn't come all the way to D.C. for a nice salad, some chit-chat, and to exchange law-practice war stories with me." She let him continue. "Here's what I think," he said. "I think you found out I just left the Department of Justice and know I was on the prosecution team, going after your husband in his criminal case. So here you are ..."

Abigail kept a pleasant, interested, but nonplused look on her face. She let him go on.

"And," he said, "you'd probably love it if I were to slip you some helpful information about your husband's case."

She was silent for a moment, then asked a simple but disarming question. "Have you found work?"

"Of course," Collingwood shot back.

"Which firm?"

He hesitated. "Consulting for a few different offices. I'm picky."

"In other words," Abigail said with steely calm, "you have not found steady work since you voluntarily left your position at the DOJ, where you were the second highest assistant attorney general in the criminal division. Harley, my point is, you'd been handpicked by Attorney General Cory Hamburg himself, and you left all that — voluntarily — so you could be picky in looking around for other employment?"

Collingwood stiffened. "My law practice is really none of your business."

"True," she said, "but justice is. And so is the truth. If I know anything about you, the truth is your business too. You're regarded as one of the most aggressive prosecutors in Washington — and one of the most ethical. I need your help. My guess is that you discovered something rotten in the prosecution of my husband — so rotten that it led you to report it to DOJ's Office of Professional Responsibility." The former prosecutor was stone-still, listening. Abigail continued, "But knowing what I do about Attorney General Hamburg and his deference to the Tulrude administration, I'm betting he made sure that OPR stuck your ethics complaint in the permanent out basket. Which put you in a real dilemma."

Collingwood still didn't move a muscle.

"Now that you're out of the DOJ, either you can keep what you know to yourself and see an innocent man — my husband — hunted down around the globe for the rest of his life by federal authorities and railroaded with phony criminal charges ... and maybe you could salve your conscience by saying that by your silence you're actually protecting DOJ's privilege of lawyer's confidentiality. Or else, and here's the kicker, you will actually have to *do* something about what you know — tell someone — someone who can take your information and do what ought to be done. For justice and for truth."

Abigail looked Harley Collingwood squarely in the eye. "Have I stated the matter accurately, counselor?"

FIFTEEN

In the Desert of Southern Israel, Near Eilat

Joshua's mind had been fixed like a metal rivet on the test he had just witnessed at the IDF weapons site. His RTS system had failed. Again. Not that it hadn't reversed the test missile and sent it back to its point of launching. The problem was, for some reason, it had not captured the guidance system in the nosecone completely, so that the ground crew could manipulate its flight and send it in new directions. He had already been on the phone with Ted, his senior engineer at the Jordan Technologies headquarters in Manhattan, trying to work out the glitch.

"Don't worry," Ted assured him, "we'll get the kinks out."

"Without three-sixty capture of the guidance systems of incomings," Joshua said, "we'll be slaves to any bad guys who launch from civilian areas, knowing that we wouldn't send missiles back to a spot where they would wipe out innocent people."

Joshua rode away from the test site, jostled in the Jeep driven by Colonel Clinton Kinney, his close buddy from the Israeli Defense Forces.

Soon Kinney took a turn in another direction, away from Jerusalem. After a few minutes he pulled to the side of the road and turned off the engine. Joshua realized why.

Kinney pointed to a stretch of desert across the highway. Joshua nodded without saying a word. He momentarily forgot the failed missile test and everything else. For him, now, it was all coming true. Right in front of him. He was a witness to the unfolding of something incredible.

From the Jeep, Joshua saw hundreds of bearded Orthodox Jews in the distance, in neon green vests, carrying boxes and plastic bags as they wandered the surface of the desert. They were bent over, searching the rough terrain that had recently been made so ruthlessly jagged, filled with volcanic pumice, huge charred boulders, and caverns that had ripped through the ground.

An uninformed visitor might simply have said the land looked ravaged by the recent massive, unprecedented volcanic eruptions and earthquakes — so-called *natural* events. But to the Orthodox who were scouring the land for the human remains of their enemies so that they could arrange the burials — and in fact, for almost every citizen of Israel — it had been a supernatural miracle brought forth by the hand of God.

"What are they called?" Joshua asked, pointing to the men who were collecting the last remains of dead Russian and Turkish soldiers, as well as Sudanese and Libyan.

"They're part of the ZAKA — a group of Orthodox Jews who for years take on the job of cleaning up the bodily remains after disasters and terrorist bombings. To keep the land ceremonially clean. But this is the largest job they've ever had — or will ever have."

As Joshua surveyed the scene, his mind traveled back. He himself had been caught in the thick of that war, on the border of Israel, just on the other side from Syria when it happened. He remembered how the Russian-Islamic coalition had swept down from the north against the tiny nation of Israel like a rolling storm. At the same time they came up from the south through the Sinai Desert, with their hundreds of thousands of troops, tanks and mobile missile launchers, and hundreds of jets launched from the Russian aircraft carriers anchored off the coast in the Mediterranean.

The invasion looked unstoppable. The IDF headquarters was bracing for a fight to the death, and Israel's military commanders were convinced that all was lost.

Then the unimaginable had occurred. The earth itself rocked, cracked open, and exploded with a force greater than multiple megaton nuclear detonations.

Joshua had been there, an eyewitness to the awesome display of divine intervention. How could he not believe that this was the long-promised reckoning?

Colonel Kinney eyed the scorched wilderness. "Now that you're a believer in the prophecies and promises of the Bible," he said, "you have to admit … this is an incredible sight."

"I know," Joshua said, shaking his head, "I was there. Saw it all. Felt it. And barely survived it. Fire in the sky, tremors in the earth. Everything God predicted in Ezekiel 38 and 39, when He described thousands of years ago how he would vanquish the Russian-Islamic invasion of Israel. And that's exactly what happened. And I lived through it to tell the tale." After a moment, Joshua continued. "And then this," he said, pointing to the ZAKA, "just one more proof …"

"Ezekiel 39:12," Kinney replied. Then he recited it from memory. " 'For seven months the house of Israel will be burying them in order to cleanse the land.' "

"And by my calendar, we're now in the seventh month, aren't we?" Joshua asked.

Kinney nodded and touched his finger to the ignition pad on the steering wheel. The Jeep's engine fired up. "I'm one of those rare things in the IDF — a Jewish follower of Jesus Christ the Messiah — Yeshua … though there are more of us since all this happened," he said, pointing to the landscape where volcanic cones rose from the desert floor in the distance. He turned toward highway 90 to head north, first along the Dead Sea and then to Jerusalem. Kinney added, "It's nice to be able to talk about this with someone who understands." Then he asked, "Your young protégé, Ethan March, he'll be waiting for us where we dropped him off … back at the bottom of Masada?"

"Right. He wanted to hike to the top. Knowing Ethan, he'll do the whole thing at a jog. The guy's a terrific athlete."

Kinney glanced over at Joshua. "Okay, so, you said you had a high-level political question to ask me. Fire away."

"Prime Minister Benksy ..."

"What about him?"

"How well do you know him?"

"Only casually," McKinney replied. "I'm just a colonel, not a general. I don't sit in on security meetings. Just the operational stuff. On the other hand, this is a small country. Everyone knows something about everyone."

"Gotcha."

Kinney shot another look at Joshua as they picked up speed on highway 90. "Okay, what gives?"

"I've got a theological question, which is also a philosophical one, so I need you to put on your philosopher's hat for a moment."

"That's interesting," Kinney said with a smile. "You're a former test pilot and a spy-plane hero for the U.S. Air Force, with an engineering degree from MIT and a defensive-weapons designer of some of the most advanced hardware and laser gadgets any military could ask for. You're one of the bravest guys I've ever met ... and one of the brightest. But in a mechanical kind of way. You're a hyperadvanced sort of technical fix-it guy, an action hero, Mr. Wizard with laser shields. But frankly, not exactly the philosopher type."

Joshua smiled. "Take away all the superlatives, and I'd say you had me nailed." Then his face dropped and his eyes fixed on some unseen point on the horizon. "There's a time and a season for everything."

"So, ask your question," Kinney said.

"As followers of Jesus Christ, we believe in the Scriptures. And as one of the few Jewish followers of Jesus in the IDF, you can appreciate that."

"Sure. Psalm 119 reminds us of that. And several verses in the New Testament."

"And that includes the prophecies foretold by God," Joshua added.

Kinney nodded. "Absolutely. First epistle of Peter, chapter one, says the Spirit of Christ moved within the Old Testament prophets and they 'predicted the sufferings of the Messiah and the glories that would follow.' The first chapter of the book of Revelation says, 'Blessed is the one who reads aloud the words of this prophecy, and blessed are those who hear it and take to heart what is written in it, for the time is near.' So, yes, I think followers of Christ need to study the *whole* counsel of God in the Bible, prophecy included."

Joshua chuckled. "Remind me not to play Bible Trivia with you."

Kinney smiled. "Okay, out with it. What's up?"

"What if you know that God has foretold something and told us clearly in Scripture that it's going to occur? You would consider that an expression of His sovereign will, right?"

"Agreed."

"Unchangeable."

"Correct."

"We accept it?"

"You mean as in — don't take any action that opposes it?"

"Right," Joshua bulleted back. "Let's say that something evil, horrendous, is about to happen, and God inspires His prophets to predict that very thing, thousands of years ago in Scripture. And suddenly, you start to see it unfolding — right in front of you. But you have the opportunity, within your sphere of power, to try and stop it, this nightmare. And you are in a situation at the epicenter of converging events to do something about it. So the question is this — do you take that chance?"

Kinney shot back. "You're still hedging. I've never known you not to get to the point, Josh. What's going on in your head right now?"

"You've seen the news, about the United Nations negotiations with the Bensky administration?"

"Sure, more peace proposals."

"Well, along those lines, Joel Harmon contacted me recently."

"The fighter pilot from the Knesset?"

"Right."

"Contacted you about what?"

"He's a member of a coalition party, the Hamonah. You know, I've heard of the other political parties over here: Likud, Kadima, Shas, Labor. But not that one, until Harmon got hold of me."

"That's because it's new. Just formed after the dust settled from our recent war — the one they're calling the War of Thunder ..."

"Yeah, I heard that."

Kinney nodded. "... After the verse in first Samuel, chapter two. 'Those who oppose the Lord will be broken. The Most High will thunder from heaven.' Anyway, this new political party was named Hamonah based on the verse in Ezekiel about the cleansing of the land. So, Joel Harmon talked to you?"

"We met once. He told me he's leading the effort to stop Bensky from going along with this U.N. initiative being pushed by Secretary-General Alexander Coliquin."

"And he's enlisted you," Kinney remarked with a studied look on his face. "Smart move. You're a national hero to a lot of folks-in-the-know here. Your RTS system averted a nuke attack from Iran. They *ought* to love you. So what's the problem?"

"He wants me to be present when he and his political group meet with Bensky, to convince him to reject the U.N. deal."

Kinney thought for a moment. "Okay, here's another verse for you — Psalm 119:46 — 'I will speak of your statutes before kings and will not be put to shame.'"

"Great verse. Only one problem. For me, it's not a matter of shame."

"Then what?"

"Fear."

"You've got to be kidding. You? Afraid of the prime minister of Israel?"

"No. Something else."

"What?"

"God."

Kinney fell silent.

Joshua explained. "I don't want to do anything that would go against God's sovereign plan. I don't want to get in the way. There's something dark and evil coming. It's almost here. I'm not talking politics or international policy. It's much different. We both know that. Something more monstrous than anything the world has ever witnessed. And for the first time in my life, I feel paralyzed. Conflicted. Undecided which way to turn. I'm afraid of making a colossal mistake — of biblical proportions."

Then he motioned toward the huge boulders on the desert floor on the other side of the highway that were covered with a thick layer of volcanic lava from the recent upheaval of the earth.

"I feel like I'm turning to stone."

SIXTEEN

Tel Aviv, Israel

Prime Minister Solomon "Sol" Benksy was seated at his usual place at the head of the long conference table. The security cabinet was there, along with the chief legal counsel and the head of economic advisors. The meetings were always lively, occasionally combative, but in a cordial kind of way. Today, however, the gloves were off.

Normally the meeting would take place at the NSC headquarters at Ramat Hasharon. But on Thursdays, following long-established custom, the prime minister always conducted his business at the IDF compound in Tel Aviv, in the conference room just down the hall from the big bronze bust of David Ben Gurion.

The secretary raised her voice above the din, trying to quiet the argument that was in full swing.

"Ladies and gentlemen, attention, please. We will now hear, once again, the short executive summary of the proposal—"

But the head of counterterrorism wouldn't quit. "You call that offer from the United Nations a *proposal*? I call it a Trojan horse!"

Prime Minister Bensky stepped in. "Please, everyone, quiet. Bring yourselves to order. Mrs. Kiryas, read it."

The NSC secretary proceeded to read aloud from the government bulletin: "'Summary of the communiqué from the secretary-general of the United Nations, the most Honorable Alexander Coliquin, to the Honorable Prime Minister Solomon Bensky. Key Points. Number one.

The Temple Mount plateau in Jerusalem shall be divided according to those coordinates on the attached addendum 6, with the Islamic Waqf Trust to continue its current control over the Al Aqsa Mosque and the Dome of the Rock in that portion marked "section A," and with the Nation of Israel to possess the right and title and full control over "section B," on the Temple Mount, including but not limited to the right of Israel to construct sacred buildings, synagogues, or a temple for worship — ' "

The chief of security policy interrupted. "We have concerns about the accuracy of the measurements necessary for any kind of Jewish construction on the Temple Mount. We need to avoid a violent reaction later from the Muslims over that. After all, they've had possession of that plateau for a long time. They're not going to give any of it lightly."

But the head of foreign policy stopped him. "We've been in touch with the IAA, our antiquities experts, as well as geologists, engineers, surveyors — all of them tell us that if you take that one-million-square-foot plateau on the Temple Mount, and you take the U.N.'s measurements, and look at their attached diagram, it certainly looks to all of us that the section they're giving us would be more than ample for the construction — "

A voice boomed from the corner, "*Giving* us?" It was the chief rabbi for the city of Jerusalem. "Did you say the U.N. is *giving us* a section of the Temple Mount? That's blasphemy! The Most High King of the Universe — He is the one who gave it to us. The *whole* of the Temple Mount. It is only because of our cowardice and lack of faith that we have not resolved this issue long ago."

Prime Minister Bensky jumped in. "Gentlemen and ladies, please. Let's not argue over semantics. The point here is that the United Nations, and, I might add, the Palestinian Authority and the entire Arab League of Muslim nations — they have all supported this proposal. And President Tulrude is an enthusiastic advocate for this approach, as well as the entire U.N. security council. This is historic ... the opportunity to take control of a large segment of the Mount. And as our chief of foreign policy was about to describe, the construction ..."

The prime minister paused and lifted his hands up for just a half second, enough for the Rabbi to intervene.

"Construction of our Temple," the rabbi pronounced with the passionate tone of an epiphany, "the central place for holy worship on Mount Moriah, to become the epicenter of all Judaism, after two thousand years of waiting." Then with eyes half closed and hands outstretched he said, "Finally, in my lifetime, it may yet come to pass ..."

"With all deference to our chief rabbi," the security-policy leader added, "there is the reality of the secular, nonreligious segment of the Israeli population. To them, the rebuilding of the Temple on the Mount may have some historical and cultural interest, of course, but it will certainly *not* be a religious priority."

The prime minister's economic advisor tapped his pen on the table. "You are forgetting two things. First, the construction of the Temple would not only be a religious, historical, and cultural event, it would also be an economic benefit of monumental proportions. My staff has already done the calculations. Tourism would double in the first twelve months and increase exponentially each year thereafter. The construction effort alone would be a tremendous asset to our economy in terms of job creation, both primary and secondary employment, and contract labor. We have estimated that international nonprofit groups, many of them religious, would contribute up to sixty percent of the building costs. And then there is the second point: increased internationalization of Jerusalem through this peace plan will actually *lessen* the risk of violence in Jerusalem."

Prime Minister Bensky jumped on that. "This is why I am in support of this proposal." He looked directly at his scowling chief of counterterrorism as he continued, "The Palestinians and the Arab League are calling for the cessation of hostilities against Israel in the future as part of this plan. And look at point number two in the Coliquin proposal — the United Nations becomes a permanent board of mediation on any disputes within Jerusalem. By agreeing with the U.N. plan, we put on the white hats. We are the good guys. We start winning back much of the esteem that we have lost over the last few decades in the international community."

The chief of counterterrorism was not convinced. "I am not as concerned about what color our hats are as I am about the explosive belts and missile launchers that some of our enemies will be carrying. This plan does nothing for my concerns — except to invite the United Nations to exercise control over the nation of Israel."

"And yet," the prime minister's female media advisor added, "the polling data tells us something different. The majority of Israelis want a peace plan. Even with the miraculous victory we just won against the Russian-Islamic invaders, our citizens are tired ... tired of war, tired of waiting for their cell phone to ring, wondering if a loved one has just been blown up in a bus attack or in an explosion at a sidewalk café. Fatigue and fear, ladies and gentlemen — those are powerful emotions. And they are powerful political realities."

On the Top of Masada, Near the Dead Sea

"I still can't believe we ran into each other." Ethan smiled at the athletic and attractive Rivka, who was dressed in hiking shorts, with a water bottle dangling from her belt. They were both looking out from a spot near the ancient ruins on top of the sandy plateau down to the desert floor far below. Then he added, "First, that planning meeting in South Korea, and now here, at this spot, with you, actually hiking and taking it easy."

"Why does that surprise you?" she asked. She had a mischievous smile.

"Okay, look, I'm former military myself, so I understand downtime, and furloughs ..."

"But you just don't picture people like me taking time off, is that it?"

"Maybe, yes. Military is one thing. But your outfit, Israeli's spy shop — the Mossad — "

"Who told you that's where I work?" she said with a sudden flash of anger. "I work as a clerk in the statistics department of the IDF."

Taken aback, Ethan studied the athletic, pretty Israeli woman. Then he noticed a flicker of another smile. "Okay," he said, "now you're playing with me. So, are you or aren't you? I suppose you can't say anyway, even though you and I were both in that North Korean deal together — or, well, actually you were, I was just sitting back in South Korea with my hands in my pockets. Though I wondered why Israel was involved in that deal in the first place."

She dodged his first question, about which agency signed her paychecks, but she answered the second one. "The last few years, Israel and South Korea have become very close diplomatically. We have more in common than meets the eye."

"Like?"

"They send a high number of tourists to Israel each year, and, like Israel, they have learned to live their lives under the shadow of enemies who are very close. And then there is the matter of our past historic alliances with the United States."

"*Past historic*? You're making a point, I take it?"

"American foreign policy is different now and impacts both Israel and South Korea in similar ways. Your country used to be smart about picking its allies, and even smarter about choosing its friends. Things have changed considerably."

Rivka shrugged off that topic and took a step toward the edge of the high plateau, looking out over the desert. "So, you're here in Israel with Colonel Jordan?"

"Always glued to his side."

"But not right now?"

"Well, almost always. I get some free time."

"I'm glad for that," she said with a smile. She pulled out a water bottle and uncapped it. She raised it to her lips, but instead of drinking from it, she gave it a shake in Ethan's direction and playfully splashed water on his face, and they both laughed loudly. Rivka took an extra T-shirt from her belt, pulled it out, and dabbed the water from his face.

Ethan took a long look at Rivka, all five feet six inches of her, as she grinned back at him. And he thought how things seemed just a little bit bizarre at that moment. It was almost laughable.

Is this woman who's flirting with me really the same Rivka I met in Seoul? The same one Josh said had kicked a North Korean guard into unconsciousness?

Apparently she was.

They started the steep climb down from the high cliffs of Masada, the place where the ancient stone walls and crumbled structures testified to the siege that took place there two thousand years before — the last desperate stand of the Jewish rebels against the legions of the Roman Empire. As Ethan and Rivka began to hike down to the desert floor, Ethan had another thought. *Okay, Rivka, let's see where you and I go from here.*

SEVENTEEN

Baden-Baden, Germany, Emperor Hadrian Hotel, Headquarters of the Order of World Builders

Faris D'Hoestra adjusted his steel-gray glasses with two fingers and maintained his expression of calm satisfaction. The session was progressing well.

He had traveled from Brussels, where the largest of his mansions and office complexes were located, to attend the quarterly meeting of the Order of World Builders — or simply "The Builders," as its members referred to it — and to preside as its permanent chairman.

The fifty members were seated around a mahogany table on the top floor of the hotel — the entire level of which had been reserved for the Builders on a hundred-year lease. Four similar leases stretched back to the eighteenth century, when the hotel was founded, but the history of the Builders went back much farther than that.

D'Hoestra's last motion had been carried unanimously, just like all the others that day.

Now for the last one.

The secretary of the Builders read it aloud — and it was moved and seconded — that "action be taken immediately to circumscribe and limit, by any means necessary, the international authority of the office of secretary-general of the United Nations, while creating an alternative international organization that shall be more receptive to the membership and influence of the Order of World Builders."

A small red light on the polished table, directly in front of one of the attendees, lit up.

D'Hoestra called on the deputy prime minister of India.

"Mr. Chairman," the Indian representative said, "I question the wording of the phrase 'circumscribe and limit.' You want to reign in the power of the office of the secretary-general when in actuality, you want to reign in the charismatic secretary-general himself, Mr. Alexander Coliquin, perhaps even to depose him. Am I correct?"

Several heads were nodding.

"I'll answer that," D'Hoestra said. "Because each of us pledged to keep these proceedings secret, as has been our honored tradition, and each of us understands the consequences that come with any violation of that pledge, I can be candid." D'Hoestra stood up from his executive chair and began to stroll slowly around the circumference of the mammoth table. "Mr. Coliquin has played the game of global chess quite well, squaring nations off against nations, constructing international coalitions behind the scenes to do his bidding. And he possesses what no prior secretary-general has ever had before — a lock-grip over the U.N. Security Council, including having Madam President Tulrude at his beck and call. A singular, titular head of global power like this — resting in the person of one man — is simply not good for the future world order. It is certainly not good for us. It is ruinous for the Builders. Our heritage stretches back through the annals of time. Yes, Coliquin must be dealt with. Quickly and decisively."

Another red bulb lit up. Lord Raxtony, an English Lord from the Royal Society, was leaning forward to speak. D'Hoestra recognized him. "Yes, well, if I may, this raises, rather well, I think, the problem I see with the other phrasing in your motion. You say we will limit Mr. Coliquin 'by any means necessary.' There is an implication there, clearly, that we will limit him without regard for any moral or legal limits. It has, Mr. Chairman, been a rather long time since this body has been asked to authorize the use of extreme sanctions."

D'Hoestra motioned to Deter Von Gunter, the controlling head of the large industrial and military armaments company the Von Gunter Group. He clearly wanted to address Lord Raxtony's comment.

"You accurately point out," Von Gunter said, his voice as smooth as warm honey, "that it has been a long time since extreme sanctions were authorized by this body. Those sanctions are called 'extreme' because they are exceptional and to be used sparingly." He paused. Then his voice suddenly jumped up a pitch, as he slapped his hands on the varnished table top. "But *extreme*, exceptional sanctions must sometimes be used! Is this not true? Otherwise we should call them *unusable* sanctions. Or *unimaginable* sanctions. Personally, I have tired of Mr. Coliquin and his antics. His international treaties entangle the world and have made life difficult for our companies — mine in particular. He is a wasp in our house. Let's get some bug spray and rid our houses of this bothersome pest."

D'Hoestra was surprised by Von Gunter, not by the outburst itself — which was typical of him — but by the degree of his passion. Then again, some intrigues obviously existed within Von Gunter's world that D'Hoestra could not possibly know about.

The chairman permitted the discussion to continue for another hour. He was in no rush. He could see the dynamics of the meeting slowly bending to his will.

In the end, although two members abstained, the rest of the World Builders voted in favor of the motion.

With his motion passed, Faris D'Hoestra adjourned the meeting. After a few pleasantries with the members, he had his driver take him to his palatial thirty-thousand-square-foot villa on the edge of the Black Forest, outside Baden-Baden. There he would be attended to by his staff of seventy. First, a soaking bath while music from a live baroque quartet in the drawing room would be piped down to his steam room. Then a massage, facial, and manicure from a bevy of female attendants. After that, a sumptuous banquet at which he would entertain six Hollywood celebrities, the president of a small island nation, a Nobel Prize winner, and a news anchor and his wife from the American Internet News Channel.

Finally, at the end of the evening, he would slip into his silk sheets. There, before drifting off to sleep to the scent of rose petals, he would contemplate his expanding empire. And Faris D'Hoestra would wonder at his place among the powerful Roman emperors like Hadrian, who had once trod those very same woods outside his villa.

EIGHTEEN

Manhattan

She shouldn't have been so stunned. After all, Abigail had reviewed the reporter's file once before. Yet there was that one little detail in those materials that she must have tucked away somewhere in her memory. Then it came back to her when she was in Denver, attending the Hewbright-for-President campaign event. Now that she was back in New York and had the big manila envelope in hand with all the documents, she checked it again — just to be sure. She had to be absolutely certain.

Now she was. It was right there in the photo — that unusual ring on Coliquin's finger. Her head was reeling. Abigail was seated on the wraparound couch in the living room of her Manhattan penthouse with her feet up on the coffee table. She normally would have taken time to gaze through the big windows and enjoy the sunset over New York. But not today. Not with what she had just seen in the file photo. She had been leafing through the unpublished article on Alexander Coliquin by the late Curtis Belltether, the eccentric online journalist, and his other materials. It was the same piece that had been mailed to AmeriNews and the Jordans by Belltether, apparently right before he was shot to death in his hotel room two years before. With a landslide of ever-breaking news to cover, the AmeriNews staff sat on the article. But then, when Coliquin was elected secretary-general of the United Nations, his nasty background suddenly became newsworthy.

Now, as Abigail poured over her copy of the dead journalist's notes and his draft article, and the photo, it all came back to her. She realized that the contents of the reporter's file had become important in ways she could not have imagined.

Just then, Deborah, who was in New York for the weekend, swung open the front door of the penthouse and announced herself. She strode into the room with Cal. She was slurping a huge plastic cup of soda.

"Well, howdy," Abigail called out, perking up a little. "How was the movie?"

"Pretty good," Cal said.

"Average," Deborah said, then added, "I'm jumping into the shower. I feel grubby."

Cal dumped himself down on the couch and looked at his mother hunched over the Belltether file.

"Homework?"

"Always."

"Dad's case?"

"In a way."

"That's a shocker!" Cal said sarcastically and gave a bright smile.

Abigail chuckled and set the file on the coffee table. "This might be tangentially related. It's the investigative report by Curtis Belltether."

Cal thought for a moment. "The reporter we talked about at the Roundtable meeting … the one who was murdered?"

"Yep." Abigail nodded.

Cal studied his mother's face. She wasn't doing a good job of hiding her feelings. "Okay, Mom, what's up?" he asked.

She motioned to the file. "When I met with Senator Hewbright in Denver, something triggered a suspicion. So I did some digging on my computer when I got back to Hawk's Nest that night. Then I had even more suspicions. And then this. For me it was confirmation." She turned on the couch so she could look straight at Cal. "Every once in awhile in life you stumble across something, and once you see it, you can't get it out of your head. Something bad. Evil perhaps. And you know that once you see it, you can't just sit by like a passive observer, as if you're in a theater watching a movie. You have to do something. You have to take action."

"You've completely lost me ..."

"Senator Hewbright," Abigail said. "He's a good man. This country needs him as president. We discussed all this during the Roundtable."

"Right."

She chose her words cautiously. "I think he's in deep trouble."

"As in ..."

"Personal danger."

Cal thought for a few seconds. Then something registered on his face, and he quickly pulled out his Allfone. "Don't know if this has anything to do with it, but saw this blurb on AmeriNews."

"I confess," Abigail said, "I've been so busy I haven't had time to read it recently."

"I got you covered, Mom." Cal tabbed through the recent news releases until he found the article. He handed the device to his mother. "Here it is. Story out of Wichita. The head of Hewbright's campaign for that city was found dead. It's pretty clear it was murder."

"What is going on here? Two politically related murders. Things are definitely not right." Abigail read the article. When she was done, she turned to her son. "Cal, we need to get hold of John Gallagher. Immediately."

NINETEEN

Casper, Wyoming

John Gallagher was seated in a small roadside diner, reading the plastic menu. He knew what he really wanted to eat — blueberry pancakes slathered with real butter and real maple syrup, a large side of hash browns, a side of sausage links and bacon, and a breakfast steak, cowboy style.

But alas, that was pure fantasy. He was watching his weight. The waitress finished waiting on several fellows in jeans and cowboy hats, then sauntered over to Gallagher. "What's yer desire, darlin' — breakfast or early lunch?"

"My desire, darlin'," Gallagher cracked, "is a breakfast big enough to choke a horse. And this looks like the kind of place that could accommodate me. But instead, I'll take coffee, black, no sugar, and an English muffin, no butter, and sugar-free strawberry jam."

She jotted it down and threw him a smile. "Live long and prosper, city slicker."

Gallagher leaned toward the plate-glass window and took in the view of the North Platte River and the mountains in the distance. A moment later, the person he was scheduled to meet was standing next to the table.

FBI Agent Ben Boling reached down and shook Gallagher's hand.

"Sit down. I'll buy you some coffee and breakfast," Gallagher said.

Boling sat but shook his head. "Thanks, but I'm all caffeined up and had something to eat already."

"Not surprising. You strike me as an early riser, Boling."

"And you strike me as a nonriser."

Gallagher guffawed. "Gee, didn't think you knew me that well."

"Your reputation precedes you. So, how have you been since leaving the Bureau?"

"Well, how do you think I look?" he said, stretching his arms out to exhibit his slimmer torso.

"Honestly, Gallagher, I can't remember how you used to look. Remember, I didn't work counterterrorism with you guys in New York. I've always done the mundane stuff—kidnapping over state lines, murder, mayhem. A little fraud on the side."

"Well," Gallagher said, "I wouldn't call that mundane. Your investigation into the death of Perry Tedrich, Senator Hewbright's Wichita campaign manager, sounds an itsy-bitsy bit exciting."

"So, that's what this meeting is about?"

"Bingo. I'm doing some checking, a favor for some friends, people who care about Hewbright's health and personal safety."

"Like the FBI doesn't?"

"I didn't say that."

"So, let me guess. You're here at the behest of that bunch of gun-twirling vigilantes known as the Roundtable?"

"Ben, they're good people who've been given a bad rap."

"All I know is what I read in the Bureau's 302 reports."

"And you believe those?"

"Gallagher, I know you had a reputation as a maverick, bucking the system, pushing the boundaries. But don't expect me to trash the Bureau."

"'Course not. You got a kid in college and another in grad school. Rocking the boat doesn't make sense for you. You see, I've done my homework too."

"I'd be very careful. I could stand up and walk out of this place."

"I know you could, but I don't think you will."

"Why not?"

"Because as special agents go nowadays, you're one of the good ones. Staying on even though you're hamstrung by Tulrude's insane rules and restrictions. And even with Attorney General Hamburg turning the Bureau into a politically correct day camp, you've managed to stick it out and still do your job well—which makes us different."

"Oh?"

"Yeah. Because I was never smart enough to figure out how to do that. So I just left. But then again, for me it was time."

The waitress came with Gallagher's English muffin. When she left, Boling gestured to Gallagher's skimpy breakfast. "Pretty Spartan."

"My doc says I need to change my nutritional habits if I want to stay around for a while, which I definitely do. I've got some unfinished business."

"Like?"

"Helping you catch the person who's stalking Senator Hewbright right now ... and planning his death."

"You talk like that, and it makes my heart go all pitta-pat, makes me want to whip out my little pocket pad and start taking notes. After Miranda-izing you first, of course, seeing as you just inferred a threat against a candidate for the presidency of the United States."

"But you're not going to."

Ben Boling leaned back in the booth. "No, I'm not. Instead, I'm going to ask you what you know, and where you got the information."

"What I know is that there may be a risk to Hewbright from within his own campaign. And I got the tip from Abigail Jordan."

"Ohhh ...," Boling said, rolling his eyes. Then he added, sarcastically, "At least you've got a source that isn't controversial."

"She's top notch. Controversy doesn't mean she doesn't have credibility. I can't tell you details yet, but she has some strong suspicions, and I think she may be right on target. So the question is—do you want to save the senator?" Gallagher raised a toasted English muffin, shook his head with a sorrowful look as he examined it, and took a large bite.

Boling leaned forward and folded his hands on the table. "Okay. I need to trust you here. Which is probably my first mistake."

Instead of giving another smart-aleck zinger, Gallagher just listened as Boling continued.

"You probably figured out why I'm up here in Casper, Gallagher. Hewbright's Senate seat is from Wyoming. His local office is here in Casper. So I'm doing the obvious."

Gallagher offered his take on that. "Obvious as in, scrounging for leads among the locals from Hewbright's stomping ground. And as in, questioning Hewbright's local office for details on the campaign worker killed in Wichita?"

Boling smiled.

"Any leads?" Gallagher asked.

"Not yet. And if I had any, I couldn't tell you the gritty details. You're a civilian now, Gallagher. Sorry."

"And of course," Gallagher said nonchalantly, "you checked the records for the visitors to the Wichita campaign office where the victim worked. To see who, from Hewbright's circle of confidants, may have visited there shortly before Tedrich's disappearance?"

"Did you even consider the fact," Boling shot back, "that the murder may have been purely random — with no political connection to Hewbright's campaign at all?"

"Could be," Gallagher replied, "but I'd still check it out, people in — people out."

"Don't worry. The local police are already doing the spadework."

"I'd check it yourself. Real close. Find out who from Hewbright's national staff may have visited Tedrich unofficially right before he vanished."

Boling squinted. "I just might do that." Then he added, "So, Gallagher, I just have one question."

"Yeah?"

"What's Abigail Jordan's interest in all this?"

"Seems clear enough to me," Gallagher said with a shrug as he popped the rest of the English muffin into his mouth. When he was done and his mouth was empty, he wiped it with a napkin and then finished his thought.

"She wants to save America."

TWENTY

As she sat with her mother in the family's New York penthouse, Deborah Jordan felt particularly low. She had just realized that she was like her father in one way — she too could bury her hurt and pretend it wasn't there. But only for a while. Eventually it would come bubbling out. Like now.

Deborah had to admit her mother was right. "Okay. Sure. At the time, yes, I was devastated."

"I know you were, dear," Abigail said, "but what about now? How do you feel about Ethan?"

"I know it was the right thing to do," Deborah said. She was pensive but sure she was right. Outside, the night had fallen and the lights of the New York City skyline outlined the skyscrapers, as if they were studded with tiny blinking jewels.

Deborah rested her foot on her overnight bag, which was already packed on the floor in front of her. "I like Ethan," she said. "He's a good man ... just not the one for me. Since we broke up I've been absolutely convinced of that. But I owe him some contact. I want to find out how he's doing."

There was a flicker of a smile in the corner of Abigail's mouth. "Oh, he's probably been dragged into a world of trouble, considering that your father's his boss now ...."

Both of them burst into laughter.

Deborah reached out and rubbed her mother's hand. "You really miss Dad, don't you?"

"Honey, I ache for Josh. I know the Lord is allowing this for some reason. But it does hurt being away from him."

"I miss him too," Deborah said. "My constant prayer is that all of us — you, Dad, Cal, and I — can have a grand reunion sometime. Very soon, I hope."

"I feel in my heart it's going to happen. You may be too young to think this way — but I also feel this wonderful peace — about all of us being together with the Lord. Heaven is going to be the ultimate reunion."

"Lately you and Dad seem to be talking end-times stuff constantly. It's pretty clear you think things are rushing toward the last days, don't you?"

"I know some of the media coverage makes us look like we're running around crying that the sky is falling. But when God lays it out in the Bible, and you see the pattern of world events converging — lining up the way that Scripture describes — I think it would be wrong to keep quiet about it."

Deborah tapped the back of her mother's hand with her finger. "This," Deborah said, "is going to be a problem for you, Mom. I'm hearing all kinds of stuff at the Pentagon about how the feds are going after nontaggers. That's what they are calling you people who didn't get the BIDTag. On the other hand, there's something else … maybe good news."

"What's that?"

"There's this guy, Tom Birdow, he works at DISA, the defense information agency. He's always stopping by my desk — "

"My daughter, the man magnet!"

Deborah tried not to smile but found it impossible. "Oh, you are such a mom …"

"Alright, so this Tom guy …"

"Yeah, he's always dropping tidbits of information about what's happening with the Security Identification Agency and Homeland Security regarding the BIDTag. Right before I came up here, he mentioned a possible amnesty program for nontaggers. President Tulrude shot it down, but Tom heard it may come up again."

Abigail smiled and looked out at the black sky and the twinkling lights of the city. "Don't worry about that, darling," she said to her daughter. "I won't be getting a BIDTag. That's all there is to it."

Deborah's eyes flashed like she wanted to pursue it, but instead, she switched to something else. "What were you and Cal talking about earlier — after we got home from the movie?"

"About some concerns of mine, about Senator Hewbright's campaign and the senator himself."

"Concerns ... like what?"

Abigail leaned over and pulled her daughter close. "My dear, have I told you lately how proud I am of your position at the Pentagon?"

Deborah rolled her eyes and smiled. "Nice dodge, Mom."

"No, not dodging. The fact is that you work in the Department of Defense. Given that, I have to be careful about the things I can share with you."

"Come on ..."

"I'm serious. I don't want to put you in a compromising position because of information you learn from me. You know, about the Roundtable. Things like that."

"So — you're shutting me out?"

"No. I'm protecting you."

"I still think that's a lame excuse, pardon my bluntness."

"Once in a while you remind me so much of your dad. Blunt is okay. Sometimes."

Abigail looked down at Deborah's overnight bag on the floor. "I'm sorry to see you leave, but you'd better get going so you can catch your cab to the station. The zip train isn't going to wait."

As Deborah stood up and gave her mother a long hug, Abigail whispered in her ear, "Who knows, dear, how God might use your position at the Pentagon."

Los Angeles, California

The banquet hall was filled with fourteen hundred campaign contributors, who had all given at least $20,000 apiece. In the soft glow of the crystal chandeliers that hung from the ceiling, President Tulrude was wrapping up her address to her party faithful.

The waitstaff hurried the plates from the table, careful not to intrude on the president's address. In the back of the room, one of the smiling waiters had his Allfone turned on video function and was holding it discreetly under a towel with the lens pointing at the president.

"And no one can deny," she said, "my impressive record on national security. Since my succession to the White House and the implementation of my BIDTag program, not a single act of terrorism has been perpetrated against this great nation. When I took over, we had domestic airplanes being shot at and a nuclear nightmare in New Jersey. Today we are safer than we have ever been. Terrorists like Anwar al-Madrassa and his ilk are on the run, hiding in their caves. We have them stymied because they cannot sneak their operatives across our borders. They can't have their thugs show up at airports, malls, public buildings, sports stadiums, or train stations — because if they do, our BIDTag scanners will pick them up. If they have been tagged, then we have access to their data. And if they haven't been tagged, our nation-wide scanners in every public place will alert us — so either way, in a heartbeat, we've got them!"

That provoked a standing ovation. It lasted a full minute. When the crowd finally returned to their seats, Tulrude continued, "We have answered the pundits who said my program wouldn't work. We have responded to the civil-liberties advocates — I know many of them personally and respect them — and the courts have upheld the constitutionality of my identification program. As for the fanatics who wail and moan about my bringing about the end of the world, wondering whether I have a 666 on my forehead ..." The room erupted in raucous laughter. "As for them," she continued, "if they say I'm the devil, well, then I say to hell with them!"

Gleefully, the audience rose again to their feet, laughing, shouting, and applauding wildly.

Islamabad, Pakistan

In a sparsely furnished apartment off Ibn-e Sina Road, the reigning terror king, Anwar al-Madrassa, was holding court. His three deputies sat on the floor in front of him. Madrassa was lounging on a worn couch next to a tea table, on which stood a tarnished brass hookah. The screen on Madrassa's personal laptop was illuminated. They had just finished watching a video on YouTube.

Madrassa smiled beneficently. "So, you all paid close attention to President Tulrude's remarks?"

The deputies on the floor nodded in unison.

"And what did you notice?"

One lieutenant offered a thought. "She is arrogant."

"Of course, of course," Madrassa said, brushing it off. "She is an American infidel."

Smiles and chuckles from the men on the floor.

Another deputy shouted out. "She is very proud of her BIDTag program."

"Ah, yes," Madrassa said, nodding, "boasting that there have been no attacks on her homeland since it began. What she does not know is that we take our time. And now, my beloved friends, that time has come."

He reached down to his laptop and tapped a corner of the screen, then waved his finger over the menu until two photographs appeared. Under each was a name in Arabic.

Madrassa explained, "I have been in touch with certain intermediaries. They, in turn, have been in contact with the highest political powers. You see? From this humble little apartment, Allah be praised, our influence has now reached all the way up to the meeting places of world leaders. By using their blind assistance, we will begin to mount our most dramatic campaign of all. The first stage is ready to begin. Would you like to see for yourselves who will be the first targets of our fiery retribution?"

The eyes of the men on the floor flashed.

Anwar al-Madrassa turned the screen so they could examine the faces. "Two infidel enemies of our most holy jihad have set themselves against us … but not for long."

On the screen was a photo of a man and of a woman. Under the pictures were names.

Joshua Jordan. Abigail Jordan.

TWENTY-ONE

Haifa, Israel

From his position high on the exterior metal safety walkway of Israel's new energy facility, Joshua had a spectacular view of Haifa Bay and the azure waters of the Mediterranean. He could see flames shooting up from Israel's oil and gas platforms off the coast and the large blades of wind turbines that had been constructed along the shoreline.

His guide, Joel Harmon, one of Israel's rising political stars, had connected with Joshua a few days earlier. He had invited Joshua to join him on a tour of the Haifa energy reprocessing plant today. It was under tight security, but Harmon, with his credentials, was able to whisk his guest through the double gates guarded by armed security and onto the grounds of the facility without a problem.

Harmon nodded to the display of energy infrastructure that stretched out along the coast. "Israel has been blessed with energy resources and the advanced technology to develop them. But what I am about to show you now is the most startling resource of all. No one saw this one coming. Of course, when we were able to turn back that incoming nuke from Iran with your RTS system and it dropped on the Golan Heights for lack of fuel, we all had the same thought — to retrieve the thing before our enemies got their hands on it. Which we did. But then there was a second thought — get the nuclear material, the uranium and plutonium, out of the warhead. As you know, under Prime Minister Bensky we've been tied into treaties that prohibit us

136

from developing defensive nuclear weapons. So, forget the military uses of the material."

"So you're using it for nuclear energy."

"Exactly," Harmon replied. He was pumped now, and Joshua saw it in his face. "As the newest member of the energy committee for the Knesset, I was all over that one. But this," Harmon said, pointing to the metal door next to them on the fourth-story entrance to the massive building, "this was the crème de la crème." He swung open the heavy door.

Inside, Joshua found himself on a metal catwalk several stories above the energy-processing operation. Below he could see a truck dumping a load onto a platform, with another right behind it in line.

Harmon explained, "When the invaders came at us two years ago, led by the Russian army, they were all using the hardware developed by Moscow. Very ingenious. Israel's military radar is usually very effective, but the Russians built troop carriers and missile launchers, even tanks, not out of metal — but with lignostone."

"Right," Joshua added, "super-compressed wood. I've followed the research for years. In fact, I personally saw a handgun made out of it back in Seoul ... at an uncomfortably close range. Impressive stuff."

"You bet. Hard as steel but easy to cloak from radar because the material absorbs the radar pulse rather than reflecting it back like metal does. That gave our enemies a considerable advantage when they placed their troops near our borders. The couple extra hours of antiradar cloaking gave them a huge head start." Harmon pointed to the truck down below. "After the war, when the dust cleared, we discovered we had our hands on massive amounts of lignostone. Tons and tons of it. The bright guys at the Technion Institute and several energy companies got to thinking — why not convert all this lignostone to combustible fuel?"

They walked along the catwalk, watching a load of scrap material being fed onto a conveyor belt that was moving it toward several grinding stations and then on to series of low-temperature furnaces. Joshua was already thinking about the remarkable fulfillment of a centuries-old biblical prophecy.

"The key here," Harmon said, "was to create a usable material that can fuel Israel's energy needs. So, how long do you think all of these lignostone armaments will provide energy for Israel?"

Joshua laughed. "Let me guess — seven years' worth of burnable energy, precisely. Exactly as predicted in the book of Ezekiel ..."

"Chapter 39, verses 9 and 10," Harmon added with a grin. "So, as I was saying, we've been burning this material for the last two years at this new facility and processing it into reusable energy cells. According to the Old Testament, we've got another five years of home heating left for Israel. Josh, you are a Christian, and I am a Jew. We have that between us. But we are joined by something important. We both revere the Bible as the Word of God."

"Yes, and something else."

"Oh?"

"We both believe in the Messiah and know that He's coming," Joshua said. "I know His name to be Yeshua — Jesus, the Christ. You, on the other hand, still have to figure out whether your Messiah's coming to this world will be His first time or His second."

Harmon chuckled and waved an index finger at Joshua. "A discussion to be continued later."

They walked down the metal stairs to the third level, where Joel Harmon led them to an elevator to the ground floor.

"The helicopter is waiting on the helipad," Harmon said as they walked outside. "Since you're an MIT grad and a world-class engineer, I figured you'd appreciate a tour of our facility here. Also, you're getting a peek at some good news about Israel's future."

Joshua thanked him as they rounded the corner of the massive building.

Harmon suddenly became somber. "Now for the tough part about our future. When you arrive in Jerusalem and meet with Prime Minister Benksy, you will find him surrounded by vipers."

"That's a pretty harsh assessment."

"I'm being frank. Bensky's a good man, but he's living under a geopolitical delusion, as if he's been bewitched by advisors who have sold him on this crazy plan of the U.N.'s secretary-general."

"I already have strong feelings about Coliquin."

"Sure," Harmon said shrugging, "I read the quote in the *Jerusalem Herald* where you called Coliquin 'an impressive voice full of reason, hope, and peace, but with an agenda straight from hell.' And you call *me* harsh!" Joel Harmon capped it off with a snicker.

Joshua gave him a befuddled look. "Joel, that's why I questioned your decision to have me join you and the members of your Hamonah party when you meet with Bensky this afternoon. I'm nothing but a lightning rod."

"So maybe we need a lightning strike." After a moment, Harmon added, "Look, Josh, whether you like it or not, when your RTS system saved Israel from that Iranian nuke attack the year before last, you became a hero to a lot of Israelis."

Joshua shook his head. "Not all Israelis . . ."

"Okay, true," Harmon shot back, grinning, "but you've read the Old Testament . . . our wandering in the desert under Moses . . . arguing, squabbling. Since when have Israelis ever been able to agree on much of anything?"

Joshua chuckled. "Seriously, Joel. I think you need someone else to plead your position to Bensky. Not me. This is when I wish I could substitute my wife, a brilliant lawyer with terrific negotiation skills. But not me. I've never been strong on diplomacy. If I open my mouth, I'll be a bull in a china shop."

Harmon halted and lifted his index finger into the air. "We need a real hero like you, who loves Israel, who has already helped to defend her." Then, after pausing and lowering his hand, he added, "And a man who has connections . . ."

"What kind?"

"Let's be honest, if Tulrude wins your presidential election, Israel will be in serious trouble. Tulrude has abandoned all support for our nation. On the other hand, if Hewbright wins, our future looks a lot brighter. When Hewbright was in the United States Senate he consistently backed Israel on security and terrorism issues. And we happen to know, Josh, that you, your wife, and your entire Roundtable group are backing Senator Hewbright. And we also know that the senator admires you."

"And here I thought I knew something about clandestine surveillance," Joshua remarked. "You Israelis always impress me with the accuracy of your covert intelligence."

By now the helicopter was in view. As the two men approached it, Joshua still didn't feel any differently about the upcoming meeting with the prime minister.

He said a silent prayer.

God, help me keep my feet on the ground during this meeting . . . and my foot out of my mouth.

Office of the Prime Minister of Israel, Jerusalem

The meeting lasted over an hour. Some heated words were exchanged, but Harmon and the three other members of the Hamonah Party kept the rancor to a minimum. Prime Minister Bensky listened throughout but talked little. He left that up to his two advisors, Chad Zadok, his chief of staff, and Dimi Eliud, his press secretary.

Near the end of the meeting Zadok looked up from his digital clipboard and said, "The prime minister appreciates your thoughts on the U.N. peace proposal. Thanks for dialoguing with us. However, the prime minister has another meeting."

Joel Harmon leaned forward in his chair, his hands open, as if he was going to grab someone by the shoulders. "Please, Mr. Prime Minister, can you at least share with us that you are open to our concerns, that you are willing to delay this dangerous deal with Mr. Coliquin and his envoy?"

"Why?" Zadok shot back, "so you and your fledgling little Hamonah Party can have more time to muster coalition strength behind your weak position?"

"This treaty with Coliquin and the U.N. is bad for Israel. Some truths are self-evident," Harmon said, shooting a quick glance at Joshua.

Now Dimi Eliud jumped into the fray. "Quoting from America's Declaration of Independence isn't the right answer for an Israeli problem." Then she directed her attention to Joshua, who had been silent. "Or does Colonel Jordan think differently?"

Joshua smiled but didn't bite.

Chad Zadok joined in. "Yes, why don't you share your thoughts with us, Colonel Jordan?"

Joshua's smile quickly evaporated. Instead of answering, he looked at Prime Minister Sol Bensky, who gestured for him to speak.

"I would rather not," he said, hedging.

"And I would rather you did," Bensky said in a soft voice. "I have heard many things about you, Colonel Jordan. Some good and some not so nice. So please speak freely. What do you think about this peace proposal? About Secretary-General Coliquin?"

"I tremble," Joshua began.

Chad Zadok latched onto that. "You what?"

"I said I tremble."

"You? The great Colonel Joshua Jordan, trembling with fear?" There was derision in Zadok's voice.

"I tremble," Joshua continued, "because of what I have read."

"About what?" Bensky asked.

"I have studied the Bible for the last two years," Joshua replied. "I am no scholar, but I tremble at what it says in 1 Kings 11:1."

Benksy's face looked as if he were searching his memory, but coming up blank.

Joshua quoted the verse from the Old Testament. "'Solomon, however, loved many foreign women — '"

"How dare you!" Zadok cried out.

"Mr. Prime Minister," Joshua said, disregarding the chief of staff, "adultery can come in many different forms, don't you agree? I know you must see that God has warned Israel throughout Scripture about entering into political treaties and intrigues with foreign powers — political adultery — when it can cause the nation to depart from God's purposes."

Dimi Eliud jumped to her feet. "Gentlemen, this meeting is *over.*"

Sol Bensky said nothing. He sat motionless in his high-backed chair, glumly staring straight ahead, as Joshua, Joel Harmon, and his small entourage tentatively rose to leave. Then the group was briskly escorted from the room. Zadok and Eliud closed the door and quickly returned to their chairs across from the prime minister.

Zadok led off. "Now you see, sir, exactly what we are dealing with.

Joshua Jordan is the foreign enemy here. He is the agitator. And our young, impressionable member of the Knesset, Joel Harmon, has been taken with Jordan's radical views."

"You still have a strong coalition in the Knesset behind you," Dimi Eliud added, "for a while. We don't know how long that will hold. The treaty with the U.N. must be signed immediately."

"And," Zadok added, "Colonel Jordan must also be neutralized before he wins any more converts to his anti-Coliquin views. Sadly, he does have a certain influence among some Israelis."

"But he is a defender of Israel," Bensky said limply, "and I for one appreciate the RTS technology he designed … and for his zeal for our nation. This is so difficult." Bensky put a hand to his forehead and rubbed it slowly.

"Of course, Mr. Prime Minister," Zadok said in a voice that was soothing, almost musical, like chimes in the wind, "we understand. That is why you must allow us — Ms. Eliud and myself — to take care of this Colonel Jordan business. You needn't worry about it anymore."

"Yes," Dimi Eliud added, "Joshua Jordan can be taken out of the equation. And very quickly."

Eliud and Zadok locked glances. Without a word, all three knew what had to be done.

TWENTY-TWO

Washington, D.C.

When Abigail received the text message, it was a jolt. It was from former Department of Justice Prosecutor Harley Collingwood. His text simply said "Meet me at Jefferson Memorial" and gave the time.

So once again Abigail chartered the family's private jet from the hangar at JFK and flew down to Washington. And once again, Cal went along for the ride. Abigail had been so absorbed in trying to dig up further information on the potential threat against Senator Hewbright that she had been able, for a few hours at least, to put her husband's excruciating legal dilemma out of her mind. But not entirely. She couldn't forget that Collingwood's inside information about the activities of the prosecutors in Attorney General Hamburg's Department of Justice office might be her only hope. Collingwood might know how they had managed to get Attorney Alan Fulsin to spin his false story about Joshua's alleged plan to create a takeover of the defense and security apparatus of the U.S. government.

Abigail and Cal had just landed at the private hangar at Reagan International, and she was about to step into the limo when she said to Cal, "So, you'll be all right?"

He nodded with a smile. "Mom, I'm old enough to take care of myself. Don't worry."

"What are you going to do?"

He shrugged. "I'll fill you in later. I'll be okay. Really."

She hesitated. "Something's going on. Anything you want to share?"

"Mom, get to your meeting. You're going to be late."

Ignoring her maternal instincts, Abigail ducked into the backseat. The driver closed the door and hopped behind the wheel.

After ten minutes of heavy traffic along the Potomac, Abigail's Allfone lit up. It was John Gallagher. When she answered, he gave her the update on his Hewbright investigation. "Okay, Abby. Here's the dope. I've been in contact with the FBI agent, as you know."

"Right. Agent Boling."

"We've been talking. I got him to open up. No small miracle, by the way. It turns out that shortly before the disappearance of this Hewbright campaign worker, this Perry Tedrich guy, he had a visit from someone on Hewbright's national campaign staff."

"And?"

"Hewbright's assistant campaign manager. Woman by the name of—"

"Katrena Amid."

"Abby, you take all the fun out. Right. That's her. You know her?"

"Just met her once. In Denver, after one of the Senator's speeches." Abigail didn't yet elaborate about the sixth sense she had around Katrena. After reflecting a moment, Abigail followed up. "But you're sure it was her—Katrena Amid—who visited Perry Tedrich right before he disappeared?"

"Sure I'm sure. Why?"

Abigail didn't respond.

Gallagher went on. "You know, Abby, you never told me why you thought that Hewbright might have some kind of mole or dirty operative within his staff. Wanna share that with your good buddy John Gallagher?"

"Not yet, John."

"Any reason?"

"I don't want my ideas to color your investigation."

"Wow. Now you're sounding like my old supervisor at the Bureau. Always went by the book."

"It's just that I have such a high regard for your ability, John. I need your untainted impressions. All of this could be just a wild-eyed theory. Maybe I've got you chasing a fantasy."

"On the other hand, one thing is not fiction."

"What's that?"

"Hewbright's Wichita election guy was murdered and dumped in a shallow grave. Nothing make-believe about that."

Bethesda Convalescent Center

On his second visit, Cal could see a remarkable change. Former President Corland was sitting up straight, his eyes bright and clear, and his speech — while still slow — was intelligible and coherent. When Cal arrived, Corland's wife had told Cal that her husband was having "one of his better days." Then she headed down to the cafeteria, leaving Cal and Corland alone with a nurse nearby.

Corland asked Cal, in a series of strained words, about his plans for the future.

"Law school," Cal said.

Corland smiled and nodded. "Following your mother ..."

"Sort of. Though she never pressured me. I was going into art at first. Actually had some of my paintings shown in a gallery up in Boston. But things changed, and I decided to go in another direction."

"Happens sometimes," Corland said and then nodded to the nurse to leave them alone. She smiled and dutifully left that area of the day room.

He noticed that Corland followed her with his eyes too. Now the only person in sight was a Secret Service agent seated on a chair just outside the room, out of earshot.

Corland immediately opened up. "I wanted you here ... to tell you ..."

"What?"

"Secrets."

Cal didn't know how to respond.

"Can I trust you?" Corland said.

"Yes. Absolutely. But why me?"

"I trusted your dad. And he was right about what he told me in the

White House. About threatened attack. But my people wouldn't listen. They undercut me. Nuclear attack ... New Jersey ... never would have happened ... if they had believed your father. I'm glad his Roundtable ... tried to help. At least New York was saved. I wish your Dad was here for me to tell this to ..." Corland stopped. Then after thinking something through, he continued. "But he's not."

"No," Cal said with emotion in his voice that had suddenly arisen and surprised even him. He struggled to say it. "I wish he was here too."

"So," Corland said with a smile, "I have to trust someone. I'll tell you then. Trust you. Maybe you ... are like your dad?"

Cal smiled. It was an accolade he didn't think he had earned, but he nodded and leaned back in the soft chair in the sunroom to listen.

Corland proceeded to explain about his White House physician having health problems himself, and how his personal doctor had to resign. President Corland had been treated for his condition of transient ischemic attack, a syndrome that threatened his ability to continue in his duties if not kept under control. The public had not been told about it up to then. When Corland's own White House physician left, Jessica Tulrude insisted that until a new White House doctor was appointed, Corland ought to use the vice president's personal physician — Dr. Jack Puttner. Up to that point, Corland pointed out to Cal, his own doctor had prescribed only blood thinners to decrease the risk of blackouts.

"But Puttner gave me something else," Corland said, "and right after that ... after a speech in Virginia, I had that terrible attack in the limo. Almost died."

"What kind of medicine?"

"Not sure," Corland said. Then his face took on an intense, twisted grimace. "But I think ... Dr. Puttner and Tulrude ... tried to kill me."

TWENTY-THREE

"The idea was easy to understand. Elegant in its simplicity. Joshua Jordan was a domestic terrorist."

Former federal prosecutor Harley Collingwood spoke matter-of-factly as he stood on the bottom steps of the Jefferson Memorial. The crowd was sparse that day. Even so, he kept his voice low.

He continued, "I looked over all the evidence we had to support that theory of the case against your husband. I was given the file by the DOJ lawyer supervising the whole case — not just the charges against Joshua, but those against you and all the members of the Roundtable. That attorney was Assistant Attorney General Dillon Gowers. So I read it all through. Several times. The theory was that when your Roundtable group hired those ex-special-ops guys to stop the portable nuke from entering New York City, that was a powerful piece of evidence we could use to convince a jury that you were running a private vigilante force, bent on usurping the United States Government. Sure, you intercepted the truck and kept it out of New York. But your special-ops volunteers paid a dear price when the terrorists detonated it along the New Jersey shore. And so did the thousands of people in the nearby town who died in the blast. It was just blind luck that the heavy winds blew the radioactive cloud out to sea and more people didn't die."

Abigail interjected, "Harley, we tried to warn the federal authorities through multiple avenues about the nuke. Our private intelligence sources told us the bomb was bound for New York, and we told the government that. But they did nothing."

"Sure, we knew you'd probably assert a Good Samaritan defense. On the other hand, as I viewed the case, I felt we could overcome that defense, but it required one important piece that was still missing."

Abigail put her finger on it. "Attorney Allen Fulsin."

"Right. Of course, we had Fulsin in our corner already, but the stuff he gave us in the FBI 302 reports — that Joshua was talking about revolution and all that — could all be explained away logically. It was clear Joshua was talking politics and social change, not armed uprising. So I told Assistant Attorney General Gowers — I said, 'Look, you need something stronger from Fulsin, if that's possible, or you'd better contemplate ditching this case.' A week later, he sent me an email. In the attachment was a second statement from Fulsin, and what Fulsin alleged in this new witness statement was incredibly powerful. He claimed Joshua had said it was time for an armed militia to arm-wrestle our national defense out of the hands of the Defense Department — by force if necessary — and that he was creating his own private army. But as I looked at Fulsin's second statement I noticed it was not an FBI 302. It was a supplemental statement from Fulsin, which had been transcribed directly by Gowers himself during his own interrogation — with no other witnesses present. That's when I got suspicious."

A couple of joggers appeared on the walkway along the Potomac, heading their way. Collingwood stepped further up the stairs toward the Jefferson Memorial, and Abigail followed.

"So I started digging around," he continued. "I found out that in the intervening week when the second interrogation took place and his second statement was obtained by Gowers, Fulsin had been threatened with a phony criminal charge of 'human trafficking' by Gowers. Apparently, Fulsin had a girlfriend from Canada living with him who had entered the United States illegally. So Gowers railroaded Fulsin with this ridiculous criminal charge, alleging that Fulsin was running a business of bringing prostitutes into the country. Fulsin got scared. That did the trick."

Abigail scampered up a few more stairs ahead of him, until she was standing over Collingwood and stopped him in his tracks. "So Fulsin was coerced into making up false testimony against Joshua by being threatened with a phony criminal charge himself?"

Collingwood looked visibly uncomfortable. "Look, Fulsin's no saint. He just wanted to get close to the Roundtable so he could spill the beans to Tulrude's staff in hopes of currying favor. They took the information and gave it to Hamburg so it could be used in a prosecution, but Fulsin ended up getting nothing out of the deal."

Abigail shook her head, astonished. "I knew Tulrude's people were corrupt, but I had no idea how corrupt. And Assistant Attorney General Gowers — he was part of this?"

"He as much as admitted to me that after Tulrude became president the gloves were off — no limits — Joshua Jordan was to be destroyed. Your Roundtable and your media outlet, AmeriNews, has made life a nightmare for Tulrude, with all of your investigative reports, starting with her longstanding objections to your husband's RTS system when she was vice president. Then, when President Corland had one of his blackouts and the North Korean ship launched the nukes at New York and the Pentagon utilized the RTS anyway and saved the entire city, Tulrude came out and said that yes, of course she authorized it and tried to take the credit. She even repeated that lie to Congress in the aftermath. AmeriNews was the only source that ran with that story about Tulrude's false statement, and the exposé AmeriNews ran about Tulrude violating the law by directing A.G. Hamburg to launch politically motivated criminal prosecutions. Your husband's, as an example.

"Anyway, Gowers distinctly told me that word had come down from the White House through A.G. Hamburg, starting from day one, that a case had to be made against your husband — at all costs. And then, when you were able to get the case against you and all the other members of the Roundtable dismissed, all except Joshua of course, Tulrude went completely crazy and called Hamburg. She screamed at him to chase Jordan 'to the ends of the earth if necessary — to apprehend and convict him.' That's a direct quote by the way. This has become very personal for President Tulrude."

The Jefferson Memorial was now empty of visitors, so Abigail and Collingwood strode up the steps and into the circular rotunda. Abigail had visited it a few times when she practiced law in Washington many years before. She gazed up at the huge marble panels inside, covered with quotes from Thomas Jefferson, chiseled in stone.

"Harley, you're an experienced prosecutor. You understand what's going to happen now. I will take this information and present it to the U.S. District Court here in Washington, where Josh's case is pending. This is the most shocking example of government misconduct in a criminal case that I've ever heard. This is what I've suspected but couldn't prove — waiting for and praying for — and now it's here at my feet. This could result in Josh's case being dismissed. But I have to ask — what made you come here today to tell me all this?"

Harley Collingwood tilted his head and nodded toward the inscriptions on the wall in front of him. "I was just hired by a great criminal-defense firm here in town, Draeger, Proxy, and Lugot. When they told me two days ago they wanted me not just as an associate, but as a partner, I came over here to the memorial to spend some time mulling it over."

Collingwood pointed to a familiar text inscribed in marble and read it aloud, word-for-word, " 'God who gave us life gave us liberty. Can the liberties of a nation be secure when we have removed a conviction that these liberties are the gift of God? Indeed I tremble for my country when I reflect that God is just, that his justice cannot sleep forever.' " He turned to Abigail. "My conscience wouldn't let me sleep. And these words of my hero, Jefferson, kept haunting me."

"So, because of that," she replied, "you decided to disclose this to me?"

"That," Collingwood said with a half grin, "and also the fact that my new law partners can't stand Jessica Tulrude, and they told me that I had their blessing to blow the lid off of this."

TWENTY-FOUR

Jaffa Street, Jerusalem

Chad Zadok and Dimi Eliud, Prime Minister Bensky's top staffers, arrived at the address in Jerusalem. It was a small, nondescript office with a sign outside that read, in Hebrew, TRAFFIC SAFETY OFFICE. When they entered, they identified themselves to a secretary who then showed them to the back office. Seated at a desk, a solid-looking bald man in a black T-shirt and a tan suit instructed them to close the door and sit down.

Zadok and Eliud were now sitting across from an operations member of Shin Bet — Israel's domestic security service. He called himself Ram, though he never gave his last name.

Ram asked them to confirm the reason for the meeting.

Zadok did the talking. "As I explained on the phone, Prime Minister Bensky wants this. The official at your agency told me to come here."

"If you don't mind my saying, on internal security matters like this, especially where it originates from the PM's office, it usually comes to us from someone in the IDF or in the cabinet — not a chief of staff like yourself."

Zadok wasn't flustered. "No offense taken. This is highly sensitive."

Ram raised an eyebrow, but his face was stone. "Everything I do here is highly sensitive. Tell me something I don't know."

Zadok straightened his legs and crossed them casually. "The prime minister wants this action taken immediately. I have already made the necessary contacts with the requesting nation. This transfer can be made very quickly."

Ram had a thin file on his desk. He opened it just long enough to give it a quick glance. "You have anything personal in all this?"

"No. This is strictly a matter of national security and public safety. At the prime minister's request."

After flipping through a few more pages of the file, Ram looked up. "You realize that the authorization for this — the legal hook — is that you say this guy is suspected of anarchist connections. You understand that?" Zadok smiled easy and nodded. "You swear that the information you gave the intake officer is true and correct, under penalties of law?" Again Zadok nodded, a little more eagerly. "How about you, Ms. Eliud. You agree with all this information?"

She nodded yes, but less enthusiastically.

"Do you have a problem with my executing this order, Ms. Eliud?"

She shook her head no and directed her gaze toward Ram's neck.

"Look at me when I ask you a question, please," Ram said.

"No," Dimi Eliud said, looking him in the face. "No problem."

"Very well," Ram said.

Chad Zadok began to stand up.

"Not so fast," Ram instructed him. "One more thing."

"Oh?"

"I want you two to approach my desk."

They followed his directive.

He twirled the file on his desk around so it was open and facing the two of them. There was a photograph in the file.

"Is this the anarchist you are referring to?"

They examined the photo of Joshua Jordan. They nodded. "Yes, absolutely," Zadok said.

Ram pulled the file back and closed it.

Zadok asked, "How long before Jordan is captured and turned over to the FBI for extradition back to America for trial?"

"When it comes to this office," Ram said, "there are no back burners."

□□□

In the City of David section of the Old City of Jerusalem, Joshua made his way through the buckets and shovels on the ground and ducked under metal scaffolding. He turned to Pastor Peter Campbell, walking next to him. "So, I get the feeling you've brought me here for a reason. And it obviously doesn't involve our favorite sporting rivalry on the links."

Campbell chuckled. "When I left my church in Manhattan to set up shop here in Jerusalem, it was serious business. You know the story, Josh. I'm convinced the return of Christ is imminent. Having been the head of the American Prophecy Council of Pastors, I felt led to relocate to Israel and share the gospel right here at the epicenter of prophetic events. But on the less serious side, yes, I did look for a good golf course in Jerusalem, but there aren't any. Up in Caesarea, yes, but that's a long drive. You and I need to take a day trip up there just to try the course sometime. Maybe I can actually beat you for a change!"

Joshua smiled, tipped his head, and remarked, "You just may do that, my friend. My game hasn't been the same ..."

But he didn't need to finish the sentence. Campbell nodded and said, "Right. Your injuries from Iran."

"On the other hand," Joshua said, "I may have lost my golf handicap, but I sure gained something even better in that hellish jail cell in Tehran."

Campbell patted him on the back. "Josh," he said pointing up ahead, "that's why I think you're really going to appreciate this."

They turned a corner, still underneath the scaffolding, and suddenly Joshua was looking at a set of stone steps that had been uncovered in an archaeological dig. They led straight up to a point where they disappeared into the side of a hill.

"I know the guys involved in this excavation. This is incredible. They tell me that during the time of Christ these very steps led up to a corner of the first century Herodian Temple."

"Okay," Joshua said, "what's the rest of the story?"

"These steps led up to the section of the Temple where the Jews who wanted to make a sacrifice would purchase an animal. That was the area where the trades were made. The place where the tables of the moneychangers were located."

Joshua felt the shiver of recognition run up his spine — a feeling of awe and suspension of time, as if all the world's activity had ceased.

"I get it," Joshua murmured, shaking his head in disbelief. "These are the steps?"

Campbell nodded and pointed to the edges worn down by the feet of countless pilgrims who had made their way to the Temple. "These are the steps that would have been trod by Jesus as He climbed up to the moneychangers' tables, where profit had become king. Up there is where He flipped the tables and declared for all to hear that the house of God should not be turned into a den of thieves."

Even though Joshua knew the gospel account, it took several minutes to sink in. Finally he spoke, "He shook things up, the Lord Jesus, I mean."

"Sometimes dramatically. Sometimes a little more quietly. But one thing about the intersection of Jesus Christ with human history — wherever and whenever He shows up, things are never the same again."

"I can vouch for that," Joshua said, still gazing at the steps. "I've changed. Radically. Supernaturally. I'm not the same man since I received Christ." Then he added with a smile, "Just ask Abby."

Joshua then turned to face Campbell. "I caught your television interview, the one with Bart Kingston, about your ministry here."

"I miss Eternity Church back in New York — but what is going on here is epic. I felt the Lord wanted me here. It's almost too much to comprehend. It is getting so close."

"Peter," Joshua said quietly, "I spoke to you earlier about my meeting with Prime Minister Bensky, about the U.N. proposal, giving Israel a piece of the territory on top of the Temple Mount and the building of a new Jewish temple. You said you'd give me your candid reaction. So ... I'm waiting."

Campbell gazed at the ancient steps once more and explained, "After our Lord comes for His church and raptures us, darkness will fall on the earth. Eventually, the Evil One will be fully revealed. You know the Scripture. It tells us that when that happens, he will enter the temple of the Jews. He will declare himself to be god, and in so doing, will revile and desecrate that place. But all of that requires one thing to happen. Right up there — " Campbell pointed up the stone steps to the high plateau of the Temple Mount — "the rebuilding of the Jewish Temple. And now, from what you've told me, I believe it's about to happen. Oh, how the coming of Jesus Christ for His church must be so very close ..."

TWENTY-FIVE

Chicago, Illinois, McCormick Place Convention Center

A dozen Hewbright campaign staffers were crowded into the green-room adjoining the stage. Their faces revealed a positive tension, a sense of anticipation and excitement. Senator Hewbright was about to deliver a speech on the economy to the convention of small business associations, a speech that would set the tone for his entire campaign. This was his Rubicon moment.

Senator Hewbright was seated in a semicircle of folding chairs, surrounded by his top advisors: national campaign manager, George Caulfield; his assistant, Katrena Amid; his domestic policy advisors, two of whom not only had PhDs in economics but also experience in managing Fortune 500 companies; his foreign policy guru, Winston Garvey; his assistant foreign policy advisor, Zeta Milla, and several others. In the corner was Agent Owens, detailed by the Secret Service to protect the senator.

In another corner, a small portable Internet television was tuned to several news channels in the quadrants of its screen, but the sound had been muted.

"Well, friends," Hewbright led off, looking more relaxed than his staff as he lounged in the folding chair, "any last-minute advice for this old political warhorse before I deliver my five-point plan to save America from financial collapse?"

There were a few nervous chuckles. George Caulfield spoke first. "You'll knock 'em dead, chief."

One of his economic advisors said, "Senator, this plan is wonderfully simple — voters will grasp it immediately — yet keyed to the five most important areas of our failing economy. I think we've got a winner on this." Then he added with a smile, "And not just because I helped draft it ..." A few polite laughs followed.

Caulfield pointed to the door leading to the mammoth convention hall. "We've got media from every news outlet out there. They can't ignore us this time. Your plan to rescue America's financial health is going to be the tipping point. Tulrude's going to have to really scramble after tonight." But as he spoke, the campaign manager pointed to the portable web TV in the corner. "Hey, Tulrude's speech in Omaha is about to begin." He called for someone to turn the sound up. The group turned their chairs around to face the television set.

President Tulrude was mounting the podium to an explosion of applause in the union hall. She made a few comments about her love of Nebraska and cracked a joke about the mayor of Omaha, who was seated on the dais behind her. When the laughter died down she began in earnest.

"I know the press reports indicated that I would be talking about national security tonight, but I have something more important to discuss — the state of our national economy."

George Caulfield whipped around and threw a quick glance to Senator Hewbright, but the candidate looked relaxed, a little amused at the seeming coincidence.

Tulrude continued, "Tonight I am revealing the solution for our national financial tragedy. I inherited this state of affairs when I entered the Oval Office. But no matter — I am here to fix it. I assure you," she said, clasping her hands across her chest as if in prayer, "that my five-point plan to save America's economy will create a new financial renaissance in our nation."

Caulfield thrust an index finger at the television screen and mouthed a word, but nothing came out. Then a look of fury burst over his face.

"Hold on, George," Hewbright said, "give our opponent a chance. We don't know what five points she's talking about."

As Tulrude delivered her version of the first two parts of her plan, it became apparent that they were the same as Hewbright's, as if she had read it verbatim from the confidential Hewbright campaign playbook. Caulfield leaped to his feet, yanked his Allfone out of his pocket, and hit Multiple Quick-dial.

Hewbright was frozen. In an instant, his national campaign-intelligence manager in Detroit and his two assistants in Des Moines were all conferenced in.

Caulfield yelled into his cell. "Tell me how this happened!"

His intel manager in Detroit screamed back. "I'm watching right now. This is outrageous. I have no idea how Tulrude stole our five-point economic speech, but we're going to find out."

After clicking off his Allfone, Caulfield paced the room, waving his arms. "There's a massive security failure in our organization. I'm telling you, there's a strategic leak somewhere. This is criminal."

Hewbright was no longer lounging in his chair. He was straight-backed and leaning forward with his forearms tightly on his thighs, his fists clenched. "No question about it, George."

Katrena Amid was blinking and shrugging her shoulders. "Okay, is this some kind of Watergate break-in? Did someone from Tulrude's outfit break into one of our rooms and get hold of our notes?"

Still stunned, Hewbright could feel the tension mounting.

Zeta Milla laughed coarsely at Amid's comment. "Katrena are you kidding? This is the twenty-first century. Political operatives don't have to do burglary anymore. Wake up—"

"Oh?" Amid shouted back, "then why don't you tell us how they could have done this."

"Everything in politics is driven by new media technology. Even in the so-called Third World countries, geopolitical movements are being formed at the speed of light through Allfone links and insta-news feeds. First in the Middle East and now in South and Central America. By the way, Katrena, that's my area of expertise."

Hewbright's brow was wrinkled. He was riveted to Zeta's every word. "So, what's your theory?"

"If it was up to me," Zeta said softly, "I would have your IT chief check every one of your key media-tech devices, starting with your All-fones. Hank, did you put those five points onto the memo-memory-drive of your Allfone?"

"Yes," Hewbright said, finally breaking his silence, "but it's en-crypted — super secure."

Caulfield hit his Quick-dial again. In a second he had their travel-ing media-tech man on the line. He had been eating a fast-food burger out in the hallway of the convention center. In three minutes he came huffing and puffing into the greenroom, his tie loosened and the re-maining half of his burger in a wrapper in his hand.

In twenty minutes, after working on the senator's Allfone, the IT guy summoned Hewbright and George Caulfield to the corner of the greenroom to talk. Speaking in a terse whisper, he said, "Okay. Sena-tor, I've run through all the programs on your memo-memory-drive, and here's the deal. I'm pretty sure — no, cancel that — I'm absolutely sure that your Allfone's been hacked."

Caulfield looked around the room until he spotted the Secret Ser-vice agent. He said to Hewbright, "Can we bring Agent Owens in on this? I think it's a criminal matter."

Hewbright shook his head. "I don't think so. Secret Service is solely for physical protection. They don't get into criminal investigations of political dirty tricks. That's the FBI's territory."

The IT guy handed Hewbright back his Allfone. The senator looked down at the device. "Well, George," he said to his campaign manager, "we've got an enemy in the camp — and I'm talking very, very close by."

TWENTY-SIX

Mayflower Hotel, Washington, D.C.

Cal had been down in the hotel's fitness room, working out with free weights. Physical conditioning had been one of his regular routines for the last few years. After that he stopped by his hotel room to check his Facebook page on his laptop. A Captain Jimmy Louder was reaching out to him. Cal had to think a minute. Then he remembered. *Oh, yeah, you're the pilot that my dad helped to rescue. You just got the Medal of Honor. Cool. I'm absolutely friending you.*

After Cal finished adding Captain Louder to his Facebook, he ambled over to his mother's room and turned on the Internet TV. After all, of the two televisions in their suite, hers had the bigger screen. Now he was standing in his sweats in front of it. He and Abigail had extended their stay after her meeting with the former federal prosecutor. She asked her former law firm in D.C. if she could use their offices to crank out some quick legal papers on Joshua's case while she was in town, and her former senior partner and sometime personal lawyer, Harry Smythe, was glad to oblige.

Silently, Cal had been struggling with something. After Virgil Corland had shared his suspicions that Tulrude's physician — and probably Tulrude herself — had plotted to sabotage his medical recovery, Cal planned on sharing the information with his mother. But things kept getting in the way. He hadn't told his mother about his meetings with Corland. Up to now Cal didn't think he needed to check in with Abigail before responding to Corland's surprising invitations to meet. But now that a former president was accusing his successor of attempted murder, Cal thought now might be the time to consult with the acting chair of the Roundtable — even if that person was his mother. He also thought he should mention his Facebook contact from Captain Louder.

Just then something jumped off the TV screen. Cal couldn't believe it. "Hey, Mom — look at these pictures. Another earthquake …"

Abigail glanced over. The camera was panning over downtown Minneapolis. Then it focused on a skyscraper — the fifty-seven-story IDS Tower. The tower swayed and shimmied, and the upper floors began to collapse. The video camera caught the very moment when the windows began to shatter, sending a shower of glass onto the street below.

"Can you believe it?" Cal asked. "Earthquakes in Minnesota!"

Abigail's face looked grim, but she was surprisingly unperturbed. "Yes, I can," Abigail said quietly from the wrap-around couch. Her eyes darted back to her Allfone. "I certainly can believe it. We're going to see more of it, Cal. Add it up. We've had three major earthquakes in the U.S. in the last two months."

She reread the text in the little window of her Allfone. There was a tilt to her head, as if it had grown heavy from some invisible burden. Cal glanced away from the TV long enough to notice that. He asked what she was reading. Abigail explained, "First, I've got a copy of the motion papers filed by the Department of Justice, asking the court of appeals to strike the affidavit I just filed with this new evidence of prosecution misconduct in your dad's case — moving the court to disregard it completely. You know, all that information I received from Harley Collingwood."

"That can't be a surprise."

"No, not really," Abigail said. "They're arguing that the information is blocked by attorney-client privilege between Collingwood and his prior employer — the United States government."

"So, is there more?" Cal asked.

"I also just received an instant-memo from the court, an order for a hearing."

"Is there a date for oral argument?"

"Yes. I filed for an expedited hearing, asked that the date for oral argument be moved up as quickly as possible." But there was a look of desperation on her face. "Now I feel pretty foolish. I filed that request yesterday with the court. At the same time I filed the affidavit from Collingwood about the blatant corruption by the attorney general's office."

Something didn't make sense to Cal. "Wait a minute. What's the problem?"

"I didn't think it would come so soon. I thought I would have some time to figure things out."

"Like what?"

"The security entrance at the U.S. Courthouse in Washington. How am I going to get into the building, get past security, to argue the case? I don't have a BIDTag. They'll stop me at the scanner, and I'll be taken into custody. I'll never get into the courtroom."

Now it was starkly clear to Cal. He had been an informal law clerk for the Roundtable while he was waiting to start law school. So his mother had brought him into the inner workings of her wrangling with the first criminal-defense firm that had represented Joshua. Now he saw the handwriting on the wall. He wondered whether his mother regretted having terminated her husband's last set of lawyers. Yes, they had been begging her to talk to Joshua and to pressure him into accepting a plea deal. When Joshua learned about that, he instructed Abigail to dump all of them. But now Cal realized that those lawyers would at least be able to appear before the hearing that was now only three days away.

Cal thought out loud, "Mom, without a BIDTag, you'd have to be a Houdini to appear at the oral arguments yourself, seventy-two hours from now." Cal grimaced. "Wow."

Abigail hit the Quick-dial function on her Allfone and called her husband's previous lawyers. She asked to speak to the partner in the office who had been handling Joshua's case until Abigail had fired him.

She drummed her fingers while she was on hold. She motioned for Cal to conference-in with his own Allfone. He snatched his cell and clicked into the call. After listening to a few more minutes of Muzak, the lawyer picked up. He asked Abigail why she was calling. She explained about the appeals hearing coming up in seventy-two hours. "Things have changed dramatically. I've filed an affidavit from Harley Collingwood, a former member of the prosecution team. This is what we've been looking for. A confession, proving that the attorney general's office coerced false testimony from a key witness."

"And now you want us back on the case?"

Abigail swallowed hard. "That's why I called. I need you to argue it. Oral argument is scheduled in three days. I realize this is extremely short notice, but you're the only ones — besides me — who know the details of this case."

She didn't have to wait long for the answer. "My partners and I half expected something like this, Abby, a last-minute plea to come back in. I just don't think this is going to work."

"You mean you're not willing to make it work ..."

"Something like that." Then the lawyer halfheartedly added, "Why not ask for an extension?"

"I can't. I'm the one who had asked for this hearing to be expedited. Now that they granted it — beyond anything I could have anticipated — I can't retreat. It would make our case look shaky."

"Sorry, Abby. Wish we could help you. But no one in this firm wants to touch your husband's case with a ten-foot pole anymore. It's too messy."

Abigail said good-bye and clicked off her Allfone. She turned to Cal. "I suppose you're going to say, 'I told you so ...'? You and Deb have questioned my decision to not get tagged."

"I know you think it's a biblical stand," Cal said. "Don't you worry that Deb and I did get tagged?"

"I explained it to you. You need it to get into law school and Deborah for her work."

"So, what are you going to do now?"

She shook her head. "Pray and then show up at the courthouse in three days. If I'm blocked from arguing your dad's case, I'll go to jail, I suppose."

Cal stood up straight. He ran his hands through his hair. A thought occurred to him. An all-important magic act was now starting to formulate in his head. "Mom, listen. I've got an idea. First, my mother's *not* going to jail. Neither is my dad — especially for a crime he didn't commit."

Abigail gave a smile that was half pride, half wonderment.

Cal strode toward the door.

"Where are you going?"

"To get my laptop."

"And?"

"I'll tell you when I find what I'm looking for."

At the door, he stopped as one more thought struck him. "Just answer this — are you willing to go all the way on this?"

"Meaning what?" she asked.

He shot back an answer that made sense only to him. "I mean — are you willing to consort with the *underground*?"

TWENTY-SEVEN

The Pentagon

Deborah Jordan stood silently in her cubicle, staring at the document she had just been given. Corporal Tom Birdow was next to her, rocking on his feet and looking up and down the hallway to see if anyone was coming.

Deborah realized she could spend all day looking at this paper, but it wouldn't change a thing. She had known her mother's name would be put on the list of nontaggers, all those who had refused to be BIDTagged, but that alone didn't mean she would be apprehended as a violator. Another step was necessary. Someone high up needed to authorize a specific warrant for her arrest. Deborah had hoped and prayed that step might be delayed — or even overlooked in the morass of government red tape.

But her hopes had now been dashed. The notice read: "ORDER FOR IMMEDIATE SEIZURE — FAILURE TO COMPLY WITH IDENTIFICATION PROCESS — BIDTAG WARRANT LIST."

Now, it seemed, nothing would be able to remove one special name from that warrant list: "Abigail Jordan."

"You realize," Tom said, snatching the paper back from Deborah, "how much trouble I could get into if my boss at DISA or the people at the Security ID Agency found out that I shared this with you."

"Don't worry. Your secret's safe with me."

"Which means ..."

"I won't tell anyone — except my family."

165

Tom shook his head violently. "That's what I mean."

"Put yourself in my position, Tom. Tell me that *you* wouldn't tell your own mother if she were about to be arrested."

Tom tucked the document back into his DISA folder. "Fine. But just remember — you didn't get this information from me." Then he strode off.

□□□

In their downtown Washington hotel suite, Abigail was looking over Cal's shoulder as he pulled up some data on his laptop.

Her phone rang. She checked the caller ID. It was John Gallagher.

"John," she said, "what's up?"

"Got some news on several fronts. First, I encrypted an email to you yesterday on that digging you wanted me to do in the public records in Miami-Dade. You know, on that refugee situation down there from years ago. I think I found what you were looking for. Not sure what that's all about ..."

"I read it late last night," Abigail shot back. "Thanks. When I get a breather, I'll explain. Life has been a whirlwind wrapped in a tornado around here. But a picture is starting to emerge. I've got a person of interest I'm looking at."

"You know, Abby, you're starting to sound more like my old buddies in clandestine services. Vague, intriguing — and smarter than me. Maybe you missed your calling." Abigail chuckled. Then Gallagher gave her the rest of the story. "On the main investigation, the murder of Perry Tedrich, I'm afraid we're at a dead end. I shadowed Ben Boling, the main FBI agent detailed to the Wichita killing, and dropped your hint that maybe it was an inside job. So Ben interviewed Katrena Amid, the only staffer who seems to have visited the victim. But she's got an air-tight alibi. She met with Perry Tedrich all right, but she had left two days before he went missing. She flew out of Wichita while the guy was still very much alive and well." After a pause, Gallagher cleared his throat. "So, Abby, where are we going with this?"

"Actually, that's not bad news at all."

"Oh?"

"No. I never suspected Katrena Amid."

Another pause on the line. "You didn't?" More silence. "Hey, maybe it's time to spell it out for your pal John Gallagher. You know I'm a slow learner."

She laughed. "Okay, maybe it is time."

Just then, the call-waiting lit up on Abigail's Allfone. At the same moment, Cal pointed to something on his laptop. Abigail trotted over and nodded as she read it too. Then she asked Gallagher to hold while she took the other call.

It was Deborah.

"Mom, Debbie here. I'm on a secure line."

"What's wrong? You sound stressed."

"I am. I just saw your name on a list for immediate apprehension as a nontagger. It's just a matter of time before they track you down."

Abigail took a moment to process that.

"Mom, did you hear what I said?"

"Yes, darling. I did. It's just that there's a lot coming at me right now. The Lord is going to have to give me patience, to keep my feet on the ground in the middle of all of this."

"Well, what I'd like the Lord to do is to give you a pair of wings because you need to get out of sight for a while."

"Can't do that."

"You're kidding. Why not?"

"It's complicated. I've got to argue Dad's case in three days ... in the federal court of appeals here in D.C."

"Oh, that's great!" Deborah exclaimed. "You're going to walk into a federal building that's crawling with U.S. marshals and FBI agents. You'll be toast within five minutes."

"Maybe not."

"How's that?" Deborah asked.

Abigail glanced again at Cal's laptop screen to a posting on a blog called *The Underground*. Abigail's reply was cryptic. "Because I may learn a sleight-of-hand trick."

Cal smiled when she said that.

"I still don't understand," Deborah said.

"I'll explain later. Hang on, Deb ..." Abigail clicked back to John Gallagher.

"Okay, John, one question: did you ever check into that health club like I asked? The one Perry Tedrich belonged to?"

"Yeah. I was able to wrangle a look at his records. He worked out at the fitness center early in the morning on the day he disappeared."

"Anyone else check in with him?"

"Nope."

"Bring any female guest to the gym?"

"Nope. Look, Ben checked all this out too ... the member list ... the whole bit. I shadowed his investigation to make sure he didn't drop the ball."

"How about anyone who might have seen him in the workout area?"

"You shoulda' been an agent, Abby," Gallagher cracked. "That'll be my next assignment. Not that I expect anything to break on this. I can smell a cold case a mile away. This may be one of them. Anyway, I'll check the list to see who else was there at that time. After that, I got to fly out of Wichita and get to Northern California. I've got an uncle getting married —" After a moment, Gallagher added — "for the third time. He ought to know better by now. I met his fiancé. I'll just say that three times is definitely not a charm."

"Do me a favor, John," Abigail said. "The minute you find out anything, call me."

"Will do, Señorita."

Then Abigail clicked back to Deborah. "I need to see you right away. Can you come to my room here in the Mayflower Hotel after you leave the Pentagon?"

"Sure."

"One more question. Do you still have some time off coming?"

"Yeah. Why?"

"Is there any way you could take it right away ... like starting tomorrow?"

"Well — I suppose I could put in for it before I leave. I could say 'family emergency,' that sort of thing."

"Exactly," Abigail said. "I couldn't have said it better myself."

TWENTY-EIGHT

"What am I supposed to be looking at?"

Abigail directed her daughter back to the photo. It was laying on the hotel coffee table next to a file of papers. "Look again."

"All right," Deborah replied, "but all I see is a photograph of a guy sitting in a room with his back to the camera."

"What else?"

Deborah raised an eyebrow and tucked up the corner of her mouth. She stared hard at the picture. "Well . . . he's got his hand outstretched to the left, reaching, I guess, for a cup on a saucer on the end table next to his chair. It was shot from the back. Whoever took it was behind him."

"Now, look at the next photo."

Abigail slid another photo out of the file and laid it on the coffee table. After studying it, Deborah said, "Looks like a blow up — magnified several times. It's focused just on the guy's left hand."

"Right," Abigail said, "these were taken by an investigative journalist named Curtis Belltether. He mailed all this to the Roundtable, along with his article, just before he was murdered."

"What are the pictures supposed to prove?"

"The man in the photo is Alexander Coliquin. At that time he was at the end of his tenure as the Romanian ambassador to the United Nations. But he was also the head of a global movement to enforce universal controls over all of the industries of the world."

"The One Movement, right?"

Cal jumped in. "Actually, that's just the religious aspect of it. I've

169

been studying this for the Roundtable." There was audible pride in his voice. Deborah tossed him an older-sister look as he continued, "Coliquin has managed to create an international coalition of major religions to get behind his initiative. That gives him the moral and religious cover for his plan to regulate global business in the name of preventing catastrophic climate change. He was the architect behind the international treaties that created the world climate agency. By the way, the guy that's been running that particular agency — this zillionaire from Belgium, Faris D'Hoestra — is one scary dude. They're seizing control of industries that are supposedly out of compliance with their super technical green standards, including companies in the U.S."

"I've missed a lot of that," Deborah remarked, "buried in the Pentagon everyday at my desk. But I haven't seen any of this on the news."

"Apparently you haven't been reading AmeriNews," Abigail said. "That's the only information source on the web that's covering it."

"All thanks to Mom, by the way," Cal said. "She chased that FCC commissioner's limo down I-66 just to get his attention."

Abigail chuckled. "Actually, it was God's doing. A miracle, the way it all transpired. But when Tulrude succeeded Corland, she appointed one of her cronies as the new chairman of that federal agency. Now AmeriNews is the only show in town in terms of alternate communications and news. Until we get another president, of course, which is what we are praying for and working toward."

"Well, as much as I appreciate the political science lesson, I still don't get it. These pictures. Where are you going with this?"

Abigail nodded. "Okay, so you know where Coliquin is now."

"Sure. He's secretary-general of the United Nations."

"And very much supported by President Tulrude," Abigail noted.

Cal had wandered off into the kitchenette to look for a snack in the fridge. He yelled out to them, "They're like kissing cousins."

Abigail nodded. "The point is that Coliquin is dropping obvious endorsements in the press for Tulrude, saying that if Tulrude wins the upcoming election it will not only be good for America, but for international peace, security, unity, and environmental safety around the world. The fact is, Tulrude's victory in November is a political necessity for Coliquin — it will be the glue that holds together the global power base that he's built for his agenda."

Deborah pointed back to the enlarged photo of Coliquin's hand. She waited for the punch-line. "And this picture?"

"Okay," Abigail continued, "look at the ring on Coliquin's left hand. Very unusual. I've checked the design on it in several anthropology texts. It's based on an ancient Egyptian design. Full of occult, pagan symbolism. Belltether must have thought this was highly significant because he obviously snapped the picture when Coliquin wasn't looking. Then he enlarged it. The article he sent us documented the corruption — even allegations of conspiracy and murder — involving Coliquin back in his native Romania. Now that Belltether is dead, the AmeriNews staff is working overtime, double-checking his sources so we can publish it. But Belltether also included a note in the packet. He said he planned on a second exposé against Coliquin, a story he thought would have, in his words, 'even more astounding revelations.' But with his murder, we may never know what he had in mind."

"Okay," Deborah shot back, "maybe Coliquin's a bad actor. So what?"

"Listen carefully to what I'm about to tell you," Abigail said, "and then decide if you can do what I'm going to ask you to do."

She had Deborah's attention. Her daughter had her head forward, eyes glued on her mother.

"Senator Hank Hewbright is in jeopardy. There's evidence that he's threatened, and I mean personally. I'm talking assassination. His chief campaign manager in Wichita was murdered. John Gallagher has heard rumors of Hewbright's Allfone being hacked."

When Abigail paused momentarily, Deborah cut in. "That's all you have? That's pretty sketchy."

"No. There's more. One of Hewbright's closest advisors may be a fraud." Deborah cocked her head and waited. Abigail finished the thought. "The name the traitor goes by is Zeta Milla. She's an attractive foreign-policy expert on Hewbright's campaign," Abigail explained. "Supposedly a refugee from communist Cuba as a child, escaping with her family on a small boat. After I met her in Colorado following one of Hewbright's speeches, I asked Gallagher to do some background investigation into the records down in Miami. There were news reports back then about a family escaping Cuba on a little rowboat with a makeshift sail. The parents died on the trip over, but a young girl survived. Her name was kept out of the article because she was a minor."

"Okay, so it checked out?"

"Not really. John told me he found a death certificate online in the Miami-Dade records for a young girl of Cuban descent, of the same age, who died about a week after the article was published. She was listed as 'Jane Doe.' The cause of death was listed as exposure, but John kept digging and found out that the birth certificate was a double. The original had the name of the girl on it, but someone had it destroyed and replaced it with Jane Doe."

"All right," Deborah shot back, "let's say this Zeta Milla stole the identity of this dead Cuban girl and used the story for her own purposes. Even assuming that's the case, it may prove she's dishonest, but not that she's a threat to Hewbright."

"When I met Zeta Milla in Denver," Abigail said, "I noticed something." Abigail held up the enlarged photo of Coliquin's hand. "She was wearing the same ring that Coliquin is wearing in Belltether's photo. I think these two are part of the same little club."

Deborah took the photo from her mother's hand, a look of shock on her face. "Okay ... I see. Right. What do you want me to do?"

"I need you to contact a friend of mine named Pack McHenry. He runs a private counterintelligence group, the Patriots. You've heard Dad and me speak highly of him. He has super-secret security clearance and has worked with American intelligence services." Deborah nodded slowly. "First, you need him to supply you with a fake ID. Let's call you Deborah Shelly. Use your middle name as your last."

"Mom, what's going on?"

"I need you to get close to someone important."

"But I'm already BIDTagged. A fake ID won't match my bio in the BIDTag system."

"Another reason you need to contact McHenry. While his computer guys haven't been able to duplicate the actual BIDTag laser process — to our knowledge there is only one person in the world who has managed to achieve that — Pack's IT team can do the next best thing — they can substitute personal data information in your government database. Look, Deb, the people you are going to be dealing with can't know you're part of the Jordan family. That's crucial. Now, when you get hold of Pack McHenry, you also have to ask him something else. We need him to access the passport records of this Zeta Milla. See if she has a history of travel to Romania while Coliquin was ambassador."

"And if she did?"

"Deb, I need you to undertake a dangerous assignment, and it can't wait. I would do it myself, but for the next forty-eight hours I'm going to be otherwise occupied."

"Occupied? Doing what?"

Abigail and her son gave each other a knowing nod. Cal filled in the blanks.

"Backpacking in the Northwest. Locating rebels."

TWENTY-NINE

Jerusalem

At the outdoor café Ethan was tilting up the little cup of Turkish espresso to catch the last drop, but in the process he caught a mouth full of grounds. He made a face as he swallowed them, then took a swig from his water bottle. "Josh," he said, "I know there must be a way to drink that stuff without swallowing the grit, but I still haven't learned it."

Joshua pointed to his cup of tea. "I'll have to convert you to this stuff, just like Abigail did for me. I used to be a coffee addict, but Abigail kept after me — even from the other side of the planet — to change my diet, food, drink, everything. I think she wants me to live to a hundred! Frankly, I think I won't make it — because I have the feeling Jesus is coming any day now." He swallowed the rest of his Madagascar tea, set down his cup, and pointed a finger at Ethan. "And when that happens, if you haven't put your faith in Christ, while I'm up there with Him, you're still going to be down here picking up the pieces — living in a shattered world that'll be run by the Devil himself. Something to think about."

Ethan tossed his boss a halfhearted smile. By now he was used to Joshua exaggerating about religious stuff — particularly the "Jesus is about to rapture his church" bit. Since they were both living in a kind of exile now in Israel, at least until Joshua's legal case got straightened out, it was almost a daily occurrence. Something was constantly grabbing Joshua's attention — a news item in the online *Haaretz* or *Jerusalem Post* or an archaeological discovery or just the sight of some tourist spot 'where Jesus once walked' — that's all that it would take to launch his mentor into a full-length sermon. When Ethan accepted the offer to work as the personal assistant to Joshua Jordan — world-class spyplane pilot, engineering genius, and American hero — he never expected to be accompanying a traveling evangelist.

But that wasn't the only thing on Ethan's mind. As Joshua got up and rather stiffly reached his arm around to grab his wallet and pay the bill, Ethan was struggling with something in his own head. *Maybe this gig isn't all it's cracked up to be. I've been in Israel for months. What am I really doing here? My job description changes every day. It's almost like Josh wants me close to him, but why, I don't know. Okay, so maybe he has to stay here because he's got a hairy criminal case hanging over his head. But not me. I'm free to go back — anytime I want to.*

I wonder if it's time to head back to the good old U.S.A. Spruce up my résumé. See if Raytheon is hiring again. I'll think it over. Start breaking it to Josh slowly.

Joshua pulled a piece of paper out of his pocket with the same rigid movement that Ethan knew well — the shoulders seemed to limit his movement. "My grocery list," Joshua said waving the emailed note. "Abigail's got me on this Mediterranean diet of vegetables and fruit. Says she thinks maybe it's going to help my headaches and the other stuff."

Yeah, Ethan had witnessed the "other stuff." The injuries Josh had received at the hands of his sadistic Iranian captors two years before were still apparent.

"Let's head over to the Souk," Joshua said, pointing across the street to the Mahame Yehuda Market. "I'll pick up some veggies."

"Just don't invite me over for dinner," Ethan said. "I'm still a meat-and-potatoes guy. And I've developed a taste for Argentinean beef over here."

As they approached the entrance of the open air market, flanked by trucks that were unloading, Ethan's Allfone vibrated. It was a text. He opened it up, surprised to see that it was from Deborah Jordan.

Hi, Ethan. Deborah here. Been meaning to connect. How's life in Israel? Maybe we can talk sometime. Catch up on your life. Is my dad keeping you in line? Ha. Ha. DJ

"Huh," Ethan muttered under his breath as they walked. Joshua gave him a quick glance but didn't ask about it. Ethan slipped the Allfone back in his pocket. Ten seconds later, it vibrated again. Was this another message from Deborah? *Man, she must really be thinking about me*, Ethan thought.

As the two of them entered the noisy crush of local shoppers meandering through the long single aisle of the outdoor market with food stands on each side, he read the newest text. But it wasn't from Deborah.

Two Shin Bet agents coming to arrest Joshua. Then extradite him to USA. Get out quick.

He tapped the Source function to see who sent it.

Sender not identified.

Ethan pushed the tab on his Allfone for a special application and turned on the function that said, "All Sender Data Fields." But the screen read:

Sender's identity is hyper-blocked.

At the vegetable stand, Joshua had a plastic bag in his hand and was putting an eggplant and a few green peppers in it. Ethan stepped up next to him, his heart pounding and his adrenaline pumping.

"We got to get out of here, Josh," he said quietly.

"What's the problem?"

"Just keep cool. I got a text from an anonymous source, telling me two agents from Shin Bet are coming to arrest you, to extradite you back to the U.S."

"Must be a mistake—"

"I get the feeling it's not. And it's my job to protect you."

"But my relationship with the Israelis has been good here."

"You mean — like the meeting you told me about with Prime Minister Bensky, when you insulted his favorite peace plan right to his face?"

Joshua stepped over to the vendor and paid him a couple of shekels. Ethan scanned the market in all directions. "Let's not take any chances. Okay? Gotta go now. Quickest way is the entrance we came in."

But as they turned, Ethan spotted two broad-shouldered men in sunglasses, one a bald guy wearing a black T-shirt and a tan suit, and the other, a muscular guy in jeans and a tank top. He turned to Joshua. "I think I've spotted them. They don't exactly look like French chefs doing their grocery shopping," Ethan whispered. "We need to get down to the other end — fast."

Joshua tried to look casual as he picked up the speed, but soon he and Ethan were jostling customers as they made their way through the congested market.

"Switch on the afterburners," Ethan grunted, "they're getting closer." Ethan half-glanced to the side and noticed that the men were about twenty yards behind them, coming straight in their direction. "Run!" Ethan yelled. They sprinted down the aisle toward the daylight at the end of the market ahead of them. Ethan could hear the commotion behind him as Ram and his other Shin Bet agent were barreling through customers, knocking them to the ground and tipping over trays of spices and tomatoes as they went.

The two agents were now ten yards away and closing fast. Ethan spotted a truck at the end of the market, just beyond the big metal door that was being rolled down by a food manager. Next to that was a small entrance doorway leading to the outside. A forklift was parked out front.

At the end of the Souk, Ethan shoved Joshua through the open doorway and turned to look behind him. He caught a glimpse of a young female in a green grocer's apron and a scarf wrapped around her head. She looked so familiar he could only ask in that instant — *Could it be?*

The woman was carrying a large tray of fish heads swimming in juice. She tossed the slimy contents onto the ground in front of the two agents. Their feet flew up into the air as they landed on their backsides on the slippery walkway.

Outside, the engine of the produce truck revved up, and Ethan pointed to the empty cargo hold in the back and yelled to Joshua, "Jump in!"

While Joshua climbed stiffly into the back of the truck, Ethan hopped onto the forklift, hit the start button, shifted it into gear, and rammed it into the door opening, blocking it completely. Then he sprinted after the truck as it started to rumble down the street. Joshua was holding on to the metal tie-off loop on the side of the truck with one hand while leaning out of the back of the truck with his other hand outstretched.

He was yelling to Ethan. "Faster!"

Ethan was pumping his legs like a machine, until he reached out and felt Joshua's hand. Joshua yanked hard. Ethan pulled himself up into the truck while Joshua bit the side of his lip and gave a wincing grimace of pain. They pulled the two canvas tarps down over the back of the truck and peeked out through the space between them.

Ram and the other Shin Bet agent had rolled up the big metal door by then. They were now standing in the middle of the alley staring at the truck as it picked up speed and headed out onto Jaffa Street, in the direction of Allenby Square.

On a folding chair on the driveway, on the other side of the door leading into the market where the two angry agents had now disappeared, a food vendor was taking a break. On a table he had his tiny wireless Internet TV tuned to the news. A reporter was standing outside of the Knesset building in Jerusalem. The man turned up the volume. "It was just announced today," the reporter said, "that in a show of political brinksmanship, Prime Minister Sol Bensky has mustered his coalition behind the multifaceted United Nations peace plan for Israel, the Palestinians, and the Arab states. The treaty will be signed tonight in an historic ceremony in the prime minister's residence ..."

The reporter glanced down at his notes, raised his face to the camera again, and concluded. "United Nations Secretary-General Alexander Coliquin has said that the signing of his treaty proposal by Israel marks a new era of peace and prosperity — not only for Israel — but for the entire planet."

TH1RTY

Edinburgh, Scotland

Bishop Dibold Kora was at the podium in the outdoor arena, just off of the Royal Mile and within a stone's throw of Edinburgh Castle, the dark medieval structure perched up high on a solid rock cliff, over-looking the city.

On the dais behind him was the Archbishop of Canterbury and the head of the Church of Scotland, along with the young Dalai Lama, two Hindu priests, a special emissary from the Vatican, an American Indian chief, the president of Wiccans International, several represen-tatives from tribal South American and African religious groups, and the Chancellor of the Gnostic Church of the European Union. Seated directly behind the podium was the head mufti of the Waqf, the Is-lamic trust that had, up to that day at least, exclusively controlled the Temple Mount plateau in Jerusalem.

The arena was filled. Special box seats had been constructed for royalty from Jordan, Saudi Arabia, England, Morocco, Belgium, and a dozen other nations. The international press was granted access to the first ten rows. Two television platforms had been set up to accom-modate the Internet television coverage that was being disseminated, live, over every network on the globe.

Kora, the special advisor to Coliquin, was finishing his introduc-tory comments.

"Last night, Israel signed the historic peace treaty that has been painstakingly forged by my hero and my good friend — Alexander

Coliquin, secretary-general of the United Nations. This was an astounding achievement of historic proportions: Israel, the Palestinian Authority, and the entire Arab League, all in agreement, all in good faith, walking together, into a future of peace. But as significant as that is, the Charter of Common Belief signed here at Edinburgh Castle today is equally monumental — a document that will go down in history as a stunning, evolutionary development — a Magna Carta, if you will — of jointly held values. A pledge of the world's religions to preserve earth from the ravages of carbon emissions that cause global warming; to insure the rich will be held accountable to provide for the poor through an internationally uniform system of enforced cooperation and equalized property ownership; to oppose the spread and dissemination of absolutist religious dogmas and rigid doctrinal beliefs that damage the spiritual harmony of our world; and most importantly, to rejoice because we have discovered a common god that everyone, everywhere, can now worship in peace and tranquility."

After the echoes of the ovation in the arena ceased, Bishop Dibold Kora motioned for a priest from the New Aztec Tribal Union to approach the podium. The priest lit a "unity" torch and waved its flame back and forth in front of him as he chanted.

The crowd, excited by the idea of a new world dawning, rose to its feet and cheered — and kept cheering for several minutes, clapping and voicing their approval in a sea of many languages.

Annapolis Junction, Maryland,
Headquarters of the Security and Identification Agency (SIA),
Near the National Security Agency

At the SIA headquarters, Jeremy, the night-data manager, had just sent an insta-memo to the assistant managing director for the Division for Exigent Requests for the TagWatch Surveillance Program. Jeremy knew his boss was at home, probably finishing his dinner, but this was urgent. The message simply said:

Have received Red Notice from AG, seconded by Homeland. Please call.

Jeremy's line rang a minute later. The assistant managing director said, "What's this about a Red Notice?"

"Yes sir. Signed by Attorney General Hamburg."

"Homeland Security wants this too?"

"That's what it says."

"Who's the subject?"

Jeremy hunted for the name on his screen. "Female. Married. U.S. citizen. Abigail Jordan."

The assistant director took a moment to respond. "Why does that name sound familiar?"

"Don't know, sir."

"All right, then. Start trolling. When you get a good fix, alert the SIA agents or maybe the FBI for an apprehension."

Jeremy clicked off his Allfone and whirled in his chair until he was in front of another screen. He placed the palm of his hand on the screen for two seconds until a green light lit up in the corner. He typed the Red Notice case number and Abigail's name, date of birth, social security, driver's license, and passport numbers into the blank. Then touched the screen where it said Extrinsic Data Location Commencing.

After thirty seconds, he received a message that read, "Subject's Last Verified Location — Mayflower Hotel, Washington, D.C."

"Okay," Jeremy said to his computer screen, "let's go trolling." His screen lit up with ten smaller screens arrayed along the margins, five on each side. Each image was in grainy black and white, the kind produced by remote video cameras.

A female face appeared in another small box on the screen. It was the District of Columbia Sector clerk speaking. "Jeremy, this is the D.C. Sector here. We've got a black vehicle we believe to be a private limo — Lincoln Navigator — driving the subject down Constitution Avenue. Video will follow."

"Copy that," Jeremy said.

□□□

Inside the Lincoln Navigator, the driver, silver-haired attorney Harry

Smythe, glanced up at the green light of the traffic camera that had just captured the image of his vehicle as it passed through the intersection. He spoke aloud but didn't turn around to his occupants. "Abby, after all these years you've known me to play it close to the vest, cautious, careful, I bet you're shocked to see me aiding and abetting a public enemy like you." He guffawed. "I read your affidavit from Harley Collingwood. Finally I told myself, that's enough. The Gestapo kind of tactics I've seen from the Tulrude administration is the last straw. So — I guess I've just become an honorary member of your Roundtable."

In the rearview mirror, Harry could see Cal turn to his mother and say, "Deb said they probably located you at the Mayflower Hotel through the extrinsic data system … public records, like hotel registrations. So we can assume they're already following us with the traffic cameras here on Connecticut Avenue."

Abigail looked ahead, and Harry followed her gaze to the sign for the National Zoo on the right. "Harry, try going in here," she said, pointing to the sign. He took a sharp turn into the zoo entrance.

Moments later, Harry was wheeling the Navigator back onto Connecticut. After several miles, he turned sharply off to the right, heading toward Rock Creek Park. But the cameras at the intersection caught the vehicle again.

□□□

At SIA headquarters, Jeremy spotted the image of the Navigator speeding through an intersection, then turning toward the park. He touched the SIA agent button on the screen and then the FBI button. A message flashed: "Closest agents — 35 minutes."

So he touched the Metro Police square on his screen. The message flashed — "5 minutes." Jeremy touched the button on the screen that read: "Authorize Metro Police Stop."

□□□

Four minutes and twenty seconds later, a D.C. metro police car, with its blue lights flashing, pulled the black Navigator over.

Two patrolmen with their guns drawn ran up to the car, yelling for the driver to put his hands up. When Harry Smythe calmly lowered his electric driver's side window, one of the officers screamed, "Hands up where I can see them. Step out immediately!"

Harry stepped out of the car, and the officer slammed him face forward against the side. The other officer was already on the other side to arrest Abigail. As he swung the passenger door open with one hand, grasping his sidearm in the other, he screamed into the vehicle, "Come out with hands raised — now!"

A few seconds passed. From the driver's side, the officer who had Harry Smythe pinned against the car called out to his partner. "Officer Baker, confirm that you have the subject in custody." Several more seconds passed, and the first officer repeated, "Officer Baker, confirm apprehension!"

The other officer appeared at the driver's side now with his revolver holstered. "No subjects in the car, sir."

The officer stepped back, and Harry Smythe lowered his arms and brushed off his silk shirt. "Do you know who I am, officer?"

"I was about to ask for your driver's license — "

"No need. I'll tell you. I'm a lawyer who has personally represented two former presidents and half a dozen U.S. senators and congressmen. I've also had one other client you ought to know about — your boss — the chief of police of the District of Columbia."

The officers gave each other a quick look. Then they tipped their hats and began to walk away. One of them added, "Sorry to have troubled you."

On a bus that was now leaving the National Zoo, Abigail and Cal sat next to their suitcases on the bench seat in the back. They glanced up at the camera above the driver's head. Cal whispered, "In two blocks we'd better hop off, get a cab. I don't think they're all equipped with cameras yet."

□□□

At SIA headquarters Jeremy was on the cell phone with his boss, explaining that the apprehension had not been successful — yet.

"I wouldn't worry sir," he said. "We'll get our subject eventually. First, she'll hit the trip wire of our BIDTag scanners and register a nontag alert. Then she'll be tracked with facial recognition cameras in every public place — restaurants, gas stations, airports ..."

"Yeah, yeah," the assistant director bulleted back. "I help run this outfit, remember?"

"Just saying," Jeremy replied, "she's in the matrix now. Just a matter of time."

TH1RTY-ONE

On the Campaign Trail Somewhere in the Northeast

Special Agent Ben Boling was ordering a sandwich at the outside counter of a roadside deli. "I'd like the pastrami on rye. No chips with that, but I'd like it heated."

Senator Hewbright was next to him. His entourage of staffers were milling around the campaign bus, out of earshot. "Don't mean to hurry you, Agent Boling, but we have an incredibly tight schedule. What can you tell me so far?"

"First — I don't have much on Perry Tedrich's death — yet. We just don't know if it was connected to your run for president. The autopsy indicates he was poisoned. That's all I know."

"I'd like to reach out to his family ..."

"I know you would. But I recommend that for the time being you let me express your heartfelt regrets. There'll be time for you to talk to his relatives when our investigation gets a clearer picture of why he was killed."

"And my Allfone being hacked?"

"That's a different story, though it may be connected. Just can't tell. What our IT forensics people say is this — it was hacked through a source in China."

Hewbright was nearly speechless. "What in the world ..."

"Do we have any reason to believe that China has any particular interest in your campaign?"

"Certainly. I've traveled there several times, spoken out against

186

their abuses of human rights and violations of religious liberties of Christians and other religious minorities. And I've argued against President Tulrude's attempt to expand our national debt that's owed to China. I've publicly argued that she's enslaving us financially to that nation."

"Anyone on your staff have any special relationship with Beijing?"

"No, sir, other than my foreign-policy advisors being knowledge-able about China in general."

Agent Boling threw some cash onto the counter and plucked up his pastrami sandwich, wrapped in paper. "We'll keep looking at this," he said. "Meanwhile, be careful who you have around you. I've talked to Agent Owens, your Secret Service man. He'll help you keep your circle tight. Can't afford too many people getting close to you. Limit yourself to those who are air-tight, as pure as the driven snow."

Ben Boling smiled at his own comment as he took a bite of his sandwich. How pure could anyone be who was knee deep into the dirtiest blood sport of all — a run for the presidency of the United States? On the other hand, after being around Hank Hewbright for a few days now, Ben had a feeling about him. There was a kind of common decency about the guy. Maybe he was the exception.

"You know, Agent Boling," Hewbright said strolling toward the campaign bus, "you want me to restrict my circle, but that's impos-sible. People want to — have a right to — shake your hand. The voters ought to be able to look you in the eye, find out what makes you tick."

"Sure," Boling said, walking beside him and using a paper napkin to wipe the mayo off his chin. "But I'm not talking about that. I mean your staff," and he tossed a nod toward the campaign workers by the bus. "They're the ones who know your every move."

Cairo, Egypt

U.N. Secretary-General Alexander Coliquin stopped at a glass case containing the mummy of an ancient Egyptian prince. He gazed into the display and studied the smooth facial features, worn by thousands of years but still preserved enough to give the impression of his brow, nose, and jaw line. The tour guide droned on about the collection in the Museum of Antiquities, lecturing his audience — representatives from the Arab League nations and the OPEC countries who had gathered to celebrate Coliquin's great coup in negotiating the treaty agreement with Israel. Meanwhile, the tour guide gushed enthusiastically about how the museum had been gloriously rebuilt since its desecration during the so-called Arab Spring revolts of 2011.

U.N. Deputy Secretary-General Ho Zhu was standing next to Coliquin. He looked at the mummy too. "Once a ruler of a great civilization," Ho remarked. "Now, just some bones in a glass box. A museum piece. How is greatness measured, truly?"

"By becoming more than even that," Coliquin replied.

Ho Zhu wondered at that. "More than what?"

"Than merely a ruler of a civilization."

Before his deputy could pursue that further, Coliquin changed the subject. "Did you get the polls after the Tulrude speech on economics in Nebraska?"

Ho smiled and bobbed his head up and down. "Yes. She gained twelve points. The bump probably won't last, but it's a good start. An excellent speech. This is good momentum leading up to the convention. Meanwhile, Senator Hewbright's party will have its convention first."

"In politics," Coliquin added, "a few days, or weeks, is an eternity. Anything could happen to Hewbright. Don't you agree, my friend?" The two men shared a knowing look.

As the crowd was led to the other end of the hall, Coliquin and Ho Zhu dropped back. The deputy whispered to the secretary-general, "Also, you should know that we have been contacted by Faris D'Hoestra's people. The World Builders."

Coliquin stopped in his tracks. "Concerning what?"

"They want a meeting."

"You still haven't answered the question."

"Concerning your 'agenda for the future.' That is how they put it."

Coliquin took a few steps and then turned to Ho Zhu. "Arrange the meeting."

"Really?"

"Of course. And I want Faris D'Hoestra there personally. Is that understood?"

Ho Zhu gave a tight-faced nod of understanding. "It will be done."

Philadelphia, Pennsylvania

President Tulrude had just finished a photo op and a quick public appearance at the Liberty Bell. Nearby was her former chief of staff, Natali Traup, who had taken a leave of absence from her White House job to help with the campaign. Traup had her Allfone in her hand and was waving it at Tulrude, as her Secret Service entourage led her to the limo. "Madam President, this has to be addressed."

"I don't see why."

"Because there are allegations that your speech was stolen from Hewbright, as a result of the Chinese hacking into his computers."

"I have no personal knowledge about Chinese computer hackers. Do you?"

Traup followed her into the backseat of the limo. "No, but it's going to look bad."

"Screw what looks bad," she replied. "How do they know that Hewbright didn't try to steal the speech from me — but I just happened to deliver mine first? That's the story that needs to get out."

"But there isn't any evidence of that."

"Then find it," Tulrude said. "Look, in the melee leading up to Nebraska, we go into a prep meeting before my speech. And when we come out, I've got a five-point plan to save America from a final, devastating financial depression. That's the fact, Natali. Now, who gave me what regarding those five points for my speech I honestly don't recall. My staff is gathering research, data, and policy ideas from the four corners of the earth. That's what they're paid to do. I'm simply not going to agonize over this. Oh, and another thing," Tulrude said, remembering a PR idea. "Get Coliquin to set up his schedule to do a public event with me while he still has the glow on from this peace deal with Israel. He may be the hero for the day, but he needs me and he knows it. Time to pony up."

"Speaking of Israel," Traup said, "Attorney General Hamburg said to tell you that Colonel and Mrs. Jordan will soon be in custody. Israel will extradite Colonel Jordan back to the U.S. and Mrs. Jordan is being arrested for violation of the BIDTag Act."

"I smell baseball in the air," said Tulrude, a die-hard White Sox fan, with a smile. When Traup flashed a confused look, the president added, "You know, a double-play."

Jessica Tulrude nursed a satisfied grin as the limo gunned away from historic Independence Hall.

THIRTY-TWO

Reagan National Airport, Private Jet Hangar

Cal paced in the lounge as he waited for the pilot of the Jordan family's private jet, the Citation X, to finish his preflight check. While waiting, he put a call in to the Roundtable's media leader.

The voice of Phil Rankowitz finally came on the other end. "Cal, buddy, what's up?"

"I'm in D.C., about to leave on a trip with my mother."

"Anywhere interesting?"

"Yeah, but I can't tell anyone where or why."

"Now you've piqued my curiosity."

"I have something even more important."

"Shoot."

"I got a story that, if we can back it up, will blow the roof off this presidential campaign."

"Sounds like a category-five hurricane news-wise ..."

"At a minimum. This is going to make Watergate and Monica-gate combined look like stuff that belongs in the lifestyle section."

"Spoken like a true tabloid journalist," Phil cracked.

"Okay," Cal continued, noticing that the pilot was exchanging pleasantries with Abigail. "I got to talk fast. You need to find some high-caliber forensic pharmacologists who are not afraid of stepping on political toes. No — strike that. Make that — not afraid to amputate some political feet."

"Ouch."

"I made a few inquiries into the National Institutes of Health and just sent you a qwiktext with the name and contact information of one doctor in particular. According to my research he did a documentary with this guy, but we may need more than one."

"We'll jump on it."

"Also, we have a blood sample that can be sent to any of them to analyze at a moment's notice."

"All right. So, can you give me a hint what we've got here?"

"Remember the *Wizard of Oz*?"

"Let me guess," Phil said, filling in the blanks. "Uh … let's see. A house is about to land on the Wicked Witch of the West …"

After chuckling at Phil's quick pickup, Cal said, "Yeah, something like that." He began to stroll in the direction of the pilot and Abigail.

"Makes me think," Phil said in a voice that was now changing tone, "that God might be moving the chess pieces in a huge way. This is all child's play for the Lord, of course. I was in the book of Haggai recently. Not where I usually spend my Bible-reading time. I'm kind of a New Testament guy. But it pays to keep one foot on each side of Malachi, I think. Anyway, I ran across a verse in chapter two. Just a few words, but it struck me in a powerful way in light of what's going on in America. The dark days we're in. The election. And the tidal wave of change around the world … It said, 'I will overthrow the thrones of kingdoms and destroy the power of kingdoms and nations …'"

"I need that reminder," Cal said, "about who's really in control. Especially now, in the middle of this chaos. And listen, Phil, Mom and I need prayer. Like right *now*. I'll fill you in later."

Cal clicked off his Allfone, greeted their longtime family pilot, and climbed into the Citation X.

When he and Abigail were buckled in, he turned to her. "Did our backpacks get loaded?"

"Check," she said, nodding. "Did you contact Phil?"

"Yes. He's going to line up some medical experts with steel in their spines."

"By the way," she said with a smile, "nice of you to finally fill in your mother with the news story of the century you've dug up — 'Vice President Poisons President and Steps into Oval Office.'"

Suddenly hearing it phrased like that, the full weight of the revelation bore down on Cal. "Almost sounds like a Shakespearean tragedy, doesn't it?"

As the jet slowly turned toward the runway, Cal glanced back and caught a glimpse of the tiny green light of the surveillance camera mounted on the top of the hangar. He said aloud, "I wonder who's watching us now."

THIRTY-THREE

Through the jet's windows, Abigail and Cal could only see the pitch black of evening. The pilot clicked on the intercom, "Jackson Hole, Wyoming, folks, straight ahead."

○○○

Down at the airport, just out of sight, an SIA field agent sat in one vehicle, and four local police officers were in two squad cars, all poised in the shadows to rush toward the incoming jet. The plan was to wait until the plane had taxied to a stop, and then to roar up to it from three directions, pinning it in, so the jet couldn't attempt a turnaround and a quick takeoff.

"Remember," the SIA agent said to the two squads, as he leaned toward his dashboard audiofone, "I take Mrs. Jordan into custody. You four take the pilot and her son. Keep your subjects in custody in separate squads for interrogation. I'll take Mrs. Jordan to the plane that I've chartered and have standing by. Remember, I won't be able to hang around your lovely city. I'll have my charter take off immediately for Washington — just me and my subject in cuffs."

"Anything else we ought to know?" one of the local deputies asked.

The SIA agent flicked on his dash light and glanced at his digital data pad. He tapped on the little window of his screen that said Extrinsic Data Field and answered, "It says here the subject may have picked Wyoming to land because she is believed to have personal contacts here, maybe people who will aid and abet her. This is Senator Hewbright's home state, and she's a supporter. Extrinsic database says she gave money to his campaign and has met with him personally. She and her husband have visited here three times in the last five years for recreational purposes."

The SIA agent clicked off his dash light and radio, then said to himself, "Looks like we've got you figured out, Mrs. Jordan."

□□□

The pilot started the descent.

"Citation X," the tower called in, "you're cleared to land."

"Roger," the pilot responded. Then he brought the private jet perfectly in line with the airstrip ahead and continued to drop.

Ten seconds later the pilot clicked on his transmitter again. "Stand by."

"Tower standing by."

"Okay ..." was all the pilot said at first. Then, a few seconds later, he said, "Landing gear ..."

"Sorry, Citation, didn't catch that. Say again ..." Silence. The tower radioed again. "Say again, Citation. We're tracking you, and you're cleared for landing."

"I said, landing gear."

"Oh, okay. Landing gear," the man in the tower responded with a lighthearted laugh. "That's always a good idea."

"No," said the pilot, "landing gear light ... not up yet ..."

Down below, just off the tarmac, the SIA agent who was looped into the tower's conversation was staring at the little audio screen on his dashboard.

"Clear to land, Citation," the tower barked again.

"My landing gear light isn't lighting up," the pilot explained.

"Toggle it," came the sharp reply from the tower.

"Did that."

"Do a flyover," the tower responded. "With our big spots we'll give you a visual of your underside, to make sure your landing gear is completely down and in place."

The pilot of the Citation X clicked off his external radio control and calmly announced over the intercom, "Abigail, Cal, hold on tight now ..."

Suddenly, the Citation jolted upward at forty degrees. The jet soared off in a westerly direction, over the mountain range that ringed Jackson Hole.

"Citation, this is tower. Please make a flyover immediately! This is the tower. Bring your jet ..."

But the pilot was no longer listening. "Folks, we'll be getting some slight turbulence over the mountains," he said to his two passengers. "You can sit back and relax. Next stop, Washington State."

SIA Headquarters

The sun had not yet risen in Maryland, but it would be up in another twenty minutes. An early-shift Tag Enforcement officer was standing over Jeremy's screen, drinking from a large paper cup of coffee. He was looking at the big red box with two Xs in it in the upper right-hand corner of the monitor.

"Hey," he said to Jeremy, who was hunched over the screen, "I see you got a big fat double-failed notice on your locator status window ..."

"Gee, thanks," Jeremy grunted. "'Cuz until you mentioned it, I hadn't noticed the huge red Xs staring me right in the face ..."

"Maybe you need Sheila to come down here."

"Negative. I can handle this," Jeremy snapped back.

Fifteen minutes later, the director strode in with a Red Notice Status Memo in his hand. He usually didn't arrive until well after dawn. Jeremy had been frantically swishing his hand across the screen, moving from menu to menu to try to insure the location of his subject. But when he saw the director, his hand froze.

The other Tag Enforcement officer slinked out and down the hall to his cubicle, clutching his mocha latte.

The director approached Jeremy, holding a crumpled email in his fist, his face radiant with flushed heat. He stood directly over Jeremy.

"This is a major malfunction, Jeremy," he growled.

"Yes, sir."

"You will consummate positive location and apprehension of the subject Abigail Jordan — and I mean in a hurry. You understand?"

"Absolutely."

"Which is why I've instructed Sheila to come down from master control and make sure it happens. The efficacy of our BIDTag protocol is on the line. The White House is watching me, and I am watching you. And you know what else?"

Jeremy shook his head.

"I'm watching your descending career path. I'll make sure the odds of your holding onto this or any other meaningful job for the rest of your life will be about the same as a porpoise playing first base for the Nationals if this snafu doesn't get turned around."

The director stormed out.

Five minutes later, a woman with stringy, slightly disheveled hair, came strolling into Jeremy's room while munching a candy bar.

When Jeremy spotted Sheila he was about to make a crack about her eating a Snickers bar before six in the morning but decided against it.

Without expression, Sheila shooed Jeremy out of his swivel chair by wagging the fingers of both hands like the maître d' in an expensive restaurant might do to a homeless visitor.

Once planted in the chair, which she first adjusted to her taller height, Sheila proceeded to display programs on Jeremy's screen with lightening speed.

"I've never seen those properties before," Jeremy muttered as he watched the master at work.

After another fifteen minutes or so, Sheila tapped a lower quadrant of the screen that read, "All National Systems Synced."

Then the red X box in the upper right section of the screen disappeared. It was replaced by a display that said, "Reboot Completed — Advanced Search Commencing."

"You know," Sheila said with mild irritation, "I told the guys here at SIA I didn't have time to train you humanoids on the second floor." Then she sighed and got up from the chair.

Jeremy pointed to his computer. "What did you do?"

"It's what you *didn't* do," she said with a lilting whine, "like integrating all the systems. What good does it do for us to spend billions on all this stuff — voice- and facial-recognition monitors, BIDTag scanners, the Personal Profiler EX-3, All Extrinsic Database and Likely Route Estimator programs, and all those cameras and mics planted in every corner of the country — when morons like you forget to synchronize them during your subject location search?"

When Sheila reached the door she tossed one last comment over her shoulder. "Now hit Start," she said. "Your Red Notice subject, whoever she is, won't have a chance."

TH1RTY-FOUR

Olympia Airport, Washington State

As the Citation X rolled to a stop on the tarmac, Abigail and Cal had already unbuckled themselves and were reaching for their backpacks. Abigail tucked her legal file in the center zip pocket.

"You didn't catch any Zs on the flight over, did you?" Cal said.

She shook her head. "I had to go over my notes, getting ready to argue your father's case." Then she looked down at the atomic-clock function of her Allfone. "Which is now less than forty-eight hours away." She closed her eyes, contemplating the enormity of the mission ahead of her. She muttered something aloud—a prayer, mixed with exasperation—"Dear Lord, all things are possible with You. But this is really coming right down to the wire ..."

As they deplaned, the pilot shook their hands. "I'll take care of the FAA and SIA inquiries. But just remember—there are four webcams here on the tarmac. So you've already been logged into the system. The clock is ticking. It won't be long before SIA catches up to your location here. A personal car, not a rental, is waiting for you in the parking lot," he added, "courtesy of your friends at the Roundtable." He handed Cal a piece of paper with the parking-lot location and the make and model. "The car's unlocked. The keys are wedged between the retractable headrest and the top of the passenger side front seat." The last thing their pilot said before disappearing into the hangar, was, "Godspeed, Mrs. Jordan. And you too, Cal."

Abigail and Cal lugged their backpacks through the small regional airport, leaving through the security exit doors. They knew the cameras up at the ceiling were catching them from several angles. All they could do was to hope and pray that they would be able to arrive at their destination before the SIA agents tracked them down. The blessing was that the little airport was not close to any major federal law enforcement offices.

While the element of time was not on their side, something else was — the primeval kind of environment ahead of them. The long arm of government scanner surveillance had not yet reached the remote wilderness area they were about to enter.

In the parking lot they located the green Land Rover. As planned, the car was unlocked, and the keys were under the passenger headrest.

Cal jumped behind the wheel, and Abigail sat in the passenger seat with Cal's micro laptop open. They headed north on the 101, toward Skokomish. After forty minutes, they were surrounded by dense forest and mountains. While Cal pushed the Land Rover as fast as they could afford to go, Abigail opened the extensive trail of emails between Cal and the clandestine group they hoped to meet.

"Cal, you've been connecting with them for five months. No," she corrected herself, paging down more emails, "almost six months."

"Ever since you started talking about not getting BIDTagged," Cal replied.

"And you did all that for me?"

"I had a feeling you were going to need something like this. Without your BIDTag, I knew this was your only chance."

"Thank you," she said, reaching over and squeezing his arm. Suddenly she was aware of the strength in his arms. He hadn't shaved, and his face had the same kind of dense bristles that Joshua would get. And there was a rugged maturity now to his profile, no longer the baby-faced teenager.

"Your dad would be so proud of the man you've become," she said. "He *is* so proud, Cal."

Cal tightened his face and didn't respond. After a while he said, "I miss him. We have to get his case turned around so we can all be together again." Then he added, "For however long we've got down here."

That took Abigail by surprise. She and Joshua were the ones who had been talking about the approaching apocalypse. They never hid their strong belief that Jesus Christ was poised, any minute now, to enter human history once again — to whisk his believing flock off the face of the planet, just before the beginning of the end.

But now, hearing Cal open up about that same thing — about the imminent return of Christ — it brought home what she had always believed in her heart, that the truth that had so spiritually revolutionized the lives of the parents had been quietly observed and absorbed by their son and their daughter. She silently spoke it in her mind. *Your word never returns void, O Lord. It always bears fruit in the right season.*

Then she went back to the email trail on the screen.

"Who is this Chiro Hashimoto they're talking about?"

"A software technology genius," Cal said. "I've read about him over the years. He was hired by Introtonics in Seattle when he was only a sophomore at Stanford, put in charge of high-tech research for the corporation. According to one article, he was developing a really advanced laser process for encoding and storing information when he left Introtonics."

"Why did he leave?"

"He found out that the White House had cut a deal with Introtonics to use his laser process to create the human BIDTag process. He's a privacy freak, totally against information systems collecting data about people. So one day he packed up his personal stuff from his impressive glass office on the floor just below the corporate president's suite, grabbed his little sculpture of Rodin's *The Thinker*, and walked out. Totally disappeared. Like vapor."

"And you know for a fact he's up here in the Olympic National Forest?"

"Not *in* the forest. Right on the edge. In a private compound."

"And you tracked him down?"

"Took several months. I had to send some fishing bait out. Posted some things on obscure, hi-tech computer networking sites. The kind of ultra-advanced technology blogs I figured that a guy like Chiro Hashimoto might be reading from his hideout, wherever that was. A lot of rumors about him — some said that he was dead. Others said he had been hired by China to hack into American security systems. Another said he brought down Wall Street's digital trading system a few years ago."

"He sounds like an anarchist," Abigail said.

"I don't believe all the rumors, but one thing's clear — he's not your average computer geek."

"Why does he trust you?"

"I'm not sure he does."

Abigail had a stunned look on her face. "Wait. I don't understand."

"I've only communicated with his group — they call themselves the Underground. A super-secret group that protests the BIDTag program — and they don't use the new international currency — the CReDO — either. But I haven't connected directly with Hashimoto."

"Why would they trust you? How do you know they're not just taking you for a ride?"

"I told them my father developed the RTS system and that my mother was the ringleader of the group that singlehandedly tried to stop the terror plot to detonate a nuke inside New York City."

"*Ringleader*? You called your mother a 'ringleader'?"

"Hey, Mom, don't be such a … a *mom*. I had to make you sound exotic. You know, rebellious."

"I consider myself a patriot — not a rebel. There's a difference."

Cal laughed.

"It's not funny," Abigail said. "What kind of impression do they have of me anyway?"

Cal laughed louder. "I love the way you are always Miss Manners, Mom — except when you're on the other side of a legal argument, and then you really go for the kill. You forget, I've seen you in action."

They fell into a comfortable silence.

Two hours later they saw a sign: "Skokomish 10 Miles." Cal checked his odometer and turned it to zero. Two and a third miles later, he saw a fire trail cut into the deep forest on the left.

"That's it," he said.

"You sure? It looks like it leads up the foothills and into a dead-end."

"This is exactly what they told me."

Cal checked his rearview mirror to make sure no other cars were around. Then he wheeled the Land Rover across the highway and onto the rough fire trail.

They began to bump their way up the path, jiggling the car so violently that their voices quivered when they spoke.

"I was just thinking about Dad," Cal said, "wondering how he's doing, whether he's safe."

"This may sound odd," Abigail said, "but I've learned not to worry about your father. At least not too much. God gifted that dear man with an uncanny ability to get out of the worst kind of trouble." Then she added, "I've actually been sitting here thinking about something else."

"What's that?"

"I've been wondering, down to my soul, what in the world has happened to my country."

The screen on Cal's Allfone, which was lying on the dashboard, lit up with a video email. He pulled the car to a halt. "This could be important," he said and tapped the Receive key. "This may be our rendezvous."

But it wasn't. The image of Captain Jimmy Louder was on the screen. The text said,

Thanks for friending me on Facebook, Cal. I'm trying to connect with your dad but can't get any intel on his current whereabouts — for obvious reasons now that I know all about his situation. Any suggestions? Capt. J. Louder.

Cal handed the Allfone over to Abigail who glanced at the message and smiled. "Okay, give him Ethan's email. He's screening incoming communications for Josh."

After tapping in Ethan's email address, Cal hit Reply. "I wonder what that's about," he asked aloud. Abigail shrugged.

Cal redirected his attention to the steep path through the woods ahead, and he hoped, after all this effort and risk, they would be able to meet with the secretive Chiro Hashimoto and his Underground. He put the Land Rover into low gear and continued the rough, jostling drive up the fire trail that cut deep into the wilderness.

TH1RTY-F1VE

Headquarters of the Central Intelligence Agency, Langley, Virginia

That same morning, as usual, William Tatter, director of the Central Intelligence Agency, had been picked up at his brownstone mansion in Old Town Alexandria by his sedan driver. Now the black sedan was pulling off of Dolly Madison Boulevard and into the familiar entrance leading to the two-hundred-and-twenty-six-acre intelligence compound.

But one thing was utterly unusual — the encrypted iGram message he had received in the early morning hours on his digital Com-Pad from one of his inside sources. He had to read it twice while shaving just to make sure he wasn't dreaming; then he swore so loudly that his wife thought that he accidentally sliced his neck with his razor. From home, Tatter immediately called his special liaison to the National Security Council and, after that, his deputy in charge of communications with the congressional intelligence oversight committees. Tatter was not a man to be blindsided. Apparently, on that day, he had been. An embarrassing realization for a spy chief. The classified iGram message proved what William Tatter had been famous for saying among his colleagues privately — that domestic spying was now the primary province of SIA, Homeland Security, and whoever happened to be Jessica Tulrude's pal.

When Tatter blustered into his office suite on the top floor, directly above the entrance doors of the agency building, he was informed by his executive assistant that the secretary of state would be visiting him that morning. Fifteen minutes later, the secretary arrived.

"Vance," Tatter said to him with visible distress, "I already know about this outlandish development. It's absurd. Maybe even treasonous."

"Oh, come on, William," the secretary said, "you had to know this was coming."

"Tulrude is — excuse my bluntness — stark raving crazy if she thinks that the CIA is going to be subject to international control of the Security Council of the U.N. This is insane."

"It's nothing new —"

"I really thought this was just some nutty idea of a bunch of radical political scientists who must be doing dope on the side —"

"You're overstating it," the secretary said calmly. "All the treaty requires is that the U.S. government must disclose to the U.N. security council, in advance, any American clandestine operations of the CIA prior to actually taking hostile action against any other nation that is a member in good standing of the United Nations."

"I got the memo. It doesn't change my mind. Well ... okay, maybe. I'll retract my comment about the proponents of this absurdity doing dope on the side. Instead, how about this — they must be on hard drugs. How about that?"

The secretary rolled his eyes. "We may not be able to do everything over at State," he said, "but we can do one thing well. We can count. And we know we've got the votes in the senate to ratify this treaty. We both know it."

Tatter's face expressed no displeasure, but his voice told a different story. His tone carried a message of total disdain. "Where is Roland Allenworth in this discussion? The secretary of defense should be here right now. He'll be equally disgusted at this act of total betrayal of America's interests."

"As for Roland," the secretary of state said as he rose to leave, "he is announcing his resignation later today."

Tatter was a Washington veteran. He knew the rules. He shot back, "But that's not what's *really* going on. What's really happening is that

Tulrude is cleaning house before the election, kicking the honest ones out of her administration so they can't spill the gory details of what has really gone on during her tenure in the Oval Office. Honestly, Vance, is there anything our president would not do for political gain? Does she have any honor left at all?"

As the secretary of state strolled toward the door he stopped long enough to ponder William Tatter's indictment of the president. "Honor? Yes, that noble, if not antiquated, value mentioned in the Declaration of Independence. *Our sacred honor* ... Well, Bill, I'll tell you what's sacred. Global peace and harmony. We are witnessing a new world unfolding before us."

Tatter had a look of resignation now, as if he had just glimpsed the future. Behind the happy placards and politically correct billboards, he could see the black smoke rising up from a dawning empire of destruction. "A new world order?" he called out to the secretary of state. "Maybe. But still guided by human corruption. That's what is going to be pulling the levers behind the curtain."

Georgetown, Washington, D.C.

Deborah Jordan was hustling breathlessly down the sidewalk along the shopping and restaurant district. She had been given the message about a secret rendezvous point, but she wondered, *I don't remember a magazine stand in front of Charley Beck's Restaurant.*

She strode down the sidewalk from the parking garage until she approached the restaurant. "Can't believe it," she said under her breath as she brushed past pedestrians. There, off to the side of the entrance to Charley Beck's, was an old-fashioned magazine and newspaper stand. Ever since the migration of all news publications to the Internet, those relics of the old print world had slowly become extinct.

The guy manning the booth was middle-aged with sunglasses and a Washington Redskins cap.

Deborah remembered the routine given to her by Pack McHenry, the shadowy black-ops manager of private intelligence services. His group — known only as the Patriots — was the stuff of legend among the members of her parents' Roundtable. She got the drift from her father that Pack McHenry, a former CIA foreign operations director, had really never left the Agency, that he and his team of special operations veterans were still assisting the United States government — but very discreetly. Not just under the radar — but practically invisible on the map.

After talking to her mother in her suite at the Mayflower the day before, she did as she was asked. She had called McHenry's number. He had answered with one word: "Patriots."

Deborah had introduced herself and said she was carrying a request from Abigail Jordan.

"Anything for the Jordans," he had replied.

She put in the request for a passport check on Zeta Milla and gave all of the background information she had about the Cuban beauty.

"Done," he said on the other end.

Then Deborah broached the other request. "I need a reliable, authentic-looking driver's license ID for myself. My picture and address. But identifying me as Deborah Shelly."

"Who's going to be checking it?"

"Some very official people ... who carry guns."

"Gotcha." Then, Pack McHenry sobered. "I have such respect for your dad and mother. Worked on some pretty important projects together behind the scenes. Saved lives. Protected the country. Tell them that I wish them God's speed, won't you?"

There had been a final good-bye kind of tone to his comment that sent a chill up Deborah's spine.

"I certainly will, Mr. McHenry," she simply said in return.

"My friends call me Pack," he had said. "Young lady — I know your position over at the Pentagon. How hard you worked at West Point to get where you are. And I also know how you must be risking all of that with what you've got planned. Your parents will be very proud."

That struck home. She stammered for just an instant, then recovered. "Yes ... sir. I appreciate your thoughts."

Before clicking off, Pack had issued a final word. "The daylight is waning, Deborah. Night's coming. A long, terrible night, I fear. What your parents believe — the coming end of days. Wrapping up of human history. The coming hand of God Almighty. Victoria — my wife — and I … haven't been the religious type, but the more we look around, we find it pretty hard to deny it now. It's all coming to pass. Josh and Abby have been right all along, you know. The Bible. The prophecies. Everything."

"Yes, sir. I believe it too."

"Well," he said finishing the thought, "you can tell your folks that I said that. I'm doing a lot of thinking lately."

That was yesterday, and now Deborah reflected again on his words as she approached the vendor on the sidewalk, the guy with the Redskins cap.

She recited the script. "I'm looking for a Superman Comic book from 1985. The one with Supergirl."

"I'm all out," the man grunted, "but I thought you'd like to see this."

He handed her an old tattered tour guide for visiting Cuba, which must have been printed before Castro came to power. Deborah smiled. Pack McHenry had a sense of humor, that was clear.

She reached in her purse, but the man frowned and shook his head. "It's on the house."

When Deborah reached her car, she opened up the book, and inside was a pristine-looking driver's license for "Deborah Shelly" with her photo on it. She drove out of the parking garage and back onto M Street North West. But when she drove by Charley Beck's, the guy with the Redskins hat was gone. And so was the magazine stand.

TH1RTY-51X

Israel

Joshua had been talking about risk at the beginning of their ride out of Jerusalem. Now Ethan, sitting in the back seat, listened as Josh mentioned it again.

"You're taking a big risk," Josh said, turning to Joel Harmon who was driving the Volvo. "Or did you forget that in Israel I'm now an enemy of the state?" Ethan saw Josh's face grow momentarily solemn. He knew how weary his friend had grown over his troubles in the U.S. Now Israel, his so-called safe harbor, had turned against him too.

Joel didn't look worried. "I may be a freshman legislator in the Knesset, but I know my way around these Shin Bet security issues. We'll get you to a safe house, Josh. If I'm asked by anyone where I'm going, I've got an answer handy."

Ethan said, "I'd like to hear that one."

"Simple," Joel shot back, "I'll tell Shin Bet, thanks to me, they don't have to worry about Joshua Jordan being inside Israel anymore." Joshua and Ethan waited for an explanation. "I'm taking you to the Palestinian Authority side," Joel added. "Because of the deal cut with the U.N. by our prime minister, that area is becoming part of the new Palestinian State — off limits to Israel."

Josh had a curious look on his face.

Joel laughed. "You think I'm taking you out of the pot and throwing you into the fire?"

"Now you're sounding like an American. I would have thought you'd have a clever Hebrew phrase for that," Josh tossed back.

"We do. But now that Sol Bensky is forcing Israel to be absorbed into the international community," Joel said with a sneer, "I'm working on trying to sound non-Jewish."

Joshua nodded. "You did a brave thing, Joel, opposing the prime minister on his U.N. plan, but I still don't know how smart it was bringing a flame-thrower like me into that meeting."

"I wasn't trying to be smart," Joel remarked, "just right. And true. When I think of those two qualities — who else besides you could I possibly bring to that meeting?"

In the back Ethan was smiling. In his private moments he had thought about the unique chance he had been given to follow Joshua through his travels, watch him in action, to hear firsthand the respect he had engendered from other men — men who were themselves accomplished and courageous. It made Ethan feel a flush of shame — for just an instant — about his potential plan to leave Joshua and head back to the U.S. He thought he had settled the issue, but lingering doubts kept popping up. He had just helped rescue his mentor back in Jerusalem, and he felt good about that. On other occasions, he felt like a piece of excess baggage on Joshua's bullet train, but not then.

Then Ethan was struck by something else. *Here I am, an ex-Air Force pilot, out of work, and what happens? I get onto a flight and run into Deborah, the daughter of Joshua Jordan, the man who is the envy of the entire defense industry and my own personal hero. The next thing I know I meet him and he offers me a job. So, am I supposed to think this is all coincidence?*

That triggered another thought, something that Joshua was always saying: "In a universe governed by God, there are *no* coincidences."

Why did it always come back to God? For most of Ethan's life, he hadn't given Him much thought. But then the Jordan family swept into Ethan's life, and ever since then, it was as if he was on one of those bumper cars at the carnival — constantly bumping into the Bible, sermons about Jesus, and Joshua's talk of his own encounter with Christ. Now Ethan was living in Israel, tripping almost daily over ancient places where Jesus walked, that Christians point to and say, "*Here* is where God did this ... or that." Ethan felt surrounded by it all, and he didn't know whether it was that bad a thing or not. Was this some kind of "Custer's Last Stand" for him on the religion issue, with the hostiles all around him with their arrows? Or was it simply a surprising turn of events, where he had a chance to smarten up and maybe learn something about himself or discover something much bigger than even that?

As they drove northeast through the remote desert suburbs of Israel, Ethan had one more question — one that had been pestering him nonstop. *Why do I get the feeling that Joshua brought me with him for reasons he hasn't bothered to explain yet?*

Joel Harmon pulled through a subdivision of Jewish homes in a desolate area. The signs on the outskirts read, "Nablus." The sun had just set.

Joel put the car in Park and turned to face Joshua and Ethan. "We're about fifty feet from the wall separating Israel from the Palestinian Authority. Obviously, you can't exit from the Israeli side through one of the regular checkpoints. There's an alert out on you, Joshua, and it's being passed through all the channels. They'd grab you immediately."

"Let me guess," Joshua said, eyeing the twenty-six-foot-high concrete wall. "We're going to leave Israel *creatively* ..."

"That's the plan," Joel replied.

"These old joints of mine aren't what they used to be," Joshua said. "Haven't scaled a wall like that in a while."

"Oh, don't worry. No repelling. No ropes. Nothing like that. That's not the dangerous part."

Ethan jumped in. "Then what is?"

"See that part of the wall — that concrete slab — that juts out a little?" Joel pointed to a point in the wall about seventy feet away. "See how it's not flush with the rest?"

They nodded.

"That's where two big concrete slabs were dropped into place by the IDF contractors. But the two ends don't exactly meet. There's a space about two-and-a-half feet wide."

"I can't believe they'd leave that open," Ethan said.

"They didn't. Razor wire's been bolted into the gap — but it can be unbolted too ... if you know the right people."

Ethan thought he had it figured out. "So, that's the hard part?"

"Afraid not. Time was when Israel would have roads on the other side of the wall where IDF patrols would cruise. But Sol Bensky ordered those stopped. So now, once you get through our wall, there is DMZ strip about one hundred feet wide until you get to the Palestinian side. You'll have to run like wild men across that strip. It's open ground. When you get to the other side, all they have is a chain-link fence with barbwire on the top. I'll give you some big wire cutters."

Joel glanced in his rearview mirror then checked his side mirror. "Okay, all clear. Everybody out."

There was only one part of the plan that Ethan didn't feel good about. As he climbed out, he asked, "Joel, we're about to enter an area riddled with Arab terror groups, and Josh's RTS system has been used to wipe out a number of those kinds of groups who have launched Stinger missiles and who ended up swallowing their own missiles — like Iran, when they got nuked by their own warheads. So, you're sending us to the Palestinian side ... Why?"

"You'll be staying with Ibrahim Kalid," Joel said as he popped open the trunk, seeming to ignore Ethan's comment.

That didn't sit well with Ethan. Not hiding his sarcasm, he kept it up. "Oh, great. You've got us under the control of some Arab guy?"

Joel reached in and pulled out two red-and-white-checked Arab headdresses and handed them to Joshua along with the wire cutters. "I know we've already gone over this, but here's the plan one more time. You will wait about ten minutes. As it starts to get dark, crawl through the open space. I've arranged for the spotlights to stay off for a few minutes to help you get across." Then he bent into the trunk and pulled out something that looked like a modern version of a long Roman shield, with a handle grip on the backside.

He gave it to Ethan. "High-impact Kevlar riot shield. You're going to want to hang on to this," he added.

TH1RTY-SEVEN

Joel told Joshua and Ethan to wait until he gave them the signal by flashing his headlights. As promised, the gap between the slabs of concrete had been left open. The razor wire had been unbolted from the concrete and pushed aside. They squeezed into the space, while Ethan clumsily clutched the bulletproof shield and Joshua held the wire cutters. It was almost dark.

Then the headlights flashed.

"Go time," Joshua whispered hoarsely.

They bolted out of the space and began to run. Ethan knew he was faster than Josh, so he slowed down a bit to let him keep pace, while holding up the Kevlar shield to protect them from any shots being fired from the right, where Palestinian border guards might be watching.

As they dashed across the first twenty feet, the big floodlights were still out. Better still, no shots were fired. Then, about thirty feet in, the lights blazed on. The whole DMZ strip lit up like a department store.

At forty feet, shots rang out from the guard tower on the Palestinian side. They pinged off the rocks and stones, then started raining down on the shield.

Fifty feet from the goal line, there was a loud boom and a large chunk of dry ground exploded three feet beside them.

"Fifty caliber," Joshua grunted as they kept up the sprint. Ethan hoped the sharpshooter wasn't too sharp. *Will this shield hold off a fifty caliber?*

Ethan kept the shield high enough to guard Joshua's upper body and head. One shot could blast his skull wide open.

Then, twenty feet from the goal line, they heard it.

Boom!

The fifty-caliber bullet struck home, punching into the center of the shield. The force knocked Ethan sideways into Joshua, and they both tumbled to the ground with the shield clattering on the hard sandy soil next to them.

Now someone on the Palestinian side began firing an automatic weapon at them. The bullets raced up the sand in a line toward them.

Ethan picked up the shield and planted it on the ground lengthwise and pulled Joshua up close. A hale of ping-pings sounded as the bullets struck the Kevlar.

"Now," Ethan yelled when the shots stopped momentarily. But as they leaped to their feet, the floodlights shut down. The DMZ strip was plunged into shadows.

The two men ran pell-mell toward the chain-link fence. More shots were fired randomly all along the strip. Ethan worried that a stray bullet would find its mark. He wondered if they were simply going to spray the fence line with bullets, knowing that it was their destination, shooting at that spot until the two reached their goal.

So Ethan decided to take Joshua farther down the strip of sandy ground. "Don't go to the fence yet. Keep running away from their sentry tower." Ethan now held the rear position, keeping the shield high and slightly upward to protect Joshua who ran a few feet ahead of him. They sprinted parallel to the fence for another twenty feet. Three more bullets pinged off the shield. Ethan's arm was getting tired. *Keep holding it up. Don't let it down.*

Then the shots stopped. The two men veered toward the fence. With his wire cutters, Joshua snipped through the metal link until he had opened a space big enough for them to squeeze through.

They dropped the cutters and the shield and donned their Arab headdresses. They ran between two concrete-block houses, trying to tread as softly as they could. Somewhere a dog started barking. Ethan swore quietly under his breath.

"Don't worry," Joshua said. "The Lord has brought us this far."

But Ethan was thinking something else. Like — what's so great about where we are now? In enemy territory — crawling with assassins.

Chased by the Israelis and shot at by the Palestinians. Supposedly, they were here to find refuge in a safe house, but for the life of him, Ethan could not see a safe place anywhere.

As they hit the street leading through the Palestinian suburb, trying to look calm as they strolled, a car approached with its headlights on. It slowed, training the beam on the two of them.

Ethan wished they had taken the time, before meeting up with Joel Harmon, to arm themselves. Now they were sitting ducks.

The late-model Citroen pulled up next to them. With the engine still running, the driver turned off the headlights and said, "Good evening, Colonel Jordan and friend."

Joshua strode up to the driver's side and reached his hand into the car to shake.

The driver was an older man with a close-cropped beard. He enthusiastically took Joshua's hand and said, "I am Pastor Ibrahim Kalid. In Jesus' name, I welcome you to the safety of my car and to the sanctuary of my home and to the friendship of my family."

The men looked at each other with a shared look of surprised amusement, as they jumped in the back of the car.

Pastor Kalid turned around and grinned at Ethan but said nothing. He just kept smiling as if he was waiting for Ethan to give him a greeting, but none came. Finally, Ibrahim Kalid said to Ethan, "And I welcome you also, my friend." As he turned his headlights back on, he added, "My wife has prepared a good meal. We must not be late."

TH1RTY-E1GHT

City of Jenin, Within the Territory of the Palestinian Authority

Anwar al-Madrassa's route from his headquarters in Islamabad to this particular patch of former Israeli geography — now in the hands of the Palestinian Authority — had been a long and tortuous one. His reputation as a major figure of Islamic terrorism made it necessary to take a circuitous route, first in the back of a freight truck to Turkey, then into Syria, and over to Lebanon. That is where a Hezbollah cell rolled him up in a Persian rug and loaded him into a van owned by a carpet store. The van then crossed into an area of Israel now controlled by the PA.

The city of Jenin was a good choice for his new center of operations. It had been the site of bomb-making for suicide terrorists. But now they were working on something that would have been unimaginable in scope so many years before and would make the former efforts of men with their bulky explosive belts under their shirts quite obsolete.

The day after Joshua and Ethan had reached the safe house in Nablus and not far from that city, in an underground laboratory beneath the basement of a children's clothing store, Dr. Ahlam was getting ready to demonstrate his weapon to Anwar al-Madrassa. In his younger years Ahlam had been one of Saddam Hussein's many chemical-warfare researchers. Now he was waiting for al-Madrassa to arrive. When he finally did, Ahlam could hardly control himself.

"Such an honor, may Allah be praised!" he gushed.

But al-Madrassa was in no mood for pleasantries. He wanted to see the experiment.

Dr. Ahlam shuttled him into an adjoining room with a glass-enclosed sub-room that contained a wire cage with a dog in it, a German shepherd. Dr. Ahlam offered al-Madrassa a chair, but the chief of the al-Aqsa Jihad terror group waved it off. He stood right up to the glass. He could see everything that way.

Dr. Ahlam donned a triple-layered haz-mat suit and screwed down his protective helmet connected to an oxygen tank. He typed the password into the airlock, and the thick glass door clicked open. He entered the glass room and pushed a button to close the door behind him. Once inside, he stepped over to an iron pipe, which was closed at one end and open at the other, which extended into the wire cage.

On a table was a heavy metal tube, and Ahlam unscrewed it and removed an interior steel lining. Then he took an unusual, industrial-looking syringe and he drew out a single drop of a yellow chemical fluid from the inner container. Ahlam then connected the tip of the needle into a pin-sized hole in the closed end of the pipe, and squeezed the end of the syringe to express the single drop into the pipe.

Two seconds later, the dog gave a worrisome look, then immediately began convulsing in pain, yelping, and vomiting blood. Within ten seconds its fur and skin began to emit smoke as it burned off of the dog's frame, falling away from its skeleton.

Dr. Ahlam looked at his watch. He held up ten fingers and flashed them twice to signify the twenty minutes he would now wait.

Al-Madrassa wasn't overly impressed. VX gas was known to have similar ghastly effects. But this little demonstration had two acts. It was the second act that he was waiting for. He strolled back and forth in front of the glass, hands behind his back.

When the twenty minutes was up, Dr. Ahlam strode up on the other side of the glass, directly in front of al-Madrassa. Then he spread out his arms dramatically, to signal his next move. With a flourish, like the impresario at the center of a miniature circus of horrors, Ahlam pointed the index finger of each hand toward his helmet.

Taking a step closer to the glass, al-Madrassa was transfixed and dropped his hands from behind his back. He stared at the chemist in the glass room.

Ahlam placed his hands on his helmet and began to screw it off the collar of his protective suit. Until the very last turn. When he was at that point, the chemist half bent a knee down as he turned the helmet one last half turn, then popped it off his suit, fully exposing his face and head to the air of the enclosed toxic room. Dr. Ahlam flashed a ghoulish grin. He then scurried up right next to the wire cage that contained the smoldering remains of the dog and placed his face against the wire, holding his hands up into the air for effect.

This was what al-Madrassa had come to see — and he was not disappointed. The implications were staggering. Whole populations of Jews, infidels, and other undesirables could now be gassed in Tel Aviv, even in Jerusalem, and almost immediately the city could be occupied without toxic effects to the Islamic conquerors who could then march in and take over. Buildings, cars, businesses, even food and water supply, would be untouched by the gas — and after twenty minutes of exposure to the air the toxin was designed to completely dissipate.

Al-Madrassa was not one to lavish praise on his deputies. After all, only Allah deserved that. But this — the triumph he had just witnessed — nearly overcame him. On the verge of tears of joy, he slowly clapped his hands together in celebration.

On the other side of the glass, Ahlam took a slow bow and threw a kiss to the terror chief who was applauding.

"Genius," al-Madrassa whispered. "Genius."

Now they could move to the next stage. He would talk to his missile men, after which the planning would begin. He had not forgotten the faces of the people he had planned to be his first two victims. The infidel Jordans from America. Indeed the Jordans, America's most zealous patriots with their detestable Roundtable group and enemies of the great Islamic Jihad ... they would be the perfect targets to start with.

TH1RTY-N1NE

Jerusalem, Temple Mount

The sun was shining, and Alexander Coliquin enjoyed the feeling of warmth on his upturned face. He was standing next to Prime Minister Sol Bensky, who had the aged chief rabbi of Jerusalem next to him. Bensky's two main staffers, Dimi Eliud and Chad Zadok, were hovering in the background.

Because of the threat of an Islamic intifada from a few of the noncooperative Palestinian groups, the mount had to be ringed with soldiers that day for the ceremony. The security measure was a joint effort by the IDF and the blue-helmeted United Nations troops. That was more than symbolic. It was a preview of the new Jerusalem under Secretary-General Coliquin's peace treaty with Israel. That city would be a truly international province, jointly ruled by both Israel and the U.N.

On the other hand, Coliquin had much to be happy about. Most of the Islamic clerics were on board with his treaty because of the designation of the Palestinian Authority territories within Israel as sovereign, and the international status of Jerusalem, which took it out of the exclusive grasp of the Israelis. After all, the Arab leaders felt assured that when conflicts broke out — which were certain to happen — the U.N. would side with them against Israel.

On the other hand, giving the Jews control over a portion of the Temple Mount was a sticking point, even with the wall that was being constructed to keep them entirely separate from the Muslim Dome of the Rock and from the Al Aqsa Mosque that had been on the plateau for centuries. But then the Palestinian leaders and the Arab League took comfort from the private assurances of Coliquin, though he knew they were not quite sure how he was going to be able to accomplish his audacious plan. He was glad for that.

Coliquin gave the signal and an international band struck up the Israeli national anthem.

When the music stopped, an old rabbi among twelve Jewish leaders at the ceremony watched as Sol Bensky stepped up to the raised podium laced with wireless microphones from every major news organization on the planet. He pointed down to the large cornerstone that was the star attraction for the final and most dramatic feature of the monumentally historic event.

"For two long millennia," he said, "the Jewish people have waited for the rebuilding of their great temple. It was destroyed in AD 70 by an act of violence, during a time when the Roman Empire was at war with the Jewish people. But today," he said, his voice ringing out from the Temple Mount and echoing down on the city of Jerusalem, "today we see the rebuilding of that temple taking place in an epoch full of promise — of peace, not war — of cooperation, not enmity — with two great faiths each agreeing to worship God side-by-side, with mutual respect on this sacred piece of ground. As in the days of Ezra, we raise our hands in praise for the construction that is taking place — and it is marvelous and wonderful in our sight."

The twelve Jewish leaders then strode to the industrial lift that held the white stone monolith. The construction had already begun. Backhoes and tractors had been busy in the Jewish sector of the plateau digging the foundation. Cranes had lowered the first row of stones, all but one — the cornerstone. Now the twelve men stepped back to allow the old rabbi to totter forward to the lever on the industrial lift.

And as in the days of Ezra, the old rabbi covered his eyes and wept. He did not weep with grief. He did not see this as a time that might soon be ripe for mourning, like the fig tree bearing fruit that was pleasing to the eye yet poisonous to consume. Instead, he wept for that which he believed had been fulfilled from the dark, dusty corners of time forgotten.

The rabbi pulled the green lever, and the engine of the lift began to grind and whir as the great stone was slowly tilted with hydraulic precision at the perfect angle so that it would slide down the smooth steel rollers. As it did, the cornerstone dropped into the space between the adjoining stones. A ground-shaking thud was heard when it found its resting place. But there was half an inch of space between the cornerstone and the neighboring stones.

The rabbi and his fellow Jewish historians and engineers and experts in the Talmud had disputed that fact bitterly with Sol Bensky. The engineers had told the Prime Minister that this was the most efficient method to accommodate the ceremony, as the project had been rushed by Bensky, with the first row of stones being laid in a tireless effort with contractors working around the clock. Bensky had ordered that the foundation be laid in a hurry, before any kind of uprising occurred from Palestinian protestors. The religious scholars told him that this design would require that mortar be placed around the cornerstone to fill in the space, something the ancient engineers two thousand years before had avoided, having brilliantly placed the stones of the Herodian temple in perfect symmetry without the use of mortar.

"But back then, thousands of years ago, they didn't have the political problems that I have," Bensky said in reply. And that was that.

The group of twelve rabbis, together with the chief rabbi, each recited a portion of Scripture and prayed over the row of mammoth white stones that were the foundation for the new global center of Jewish worship. With the foundation now laid, the rest of the construction could be finished with lightning speed. The engineers had assured Bensky of that.

But in the midst of the honored guests on the Temple Mount that day, Coliquin was not thinking about engineering details or Bensky's political problems. He had his own agenda. As the last prayer was being recited, Coliquin heard in his Allfone earpiece the chimes of an incoming message. He tapped the tiny ear bud to listen. It was the Deputy Secretary-General Ho Zhu.

"Mr. Secretary," he reported, "I have been in personal dialogue with Faris D'Hoestra. It took some time. Many layers of protection surrounding him. But I got through and spoke with him about your desire for a meeting."

Coliquin, in a hushed voice, asked to hear the specifics.

"D'Hoestra wanted to meet on neutral ground. I expressed your similar thoughts."

"You'd better have done this right, Ho."

"I said you wanted Abu Dhabi. Specifically Dubai."

"Perfect."

Coliquin tapped his ear bud to turn it off. It had been a very satisfying day. The U.N. secretary-general's agenda was far bigger than some temple building on a hill in Jerusalem. And now Coliquin could see that it was getting very close to completion.

FORTY

Washington State, on the Edge of the Olympic National Forest

Two miles up the rough forest trail, Cal pulled the Land Rover to a sudden halt. He had spotted something. He got out and trotted to a large tree just to the left of the lane. After studying it and running his finger along a marking on the bark, he said, "This is it!"

Abigail was reading something on her Allfone, but she clicked it off, hopped out, and joined him. She stared at the bark where someone had carved an intricate image — the shape of a light bulb. Inside the outline, a lowercase *i* had been cut into the center. She asked, "What is it?"

He gave a knowing nod. "The logo of IntraTonics, the software and laser logistics company where Hashimoto used to work. Must be an inside joke. We've got to be close."

Abigail wasn't convinced. "I know you emailed your contact that we were coming, but we can't wait for them to find us. I'm running out of time. Josh's case is being heard in a federal court on the other side of the country tomorrow, and I'm the only one who can handle it. I had hope that Harry Smythe would be my backup, but I just got a text that he's been hospitalized. It may be his heart again. I hope not. So, I have no other legal counsel who can pitch in. I'm it. We have to find these people *now*."

They climbed back into the Land Rover and drove up the trail a quarter of a mile. Cal slowed the car again, then stopped. He gazed out at the woods to the left. "Not exactly a road," he said, pointing to a spot where the underbrush looked less dense, "but wide enough for a four-wheel drive ... maybe." He rolled down the window and clicked off the ignition so he could listen.

"I hear something," Abigail said, "like some kind of vehicle approaching."

"Someone's coming," Cal said, pointing to the cleared space. Moments later, a black Hummer bounced into sight, winding slowly around trees and hitting ditches and rises in the forest floor. It stopped. Four men with beards, sunglasses, and stocking caps on their heads jumped out, mostly decked out in dirty lumberjack shirts and overalls. Two were carrying shotguns.

Abigail had a sudden, fearful thought. *What if these men have nothing to do with the Underground? Maybe they're simply thugs living in the wild, running from the law.*

One of the unarmed men approached them first.

"We've been looking for you — ," Cal started to say.

"Shut up," the man barked, "until we ask you to talk."

"What's your name?" he asked Abigail. She identified herself, trying not to tremble.

He stepped up closer, grabbed her, and forced her to the ground as he pulled long plastic zip ties from his pocket. He looped them around her wrists. Cal leaped at him, jamming his forearm under his neck and locking it until the man started gagging and let go of Abigail. Cal then yanked him off of Abigail and tossed him sideways to the ground and shouted, "What are you doing? You know who we are and why we — " But Cal didn't have a chance to finish his sentence. Two of the other men jumped him from behind, and one of them slugged him twice in the side of the head. Abigail screamed, but they ignored her. The two men pinned Cal and zip-tied him while the other secured Abigail.

At that moment a small all-terrain four-wheeler came rushing out of the woods and slammed on its brakes next to the Hummer. Another bearded man hopped out, this one dressed in dockers and a clean sweatshirt. He had a photocopy of the headshots that Cal had emailed the group when he had first set up the meeting. The man compared the faces in the picture with Cal and Abigail on the ground. He said, "Okay, men, no need to get rough. These are the ones." He bent down to Abigail. "Sorry about the inconvenience, Mrs. Jordan, but we can't be too careful. The government would love to know our location." Then he ordered the men to cut the zip-ties.

As Abigail and Cal stood up, the leader added, "But I'm going to insist that you wear hoods over your heads until we reach the compound."

An hour later, Abigail found herself sitting across from the mysterious Chiro Hashimoto in a forlorn camping lodge. The front yard was filled with tall weeds, and the main building, constructed of split logs, had moss creeping up its outside.

Hashimoto was a slim Japanese man in his early forties, but he looked younger with his head of wild, untamed black hair, which seemed to sprout in all directions. Now that Abigail had her personal audience with the iconoclastic computer genius, she was going to give him a piece of her mind. "You men are outrageous! Cal gave you notice that we were coming, and why. Roughing us up was uncalled for!"

Hashimoto seemed nonplussed. "You're the one who needs me, not the other way around. So we can treat you any way we want."

"You should be ashamed of yourself!"

Hashimoto laughed loudly. "So, you're going to act like my mother now?"

She glanced around at the dirty dishes stacked on a table in the corner. "You clearly need one around here."

"Look," Hashimoto shot back, "the way your son went after my guy, you should be glad that neither of you got shot. And you know what else?" Hashimoto stiffened his back and tilted his head slightly. "I think your son is a punk."

Abigail went snake-eyed and blurted out, "You may think he's just a computer geek because he managed to hunt you down, but if it was just the two of you in a fair fight, he'd break both your arms."

Hashimoto grinned back. "And what makes you think I fight fair?"

He gave a loud guffaw as he sat cross-legged, jiggling his foot. His face turned. "Okay. Chitty-chat is over. I know what you want. You got a problem. No BIDTag. And you want Chiro Hashimoto's magic solution."

"I'll be frank with you," Abigail said, "because I'm desperate. In about — " she glanced at the atomic clock on her Allfone — "nineteen hours, I've got to be in a federal court of appeals in Washington, arguing my husband's case."

"You're not going to make it, lady. How you going to get there in time from here?"

"Don't worry about that. I've got my travel plans set. But what I can't do is pass through a BIDTag scanner without your help. I'm a nontagger."

"When chips are down, you need Chiro Hashimoto," he said with a sly smile.

"That's right," she said, "but first I want to make sure Cal is okay. Where did they take him?"

Hashimoto waved to a man standing outside who had been peering in through a dirty window. The man disappeared, and in a minute Cal was led into the room. Hashimoto dismissed his man and pointed to a chair next to Abigail. He asked Cal to sit. "I've read up on you guys," Hashimoto said, "all of you. You Jordans are some kind of wild, wacky family." He tittered. "Don't really know, though, if I like your Roundtable. Maybe some of your agenda is okay. Other stuff, not quite so sure. But I like the way you tell the big fed power tyrants they got to watch out."

"I think you're the real rebel here," Cal said. Abigail could see that Cal was trying to win Hashimoto over. "You masterminded the biggest global computer network hacking job ever accomplished. If, in fact, that was you — "

Hashimoto grinned. "Kid's stuff. I just used some advanced spearphishing emails contaminated with malicious software and spread through botnets — my own design — aimed at worldwide organizations and several countries. They click onto my infected link and — presto — I get an open door into their entire network. I was on the verge of an attack even bigger — an instant entrée into all thirteen root servers that control the entire Internet."

"So, why'd you leave China?" Cal asked.

"The IT bureau guys in Beijing said they would hurt me bad if I didn't do everything they wanted. That was like a big poke in the eye. I kind of woke up, you know? I decided to get out fast. Next stop, Seattle, and IntraTonics." He turned to Abigail and added with a grin, "Also lady, I don't really think Cal is a punk. I was just playing with you."

Cal jumped in. "Chiro, can my mother get one of your masking BIDTag facsimiles?"

He rubbed his chin and turned his attention to her. "So, your husband, Colonel Jordan ... I've read some of the tech journals on his RTS invention. Nice little system he's developed. So, this legal case he's got ..."

"He's been charged with treason. The real story is he's a patriotic American hero who has done nothing wrong, but President Tulrude is bent on using the attorney general's office to destroy him. This goes all the way back to when Tulrude was vice president. Josh's AmeriNews Internet service started to expose her corruption. She knows that the Department of Defense is resentful of her sellout of our country and sympathetic to what the Roundtable is trying to accomplish — to educate the American people about the garage-sale giveaway of American national security and sovereignty by Tulrude's administration."

"Okay, yeah," Chiro said, "interesting. But I don't get why you need my help, lady."

"I'm my husband's attorney. I've got to plead his case tomorrow. If I don't, he and I will be forced to stay on opposite ends of the earth, and Josh will never get a fair trial. Ever. But I can't take a single step into that federal court building — through the scanners — unless I've got something that looks and acts like a BIDTag on the back of my hand."

"I guess you and I have something in common," Hashimoto said. "Neither of us wants to be a tagged chicken in the government's henhouse. But I always wondered why the government wouldn't let people get tagged after the deadline ... you know, for people who change their minds. Just make them pay a fine, that kind of thing. It didn't make sense."

"I could speculate," Abigail said. As she looked at Hashimoto's widening eyes, she could see he was interested. "It's my guess that Tulrude's tough, no-amnesty for nontaggers was part of some deal she made with international leaders. Part of a global plan she's tied into. There's somebody at the very top — higher even than the president — who needs every human on this planet to be controlled through BIDTagging."

Hashimoto leaned back in his chair. "Yeah, yeah. The big plan. Right. The worldwide game. I've been thinking about that." Then he broke into a big grin. "But I got my own plan. I can outsmart the global people. I have a plan for gaming their own game."

"I came to you for help," Abigail said. "So, in return, I'm going to help you. I'm going to tell you something important. You may be a computer genius, Chiro, but you need to know that some systems can't be gamed. The prophetic events that God is about to unfold can't be sidetracked or avoided. I'm here because I believe God is about to allow Planet Earth to be shaken in a very dramatic way. Titanic events — horrible catastrophes — human suffering, yes, all of that is about to come to pass. But in the midst of it all, a chance for everyone, including you, Chiro, to consider the most important figure in the history of the world — Jesus Christ. What He did for us in the past — His death on the cross for your sins, and His promise of eternal life for everyone who believes in Him and receives His forgiveness as Savior and Lord. And then there's what He's going to do in the future — when a few years of worldwide suffering have passed, Jesus will come back to establish His reign on earth. His kingdom. I'm telling you this because, when these events are ready to burst upon the scene, my son, Cal, and I, and many, many others — all of the followers of Jesus Christ, we will all be taken off the earth."

Chiro gave a funny look, jutting his head backward. "You taking a space ship or something?" And then he gave a nervous laugh.

Abigail gave him a warm, mothering smile. "Jesus is calling His own, His true followers to Himself, those who have believed in Him and whose spirits have become born again as a result. In one, fleeting blink of an eye, we will be gone and will be in the presence of the King of Kings. I hope by that time you will be one of those, Chiro. But if not, then just remember what I told you today. If you find yourself left behind, surrounded by an unbelieving world full of chaos, and violence, growing cold, and loveless, and dark, then remember this conversation. Whatever else you do, remember what I just told you."

Chiro was now wrinkling the side of his mouth, not smiling, not sneering, but considering the unthinkable. "You're talking about the end, aren't you? The end of the world."

Abigail nodded and smiled in a way that looked into his eyes and way beyond. Then Chiro jumped to his feet. "Okay, lady, I'll help you. Quick, quick. Follow me."

FORTY-ONE

Special Agent Ben Boling was in his office, finishing up reports at his desk. He was summarizing his investigation into the possible threat against Senator Hewbright. He had been walking a razor-thin line with John Gallagher, collecting tips and dropping hints himself, but just short of violating Bureau rules.

When Boling was in Wichita, he scoured the records of the Better Body Health and Fitness Club where Perry Tedrich was a member and had worked out the day of his disappearance. Boling learned something intriguing. On the day that Tedrich had been there, a woman member said that, after her workout, her membership card went missing, apparently when she was in the shower. At first she thought she had misplaced it but realized it had probably been stolen. While the locker rooms were open to the public, a card was required to get into the gym itself. For some reason the owner had set up a system where the membership cards had RFID chips and ID numbers in them but no other identifying data — no picture, no name. According to the fitness center, that was to protect the privacy of their members.

When the manager of the center found out about the possible theft, he made a general announcement over the PA, warning the people in the gym to make sure their cards were secure. Boling figured that Tedrich must have heard that and placed his card in his shoe for safekeeping.

Boling asked the owner to check the computer registration log. It showed that the woman whose card was stolen entered the gym at 12:30 p.m. that day. She left at 1:20 p.m. when she had finished her workout. But someone, using the same card, went back to the gym at 1:28 p.m., about three minutes after Perry Tedrich had arrived.

One thing that had not been made public was the fact that Perry Tedrich wasn't just the head of Hewbright's Wichita campaign. He had also been an integral part of Hewbright's Washington senate staff for several years, before returning to his hometown of Wichita to run that city's campaign headquarters. He knew Hewbright as well as anyone in the capital, including a lot of personal contact with Hewbright's late wife, who had died of cancer two years earlier. Did Tedrich have some personal or political information about Hewbright that his enemies wanted to learn?

That was when Boling put in a city-wide request for hotels, restaurants, bars, and movie theaters — all of which now were using RFID scanners as well as BIDTag scanners — to see if the computer chip in the membership card registered a hit at any one of them that day. He received one result. The card carrier had entered the Red Steer Bar and Grill at 3:00 p.m. At the exact same time, the RFID chip in Tedrich's membership card also registered a hit as he also walked into the restaurant. At 4:50 p.m., Perry Tedrich's credit card was hit for a lunch for a party of two. No one at the Red Steer remembered Tedrich or the mystery woman, but the cards showed that they left together.

Boling felt he was closing in. He was about to put it in writing when a flag showed up in the corner of his computer screen. It read: "Assignment Status Report."

He read it over, groaned, and shot back an insta-memo to the sender. "Is this true?"

The reply showed up on his screen five minutes later. "Yes. Effective immediately."

Boling sat at his desk, staring out the window for nearly half an hour. Then he called his wife. "Hey, it's me. Okay, honey, how about dinner out tonight? Your choice of restaurant."

"Sure, but I've already thawed some pork chops."

"Feed 'em to the dogs."

"Something wrong?"

"I just need to get out and get my mind off my job."

Wichita, Kansas

That same day, John Gallagher had managed to persuade the manager of the Better Body Health and Fitness Center to let him roam among the clients in the gym. Gallagher had simply explained that he was "working the case with FBI Special Agent Ben Boling." Technically true, he mused. Sort of.

He arrived on the same day of the week — at the same time — as when Perry Tedrich had last been there. Gallagher interviewed every woman in the gym, but none of them could remember a thing about that day. He strolled over to a man on the elliptical machine. He flashed a picture of Perry Tedrich, and the man stopped his routine and took a look. "Yeah, he looks familiar. I've seen him here."

Then Gallagher asked whether he recalled the day of the incident and gave the date and added, "The desk records say you came in that day."

The guy became a little ill at ease, but Gallagher assured him he wasn't the focus of any investigation and had nothing to worry about. So he started opening up. He said he vaguely remembered Tedrich being there that day.

"Do you remember any new faces that day?"

The man smiled. "Oh, yeah. A real looker. A really fine-looking woman working one of the ellipticals down the row there."

Gallagher asked for a description, after which he pulled out pictures of some of the women on Hewbright's staff, together with a few wildcards thrown in for good measure. He showed them to the man and told him to take his time.

"This one," he said, pointing to one of the photos. He picked that photo out in an instant, and Gallagher knew why. He thanked the man, trotted out of the fitness center, and immediately speed-dialed Ben Boling.

When the FBI agent answered, Gallagher skipped the pleasantries. "Ben, hot off the press. I know you don't want any official help from us Roundtable types, but I also know the politics of the new FBI since Tulrude took over — and how you guys have your hands tied behind your back. So I'm about to give you some really sweet unofficial help on this Hewbright case. You can thank me later. I've just made a positive ID on one of Hewbright's national advisors — Zeta Milla — as the woman Perry Tedrich was with on the day he vanished."

Boling was in the lunchroom of the FBI field office where several other agents were milling around. He asked Gallagher to hold on as he went back to his desk.

When Boling got back he said, "Okay. That fits with what I've got. I found out that our victim was with the same person both at the gym and then at a restaurant later that day."

There was silence on the other end. Finally Gallagher replied, "Awfully nice of you to share some information with me, Ben. Really appreciate that."

Now Boling was the silent one, as he was figuring things out.

"So, listen," Gallagher continued, "I've also found out something else. Zeta Milla's got this cover story about being a heroic survivor who escaped Cuba as a little girl, but I believe she stole the identity of that Cuban girl."

When he didn't get a reply, Gallagher added, "Still there, Ben?"

"Yeah ..."

"Anyway, I know the really rotten-to-the-core politics in the Bureau. One of the reasons I left. But Ben, I'm telling you, watch your backside. You don't know where this will lead. One thing, though — if you get the pink slip telling you you're off this case — you can pretty well guess that something is really rotten in Denmark, so to speak — and in Washington too."

"Thanks for the tip, John."

"So — where do we go from here?"

"Nowhere in particular."

"What?"

"Yeah, look," Ben said, "I gotta go. Good talking to you."

After clicking off, Ben Boling scrolled his screen up to the Assignment Status Report he had just received and read the notice again:

Please be advised that Special Agent Ben Boling is being transferred from the Hewbright Investigation — Case No. WK-1377 — SA Boling's authority to inquire and access investigative data on this case number is hereby terminated.

FORTY-TWO

Charleston, South Carolina

Outside the barbecue joint, the parking lot had been rigged up with a platform that had "Hewbright for President" banners everywhere and was filled with long tables heaped with food. Deborah Jordan was waiting patiently off to the side. She had been standing there for two hours, first listening to Hewbright's stump speech, then watching him shake hands under the watchful eye of his Secret Service agent. A parade of well-wishers lined up to fill their paper plates with barbecued chicken, baked beans, and cornbread.

Finally, she spotted Katrena Amid with her staff credentials swinging around her neck. Deb strode up to her. "Sorry to bother you, Ms. Amid, but I'm Deborah, and I spoke to you earlier today about working as a volunteer on the national staff, remember? I came recommended from Abigail Jordan. She's a personal friend and supporter of Senator Hewbright. I've got Pentagon experience in information services, and I graduated from West Point."

"Yes," Amid said, "I remember. You're Deborah Shelly. We were waiting for our security folks to clear you. I haven't heard back. Sorry."

Deb persisted. "I've got my own car. I'll pay my own expenses — "

"That's nice, but we've got a lot of folks who want to work in the campaign, and we can't fit all of them in. Perhaps you can work for us in your local precinct — that would be a great help to the senator."

Just then, Deborah noticed that Senator Hewbright had worked his way down the end of the food tables and was shaking hands with a couple. He was just twenty feet away. Deborah excused herself and hurried off in his direction before Amid could protest. The Secret Service agent stepped in front of her when she was about ten feet from Senator Hewbright.

Deborah stopped, smiled cordially, and called out to the senator. "Senator Hewbright — Abigail Jordan says hello!"

Hewbright turned and squinted in her direction. He started moving toward Deborah as Katrena Amid stepped quickly in her direction to play interference. But Deborah beat her to the punch. Hewbright was next to Deborah and tossed a relaxed nod to his security guard. Deborah explained, "Abigail Jordan recommended me as a volunteer on your staff."

"Oh? So, how is Abigail these days?" the senator said as he shook Deborah's hand.

"Doing well, Senator. Working on her husband's case, I believe, trying to reverse the nonsense caused by the Tulrude administration."

Deborah pulled a letter out of her pocket and handed it to Hewbright. "Here's Mrs. Jordan's letter of recommendation."

Hewbright scanned it while Katrena Amid grimaced.

"This young lady is Deborah Shelly," Senator Hewbright said, holding up the letter and handing it to his staffer. "It says here you graduated with honors from West Point and work at the Pentagon."

"Yes, sir. I applied for an extended leave with the hopes of being able to help with your campaign."

"Of course, security is getting tighter these days. They'll have to screen you."

"Ms. Amid has already put my name in several hours ago. I filled out your security form. We're just waiting now."

"I'll tell you what," Hewbright added. "I have great admiration for Abigail and Joshua Jordan. If they say you should be on my national team, and you get clearance from security, then I say come onboard." He turned to his assistant campaign chief of staff. "Katrena?"

She smiled tightly. "Yes, Senator, we could use her, absolutely."

"Well, this is the last whistle-stop for me before our national convention, which starts tomorrow in Denver. I'm flying there tonight."

"And you have the sufficient delegate count from your primary victories," Deborah said brightly, "to sweep the convention." She was silently thankful she had done her homework.

"On the other hand," Hewbright said, "anything can happen at a political convention." He waved to her and started to step away as his national campaign director beckoned to him. Hewbright stopped and took a step back toward Deborah. "I'm sure you know I'm an old military guy myself and a member of the armed services committee for more years than I can count. I'm really happy to have someone like you onboard."

After stopping for a moment to say something to George Caulfield, Hank Hewbright headed to the big campaign bus to get some down time.

□□□

In the campaign bus Zeta Milla was pouring a cup of coffee for Senator Hewbright. She mixed in some creamer and a packet of Sweet'N Low. "Hank, here's your coffee, just the way you like it."

"Wow, that's real service. Thanks, Zeta."

He dropped into a soft swivel chair and loosened his tie. "I know your focus is South and Central America and the island nations, but that briefing book you put together on the Russian Republics and China for my future debates with President Tulrude was exceptional."

"Glad it was helpful. I've told you a million times, I'll do whatever I can to help. You're very special."

He nodded humbly. "It's been a long primary season," he said, rubbing his eyes, "but now the convention. Then the debates, and then the home stretch to the election."

Milla sat next to him in the other swivel chair. "If you allow me to say so, Hank, I know that Ginny, from what I knew of her, would have loved to have been here to see this. She would have been so proud of what you've accomplished — and all that you will accomplish as the leader of the Free World. This is your time, Hank. Relish it."

"Funny you should mention Ginny. I haven't said this to many people — but she's been on my mind because of what she said shortly before she died, about her wanting to see me run."

Zeta reached over and rubbed his hand. He squeezed back. He looked her in the eyes, then broke the gaze and slowly released her hand. "We have to be careful, Zeta. About mixing the personal with the political. Sometimes the lines get blurred. It's not about Ginny either. She told me pointblank that I would need a woman in my life when she was gone."

Zeta smiled and nodded, but she wasn't surprised to hear Hank's confession. She replied, "Whoever that woman is, she'll be very lucky. I've never met a man like you, Hank." Then she pulled his hand to her lips and kissed it. Standing up to leave, she said, "You need time. Today was a long day. I'll be around ... anything you need ... anything. Just ask."

As she walked out of the bus, she ran into George Caulfield who asked where Hewbright was.

"In the bus," Zeta answered. "We were having some private time together."

The campaign director stopped in his tracks and gave her a withering look. Then he mounted the steps into the bus.

Zeta continued on. There was a lot of work to do.

□□□

An hour later, Katrena Amid, holding her Allfone, strode up to Deborah. "Right. Just heard. Got an expedited approval from the security people. Looks like we'll be seeing you in Denver. You'll have to get your own transportation though. We'll have your credentials by the time you arrive."

Deborah breathed easier and thanked Katrena. In her peripheral vision Deborah caught Zeta Milla. As Katrena hurried off, Deborah casually jogged over to Milla, who was putting some papers into a briefcase. "Excuse me, but aren't you Zeta Milla?"

The Cuban woman smiled politely. "Yes, I am."

"I'm Deborah. New campaign worker. Volunteer. I know you're one of the shining lights among the senator's foreign relations advisors, and I just wanted to introduce myself."

"Kind of you to say so," Milla said, going back to her papers.

"I'm a West Point grad with a strong interest in foreign relations. So I'm thrilled I might be able to work with you."

Zeta Milla turned quickly to face her. "I'm afraid not. Campaign staff—especially volunteers—don't consort with professional policy advisors. Now, if you'll excuse me ..."

Milla gathered up her reports, stuffed them in her briefcase, and walked quickly away.

FORTY-THREE

Abigail and Cal were in the Citation X, winging their way through the darkness back to Washington, D.C. Abigail was relieved she might be able to get to her court appearance on time after all. She glanced over at Cal, who was fast asleep and snoring loudly. But she couldn't sleep. Her mind kept clicking despite the fatigue that threatened to overwhelm her.

The reading light above her head was on. She was cramming for the oral arguments that would commence in just a matter of hours. She knew the laws related to the issues in the case, of course, and she had the facts down cold. But she didn't know what was on the mind of the three appellate judges who would be hearing the case. She wouldn't know that until she was standing at the podium in the federal courtroom. The green light would flash on, signifying her turn to start her argument, and then — if everything had gone perfectly up to that point — she would argue the wrongness of the case against Joshua and field a raft of questions from the judges.

Before getting to that point, however, she had to get inside the courthouse, which meant getting past the security guards with their BIDTag scanner just inside the entrance. She lifted the back of her right hand to the light. The laser tattoo was invisible — just like the real BIDTags.

When Chiro Hashimoto had escorted her and Cal out of his lodge and down a path through the woods to a lonely cement building that had a huge satellite dish mounted behind, he assured them his system would work. "My BIDTag facsimiles are the closest counterfeit you will ever see," he bragged, "perfect in every detail. I was able to duplicate the government's laser imprint system. You know why?"

Before Abigail or Cal could respond, Hashimoto answered, "Because I'm the one who designed it for IntraTonics, who then sold it to the government!" And with that he laughed raucously. "I consulted with bioengineers and medical experts about using nonlethal lasers to imprint permanent, invisible code matrices on human skin. Not easy. But I did it. You have to admit — the idea was pretty cool, right?"

"Now the question is," Cal replied, "will your counterfeit BIDTag, created out here in the forest, simulate the government's system? Is it close enough that the tag screeners at the courthouse will give her a pass?"

"I've built my own scanners," Hashimoto said as he unlocked the door to the cement building, "very close to the ones the government uses. So I can test the result. Passes every time."

Once inside, he flicked on the florescent overhead lights. What Abigail and Cal saw was a fully functioning tech lab, complete with rows of computers linked together, laser guns inside glass tubes, and a table with microscopes. But there was more. Cal drifted over to the other side of the room where a row of chairs were lined up behind a long metal table. On the table there were rows of zephyrs, receivers, shortwave transmitters, voice analyzing screens, cryptographic cipher machines, and monitors — all cabled together in a massive tangle of electrical cords.

"This is your own listening station, isn't it?" Cal said, pointing to the strange collection of electronics.

"We're not finished yet," Hashimoto said, "but when we are, I'm going to watch the government's surveillance just as closely as they watch the citizens of America."

"Why?" Abigail asked.

"Well, why are you here, right now with me, in the Olympic National Forest?" he shot back. "Because we don't trust how our government has morphed — turning into a predator, devouring information about everyone in the nation. I don't trust how it's going to use that data. We are entering a new ice age, where freedom will be extinct. The big freeze. And so, this," Hashimoto said, gesturing to his makeshift surveillance laboratory, "is my Ice Station Zebra."

Cal chuckled at the movie reference. Chiro took Abigail over to one of the laser tubes. "The key," he continued, "was to take the basic laser-imprint system I devised and refine it. Changed it so in my version the imprint is only temporary and would fade from the surface of the skin. That was really hard to do, but I did it. That way if we have to venture out into society we can laser-tag ourselves with a little invisible QRC box on the skin that contains harmless basic bits of information that will satisfy the government scanners but won't give away anything. Then, after a few days — poof — the laser tag starts to dissolve."

Hashimoto dumped himself onto a lab stool in front of a computer. He started typing in a flurry. "I'm creating your QRC pattern that will contain only a little bit of data about you, which I will put into the system." When he had finished, Abigail placed her hand into a brace that lined up the back of her hand against the glass-enclosed end of the laser tube. "Okay. Now your own personal QRC matrix has been loaded into the laser for transmittal in the form of a little invisible pattern that will be lasered onto your skin. Don't move," he said. He typed in a code that was connected to the laser and flipped a switch. "In twenty seconds you'll feel it," he said. "Unlike the government's version, you will feel mine, and it'll hurt a little."

The laser whirred — first softly; then, with a minor roar, a stream of light as gossamer thin as a spider web shot through the tube onto Abigail's hand. She winced. Then it was over.

As the three of them walked back to the lodge in the dusk, Cal thought of something the tech genius had said. "You described your scanners as 'very close' to the kind used by the government. Which is fine as far as it goes. But have you ever sent your temporary laser tags — like the one you just gave my mom — through the government scanners to see if they will pass security?"

"Ha, ha," Hashimoto replied.

"That doesn't answer my question," Cal pressed.

Hashimoto's reply left a cloud of uncertainty hanging in the air.

"Do you think I would leave my compound to test it out on the federal government?"

Now, airborne in the Citation X, Abigail stared at the back of her hand, wondering what was there. Would it be her passport into the court building in Washington? The rest would have to remain as it always had remained, in the sovereignty of God. She tried to review her notes for the case, but her eyes were too heavy. Before long she was fast asleep.

FORTY-FOUR

Jerusalem

Pastor Peter Campbell staked out a spot on the Western Wall plaza to preach. He knew it would be controversial, but he fixed his eyes on the earthmoving equipment, tractors, and cranes on the Temple Mount just above the plaza. It seemed clear that the climax of history was rushing up. How could he wait? This was a time for boldness. He had left his Eternity Church in Manhattan in the hands of his assistant pastor so he could come to Jerusalem for exactly this moment. He thought about runners who had trained and prepared all of their life for the Olympics and had one chance to compete. Would any one of them balk when it was time to stride up to the starting blocks?

Forty members of his small Jerusalem congregation gathered around Campbell as he started to preach. Onlookers started drifting over to hear him. Soon the group swelled to over a hundred. Campbell had a small portable amplifier and a wireless mic headset. As he spoke, his voice was calm, unrushed.

"Two millennia ago, a fisherman-turned-disciple by the name of Peter walked into the center of this city. Filled with the Spirit of God, he told the crowd what he himself had seen and heard about the person of Jesus Christ. Peter was an eyewitness. And he gave testimony that Jesus, his beloved friend, rabbi, Savior, and king — the very Son of God — died on a bloody Roman cross not far from here. But he died for an incredible purpose — to take away the sins of everyone standing here today—me and you—everyone who ever trod these stones and everyone who ever lived. He paid the price that only the sinless Holy One of God could pay—the man who was truly God in the flesh and who had dwelled among us. He took on Himself the punishment destined for us and willingly accepted the sentence of torture and death. Right here in this city.

"But it didn't end there. Jesus walked out of the tomb three days later, just as He said He would. And Peter was an eyewitness to that too. Possessing such earthshaking news, Peter could not be silent about it. And neither can I. Many years ago my life was transformed by the power of Jesus Christ who walked out of that grave—it started on the day I confessed that I was a sinner and that Jesus, the Son of God, was my Savior and Lord, and that I wanted Him to live and dwell in my heart—that is when everything changed. And it can change for you. Thousands responded to Peter's message that day in this city two thousand years ago. But God is not interested in thousands or millions or billions. Numbers don't impress Him. He is the one who cast a trillion stars across the universe. God will soon enter this planet and bring an end to human history. His Son, Jesus the Christ, will establish His kingdom. But there is one particular number that does concern the heart of God." Peter Campbell pointed his index finger up to heaven. "That number is the number one. Which means you," and he pointed to a young man wearing a UT Longhorns football sweatshirt in the crowd. "And you." He pointed to a mother with her hands on a baby carriage. "And you, my friend." He gestured to a bearded Hasidim in the very back of the crowd, who was wearing a black hat and long coat.

"Today, you are building a great temple," Campbell said, pointing to the construction on the Temple Mount. The sounds of tractor treads and diesel engines could be heard. "But know this—that God is building His temple. And it is not a thing made by human hands. It is an assembly of people who have chosen to believe in, receive, and follow Jesus. They are His temple, the work of the hands of God. And today God welcomes you to become part of His great spiritual assembly. He holds the door open. And when God opens a door no man can close it. You can walk through that door right now. Jesus is that door. And He wants to welcome you, like a prodigal son or daughter, and to lift the burdens from your soul. But also know this — a day will come when that door will close. And when God closes the door, no man can open it."

☐☐☐

The commanding Shin Bet agent, who was surveying the scene from his position on the edge of the large open plaza, radioed the Jerusalem police and gave his order in Hebrew. "We need armed officers to disperse an illegal assembly at the Western Wall plaza, over."

"This is police dispatch. What is your situation?"

"A Christian religious leader is preaching in violation of the prime minister's emergency order regarding religious incitement of civil unrest."

"Confirmed. Officers are being dispatched, over."

☐☐☐

Beyond the outer ring of listeners, GNN reporter Bart Kingston was ready to do a stand-up with his single cameraman. When he had heard from his sources in the city that Pastor Campbell planned to defy the prime minister's emergency orders to prohibit "public displays of extremist religious language," he rushed to the scene.

His timing was perfect. At the other end of the plaza, a dozen Jerusalem police were entering the wide space, heading directly toward the crowd. A loudspeaker boomed over the area, commanding the crowd to disperse. People moved in all directions. Soon, the only people left were Campbell, a handful of his devotees, and the police.

Kingston motioned for his camera guy to follow him closer to the Western Wall area. Then the unexpected happened — four Jewish men, who appeared to be lawyers or some kind of businessmen, appeared and rushed headlong toward the police.

They held papers in their hands, shouting, "We have a temporary restraining order from the Israeli Supreme Court to protect the rights of these Christian worshipers ..."

Kingston, standing a good distance away, watched as the guards disregarded the paperwork. One of the officers lobbed a canister of tear gas into the air, which fell a few feet away from Campbell, spilling white smoke into the area. A young woman collapsed, coughing and gagging. Campbell stumbled over to her and picked her up in his arms and tried to walk her away from the area. But his eyes were streaming with tears, and his throat was closing as if a boa constrictor was squeezing his windpipe.

From his safe position, Kingston was about to ask his cameraman if he had caught all of this, but the guy was a pro, and Kingston knew it. At some point — perhaps only an instant later — it ceased to be a news story for Bart Kingston.

He surveyed the scene. Pastor Peter Campbell was overcome by gas and down on his knees with a young woman cradled in his arms. Kingston looked up at the Temple Mount, where the construction workers were peering down at the melee on the plaza below.

Apocalypse was one of the words that flooded Kingston's mind.

And he thought of another word, one that Campbell had shared in their television interview a week before. It was a word that he couldn't admit to anyone else. He barely was able to admit it to himself, but he was seriously entertaining it and what it meant. The thought of the ultimate divorce — of some taken and some left. A God who rescues those who have accepted his lifeline and leaving behind those who have refused. As the police with their gas masks waded into the smoke to arrest Campbell's small but disabled group, Kingston could not shake the almost palpable force of that word.

Rapture.

FORTY-FIVE

Washington, D.C.

It was after hours and Supreme Court Justice Carter Lapham was in the back of the limo that was pulling out of the underground parking deck of the Supreme Court building. For some reason his driver turned onto the avenue that ran past the front of the tall marble courthouse with the words "Equal Justice Under Law" chiseled in stone over the columns. After stopping at the corner, the driver turned right onto Second Street and slowly eased into traffic as it passed the Supreme Court building. It looked like a traffic tie-up ahead and some flashing lights from two squad cars.

Lapham peered at the tangle of traffic. "Hey, Brock," he said with a wry smile, "would you like me to drive tonight? I could teach you some techniques on avoiding traffic jams."

Brock, his longtime driver, smiled into the rear view mirror but didn't respond, as if he had chosen this route on purpose.

The justice glanced from the window as the limo snaked past the steps leading up to the Supreme Court. He could see several capitol police officers handcuffing a man and a woman who were holding signs. One read: "Christ = Truth / Allah, Buddha, Sidharta = Liars." Another read: "Jesus Is Coming to Judge the Judges."

Justice Lapham had dissented bitterly in Marquis v. United States of America, but he could only woo three other votes to his side in that case. His dissent went beyond the bounds of anything he had ever written before in a decision — calling it a "constitutional atrocity" for the majority to have upheld the hate speech provisions of the international treaty pushed by President Tulrude and ratified by the senate. He was now witnessing the toxic aftermath of that treaty with his own eyes. But there was something worse, and it made him cringe. Lapham considered the court's decision in Marquis to have been a betrayal of the oath taken by the five other justices who formed the majority in that court opinion. After all, there was that matter of an oath taken by the justices — all of them — to uphold the Constitution. When exactly, he wondered, does bad judicial reasoning drift into treason, like a wayward youth who finally takes up the enticing invitation to join the local gang?

For a fleeting moment he entertained, once again, the idea of retirement. To go fishing in the Gulf on his forty-footer; going after that worthy fighter, the yellow-finned tuna, or the elegantly powerful sailfish that he would catch and release; traveling the world slow and easy, with his wife at his side ... Perhaps he would accept the permanent invitation to become an elder in his hometown Bible church in Wilmington, North Carolina.

Now it almost seemed as if he had the taste of vinegar in his mouth as the limo cruised away from the scene. It was the bitterness of gall, that his own country seemed to be slipping into legal oblivion. But then, this was not just a legal issue, and Lapham knew it. By and large, most judges he knew expressed little compulsion to honor the great Lawgiver. The words of one of his favorite poets, William Butler Yeats, haunted his mind more than ever lately. Its harrowing vision of the disintegration of civilization seemed to be ever before him — just as in Yeats's poem "The Second Coming," which he knew by heart:

Turning and turning in the widening gyre
The falcon cannot hear the falconer;
Things fall apart; the center cannot hold.

FORTY-SIX

SIA Headquarters

In his office, Jeremy was back on duty. Taking tentative sips of his still-too-hot paper cup of French vanilla coffee, he read the tracking report on Abigail Jordan. The surveillance chain had broken temporarily in the state of Washington. Then it was picked up again when the SIA facial recognition software made a match, verified by the Likely Route Estimator program: she had boarded her private jet in Seattle with a flight destination of Reagan National Airport in D.C.

Jeremy tapped in the search for FAA radar results. The jet was now approaching Columbus, Ohio.

The radar read: "Permission to land received by the tower in Columbus."

He took another sip. Better now, the coffee was hot but not scalding.

"Permission to land granted."

Ten minutes later, another posting on the FAA update quadrant of his screen.

"Citation X cleared to land at the Rapid Air commercial delivery hangar."

On the jet, Abigail put down her legal file and stretched. Cal was awake next to her. He looked out the window at the Ohio landscape. "You know they'll be waiting for you," he said, still gazing out the window. There was a resignation in his voice.

"Yes. They won't give up." As he turned his face from the window to face her, she added, "And neither will I."

"Abby and Cal," the pilot said, adjusting his sunglasses and donning his cap, "we'll be landing shortly. We're going into our final descent."

Abigail knew what that meant. And what she had to do.

At his tracking desk Jeremy touched the screen to view all the camera shots at the Columbus airport. He saw three angles. A small Rapid Air jet was being loaded with boxes. Some members of the ground crew were hovering around the jet, finishing the preflight check.

Jeremy hit the local police alert. A few minutes later the Columbus airport police said they would dispatch two squads to the hangar as soon as they finished the execution of a warrant on a fugitive who had just entered the passenger terminal.

The Citation X was rolling down the runway into view. It taxied up to the hangar and stopped.

"Better hurry," Jeremy said into his voice monitor. "They've landed."

The airport security officer responded, "Your subjects will not be leaving the airport—at least not on the ground," the officer replied. "We've relayed your request to every road leading from the commercial hangar. Tollgates are all shut now. Your subject can't get past any of them."

One of his fellow SIA staffers strolled in and began asking him about the upcoming agency bowling tournament, but Jeremy's eyes never left the screen. He shot his left hand up in the air. "Can't talk. Following a Red Notice here."

"Oooh," came the cynical response, "excuse me, Mr. Bounty Hunter of cyber space," and he left.

The camera shots on Jeremy's monitor showed the door of the Citation X opening. He saw the pilot, in his sunglasses and cap, and his flight case in hand, walking down the steps and darting quickly into the hangar.

"What's this?" Jeremy shouted. He waited a minute, then decided to hit the speed dial number for the hangar desk clerk. But before he could, the pilot, with his flight case, came striding back out of the hangar and quickly mounted the stairs and entered the Citation X, closing the door behind him.

"What's the matter," Jeremy said, questioning the image on the screen, "don't those expensive private jets have their own bathrooms? This doesn't look right."

The two pilots and a navigator of the Rapid Air commercial jet walked out and climbed up the stairs. The pilots could be seen strapping themselves into the cockpit. Jeremy hit the airport tower alert line. "Request a stop on a private passenger jet on the tarmac."

The Citation X was already taxiing down the runway.

"SIA, you need to give us the FAA stop order number" came the response.

"Forget it," Jeremy grumbled, "too late. Bathroom break completed. Or whatever ..." It was the *whatever* that bothered Jeremy.

"Say again?"

"Never mind. The private jet is already back in the air." Then Jeremy said to himself, "Okay, now I'm bringing it, Mrs. Jordan. The full force of the SIA's coming down on you at Reagan National. Last stop. We'll be waiting."

Jeremy touched the All Agency Enforcement tab on the screen. Boxes for FBI, SIA, Homeland Security, D.C. Police, Secret Service, and Airport Security appeared. One by one, Jeremy touched every box on the screen. Each time, he typed the Red Notice file number to authenticate his request.

It took only fifteen minutes for each of the agencies to respond. All but the Secret Service and Homeland Security verified that officials were on the way to the private charter flight section of Reagan National Airport. Two FBI agents, two SIA officials, two squad cars full of D.C. police, and an armed airport security officer had been dispatched. The full fire power would arrive at the tarmac within thirty minutes. More than enough time. The Citation X would not land for at least forty-five minutes, maybe longer.

FORTY-SEVEN

Nablus, Palestinian Authority

Ethan sat exhausted at the dining room table. He slept little the night before, tossing and turning as if electric currents were racing through his body. He couldn't shut his mind down. Pastor Ibrahim Kalid and his quiet, pleasant wife and their two daughters had all been cordial — overly accommodating, in fact, during his stay in their modest cement-block house.

The pastor's wife was now serving Ethan another enormous meal, this time a midafternoon snack of tea, falafel, hummus, dates, and olives. Joshua was in the other room with Pastor Ibrahim, praying. Ethan gave the woman a weak smile.

"Eat, please," she said. "You are a big man; you need much food."

"Any more, Mrs. Kalid, and you will make me too big." He patted his stomach, and she smiled and shook her head.

He reached out and picked up a soft date and popped it in his mouth, pulling the sweet fruit away from the seed with his tongue and then plucking the seed out of his mouth with his fingers and putting it on the brightly painted plate in front of him.

"Good dates," he said.

She smiled. Ethan felt awkward alone in the room with this woman, so he tried to make conversation. "So, have you — and your family — always been Christians?"

"No," she replied, "we were Muslim, like most here in Nablus."

"So, you changed?"

"Yes, took Jesus into our hearts."

"Has that ... caused you problems? With your neighbors, I mean?"

She shrugged and said, "A little, yes."

Ethan was tempted to explore that. He knew enough to understand that these people must be viewed as infidels by others in their town. Now they were harboring Joshua Jordan, a man targeted by Islamic terrorists — in fact, one of their Imams had issued a fatwa against him. He wondered if the Kalid family had ever received death threats for their new faith or had even been the targets of violence because they were now following Jesus.

But Ethan decided not to pursue it. Instead he said, "Mrs. Kalid, you are very brave to have us stay with you. I really appreciate it."

She said something in return, but he couldn't decipher it through her thick Arabic accent. His face must have registered a question because she articulated the comment once again, but much more slowly: "I am being the Good Samaritan, like Jesus say."

"I see."

Ethan felt a flush of embarrassment, though he wasn't sure why. Maybe it was because, looking at this quiet woman now, he was in the presence of an astounding mixture of character traits — simple purity of motives coupled with some incredibly big-time courage. How could he explain that? He didn't know. But it seemed to amplify his own shortcomings.

The door to the adjoining room opened and Joshua and Pastor Ibrahim walked out. Joshua had his Allfone in one hand and with his other shook hands with the pastor. He then glanced over at Ethan. The look on Joshua's face seemed to possess an answer to a question that Ethan hadn't even asked yet.

Josh motioned for Ethan to follow him over to the other side of the room, and lowered his voice. "I just received a message from Joel Harmon," he said. "IDF command wants to talk to me about finishing our RTS refinement after all."

"What? Israel was tracking us down. I thought the prime minister wanted you in custody and turned over to the FBI for extradition?"

"He did. But then things changed, and they're willing to let bygones be bygones if I help them now."

"What happened?"

"I don't have all the details. But it seems the threat level has just been raised."

"What kind of threat?"

"Biological. In the hands of bad guys. That's all I know. The IDF's begging for us to help them to achieve full redirection capacity for the RTS defense system. So, I'm guessing that they anticipate a missile strike with some kind of nightmare biological warhead. They must want to make sure they can redirect the missiles to a full spectrum of alternate destinations — away from population centers."

"That's good news, then," Ethan beamed. "We can come out of hiding."

"Good news and bad news."

"What's the bad part?"

"The RTS tests I've run here in Israel haven't done the trick yet, to accomplish the higher level of control over the guidance systems of incoming missiles. That's what the Israelis want. But I've got an idea on how to get that RTS enhancement to happen. I hope ..."

"You'll figure it out," Ethan said, worried but trying to sound convincing.

"I just hope by the time I figure it out," Joshua said, "it's not too late."

FORTY-EIGHT

In the early morning hours, around 6:45 a.m., the nurses at Georgetown University Hospital were making their rounds. One of them was attending to attorney Harry Smythe, who was hooked up to a heart monitor. He had not been a happy patient. He kept talking about a case he might have to argue in court for some lady named Abigail Jordan. The nurse assured him he was going nowhere. He would have to remain in the hospital for several more days at least.

□□□

At 6:45 a.m., Jeremy was looking at his monitor, which was full of video images of the hangar and part of the D.C. Reagan Airport tarmac. The director was standing next to him, and behind him were several SIA staffers who had heard about the upcoming arrival.

Jeremy saw that the area around the hangar where the charter flights and private jets would dock was surrounded by armed federal agents and local police. On his audio hookup, Jeremy could hear the Citation X radio the tower for permission to land. It was quickly granted. The jet was descending. The FBI had taken the lead in coordinating the task force on the ground and would soon give the go ahead to approach the jet. "Hold positions," the senior FBI agent said over the radio.

The Citation X slowed as it approached the tarmac apron in front of the hangar. Then it halted.

"Perfect position," the FBI agent said to his team members. "Wait till we verify the engines are off."

The engines of the Citation X were cut, and the roar began to wind down to a whine and then a quiet whirring. The FBI agent counted down slowly from ten. When he got to one, he shouted into the radio, "*Now*, go, go, go!"

Several officers, with guns drawn in point-and-aim position, sprinted forward to surround the cabin of the jet. Over a bullhorn a voice advised the occupants to exit the plane with their hands raised high. Moments later the door opened. The pilot, still wearing his sunglasses, appeared with hands up and slowly descended the steps.

Next came Cal with his hands up as well. When they were on the tarmac, the officers grabbed them and cuffed them. All eyes were on the open door of the jet.

"Abigail Jordan," the voice on the bullhorn announced, "exit the airplane immediately with your hands up or we will come in after you."

In the SIA headquarters, watching the arrest scene play out on the monitor in Jeremy's office, the director was muttering, "Doesn't this lady know the jig's up?"

There was movement in the cabin near the open door. Someone was preparing to exit. A woman's hand appeared through the door and grabbed the handrail.

"Hands up!" the bullhorn boomed. Then the person exited the plane in full sight of the law enforcement team on the ground with their weapons drawn.

"What?" was the first word that came out of the SIA director's mouth. And then several profanities quickly followed.

Descending the stairs was a blonde middle-aged woman dressed in a pilot's uniform with a pair of sunglasses perched carefully just above her hairline so as to not muss her elegant coiffeur. When she reached the bottom of the stairs, she raised her hands but with a maintained gait and look of relaxed confidence, the kind of expression belonging to someone who had grown accustomed to high-stress intrigue.

As the FBI special agent in charge holstered his weapon and approached the woman, he ordered his fellow agent and two D.C. cops to enter the plane and search for Abigail. They scrambled up the stairs.

The agent, now directly in front of the woman, squinted in the early morning sun, shielding his eyes with his hand. "Victoria?" he stammered. "Victoria McHenry? What in the world are you doing here?"

She smiled and replied, "Hi, Fred. Yes, it's me."

"You aren't," he began and stepped closer, "still in the Agency ..."

She shook her head. "No. Pack and I've been out of the clandestine services division for a number of years now."

"Then what in the world are you doing here? In a pilot's uniform?"

"Can't a girl play dress-up once in a while?"

From the top of the stairs, the other FBI agent shouted down, "Fred, there's no one else in the plane."

Fred straightened up into a posture of official business. "Sorry, Victoria, but if you're a civilian, then I'm afraid you've just walked into a world of legal troubles."

"And what would those be?" she asked nonchalantly.

He bulleted back his reply without taking a breath. "Assisting a citizen who has refused to submit to federal BIDTag identification procedures as required by federal law."

Cal spoke up. "That's where you're wrong ..."

The FBI agent whirled around toward Cal. "And who are you?"

"Cal Jordan. You need to know, agent, that in the rush toward passage in Congress, the federal act making it a crime to refuse to get tagged contained one technical mistake. It was drafted in such a way as to prevent someone — like Victoria McHenry, or me for that matter, or even the pilot of our Citation X — from being prosecuted for aiding and abetting or even being a party to conspiracy to aid someone who has refused to get tagged. In other words, the only person you could prosecute would be someone who actually refused to get BIDTagged. And I presume you think that person is Abigail Jordan, my mother. Am I correct?"

The FBI agent strode up to Cal. "Are you a lawyer?"

"No, but I'll be a law student in a couple of weeks."

The FBI agent narrowed his eyes as his face faded into a scarlet color.

"Wanna bet?"

FORTY-NINE

Dulles International Airport, Virginia

John Gallagher had received the message from the Roundtable that Abigail needed his help. So he flew to the East Coast, having just arrived at the Dulles airport, west of D.C. He used his ex-fed-agent contacts to get a big SUV with tinted glass, hoping that would limit facial-recognition systems from getting a peek at Abigail, who was now sitting in the backseat. The license plates had special reflective plastic covers that made them unreadable from intersection cameras.

In a matter of minutes he would have to pass through the Dulles Toll Road. As part of the BIDTag program, the highway folks had discontinued the quick-pass system. Now, all drivers had to stop at the tollbooths and hold out the back of their hands to the scanners. He half-turned around to alert Abigail. "Okay, tollbooth ahead. We're about to see if I'm Mr. Clean with the feds or not."

Abigail leaned forward with her forearms resting on the seat in front of her. "John, this is the only route that will get me to the federal courthouse in time for my argument. We both heard the traffic report on I-66. The Dulles Toll Road is our only hope. So, friend, you do the driving up there, and I'll do the praying back here."

When they arrived at the booth, Gallagher held out his hand so it could be examined by the scanner housed within the little plastic hood that jutted out toward the driver's side.

The tollgate stayed closed in front of him and the red light was illuminated.

Gallagher waited, shifting in his seat. He could hear Abigail's voice softly speaking behind him. He raised his eyes to catch the reflection in his rearview mirror. He saw Abigail in the rear seat, hands clasped, head bowed, praying.

Come on, come on, Gallagher thought.

Then the gate lifted and the light turned green. Gallagher rolled to the tollbooth. A clerk sat in her little window. He took out a couple of international CReDO coins — the only ones that were accepted at tolls, and handed them to the woman. She counted the coins. The final light was still red ahead of them. The toll woman seemed to be studying her BIDTag scanner screen. Gallagher shifted in his seat, staring at the red light. Another half minute passed. Finally, the red light turned green and Gallagher eased his car forward, and then immediately merged into the crush of traffic on the Dulles Tollway heading toward downtown Washington.

□□□

In the Security and Identification Administration headquarters, Jeremy was working the same Rubik's cube he'd been working on all day. And he was about to twist the last colored square into place.

He reviewed the footage from the cameras at the Columbus commercial hangar. It showed someone — obviously Abigail Jordan, he now knew in retrospect, dressed as a pilot and walking from the Citation X into the hangar. Then, shortly after that, Victoria McHenry, also dressed as a pilot, left the hangar and then headed back to the Citation X.

Jeremy asked the obvious question: Where was Abigail Jordan now?

He was more than a little embarrassed and nervous to have to put in yet another apprehension request. This was his third request for the same violator, and now he had to get the approval of the director. He ran upstairs to the executive level and waited outside his door in the lobby. This particular apprehension was giving him heartburn. After fifteen minutes he stepped over to his secretary and asked her to move things along. Five minutes later, the director stepped out. Jeremy had the order for apprehension on an e-pad and a digital pen in his hand. The director scribbled his signature on the screen, gave him a look of disappointment, and reentered his office.

This was Jeremy's last chance — and he knew it. He returned to his database and tried another search. This time, the computer revealed just the information needed. Abigail Jordan, attorney-at-law, was scheduled to present an oral argument that morning at the U.S. federal court building in Washington, in the case of *United States v. Jordan*. Jeremy typed the courthouse address into the notice and hit Send, delivering it electronically to "all available law enforcement personnel within the District of Columbia." Then he crossed his fingers.

FIFTY

Abigail was as ready as she would ever be.

She clutched the brown expandable case file in her hand as she rode in the back of Gallagher's SUV. During the flight, she had changed into a dark blue suit and white silk blouse — the one she had stored in the flight case that she had carried off the Citation X and onto the commercial delivery plane. It was the outfit she often used for appellate arguments back when her law practice had her appearing in court regularly. That was when she would be able to jog several miles a day and would log three days a week at the gym. She giggled to herself in the jet's cramped bathroom when she put on the suit, skirt, and blouse and realized that they all, mercifully, still fit. Life had become so complicated recently. Almost no time now for the gym or running or so many other seemingly mundane things she used to take for granted. Sometimes she yearned for them.

As she buttoned up the suit, she wondered, *When, exactly, did the journey of life transform itself into such a hair-raising mountain climb?* She used to chuckle when friends would talk about slowing down and preparing for a future of relaxation and recreation. For her and Joshua, the days had sped up, not slowed down. The risks were more dangerous, and the stakes had become almost too high to calculate. In a short time she would be trying to enter a U.S. courthouse with a forged BIDTag to defend her husband in court. It was as if a spider web with the tensile strength of steel had entangled them both.

As she continued to get ready in the SUV, now brushing some lint

263

off her sleeve and trying to work the wrinkles out of her suit jacket, Abigail looked ahead at the traffic on Constitution Avenue. Just a few more minutes and they would be at the courthouse.

She thanked God for the miracles that had popped up every step of the way. That ride from Columbus to Dulles airport on the commercial transport plane had been arranged courtesy of Rocky Bridger, retired Pentagon general and devoted friend on the Roundtable. Rocky knew the president of Rapid Air personally. He hadn't filled them in about all the details of Abigail's desperate plight, but Abigail and Cal had researched the law and knew that Rapid Air employees couldn't get into any criminal trouble by helping her avoid the SIA surveillance. Another Roundtable member, Judge Fort Rice, also checked out the BIDTag authorization act hurriedly passed by Congress. Because of a glitch in the law he had come to the same conclusion. Of course, none of that affected the ability of the U.S. government to come after Abigail.

Gallagher slowed the SUV and pulled into a parking spot reserved for "authorized vehicles only."

"Okay," the ex-FBI agent said, turning off his car. "I'll get a parking ticket here, so I'll have to send you the bill." He cocked an eyebrow. "But it avoids all the cameras and scanners in the public parking area. Also, here's some good news for you. I checked and the facial recognition cameras inside the courthouse had to be yanked out. Got some kind of computer virus. Come on, Abby. Follow me."

Gallagher and Abigail moved along the perimeter of the courthouse building until they arrived at a rear service entrance. Gallagher hit the speed dial on his Allfone. "The agent is outside," he announced into his cell and clicked it off.

"So I'm an agent now?" Abigail asked.

"I know the courthouse security guy. Did him a few favors when I used to be a frequent government witness here in D.C.. Anyway, I told him you're operating undercover. You are, aren't you?" Gallagher half smiled. "Anyway, this'll get you past the front door X-ray machines and cameras, but it won't get you past the BIDTag scanners they've set up on every floor. Which courtroom are you heading to?"

"Courtroom 11, fourth floor."

"You remember the back stairway leads up to each of the floors?"

"Yes."

"It should be smooth sailing to your floor. But from that point on, SIA agents are at the scanners. I'm sorry, but I can't help you there. You'll be on your own."

Abigail nodded, then checked the time. Ten minutes left. She hurried to the stairwell.

A bailiff and a court clerk with her hands full of files stepped into the stairway, then passed by her, complaining about the crowded elevators.

Abigail tried not to look too rushed as she climbed the stairs to the fourth floor. Arriving at the door that led to the open hallway, she prayed, *Lord just give me the chance to argue Josh's case — I will accept whatever happens after that.*

She opened the door. Fifteen feet ahead was the SIA security station, blocking the hallway leading to Courtroom 11, which was halfway down the corridor on the left. Two SIA agents were in position, one on each side of the scanner, which was a larger and presumably more sensitive version of the one that was in the tollbooth on the Dulles Toll Road.

A lawyer with a fat briefcase was standing in line ahead of her. He placed his right hand into the scanner. Ten seconds later the bulb on top flickered green. The SIA agent nodded, and the lawyer strolled ahead, briefcase in hand.

Abigail stepped up. She smiled. "Good morning," she said brightly.

"Right hand please," one of the agents told her.

Abigail inserted her right hand into the open space in the big square scanner, palm down. She was glad it was only a BIDTag scanner and not a facial recognition camera. But that was only cold comfort now as she waited to see if Chiro Hashimoto's substitute BIDTag was as good as he had claimed.

The SIA agent squinted at his screen. A few seconds passed. The light on the scanner was not lit. "Withdraw your hand please," he barked.

She did as she was told, but her heart was racing.

"Reinsert please," he said bluntly.

Abigail placed her hand in again, palm down. Two seconds passed. The SIA agent staring at his monitor gave a nod toward the screen but seemed surprised when he looked over at the unlit bulb. He reached over and tapped the bulb with his finger.

The bulb lit up green.

Abigail, still clutching her file, strode between the SIA agents and picked up the pace. Courtroom 11 was only thirty feet away, but there was a sudden noise behind her in the hall. An FBI agent and an SIA official had just blown into the hallway from the stairwell.

"Stop her!" one of them shouted.

At the opposite end of the hallway, at the other SIA station, the two agents posted there left their position and started charging toward Abigail. She broke into a flash of speed, sprinting with legs churning.

I haven't come this far ...

She skidded to a stop at the open doorway of courtroom 11 and dodged in. A court clerk with an electronic clipboard was standing just inside the courtroom. Abigail could see that a dozen other lawyers were already seated in the benches, waiting for their cases to be called.

"Abigail Jordan, arguing for the defendant. *United States v. Jordan*," she said hurriedly to the man.

An instant later, one of the armed SIA agents grabbed her by the arm.

"What's this?" the bailiff said with a stunned look.

"Illegal entry into the building," the agent barked, "and an outstanding SIA warrant."

Abigail stretched forward, getting as close to the bailiff's ear as she could, and whispered, "Sir, I am an attorney, and I need to argue my husband's case today. *Please*."

The court officer held up a hand and looked at the SIA agents. They were immediately joined by the FBI agent, who grunted, "No offense buddy, but you're just a court bailiff. We're federal agents with a warrant. So step aside."

The bailiff's eyes lit up. "Excuse me, what did you just say?"

The SIA agents ignored him and began to tug Abigail out of the courtroom.

The bailiff was fuming. "You may be federal agents, and I may be *just* a bailiff, but you have just stepped inside the courtroom of the United States Court of Appeals. The judges are in charge here — not you. And those judges have delegated authority to me — that's right — to *me* — to exercise absolute control over the conduct of all persons entering this place. So I say to you, gentlemen, please unhand this attorney. Take your seats quietly in the back if you wish, but you'll have to wait until after her case has been argued to execute your warrant. If that's not acceptable, I'll call the U.S. Marshal's office downstairs, and you can have it out with them."

The SIA agent loosened his grip, and Abigail quickly pulled away, striding up to the counsel table in the front of the courtroom.

The opposing attorneys from the Department of Justice were already in their seats. All three government lawyers were bug-eyed, having just witnessed the spectacle in the back of the courtroom. Abigail pulled her notes out of her file and laid them on the table with precision, trying to calm the thumping in her chest. She turned to the three opposing attorneys.

"Counselors," she said with a nod of greeting. She turned to face the door where the three judges would soon enter.

Lance Dunny, the lead prosecuting attorney at the other table, returned her greeting. "Counselor," he replied. And then with a twisted grin added, "This is perfect. A criminal for a lawyer, comes in to defend her criminal husband."

A thought suddenly occurred to Abigail, and she turned back toward her abrasive opponents to share it. "As John Adams once argued in the most famous case of his career — 'Facts are stubborn things.' And just for the record, Mr. Dunny, so am I. I trust you're prepared for both."

FIFTY-ONE

Lance Dunny was the government's choice to argue against Abigail. A smart move, Abigail knew. The DOJ lawyer who was standing at the lectern addressing the three judges was the head litigator in the government's criminal division, and when Dunny won — which was often — he didn't just edge out the opposition by a nose. He would usually crush them. His argument that day in *United States v. Jordan* had been commanding and elegant in its simplicity, perfectly attuned to the three judges, two men and one female, who sat, black-robed, in front of him and peered down from the bench.

Of the three appellate judges assigned to hear this case, none had been appointed by President Tulrude. Abigail considered that a plus. On the other hand, all three had reputations for pro-government toughness when it came to criminal prosecutions. Rarely did any of them vote for reversal of criminal convictions. Agnes Lillegaard, the chief judge on the panel, had been a former federal prosecutor, as had Judge Turkofsky, who sat to her right. Judge Preston on her left had a stint, before appointment to the bench, as counsel to the Senate judiciary, where he helped draft stringent anti-crime legislation.

In his oral presentation, Lance Dunny did an artful job pulling apart what he expected to be Abigail's chief arguments.

During her own opening argument, Abigail made two main points. First, that the "material witness order," which the trial judge had imposed against her in Joshua's case, was improper. That order, she pointed out, prevented her from leaving the United States while

Joshua's case was pending, supposedly on the basis that she was an important witness for the prosecution, and that without such an order she might be a flight risk, leaving the country to join her husband overseas and thereby placing herself beyond the jurisdiction of the court. This, she said, violated due process, constituted cruel and unusual punishment for a witness, and further violated the constitutional right to travel.

Dunny called those arguments "absurd." At one point Judge Agnes Lillegaard, nodding as Dunny continued to denigrate Abigail's reasoning, added her own comment: "Some wives might feel that being forced to join their husbands would be the real cruel and unusual punishment — " The courtroom broke into cordial laughter.

Then Judge Turkofsky asked, "Mr. Dunny, isn't it a fact that the defendant, Mr. Jordan, has already been residing overseas, placing himself outside of the jurisdiction of the United States?"

Dunny nodded vigorously. "Precisely, your honor. In Israel. And he has successfully avoided extradition back to America. So we have already been stonewalled by a criminal defendant who has committed acts of treasonous interference with the U.S. government. It is outrageous that his wife is trying to get this order overturned so she can flee this country too."

Abigail then argued her second point, that the case against Joshua had been based on false and contrived evidence, which, she said, she would soon reveal.

At that point, Dunny's invective became white hot. "Mrs. Jordan comes into this courtroom, telling us that honorable, high-ranking members of the Department of Justice have deliberately manipulated a witness into presenting false testimony. This is astonishing! Does this woman have no shame? But look at what she has produced — an affidavit from a former low-level assistant U.S. attorney, clearly a disgruntled former prosecutor who — for whatever reason — has invented this tale of prosecutorial misconduct. This attorney, Mr. Collingwood, by the way, has now joined one of the most well-known criminal-defense firms in Washington. His affidavit admits that. Apparently, now that he's defending criminals rather than putting them behind bars, Mr. Collingwood is showing a different side of his character — a side that doesn't blink at defaming the very legal agency he once worked for."

But Dunny saved the hardest blow, the punch in the solar plexus, for last. He argued that Abigail was ethically disqualified from even appearing in front of the judges as her husband's attorney "in light of the clear ethical rule prohibiting a lawyer from representing a client in the same case where the attorney is called as a witness. The material witness order recognizes that the government intends to call Abigail Jordan as a witness against her husband," Dunny said. "Case closed. Mrs. Jordan's appearance here is an insult to the rule of law."

When Dunny sat down, Abigail approached the lectern for her rebuttal. As she took a moment to collect herself, she felt the volcano of emotions threatening to be loosed within. She knew the risk she had taken in even defending her husband in the appeal — trying to argue with cold analytical precision a case that had so torn their lives apart and had separated Joshua from her by the full expanse of an ocean. But now she had no choice. She had to become someone else — Lady Justice herself, dispassionate, objective, and truthful.

"As to counsel's argument," Abigail said, "that I am a material witness in the case against my husband, and am therefore disqualified from appearing here, note that the word *material* implies relevance and materiality, that I have something relevant and significant to say in court that would tend to incriminate my husband. Where is that materiality? Where is that relevance? I have filed an affidavit proving that I have nothing whatsoever to say that could possibly show my husband — a true American patriot and hero — to be a criminal. Curiously, the government has failed to advise you judges exactly what they would expect to elicit from my testimony that could possibly be helpful in their case, which leads us to two conclusions: either the government lawyers are sloppy — or they are devious. Sloppy in mistakenly assuming that I have something to add to their empty case. Or, the more likely explanation, devious in deliberately obtaining a material witness order against me just to keep my husband and me separated, thus applying psychological pressure to get Joshua to return to the United States to face a wrongful and contrived prosecution."

Judge Preston, who had been quiet during oral argument, now came to life. "Mrs. Jordan, those are serious charges. Why should we believe you and not the United States government?"

"Because, Your Honor, as I've often said, facts are stubborn things. They call out to our sense of justice and reason and appeal to our moral conscience. So let's look at the following facts. First fact — a respected assistant United States attorney has signed an affidavit — under oath — indicating that the assistant attorney general coerced a witness — a lawyer no less — into making false allegations against my husband, allegations that are the core of the government's case. Fact — the government lawyers have failed to counter that affidavit with one from the assistant attorney general disputing those allegations. Now that is truly astounding. Another fact — Mr. Collingwood, in his affidavit, implicates the Tulrude administration in trying to railroad Joshua into prison for purely political purposes. And a final fact — the government has refused to produce a single piece of evidence disputing those facts."

Judge Agnes Lillegaard took her reading glasses off her nose and stared directly at Abigail Jordan. "You are asking this court to dismiss this case against your husband before it ever gets to trial, based on a single affidavit. As long as I've been on this court we have never done such a thing, Mrs. Jordan. You are asking for something extraordinary here."

Abigail's voice quivered. "This case *is* extraordinary. We live in extraordinary times, when extraordinary injustice has taken place. And in this courtroom we have presented extraordinary evidence of political and legal corruption of the most astonishing kind."

As she prepared to collect her papers, noticing the red light on her lectern, Abigail finished. "There is a reason that in the familiar statue, Lady Justice is always blindfolded," she said. "That is so she will not be dissuaded — not be tempted — by the faces of high and powerful figures, even those in the attorney general's office, and the Oval Office, those who would wink at her, suggesting slyly that their corruptions be overlooked so that they might continue persecuting those who expose their corruption."

Abigail gathered up her papers and walked back to the counsel table. As she did, she saw the contingent of armed federal officers in the back of the room who would soon be placing her into custody.

FIFTY-TWO

Denver, Colorado

The task was to keep Senator Hewbright alive.

Deborah Jordan momentarily thought this was an audacious assignment — bordering on crazy. But with her military training at West Point in clandestine operations, and her desire to work in national security matters, did she really have a beef after all? She would have been happier if John Gallagher was closer, but Abigail had assured her that the former FBI agent was out of pocket. Even if he wasn't, his past government profile and current association with the Roundtable disqualified him from trying to pose as some nondescript campaign volunteer. Besides, he was not the kind to quietly blend in.

As Deborah wheeled her rental car off Auraria Parkway and headed to Chopper Circle to park as closely as possible to Denver's massive Pepsi Center, she wasn't thinking about the frenzied political convention about to take place there. Instead, she thought about her mother's final instructions. "Stay as close as possible to Senator Hewbright — but even closer to Zeta Milla. Milla was the most likely threat against Hewbright, but only when we get clear evidence against her can we afford to blow your cover and reveal it all to Hewbright."

Everyone in the family said that Abigail had the gift of spiritual discernment when it came to people. *Okay,* Deborah thought. *True enough. But the initial facts were sketchy.* A dead campaign director in Wichita. The fact that Milla was wearing a ring that matched the one worn by U.N. Secretary-General Coliquin. Plus Milla apparently lied about being a refuge from Cuba as a child. And Hewbright's economic plan had been stolen by someone, apparently in China, who had hacked into his Allfone. That was all they knew.

Until, that is, Gallagher dug around in Wichita and learned that Zeta Milla was the last person who was with Perry Tedrich at his health club, then at a restaurant for lunch, shortly before his disappearance. In Deborah's mind, that blew everything wide open.

Gallagher had shared the news with FBI Agent Ben Boling, with whom he had been working, but then, incredibly, Boling had gone silent. Maybe it was because the Secret Service had already checked Milla out, along with other staff, and had given her a clean bill of health.

Or maybe it was something else.

So Deborah had decided to do some digging of her own. She checked into Milla's position on the campaign team by making a few calls and using some of her contacts at the Pentagon, hoping to cinch the case against Milla as some kind of saboteur. But the stuff she came up with was pretty benign.

Not surprisingly, Milla's job with the campaign was to help Hewbright bone up on issues relating to Central and South American affairs, including Mexico and the island republics in the Caribbean. She wasn't hired to give immigration advice, however; that was strictly the territory of Hewbright's domestic advisors.

Deborah learned that Milla had a master's degree in international affairs from American University, with credits toward her Ph.D. She worked for a while in the State Department, first during President Corland's tenure, and then in President Tulrude's administration. She was a middle-level staffer, and as far as Deborah was able to determine, she had not distinguished herself. She had kept a low profile. Milla had joined Senator Hewbright's staff just in time for his decision to run for president.

As Deborah made her way through the crowds that swarmed the cavernous lobby of the ten-story glass convention center, and headed toward the Hewbright staff registration desk, she kept asking herself the same three questions. No matter how many times she turned them around in her head, they all seemed hopeless, particularly as she stepped into the monolithic chaos of a presidential convention. *First, why would someone like Zeta Milla pose a threat to Hewbright? Second, even if she is a threat, how am I going to find out about it? And third, if I find out — how am I going to stop it?*

A political volunteer, a tall, blond, athletic-looking guy was behind her in line.

"Hi, there," he said, bending forward to catch Deborah's attention.

She broke out of her mental distraction. "Oh, hi."

"Diehard or newcomer?"

"Pardon?"

"I'm a diehard Hewbright supporter. Helped him in his last senate race. Just local canvassing stuff. My home state is Wyoming. How about you?"

"Oh, yeah I'm pretty diehard. I work in Washington."

"State?"

"No, D.C."

"So you've jumped on board recently, I bet."

"Something like that." She smiled politely but wasn't in the mood for small talk.

"There's already some trash talking from Governor Tucker's group," he said.

That got her attention. "Oh?"

"Yeah, they want to disrupt the ballot and to throw it into a brokered convention. Maybe these lamebrains can't add, but Hewbright's already got the delegates sewn up. He swept almost all the primaries, but the Tucker Troops just won't give up. Just thinking about it makes me sick. What a rotten deal if Tucker actually wrangles the nomination. He's like Tulrude lite, don't you think?"

She was mildly impressed. "Absolutely," she responded.

"The guy's cut from the same cloth as Tulrude ideologically; so why doesn't he just switch parties? And he came across on the TV debates like a college professor. Practically put me to sleep every time he opened his mouth. Reminded me of my history prof at Colorado State.

Anyway, Tucker's so totally unelectable it's tragic. No sweat though. Absolutely no chance of him pulling it out. Hewbright's got this locked up. I mean, really, Hewbright would have to get hit by an asteroid to lose this."

Deborah's head snapped. She thought, *Whoever you are, you have no idea what you just said.*

Then, almost as an afterthought, he added, "I'm Rick. And you're..."

"Deborah."

He shook her hand. He had a strong grip.

"Maybe we'll run into each other during the convention. Tell you what, if we do, I'll buy you coffee."

"Sure, but I have a feeling we may be pretty busy," she said, keeping a poker face. "You know, coming to the rescue of our candidate."

FIFTY-THREE

Washington D.C., Office of the United States Attorney

As soon as Abigail finished her oral argument she snatched up her file and made her way to the back of the courtroom, preparing for the worst. It was every bit as humiliating as she had imagined. In full view of the court, the federal officers jumped to their feet. Then, one agent on each arm, they escorted her into the hallway — where they cuffed her.

Abigail had a single, dismal thought. *Ball game's over. Now we just wait for the score.*

She had expected to be hustled to the federal detention center and booked and put into a cell. And she may have been heading that way. But while she was in the back of the agency car with her hands manacled, the SIA agent in the front seat received a call. When he hung up, he then turned to the driver and said only, "Change of plans. We're going to the U.S. Attorney's Office." On the way they perfunctorily advised Abigail of her Miranda Rights. She knew what that meant. *Here we go*, she thought, bracing herself.

The new U.S. attorney for the District of Columbia, Tanya Hardcastle, was a recent appointee of President Tulrude's. That was all Abigail knew. But that was enough. When they arrived at the building just off of Second Street, the squad drove down into the underground parking. Surprisingly, the cuffs were removed and Abigail was walked through the structure and up into the lobby. She couldn't help but smile when the BIDTag scanner gave her the green light. Her captors were not amused.

She was taken to a small conference room on the same floor as U.S. Attorney Hardcastle's expansive office. She was offered coffee but replied that she preferred tea. They brought her some in a cup with a saucer, and whatever it was, it wasn't bad. Several hours passed. Assistant U.S. attorneys and their staffers scurried by. She caught glimpses of them through the window in the door. And she waited.

When Tanya Hardcastle, a short, bony woman with a smoker's voice, finally entered, she smiled and sat down across from Abigail at the conference table.

Tanya Hardcastle knew that Abigail had no clue that the three federal judges in her case went into their standard closed conference immediately after the morning's oral arguments to consider their votes. And she would not have known how they had made such quick business of the case in *United States v. Jordan*, that it only took one vote to secure a decision among the three appeal judges. It was unanimous. Hardcastle also knew how Judge Agnes Lillegaard had drafted an order. When that judge emailed that order to the court clerk, it was read by another clerk, who called a friend at the Department of Justice. Swearing the friend to secrecy, he disclosed the contents of the order. But the word spread rapidly, and then a deputy attorney general called Hardcastle's office to alert her to the rumor, knowing that she already had Abigail in custody in the high-profile case. So Hardcastle knew the end of this legal story and what the court order said. And Abigail knew none of it.

Sitting across from Abigail, Hardcastle started off with a good-cop routine. "I've checked you out," the U.S. attorney said in an even, pleasant tone. "You have a reputation as a very sharp attorney here in the District. Some impressive victories. And, as you and I both know, it's a man's world, Abigail ... may I call you that?"

Abigail smiled tightly and nodded.

Continuing, Hardcastle said, "It's been a man's world in the practice of law. Back when I graduated from Princeton law, the partner in my first firm had me working in the secretarial pool. Can you imagine? But women like you and me, we've changed things — for the equality of women. Don't you think?"

Abigail took a sip of tea. "Are you trying to turn me into a feminist, Ms. Hardcastle?"

"I think you're already one. You just don't know it."

Pushing the cup and saucer away from her, Abigail replied, "What I am, madam, is a believer in the U.S. Constitution. When the Fourth Amendment says that every citizen has a right to be 'secure in their persons,' it means what it says. It means that the federal government cannot force Americans to receive a laser-tattooed tracking device imprinted onto their skin, even if it doesn't hurt and even if it's invisible to the naked eye."

"Federal courts have disagreed with you, Abigail."

"Only because the Supreme Court has refused to take the issue up. I'm guessing that Justice Lapham can't muster the necessary four votes to grant a writ of certiorari on all those appeals from nontaggers."

"Well, I'm not here to debate the finer points of the law ..."

Hardcastle paused, but Abigail didn't fill in the blanks for her, so the U.S. attorney continued, "I'm here to offer you complete immunity from prosecution if you simply give me some facts."

A brief flash of shock registered on Abigail's face before she returned to a neutral glare. "Such as?"

"Who gave you your fake BIDTag. It's pretty impressive. It passed all our scanners."

"Does it matter? I've been BIDTagged one way or the other."

"Oh, I think we both know you haven't. Not legally. The point is that we know someone out there is minting this counterfeit version. Just tell us who, and we'll grant you immunity."

Abigail had suspected that Chiro's forgery would be of interest to the feds, but she didn't expect they'd offer her immunity in return. Surely, they'd lock her up anyway and try to force the information out of her. But something wasn't right. Abigail thought back to the eccentric Chiro Hashimoto and her pledge to him before leaving his compound that she would keep his identity and his location confidential. "You're asking me questions that are covered by the Fifth Amendment of the Constitution," Abigail replied. "And I recall being given my Miranda rights earlier today," she added.

Hardcastle bristled. "Go ahead and try to play tough with me. But remember — all I have to do is make just one call and guys with guns show up here and lock you in a metal cage."

"Sounds unpleasant."

"Jail cells generally are."

Abigail could smell a rat. Tanya was trying to sneak something past Abigail. Her best guess, and greatest hope, was that Hardcastle had already heard some inside information about the court's ruling in her case. Abigail was banking on that. And she was now also banking on the fact that Hardcastle knew that the government's case against Joshua may have just gone down in flames. "I'll have to respectfully decline your offer," Abigail said.

The U.S. attorney fluttered her eyes. "The thing about smart people," Hardcastle said, this time not trying to hide the edge in her voice, "is that they can sometimes outsmart themselves." Then she got up and headed to the door, but halfway there she halted, as if tempted to try again to manipulate Abigail into yielding information, but then she thought better of it. To cover her abrupt stop, she bent down and scooped up the teacup and saucer off the table. Abigail had to stifle a laugh. She'd made the right call.

"Thanks for the tea," Abigail said brightly.

"Don't move," Hardcastle said, irritation all over her face.

Outside the room, Hardcastle shoved the teacup and saucer into the hands of an assistant and then stormed into her office. She snatched off her desk the hard copy of the Per Curiam Order of the D.C. Circuit Court of Appeals that she had printed out from her email just before talking to Abigail. Now she read its infuriating contents again. One more time. Just to make sure.

Judges Lillegaard, Turkofsky, Preston.

ORDERED: That the Material Witness Order entered against Abigail Jordan by the U.S. District Court, requiring her to remain within the territorial boundaries of the United States during the pendency of the criminal action titled *United States v. Jordan*, is hereby reversed and vacated, on the grounds of the Due Process Clauses of the 5th and 14th Amendments to the U.S. Constitution.

This Court further Orders the government to show cause to the U.S. District Court, within seventy-two hours, as to why the criminal action against Joshua Jordan should not be dismissed on its merits in light of the affidavit evidence of prosecutorial misconduct submitted by defendant's counsel, Abigail Jordan.

Still in the conference room, as Abigail wondered whether she would be spending the night on a metal cot, an agent entered the room and asked her to follow him. Five minutes later, she was outside on the public sidewalk, unaccompanied and smelling the welcoming though automobile-congested air of Washington, D.C. Her only guess was that Hardcastle, having suffered a humiliating defeat in the case against Joshua, was not going to risk charging Abigail with her apparent failure to get a timely BIDTag, especially since she now appeared to have one that inexplicably passed through the federal scanners.

But Abigail was struck with the question she did not have a chance to ask Hardcastle. For Abigail, it was the most important question of all. *Where is Cal?*

But that thought was interrupted by her Allfone. She opened her email and noticed a message from the D.C. Circuit Court of Appeals. The Per Curiam Order was attached.

She took a deep breath and read it with a trembling hand. For good measure, she read it again. That is when, there on the sidewalk, Abigail burst into tears. She continued to cry and laugh amidst the busy pedestrian traffic, murmuring a prayer of thanks about the goodness of God and His love of justice. She didn't care about the passersby who gawked at her. She was finally able to vent the emotions she had carefully managed for so long while she had waited for God's vindicating hand.

Abigail spoke out to no one in particular, "Josh, I miss you." She had been out of contact with him for a while. She knew it was necessary — avoiding phone calls and even encrypted emails while she was dodging the government surveillance — but soon the waiting would be over. "Josh, I can't wait to fly to Israel to see you, darling …"

A voice behind her broke in. "How about your trusty legal intern?" It was Cal. Abigail jumped and even more tears started trickling down.

"Mom," Cal said, "you look surprised. I told you there was no way I could be charged. Victoria McHenry was released too. Man, she's one cool and collected customer. But then, considering her spy background, I shouldn't have been surprised."

"I need to thank that dear woman for sticking her neck out for me," Abigail said, wiping a tear away and not worrying about her messed-up eyeliner. "And yes, you'll join me as soon as we can get our jet ready — and Deborah too."

"I called her," Cal said, "as soon as I was released and gave her a status on what's happening here, left it on her voicemail. I got a short text message back. She said she's in orientation meetings with the convention team in Denver. Doesn't sound promising."

"Give her time. She's the right person for that assignment. We need to keep praying for her too. This could be dangerous."

Cal nodded and then glanced at his Allfone. "I got a message from Phil Rankowitz. Didn't tell me much, just that he needed to talk to us. It's about the two stories he's working on for AmeriNews, both of them shockers — the Alexander Coliquin exposé and the investigation on the possible poisoning of President Corland. Phil reminded me that I need to get Corland to sign an authorization so we can get testing done on that blood sample his family doctor took. His wife had suspicions and ordered the blood draw taken right after that last near-fatal attack he had."

"When was your last contact with Corland or his wife?"

"Last week."

"You may want to double-back with President Corland," she said, dabbing her eyes with a handkerchief. "I'm sure getting his medical consent is no problem, but we need to prepare him. If the tests show he was poisoned, the story will set off a firestorm."

"Right," Cal said, "but first, I'm starving. Let's grab something to eat. Backpacking in the Northwest, escaping SIA agents, and facing federal arrest has given me a monster appetite."

FIFTY-FOUR

Fair Haven Convalescent Center, Bethesda, Maryland

Winnie Corland was sobbing. She stood over the body of her deceased husband, but her knees weakened and she fell against the bed, reaching out and touching his cold face. This was not just a former president she was embracing. It was her husband of fifty years. A nurse came up next to her and helped her into a chair.

"He just passed in the night," she explained to Winnie. "I'm sure it was peaceful. I am sorry about your loss."

She knew his health had been fragile, especially when he collapsed in the Oval Office after one of his worst transient ischemic attacks. But after the succession of power to Jessica Tulrude, and Virgil's transfer to the convalescent center, he seemed to be doing better. Slowly, to be sure, but improving.

The nurse stepped out as Winnie tried to catch her breath in a short, gasping effort. She dabbed the tears from her face and took a deep breath. The Allfone in her purse on the floor started humming. But she ignored it.

She thought back to her time with Virgil the night before. She had spent the evening with him, just talking quietly. She was grateful for that. They had laughed at memories of their life together, like their honeymoon. Being nature-lovers, they had gone rustic, camping in a state park in Maine. They had pitched their tent on the low ground, and when a nasty rainstorm broke in the middle of the night, the waters rushed through their tent, nearly floating them away. Her eyes filled with tears again, but a smile started to break in the corner of her mouth as she remembered that.

She recalled how last night, one more time, Virgil shared with her the story of his devoted Secret Service agent, a Christian man, who had such an influence on him, and how Virgil had made the decision, in his words, to "personally trust his soul into the hands of Christ." It was the day that Virgil had been alone in the Oval Office, shouldering the usual, ever-present burdens of the presidency. But he said that something that day actually outweighed all of that: the burden of his heart, the "empty hole there, and my longing for a touch from God, to repair me, forgive me, and to bring me some peace." So, as Corland related it to his wife, he slowly eased down on his knees, behind the famous nineteenth-century Resolute Desk, and began to pray, pouring out his heart of repentance and faith in Jesus, trusting his soul and his life to Christ, God's "Divine Commander-in-Chief," as he put it in his prayer, "My Savior. My King."

Despite his pleas, Winnie had never been able to make that decision for herself. What was it that had kept it all so distant — at arm's length? Virgil was always such an external person. She, on the other hand, was the private one. She would ponder what Virgil said, but then would silently push it back into the closet and close the door.

Virgil often took her hand gently and asked her, in a voice that, for him, was unusual in its pathos, to "please, please, consider where you stand with the Son of God."

But now he was gone, and there was nothing that would change that. And she was alone.

She slowly fished her hand into her purse, pulled out the Allfone, and hit the voicemail function. The voice message was from Cal Jordan, the young man that Virgil had so enjoyed. He was asking to talk to Virgil or Winnie as soon as possible, and Cal added, "I sure hope you both are doing well. I really appreciated my talks with President Corland. Good-bye."

She clicked off her Allfone so she wouldn't be bothered again and dropped it into her purse. All she wanted to do now was to sit in the room and stay close to the last physical likeness of her late husband. Nothing else seemed to matter.

Pepsi Center, Denver

In the middle of the frenzied political theater unfolding around her, Deborah was obsessing over a question — a very politically incorrect one: *How do I trap our candidate's advisor and slam the cage shut before she bites?*

The volunteers, having paraded to the middle of the cavernous arena, were now seated while the roadies and tech guys finished erecting the sets on the stage. On either side of the presenting area, where a Plexiglas podium had been installed, tall panes of red-white-and-blue-colored glass rose fifty feet into the air. Sparkling banners and a mammoth American flag made of shimmering lights formed the backdrop.

The manager of volunteer services was on his feet at the front with a sports-mic headset. He was looking at his e-pad, getting ready to address the one hundred and seventy volunteers for the Hewbright campaign. Deborah was one of them. A few seats away, Rick was joking with a group of friends. His face brightened when he noticed Deborah.

Oh boy, she thought, as Rick got up from his seat and tripped over knees and feet to approach her. He bent down to the girl next to Deborah and said, "Would you mind switching seats with me? This is a long-lost friend of mine. Gotta do some catching up."

The girl tossed him an exasperated look but changed seats. Rick sat down and stretched out his long legs, pretending nothing had happened.

"Long-lost friend?" Deborah said with a smirk.

"Oh, that? Naw, listen, this is strictly platonic. You don't think I'm trying to hit on you, do you?" Rick's cocky smirk gave that one away.

"Okay," Deborah said, "then hit me with some platonics."

"Right. How about this ... just heard that the Tucker troops are ramping up their smear campaign."

At the front, the volunteer manager was being approached by another Hewbright staffer carrying a digital clipboard.

"Tell me," Deborah whispered.

"They're saying Hewbright's a womanizer. One-night-stands in motels with admirers. That kind of thing."

"That's crazy. Hewbright? Who's going to believe that?"

"Look, his wife's been dead a couple of years. Nobody expects the guy never to go out with women again. He's not a monk. But this stuff they're saying is so vile and false it's incredible. I heard Hewbright's going to haul Tucker before the rules committee, to either prove this stuff — which he obviously can't — or make a public apology in front of the delegates. You wonder where these rumors start anyway."

As Deborah was trying to process that, wondering if it had anything to do with Zeta Milla, the staffer at the front with the e-clipboard broke into a wide grin and waved to someone around the corner. Senator Hewbright came into view, waving to the volunteers, who stood to their feet, clapping and whistling.

After the hall grew quiet again, the senator began his remarks. "You young people who have given so much and asked for so little in return, you are the essence of my campaign. You're here not just for me, although I thank you for that from the bottom of my heart, but you're also here for America. You sense, as I do, that our nation is on a precipice, tottering this way and that — on the brink of an unknown and turbulent future. Possibly catastrophic. But I see, at the same time, another direction — that we can be on the brink of a great restoration, a recovery of something lost, a revival of the American vision. That there can be greatness still in this nation, and we can say that without apology, without embarrassment for who we are, and what we stand for. Leading the world, rather than asking the world's permission. Standing tall, rather than bowing low to international powers, refusing to be financial beggars at the economic table of global masters, but rather choosing to be the brokers of freedom that we were destined to be."

Hewbright stopped and smiled. "All right, enough of my acceptance speech ..." The crowd laughed and burst into more applause. "But," he added, "I do thank you all. Truly. And let me share something I just found out. The first televised debate will be in ten days. I'm hoping and planning to be the candidate on the other side of the podium from Tulrude." More wild applause. "That first debate will be on foreign policy." With that he turned to someone standing just around the corner, blocked by an entryway. "Come on up here, Zeta."

Zeta Milla stepped into view and strode up next to Hewbright with a modest smile. She was carrying a chic black handbag. Deborah, who had inherited her mother's taste for style, recognized the Dolce and Gabbana bag immediately.

The senator looked relaxed and energized. "My chief international-affairs advisor, Winston Garvey, isn't here right now — otherwise I'd introduce him to you. He's up in the war room, as we call it, putting together my briefing books on global issues. But this is Zeta Milla, and she is on our foreign-relations team. She briefs me on Central and South American issues. And she's even smarter than she is attractive ..." There was a burst of applause.

Deborah had her eyes on Zeta Milla. As Hewbright waved good-bye to the volunteers, Milla slipped her hand around Hewbright's arm. He moved away from her so slightly that it was nearly imperceptible.

Rick's face lit up. "He's going to make a great president." He turned to Deborah. "So, what's your assignment?"

"Tell me yours."

"I just found out. You're never going to believe it."

"Try me."

"I'm the go-for guy in the war room! Is that the bomb or what?"

"You're kidding."

"Not at all. That Zeta Milla babe we just saw ... I met her up in the war-room suite. Met that Winston Garvy dude too. I'm right there, in the middle of the action, even though I'm just a fetch-and-carry guy, but still ..."

Deborah tried not to dive in too eagerly. So she waited a few minutes. Then, she looked at Rick and spoke quietly. "Okay, Rick, you can buy me that cup of coffee."

"Hey, sounds great."

"But you have to do something first."

Rick threw her a hesitant grin, "What's that?"

"Can you get me on your team? I'd love to work in the war room. The heart of the action is right where I want to be."

Paris, France

It was 2:00 a.m. in Paris. In his apartment just off Place de la Republique, Pack McHenry was working. The former American intelligence officer had just finished reviewing several surveillance reports on terror cells in the European Union on his encrypted email system. He approved them and sent them electronically — and encrypted — over to the Paris post of the CIA, one of his contract clients. He glanced at his Allfone watch — the one with ten time zones. It was early evening in Cuba.

So he made his call to Marianao, Cuba, which was in the Old Havana section. Carlos picked up.

"Hello, my friend."

"Greetings, amigo. Where are you calling from today?"

"You know I never answer questions like that," McHenry said.

Carlos laughed hard.

"So," McHenry asked, "what have you found out?"

"I am pretty sure it's a match. These two women are the same person."

"You're sure?"

"Yes, I think so."

"Zeta Milla and ... what's the other's name?"

"Maria Zeta. Yes, same woman, I believe. But I had to do a lot of digging, Señor Pack. She's been off the island for about eight years."

"So, the question is, long enough to go to school in the U.S., get a master's degree and some credits toward a doctorate, put time in at the State Department, and then join the staff of a senator?"

"That doesn't sound like a question," Carlos said, "more like an answer."

"Yes, exactly," McHenry said. "Anything else?"

"We call her type *Buta Buts*."

"Meaning ..."

"A poisonous tree. Any contact with it hurts you, blinds you, or even worse."

"Not the kind of girl to bring home to Mom."

"As a teenager, she was recruited by Castro's staff. She was pretty and very smart, but ruthless. Killed two men I know of."

"Why?"

"It was just a test, just to see if she could." Then Carlos added, "She passed the test."

"She's only worked in Cuba?"

"No, I heard she has been reassigned overseas, but I don't know where."

McHenry thanked him and told him he would wire some money to him. Then Pack pulled out the summary of the international travel itinerary his agents had obtained on Zeta Milla, aka Maria Zeta, something he ordered as a favor for Abigail.

As he studied the data, it became clear why Abigail wanted it. The listing documented every trip that the Cuban woman had taken to Romania while Coliquin still maintained a home there during his stint as that country's ambassador to the U.N. And the list of Zeta Milla's trips to Romania — apparently to meet with Coliquin — was very long.

FIFTY-FIVE

On the Edge of the Negev Desert, Israel

The Arab school was the perfect cover for the assembly of one of the world's most grotesque weapons of mass destruction. In that remote area, just off the highway from the desolate Negev, the school was made up of three buildings, mostly classrooms for Bedouin children. There was also a large cinderblock garage fifty yards from the other structures. That windowless building would be the assembly site.

While the children played cheerfully on the playground at the end of their school day, inside the garage, Tarek Fahad, Anwar al-Madrassa's chief of weapons inspected the missile housing and nosecone, which were laid out on a long steel worktable. Then he turned to Dr. Ahlam, the terror chemist who had designed the horrifying biological agent that al-Madrassa's cell was now calling "The Elixir of Allah." "I hear your elixir can melt the skin off a dog, down to the bone. Let's just hope it can do that to humans."

Dr. Ahlam had his own challenge. "Don't worry about my biological material. It will do that and more. My worry," he said pointing to the hardware on the table, "is about your delivery system."

Laying his hand on the shiny steel casing, Fahad retorted, "Very smart missile men have provided this to us. For a very high price, of course. Have you ever heard of a company called the Deter Von Gunter Group?"

Ahlam narrowed his eyes. "Sounds familiar ..."

"Big weapons company. The owner is part of a group called the World Builders."

When Dr. Ahlam gave a blank look, Fahad shrugged. "Not important. Because Anwar agrees with me that this missile will work perfectly to carry your elixir to its target."

"But Israel still has the RTS defense system. I'm afraid it will keep my bio-weapon from reaching its destination."

"You worry too much," Fahad said smugly. "RTS will be of no consequence. We will be burning the skin off infidels one way or another."

Pepsi Center, Denver

Deborah had made a mad dash downtown to do some emergency shopping and was just now arriving back at the convention center and flashed her credentials. Her Allfone rang. It was Pack McHenry.

"Deborah," he said quietly, "I have every reason to believe that Zeta Milla is one bad actor. To the extreme."

Deborah scurried to a corner of the convention center to buy herself some privacy. "Yes, Pack, I copy that."

"I'd stay clear of her, if I were you."

"Can't do that, sir."

"Listen, Deb, this woman is like a coral snake; you don't realize how poisonous until it's too late. Leave her to somebody else."

"Like who? The convention starts tonight. I get the feeling that something is about to break — right on top of us. Maybe even tonight."

"Since none of my people are available," McHenry said, "I put in a call to John Gallagher, but he hasn't called back. Maybe he can do something, push the FBI or local cops to intervene."

"He's tied up in some kind of wedding in Northern California."

"Then you need to confer with your mother. Get someone there to help you."

"Too late. You know the hoops I went through to get inside the campaign. I'm in striking distance. The tip of the spear. I need to finish this."

"All right. I understand. I'll keep calling Gallagher."

"Fine. Just know that I'm getting close."

Then she noticed Rick, who was roaming the lobby, searching for someone. He caught sight of Deborah and trotted over.

"Very close," she added to Pack McHenry and clicked off her cell.

"Come on, Deborah," Rick said in a huff, "we got to get up to the war room suite — like right now. We're supposed to be serving drinks and running errands." He looked down at the big duffle bag on the floor next to her. "What's that?"

"Oh, it's mine. Didn't have time to drop it off at my hotel room." Then she grabbed it by the handle. "I'll just take it with me."

"Whatever," Rick said. "Let's go. I did you a favor getting you in, so let's not blow it, okay?"

IDF Headquarters, Tel Aviv

"I can't seem to get a handle on this. I've worked the problem from every possible angle and still can't get to the bottom."

Over the phone, Ted, the senior engineer at Jordan Technologies, sounded stressed. As well he should.

Joshua was standing off to the side of the R&D conference room with a high-security satellite Allfone in his hand. Several IDF officers were huddled at the other end of the room.

"Look, Ted, they're telling me there's a new threat emerging over here. They've got intel that Anwar al-Madrassa was spotted in Lebanon and may be inside Israel by now. His terror cell is working on a nightmare kind of bio weapon. We can't afford to just turn that kind of incoming missile around one-hundred-and-eighty-degrees. It may be launched from a civilian area. We need three-hundred-and-sixty-degree-capture control. And we need it now."

"I keep telling you, our computer models work perfectly, but something happens in the real-world tests that I can't pick up from here."

Joshua rubbed the back of his neck. He could feel himself tightening like a steel cable. "Well, I've checked the data from this end. Our IDF friends have suggested that we adjust the intensity of the laser beam itself. They think if we scale it down a bit we'd have a better chance at loading our three-sixty controls into the missile's total guidance program."

"Problem is," Ted said, "once you do that, you may lose the capacity to do the initial capture of the trajectory data from the guidance program in the missile cone. If that happens, you may lose all control over the incoming weapon."

"That's what I told them," Joshua said, shaking his head. "I think we keep the laser intensity where it is. My guess is there's something going wrong in the data stream between the laser and the guidance of the incoming missile. Keep working the numbers and see if you can find any anomalies. This may be a software problem. Look at the code we're using and see if that's the issue."

Joshua clicked off and looked over at Ethan, who was sitting at the conference table.

Ethan sat up straighter. "I wish there was something I could do," he said, "but you guys are the tech geniuses. I'm just a former flyboy."

Joshua sauntered over to Ethan and sat down. "This glitch is driving me crazy. But I'm glad you're here."

"I appreciate that, but I still can't help you with your RTS problem, and I've got no political clout with the Israelis."

"On the other hand," Joshua replied, keeping his voice low, "you did some quick thinking in that market, keeping those Shin Bet agents off my back."

"Which turned out to be a moot issue," Ethan said with a smirk, "because they stopped chasing you down anyway — now that they need your RTS system again."

Joshua bent closer to Ethan, and lowered his voice to almost a whisper. "Listen to me, Ethan. I know you wonder what you're doing here, but I know you're meant to be here with me. There are things that have yet to be revealed. You're in a time of preparation, I think, and I know you balk when I talk like this ... but I can see in your eyes that you're starting to believe me. The role you are meant to play is not about me. It's much bigger than that. I get the feeling you are going to be a major player in events to come." Then Joshua felt his countenance fall. "Which means, necessarily, that I fear for you at the same time."

Ethan looked confused, but Josh couldn't explain it any further.

"Colonel Jordan?" A voice came from one of the IDF officers on the other side of the room. "We have a message for you to call your wife."

Joshua nodded to them and turned to Ethan. "That's good news. I haven't heard from Abby for the last week. I wonder what kind of trouble she's been getting into."

FIFTY-SIX

While Joshua was on the Allfone with Abigail, Ethan stepped out into the hallway of the IDF headquarters. He thought about Josh's comments, and his gut did a flip. He didn't understand the meaning behind Josh's words. He was used to Josh's talk about the so-called end times, but now things were getting a little too personal.

As he walked down the hallway, he saw something that made his head spin. He tried to look nonchalant but failed. He made an attempt at a polite head nod but ended up breaking into a grin. Rivka was in the corridor, leaning against the wall with her arms folded. She looked unusually professional in a dark suit and tan blouse. She greeted him, "Hello, Mr. America."

"You look spiffy," Ethan shot back.

"Well, I'm on official IDF business."

With an attempt at bravado, Ethan cracked, "I thought you came by for me."

"And what if I did?"

Suddenly he knew this was one of the nanosecond moments — in the cockpit, stick in hand, incoming aircraft sighted. Friend or not?

"Well," Ethan said, not realizing he was blushing, "I'd say that was good to hear. Really good. If it's true."

"Let's take a walk," Rivka said, motioning them away from the cluster of Israeli officers who were mulling over something out in the hall.

He thrust his hands in his cargo pants. "The last time I saw you,

Rivka, you weren't so dressy. In fact, you were decked out like a fishmonger at the Mahame Yehuda Market, tossing a pan of oily fish guts on the floor, right in front of those Shin Bet agents."

She muffled a laugh. "Have to say I enjoyed that one. I knew that HQ here would eventually get that extradition decision of Bensky reversed, talk some sense into the PM — particularly now that the threat level is sky-high again and they need you guys."

Rivka stopped and looked around. No military staffers were in earshot. "And I noticed the neat little trick you pulled with the forklift at the Souk. Those Shin Bet guys were so ticked ..."

"Brought back memories. I operated a forklift in a warehouse, working through junior college, before the Air Force." He and Rivka leaned against the wall now. It felt good to be close to her again. She smiled but didn't respond. He kept talking. "That was you, giving me the text message that day in the market, wasn't it? Warning us about the two agents."

"I told you once that I was the best friend you could have."

Ethan looked down the hall, where the IDF officers on the biothreat task force had finished their huddle and were going back into the conference room. "Are you in on this deal too?" he asked, nodding down toward the conference room at the end of the hall.

She answered with a simplicity that Ethan recognized. It was her resolve to do her duty to Israel. "Yes," she said. "I'm involved." But then, with equal calm, she added, "And so are you."

That was a comment Ethan wasn't ready for. He took a breath and was about to dive into it with Rivka, but before he could, Colonel Clint McKinney came hustling down the hallway. "Ethan, where's Josh? I've got to talk to him, stat, about taking a little trip with me."

Ethan pointed to the open door down the corridor. "He's taking a call down there, sir. In that room."

McKinney thanked him and quick-stepped his way to the conference room. He disappeared through the open door.

Ramat Air Base, Israel

On their drive from the IDF headquarters to the airbase, Colonel McKinney briefed Joshua on what he was about to see. The idea electrified Joshua's attitude about finding a solution. Joshua said he had been working hard to use a "left field" approach to solving the RTS problem — thinking beyond the parameters of the problem — which had to do with the inability of the RTS laser system when fired from a defensive rocket, to take hostage the entire guidance program of the other, hostile, incoming missile.

"Yes, Clint, absolutely," Joshua said with a burst of enthusiasm, "this could be the answer."

Clint eyed him with a smile as they strode into the experimental-aircraft hangar.

The IDF officer finally had to ask, "Josh, for a guy tormented by your RTS problem, you seem to be in a good mood all of a sudden. What's up?" Then he flashed a grin. "Is it just my brilliant suggestion?"

"Not to take anything away from you," Joshua shot back with a smile, "but I just called my wife. I'll tell you, Clint, God is good. Abby's been punching away at that phony criminal case the DOJ brought against me. Now she's got the other side up against the ropes. And the court order keeping her from joining me over here just got kicked. She's making plans to round up Cal and Deborah and fly over here."

Inside the hangar, Joshua saw what he had come for. He walked slowly around the gleaming fighter jet and studied it. Another officer joined them.

"Josh, this is Dr. Jacob Chabbaz," McKinney said. "He's in charge of our R&D RTS in-flight program."

Joshua pointed to the fighter. "So, this is it?"

Chabbaz nodded. "The F-35 Laser Variant. We weren't planning on manning this one yet, but with the newest threat, I think we can prep it for you. You'll notice the orbital laser housing where the weapon bay door used to be. The LV has three-hundred-sixty-degree optics, capable of locating any incoming missiles. Excellent capacity also to strike them with your RTS laser."

Joshua peeked under the fuselage at the laser mounting. "I've read the specs. Very impressive." He stood and looked over at McKinney. "You know what I'm thinking ..."

"Yep. That's why I brought you here. You've flown our F-22s over here in the last few months. Our test pilots can run you through the operational stuff for this F-35 variant on the ground. But it's a canopy built for only one pilot — and that pilot has to be able to decipher the RTS laser readings during the test runs. Nobody can do that like you, Josh."

"Okay," Joshua said, "I'm in. Once your guys walk me through the drill I think I can handle taking it up for some test runs. Clint, this may be the way to crack the problem with our RTS data-stream. Starting with in-flight use of the RTS aimed from the jet at an incoming missile at a close range. If I can capture the guidance program of the enemy bird completely that way, then we just work backward to refine the ground-to-air system."

Clint McKinney nodded in agreement. But he and Dr. Chabbaz exchanged glances. Then Clint spoke up. "Our intel says that this bio-threat is imminent. So, I need to start your operational briefing immediately. That's one phase of our defensive response — but there's another."

"Am I involved in that?" Joshua asked.

"No," Clint said with a penetrating look, "but your assistant, Ethan March, is."

FIFTY-SEVEN

Pepsi Convention Center, Denver, the Hewbright War Room

Secret Service Agent Owens, wearing the usual dark suit, white shirt, and light blue tie, was munching a cookie in the corner of the five-room suite while Deborah cleared the soda cans and coffee cups from the long buffet table. The Hewbright staff had decided they couldn't trust the convention hospitality workers to set up and tear down the food service, not since the hacking of Hewbright's Allfone, and Agent Owens had made them aware of the need for heightened security.

Deborah was tossing the trash from the buffet table into a big garbage bag. She glanced over at the meeting taking place in the adjoining room, where the senator, in shirtsleeves, was leaning back in his chair, arms crossed. Beside him stood George Caulfield, his national campaign manager, and across from him was Zeta Milla, holding her black D&G handbag. Winston Garvey, the chief foreign-policy advisor, was somewhere out of sight, and Deborah could hear snatches of their conversation. Several American companies in Bolivia, they were saying, had just been forcibly taken over by government forces, and the executives had been taken hostage. President Tulrude was deferring to the United Nations to intervene. Now Hewbright was formulating his public response.

The opening ceremonies of the convention would start that night. Deborah knew that would involve a military honor guard and a musical number by a large community choir from Colorado Springs. That would be followed by a video presentation on the JumboTrons, giving a retrospective of American history, called *Our Legacy of Liberty*. Later, at the end of the evening, Senator Hewbright would appear on stage and formally present the big ceremonial gavel to the chairman of the party, who was presiding over the convention. As she thought of all this, Deborah had a feeling of impending dread — it was the timing of it all, right before the climax of the convention. If someone was going to disrupt Hewbright's nomination, wouldn't this be the time? Deborah knew she had to do something — anything — to find out what Zeta Milla might be planning. And she had to do it fast. It was time to try the plan she had formulated earlier.

Deborah tied up a garbage bag and walked out of the common room. Rick had left with a rolling cart of leftover food several minutes before. On the way out, she snatched up an empty garbage bag and tucked it under her arm. With the full bag of garbage in her hand, she jogged down the hall to the service elevator and threw it into the open elevator. She pushed the button for Basement and scooted back down the hall to the women's restroom where, around the corner from the stalls, she had stashed her duffel bag. She opened it and pulled out the handbag she had purchased that morning — identical to Zeta Milla's — which Deborah had filled with empty files and a stack of photocopy paper to give it heft. She dropped the expensive handbag into the empty garbage bag and trotted back to the war room.

Hewbright's group was still in the adjoining room. Zeta Milla was in the same spot, handbag hanging from her arm. Deborah could see Hewbright speaking and looking up at Milla. Milla nodded and walked out into the common area where agent Owens and Deborah were standing. Deborah took her garbage bag and pretended to busy herself, collecting plastic knives and spoons. Zeta placed her handbag on a chair and pulled out her Allfone. On her cell she talked quietly to someone, asking for statistics on the U.S. companies in Bolivia that had just been raided. While she was talking, George Caulfield hurriedly dashed out and told her to come back into the room, to catch the remarks of President Tulrude, who was about to deliver a live televised message from the Oval Office. Caulfield was red-faced, yelling that Tulrude was "trying to co-opt our convention" with this stunt.

Zeta Milla nodded and told the person on the phone that she would call back. She dashed back to the adjoining room with her Allfone in her hand, leaving her black handbag on the chair. A chill ran down Deborah's back. An opportunity. She knew this was it.

Go girl, charge of the Light Brigade!

She stepped over to Agent Owens and said, "Excuse me, Agent Owens, I'm not sure, but there seems to be some strange stuff going on out in the hallway. Thought you may want to know."

"Strange? Like what?"

"Like a suspicious-looking bag in the service elevator." She tried to sound innocent so that later he wouldn't suspect her of having staged a diversion.

Owens swallowed the last bite of his cookie and headed down the hall.

Deborah made her way to the chair where Milla's handbag was. Keeping her eyes fixed on Zeta, who had her back to her, Deborah snatched it up, pulled her identical bag out of the garbage bag, and after placing it on the chair, strode quickly around the corner to the kitchen galley, out of sight. Deborah opened Milla's bag and rifled through the contents. A small makeup kit, lipstick, a calendar. She leafed through it, but nothing suspicious jumped out.

She peeked around the corner. Milla still had her back turned. The group was glued to the television at the other end of the adjoining room, and the president's voice could be faintly heard in the background. Deborah kept digging. Kleenex. Breath mints. She came to the bottom where she found a piece of folded paper. It was a printout of an email from Zeta Milla to FBI Agent Ben Boling. She poured over its content. It confirmed their earlier conversation, in which Milla described to Agent Boling, in detail, her visit to Perry Tedrich in Wichita the day of his disappearance. Milla told Boling how much she appreciated his clearing her of any suspicion in Tedrich's disappearance and tragic death and how heartbroken she had been. She also mentioned that she feared for Senator Hewbright, particularly after the hacking of his Allfone, and that she urged the FBI to increase surveillance for the sake of Hewbright's personal safety.

Zeta Milla seemed to be the epitome of a non-threat. Deborah was numb with disbelief. And something else — she felt utterly stupid. She stuffed the contents back into the purse and quickly moved over to the chair. She grabbed her replica handbag off the chair, tossed it back into the garbage bag, and then placed Milla's black bag back on the chair.

When she turned, she was startled to see Zeta Milla standing in front of her.

"Sorry," Milla said with a smile, "I need to get past you."

Deborah moved out of the way. Milla smiled, casually picked up her handbag, and turned back to Deborah. "By the way, I'm glad to see you on the team. I'm sorry I sort of gave you the brush-off a while ago. Must be the stress of everything that's going on, I guess."

With a nod, Deborah said, "Sure. Understood."

Milla dashed back into the adjoining room, as Agent Owens came strolling back from the hallway. He walked up to Deborah. "I found that suspicious bag in the service elevator."

"Oh?"

"Wasn't that the same garbage bag you just took out of here?"

With a struggle to look confident and undaunted, Deborah replied, "Wow. Yes. Don't know where my head's at. Sorry."

Agent Owens sauntered over to the cookie plate and grabbed a lemon bar, still eyeing Deborah as he did.

Deborah tried to sort things.

An hour later she was standing in the top tiers of the convention arena, looking down over the scene — the human tide of political exuberance mixed with celebratory chaos. Every seat was taken. Funny hats, waving banners. Confetti flying. The signs for each state delegation posted among the crowd.

But in the midst of that massive surge of optimistic energy, she was surrounded by darkness. Doubt, like a storm cloud, had swept over her.

When the house lights dimmed, the crowd quieted. A mezzo-soprano from the Denver Opera appeared on stage in a single spotlight.

Behind her, the entire back wall displayed an enormous American flag made of tiny lights, which sparkled and began waving digitally. The woman began singing "The Star Spangled Banner."

Deborah saluted the flag, but as she did so, something flashed into her mind. Why would Milla carry such an exonerating email in her purse in the first place? In fact, why would she have so carelessly left her purse in the main room if she knew there was a mole inside the campaign? Deborah quickly worked through one explanation in her head. If Milla was a traitor, then perhaps she had left the purse within Deborah's reach so that she could deliberately plant false information about her innocence. But if that was true, that would mean Zeta Milla had discovered that Deborah was suspicious — and maybe even knew that Deborah was a plant herself.

When the singer finished, she made a quick bow, and the crowd roared their approval.

But Deborah's mind was not on what had just been sung — the familiar first stanza of the national anthem — but on what had not been sung. At West Point, Deborah had learned the second stanza as well, and as she recalled the lyrics she felt a chill run down along her spine, as if an ice cube had fallen down the back of her blouse.

On the shore dimly seen through the mists of the deep
Where the foe's haughty host in dread silence reposes,
What is that which the breeze, o'er the towering steep,
As it fitfully blows, half conceals, half discloses?

She mouthed the words to herself. "Half conceals — half discloses."

That was it. She thought about the email in Milla's purse, purporting to be from Milla to the FBI agent. But that was only half the evidence, wasn't it? Milla could easily have contrived that. Where was the evidence that Agent Boling ever received it or that she had actually sent it?

She grabbed her Allfone and typed into the little keypad a question to Gallagher.

Urgent — Did Ben Boling ever clear Zeta Milla as a suspect in the Wichita murder?

Then she hit Send. But Deborah wasn't going to wait for the reply. She was already jogging out of the arena and down to the elevator so she could get up to the war room suite.

□□□

In a small, noisy café in northern California, at John Gallagher's uncle's wedding reception, a homegrown band was playing the blues instrumental "Night Train." Gallagher was one of the groomsmen, but this definitely was not his kind of bash. When he received Deborah's text, he was glad to be able to loosen the button of his starched tux shirt and step outside onto the deck to get a breather.

He glanced at her question on his Allfone. He squinted. He dashed off a reply and hit Send. But halfway back across the deck toward the door, Gallagher stopped and typed another short message to Deborah.

Be careful kiddo.

FIFTY-EIGHT

Deborah was almost to the elevator. A few stragglers dashed past her to get down to the convention hall. In the background she could hear the echoes of the announcer and the crowd cheering in the arena.

She heard the buzz. She flipped open her Allfone. It was from Gallagher.

Her question had been simple enough:

Did Boling clear Milla?

Gallagher's response was even simpler.

No.

In the elevator Deborah punched the button for the floor of the war room. As the doors closed, she knew what she had to do, though it had all the appeal of grabbing a wasp's nest with her bare hands. She had to get Secret Service Agent Owens aside, show him Gallagher's text, and explain the phony email in the bottom of Zeta Milla's purse. She also had to explain the background information that Pack McHenry had dug up about Milla's real connection to the Castro regime and her history as an assassin-for-hire.

Okay, Deborah thought, she would have a lot of explaining to do herself — like why she was acquiring intel about Milla in the first place and how she had joined the staff under an assumed name. Yes, she knew she might even be suspected of foul play herself. But all of that was a calculated risk, well worth it if Zeta Milla could be exposed before something happened to Senator Hewbright.

The elevator doors opened, and Deborah sprinted out just in time to see Rick heading down the stairwell.

"Rick," she cried out, "have you seen Agent Owens?"

"Uh, yeah ... awhile ago. He's always hanging around the senator." Then Rick said, "I'm taking the stairs to the arena; it's faster. Don't want to miss — hey," he said as if he had remembered something, "they were looking for you in the private suite." Then he turned and headed down the stairs two at a time.

Deborah jogged into the war room. It was cleared out. No signs of anyone.

She stepped into the hallway. A second buzz on her Allfone. It was the second short message from Gallagher.

Be careful, kiddo.

At the end of the corridor, the door to Senator Hewbright's private suite opened. Zeta Milla emerged, dressed for the evening, very classy. Her hands were thrust in the side pockets of her designer suit jacket, and a Gucci briefcase was tucked under her arm.

"Hey, there," Zeta yelled cheerfully, "we were looking for you. The senator has a quick errand for you."

For an instant, as time stopped, Deborah looked down the long hallway at Zeta Milla and wished she had more time. Thinking of Gallagher's warning, she thought to herself, *Sorry, John. Can't do.*

Deborah caught her breath, manufactured a smile, and strode down the hallway toward Zeta Milla.

Milla let Deborah pass by her and walk into Senator Hewbright's suite. Deb had taken only a few steps into the penthouse suite before she was startled by the sound of the door slamming behind her. Zeta was behind her, her hands no longer in her pockets. She held a briefcase by the handle and wore latex gloves.

Deborah scanned the room. She could see a pair of feet lying on the carpet, extending from behind the cabinets of the kitchenette. She took a step in that direction and recognized the dark suit and light blue tie of the man lying there. In the middle of Agent Owen's white shirt was a small blackened hole and the blood that encircled it.

Deb lifted her eyes. Senator Hewbright was also on the floor of the kitchenette, but from what Deb could tell, he was still alive. His eyes were wide and his mouth covered in duct tape. The cabinet doors under the sink were open and his hands were handcuffed together around the pipe.

When she turned toward the door, Zeta was there, almost touching her, pointing a handgun with a silencer at Deborah's face.

"Sit down, dear," Milla said calmly.

Deborah did as she was told, easing onto the soft chair in the living room but not taking her eyes off Milla.

"You know," the woman said, "I had a plan before I knew that you were coming. Crude. But it would have been effective. But when you walked into this campaign, I knew how very perfect you would be."

"You don't have to do this," Deborah said.

"Oh, but I do."

"Why —"

"Don't bother trying to understand," Milla said. "You Jordans think you can outsmart the world. You — the young West Point graduate — did you really think you were going to outsmart me?" Zeta laughed with a guttural tone. It had the sound of something hideous and evil.

"But you should know something," Milla continued. "How your love for Senator Hewbright will not go unnoticed."

"What are you talking about?"

"How you stalked him and came here under an assumed name. Yes, I know that too. How your romantic obsession with him slowly became psychotic."

Deborah's eyes flashed. "You're crazy."

"Oh?" Then Zeta Milla, with her other hand in her briefcase, pulled out some invoices. "Then what do you think the authorities will say about these ... motel receipts with your name on them — having paid in cash each time, of course, showing your many liaisons with the good senator at those times when I know he would have been alone and without witnesses — except for Agent Owens."

Milla glanced over at the agent's body. "Oh, dear, and he's gone too. Well, they'll find the receipts in your pockets, along with the note about how enraged you were at finding out that the senator had feelings for me. A murder-suicide ... a fairly common syndrome, I'm afraid."

"No one will believe it," Deborah spit back. "My father and mother will hunt you down and expose all of this."

"I doubt that, but even if they do, it will be too late. Senator Hewbright will be permanently unavailable as a candidate, because in your rage — you killed him. Before you committed suicide, of course. They will find the gun in your hand, and I will tell them how I witnessed the whole awful bloody ordeal. Which leaves Governor Tucker as the dark horse candidate here at the convention. As you know, he doesn't stand a chance of winning, especially after his political party gets smeared with this grotesque spectacle." Then she added, "Deborah, dear — really — by being here, you really gave me the perfect gift. Thanks, darling."

A knock on the door.

Deborah froze.

Zeta calmly walked closer to the door but kept the long barrel of the gun pointed at Deborah. "Who is it?" she asked.

"Room service. Delivery for the senator."

"No, thank you. He's taking a nap right now. Just leave it outside, please."

"Oh, boy," came the voice from the other side. "My manager's going to throw a fit. All the candidates are supposed to get one of these baskets. I need to say I've passed it off to someone up here or he's going to come up here himself and blow a gasket."

Zeta Milla waved with the gun barrel for Deborah to stand up. Then she said in a hoarse whisper, "Take the basket and close the door. If you do anything I don't like, I'll blow a hole in your back."

Milla stepped to the side, out of range of the door, with her gun trained on Deborah.

Opening the door, Deborah saw a middle-aged man in a white service jacket, holding a basket. He had a pleasant smile. As she reached for it, he pushed his way forward, entering the suite and staring right into Deborah's eyes with a look that seemed to be telegraphing something. "Sorry, but I need you to sign for this," he said and looked around the room as if he were deciding where to set the basket down.

FBI Agent Ben Boling, in the room-service outfit, smiled at Deborah as she signed for the basket, and he looked around the room without moving his head.

When he looked to his right, he saw Zeta standing just around the corner. The glass cabinet across the room had caught her reflection, and Boling could see the gun in her extended hand.

Instantly, he pushed Deborah to the ground, dropping the basket, and in a swooping motion turned the corner toward Milla. He fired a shot but missed. She returned fire and hit Boling in the chest. He collapsed to the floor.

Zeta moved out from around the corner and fired again but narrowly missed Boling's neck. Before Zeta could hit him again, Deborah leaped at the gun barrel and knocked it as it fired. A lamp on the other side of the room shattered. There was a momentary struggle for the gun, but Milla kicked Deborah ferociously in the knee-cap, then in the groin, and stomped her shin, all in rapid succession until Deborah faltered. Then Zeta swung the handgun violently to Deborah's face and pistol-whipped her to the ground.

She took direct aim at Deborah's head as she stood over her.

But a blast dropped Zeta to the ground like a marionette without strings. The bullet to the side of Zeta Milla's head from Ben Boling's Smith and Wesson was fatal.

Deborah scampered over to Boling, who was trying to talk but could only emit a gasping noise because of the hole in his lung. She leaped to her feet and ran into the hallway, where a security guard and a campaign staffer were already responding to the sound of shots.

"Man down, man down!" she screamed. "Get an EMT right now!"

FIFTY-NINE

Abu Dhabi, Domain Tower Hotel

It was evening and Alexander Coliquin was in his top-floor suite, standing before the glass portico, one thousand two hundred feet and eighty-eight floors up from the pavement below. The skyline of the crown jewel of the United Arab Emirates was spread out before him, twinkling like the stars in the night sky.

He was not a man to show inner turmoil. His man servant bowed and presented a cup of jasmine tea on a solid gold platter. Coliquin took it and smiled as the servant disappeared. No one could have guessed the news he had just received. That his dear Zeta — whom he knew as Maria — was gone. Forever. He lifted his left hand and studied the ring on his finger. It was a gold-and-silver replica of a snake with ruby eyes, devouring its own tail. He recalled the day in Bora-Bora when he and Maria had been wed, with these matching rings, in a simple ceremony performed by a local Shaman.

He was not one to commit exclusively to a single lover, and he had assured her of that before their wedding night. But she had only kissed him and playfully replied, "Neither am I."

But even more than her capacity for both playfulness and cruelty, Coliquin treasured her other talents as well: her ability for artful deception and her skillful execution of targets — without hesitation. She had a unique kind of innovation and creativity. For her, the setup, the game, and the killing, was an art form. Few possessed what she had. And now Coliquin's beautiful weapon was gone.

But there was an even bigger complication. *What if,* he thought, *despite all my efforts, Senator Hewbright becomes the next president of the United States?*

Coliquin had watched the convention coverage from Denver. Every second of it. He checked every Internet news service, searching for any hint of what had transpired that night in the Pepsi Center when his precious instrument, his beautiful partner, had been shot in the head. But there was nothing. He found it infuriating that his plan, even if it had failed, would not at least have tainted the convention with the bloody tale of near-assassination. Incredibly, they had managed to cover it up, kept it from the American public.

So when Hewbright appeared on stage so repulsively triumphant, confident, and energetic, to deliver his acceptance speech, as if nothing had happened, Coliquin took that as a personal slight. It was as if the idea of a contrived murder-suicide had never existed. Yet even though the scheme failed, Coliquin was convinced that the right kind of media spin about the shootout could have imprinted Hewbright's campaign with a negative image, like an ugly birthmark. But that had been stolen from him.

Now people would have to pay. Those responsible — and maybe even those who were not. Failure never meant having to forego revenge.

When he heard the chimes from the front door of his penthouse, he knew he had business to attend to. It was Faris D'Hoestra and his powerful industrialist associate, Deter Von Gunter, a member of his World Builders group. He buzzed them both into the room.

D'Hoestra was not a man to linger. "I've come all the way to Abu Dhabi," he began, "as you requested. It seems a long trip for a very simple issue."

"You mean the U.N. charter amendment? Not so simple."

"Well, that is why we're here." D'Hoestra glanced down at the couch and asked, "Shall we sit?"

"No need," Coliquin replied. "I said it wasn't simple. I didn't say it was impossible. I know what you want — a restructuring. You want the U.N. Security Council to slowly ebb into oblivion, to be replaced by your super committee, so the World Builders can have a dominant role through your own assortment of international members."

Coliquin pulled an envelope from his suit-coat pocket. "Here's a draft agreement from a number of key nations willing to sign on to your plan and submit it to the General Assembly for a formal amendment to the charter."

D'Hoestra began to reach for it, adding, "And it has your official endorsement, I trust?"

"Of course," Coliquin replied, still hanging onto the envelope.

"And what do you expect in return?"

"Your support. And that of the Builders."

"Is that all?"

"For now."

Coliquin threw a look at Deter Von Gunter who was standing nearby with a blank expression. "Deter," he said waving the envelope, "why don't you have a seat. While Mr. D'Hoestra and I chat privately."

Then Coliquin led Faris D'Hoestra through the glass doors to the sweeping patio outside. D'Hoestra took in the panorama of the night sky and the lights of Abu Dhabi below. "Beautiful," he murmured to Coliquin who was standing on his right side, smiling.

Coliquin, glancing back through the glass toward Von Gunter, said with his hand on D'Hoestra's shoulder, "You and I can be blunt. This U.N. charter proposal was not easy for me to obtain, but I know the leverage you have. You've played the game well. Next time I won't cave in so easily."

He slipped the envelope into the inside pocket of D'Hoestra's suit coat and patted his chest. "Now," Coliquin added, "we have a few loose ends to tie up." Then he glanced down at his own left shoe. "Like an untied shoe."

D'Hoestra looked down and noticed Coliquin's left shoelace was untied. While Coliquin bent down to tie it, D'Hoestra stepped up to the white chest-high stone wall that separated the portico at the top of the sky-scraper from the thin air beyond. He took a furtive glance over the edge and straight down to the ground over a thousand feet below. Instinctively, he took a step backward. But a hand grasped his right ankle like a vise.

A look of shock spread over D'Hoestra's face as Coliquin, with his right hand still locked on to D'Hoestra's ankle, reached up with his left hand and grabbed the World Builder chairman by the back of his belt.

D'Hoestra awkwardly reached around to remove the hand from his belt, but Coliquin was too quick. In one terrible, swift motion the U.N. secretary flipped Faris D'Hoestra up and over the top of the wall, launching him into the night air.

As he plummeted toward the street below, D'Hoestra shrieked and swung his arms like a child in a nightmare, spinning and doing horrible somersaults on the long ride down.

Coliquin watched until he was sure the body had hit the pavement. Then he stepped back inside. Deter Von Gunter was smoking a cigarette, leaning back in the chair with his legs crossed. He blew out a thin column of white smoke and asked, "That wasn't really a U.N. charter you stuffed in his pocket, I take it?"

"No," Coliquin said, "it was his suicide note."

If his dear departed lover had been in the room, Coliquin would have lifted an eyebrow and instructed her, "That's how it's done."

But he turned to Von Gunter instead. "We have unfinished business. You need to have your World Builders group decide its direction now."

Deter Von Gunter tapped the end of his cigarette out in the crystal ashtray and stood up. "Not necessary. We've already voted." Von Gunter lowered his head to Coliquin's left hand and delicately kissed his ring.

Denver, St. Anthony's Hospital

John Gallagher swept into Ben Boling's hospital room and spread his arms wide when he saw the FBI agent in bed. "My hero!"

Boling gave a head nod. "Hey, Gallagher."

"Sorry I didn't spring for a bunch of flowers for you. Now that I think of it," Gallagher said, "I was just at a wedding ... I could have swiped some on the way out."

He strode over to the bedside table and picked up one of the get-well cards. "Gee, a personal card from the director of the Bureau himself. Nice. But I noticed they didn't include your reprimand slip in it."

"You know the procedure. They'll present it to me personally when I get back."

"Well, anyway, you saved the day."

Ben Boling painfully moved over a bit in the bed to face Gallagher, grabbing the metal railing as he did. "Not entirely. One dead Secret Service agent. Do you know if Owens was married?"

"Divorced," Gallagher said. Then his face took on a thoughtful expression. "You know, there was a time when I would have tried to make a joke out of that. Death vs. divorce. Sound cynical?"

"You're preaching to the choir," Boling said. "We all have ways to cover up the garbage we carry around in this kind of work. Me? I go fishing. You ought to try it."

Then a look of panic spread over Boling's face. "Oh, man, I just remembered. My wife's due here any minute. She's flying in. I needed to keep my intervention at the convention top secret, so I told her I was on a fishing trip."

"You were," Gallagher said, "and you caught a killer — and a half ounce of lead."

"You know where I took it?" Boling said. "Same place in the lung that Ronald Reagan did. So why did he look so much better than me afterward?"

"Speaking of Washington, why'd they yank you off the Hewbright assignment anyway?"

Boling just shook his head glumly.

"There's bad stuff afoot," Gallagher said. "Not just petty infighting, my friend. True rotten, dirty dealing. Starting at the top. Anytime you want to join me in semiretirement, just let me know."

"Naw. Not me. I'm sticking it out. When something's gone bad, there's always a chance to bring back the good." Then Boling's eyes widened. "Hey, you want some inside information?"

"You kidding? It's like Oreo cookie ice cream to me."

"The hacking of Hewbright's Allfone. The FBI cyber guys traced it to a Chinese hacker."

"Old news," Gallagher said.

"What you don't know is the name of the hacker's close associate."

"You got me drooling. Who?"

"Ho Zhu."

"I could make a joke out of that too, like the old 'who's on first' routine ..."

"This one's no joke."

"All right, so what's so important about Ho Zhu?"

"He's the deputy secretary of the U.N., just under Coliquin ... one of his right-hand men."

Fair Haven Convalescent Center, Bethesda, Maryland

Cal had brought the medical authorization form with him to meet Winnie Corland. She had to be there to collect some personal items of her late husband's anyway, she said. Now they sat together in the dayroom. The form was on the side table between them, but looking at Winnie and the sadness in her eyes, Cal was sure he would be leaving with it unsigned. She was grief-stricken, and the way Cal saw it, the last thing on her mind was the desire to expose an attempt to interfere with the health of a sitting President. Not now, at least. Winnie was clutching her purse as if she were ready to get up and walk out any minute.

Winnie didn't talk much. She only mentioned a few details about her husband's time in the Oval Office and the fact that they didn't have any children, but Virgil had always wanted a son.

"He followed that terrible incident you were in up in New York at the train station. He admired your father — but thought highly of you too, the way you were able to stay so calm and courageous in the face of such evil. And I think," she said, and her chin trembled as she said it, "that he would have liked a son like you."

Surprisingly she got around to talking about President Tulrude, and how she had pressured Virgil to use Dr. Jack Puttner, her own physician. Corland received one shot of something from Puttner for his transient ischemic heart condition, she couldn't recall what. Then Virgil's massive attack took place in the presidential limo after a speech in Virginia.

"I never trusted Tulrude or that Dr. Puttner," she said.

"How did your husband end up with a vial containing the blood sample that he gave to us?"

Winnie looked away from Cal, seemingly ashamed. "When we first rushed Virgil into the ER in Leesburg, I told the doctor I thought the attack may have been caused by a medical reaction to the drug that Puttner had used. He must have drawn blood immediately. Because later he gave me a plastic medical envelope with the blood sample tube in it. He gave me a funny look when he did and told me to preserve it by keeping it refrigerated. That I 'might need it as evidence' later on. He said he suspected some strange things going on — the way that federal officials were handling the medical records. That's all he would tell me."

For Cal, the trail seemed to lead not just to Dr. Puttner but to Tulrude as well.

"But now Virgil's gone," Winnie said, her voice faltering, "you have no idea how hard this is, talking about this. I just want to forget. All of it."

A realization hit Cal. If he had done the smart thing while Corland was still alive, and had him sign the medical release back then, he wouldn't be in the tough spot that he was in now. But it was too late for that.

"I think that's all for now," Winnie said and struggled at a smile. "I have to go."

"I understand," Cal said, getting up to leave. "Mrs. Corland, I'm so very sorry about your husband. I liked him a lot. I enjoyed spending time with him. I'm sorry if I've brought up some bad memories for you."

Then he turned and walked toward the entrance of the day room.

"Cal," she said softly. "Please, take this away." Winnie was holding the medical authorization that he had left on the table.

He complied and trotted up to her and took the form, but Cal noticed she was putting a pen back into her purse, and he saw her signature at the bottom of the form.

"And don't worry about my being the one who signed," she replied and snapped her purse shut. "I have power-of-attorney."

SIXTY

Four Days Later, Early Morning, on the Edge of the Negev Desert, Israel

There were no classes in the Bedouin school that day. In the cinder-block garage, Tarek Fahad and his two assistants had finished the assembly of the missile and the portable launching system provided by the weapons division of the Deter Von Gunter Group. Dr. Ahlam had been silently watching them during the process, getting so close that he occasionally got in the way.

Now it was his turn. "I have placed the biochemical agent underground," he said, pointing to a square concrete trapdoor in the floor with the heavy metal handle. "In a protective capsule within a lead-lined container. I am going to carefully retrieve it now. But after that, I will have to put on my bio-suit to load the chemical into the missile. I have suits for you in the back of my truck. You must put them on."

Fahad glanced at his watch. So far they were on schedule.

Dr. Ahlam had a question. "If you will permit me, I have worked so long and hard on this project. The Elixir of Allah is, I believe, my finest masterpiece. I know you have the target selected. You must have. Yes? Down to the square inch."

Stepping closer to Ahlam, Fahad jutted his head up a little, eying the chemist, and said, "What is it? Just say it. What is it you want to know?"

"Your target. Where will my poison do its work?"

"Oh, that?" Fahad said and turned to his two friends. They all chuckled.

319

"The missile will be aimed at the Jewish Quarter in Jerusalem," Fahad answered. "But as for the location where it will accomplish its most marvelous work," he added with a raised eyebrow, "that I cannot share. It is a secret."

Jewish Quarter, Old City, Jerusalem

Peter Campbell was striding down Bab as-Silsila, the Souk containing shops and restaurants just beyond the Western Wall plaza where he had been arrested the week before. The pastor had always been a fast walker, and GNN reporter Bart Kingston was chugging hard to keep up.

Campbell turned to look for Kingston, then slowed so he could catch up. "I never thought I'd see the day a GNN reporter would help me get out of jail."

"You're an interesting story. My editors had to okay it. You know, all that ethics in journalism stuff. Though we didn't have to post bail. Just had to convince the authorities to release you and the others because of the temporary restraining order entered by the Israeli Supreme Court."

Campbell pointed to a café. "Between the Arches," he said, "let's duck in here, if it's okay. I'm famished."

The two men stepped down the spiral stairs into the subterranean restaurant that had been built into an ancient Roman cistern. As they sat at a glass-topped table, Campbell, who knew a little of the background of the café, launched into a description of the architecture of that part of Jerusalem during the life of Christ.

After ordering sandwiches, Kingston bent forward, leaning his chin on one fist, with one elbow on the table. Campbell noticed he didn't have his notepad out. No tape recorder was running.

"Question," Kingston began. "What do you say to skeptics who say, look, it's been more than two thousand years since Jesus' time. I thought He was supposed to return."

"I'd give the same answer that the Apostle Peter gave in his second epistle. You can look it up in the New Testament. Chapter 3. He explained that mockers asked the same question in the first century.

His answer was twofold. First, God doesn't count time the way we do. With the Lord, a thousand years is like one day. But more important is the reason God is waiting until the last minute to command His Son's second coming to earth. Peter says this: 'The Lord is not slow about His promise, as some count slowness, but is patient toward you, not wishing for any to perish, but for all to come to repentance.'" Campbell sized up the reporter sitting across the table. "Bart, listen, if the Lord is patient, slow to finally break open the heavens and have Jesus Christ appear to His followers and whisk them off the face of the earth, then maybe it has something to do with *you*."

Kingston straightened up. "I don't follow that one."

"God doesn't want anyone to perish into a Christless eternity. Maybe God's been waiting for you — and others like you — to make that one decision that could change your destiny forever."

"Others? You mean members of the press?" Kingston asked with a sly smile.

Campbell tapped his finger on the table, punctuating his response. "Butchers. Politicians. Bakers. Sales clerks. Farmers. Garbage collectors. And yes, even news reporters. Hardened criminals, sure. And law-abiding citizens too. Every tribe. Every tongue. Every nation." Then the pastor leaned back, as he noticed the waiter heading their way. "Bart, I think you are a serious guy who is seriously considering the claims of Jesus Christ. His claim to be God Incarnate — the claim that His blood sacrifice on a Roman cross is sufficient to cleanse your sins and bring you into the family of God — and His claim that He is standing at the door of your heart right now, knocking. And what you need to do is open the door and invite Him in by faith. You have to ask yourself a tough question — am I honest and objective enough to admit that I hear His knuckles rapping on that door right now?"

The waiter laid the plates on the table. As he did, Campbell reached out with his knuckles and rapped them gently on the glass table top.

Tel Aviv

Abigail had taken to holding Joshua's hand everywhere. Shopping, walking in the market, going from room to room in his apartment.

This was only the second day of their reunion, and she didn't want to let go.

"I want to stay with you," she said in the hallway.

In the living room, Deborah was grabbing her purse, and Cal was checking his digital camera. They heard their mother and started to laugh.

"Just don't start kissing in front of us again," Deborah said, rolling her eyes.

"Yeah," Cal added, "rule number one — no parental PDA in front of your offspring, even if we are adults."

"Look, Abby, honey," Joshua tried to explain, "I've got another flight planned in the F-35 LV today. We're getting close to working the kinks out of the jet-mounted RTS system. We'd be separated anyway."

"But we've been apart for two years," she said with pleading in her voice. And she repeated it again. "*Two years*. I had started to feel like a widow, Josh." She knew she was being unreasonable, but she didn't care.

"I know, babe. This has been miserable for both of us," he said. Then he drew her close. As he brought his lips close to hers, he turned toward his son and daughter. "Cover your eyes," he yelled to them with a grin as they both groaned. He held her in a passionate embrace for a while. He pulled back but then went in for another kiss. More moaning from his son and daughter.

"Okay, tell me, Abby," Joshua asked, "what is the name of that legal group you're going to address?"

"The International Society of Lawyers."

"Are you familiar with it?"

"The name rings a bell."

"Who invited you?"

"I received an email from Fort Rice. He forwarded the invitation to me."

"What are you going to talk about?"

She cocked an eyebrow. "Take a guess — your case, of course. I'm the lunch speaker. They want me to address the subject of Wrongful Prosecution and Political Aspects of the American Legal System."

"I can't think of a better expert on the subject," he said. "Now that the Department of Justice has voluntarily dismissed their case against me, thanks to you."

"I think the DOJ just wanted to avoid the humiliation of our judge dismissing it in open court, so they beat the U.S. District Court to the punch."

"You know," Joshua said, "I was just thinking. I can call Clint McKinney and have the IDF escort you."

"Dad," Cal piped up, "what are you worried about? Besides, she's not going to make it in time. We've got to leave right now if we're going to make it to Jerusalem by noon."

"I just want to make sure my bride is safe," Joshua said.

"Really, Dad," Deborah said, "Mom outsmarted the entire federal surveillance system, talked her way into the wilderness compound of one of the world's most secretive recluses — "

"Yeah, thanks to me," Cal added with a grin.

"Oh, whatever," Deborah sniped. "And then she makes it back to D.C. in time to win your case. I think she can take care of herself."

"Well," Joshua said, "she's got you two. Both of you are heroes in my book. You, Cal — getting your mom across country and back again, against everything the SIA could throw at you. And Deborah — putting your neck on the line to face down that threat to Hewbright ..."

"God's hand," Deborah said, with a sudden and remarkable adulthood to her voice. "No question about it, Dad."

Cal was nodding too. "Deb and I have been talking about that, how faithful the Lord has been, watching over us. All of us."

"The sparrow," Abigail began to say, ready to recite the familiar saying of Jesus — that even a sparrow cannot fall without the Heavenly Father's notice. But this time it caught in her throat as she looked at her husband and thought about those words and what he did for so many years as a pilot and what he was about to do again. She began to tear up.

"What's the matter, darling?" Joshua asked.

"Nothing," she said, wiping her eyes. "Just full of emotions. So glad to be with you at last. All of us together. For whatever time we have."

Then she turned to Cal and Deborah. "Okay, let's get moving." As she stepped toward the door, she turned toward Joshua for one last look. "Have a good flight, my precious husband," she said. She went back for one more kiss, then turned with her son and daughter and left.

Two hours later, in downtown Jerusalem on the edge of the Arab section, Abigail was on the sidewalk with a note in her hand that showed the address of the meeting. The green door to the Society of International Lawyers was locked. Cal and Deborah peeked in the windows.

"No lights. The place is shut down," Cal said.

"Some wires got crossed," Deborah said. "I say we take off, start our sightseeing."

"I called my contact person," Abigail murmured, looking at her Allfone and at the number she had called. "No answer."

The neighborhood seemed unusually quiet. Abigail saw only one person, a shopkeeper in front of his corner grocery. In the distance was the sound of approaching vehicles. Suddenly Abigail felt the hair rise on the back of her neck. She turned to move toward their car, and she was about to shout to Cal and Deborah. But not in time.

In a single coordinated movement three vans raced in from a side street. They screeched to a halt at the curb in front of them. Doors flew open. Several armed Arab men poured out. They charged straight at the three members of the Jordan family.

SIXTY-ONE

New York, AmeriNews Network Headquarters

Terri Schultz was bolting out of her office but stopped momentarily to glance at herself in the round mirror on the wall. The news manager didn't like what she saw. *Yikes, I'm a mess.* She ran a brush through her hair, grabbed her e-pad, embedded with her notes, and sprinted down the hall.

The tech assistant outside the recording room waved for her to hurry up. "Come on, Terri, he's on the line."

As she reached the door her assistant reminded her, "Don't forget to get his waiver about our recording him ..."

She halted and gave him a withering look. "I've been doing this for a decade, remember?"

Then Terri scooted into the recording booth and strapped on the headset. "Okay, Dr. Derringer, are you there?"

"I am."

"I can't thank you enough for your willingness to give us your expertise. Phil Rankowitz speaks very highly of you."

"Phil and I go way back. He did a TV series years ago on our work here at the NIH."

"We told you that we're going to record this conversation. I sent you the written waiver. We'd like you to email that back to us, preferably right now, before we start."

"Sure. I realize, you know, how … explosive this whole thing is. Might be. I can't say I'm excited about getting sucked into what might be the political firestorm of the century. On the other hand, well, it is what it is, I guess …"

Dr. Derringer excused himself and turned to his office manager to discuss the waiver. He returned to Terri. "We can't email from this desk, the computer's down. Give me just a minute. I'll sign it. We'll get it to you stat. Then we can talk."

While Terri was on hold, she placed her finger on the fingerprint ID of her e-pad, and it lit up, revealing the outline of her questions. She wiped the palm of her hand on her jeans. *Wow, cold sweat. Steady girl. Just because you're about to break a story that's a twenty-first-century version of the Lincoln assassination, no need to unravel.*

Taking a deep breath, she took stock of the moment. Phil Rankowitz had entrusted her with the medical side of this story. She figured that ought to count for something, right? And even being hired by AmeriNews was a great boost for her, after her job at the *New York Times* folded when it shifted to an all-Internet format. And while she didn't share Phil's religious super-zeal about Jesus, they did share the desire to tell the public the truth.

Dr. Derringer came back on the line. He said he was ready. Terri checked her Allfone and saw the email. She opened the attachment. The signed waiver from the doctor was there. She gave the signal to the board operator across the glass from her to start rolling tape. Then, on the record, she asked him if he was consenting to the recording of the interview. He said yes. So she began.

"Dr. Derringer, as head of pharmacology at the National Institutes of Health, you agreed to analyze a blood sample that had been taken from former President Virgil Corland in the emergency room in a hospital in Leesburg, Virginia, shortly after he had suffered a massive episode connected with his medical condition of transient ischemic attack, is that correct?"

"Yes, that's right. I tested the blood sample, determined that it was suitable to yield results. I examined it for several different components and to see what chemical or medical agents may have been in his bloodstream at the time. I reached some conclusions and had them double-checked with my colleagues at the NIH."

"Do you personally know Dr. Jack Puttner, the interim physician for the president at the time?"

"No. I only know of him — that he originally had been the physician for Vice President Tulrude."

"Can you give me a short and concise layman's summary of what you found in the president's blood?"

"Short and concise? I suppose I can."

"Anything I need to know before you explain that to me?"

There was a pause. Terri prodded him a bit. "Doctor?"

"Only this — better buckle your seatbelt ..."

The White House

Inside the Oval Office, Chief of Staff Natali Traup stood stiffly in the center of the carpet's presidential seal as President Tulrude glared at her. The president stood behind her desk, her shoulders hunched and her hands flat on the desk top. Tulrude had a look of contempt mixed with fury as she began to yell. Bits of spittle flew from her mouth.

"What do you mean he won't return your calls? Did you say who you were — that you were calling for the president of ... the United States ... of America?"

"Yes, I told him," Traup said. "I called several times. I said this message is for Dr. Jack Puttner and that President Tulrude needed to speak with him immediately. That it's a matter of grave urgency."

"If our intel is correct, and AmeriNews is trying to do a scoop on Virgil Corland, and they're pursuing some sick, extremist, right-wing plot to tie me to some attempt to worsen Corland's medical situation ... or even ... to cause his ..." But she didn't finish the sentence. Then a thought flashed over her face, and she changed course. "You should have told Puttner in the voicemail that this is a matter of national security. You should have said that."

"But it isn't."

"It is. It's an attack on the credibility of the president — *me*. That's national security."

"No," Traup said quietly but firmly. "It isn't, with all due respect, Madam President. What it really is, I think, is a matter of political security. Yours. And your reelection."

"And that directly affects you. You'd better decide whose side you're on, because you will be called upon to apply some serious pressure on the good Doctor Puttner to play ball with us before the prosecutors sit down with him. Do you understand me?"

Natali Traup took a step backward, just off the presidential seal. "I understand," she said quietly. "And because of that, I will have to do some thinking. About many things."

Launch Site, Edge of the Negev Desert, Israel

Abigail had been beaten. Her left cheek was bruised, and her left eye nearly closed with swelling. Her Islamic terrorist captors had shown her no mercy. Cal and Deborah had been manhandled even worse. From her position strapped to a metal chair bolted to the floor, she could see them both, tied in their chairs next to her. Deborah was bleeding from the mouth and had a gash across her forehead, and both of Cal's eyes had been blackened and it looked as if some of his teeth were missing.

On the other hand, four of the nine members of the Al Aqsa Jihad terror group who grabbed them were now out of commission, thanks to the ferocious struggle put up by Cal and Deborah and the injuries they dealt out: a broken arm, a busted nose, a few fractured ribs, a dislocated shoulder, and a concussion.

But there were still five of them left, and they all had weapons. They captured and tied up the Jordans and dragged them into the van to be taken to the site of their captivity.

Abigail looked up at the roof of the garage that was part of the Bedouin school grounds. Half of the tin roof had been retracted with a long-handled pole and was now open. She could see the blue sky of late afternoon above. She thought about Joshua and prayed that he was safe. She knew that whatever was going on — whatever the horrid plan that their kidnappers had in mind — it must surely have something to do with Joshua and his RTS system. Maybe even retaliation for his system having been used against Iran two years before.

As she thought about that, she also studied an object nearby that looked like a long cylinder on a work bench, draped with a tarp.

A missile.

The five men huddled near a side door as if waiting for someone. Deborah whispered to her mother, though her speech was garbled because of her injuries. "Don't like ..." she started to say, but the rest was inaudible. She tried again. "Don't like that we're *not* blindfolded."

Abigail nodded. The captors were not concerned about being recognized. They were clearly not planning on leaving witnesses. Then the door swung open.

The terror cell leader popped in. The other men smiled and bowed from the waist. Tarek Fahad spoke to them in Arabic. The men scrambled. Several headed to the work bench where they pulled the tarp off the missile containing the Elixir of Allah. The others scampered to a corner of the garage where they retrieved a satellite television camera. They set up the camera directly in front of Abigail, Cal, and Deborah. The savage broadcast would be linked to a television station, set to broadcast the live feed of their grisly fate.

SIXTY-TWO

Israeli Airspace, over the Northern Sector of the Negev Desert

In the cockpit of the F-35 LV fighter jet, Joshua peered through his helmet visor. He focused first on the forward screen on the flight deck, then the one on the left, and the lit-up LCDs on each. "I'm checking the threat warning prime and the auxiliary right now," he reported. "They're both operational. I'm still getting used to the layout. A different configuration than I'm used to."

The voice of the test pilot on the ground at the control tower responded, "That's because it's been adapted for your RTS system. Just maintain your current airspeed. Our guys down here are going to tee-up the unarmed bird to send your way for the first test."

There was another voice. This time it was Colonel Clint McKinney. "Hey, Josh, Clint here."

"Good to hear your voice, man. You down there in the tower?"

"Yeah, stopped by to make sure these guys don't go too easy on you, you know, on account of your advanced age."

Joshua laughed. "You don't know the half of it."

"By the way," Clint added, "got a message from command that I was supposed to pass on to you."

"Oh, from who?"

"A friend of yours — Judge Fort Rice — says that Phil Rankowitz is ready to bust the big story wide open. Said you'd know what that means."

"Yes, sir," he said, "I sure do. Thanks."

To Joshua, it was a long time coming. Now it sounded as if Phil had gathered enough information to break the story about President Virgil Corland's illness, and Tulrude's complicity in a plot to take him out. Finally, he thought, the truth about her rotten administration might get out to the American people.

Clint added, "He also mentioned something about your last message to him ..."

"Right," Joshua replied, "I thanked him for passing on the invitation for Abigail to speak to that international lawyer's group in Jerusalem today."

"Well, that was why he was trying to get hold of you."

"What's up?"

"Judge Rice says that he doesn't have the faintest idea what you're talking about. He never passed on any such invitation."

Joshua spent only two seconds processing that. Then his heart sank. "Clint, do me a favor. You've got Abby's number. Give her a call immediately and make sure everything's okay. Something doesn't sound right."

"I follow you," Clint said. "Will do."

When Joshua had first lifted off in the F-35 that day, he had felt the weight of two burdens. The first was the reason he was in the sky at that moment, trying to engineer a fix for his RTS system. But the other was down on the ground — knowing that Ethan was out there somewhere acting as a decoy on a dangerous mission. Joshua's prayer that morning as he climbed into his flight suit had been for the safety of his protégé. But Clint McKinney's message had just shoved all of that to the back of the line. Front and center, now, was the wellbeing of his wife.

Abby — are you safe?

Northern Bethesda, Maryland

Winnie Corland sat in the den in her Symphony Park brownstone, the one she had purchased because it was close to her late husband's convalescent center. She was alone, sifting through some of his personal effects. She had waded through the political paraphernalia. Now

Winnie was looking through the intimate things, like Virgil's college yearbook and a love letter he had written to her during their undergraduate days. And his brown leather Bible.

His absence was overpowering. Not hearing his voice. Not seeing his face. It was as if their life together had been as fragile as a dry leaf, and a powerful wind had just rushed in and carried it all away in an instant.

That made her remember something that Virgil had read to her aloud many times. She tried to cling to it. She flipped open his Bible, which she had almost never opened herself. There was a thin silk ribbon placed at the first chapter of the gospel of John. She scanned through the first chapter but didn't find what she was looking for. It wasn't in the second chapter either. But in the third chapter she found it, the part where Jesus speaks to Nicodemus, the great Jewish teacher, imparting the secrets of the Spirit. She read it aloud. " 'Do not be amazed that I said to you, 'You must be born again.' The wind blows where it wishes and you hear the sound of it, but do not know where it comes from and where it is going; so is everyone who is born of the Spirit.' "

She closed the Bible but noticed the edge of a note card sticking out, just under the back cover. She pulled it out. She recognized Virgil's handwriting immediately.

It was entitled simply, "A Prayer."

Lord forgive me, a sinner,
By the Holy blood of Jesus Christ, Your only Son,
Which He shed on the cross in Jerusalem
*   for all of my transgressions,*
And who was proven trustworthy and Divine
*   by His miraculous resurrection from the grave;*
You, Jesus, I declare to be
*   the Commander-in-Chief of my soul,*
*   my Savior, my King.*
You have set eternity in all our hearts, Oh God,
*   so that we would search for You.*

And now I want You to fill that empty space
   with the presence of Jesus the Christ, who is my Lord,
   and whose glorious coming is my most blessed hope.

Winnie closed the Bible and put it on the table. But she still grasped the note card firmly in her hand. Her eyes were open but filled with tears. She remembered Virgil's funeral, his closed casket, and the sight of it being lowered into the ground. In a strange way, she felt she was in a casket herself, suffocating. Entombed by her failure of will. How long would she ignore the whispering in her heart — the call of the Spirit for her to be reconciled with the God she had deliberately kept at arm's length?

It wasn't for Virgil that she now reread the note card through hot, streaming tears. Instead, it was for herself, for her own destiny. This would have to be her own act of faith. She knew it was time to move out of the shadowy tomb in which she had lived. She wondered about the sunlight she longed for, which she knew awaited her. She read out loud each word in Virgil's prayer now — no longer just his, but hers as well.

And when she was done, she closed her eyes and wept for the wasted years she had spent neglecting the call of God to her heart. But she also wept for something else. Funny, she thought, but her tears were also for the joy that she felt washing over her like a flood. Winnie suddenly realized that what had just filled her mind like a flash must be true — beyond any debate.

I think that something glorious is coming ...

In the Streets of Nablus

Ethan was behind the wheel of the armored IDF Jeep, heading slowly down one of the main arteries of the city. His hands gripped the steering wheel with white knuckles. For months he had griped to Joshua about not having a direct hand in any missions. Now he had his chance. He was silently giving himself a pep-talk. *Just don't blow it, Ethan. Keep everything under control. Don't let things go haywire.*

That location in Nablus had been chosen because Israeli intel showed that messages about an impending bio-threat had been shuttled back and forth by members of a known terror cell in that Palestinian-controlled area. It was decided that some of the terrorists behind the bio-attack must be there. The plan was to lure at least one of them out in the open, take him alive, and use extreme measures to extract the details of the attack from him.

Ethan glanced at the man sitting next to him, an IDF soldier posing as Joshua. After eye-balling him again, Ethan said, "Not a bad resemblance. But the nose is all wrong."

This prompted a response from Rivka, who was lying in the back of the Jeep holding a Jericho .9mm handgun against her chest. "If they get close enough to see that this guy's nose is different from Joshua's, it'll be too late for them anyway."

Gavi, also armed with a special weapon, was lying next to Rivka in the back, once again acting as her mission partner. He cut them off. "Stop the chatter folks. Ethan, pay attention to your earbud."

Ethan nodded and adjusted the earpiece in his left ear. "Just checking in," he said. A voice came back in his ear. "Head's up, Ethan. You're in the zone now."

Traffic was moderate. A grocery truck ahead of them. A single, older model Renault behind them. A few cars way up ahead. Shops on each side. A woman with a stroller on the sidewalk to the left. A café up on the right, where several men were having coffee at outdoor tables.

A false message had been deliberately disseminated saying that Joshua was being driven by his partner, Ethan, to a testing site for his RTS system, but that gunfire had been heard along the route, forcing them to quickly divert through Nablus. The sound of gunfire was real—it had been supplied by the IDF. They also made sure that the message was leaked to a source they suspected to be a sympathizer of the Al Aqsa Jihad group headed by Anwar al-Madrassa.

The trap had been set. Now they had to hope that the members of the terror cell would take the bait.

The truck ahead slowed. Now the café was almost directly to their right. Ethan glanced to his left. The woman with the stroller was gone.

In the window of an appliance shop two men stood, looking out. Ethan looked up at the second floor. Someone was holding something to his eyes, maybe binoculars. Then the figure quickly stepped back.

"I think I see spotters, folks," Ethan said. "Stay alert."

The truck ahead jerked forward a few yards and stopped.

It happened with lightning speed. Several men with weapons poured out of the shop on the left. The men at the café jumped to their feet, and one of them fired at Ethan, fracturing the bulletproof windshield.

While the men rushed the Jeep from both sides of the street, two Mossad agents in a van parked along the curb jumped out and fired at the assailants from a crouching position.

Rivka was up and shooting to her right. Gavi shouted, "Man in the green T-shirt." He had already picked his target — from a photo array in prep for the mission. He fired the dart and it struck the young man in the chest. The man, who seemed to be about eighteen years old, started shaking, dropped his weapon, and collapsed to the ground while other shooters around him were dropping. The Mossad guys at the van gave covering fire while Rivka and Gavi leaped out of the Jeep and dragged the young man into it.

"Go, go, go!" Gavi screamed. Ethan did a three-sixty, bumping up onto the sidewalk as bullets banged against the armored vehicle, and then he headed back down the street, straight at the Renault. The driver jumped out and started to run away, so Ethan slammed the Jeep into the left front headlight of the little car, knocking it out of the way and then speeding down the street.

In the back seat, the young man was limp from the neuromuscular agent that had been injected into his body, designed to temporarily paralyze his large muscles but not the vocal chords. Then Gavi took out a small black case, slipped out a hypodermic needle and stuck it into the man's jugular vein. Then Rivka turned him on his side so he could vomit. Ethan glanced in his rearview mirror to see what was going on. Gavi told Rivka to keep watch over him as he leaned over the front seat and began shouting out directions to Ethan.

"We need to get out of the Arab areas quick," he yelled. "Turn here!"

Ethan took a sharp right onto a road that he could see led out of Nablus.

"What was in the needle?" Ethan shouted back.

"Our own upgraded brand of SP-117," Gavi said. "We can thank the Russians for coming up with it. But we improved it considerably, speeding up the brain-blood absorption process. Only takes a few minutes now to get the subject ready to chat freely."

When Ethan flashed a blank look, Gavi said, "Hypnotic drug. Disarms psychological restraints. Especially," he added, "under conditions where the subject is experiencing a deep fear for personal safety." Then a second later, Gavi snapped, "Okay, take the highway to the left, and keep going straight. You're on the right track." Then he turned back into the rear of the Jeep.

A few minutes later, Ethan noticed Gavi again in his rearview mirror. Rivka was propping the man up, and Gavi was holding the unloaded dart gun against his forehead and yelling into his captive's face. Rivka was adding to the effect with a mock effort to dissuade Gavi from shooting. "No, no, don't!" she was saying, waving her arms at Gavi. But her partner kept the dart gun pressed against the man's head, shouting in Arabic. "Where is the biological weapon? Where's the poison? Where's the Elixir of Allah?"

The young man's eyes darted around wildly. He muttered something.

"Speak!" Gavi screamed again.

He muttered again. And Gavi brought his face down closer into the young man's face and demanded that he answer the question.

"Madrasah," the young man murmured.

"Yeah, we know you work for Anwar al-Madrassa," Gavi screamed back. "But we want to know where the Elixir of Allah is, and we want it right now."

"*Madrasah,*" the young man said again.

Now Rivka was pushing Gavi away, playing her part in the good-cop, bad-cop routine. "Say again?"

"*Madrasah hassah,*" the man muttered, a numb expression on his face.

Rivka sat up and looked at Gavi. "That's not a name," she said. "*Madrasah hassah* means 'private school' in Arabic."

The Jeep roared out of Nablus, while Rivka yelled into her earpiece, loud enough so that her commanders back at the headquarters would not miss it.

"The bio-weapon's in a school building somewhere."

Gavi grabbed the man by his shirt and screamed in his face, "What school? Where?"

But the man shook his head violently and in a pleading voice cried out in Arabic, "Don't know. Don't know."

SIXTY-THREE

A voice came over the headset in Joshua's helmet. "Colonel Jordan, we have an update on Ethan March."

Joshua had put the F-35 LV fighter in a slow circle over the northern sector of the Negev desert, waiting for the "go" sign for another missile test. But his mind had been on multiple crises. Ethan was one of them.

"What?"

"He's safe. The mission hit the mark."

Joshua breathed out, *Thank You, Lord.*

"In fact," the tower continued, "it was more successful than we planned."

"How?"

"We've narrowed the site. The bio-threat is emanating from a school building somewhere. We received that from a captured cell member. Our intelligence people are putting together a scenario of the probable locations."

"What about the delivery mode?"

"We've got that too. After further interrogation, he admitted it was airborne. Colonel Jordan, we are dealing with a missile carrying a biological toxin. And it's unlike anything we've seen."

Flying a mile over the desert, Joshua didn't want to hear that. He still hadn't been able to use the in-flight RTS laser on the modified F-35 to capture the entire guidance system of incoming dummy missiles during the testing phase. Which meant that his RTS system was drastically limited — it could still only perform the original design

task — a mirror-reversal of the trajectory of enemy missiles, returning them to their launch site. His new laser-guided data-capturing
program to redirect enemy warheads in any direction, at will, wasn't
working.

"Tell me," Joshua asked, "what does that do to our test today?"

There was a pause from the command tower. Then the answer. "It
means we wish it was last week, rather than today. Our intel indicates
this threat is imminent."

"Do we scratch our test up here?" Joshua asked.

"We're checking on that. But I have some other information —
about your family."

A strange feeling washed over Joshua, as if he had half-expected
what was next, as if this day had already been scripted.

"A witness in Jerusalem, a shop owner in Nablus, called the police,
says he saw a woman matching your wife's description, accompanied
by a young man and young woman, being dragged into three vans and
driven away at gunpoint."

Joshua had the air momentarily sucked out of him. All he could
mutter was, *"Oh, dear God."*

The voice in his helmet continued, "We have a partial description
of one of the vans. It's been matched to one belonging to the jihad
group headed by Anwar al-Madrassa."

Joshua was stunned. The tower asked, "Still with us, Colonel?"

"Roger that," he could barely say. He was crushed.

"Stay with us for further instructions, sir."

"Roger."

Joshua could now hear only the sound of his own breathing in his
helmet. In and out. Inhale. Exhale. In the upper corners of the inside
of the helmet were the green illuminated vector screens that he would
use to site incoming enemy missiles. He wanted to pray, but somehow
it was too much, and he couldn't. He knew the groaning inside of him
would be heard. God was listening. It was just that now, circling high
above the brownish desert, feeling that his guts had just been ripped
open, he couldn't put it into words.

After a few minutes, the voice came into his helmet again. But this time it wasn't the same. It wasn't the usual measured, in-control monotone he had been used to hearing as a pilot from the tower. Now it was hurried. Almost frantic. "Colonel Jordan. Stay in your pattern. I repeat, stay in your pattern. Do you read?"

"Copy. What news?"

"Radar shows an incoming heading to Tel Aviv. One of our F-16s was dispatched, but it blew past him before he could shoot it down. Our ground-to-air defenses have been launched, but this thing has a very advanced avoidance program."

"Where was it launched from?"

"We're trying to determine that. Also — " The voice stopped. Some shouting in the background. Joshua thought he could hear Clint Mc-Kinney's voice. Yes, it was him.

Now Clint spoke into the headset. "Josh, this is Clint. You have a right to know. We just launched the standard RTS-equipped missile to turn this in-coming warhead around."

"I copy that."

"But, Josh, there's video footage on the Internet. Live-streaming. Abby and Cal and Deborah. All of them tied up in some location. And . . ."

"And what? Tell me, Clint. Tied up and what?"

"The message says that all three are at ground zero of the launch site of the bio-weapon. If your RTS is successful, it will turn that monster on your family. Josh, I'm so sorry . . ."

"Have you reverse-engineered the flight pattern of the incoming, to find the site and get them out of there . . ."

"Somewhere around the edge of the Negev. There are several Bedouin schools in that area. We're trying to isolate the location and helicopter the IDF guys out there . . ."

Joshua was yelling. "At four hundred miles an hour that missile's going to get there first!"

In the background Joshua heard a voice say, "RTS just made contact with the enemy bird; it's turning around."

Inside his helmet Joshua tried to slow his breathing. *Think. Be precise. But be quick. You only have one crack at this. Oh, Lord, help me.*

Then he said, "Tower, Jordan here."

"We read you."

"Give me the flight pattern of that enemy bird and the coordinates."

"Doing it now."

Joshua checked his radar-warning receiver. It lit up in the corner of the screen, and he now saw the flight pattern of the warhead containing the Elixir of Allah heading his way, high above the Negev desert. He punched the autopilot matching control so he could intersect the trajectory and the altitude of the incoming missile.

"I'm climbing," Joshua said, jamming his side-stick controller on the right and putting the jet into a steep climb. Then he pushed the throttle grip on the left to send him streaking nose-up into the sky as fast as he could squeeze power out of the turbines.

His screen showed the blinking cursor for the incoming missile.

"Waiting for it to come into range," Joshua called out. "Waiting ..."

The blip on the screen was closing in. The missile was getting closer.

Joshua hit the button for the RTS-360 guidance capture system, and a laser beam blew out from under the fuselage. He read the RTS integrated control panel. It illuminated.

Contact.

The data-controlling laser hit the nosecone of the enemy missile.

He waited for the reading — the terse LCD that would read either "Full Capture" or "Failed."

"Come on. Come on. Come on ..."

Then the message flashed on the screen. But his world rocked.

"Failed."

A half second passed — but enough time for Joshua to calculate it. There was only one option now. He had to insure that his family was protected. His F-35 LV had no weapons other than the RTS, so now his only weapon was the jet itself. It was the only way to stop the biowarhead streaking back toward his wife and son and daughter.

"I'm going to hit it on the run. I'm intercepting," he said.

The tower squawked back, "Colonel, wait. We have no secondary verification that your family is at ground zero."

"I can't take that chance. I'm going in."

Joshua lined the nose of the F-35 with a point along the intersecting trajectory of the missile on his screen. He would have to hit the warhead on the pass. With his left hand he jammed the throttle and headed to the intersection point, and with his right hand he used the side-stick controller to arc the jet toward the endgame. There was only one chance to knock that missile out of the sky. He knew what that meant. No way to bail out before the collision. He had to ride it into the point of contact. Then a fiery crash with a missile loaded with a nightmare toxin. That was the terrible best-case scenario. But at least his family would be spared.

The blip of the missile was closing in on the intersecting vector on his screen. And so was he. Each blip approached the other. Joshua gave his final message to the control tower. "Tell Abby and the kids I love them ... and ..." His voice caught.

"Tell 'em we'll all be together in heaven."

There it was. He saw it glint into view, the nosecone of the missile approaching like a flash of light. He aimed at it by leading it perfectly, gauging its superior speed to hit it on the pass-by. He banked the F-35 directly toward the oncoming warhead.

He yelled two words.

"Now, Lord ..."

With supersonic speed, the missile's nosecone tore through his left wing. The missile exploded and the percussion ripped open the fuselage of the jet, spraying the toxic gas over the ravaged skin of the F-35. The jet began to spiral down, twisting at two hundred and fifty miles an hour, covered in deadly toxins.

He reached for the release for the ejection seat. Where was it?

In the sickening, dizzying spin toward earth, Joshua saw something, heard something, and he could only say one word at first.

"What ..."

The tower was calling to him in his helmet. But that didn't matter now.

Somewhere there was a sound. Piercing. Heart-thumping. A trumpet sounding? Incredible. Unfathomable. It had the power of the sound of a cosmos being birthed.

"Oh!" Joshua exclaimed, as a boy might say if he witnessed something awesome, as the sky seemed to fill with a golden note, like the unison of all the world's trumpets. All around him. Thrilling, thrilling. And there was a voice above even that, and the voice had the thundering power of ten thousand oceans.

"My dream," he heard himself say. But it was not a dream. Not this time.

Somehow he was outside of the F-35, watching it as if he were a spectator. The jet had no pilot, yet its canopy was still intact — the ejector seat had never activated — and it was spinning and smoking and careening farther and farther away from Joshua on its gravity-bound descent toward earth. And it kept falling. Until it hit the earth. A tiny red flash of an explosion could be seen far below.

Joshua had never ejected. Yet he had not gone down with the jet. He was not in the debris of the crash. Or anywhere on earth.

SIXTY-FOUR

If he hadn't already been transformed, he wouldn't have understood it. While his jet plummeted to earth without a pilot, Joshua rocketed up through the atmosphere, confounding the laws of nature. Yet his mind was able to fully comprehend it. It had been changed too.

What was happening was not a matter of science. It couldn't be contained in the theories of man. What Joshua was seeing at that moment, and where he had found himself, had reduced all of those things of earth, the human achievements, the fanfare, the struggles for glory and power, to a pale world of shadows.

Joshua was walking in a place that seemed warm and familiar, yet surprisingly spectacular. There was the instant experience of belonging there. This brilliant pavilion was the home of God. And Joshua was part of it. There was calmness inside. Peace. No racing heart. No sweating palms. No gut-wrenching decisions to make. Not anymore. Everything around him seemed so new, like the birth of a new world, yet not bound by the old laws of nature of the old world he had come from. There was a light more radiant than the sun and it was brightening the landscape. It seemed to be coming from a focal point in the distance. Yet it illuminated everything, while at the same time cast no shadows.

Joshua looked around and was suddenly aware that there was a vast ocean of people all around him. Millions and millions of them. From ages past to the present. Their faces, like his, reflecting something. But he didn't have to guess what that was, for he knew what they knew — a miraculous kind of understanding and an expectation of what would

344

happen next. And a joy that surpassed any method of calculation or description.

And here was the amazing thing — Joshua was able to visualize everything around him, both near and far, simultaneously, things in the closest detail and yet at the same time able to take in a bird's-eye view of the entire assembly. Joshua laughed and shouted out in astonishment at the miracle of it. And at the fulfillment of it — God's promise — that at just the right moment in human history the Lord of the universe would rapture — would call to Himself — every follower of the Son of God, and remove them from Planet Earth in an instant.

Joshua looked to his left. There was a woman, no longer aged, and no longer weeping and mourning from a broken heart. She was smiling and hugging someone. Joshua looked closer. Her joy became Joshua's. And he delighted in it as if it were his own.

The woman he was watching had the blush of a newlywed, and she was smiling and touching the youthful face of Virgil Corland, who looked then to be only in his thirties. The former leader of the Free World was now a humble citizen of heaven.

"I saw the glory of it," Winnie Corland said gently as she stroked Virgil Corland's face. "God gave me a tiny glimpse after you died, when I opened my heart to Christ that day at our brownstone condo. A snapshot of what was ahead for us. Oh, Virgil, you were so right, my dearest."

Virgil was beaming as he looked in her eyes. "All of the waiting. The aching joints and the endless medications. The flesh that didn't cooperate and aged. And the trials that tested our hearts and our bodies. All that is over now."

Joshua refocused. There was a voice of another woman, and he recognized it immediately. The one who had taught his Sunday school class when he was a wild, reckless, wayward boy.

"Josh-a-boy," the voice said. And then he knew. She was the only one who had ever called him that nickname, the name that caused him to wince in embarrassment when it was mentioned in the presence of his buddies. Joshua turned to her. He had never truly thanked her for the seed she had planted in his soul. As it turned out, she had not lived long enough to see it bloom.

Standing in front of him, the woman was now youthful and vigorous. The face bore an image that had a slight similarity to Joshua's, the eyes, maybe. That's what family friends had always said. In the final years before her passing, Joshua had only known her as the frail, bent frame that needed a walker. *There is so much to say,* Joshua thought as the flood of memories rushed through his mind, of the house in Colorado with the willow tree and the woman in the apron on the front porch calling to him to come in for dinner.

Joshua now spoke the one word that seemed to contain all of those powerful memories.

"Mom," Joshua called out to her. Then he added with a tender astonishment, "You were so young. I had forgotten how young you were."

"But you, son," his mother said as she reached up to pat his cheek, "you were always the same boy to me."

Joshua put his arm around his mother and surveyed the scene. Not far away, he recognized three members of the current U.S. Supreme Court — all of them whisked away from the conference chambers in the marble court building in Washington in the middle of a heated debate over a pending case, while the rest of the astonished justices who remained behind were left to stare, slack-jawed, at the empty chairs. Joshua noticed one of them, Justice Lapham, close to him and now shaking the hand of John Jay, America's first chief justice, who had taken up that post shortly after the nation's founding in the eighteenth century.

Beggars and billionaires greeted each other like long-lost brothers. Martyrs for the gospel who had been burned, beaten, ripped apart, and beheaded for their faith were now whole. Persons lost at sea, buried in avalanches, ravaged by hurricanes, killed in war and in peace time, victims of disease and hunger, builders of empires who, in paneled offices, had bowed their heads to the call of Christ, and vagabonds who had responded to tent revivals in the wilderness.

They were all there.

But Joshua was searching for other faces. He knew they must be there somewhere. His heart, mind, and soul told him so. His eyes kept searching. Until — right there — he told himself, there they were. He had spotted them. The three of them, calm and joyful, now almost within reach. Joshua held out his arms toward them and pulled Cal and Deborah into a crushing hug. Then he held them both at arm's length to study their faces. "You look older a bit, but only slightly," he mused with a smile. "And most certainly wiser!"

Both of them laughed.

"How proud I am of you both. You were so brave," he added. "And faithful to the Lord, right up to the end." Then his two grown children stepped aside. So he could take her in with his eyes, from head to foot. Abigail was standing in front of him, without a scar. Without a tear. Without a worry. "I wouldn't have believed it," Joshua said, gathering Abigail gently into his arms.

"Believe what, my precious soul mate?" she asked.

"That you could ever have been more beautiful than you were down there — and yet, here you are."

"I know what you did in the last moments," she said quietly, as she pulled him close to whisper it in his ear. "To rescue us. And to protect us." She laid her hand on his heart. "And our Lord knows it well too. There is no greater love," she said, "than to lay down your life for another. And you did it, Joshua, for us."

"I had a great teacher," Joshua said. "A great Savior."

Suddenly, the figure in the light, who was the light that illuminated everything, was coming closer. The multiple millions of saved souls now fell to their knees. Princes and commanders, knights and peasants, men and women of power, as well as the powerless and the forgotten of the world, all of those who had staked their souls and their eternities on the perfect blood that had been shed on an ugly, Roman cross, and who had now been gathered together from throughout the millennia, all of them were worshiping and singing to the One who had ransomed them. Their Champion. Their Lord.

Not far away from Joshua, Abigail, Cal, and Deborah, Phil Rankowitz was kneeling with several other members of the Roundtable. Every head of every person was bowed for the same reason.

Walking in the apex of the light, now clearly seen, was Jesus Christ, the King of Kings. And He was approaching.

5IXTY-FIVE

The Next Day, New Babylon, Iraq

Alexander Coliquin was in his two-thousand-square-foot suite. He seemed oblivious to the multiple catastrophes across the globe. From the windows of the top floor of the white-stoned U.N. building, he could see palm trees swaying in the wind and the gardens stretching for a half mile out to the gated entrance.

But his two closest associates, Deputy Secretary Ho Zhu and Bishop Dibold Kora, were transfixed in front of the wall of web TVs, clicking through screen after screen to collect the global coverage of the stunning events of the day.

In San Francisco, a record earthquake toppled a portion of the Golden Gate Bridge on the Sausalito side and sent cars tumbling into the bay. Quakes off the eastern seaboard created a tsunami that swept into Charleston, South Carolina, and carried off more than eighteen hundred people. There were tremors in Istanbul, Moscow, Tangiers, and Wellington. In Perth, a third of the downtown towers collapsed into the sea as massive tectonic plates deep in the earth shifted violently beneath that part of Australia's coast.

But more amazing were the "unexplained phenomena," as the press called it. Jet liners veering off course. Traffic jams caused by driverless cars. Judges disappearing from courtrooms. Churches vacant. People vanishing in the middle of meetings. Television anchors in Biloxi, Richmond, and Omaha evaporating during live broadcasts. Missing persons reports flooded into every metropolitan police department in every city. Those disappearances caused more than a dozen near crashes of airliners as copilots were forced to take over the planes when pilots evaporated from cockpits. An ocean liner that suddenly had no captain or first mate plowed into three other cruise ships in the Port of Miami and sank two of them. A 240-car pileup occurred on the 101 outside of Los Angeles when drivers were no longer behind their steering wheels. Financial experts on the television coverage were already predicting that a few insurance companies could go bankrupt just from the automobile collision claims alone.

Bishop Kora spoke first, wagging his finger at the two dozen television screens. "Now the conspiracy theories will come. The fanatics. The lunatic fringe. They will call this the judgment of God …"

"No, they won't," Coliquin replied effortlessly, turning from the window to address him. "The dangerous ones will call it the rapture."

"You will need to issue a statement," Ho Zhu said in his usual perfunctory tone. "And if possible, announce a joint effort with President Tulrude. An international plan to restore order. She needs more help."

"More help?" Kora bulleted back. "It isn't enough that you had Hewbright's Allfone hacked and handed Tulrude that five-point economic plan on a silver platter?"

"No, not enough," Ho Zhu stated in a matter-of-fact tone. "She needs a boost in the polls. Hewbright is closing the gap. And Secretary Coliquin, the world needs to hear from you."

"Yes, a statement," Coliquin said. "Don't worry. I have that well in hand."

Two hours later, Coliquin gave an address in a live global broadcast from his new Iraq headquarters. It was covered by every Internet news agency on the planet.

"Ladies and gentlemen," he began as he looked out from behind his mahogany desk directly into the camera linked to an international satellite multi-feed. His handsome face wore an expression of weighty concern. "Today we face a great quandary. So many questions abound. Natural disasters. Tragic loss of life. Why, we ask ourselves. And in the midst of it — perhaps the saddest thing of all — the death of millions of people. But we may have a partial answer. For unknown reasons, countless people have apparently, and suddenly, abandoned their homes, their places of work, their cars, and retreated to remote areas. Reports are coming in slowly that many of these people were known to be radical, fundamentalist Christian extremists, and theories are surfacing that they may have committed mass suicide in distant, wilderness areas. It may take a long time to locate and recover all the bodies. Perhaps we never will. And we may never know all the reasons for their irrational, delusional actions. In the darkness of their confused dogma, they may have thought that the end of the world was approaching. They may have taken the last, desperate leap because of their rigid, frenzied beliefs about Jesus, thinking that they could somehow hasten His coming. And so as a result, my friends, they are gone. My heart goes out to all those who mourn today."

Coliquin gave a half shake of his head and pursed his lips, in a posture of sad regret.

"But there is a light in the darkness. I have commissioned Bishop Dibold Kora, my special envoy, to commence talks with President Tulrude, in conjunction with the G-7 and the European Union and nearly a hundred international relief agencies, to commence a massive effort to meet the needs of those around the world who are suffering. Equally important," Coliquin said, "is our global plan to complete our project for unity, the One Movement, to prevent the spread of dangerous religious ideas like the ones that seem to have caused this terrible act of self-annihilation. After all, my friends, can we truly say that we love our neighbor if we allow our neighbor to suffer under the evil spell of hateful, harmful, religious propaganda? There is a better way. And you can be confident that if we follow that way, it will lead us to a better world."

Israel

The disappearance of millions of people around the world had a magnifying effect on those who had been left behind. Bart Kingston had read confirmations, which continued to pour in worldwide, that those who disappeared had indeed been Christians, and this tended to multiply exponentially the attitudes that many had already been harboring about religion, or God, or more particularly about Jesus and the book that detailed His story. Some had remained suspicious, and others seemed to consider the idea that Jesus had come to redeem the human race.

Kingston was still in Jerusalem when it all happened. He had tried to make contact with Peter Campbell, but the man was nowhere to be found. Kingston even trudged into the Old City section, making his way through the crowds that had gathered in the streets. He had checked Campbell's office and even his apartment.

Kingston had planned to fly back to New York, but he had cancelled his flight. He needed to stay in Israel for the time being. First, because he had journalistic responsibility. And second, because he had to sort out some things in his own head. If that was possible. And he wasn't sure it was.

□□□

In Tel Aviv, Ethan was now approaching Joshua's high-rise apartment. He was so deep in thought he had momentarily forgotten which street he was on. He had to stop and look around. Then he reoriented himself. The apartment building was a half block away.

His Allfone rang. It was Rivka. She sounded subdued. "Hello, friend."

"Hi."

"How are you feeling? Confused, I bet."

"Confused? That doesn't begin to explain it. I'm a mess, Riv."

"I know," she said with a soft kind of regret, "I am so sorry about losing Josh."

"Yeah, well, I can't think straight right now. But what you said — 'losing Josh'? I'm not sure about that ... not exactly."

"Ethan ..."

"Well, did he die? Or didn't he? What happened, really?"

"Ethan, Josh's fighter plane was struck by a missile."

"I'm a pilot, Rivka. I know some things about flying. The sensors in the cockpit of Josh's F-35 LV indicated that his body had evacuated the cabin — yet the canopy on that jet was never blown. The ejection seat was never activated. The ground crew found bits of his flight suit in the wreckage. But no signs of human remains. Not a single trace of his DNA. You explain that ..."

"You know what happens when a jet explodes," she said. There was regret in her voice, certainly, but also persistence. "Everything burns up. Everything."

"Not everything. There's always a human trace. Even a small one. But here, there was nothing. Zero. Zilch."

"Okay, Ethan, I know you're upset," she said.

He could tell she was placating him. Maybe that was okay, but he wasn't in the mood. Ethan was not going to let it drop. "Then what about Abby and Cal and Deborah? The IDF rounded up the terror cell that was responsible for tying them up in that school in the Negev and making them the target for the bio-warhead. But then the Israeli special ops guys located the school — you know what they found? Three empty chairs, some loose rope, and a pile of clothes. Whoosh. The rest of the Jordan family had disappeared. And then there are all those reports about the millions of other people who disappeared ..."

Rivka changed topics abruptly. "I thought maybe we could catch some dinner together. Give you a chance to talk."

"I'm talking right now," he said, as he stood in front of Joshua's apartment tower. "But you're not listening." After a pause, Ethan settled down. "Sorry. Don't mean to make you the bad guy."

"That's okay. Anyway, you're right. I'm *not* one of the bad guys. Those would be the guys who were trying to blow your head off while you were driving an armored car down the streets in Nablus."

"Right," Ethan replied, trying to stay focused. "And I guess I never got the chance to thank you for shooting straight and keeping me alive back there. So thanks."

"Don't mention it. Besides, you had the tougher job. You had to play the sitting duck. Not me."

Ethan strode up the steps to the front door of the residential tower. "Listen, I'll get back to you. We'll make plans, okay?" he said to Rivka, tenderly, before they ended the call. "I want to sit down with you. Have a long talk. But only after I've cleared some things up in my own head first."

They said good-bye and agreed to meet the next day.

Ethan stood at the front door of Joshua's apartment tower and pushed the security pad. After it buzzed, he identified himself. The security guard at the desk let him in.

"Morning, Mr. March. So sorry about Colonel Jordan."

Ethan gave a slow shrug. "Me too."

"You would like to see, maybe, his personal effects?"

"I thought maybe I'd check out his place. I'm really not sure why I'm here."

"I think that Colonel Jordan must have figured you out pretty well, yes?"

"Why's that?"

"He left instructions."

"What kind?"

"A sealed note. Left with manager. Some time ago. To be opened in the event of 'unexplained absence or suspicious disappearance.' His orders. So, with what happened yesterday, we decided that . . . hope you don't mind, but we felt we should open the envelope."

Ethan bristled. *Man, these guys didn't even wait forty-eight hours.*

He waited for the rest of the story.

"So," the desk manager said, "he left this." And with that he handed him a small key.

"What's this for?"

"Safety deposit box of Colonel Jordan. Here in the building. His note said to give this to you. That's all."

Ethan fingered the key, then asked where the box was. The desk manager led him to the second floor and into the room with the safety-deposit boxes. Ethan inserted the key and opened the little metal door. There was only one thing waiting for him. A DVD player.

The manager gave him the key to Joshua's apartment, and Ethan walked inside with the portable video pad. It was a strange feeling, knowing that Joshua was gone. But where? That was the question. He noticed that there was a half-filled cup of coffee on the kitchen counter that Joshua hadn't finished. Probably fixed himself some coffee pre-dawn, just before heading out to the airbase for what would be his last mission.

Ethan chuckled a little at that. *Hey, Josh, I thought Abby got you off coffee and onto tea.*

But the smile faded quickly as Ethan plunked down on the couch. He had never felt so utterly alone. A jumble of crazy thoughts ran through his head. For a guy who always felt he needed to control his future, Ethan was facing a bizarre, uncertain life ahead. Josh, who was not just his boss and mentor, but who had also become his friend, had just vanished into thin air. Along with his entire family. They had become a second family to him. Though he never expected things to turn out like this, especially after Deborah had broken things off.

Suddenly, Ethan was aware of the vibration of his Allfone. He plucked it out of his pocket. It was an incoming email. He touched the screen and opened it up. A text message from "Jimmy Louder."

"Huh," Ethan mumbled. He hadn't heard from the Air Force captain since the aftermath of his rescue from North Korea. Ethan had the chance to greet him at South Korean HQ after the mission. But only very briefly. Then the Air Force whisked him back to the United States for debriefing and a return to his wife and kids.

But Ethan wasn't in a mood to read it. Not now. He had something much more important to do. He waved his finger over the On tab of Joshua's video player. The screen lit up. He touched the Forward button.

What he saw next made him jump a little.

It was Joshua's face filling up the screen, looking straight at him.

"Ethan, if you're looking at this right now, I'm off the planet, my friend. And you've been left behind. I didn't want that for you. But that's the way it is. I told you that I felt that the timeline was short, that Jesus would be mustering his army of followers pretty soon, that world events were rushing to a climax. So, I'm up there. And you're still down here."

"Whoa," Ethan muttered. This was heavy. Ethan immediately hit

Pause on the video pad and caught his breath. He waited several minutes before he hit Resume on the control.

When Ethan started the video again, Joshua walked him through what he called the "half-time coach's chalk-talk." Starting with the basics, once again, about who Jesus was, why He came to earth, why He died, what His death accomplished for the sins of mankind, the proof of His divinity by rising from the grave. And how Ethan needed to confess and believe those things and personally receive the person of Christ as Savior and Lord.

Ethan had heard it all before. Ever since his "salvation event," as Joshua called his Iranian jail experience, he would drum it into Ethan every chance he got. But now, it was different. Ethan couldn't avoid it. Couldn't dismiss it either. Too much had happened for him to play games. Like the miraculous disappearance of Josh and his entire family — raptured away from the earth, it seemed — just like Josh had said, the way the Bible had predicted it would happen.

Joshua's face on the screen leaned forward just a bit. Ethan stared back. For that instant, it seemed almost as if a holographic, three-dimensional image of Joshua was there in the room with him.

No, Ethan thought to himself, *even more real than that*. As Joshua spoke, Ethan sensed that what he was hearing now was the truest thing that ever existed.

"Let's start with the facts," Joshua said. "Jesus died on a cross in Jerusalem. Now Ethan, I don't know where you are right now as you are listening and watching this, but maybe you are still in Israel. The landmarks of the miraculous life of Jesus the Christ, the Promised One, are all over the Galilee and Jerusalem. I've shown you many of them myself. But just knowing that isn't enough. You need to face up to your status as a sinner, a man who has fallen short of God's design for you, just as I had to do. You and I are alike in many ways, you know. Including this — when we measure up our lives with the specs of God's moral plan for us, we know that we've blown it. Time and time again."

Ethan nodded at that, even though he was humbled to think of himself in the same category as his mentor. But there it was, the plain fact that Ethan — headstrong, both ruthlessly sure of himself at times and yet, beneath it all, also insecure as well — now had to face up to the same reality that Joshua had.

"Okay," Ethan said. "I got it. I guess I can't deny it. Proud. Selfish. Arrogant at times. Always looking out for myself. I could go on and on ... yeah ..."

But then something happened. Ethan was no longer addressing the image on the screen. He knew that what he had to say had to be said to God Himself, and to His Son Jesus.

Ethan's voice trembled. "Okay, God, yes. I admit I'm a sinner."

On the screen, Joshua kept talking, "Jesus didn't just die on the cross, Ethan. He was the sinless Son of God, willingly dying on the cross for your sins. Yours, Ethan. The same as mine. As the perfect sacrifice — the only sacrifice that would satisfy God's perfect sense of justice."

"Yes, God," Ethan murmured. "I know that's true. For some time I've been convinced of that, down deep, but I just didn't want to come out with it ... until now ... which I guess makes me a kind of coward ..." Ethan's voice was beginning to crack.

"And then," Joshua continued, "to prove to the whole world that He was God in the flesh, Jesus defied the grave and walked out of that tomb three days later ..."

"Yes," Ethan said. His eyes were cloudy now. Moist with tears. "I remember the stories. Jesus raised others from death. He was God. Walking around, right here in Israel. Looking out for other folks. Never for Himself ... Perfect ... Of course Jesus rose from the grave ..."

Joshua added, "And the only remaining thing, after acknowledging all of that, is to open your heart, invite Christ in, as Lord and Savior ..."

"Don't know why," Ethan said, breaking down once more, "why, oh God, why You'd want Your Son to live inside of a guy like me, selfish, scheming, lying ..."

Ethan was weeping, his head in his hands. "But God, I'm asking if Jesus could come into my heart. Right now ... Savior and Lord. No more escape plans for me ... no more dodging it, trying to weasel out of it ... no, Sir. Please, Jesus, come into me ..."

Reaching out through his tears, Ethan hit the Pause button once again. He sat for a while in silence, not knowing how much time had passed.

Finally he asked a question out loud.

"Okay, Ethan . . . now what?"

He found himself staring at the ugly shag carpet on the floor of Joshua's little Tel Aviv apartment, and he couldn't help but laugh loudly at Joshua's bad taste in carpeting.

That's why you needed Abby — she always was a better interior decorator.

Right then, sitting on the couch in Josh's apartment, Ethan was able to reflect. He was beginning to figure something out. Like why Joshua had invested so much into him. Keeping him close. Talking endlessly about preparation. Yes, as it turned out, Joshua had figured Ethan out pretty well. Joshua must have known he would probably miss the first train when it came roaring past, and after the rapture he would be left back on the platform of the station with the rest of the human race.

He hit Resume.

Joshua's face appeared again. And what he had to say was hard and tough to hear. But Ethan wanted it all, the good and the bad. And that's what he got.

"Ethan, I hope you've accepted Jesus Christ into your heart. If so, you've been born again. So now, what you have to do next will be up to you. The world is about to start exploding around you. The forces of hell are going to be mounted against you. I guarantee it. That's what you're up against."

Then the image of Joshua's face on the screen broke into the kind of smile that Ethan recognized. Some people might even think it was a look that was a little brash on the surface. But Ethan knew better. Deep down Joshua had been a man who simply knew who he was and what he had to do.

"In the beginning you'll feel pretty much alone, Ethan. You'll have to stand strong." Joshua said, "I'll walk you through things in this video log as much as I can. But that's just the start. After a while you'll be able to handle things on your own. You'll be able to decipher for yourself what God has already described about the last dark night of the world that is coming, even if you can't see it yet, because you'll have His road map. So when the very worst comes — when the enemy tries to cripple you and destroy you, there won't be any surprises."

Ethan had been bracing himself, but now he muttered back to the screen, "Hey, Josh, thanks for the good news."

On the screen, an ever-widening grin spread over Joshua's face. It was the look of a man who had been gripped with an amazing story, and because he knew down to his soul that it was all true, he couldn't wait to tell it.

"But listen, Ethan, it's not all gloom and doom. There's the rest of the story, and it's magnificent. I'm going to share that with you too. Just wait until I tell you exactly what's going to happen at the end. But I don't want to get ahead of myself. I'm going to lay this out for you. The same as if you were being given a pre-mission flight check. But, Ethan, this is going to require that you take each step as a walk of faith."

Ethan found himself nodding at the screen. "Okay, Josh. What you got for me?"

Joshua's image continued to speak. "You need to know two things. First, I believe in my heart that God has picked you to shake things up down there on earth. To help lead an incredible, worldwide spiritual revival. There's still hope for folks down there. And you're the one to tell them that."

Ethan shook his head. "Oh, man. Are you sure you've got the right guy, Josh?"

"Second thing, Ethan," Joshua continued. "You may feel alone, but you're not. God will bring you into contact with an army of people who are ready to claim Christ for themselves — and to stand fast against the darkness. Against the Evil One. The hideous force that will temporarily be running things down there. You need to start searching for fellow compatriots to help you with this mission."

Ethan hit the Pause button, shook his head, and spoke out loud. "And where am I supposed to find them?" He thought about that for a few minutes. Joshua's words *walk of faith* rang in his ears.

"Okay, God," Ethan said. "Where do I start?" Then there was another minute of thinking. That is when Ethan became aware of his Allfone that he had put back in his pocket. He pulled it out and flipped it open. Then he hit the Display button for Captain Louder's email that he had received just minutes earlier. Ethan began to read it. It said:

Ethan — Captain Jimmy Louder here. I wanted to connect with Joshua Jordan. But things being as they are — I guess that isn't in the cards now. So I'd like to talk to you. If you're still here, that is. It's about something that Josh had told me during the rescue over in North Korea. And a few things too that my grandfather used to tell me. Why do I get the feeling that things in this old world are never going to be the same? I think I know what is going on, and I want to make sure that I line up with the right side on all of this. Time to make some mission-critical decisions. Can we talk? Here's my cell number, and you've already got my email ..."

Ethan March smiled. Then he laughed out loud and kept laughing. It felt good to let loose. Yes, Ethan decided, in a little while, right after finishing the video message from Joshua, he would make contact with Jimmy Louder. Maybe he would be his very first partner in his new mission.

Things were already happening quickly. For a guy who had always maintained an outward bravado while inwardly grappling with the fear of losing control — whether it was pitching a fastball, keeping a girlfriend, or flying the newest Air Force fighter — Ethan realized that he had now chosen a different path. A few minutes ago he had just told God that it would be God, not Ethan, who would be in charge of his life and directing the trajectory. If that was true, then his future was strangely settled, even if he didn't know exactly what that meant or what his life was going to look like.

Yet somewhere inside, Ethan already felt a newfound sense of certainty, as if he were about to launch a flight into the turbulent center of something dark, dangerous, and unfamiliar. But he was okay with that. Only this time there would be no computerized flight deck in front of him. And while it might be his hand grasping the side-stick in the cockpit, Ethan was already sensing that it would be the power of God within him that would have to control the flight pattern.

So he returned to the video player and hit the Resume button again. The image of Joshua's face came to life again on the screen. When that happened, Ethan spoke out loud from a heart that had been humbled, yet his voice was also decisive and immovable, like chiseled rock.

"All right. I'm here. And I'm listening now. I'm ready for my orders."

DISCUSSION QUESTIONS FOR *BRINK OF CHAOS*

by Craig Parshall

1. Joshua has been separated from his country, his wife, and his children, for two years since the end of the preceding novel, *Thunder of Heaven*. He has been living in exile, primarily in Israel, a nation that has given him sanctuary while unjust criminal charges are being pursued against him by a corrupt White House administration. His wife, Abigail, has counseled him to stay abroad — out of the jurisdiction of the U.S. courts until she can prove his innocence. Do you think that was good advice?

2. In *Thunder of Heaven*, and the preceding novel, *Edge of Apocalypse*, the risks of nuclear weapons in the hands of terrorists or rogue nations is presented. Now, in *Brink of Chaos*, we see the threat of a horrendous biological weapon under the control of a terror cell. Which threat do you believe is a greater risk?

3. The lives of Ethan March and Rivka, the Israeli spy, keep intersecting. Where do you envision their relationship going in the future? What impediments would there be to a romantic relationship?

4. In the futuristic view of America in this novel, the government is exercising a surprising amount of electronic surveillance over its citizens. How close, or far away, are we from that kind of scenario actually happening? What are both the arguments for and those against this kind of electronic surveillance of citizens that are mentioned in the novel?

5. *Brink of Chaos* presents one possible picture of a future rapture of Christians off the earth. If God were to remove His church from

the world today, what kinds of repercussions do you think would occur for those "left behind" on the earth?

6. Alexander Coliquin's ambition for global power is expanding in *Brink of Chaos*. Do you see any roadblocks to his goal?

7. *Brink of Chaos* begins with a startling dream. Do you think that God speaks to his followers today in dreams? Has He done so in the past? Is there any support in the Bible for this to occur in the future?

8. Was Abigail Jordan wise or unwise, right or wrong, in refusing to receive the government mandated BIDTag? How does that square with the Bible's mandate for Christians to obey the government? Does the Bible give examples of exceptions to the general rule of obedience to rulers?

9. Of the five main characters in the novel, Joshua Jordan, Abigail Jordan, Deborah Jordan, Cal Jordan, and Ethan March, with which character do you most closely associate? Why?

10. How do you visualize God's "heavenly realm" now, before the coming of Christ to the earth? What parts of the Bible would support that image?

Edge of Apocalypse

#1 New York Times *Bestselling Author Tim LaHaye and Craig Parshall*

The End Series by *New York Times* bestselling author Tim LaHaye and Craig Parshall is an epic thrill ride ripped from today's headlines and filtered through Scriptural prophecy.

In this adrenaline-fueled political thriller laced with end times prophecy, Joshua Jordan, former U.S. spy-plane-hero-turned-weapons-designer, creates the world's most sophisticated missile defense system. But global forces conspire to steal the defense weapon, and U.S. government leaders will do anything to stop the nation's impending economic catastrophe — including selling out Jordan and his weapon.

As world events set the stage for the "end of days" foretold in Revelation, Jordan must consider not only the biblical prophecies preached by his wife's pastor, but the personal price he must pay if he is to save the nation he loves.

Available in stores and online!

Thunder of Heaven

A Joshua Jordan Novel

#1 New York Times *Bestselling Author* Tim LaHaye and Craig Parshall

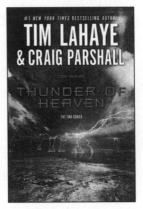

The End Series by *New York Times* bestselling author Tim LaHaye and Craig Parshall is an epic thrill ride ripped from today's headlines and filtered through Scriptural prophecy. As world events begin setting the stage for the "end of days" foretold in Revelation, Joshua Jordan must weigh the personal price he must pay to save the nation he loves.

Thunder of Heaven will appeal to the tens of millions of readers who have already made Tim LaHaye a household name and one of the bestselling authors of all time. This book is a return to form for Tim LaHaye whose previous prophetic fiction series, Left Behind, has sold roughly 70 million copies. Those who have read Left Behind and are eager for more highly charged fiction based on biblical prophesies will embrace *Thunder of Heaven* for the same reasons that turned Left Behind into the world's most celebrated publishing phenomenon of the last two decades.

Available in stores and online!

Revelation Unveiled

*Tim LaHaye,
coauthor of the bestselling
Left Behind Series*

The biblical foundation for the bestselling Left Behind Series ... In *Revelation Unveiled*, Dr. Tim LaHaye, coauthor with Jerry Jenkins of the bestselling novels *Left Behind* and *Tribulation Force*, reveals the scriptural foundation of this series. *Revelation Unveiled* explains such critical topics as: the Rapture of the Church, the Return of Christ, the Great Tribulation, the Final Battle against Satan and His Hosts, the Seven Seals, the Millennial Reign, the Seven Trumpets, the Seven Bowls of Wrath, the Great White Throne, the Destruction of Babylon, the New Heaven, and the New Earth. Previously titled *Revelation Illustrated and Made Plain*, this revised and updated commentary includes numerous charts. With simple and accessible language, *Revelation Unveiled* will help you better understand this mysterious, final book of the Bible and its implications.

Prophecy Books by Tim LaHaye

Are We Living in the End Times?

Charting the End Times

Charting the End Times Study Guide

Revelation Unveiled

The Popular Bible Prophecy Commentary

The Popular Encyclopedia of Bible Prophecy The Rapture: Who Will Face the Tribulation?

Tim LaHaye Prophecy Study Bible

Understanding Bible Prophecy for Yourself

These and other LaHaye resources are available at:
www.timlahaye.com

Share Your Thoughts

With the Author: Your comments will be forwarded to the author when you send them to *zauthor@zondervan.com*.

With Zondervan: Submit your review of this book by writing to *zreview@zondervan.com*.

Free Online Resources at
www.zondervan.com

Zondervan AuthorTracker: Be notified whenever your favorite authors publish new books, go on tour, or post an update about what's happening in their lives at www.zondervan.com/authortracker.

Daily Bible Verses and Devotions: Enrich your life with daily Bible verses or devotions that help you start every morning focused on God. Visit www.zondervan.com/newsletters.

Free Email Publications: Sign up for newsletters on Christian living, academic resources, church ministry, fiction, children's resources, and more. Visit www.zondervan.com/newsletters.

Zondervan Bible Search: Find and compare Bible passages in a variety of translations at www.zondervanbiblesearch.com.

Other Benefits: Register to receive online benefits like coupons and special offers, or to participate in research.

The Distance from Normandy

Also by Jonathan Hull

Losing Julia

The
Distance from
Normandy

Jonathan Hull

ST. MARTIN'S PRESS ≈ NEW YORK

www.stmartins.com

ISBN 0-312-31411-6

First Edition: September 2003

10 9 8 7 6 5 4 3 2 1

In memory of my father,
who showed me the wonder of books
and the wisdom of kindness.

Morton D. Hull
1927–2003

Sorrow makes us all children again.

—*Emerson,* Journals, *1842*

Part One

Chapter 1

They were late. Mead peered out the living room window again and checked his watch. Already an hour late. That was Sharon for you. It was, he'd decided long ago, a genetic flaw like baldness or myopia, only more irritating. Even as a child she'd been chronically late—pleading for a ride after missing the school bus, lingering dreamily on the jungle gym long after the school bell rang, prancing down the stairs to the dinner table at the very last moment, her sunny round face disarming his anger. She'd even been two weeks overdue at birth as Sophie swelled like a manatee and finally had to be induced. Mead dropped back down into his dark blue overstuffed chair, shuffled through the paper, then stood back up and peered out the window again.

After realigning the magazines and books on the large oak coffee table, he gave the brown sofa pillows a few dutiful whacks, then adjusted the gray dustcover draped over the telescope that sat on a tripod in the corner. Crossing the light blue carpet again he entered the kitchen, wiped down the counters one last time, then refilled his coffee mug and held it to his lips, taking small sips as he surveyed the empty sink and the neatly folded hand towels that hung from the oven door handles and the tidy row of spices and medicine bottles on the windowsill. So damn many medicines. He tapped the fingers of his right hand against the tip of his thumb, counting off the last dosage: next batch at 4 P.M. (A complete waste of money, he suspected, hating the frailty they implied.)

He set his mug on the counter and walked down the short and dimly lit hallway to the first bedroom on the left, peering inside. Sophie's room, the 1960s Singer workhorse still sitting on a small white table, waiting. "Just give me one little teeny, tiny place where I can make my mess," she'd said when they began looking for their first house in 1954. And finally, after Sharon went off to college and they purchased their third house in 1974, he'd been able to oblige. "It's *perfect*," she said as they surveyed the small extra bedroom. "Just wait until I'm finished with it." Once they'd fixed it up with some new carpeting and paint she'd disappear for hours to sew and hum and iron and do her decoupage and putter—or just sit like a queen in her hand-painted rocking chair by the window, gazing proudly at her small vegetable garden, now untended, overgrown and reclaimed by nature. Like Sophie.

For the first three months after she died Mead kept the door closed, unable even to set foot in there, as though afraid he might see her, afraid that she'd have to go through it again. The unbearable thing. So he kept the door closed and walked quickly past, some days wondering whether he had heard a sound, a sigh or rustle of fabric.

When Sharon visited that first Thanksgiving—nearly three years ago now—she tried to clean things up, making big piles of her mother's clothes to give away. But while she went to the grocery store to restock his refrigerator, Mead quickly rescued several of his favorite items and returned them to Sophie's closet, where her best shoes still hung from a pink wire rack on the left. And her slippers. Her worn, old yellow slippers, which still bore the impressions of her narrow size-six feet. Mead could never bring himself to throw out her slippers.

He listened to a car pass, still standing in the doorway, then checked his watch again. He'd spent three days trying to ready the room for his grandson, removing some of the pictures on the dresser—but leaving enough to remind the kid of his roots, of where he was. He stored all the plastic boxes of thread, pins, fabric samples, knitting needles and patterns beneath the twin bed. And buttons. There were jars and jars of buttons stashed everywhere, like acorns for winter. Sophie loved buttons. She adored the shiny, small, matching cuteness of them. Whenever Mead lost a button, a look of singular purpose shone on her face as she'd snatch off his shirt or coat and whisk it away to her room. "I can match it *perfectly*," she'd say as she foraged noisily through her button jars.

When he tired of trying to organize the room he'd sit in the rocker thinking of her sitting in the rocker and he'd steep himself in as much of her as still remained in the room. There was plenty. Enough, he thought, to survive on. At least for a few years. He didn't think of it as a memorial or a mausoleum—nothing quite so morbid; it was simply the place where she was more present than anywhere else, where her scent was the strongest. And so he'd gotten into the habit of spending a few minutes each day in the rocking chair, telling her things and imagining what she'd say and how she'd laugh or scold him, or just give him that look of hers where her eyebrows came together. After three days of moving things back and forth he'd finally made what he considered adequate space for his grandson. Just enough for a few weeks, then he'd put everything back exactly as it was.

He smoothed down the bedspread one more time before returning to the kitchen where he finished his coffee, washed out the mug, dried it and re-shelved it before wiping down the counters once again. Then he checked the refrigerator: plenty of sandwich meats, orange juice, milk (whole, as well as Mead's one percent), two flavors of Gatorade—terrible stuff, he thought, after a taste—two packs of all-beef franks, several pounds of lean hamburger meat, Swiss cheese, eggs, bacon, sausages in both links and patties. Even ice cream bars with nuts, which he'd selected after much consideration. (He'd been off ice cream for two years after noticing a certain softness around the midriff.) Plenty to get started. Who knew what the boy would eat?

He went back into the living room and peered out the window, then sat back down in his blue chair and waited.

A knife. A goddamn pocket knife.

•   •   •

Andrew sat in silence next to his mother, arms wrapped around his backpack. Crazy stupid thing. Crazy stupid world. And now this. He tapped his toe against the floorboard. And the thing was, he'd do it again if he had to. He'd push back again. He squeezed his backpack to his chest. *Push, push, push.* That's what it was all about. Getting pushed and pushing back. So he'd finally pushed back. Hard. And now everybody wanted to destroy him.

They always had.

It wasn't hate he felt, not the usual hate that seemed to pressurize everything until his ears ached. More like a sort of burning in his pimpled, freckled face. He kept thinking about what his best friend Matt used to say, about how sometimes it felt like life was gonna bust his head wide open. And then one day Matt decided he couldn't take the pain anymore;

he'd had enough. *How could you leave me like that?* Now Andrew was no longer sure that he could take it either.

He stared out the window at a passing silver Porsche convertible, watching the middle-aged driver talk smugly on a cell phone. Sixteen, and still the fucking helplessness of it. Can you will yourself into someone else's skin? But who'd want to switch with him? No one. He watched the driver, one hand resting lazily on top of the steering wheel, world by the balls. Probably talking dirty to his horny girlfriend. And with a silver Porsche convertible hauling his rich ass anywhere he wants to go. Andrew couldn't imagine the freedom of it, the absolute independence; doing only what you want to do, going wherever you felt like going. Just being able to pick up and *move*. Was it just a matter of waiting long enough? Learning when to push? But he'd always been waiting. He was tired of waiting. He slipped on his headphones and turned up the volume on his CD player. Fuck waiting.

They'd left the house at nine that morning for the flight from Chicago to San Diego, landing just after lunch. But his mother took the wrong bus to the wrong car rental agency and it was another forty-five minutes before they arrived at Thrifty, where they were given a tiny, white two-door with the smallest tires Andrew had ever seen. Typical, he thought, squeezing into the front seat and putting his headphones back on. The cheapest everything.

He looked quickly over at his mother, then back out the window, forwarding to the next song. He'd have to wait a lot longer now. Maybe forever. Okay, so he'd wait forever. What did it matter, really? What did anything matter? Because the thing that he could never stop thinking about was: *nothing* really mattered. The vast stupidness of everything was always there laughing at him: when he took a test, when he studied, when he stood before the mirror in the bathroom for twenty minutes each morning struggling to conceal his acne with his mother's makeup. It was all so amazingly pointless. All of it: grades and sports and theorems and diagramming sentences and always having to pretend to be what you weren't, and—most of all—the way everybody worked so hard trying to impress everybody else. *Pointless.* Yeah, he understood that. He understood a lot of things. That's what made it harder: *knowing*. And no one thinks you know. They don't have a clue that you can see through it all. Or maybe they've forgotten that they could once see through it all, too. (Is that it? He was never quite sure what happened to adults, how they became so pathetic.) He turned up the volume on his CD player. But still he'd have to get through the next three weeks. Twenty-one days with his grandfather. Mr. D-Day himself. The great Nazi slayer. Just thinking about it scared him, knotting up his stomach. And Andrew hated being scared more than anything. He was tired of being scared.

His mother tapped him on the shoulder. "How are you doing?"

Andrew shrugged.

"We should be there in fifteen minutes."

Another shrug.

"But you'll try?"

Andrew remained silent.

"Please?" Her features drew up with concern, which always got to him.

"Yeah, I'll try."

He didn't hate his mother. He never could, not like some guys hated theirs—a deep, primal sort of hatred. His mother was simply too stupid to hate. Nice but stupid, always losing things and leaving the car lights on and forgetting to pay the phone bill and dating the biggest jerks in the world. And then there was all her crying, which seemed to get worse and worse so that her mascara was always smearing, which drove Andrew nuts. She cried over everything: television shows, his grades, boyfriends, burning dinner, being poor. No, he didn't hate her. She was too fragile to hate. But he couldn't tell her anything. No way. There was a time when he wished he could, when he wanted her to understand what was happening to him, when he desperately needed her help. But not anymore. Who wants their mom to know the truth, to know that their son is silently drowning—that every morning when he goes to school and walks down those cold, echoing corridors with the jeering faces and the impenetrable circles, he just *dies?*

He changed CDs.

And that was the worst thing: hurting her. He still couldn't shake the look on her face when she arrived at the principal's office and saw him sitting there with the knife on the table and the cop and the flushed angry faces and the accusations. Like he was crazy, one of those wackos on TV in combat black, taking the whole fucking football team down with them.

No, he wasn't the crazy one. It was the rest of them that were crazy. All he wanted was for the pushing to stop.

Just please stop pushing me.

. . .

Sharon had called her father that night.

"Oh God, Dad, you'll never believe what's happened . . ."

"Try me."

"Andrew's been expelled. He brought a *knife* to school. He pulled it on a classmate. He didn't hurt him but—"

"Now slow down a minute. A *knife*? You sure they got the story straight? Andrew hardly seems like—"

"Of course I'm sure. He's been expelled. Andrew's been *expelled.*" She burst into tears. "I can't handle him anymore, Dad. I know he's a good kid inside but I can't handle him."

"How long is he out of school?"

"At least three weeks, which is all that's left until summer break." Sharon's voice wavered. "I don't know what's going to happen in the fall. There's a hearing. They could press charges."

"Just back up a minute. What kind of knife?"

"A pocketknife. The one you gave him when he went to that camp you sent him to."

Mead recalled the small buck knife he had engraved for Andrew's tenth birthday, just like the one that his own father had given him and that he'd kept all through the war. Did he still have it somewhere? "And you're saying he *pulled it* on somebody?"

"An older boy named Kevin Bremer. All I know is that he's on the football team."

"Maybe Andrew was just trying to show it off, impress the guys." He couldn't imagine his grandson trying to hurt anybody. Being hurt, yes.

"No, he was going to . . . stab him. That's what all the other kids said." She tried to stifle another sob. "I just can't believe it. I've completely failed. I'm just a mess, Dad. I don't know what to do anymore. Ever since the suicide, Andrew's been . . . oh God, Dad, what am I going to do?" She cried even harder.

Six months earlier, Andrew's best friend had killed himself by overdosing on alcohol and a bottle of his mother's tranquilizers. Mead had offered to send Andrew away to a boarding school, thinking it might give him a new start, but Sharon wanted to keep him close by.

And now this. Mead shook his head. To hell in a handbasket. And he'd seen it coming for years. The riots, race problems, drugs, violence, promiscuity. Christ, the filth on television. Pure pornography at family hour. At least all those young soldiers who never came home didn't have to see what became of the country they died fighting for. Freedom? More like anarchy. But he'd be gone soon enough. And frankly, that was just fine with him. He'd seen plenty, thank you.

"It's the goddamn television," he said finally. "That and the music and those computer games they play and the general lack of respect. You throw your TV out the window and tell that boy to straighten up and mind his Ps and Qs, or I'll do it for him. Better yet, tell him he'll go to military academy and I'll spring for it."

"This is Andrew we're talking about," said Sharon. *"Andrew."*

Mead looked over at the photograph on the coffee table: Sharon and Andrew at the boy's middle-school graduation. A nice enough kid, Mead thought, but shy and small and underfed-looking, with oily skin and a droopy, introverted face. A disappointment, frankly. Four-F. And as for teenagers, Lord, Mead could hardly bear the sight of them lurking in the malls, the girls dressed like hookers and the boys with their pants practically at their knees, cracks showing for all to see. "Pull up your trousers, sonny," he'd mutter to himself, never quite able to figure out how they stayed up at all. Every Christmas he made sure to give Andrew the finest belt money could buy. But the kid never wore one. None of them did.

Still, he'd always had a soft spot for Andrew, the only child of his only child. How Sophie used to dote on the boy, making him little outfits, buying him more presents than he could ever need, puddling up at the mention of him, as if having a grandchild was her life's crowning triumph. And Mead knew it hadn't been easy for the kid, whose father, Carl the Creep, ran off with some floozy when Andrew was just eight, and hardly bothered to call except when he was crocked. Mead had felt something funny on the back of his neck the first time he met The Creep, and he had sat distraught during the wedding wondering what in God's name he'd done wrong to cause his daughter—his sweet, precious Sharon, the only child Sophie had been able to have—to seek out a lazy son of a bitch like that. (Though she'd always had terrible taste in men, like the color-blind choosing a wardrobe.) Oh yes, he'd been onto The Creep from the start, and every time he was forced to talk to his son-in-law he'd find himself fantasizing about where on that big, mushy, arrogant face he might plant a decisive punch.

"Why'd he do it? There must have been some reason."

"How do I know why?"

"You ask him, that's how."

"He won't tell me. He won't tell me *anything*."

"Well then you lock him up in his room until he will tell you."

"You don't know him, Dad. He'd stay there until he starved. He's . . . he's changed. He's just boiling inside." She paused to blow her nose, making a loud honking sound. "I know he hasn't had it easy—I'm doing the best I can—but this?"

"Wasn't he seeing some sort of therapist?"

"He went for a while. Then he wouldn't go anymore."

"You don't give him a damn choice."

"Dad . . ." her voice broke. "I just can't handle him anymore. I took tomorrow off from work but I just started the job and . . ." She began to cry again.

Mead winced at the sound of her tears. What had happened to her? How had she become so beaten down and overwhelmed by life that he feared what each phone call might bring? Without thinking, Mead said, "Why don't you let me take him for a few weeks?"

There was a long pause. "You?"

"Why not? Maybe I can knock some sense into him."

"You know you'd go crazy in about five minutes."

"Give me some credit."

"Let's just say that teenagers aren't exactly . . ."

"Aren't exactly what?"

"You're serious?"

"Sure I'm serious."

Was he? Already Mead wondered whether it was too late to retract the offer.

There was another long pause. "Maybe it would be good for him. God knows, he needs a man around. But you're really serious?"

Mead swallowed hard. "Of course I'm serious."

•   •   •

Mead was on the front walkway of his small, white, one-story ranch house when the car pulled up. Three years in the service and the one lesson that stuck with him was: never volunteer. But Sharon needed him. Frankly, she needed a lot of things. Poor girl, always reeling from one disaster to another. Sophie had been right, their daughter just wasn't a natural when it came to motherhood. Or men. But did I really say three weeks? You're getting soft, old man. The thing is to lay down the law from the start. State the rules and consequences. And there would be consequences.

But exactly what consequences? He'd given that question considerable thought over the past few days. He couldn't just take the boy over his knee and smack him (though it might do him some good). He could always ground him, but ground him from what? It wasn't like the boy had any friends in the area. And what the hell would they *do* for three weeks? He was stumped on that one. At least there was the basketball hoop he'd purchased in a panic the day before and spent four hours assembling in the driveway. So—he could take away the boy's basketball privileges. And no Gatorade. Any back talk and down the drain goes the Gatorade, which is where it belongs anyway.

Across the street his neighbor Evelyn came out to water her flowers, stopping to wave enthusiastically. He waved back politely, hoping she wouldn't bring him over another batch of her nefarious raisin cookies. He wasn't quite sure what to make of Evelyn. A few years younger than Mead, she'd been widowed ten years previously and seemed to spend most of her time tending her garden and cooking raisin cookies or brownies or muffins, which she'd leave on Mead's doorstep in little decorative tins, returning every so often to collect the empties and chat. She and Sophie used to gab about gardening, sharing tips and an occasional recipe, but they'd never been close. Mead always suspected that it was because Sophie thought Evelyn was excessively attentive to him. (She didn't miss a thing.) It probably didn't help that Evelyn's bougainvillea scrambled enthusiastically up her trellis while Sophie's seemed paralyzed with a fear of heights. Indeed, Evelyn's flower garden put the entire subdivision to shame, exploding in riotous reds and yellows and oranges and blues long after every other garden—including Sophie's—had expired in the summer heat. "I think she *uses* something," Sophie would say accusingly.

She wasn't at all bad-looking—for her age (no small qualification). But Mead certainly didn't think of her *that* way. Indeed, he was careful always to be extremely circumspect in her presence, not wanting to give her any encouragement. The thought of Sophie rolling jealously in her grave was simply unbearable. Besides, Mead had little confidence in his ability to correctly interpret the subtle signals that guided male-female relations. Years earlier he'd been the unwitting and mortified subject of a vigorous pursuit by a chain-smoking, six-foot-three divorcée named Frances who worked in the accounting department of his engineering firm. At first he thought it a mere unfortunate coincidence that she always appeared at the coffee machine whenever he went for a refill, but when she goosed him at the Christmas party after imbibing too much punch he knew he was in trouble. The next day he went out and purchased his own coffee thermos, and from then on he took elaborate precautions to avoid being in the same room with her. Yet two months later an envelope with no return address arrived in his office mail. Inside was a one-page poem, which, as far as he could tell, had something to do with the different shades of light on a Sunday afternoon—though he suspected it might be some sort of coded proposition. He received three in all, and though he shredded each one on the spot, they left him feeling sullied and traitorous (despite a flawless record of fidelity). Should he tell Sophie? But how could he? *You must have been leading her on.* And yet if he didn't, he'd have something to hide. A secret. He never did tell her—despite several aborted attempts—and thankfully the pursuit ended as suddenly as it had started. Still, the experience convinced him that one could never be too cautious in dealing with the opposite sex. He glanced over at Evelyn across the street, then quickly looked away, pretending to be busy adjusting his sprinkler.

Finally a small white car—so small he thought it might be electric—turned the corner and came down the street, popping the curb as it pulled into his driveway.

"Hi, Dad." Sharon jumped out and gave him a big hug. He'd forgotten how familiar she smelled. Even with her lotions and shampoos and the awful perfume that always made his and Sophie's eyes water—*are you sure it's not tear gas?*—he could still trace her original scent, the one that drifted into his being the day he first kissed her fuzzy little scalp at the hospital in Tampa, where they had lived for three years after the war.

"You're late."

"Sorry. We had a small problem with the rental car."

"Mom went to Hertz by mistake," mumbled Andrew. "This is from Thrifty." He pointed disgustedly at the car. "We should have gone to Hertz. Everybody else goes to Hertz."

What a punk, thought Mead, studying his grandson, whose enormous jeans could easily have fit on the biggest man in Mead's old rifle company. He wore dirty, unlaced sneakers, walking on the flattened back heels as though they were slippers, and a large and rumpled black T-shirt with some sort of Satanic omen painted on it. He had a small, gold hoop earring in his left earlobe and his hair—once brown but now streaked with yellow along the top—looked like it had been cut with shears, then fermented under a helmet for several weeks. In short, the boy looked like a refugee or drug freak.

Mead felt a chill of repugnance. My own grandson. And a hooligan as well. He reached down and tapped the roll of antacids in his front pants pocket. What the hell was Sharon thinking, letting him travel dressed like that? It was no wonder so many friends had retreated into elderly compounds over the years, safe in their snug little time capsules, oblivious to their irrelevance. Mead would never do that. He wasn't about to hide behind some damn guard and gate. Finally he stepped forward and put out his hand. "How are you doing, son?"

The boy shrugged and took his hand, offering a limp, moist grip, so that Mead feared he might break the boy's bones if he squeezed too hard.

"Well, get your things and come inside."

Andrew returned to the car for his backpack, duffel bag and skateboard. Sharon stood staring at Mead, her eyes moistening. "Thank you," she whispered. "I don't know what else to say."

Mead watched the boy for a moment, wondering if he should help—naw, let him carry his own load—then turned and went inside, hoping Sharon wouldn't get weepy.

"Well, this will be your room," Mead said, standing awkwardly at the doorway to Sophie's room.

"It was Mom's," said Sharon.

"You guys had separate bedrooms?"

"Of course we didn't have separate bedrooms," Mead said with a scowl. "This was her . . . workshop."

"Mom loved this room."

"What did she make?" asked Andrew, eyeing the room suspiciously.

"What didn't she?" said Sharon. "She was incredible with her hands. I think I must have been adopted."

"Your grandma made half the stuff in this house," said Mead proudly.

"Take that mirror with the shells, for example. She found every single one of those shells herself."

"When they lived in Tampa," explained Sharon. "Mom loved beach-combing."

"And look how she glued each one on just perfectly," continued Mead. "You could get some money for that one. And those curtains, made them herself, and this quilt . . ." Andrew eyed the bright orange and brown bed-spread. "And that plate on the wall."

"Decoupage," said Sharon.

They stood in silence, shifting from foot to foot.

"So, why don't you unpack your things and your mom and I will be in the living room," said Mead finally. The moment they walked away Mead heard the door close.

After stopping in the bathroom to down two antacids, he offered Sharon a soft drink—Fresca, his favorite—then took a seat in his blue, overstuffed chair and looked closely at her. She looked thinner than usual, with a puffi-ness around her large hazel eyes and lines on her oval face that he didn't remember seeing before. Even her hands looked thinner, veins showing. *Where did you go, Princess?* It broke his heart to see what had happened to her, how she never seemed to get her footing, going through jobs and men like tissue. What had they done wrong? Nothing. Sophie had even offered—much to Mead's horror—to move out to Chicago to help with Andrew after The Creep first walked out. (Thank God Sharon wouldn't hear of it.)

She had a big enough heart; maybe too big. It was common sense that she lacked. He looked at the gray roots of her thinning, dark brown hair, remembering how full and shiny it once was and how Sophie loved to braid it into all sorts of designs before sending Sharon skipping off to school in the morning. "Look at me, Dad!" And what a beauty she'd been, beauty that gradually had been washed away by heartbreak and circum-stance. Mead took a deep breath, fighting back a tightness in his chest.

"How have you been, Pumpkin?" he asked softly.

"The truth? Awful." She sat on the sofa across from him, leaning over her knees. "I just don't know what to do about Andrew. He's . . . he's not a bad kid, Dad. You know that. But he's got so much stuff inside and I don't know how to get it out. Ever since Matt's death he's been . . ." She raised her hands into the air, eyes welling up.

"Any more word from the school?"

"I'll find out more next week. They're considering whether to let him back next fall."

"How are his grades?"

"Terrible. In the last couple of years he's just stopped trying. And he's such a smart kid. I know he is." She wiped her eyes.

Mead leaned forward and took Sharon's hand. "Are you taking care of yourself?"

"Oh God, don't worry about me."

"But I do. You look thin."

"I've never been thin."

"Baloney. You getting any exercise?"

She shrugged. "I was working out a couple of times a week until I started this new job. I've just got to get a routine going."

"You're not still smoking?"

"I stopped—for *good*."

Mead raised his eyebrows.

"It's been a month. Promise."

"You two could move out here. Get some sunshine." Mead surprised himself with the offer, half hoping she'd decline.

"Dad, I *like* Chicago."

"Can I give you some money?"

"You just sent me a check."

"I have more than I need."

"I'm not your charity."

"You're my daughter."

She leaned toward him and kissed him on the cheek. "So how are you?"

"Fit as a fiddle."

"I hope I have your genes, but I'm starting to have my doubts."

Mead considered inquiring into the latest developments of her tumultuous love life, but then thought better of it. "So, uh, how does Andrew feel about . . ." he gestured around the room, "this?"

"Coming here? Well, it wasn't exactly his idea. He's a little nervous."

"Of course."

"I don't know how to thank you. With this new job and—"

"Don't think about it."

She wiped her eyes, smudging her mascara. "I think you'll be good for him. He needs a man, Dad. I really think he needs a man to reach him."

Mead took a deep breath and finished off his Fresca. "Well, we'll see." He heard noises coming from Sophie's room. Christ, was the boy rearranging things? Mead wouldn't stand for that.

Sharon glanced at her watch. "Yikes, I'm supposed to meet Cindy in half an hour. You remember Cindy? She's letting me sleep at her place tonight and I've got a flight home first thing in the morning."

Mead tensed. "You could have slept here," he said, trying to keep the hurt from his face.

Sharon looked around the living room, simply furnished with a dining room table at one end, and at the other a sofa, two chairs and a coffee table set around a small gas fireplace with three artificial logs.

"I would have slept on the couch."

"You're sweet, but I haven't seen Cindy in years." She got up and gave him a hug. "Thank you for paying for the tickets. I'll pay you back. Promise."

"You know I won't let you do that."

Sharon tried to smile, then gestured toward the hallway. "I'll just go say good-bye."

Mead nodded.

"He's really a good kid, Dad. He's just . . ."

"We'll be fine."

Mead stood on the front porch watching Sharon drive off, waving until the car turned down the block, then waving to the memory of her being there. He lingered for another moment, making a fist at his side to keep hold of himself, then pulled the mail out of the box and went back inside, bolting the door before returning to his chair where he sat leafing through the bills and catalogs and wondering what to fix for dinner. He heard more noises coming from Sophie's room. What the hell's going on in there?

When Andrew failed to emerge after half an hour Mead finally got up, walked down the hallway and stood outside the door listening. Not a sound. Was he taking a nap, for Christ's sake? Mead would have to put a stop to that, put the boy on a firm schedule. He returned twenty minutes later and listened again. "You want some Gatorade?"

"What?"

"I said, do you want some Gatorade? Got orange and red."

"No thank you. I don't like Gatorade."

Mead stood at the door for a moment. "Neither do I," he grumbled, heading back to the kitchen where he removed both jugs of Gatorade from the fridge, opened them and poured them down the sink.

An hour later he returned to the door and listened again. "You coming out of there sometime?" No response. Mead knocked. "I said, are you ever planning on coming out of there—or shall I just slide the food under the door?"

"I'm sorry, I was listening to music. Sure, I'll be out. When do you want me out?"

Mead stared at the door, noticing how faded the paint looked. Come to think of it, the whole house could use a fresh coat. Mead remembered how he and Sophie had spent weeks repainting it themselves, using the savings to go to Hawaii. Must have been fifteen years ago. "When would you want to come out?"

"Whenever."

"When's that?"

A minute later the door cracked open and Andrew peered out, all the shyness gathered around his eyes. Damn if he doesn't have the saddest eyes. Mead took a step back. "Well, I'll be in the living room. Dinner's at six. *Sharp*." He turned and headed back down the hall. The door closed behind him. Three weeks, Mead thought, shaking his head as he settled back down in his blue chair and shuffled through the newspaper. Better restock the bourbon.

•   •   •

First, the orange and brown bedspread would have to go. Pathetic. It was like rooming with an orangutan. He folded it up and stuffed it onto the top shelf of the closet. After contemplating the layout of the room for several minutes, he switched the rocking chair with the dresser, then back again. Maybe the bed should go against the window. He tried four different arrangements, finally settling on the bed in the corner by the window, next to the dresser, with the small rattan desk at the foot of the bed and the rocking chair in the opposite corner. He considered unpacking his bag, but all but two of the drawers were full, crammed with sweaters and bracelets and earrings and balls of yarn and socks and shawls. Grandma's stuff. He picked up a yellow sweater and held it to his nose, then put it back and closed the drawer. Creepy. So he'd just keep his things in his bag. No need to unpack anyway. Only three weeks. Any luck and he'd go home early. The thing was just to get through it.

He sat on the bed wondering whether to take down any of the photographs and cheap-looking artwork, the kind sold at garage sales, then drummed his fingers on his kneecaps. Day one. Should he make a scratch on the wall? At least he'd finish *The Two Towers* and maybe even *The Return of the King*. But man, three weeks with GI Joe? He got up from the bed and stood at the dresser studying the framed photographs of his grandparents that were neatly arrayed in rows. As he looked closely at them he realized for the first time that both his grandfather and grandma had once been okay-looking, at least in black and white. He picked up a photo of his grandfather in uniform, surprised by how young he looked, like he barely shaved. Definitely good-looking: powerful eyes—deep blue in real life, which always made Andrew wonder why his own were dirty brown—good nose, all-American face. Frankly, way better looking than me. And the thing was, there was no similarity at all. He tried to see himself in his grandfather's eager young face but couldn't. Not even a trace. Grandfather the Kraut killer. Probably killed dozens of them. He'd seen plenty of shows on late-night television about the big war, the German dive bombers screaming downward and the guys jumping into the water and wading to the beach and then the grand finale with the mushroom cloud and then all those white crosses that went on forever. *Saving Private Ryan* was definitely intense, especially the scene where the Jew gets knifed by the German. Nasty. But he could never place the old guy in the green, button-down sweater sitting in the living room with those battles in Europe. That was like, *fifty* years ago.

He carefully placed the photograph back on the dresser, then knelt over his bag, opened a side compartment and pulled out the extra large Ziploc bag containing Matt, or what was left of him. He'd been surprised that the ashes weren't exactly ashes—not like what's left from a campfire—but more like little coarse white and gray pieces of ground shells from the beach. He had spent hours imagining Matt's body being placed on a big grill and then slid into a hot furnace and cooked to a crisp. (Heat for two hours at up to 1,800 degrees Fahrenheit, then pulverize—according to a

Web site he checked out.) Even dead, how could that not hurt? And how did they catch the ashes and keep them from being mixed with other people's ashes? What if it wasn't Matt at all that he was holding but some big-butted Bertha from the South Side? He carefully opened the Ziploc and put a finger in, stirring the little pieces of bone. Was it a crime to transfer stolen ashes across state lines? He didn't care—stealing Matt's ashes was the single best thing that Andrew had ever done. Once he heard that Matt was going to be taken to some family plot in Indiana he knew he had to do it. Matt *hated* Indiana, where he had to spend every Thanksgiving and Christmas on a farm visiting relatives, all of whom were seriously religious. Everyone suspected him, but they couldn't prove it. *The perfect crime.* He smiled and placed Matt in his lap.

Actually, he didn't really think of the ashes as Matt. He figured Matt had already been reincarnated into something else. He was always on the lookout, scrutinizing cats that rubbed against him and dogs that licked him and babies wailing at the grocery store and any stranger who gave him a second glance. He knew that Matt was out there somewhere; it was just a matter of time before he made the connection.

He put the Ziploc on the dresser and pulled out a smaller baggie containing three joints, which was all he could scrounge up for the trip. Would his grandfather search through his things? (Didn't everybody?) He looked around the room, then went over to the closet, chose one of his grandma's shoes at random and stuffed the baggie containing the joints into the toe, smiling to himself at his cunning. Then he gently flattened Matt's ashes and placed them under the mattress near the head. When he finished he sat back down on the bed and checked his watch. Is the old man expecting me in the living room? But what the hell are we going to do sitting in the same room?

He'd never felt comfortable around his grandfather (it was never *grandpa*). Not the way he had with Grandma, who played hours of cards and checkers and Parcheesi with him and always brought him homemade cookies and brownies when they came to visit. He hardly knew his grandfather, who always seemed to sit watchfully in the largest chair like the teacher during an exam. Sure he respected him, at least in the reflexive way you admire an astronaut or Olympic athlete, or show reverence for the dead. But he felt more intimidated than anything, hating the sweaty smallness he felt in the great man's presence. GI Joe's generation saved the world and there's been nothing but riffraff ever since. And basically, hero or not, the guy was wound up tight as an asshole. It was like having a cop, a priest and a principal all wrapped into one. And what's with the big American flag out front? It's like staying at the fucking post office.

He got up and looked at the photographs again, trying to figure how the young man in the uniform mutated into the cranky old headmaster sitting in the living room. What the hell did he do for kicks? Fondle his medals? Andrew tried to imagine his grandparents having sex but the idea made him cringe like he'd just sucked on a lemon. He sat back down on the bed, feeling edgy. Oh man, three weeks.

· · ·

Mead settled on hamburgers. Top-grade, mixed with his own special seasoning. He scrubbed his hands, dried them, then carefully laid out a sheet of wax paper on the kitchen counter and began to knead the meat, shaping the patties until they were just so, plump but not too thick in the middle. Four patties should do it. These kids could eat entire livestock. He added a bit more pepper, then another dash of Worcestershire. Nothing like Mead's juicy burgers. (To hell with doctors.) After putting on his apron— the black one with the white chef's hat on it that Sophie made for his sixty-fifth birthday—he grabbed a box of Ohio Blue-Tip Matches from the top of the refrigerator, opened the screen door and went out to the side of the house to light the grill, suffused with a rare sense of contentment.

Once the burgers were on, he sliced up some onions, tomatoes and lettuce, then readied the condiments—ketchup, French's, Grey Poupon and horseradish spread—as well as cheddar cheese. He'd make two cheeseburgers and two plain. The boy could take his pick. But where to eat? Mead usually had his breakfast at the small table in the kitchen, then ate lunch and dinner on a TV tray in the living room. *Hmm.* They could eat at the table outside, enjoy the evening air. But it might be buggy. He stared at the little kitchen table, imagining them sitting face-to-face. Not a chance. There was always the dining room table; certainly plenty of elbowroom. But no, too formal. Besides, Mead never ate at the dining room table. As far as he was concerned, that was for entertaining, and he most definitely was not entertaining. Well then, they could eat from trays in the living room, keep it casual. He glanced down at the condiments, imagining his grandson dribbling ketchup and mustard all over the sofa and carpet. To hell with the bugs, they'd eat outside. He went back out and checked on the burgers, delighting in their freshly-singed smell. As he flipped them one last time—nearly perfect—Andrew appeared.

"What are those?"

Mead looked down with pride at the sizzling patties, adding cheese to two of them. "Well now, cut off my leg and call me Shorty, but in these parts we refer to them as burgers. *Hamburgers.* And they happen to be my specialty."

"Are they meat burgers?"

"I don't think I follow you, son."

"Are they made of meat?"

Mead put down his spatula. "Now what do you think?"

"I mean, *real* meat?"

Mead sized up his grandson, wondering if the boy was on drugs. It would explain a lot of things. But his eyes were clear enough and he seemed steady on his feet. "Yes, you're looking at real, honest-to-goodness hamburgers. Top grade. Ol' Daisy herself gave up the ghost so that we might eat." He picked up his spatula again. "Grab a plate."

"I thought they might be veggie-burgers."

"Now why would you think a thing like that?"

"Because I don't eat meat."

Mead stood motionless. "You don't eat . . . meat?"

"I'm not like a total vegan. I like cheese and tuna fish. But no land-based animals. It's been almost a year now." Andrew shoved his hands into his front pockets. "Farming's like the biggest polluter in the country," he mumbled. "And the energy that goes into raising one cow could feed thousands of people. Cows are even considered holy in India. Did you know that? They're practically rock stars. Man, if I was a cow I'd definitely want to live in India."

Mead looked down at the burgers, then back at the boy. "You don't eat meat?"

"Nope. But with tofu—"

"By God, it's no wonder you're so damn scrawny. You're not getting any protein."

"Beans have tons of protein."

Mead stared at the boy, then down at the grill. The burgers were now overcooked. Nothing Mead hated more than overcooked burgers. He grabbed a plate and took them off.

"I figured Mom would tell you."

Mead considered forcing his grandson to eat a cheeseburger on the spot, double time. Might be just what he needs. "You come with some sort of instruction manual?"

"I'm not that hungry anyway," Andrew mumbled.

"And for God's sake, stop mumbling." Mead carried the hamburgers to the kitchen while Andrew held open the screen door. "I've got some tuna fish. You said you like tuna fish?"

"Yeah, I guess I'll have some tuna fish."

Mead set the burgers down on the counter. They'd be cold by the time he ate. Tough and cold. He thought of all the meat sitting in the fridge. Enough for a platoon. *Damn.* He'd have to freeze some or it would spoil. Or was it too late to freeze meat that had been in the refrigerator for two days now? Better freeze some anyhow, give it the sniff test when it thaws. He looked back down at his burnt burgers. *Patience.*

"I make great tuna fish," he said finally, trying to sound pleasant. "Your grandma taught me the secret. Gotta mince it up real fine with your fingers. Then a squeeze of lemon, some Grey Poupon, mayonnaise and relish."

"I just like mayo, thanks. If that's okay . . ."

Mead stood looking at the boy, who was a good five inches shorter. (Mead was six-foot-one, or liked to think he still was.) "Fine. You make the tuna. It's there in the cabinet." Mead pulled out a bowl, a can opener and the mayonnaise, then covered the hamburgers with tin foil. "I'll be in the living room."

"You can go ahead and eat," said Andrew.

"I'll wait," said Mead, heading for the bourbon and feeling his stomach growl. He could hear Andrew rummaging through the cabinet.

"There should be a couple of cans right there in front, second shelf," Mead called out, knowing full well there were five cans of Starkist stacked right between the jar of Prego pasta sauce and the two cans of sliced Dole pineapples.

"I was just wondering if you had any packed in water?"

"Excuse me?"

More sounds of cans and jars being moved. Damn it. Mead rose from his chair. "Is there some sort of problem with my tuna fish?"

"It's just that it's packed in oil."

"It's Starkist, for Christ's sake."

"You can get it packed in water—but that's okay."

Mead sunk back down into his chair wondering if he should just call Sharon and tell her the whole thing had been a mistake; that Camp Mead was closed for the season and that little Sad Sack would be on the first plane home in the morning with a bag of carrots to see him through.

Several minutes later Andrew appeared in the living room. "I'm ready to eat when you are."

After Mead toasted a bun he slathered his hamburger with condiments, touched up his bourbon, then sat down at the small, white kitchen table across from Andrew and ate in silence.

Midway through his burger the doorbell rang. The raisin cookie lady, thought Mead, shaking his head.

"I'll get it," said Andrew.

Mead rose to stop him but Andrew was already halfway to the door.

"You must be Andrew," he heard Evelyn say. "Every bit as handsome as your grandfather." Who is she kidding? "I hope I'm not interrupting . . ."

"No, please come in. Hey Grandfather, you have a *visitor.*"

Mead quickly wiped the mustard from his mouth and grabbed the three empty tins from the top of the refrigerator. "Hello, Evelyn."

"Hello, General."

"General?" Andrew looked at his grandfather with a grin. "I didn't know you were a *general.*"

"I'm *not* a general."

"But he seems like one, don't you think? Must be that commanding presence." She winked. "Anyway, I've brought you some muffins." She took the three empty tins from Mead and handed him a full one. "I would have made more if I'd known your grandson was in town."

"This looks like plenty," said Mead.

"How long are you visiting for?" she asked Andrew, who was still grinning.

"A couple of weeks—maybe." Andrew took the tin from Mead, popped it open and selected a muffin. "This is *good,*" he said, taking a bite. "And I love the raisins."

Oh, God, thought Mead, she'll bake up a storm. She gave him a big smile. He had to admit she had a nice smile, which after so many years had been etched into her face as a kind of testament to her pleasant nature.

Taller than Sophie, she had warm hazel eyes, sun-freckled skin—a bit wrinkled but not yet lifeless—and good posture. Her gray hair was cut short and styled simply and she wore khakis, sneakers and a plain lavender shirt. Either good genes or healthy living or maybe even both. (How quickly Sophie had aged those last years, shrinking so fast that he had the illusion he was getting taller.)

"I try to keep your grandfather from wasting away," she explained to Andrew as he stuffed the remaining half of the muffin into his mouth.

"Delicious," he mumbled.

"Evelyn lives in the white house across the street," said Mead.

"Oh, I see," said Andrew with a knowing smile, which made Mead blush. "Well, it's really nice to meet you."

"I'll leave you two to finish your dinner," said Evelyn, sending Mead another one of her smiles, which wafted toward him like an enormous smoke ring. Sophie would have had her neck, he thought.

"Thanks for the muffins," Mead said, walking her to the door.

"Yeah, they're *awesome,*" Andrew called out from the kitchen.

• • •

Mead always took a walk after dinner—it kept him regular as a Rolex—but he wasn't keen on leaving Andrew alone in the house. Nor did he especially want his grandson to join him for what was his favorite time of the day, watching the colors change and feeling the heat finally break and in the winter being able to look in the windows of his neighbors and glimpse little snapshots of solitude and chaos. After clearing their plates—at least the boy cleaned up after himself—Andrew retreated to his room while Mead returned to the living room. Jesus, it's like rooming with a monk, he thought, giving the paper a final once-over while listening to the tick of the silver clock on the mantle above the fireplace. Sophie's parents had given them the clock as a wedding gift along with the brass nameplate that still hung just above the doorbell beside their front door, though Mead always felt it belonged on a much larger house (which was why he kept it hidden in the back of the closet for years until Sophie insisted they put it up shortly after their last move). "Seems a bit showy to me," he muttered as Sophie marked off with a pencil exactly where she wanted it mounted.

"Everybody has one," she said, handing him the drill.

"They do?" Mead looked around at the other houses. "Looks like someone better tell the neighbors." But it was worth it just to see the glow on Sophie's face when she stood back and admired it.

"Now isn't that the homiest thing you've ever seen?"

He listened as Andrew emerged from his room and headed for the bathroom, closing the door quickly behind him. *The kid goes more than I do.*

He looked back at the clock. The thing was to have some sort of talk. *Man to . . . juvenile delinquent. What the hell business have you got bringing a knife to school? Don't you know who you are, son? Oh, the things he could tell the boy. Goddamned vegetarian, worrying about cows when you're pulling knives on classmates.* He took another sip of his bourbon. *You know the kind of work I was doing when I was your age? Have you any idea what work is?*

"Good night," said Andrew, appearing in the hallway with his Sad Sack face again.

Mead looked at his watch. "Hell, it's only eight o'clock," he said. "Thought we might play a few darts." He gestured toward the dark wooden cabinet that hung above the small bar. Sophie had bought it for him with her first couple of paychecks after she got a job working at a fabric store once Sharon went away to college. Mead loved the way the cherry cabinet doors swung open to reveal the board and the little drawer beneath that held his six high density tungsten darts with solid aluminum shafts and feather flights. There was a small blackboard for scoring on the inside of the left cabinet door and a second drawer for chalk and the eraser. Mead had carefully mounted the board so that the bull's-eye was exactly five feet, eight inches from the ground, and he had adjusted a table and chair until he could draw a visual toe line across the carpet precisely seven feet, nine and a quarter inches from the board. Regulation.

Mead walked over and proudly opened the cabinet.

"I'm tired," said Andrew.

Mead hesitated. "Sure. Traveling and all." He closed the cabinet back up again. "Well—got everything you need, toothpaste and all that?"

"I'm fine."

"I keep a light on in the bathroom. I'm always up by six."

"Good night."

"Good night. And don't forget to brush your teeth." Mead listened as Sophie's door clicked quietly closed, then went out front, took down the

American flag, carefully folded it and placed it on the top shelf of the hall closet. Then he freshened up his bourbon, opened the dartboard cabinet again and selected three darts.

It felt strange having someone else in the house. After Sophie died he hated the quiet, which was so enveloping that he soon found himself tip-toeing about. Then one evening he dropped a glass in the kitchen and it shattered with such a loud noise that he ran from the room in a panic. For the next few months he left the radio tuned to a classical station, even at night, and when that wasn't enough he hummed to himself. Then one afternoon the power went out and the silence swept over him so suddenly and completely that he could almost hear his grief, as if loneliness was an audible thing. But he had faced it, and when the power came back on three hours later he kept the radio off, gradually acclimating himself to the hushed timbre of widowerhood. Still, he couldn't shake the awful feeling of being left behind, like a child who loses his parents at a carnival and can't remember the meeting place. Every room seemed so desolate and hungry for her presence that he even considered moving. But when the perky young realtor with a long tear in her nylons suggested that the house would show better if they rented some *happy* furniture he'd gone cold on the idea, thinking that anywhere else would just be farther from Sophie.

Mead carefully took aim and threw the darts one by one, clustering well below the bull's-eye.

Even dying she'd been stronger. As soon as she knew she wasn't going to get better she started worrying about how he'd manage.

"Now, Peanut, don't concern yourself about me."

But she had. If she could have she would have cooked him ten years' worth of meals and frozen them in labeled Tupperware containers. *Monday dinner, preheat to 325. Tuesday lunch, thaw overnight.* She'd even left him a list of simple recipes, writing everything out as clearly as possible with smiley faces drawn here and there. *No, you can't cook it in half the time by turning the oven up to 600!* (He'd tried, and sure enough she'd been right.) The last thing she'd done before she was bedridden was to make and freeze a large batch of her special pasta sauce, which he loved. But he never could bring himself to eat it. When he thawed it out two months after she died the smell was simply too much. But he couldn't bring himself to throw it out either, not until it got moldy. *Sorry, Peanut.*

After putting the darts away he turned off the living room lights and sat in the dark, thinking he'd wait until he felt a little more tired before heading to bed.

He looked over at the burgundy sofa, remembering how he'd slept there that last month when Sophie was in the hospital bed they'd set up in the living room with the IVs and oxygen.

"I've been having the most lovely dreams," she said one night as they lay in the dark talking.

"Don't keep any secrets."

She started coughing, almost a choking sound, then caught her breath. "You'll just laugh."

"Try me."

"If you insist." She coughed again, then cleared her throat. "This afternoon I dreamed that you and I were having a wonderful picnic—on the roof of the Duomo in Florence."

"On the roof? We've never even *been* to Italy."

"But I know what the Duomo looks like." And that she did. She had dozens of coffee-table books about Italy and France and Spain, planning for the trip that they never took.

"You see, we'd just gotten married in the Sistine Chapel and—"

"The Sistine Chapel? Not by the Pope, by any chance?"

"Actually, yes! It was Paul."

"John Paul?"

"No, the first Paul. Saint Paul."

"*Saint* Paul? Geez, that's some wedding, especially for a couple of Unitarians."

"It's just a dream, silly."

"Go on."

"Anyway, it was a beautiful service but your stomach kept growling."

"Probably just nerves."

"And so I decided to have a picnic on the roof of the Duomo in Florence."

"Good thinking. But isn't it a sloped roof?"

"That's why the grapes kept rolling off!"

"It's the medicine, my dear."

They lay in silence listening to a large plane rumble overhead, then suddenly Sophie let out a laugh.

"Now what?"

"I was just thinking about the night you asked me to marry you. Remember how you kept getting up from the table to use the restroom? You must have gone four times."

"Must we really—"

"To tell you the truth I thought you had . . . you know, problems."

"I was rehearsing my lines."

"You never told me that."

It was true. Mead had gone to the restroom four times to practice in front of the mirror. But it hadn't done any good. Once he took Sophie's hand and began to speak, the words had derailed right in his mouth and Sophie had to finish his sentence.

"I must be the only girl who proposed to herself," she said.

"I would have gotten to the point eventually."

Mead listened to the sound of her turning in her bed, then more coughing, which made him wince. "Can I get you anything?"

"No no, I'm fine." She coughed again. "I'm sorry to be such a bother."

"Peanut, please."

"I really don't want a big fuss made at my funeral."

Mead opened his eyes and stared at the red blinking of the monitors by her bed. "Let's not talk about it."

"I just don't like big fusses."

"Okay, no big fusses."

"You'll keep going to church?"

"Sophie . . ."

"I need to know."

Mead hesitated. "I'll keep a foot in the door."

"Promise?"

"I said a *foot*."

"That's good enough." She sighed. "I just worry about you so."

"Come on now, I'm a tough old bear."

"Oh no you're not. You're a big Pooh." She laughed again. "I'll never forget the look on your face when you walked Sharon down the aisle. Goodness, you had the whole place in tears."

It was true. Even though he loathed his son-in-law, the sight of Sharon in her wedding dress had completely undone him. There were other times, too, when he'd suddenly find himself full of more emotion than he knew what to do with: anniversaries, Christmas, New Year's Eve when Guy

Lombardo and his band played. He always fought it, disliking the feeling of being out of control. And yet every year it got worse.

"I don't know how you're going to get through my funeral," she said, her voice suddenly squeaking.

"For Pete's sake, Sweetie Pie, let's talk about something else."

But she'd been right. For when he sat there in the front row looking at her casket he thought he would drown.

Her final wish was to die at home and yet he hadn't let her. When she couldn't catch her breath one evening and the monitors started flashing he simply couldn't bear it and had called an ambulance. *Hurry!* They'd resuscitated her all right, yanking her back to life despite the D.N.R. orders she'd drawn up months before and granting her one more hideous week, which she spent behind the curtain of a small, semi-private hospital room.

"I'm so sorry," he told her over and over again, bent over her bed and trying to keep away the pushy nurse who pumped the fluid from her lungs twice a day.

She just squeezed his hand.

He used to visit her grave twice a week, bringing her yellow tulips—her favorite—and making sure the gardeners were keeping things up. But no matter what time of day he went, he always ran into an enormous widow who parked herself in a little beach chair right on the adjacent plot and yacked nonstop to her dead husband Henry.

"Should have been at the races today, Henry. All the long shots were placing. And did I tell you about the trifecta? My God, Henry, we almost won the trifecta! Five thousand dollars, Henry!"

Thousands of headstones and not a visitor in sight except the big, loud psychotic sitting three feet from Sophie and chewing the ear off her dead husband.

"Excuse me, I wonder if you could keep it down a bit," Mead finally said one sweltering afternoon.

A look of hurt came across her big, juicy face, which was heavily powdered. "I'm just talking to Henry here." She fondly patted the top of Henry's gray headstone.

"Yes, well you see I can't hear . . ." Mead started to gesture toward Sophie's grave, then dropped his arm, feeling foolish.

She winked at him. "You too? And my daughters think *I'm* crazy."

"Now wait a—"

"Not to worry." She leaned over and gave his forearm a knowing squeeze, then turned back toward her husband's headstone. "Hey Henry, you want to meet the neighbors? I mean we *are* practically neighbors." She gave Mead a big, lusty smile.

He placed the flowers on the grass beneath Sophie's name, silently apologizing for the short visit, then turned to go.

"Maybe we could go to the races or have dinner or something?" the widow whispered. "Seeing as we're neighbors."

Mead looked at her in horror. "I don't think Henry would like that," he said in a loud voice. Then he walked quickly to his car.

. . .

Andrew lay in the dark listening to his headphones for a while, then placed them on the table next to him, pulled up the sheets and rolled onto his stomach, digging his fingers into the pillow. It had him again, grabbing him in its claws and tearing at his skin. Tossing and turning, he couldn't escape the awful, cold emptiness of everything.

That was what he feared most about silence. At least the music could chase it away, scattering all the thoughts and images like a hurricane flattening trees. But silence? He dreaded silence. In bed at night in the dark was always the worst, stranded there with all the fears, squirming and batting at them, feeling embarrassed just being alive.

He could never figure how other people managed. How could they be so calm, even cheery? Were they clueless? I mean, fuck me, fifteen years of homework just so you can get a job kissing up to some asshole? (All his mom's bosses were major assholes.) *Please.* And then after putting up with all the bullshit—years of it—what happens? You croak.

Very funny.

Ever since puberty Andrew had been haunted by the conviction that he had been born into a primitive and brutal stage of human evolution. The older he got, the harder he found it not to dwell on the mounting evidence that life was, in a nutshell, ridiculous; a big tease in which you could imagine and hope for wonderful things—constant sex, being able to live forever, world peace—only you couldn't have them. (Not even close.) So what was the point? (And what kind of God would invent a creature with needs it had no hope of fulfilling?) And yet other people didn't seem the least bit fazed. Truckloads of bullshit every way you turned and nobody else seemed even remotely freaked out. Was he just wired differently? (Sometimes he imagined himself as one of those huge radio dishes, able to suck in all the bad vibes in the cosmos simultaneously.) Was he the only one who *was* wired?

He sat up and opened the window a few more inches. When he lay back down he could just hear the soothing murmur of a neighbor's TV, then down the block the groan of an automatic garage door. As he closed his eyes he felt the anger backing up in his veins.

He used to cry. At night when his parents would yell at each other— mostly his dad—he'd sit in the far back of his closet under a pile of clothes crying with his hands pressed against his ears.

"Goddamn it, Sharon, can't you even balance a goddamn checkbook?"

"I thought I'd—"

"Twenty-five bucks every time you bounce a goddamn check!"

"Please, Carl."

"Where's your checkbook?"

"I told you I'm not going to talk to you when you're drinking."

"Give me your purse."

"Please lower your voice, Carl." Crying. The screech of a chair being pushed aside.

Andrew pressed harder against his ears.

"Give it to me now, you dumb bitch!"

Crash.

And then the day in third grade when he came home from school and his dad was gone. At first he thought they'd been robbed. The TV and stereo were missing and the house was a mess, with all the dresser drawers in his parents' room opened. In a panic he called his mother at work.

"Oh my God," she'd said. "Your father's left us."

He didn't believe it at first. Not until he went into his room and saw the note on his bed.

Andy,
I'm not sure how to explain this to you, but your mother and I
haven't been getting along too well and I've decided to move out and
get my own place. You're just going to have to trust me that it's
better for all of us. Sorry I didn't have a chance to say good-bye, but

I'll call you when I get settled and you can come and visit, all right? So be tough and take care of your mother, okay Tiger?

Dad

But he didn't call. Not the first week. When Andrew's mom finally handed him the phone nine days later the voice on the other end sounded distant and slurred. "Now don't start bawling on me, Tiger." He called again three days later, then once a week, then once or twice a month, always promising things that never happened.

Andrew stopped going into his closet after that. Instead he'd just lie in bed and cry, not even meaning to or knowing when it would start or how he could ever stop it. But one night he couldn't cry anymore. He was *empty*.

He rolled over on his back, watching the light from a street lamp press through the curtains. He tried to imagine Grandma sitting in the corner sewing those curtains, working her wrinkled fingers over every stitch. He could recall her hands perfectly: the large brown splotches, the green veins snaking between the knuckles, the way her fingers curled this way and that like they'd all been broken a dozen times.

He put his headphones back on and turned up the CD as loud as it would go until his body rocked back and forth beneath the sheets. They understood. He could tell by the sounds and lyrics that they'd been there. That's how he knew that he wasn't alone; that there were others out there. Man, thank-fucking-God for that.

Music was basically the only thing that wasn't bullshit. It said *everything*. Ever since he got his first radio when he was eight he could hardly get enough of it. He loved singing, too. Sometimes when he was in the shower he'd sing so loud that his mother would bang on the door. "Time for school, Pavarotti." He spent hours strutting around his room with his stereo cranked, howling into his hairbrush and hitting the notes just perfectly. He knew he had a good voice; maybe even a great one. When he was little he'd been in the choir at church and sweaty Ms. Swanson frequently complimented him. "You have a gift, young man," she'd say, pinching his bright red cheek.

Only there wasn't much he could do with his gift. He quit the church choir in sixth grade after blowing his debut solo at the Christmas concert—he'd been so paralyzed with fear that he began hyperventilating—and he wasn't about to sing at school, where being in the choir was not only seriously uncool but infested with sexual implications. He thought about trying to start some sort of band—Matt played the clarinet when he was younger and could keep a beat—but Andrew couldn't imagine getting up in front of people—not unless he was drunk. (Going to the blackboard was misery enough.) Besides, he didn't have enough friends to form a band. So instead he sang in the shower and in his room and on the way to school—if no one was around—and at Matt's prodding he began keeping a notebook in which he wrote lyrics.

He'd been singing the first time he really got beat up. It was the second week of fifth grade and he was walking home from school while slowly working his way through "Sunshine on My Shoulders" (his mom was a huge John Denver fan and Andrew had Denver's entire playlist involuntarily embedded in his brain). He'd scanned the block for pedestrians, but somehow he got so caught up in the lyrics that the Laffley brothers, who were several years older and ruled a four-block area between Andrew's house and school, managed to creep up behind him. Just as he was hitting the high notes—*makes me crrryyyyy*—they pounced, locking his left arm up behind him before flagging down every kid for miles and demanding Andrew sing.

"Take it from the top, Sunshine," they said with hoots of laughter, thereby creating the nickname that would haunt him for years.

"Let me go," he cried as a swelling crowd of kids formed an expectant semicircle.

The Laffley brothers lifted his arm inch by inch until he was fighting tears.

"Sing it, Sunshine."

Andrew searched all the faces, looking for help. But he only saw smiles.

After that he seemed to get picked on more and more—mostly with words, sometimes with fists, until he felt like a target every time he passed by a group of classmates. He didn't tell his mother. Years earlier he stopped telling her things like that, not wanting to upset her any more than she already was. Even as a child he could sense that she had her hands full just fending for herself—she always seemed to be getting fired and he figured it was because of trying to take care of him, making her late for work—and he was determined to show her that he could look out for himself just fine. He didn't want her to leave too.

He'd always been a loner, keeping such a low and cautious profile that he often thought of himself as a Special Forces commando slithering through each day. But it wasn't until sometime in the middle of fifth grade that he realized he'd been ostracized; that he'd always be alone, that he could no longer pretend he was a loner by choice. As far as he could tell, it was like, one day when he wasn't looking everybody in the school had a secret meeting and paired into lifelong cliques, passing out various codes and inside jokes. Once, when he was younger, he felt like part of the class; invited to all the birthday parties, included in games at recess. Then suddenly it was nothing but tribes and packs and clans and he couldn't find anywhere to squeeze in, not until he met Matt, and even then he still felt alone because their friendship was based on loneliness.

For a couple of years he pretended that he didn't care, that when he headed down the hallway at school or crossed the yard he was going somewhere important; that he had other plans and friends. But once he went to Montrose High there was no more faking it. You can't hide your status in high school. People know just by looking at you. At first all the unspoken rules and rituals of high school completely baffled him. Just figuring out where among the bike racks an unpopular freshman should park in the morning was trauma enough; running the gauntlet between classes was almost unbearable. Can I piss safely at the urinal if flanked by two juniors? If a bunch of jocks are blocking my locker (to his horror, his locker was situated right in the middle of a hallowed stretch known as football row) should I attempt to politely squeeze through and get my books, or is it better to go to the next class unprepared, but unmolested? He spent hours trying to figure out exactly where the boundaries were, where he could and could not set foot. Then one day he got it; he cracked the code. It all came down to numbers.

It was breathtaking to suddenly see everything so clearly, to understand exactly what high school was really all about. And yet it depressed him enormously too. Because from then on, there was no escaping the *stupid fucking numbers.* Every day when he stood with his lunch tray at the cafeteria wondering where to sit he could see them; the all-important rankings that were updated hourly and written right on the calculated expressions of every student from number 1—Sue Richards, the prettiest girl in the school—to 3,000—Bill Humphrey, who at two hundred and eighty buttery pounds was the undisputed social caboose of the entire student body. The kids in the top thirty sat at one table while those from roughly thirty-one to sixty sat at another. Once the higher numbers sorted themselves—and it was an effortless, almost instinctual process—the lowest-ranked kids, the untouchables, shared whatever empty tables were left. And so every day as Andrew stood holding his lunch tray, he'd anxiously scan the tables to see where he belonged, which meant first eliminating all the tables where he didn't belong.

For years he worshipped the most popular kids, trying desperately to imitate everything they did and said, hoping that someday, somehow, he would be initiated into the elite. He studied what they wore and how they walked and even the way they laughed and scowled. But it was a joke trying to be like them. Because no matter what he did he never could. Not even close. And then he started hating them. Every time he saw them clustered at the best tables having all the fun he hated them. He hated their expensive clothing and their perfect hair and teeth and their beautiful faces and trophies and cars. But most of all he hated them for making fun of people like him.

One to three thousand, plain as day right on every student's face. There was no hiding from the numbers. Maybe you could keep it from your parents, but not from other kids. For some reason Andrew always thought of himself as number 2,888, well below Matt—not that it really mattered once you were anywhere below five hundred, which was social oblivion—but above complete losers like Phil Lubman and Beth Rodriguez and Stuart Smith, whose nervous ticks and physical deformities were surpassed only by Bill Humphrey's endless rolls of smelly fat. Yes, everyone could see Andrew's ranking just by looking at him. Even Andrew could see it.

He could still remember the morning, standing before the mirror in the tiny bathroom with the peeling yellow ceiling that he shared with his mother, when he first realized he was ugly. It was as though one day he was just this kid like every other kid, shy and quiet, but physically average, and the next he was ugly. *So that's why they don't like me,* he thought, standing there at the mirror with tears coming down his stupid ugly face. He looked at his ears from different angles, wondering why he'd never noticed just how *obvious* they were, like they belonged on a much bigger head. Then he studied his teeth, which were all bunched up in the front of his small mouth (braces in sixth grade would straighten them, but not improve the overbite that made him look like a braying donkey when he smiled). He stood back and looked at his face from one side, then the other.

No matter how he tried to push out his jaw, his chin just sort of disappeared into his neck as if he was wearing a muffler. In a panic he leaned into the mirror and examined his nose. Straight enough, but a bit short, so that the nostrils looked slightly flared. Jesus, have I always looked like this?

He switched the bathroom light off, then on again and reexamined his face. Ahhh! I can't have morphed overnight. Yet everywhere he looked the proportions were wrong. His muddy brown eyes seemed a little too far apart and lacked any of the power he'd started noticing in other people's eyes; his shoulders were small and severely sloped, like a broken hanger; his skin was getting greasier by the day. In short, he was one ugly fuck. He turned off the light again, then sat on the toilet, dropped his head into his hands and cried, feeling as if a terrible mistake had been made and he'd been assigned the wrong face. And that's when he realized that there'd be hell to pay for *years*.

Some days, standing there before the mirror after school, it was all he could do to keep from trying to peel his face right off. He came to think of it as a mask behind which he was imprisoned. People could look at him, but they couldn't see him, and that explained almost everything. Nobody picks on you if you're good looking. It's like *armor.* Good-looking people are practically celebrities. They get *everything.* But if you've got an ugly face, it's just flies to shit.

Sitting in Spanish class, he couldn't decide which was worse: having Cori Fletcher (a genetically perfect goddess he'd been tracking since fourth grade) look at him—especially when his face was all broken out—or being ignored by her. He tried to sit right behind her and he would spend the entire period staring at the back of her neck and bartering with the devil. (One minute of free reign with the soft flesh just behind her ear—oh, to bury his face in there and never come out!—for five years in burning hell. What do you say, Satan?) If she could only see him for what he could be—what he *would* be—instead of what he was! *Look at me, Cori. No, not my face, at* me. *Look all the way inside me.* But she didn't see him. None of them did. And that right there told him that God was a big, fucking joke.

He rolled back on his stomach, remembering the feel of the knife in his hand and the power that he felt shaking it right in Kevin Bremer's stupid face. *Now who's scared?* Wasn't even like it was him holding it. And yet everything in his whole life seemed to lead up to that moment; being pushed around on the playground and on the way to school, pushed in the hallway, pushed during P.E. Then one day Sunshine pushed back.

Surprise.

First he just started sleeping with it, like for good luck, wanting its power to rub off on him. He loved the smoothness of its handle and the shiny brilliance of the blade, sharp and deadly as anything. It wasn't until Matt died—until after they'd killed him with all their taunts—that Andrew started carrying it in his front pocket, desperate for the companionship. Just knowing it was there made all the difference when he set off to school each morning, bracing for blows. *If only you knew,* he thought. *If only you knew.*

He lay listening to the CD for a while, still watching the light from the street lamp creep around the edges of the orange curtain. Gradually the volume faded. He checked the dial: still on full. Must be the batteries. That's what he'd forgotten to pack: the adapter. *Shit.*

He took his palms and pressed the headphones against his ears, desperate for sound. *Why'd you leave me, Matt? Why?* And then closing his eyes he saw the whiteness of Matt's face again and felt the coldness of his cheeks as he shook his head back and forth trying to wake him. *Wake up, Matt! Please oh please wake up.*

He held the headphones to his ears until the music died, then curled up on his side and rocked himself to sleep.

Chapter 2

By 9 A.M. Mead was worried. What if the boy had sneaked out the window or done something crazy? He thought of a red-haired fellow from Pittsburgh—ammo carrier for a BAR team, strong as an ox—who wandered off into the woods near their bivouac in Germany just after mail call, let out a bloodcurdling roar, then pulled the pins on two grenades and blew himself up, after learning that his fiancée had run off with a musician. And three weeks later Hitler was dead.

Mead listened again at the door, paced the living room a few more times, then decided to knock.

No answer.

"You alive in there?"

Silence.

"Andrew?"

Finally the creaking of the bed frame, which reminded Mead of Sophie rising from one of her afternoon naps. The only time she slept there was during her naps, dozing off for half an hour after lunch, then longer and longer in the last years, until he'd wait longingly for the sound of the creaking that signaled that she was awake. And then he'd hurry into the kitchen and make an iced tea with a wedge of lemon and sprinkling of sugar and bring it to her, sitting next to her on the edge of the bed and admiring whatever she'd made that day, until finally her gnarled hands could no longer make anything.

"Yeah?"

"You still sleeping?"

Pause. "I was."

Mead looked at his watch. "Well, I'd say it's high time to get up. You eat cereal don't you? Got Cornflakes and oatmeal. Might even have some Product 19."

"Yeah, cereal's okay." Another pause. "Do you have soy milk?"

"For crying out loud." Mead leaned his forehead against the door, trying to calm himself. "We'll go shopping after breakfast, how's that?"

"Sure, whatever. I don't have to have milk. I'm not even hungry."

Mead hesitated, staring down at the door handle. "I'll be in the living room."

Andrew was polite enough during the trip to Vons, pushing the cart and offering to carry everything. But he didn't talk. On the drive to and from the store Mead couldn't get more than single-sentence answers from him, and they were barely audible. And the thing was, there was nothing to talk about. Mead racked his brain trying to think of topics. Sports, of course. But the boy wasn't interested in sports. He didn't seem to care about the Lakers or Bulls or Cubs or Cardinals. And that was a big warning light right there: a sixteen-year-old boy who didn't care about sports. Mead tapped his fingers on the steering wheel.

Girls? Mead wasn't about to go down that road with his grandson, though it was certainly the primary preoccupation when he was sixteen. He remembered the first time he saw Sophie, no sweater girl but cute as all get out in her bobby socks and skirt, with a softly waved shoulder-length bob of blond hair framing her warm and open face. Mead smiled to himself as he remembered the first time he ran his hand under her blouse, his fingers trembling at the unbearable softness, afraid he might hurt or scratch her. He slammed the brakes at a stop sign, just barely avoiding the car in front of him. Jesus, watch the road. His grandson gave him a funny look.

So what else was there? Hobbies? The boy didn't seem to have any, aside from knives. He glanced down at Andrew's small soft hands, still the hands of a child, no veins showing. Boys not much older were hurled against Fortress Europe, rolling it back one stubborn German at a time. (And those sons of bitches could fight.) Mead always thought of the war as a sort of kiln in which his generation had been fired—at least those who survived. But today? Seems like they take forever to grow up, still babies at nineteen and twenty, expecting handouts. By God, he thought, it's going to be a long three weeks.

As they pulled into the driveway Evelyn was out front watering her flowers.

"I get the feeling she likes you," said Andrew.

Mead glared at him.

Andrew smiled. "You have to admit she's nice."

"That'll be enough."

Evelyn waved as they got out of the car, then signaled for them to wait and dashed into her house. Moments later she emerged with a large red cookie tin.

"Great, I'm starving," said Andrew, trotting across the street.

Mead watched as Evelyn and Andrew chitchatted like a couple of old hens. It was the first time he'd seen his grandson so animated. Was it a raisin thing?

"These are even better," said Andrew as he returned triumphantly with the tin. After they unpacked the groceries Andrew asked if there was anything else Mead wanted him to do before he went to his room.

"Come to think of it, the grass could use a trim."

Andrew nodded without expression. "Where's the mower?"

"In the garage." Mead gestured toward the door off the hallway that led to the garage, then stopped Andrew. "It can wait another day." He forced himself to smile. "I've got a basketball hoop out front. Brand new. Ball's in the garage. I thought maybe you'd like to throw a few hoops?"

"Maybe later."

"Sure, later."

They stood facing each other.

"Listen, I know this wasn't your idea to come here. . . ."

Andrew stared down at his feet, one hand fiddling with his earring.

"I just want to say that . . . well, I'm pretty damn upset about this whole business."

"Sorry." Andrew started for his room.

"Where are you going?"

"I was going to read."

"I'm *upset,* you got that?"

"Yes."

"And I don't like you moving things around in there too much."

"I'll move everything back."

Mead hesitated. "Well, hell, you might as well not move them back now if you've got things set up the way you want them. Just don't do any more moving. Be careful with things, you got that? It's your *grandmother's* room."

"Yeah, I got that." Andrew turned and headed down the hallway. "Thanks for getting the veggie burgers," he said before closing the door.

. . .

Sixteen. Mead tried to remember what he felt like when he was sixteen but there was no comparing it. He slumped down into his chair and closed his eyes, recalling his sixteenth birthday. June, 1940—a downpour in Akron and somewhere beyond the fields and factories the world was catching on fire. Less than two years later his brother Thomas would be dead, his cruiser sunk by two torpedoes in the Pacific. After that all Mead cared about was getting into the army. He remembered heading proudly down to the recruiting station on his eighteenth birthday, destiny all over his boyish face. *I'll get 'em back, Thomas.* And then the physical and the swearing in and that first time he looked at himself in the mirror wearing his crisp new uniform, feeling a part of the biggest thing ever, ready to save the world, hometown girls falling at his feet.

He listened to the sound of Sophie's door opening, then the bathroom door closing, then the loud rush of urine.

Sixteen. Mead had killed sixteen-year-olds. Even younger. Because at the end, that's all Hitler had left to throw at them. Children.

"They're coming!"

Mead peered over the top of his foxhole in horrified fascination as two dozen screaming Germans emerged from the woods and charged across a snow-covered field. Mead began on the far left, aiming and firing at chest level. One down, then another, then a third, who tried several times to get back on his feet until Mead shot him again. But the rest were closer now. Forty yards, then thirty, then twenty. Mead heard a shout from the foxhole to his right and then cries for help. He kept firing frantically as the concussion from a grenade ripped off his helmet and momentarily blinded him, blood streaming down his nose. He blinked several times as he struggled to reload, then aimed again at another German, hitting him in the shoulder. Another concussion snapped against Mead's eardrums but he kept firing, this time at point-blank range.

And then it was over. Two dozen Germans dead and wounded on the snowy field, their bright, red blood seeping into the downy whiteness. Hitler's boys.

The toilet flushed, then a minute later the bathroom door opened and Sophie's door closed.

He'd spent years trying to forget the faces, their little bodies twisted this way and that where they fell, as if part of some enormous Aztec sacrifice. Sometimes he'd be in a store or at the beach and he'd see a face that would stop him in his tracks; a face that accused him, even in its ignorance. He particularly remembered one young German boy who looked just like a kid who lived down the street when he was growing up. He was lying in the snow on his back bleeding from his gut and crying, and Mead briefly caught his eye before hurrying on because there simply wasn't time to help. When he passed back that way the next day the boy was frozen solid, arms still reaching for the sky.

By January the Ardenne was littered with frozen bodies, some still at their guns so that you'd shoot them to be sure they were dead. Mead felt himself shiver, the memory of coldness biting through his overcoat and gloves and his double-sole woolen socks and wool-knit cap and the bed-sheets he'd wrapped around himself like a scarf. Coldest winter in years, so that you didn't dare breathe on your weapon for fear it would freeze up.

Bitte, hilf mir.

He could recall the German boy's frozen face perfectly, the way the frost gathered around the eyes and nostrils and mouth and the bluish tint of the lips and ears. There were dozens of faces that he could never forget; faces that hounded him over the years like unwelcome visitors pounding at the door. And Mead had spent his whole life leaning his shoulder against the other side, praying the locks would hold. *Just leave me be.* For years he'd managed to keep them out. By piling everything he could find against the door he'd kept the faces from breaking in and overwhelming him. But he always knew they were out there; faces of friends and enemies and the living and the dead pressed against the door, demanding to be seen.

Mead massaged his temples with his two forefingers, then got up and walked over to the couch, figuring he'd stretch out for a few minutes. Just not used to being around teenagers. Or maybe it's the new thyroid medication. He carefully removed his wire-frame glasses, folded them and placed them on the coffee table, then clasped his hands over his belly and closed his eyes. He tried to think of the latest American League West standings and then congratulated himself on how nice the lawn looked, thick and dark green. Then he remembered his retirement party and how embarrassed he'd been when he fell apart during his little speech. Finally he tried to recall in correct order the winning teams of the first ten Super Bowls. Okay, that's better. Take it nice and easy. Now let's see, was it Green Bay or Oakland in 1968? But he felt it coming. No matter what he tried to think of he felt it coming, and before he could stop himself he was suddenly back in the well-furnished chalet in Berchtesgaden, Germany, May 1945, reaching for his pistol. And then he saw him. For the first time in years he saw the young German with the brown eyes and the large forehead and small chin standing there looking at him in disbelief. *You wouldn't would you? Oh yes, but I would.* How long had they stared at each other in stricken silence? Thirty seconds? A minute? And then in a momentary fury, it was over.

Hans Mueller.

Mead could still see the angular scrawl of the German's signature on the inside page of his worn *Soldbuch*—military pay book. And he remembered the Luger and the medals and the wristwatch and the black leather wallet filled with photos; treasured little snapshots of mother and father and sister and girlfriend all waiting for Hans Mueller to return. And he could have returned. Yes, Hans, you could have returned.

Bang.

Mead opened his eyes and sat up, feeling his heart going so fast he wondered if he was having a heart attack. He took several deep breaths and rubbed the bridge of his nose before putting his glasses back on. Jesus, get hold of yourself. He got up and walked back to the kitchen and took four medicine bottles down from the windowsill, trying to still the tremors in his hands as he struggled with the tops. After parceling out his dose he poured himself a glass of water and swallowed the pills before replacing the caps. Then he rinsed the glass, dried it and placed it back on the shelf before heading out to the backyard to scrub down the grill. But no matter how hard he worked his hands he couldn't stop thinking about the chalet in Berchtesgaden and the final expression in the young German's face.

Please, just leave me be.

. . .

At least he had batteries. His grandfather had bought him an eight-pack and Matt had taught him that if you boiled the batteries in water they'd recharge a few times. (So long as they didn't explode.) Of course, he'd have to wait until Sarge was out of the house. Did he ever go out? What did he do all day besides read the paper and play darts and clean the barbecue? Talk about needing a life.

Andrew was horny and debated masturbating. It seemed a little weird to do in his grandparents' house, even potentially sinful. But three weeks? He couldn't remember the last time he went three days, except when he had the flu. (After forty-eight hours the first symptoms of an imminent nervous breakdown would appear, requiring immediate action.) Maybe later. He shuffled through his CDs, put one into the player and flopped down on the bed, wishing he had his PlayStation.

He checked his watch and thought of his classmates sitting in school. He'd be in Spanish now, staring at Cori Fletcher and thinking that if she wouldn't even bother to look at him then what was the point of existing? They'd all be talking about him still, laughing at what a mental case he was, pulling a knife on Kevin Bremer and getting expelled. He felt the burning in his face again and turned up the volume on his CD player.

Would they let him back to school next year? What if they sent him to prison, or worse, reform school? Or maybe they'd punish him by keeping him back a year? He'd kill himself, right on the spot. He wondered what kind of pills Matt had taken and where he could get some. In a way it was comforting to know that Matt was always there waiting for him; that any time he wanted to he could join him, like having a secret escape hatch. But he didn't want to join him. Not yet. He kicked his shoes off, wondering what the school would decide. No matter what, they'd always be watching him; he'd be under scrutiny forever. He clenched both fists and closed his eyes tight, wanting to smash something. Did his dad know yet? He wondered if his mom had called him. What would he say? Or would he even care?

He thought of their last conversation three months earlier when his dad had called from Texas.

"Your mother says you're failing at school."

"I'm not exactly failing."

"You don't call two Ds failing?"

"I got a C in—"

"Listen, buster, I want those grades up by next semester, you got that?"

"Okay."

"Good. You bring home some As and Bs and we'll go fishing. How 'bout it?"

He was always offering to take Andrew fishing, only they never went. Not since Andrew was a kid. He could still remember the one trip they took to Wisconsin, setting up the little pup tent and cooking the fish they'd caught right in the campfire wrapped in tin foil. It was the greatest feeling in the world, waving good-bye to Mom and sitting in the front seat of Dad's red Jeep Cherokee with his new tackle box on his lap, heading off on an adventure, just the two of them. But then he'd ruined it, thinking he'd heard a bear the first night—*something* was snorting around the tent—and getting so hysterical his dad took him home the next morning, saying he wasn't man enough to camp. "Hell, you're still a damn baby."

Fuck him too. Fuck all of them. He put his palms together and pressed as hard as he could while clenching his jaw. Anyway, none of it matters. Even the whole planet hardly matters when you think of how big the universe is, which was the best thing about getting stoned because you could really *feel* the bigness.

Matt understood that. He understood everything. They'd been best friends ever since a winter afternoon in seventh grade when Andrew discovered that his book bag had been filled with snow and Matt helped him empty it out and dry his homework, thereby destroying any chances of his own social rehabilitation. But Matt figured he'd never be accepted anyway. He had too many demons to really belong. Yeah, Matt understood all about the demons, maybe even more than Andrew, and knowing that he understood made everything bearable again.

Retaliation had been swift. Andrew and Matt were walking home together the next day when they were both hit by a fusillade of ice balls. Matt fell to the ground crying with a bloody nose while Andrew scrambled to gather ammunition and prepare a defense. Only he never saw who threw them or where they came from. The enemy was *everywhere*.

"We'll get them back," said Andrew, helping Matt to his feet. "I swear we'll get them back."

Matt was slight like Andrew, only shorter, with curly black hair and dark green eyes set close in his thin face. He was smarter too, always reading all sorts of books to see if things were really as desperate as they seemed. Whenever they got stoned together Matt would quickly pare their options in life down to two rather bleak choices.

"Look, you and I know that life is basically a lot of bullshit, right?"

"Right."

"So the way I see it, we've got two choices."

Andrew held in a chest full of smoke, then let out a loud exhale. "I remember that part, I just forget what the choices are."

"It's simple: either we pretend we don't realize what a big joke everything is, which means we've got to be total fakes like everybody else, or we don't pretend."

"So what happens if we don't pretend?"

"Then we're fucked."

"Pass the joint."

Matt's dad was as unpredictable as Andrew's. Sometimes he was the nicest man Andrew had ever met, building a model rocket with them—it blew up midflight, which was depressing but still kind of cool—and taking them ice skating and to the auto show, and other times he'd be sitting in the living room watching TV and if anyone so much as made a peep he'd start throwing beer bottles. Twice he gave Matt a black eye and by eighth grade Matt no longer invited anybody to his apartment. Instead, they hung out either at Andrew's where they could play video games and listen to music, or in the forest preserve near the freeway where they had a stash of stolen cigarettes, liquor, firecrackers and dirty magazines that they kept buried in a plastic container. That's where they'd been: the forest preserve, tucked into their sleeping bags and knowing nobody could find them.

Wake up, Matt.

They lived only five blocks apart in nearly identical ugly brick apartments with graffiti covering all the Dumpsters and scowling old ladies perched on their little patios monitoring every movement. You didn't belong in certain circles when you lived in an apartment. No one said anything, it was just understood. Matt could draw almost anything and he would spend hours sketching floor plans of great big houses with dens and TV rooms and sunken Jacuzzis and saunas and pools and patios and rec rooms with pool tables and air hockey and Ping-Pong and the latest arcade games. To Andrew, there was nothing better than sitting in the forest preserve on a warm afternoon sipping from the bottle of Southern Comfort that Matt stole from his father and arguing over plans for the houses they would build, houses that would sit side by side on a cul-de-sac in Hollywood or South Beach or Aspen.

"We're talking total soundproofing," Matt would say, putting the finishing touches on his living room. "Built-in speakers *everywhere*."

Andrew imagined himself walking room-to-room in a house full of built-in speakers, the guitars and drums and lyrics welcoming him everywhere he turned, like he was strolling around inside his own head. *Someday.*

Matt was the only person Andrew had ever met who was even more sensitive than he was, like he was always walking barefoot across gravel. Though not quite as ugly as Andrew, Matt was picked on for being short and for being different, wearing nothing but black and dying his hair green and wearing a stud in his tongue. He never fought back. When the bullying started he'd just curl up into a ball and plot his revenge. His theory was that people either went through total hell as kids or as adults, so he figured they were just getting the bullshit over with early. "You'd better be right," said Andrew as they lay side by side on their backs in the forest preserve getting stoned after school.

For a while they tried to hang out on the fringes, like stray dogs seeing how close they can get to the barbecue without being kicked. But they quit even trying after they were beaten up one afternoon by a group of jocks in the parking lot of the McDonald's where everybody hung out after school.

"Here come the Beanie Babies," said a voice as they approached.

Matt looked over at Andrew, pain in his face.

"Just ignore them," Andrew whispered, hoping for a glimpse of Cori.

They tried to casually meld in, hands shoved deep into their pockets and feet shuffling back and forth. Matt wore a black knit cap and lit a cigarette with a flick of his Zippo, which had a skull and crossbones on it. Andrew saw Cori huddled in a cluster of girls and tried to catch her eye. Jesus, she was absolutely perfect. What was it like being so perfect? He imagined kissing her right on the tip of her adorable little nose and then scooping her up into his arms. *Argh . . .*

"Hey Sunshine, what's with the Salvation Army shoes?"

Andrew pretended he didn't hear, slowly trying to move away from a nearby pack of jocks without triggering the chase instinct. But it was true, they were dorky shoes. No matter how many times he begged his mother, she wouldn't buy him the right brand.

"You think I'm spending eighty dollars on a pair of sneakers? Dream on." So he wore the cheap imitation ones, and every morning when he slipped them on his feet he felt the shame running right up his legs.

"Are you like, in mourning or something?" said another jock, gesturing toward Matt's black clothing. "Or is your mother some kind of vampire?"

Andrew and Matt backed off a little more, dropping their heads low between their shoulders and trying to look at nothing. All the girls were watching now.

"Hey Shorty, how about a couple of bucks for a burger?" said Bremer, who was an enormous junior and easily the biggest prick on the planet.

"Fuck off," said Matt.

Oh shit, thought Andrew. "Come on, let's go," he whispered.

"I think Shorty here wants to get his ass kicked," said Bremer, walking up to Matt, who was half his size.

"Leave him alone," said Andrew.

"You shut up, Sunshine." He turned back to Matt. "So how about it?"

"I said, fuck off."

Bremer shoved Matt backward a few times, then hit him in the stomach, causing him to double over. Matt didn't fight back. Instead he just buckled and fell to the ground as Bremer kept punching him. Andrew wanted to run. He wanted to run and never stop running. But as all the fear and hatred welled up in him he suddenly lunged at Bremer, swinging wildly. Instantly he was in a headlock being slowly twisted to the ground, finally dropping down like a calf, barely breathing as he caught a glimpse of Cori out of the corner of his eye. He hardly even felt the blows.

Two days later Matt called Andrew to announce that he had the perfect plan. First, they'd need lots of weed killer, which they purchased from several hardware stores in different neighborhoods to avoid suspicion. The following Saturday night Matt stayed at Andrew's for a sleepover. Once Andrew's mom went to bed they quietly played PlayStation in the living room until 2 a.m., then dressed, turned off the lights, crept outside and rode their bikes to the school where they'd stashed ten jugs of weed killer in green garbage bags they'd hidden in the bushes near the football field.

"Just do what I say," said Matt, pulling out a large diagram and tape measure from his pockets. He had also brought along a bottle of Coke heavily spiked with Bacardi, from which he took a large swig before handing it to Andrew.

"Why won't you tell me what it's going to say?" asked Andrew, carefully pouring out another bottle of weed killer as he crouched on the grass beside Matt and followed his instructions.

"You'll just have to wait and see. Now make a sharp ninety degree turn there and go down another three feet." Matt crawled along on his hands and knees, the diagram between his teeth. "Perfect!"

The next Saturday Matt and Andrew attended their first high school football game. "We are ass-deep in enemy territory," whispered Andrew as they waded through the crowds of jocks and wannabes. Cori passed right by him but he couldn't catch her eye. He stared at her butt, hugged tightly by her jeans, and tried to imagine her in just her panties. *Marry me.*

"Come on." Matt led the way up the bleachers, stopping at the last row and letting out a whoop. Andrew turned and looked out over the field where large letters of dying brown grass spelled *Home of the cocksuckers.* It was their finest moment.

Bremer pegged them right away, nearly knocking out one of Matt's teeth the next week after school and then taking a crowbar to Andrew's bike, which his mother had given him for his fifteenth birthday.

"I still say it was worth it," said Matt, lisping through his swollen lips as he helped Andrew carry the pieces of his bike home.

"I'm going to kill him," said Andrew, quaking. "I'm going to fucking *kill* him."

Andrew and Matt spent hours fantasizing about precisely how they'd kill Bremer, how they'd torture and humiliate him before throwing his big hairy ass to the sharks or crocodiles or a pack of hungry pit bulls. (Each Christmas they begged their parents for a pit bull—or at least a rottweiler—to no avail.) It was the one thing they talked about almost as much as sex: ways to kill Kevin Bremer.

Big, tall and unbearably arrogant, Bremer looked about five years older than he was, with huge arms and a dark beard always just about three days old. He was not only the star fullback of the football team but he held the school record at the bench press—320 pounds—and drove a brand new blue-and-white Suzuki SuperSport motorcycle, which everyone figured was stolen. Andrew and Matt were in study hall with Bremer both their

freshman and sophomore years—they couldn't believe their misfortune—
and somehow Bremer singled them out the first day of school. "The
Beanie Babies," he called them. "Shorty and Sunshine." And the girls
loved Bremer. They got giddy over his big, stupid shoulders and his stupid
jokes and the way he swaggered onto the football field after half time like
he was going to save the whole fucking season. Andrew never understood
why the nicest girls, the ones he fantasized about night after night until he
was sore, could be attracted to a fuckhead like Bremer. And if it had to be
that way, why couldn't that be enough? Why did Bremer still have to pick
on *them?*

"The important thing is that he feels a lot of pain before he dies," said
Matt as they sat in the forest preserve getting stoned. "We can't just shoot
him in the head."

"Maybe we could poison him?"

"I still say the best thing would be to shoot him in the balls. That way
we don't even have to kill him. It wouldn't be homicide." He passed the
joint back to Andrew.

Matt had a point. They both lay back on the leaves imagining Bremer
without any balls, then Andrew pushed aside a small log and dug out the
plastic container that held their stash.

"I'll take the *Hustler,*" said Matt. Andrew tossed it at him.

"Careful!"

"You're the one who drools all over the pages." Andrew flipped through
their tattered copy of *Penthouse,* then glanced through two issues of *Play-
boy* before settling on *Gallery,* which had a memorable scene on page
forty-three. The stash also contained two packs of firecrackers, six bottle
rockets, three M-80s, two Bic lighters, four packs of Marlboros, two Gar-
cia y Vega cigars, a quart of Southern Comfort, rolling papers and a small
baggie of pot.

"Jesus, check this out," said Matt, handing the *Hustler* to Andrew.

"She's too skinny," said Andrew.

"Skinny? Are you crazy? She's *gorgeous!*"

Andrew stared intently at a photo of a redhead bending over a desk,
trying without success to place himself in her immediate vicinity.

"Oh God, this one kills me!" howled Matt.

"Quiet, I'm trying to concentrate." Andrew looked at a photo of the
redhead slipping into a hot tub. *Come take me, Big Boy. All of me.* Finally

he put down the magazine, relit the joint and handed it back to Matt, feeling utterly depressed. "I got a D on my science report," he said.

"Don't worry about it. I haven't even turned mine in."

"But you're good at science."

"I refuse to dissect a pig."

"You have to," said Andrew.

"No way. What are they going to do, kick me out of school because I won't butcher Piglet? What am I, a sushi chef? I mean, that just blows my mind."

"Everything blows your mind."

Matt took another hit, then coughed. "Especially this stuff."

"Speaking of mind-blowers, didn't I see you talking to Megan yesterday?" Matt had been madly in love with Megan Wynn for three years running, despite the fact that she wouldn't have anything to do with him. He spent hours talking about her, describing her lips and nose and ears and knees and the way she tossed her head to the side. "God, that kills me," he'd say, frequently collapsing into despair at the thought that he'd never get to so much as touch her. Unable to contain himself, he had even started writing her poems and letters, anonymous at first, then open declarations of his love because that was just the way Matt was; shy, but gutsy as hell at the same time. She was the one part of the world that he couldn't let go of, and Andrew sometimes thought that the only reason Matt even bothered to get up in the morning and shower was in case he ran into Megan.

Matt shrugged.

"I know I saw you talking to her." He elbowed Matt. "You didn't ask her out, did you?" Andrew burst into laughter, not meaning to but unable to deal with the idea of Megan and Matt on a date, which was a *real* mind-blower.

"Actually, I did," said Matt.

Andrew sat up. "No shit. What did she say?"

Matt shrugged again.

"Tell me. Tell me what she said."

"She told me I was a creep and to leave her alone."

"She said that?"

"And she said if I didn't stop writing her letters she'd call the police."

"No kidding?"

Matt's face twisted up as he tried not to cry. "She said I was stalking her."

"*Stalking* her? Jesus, that's bullshit."

"That's what she said, that I'm a creep and to stop stalking her." He dropped his head into his hands.

"Oh shit, buddy, don't listen to the crap. She couldn't have meant it."

"But she did. She meant every word."

Two weeks later Megan started going out with Bremer. A week after that Matt killed himself.

Wake up, Matt.

. . .

Sharon called that evening after getting back to Chicago.

"How are the boys?" she asked nervously.

"Just peas in a pod," said Mead, sitting on the edge of his bed and working polish into his shoes.

"Honestly, how is everything?"

"You didn't tell me he was a vegetarian."

"Oh jeez, I thought you knew. And he's terribly allergic to strawberries and bee stings."

"Anything else I should know?"

"It's not going well, is it?"

"We're just . . . getting reacquainted, that's all."

"Are you sure? Because if—"

"Of course I'm sure."

"I can't tell you how much I appreciate this, Dad. I don't know what I would have done."

Mead held his shoe up to the bedside lamp, admiring the gloss. "No trouble at all. You know your mother and I would do anything to help."

"I miss Mom. I keep thinking she'd know what to do, that this wouldn't have happened if she was still alive."

"I miss her too, Pumpkin."

"Has he told you anything yet?"

"I've learned quite a bit about tofu."

Sharon tried to laugh.

"You'll have to give us a little time."

"I'm so worried about him." She started crying again.

"Now, you just take care of yourself."

"He's not a bad kid, Dad. I haven't raised a bad kid."

"Of course you haven't."

"I don't know what I'll do if they decide to press charges."

"One thing at a time."

"He hates me, Dad. Andrew hates me."

"He doesn't hate you."

"But he does. He's never forgiven me for his dad leaving."

"Good riddance, if you ask me."

"And he's just horrible to the men I date."

Perhaps the boy's got some smarts after all, thought Mead.

"I don't know how to talk to him anymore. I can't even find him behind all that anger."

"He's a teenager. You can't talk to teenagers."

She took a deep breath. "I love you, Dad."

"I love you, too."

"Don't forget to remind him to work on his homework every night. His teachers gave him a big packet of assignments."

"I'll get on him. Now listen, you take care of yourself, you hear? And no cigarettes."

"I promise."

After he hung up Mead finished shining his shoes, then carefully replaced the wooden shoe trees before returning them to the floor of his closet, lined up from light to dark. Then he undressed, put on the light blue pajamas Sophie made for him and went to the bathroom, filling the sink with warm water. Once the temperature was right he leaned forward, cupped his hands and gently lifted the water to his face.

•   •   •

Andrew cut the lawn the next morning, stopping several times to talk with Evelyn. Mead peered cautiously out the window. What the hell could they be yacking about? After sending Andrew to his room to put in an hour of homework Mead gave the lawn a once-over, hitting all the spots his grandson had missed and getting the rows in nice neat diagonals running left to right.

"Evelyn's a real hoot, don't you think?" said Andrew over lunch.

"What do you mean by *hoot*?"

"She's cool. She cracks me up."

"I'm glad someone does."

"Her husband's dead, huh?"

Mead nodded.

"Do you guys ever like, do anything?" An annoying grin crept across the boy's face, smearing his features.

"What is that supposed to mean?"

"I'm just wondering if maybe you guys ever went to a movie or dinner or something?"

"The answer is no." Mead ate quickly, trying to avoid Andrew's inquisitive stare.

"Just asking."

After lunch Andrew shot baskets while Mead vacuumed, which gave him an excuse to inspect Sophie's room. As soon as he opened the door he felt a sense of panic. Andrew's things were heaped in a pile on top of his duffel bag, and the bed had been pushed into the corner where the sewing machine used to be and the rocking chair had been moved to the opposite corner near the door. The framed photographs were still there, but rearranged, and in the closet one of Sophie's dresses—the flowery blue-and-yellow one she made for their last trip to Hawaii, getting all dolled up for their anniversary—had fallen off its hanger and lay crumpled on the floor. Mead bent down, picked it up and carefully rehung it, then ran his fingers slowly along the row of dresses like a harpist. When he finished vacuuming he sat down briefly in the rocking chair, then went out and closed the door behind him.

Andrew was still out front throwing baskets. Mead watched him through the bay window in the living room, enjoying the rhythmic sound of the ball striking the cement. Yet his grandson obviously had no talent for the sport: he rarely made a basket and he threw with a sort of flailing of his arms, so that it was painful to watch.

Andrew missed a few more baskets, then put the ball away and came inside.

"Have a seat," said Mead, catching him before he could retreat to his room.

Andrew looked around nervously, finally settling on the edge of the sofa, ready to spring back up.

"Nice hoop, huh?"

"The hoop? Yeah, it's all right."

"Put it together myself."

"It's nice."

Long silence, both looking at anything but each other.

Mead swallowed and sat forward in his chair. "So, I'd say it's high time you and I had a little talk."

"A talk?"

"About this trouble you've gotten yourself into."

Andrew seemed to shrink into his T-shirt. "Not much to talk about."

"Oh, I think there is. I mean, it's a goddamn stupid thing you did." Mead hadn't intended on getting so angry but suddenly he couldn't help himself. "Pulling a knife on somebody? Who do you think you are, for Christ's sake, Marlon Brando?"

"Who's he?"

"An actor."

"I wasn't acting."

"I didn't mean *acting*." Mead rubbed his forehead. "Pulling a knife at school?" He made a snorting sound and leaned back in his chair, then forward again. "By God, they can lock you up for that kind of thing."

"I'm sorry."

"Sorry? That's all you've got to say?"

Andrew sat immobile.

Mead slammed his fist against his armrest. "You know the only time you ever pull a weapon on somebody? When you're going to use it. *That's* when you pull a weapon on somebody. You understand that?"

"Okay."

"What the hell do you understand?" Mead fell back into his chair again.

"I'm sorry."

"Do you have any idea what this is doing to your mother?"

"It has nothing to do with her."

"Like hell it doesn't. She's worried *sick* about you."

Andrew fidgeted nervously. "Can I go now?"

Mead felt flushed in the face, wondering what else to say. "I want you to do another hour of homework, you got that?"

Andrew rose to his feet. "Yes, I've got it," he said meekly as he crossed the living room and headed down the hallway.

. . .

Mead sat stewing in his chair after Andrew left. Shouldn't have lost my temper. But damn the boy. Who the hell does he think he is? Mead got up, straightened out the brown sofa pillows, then sat back down. Sharon had been far too soft on him. Sure it was hard without a father around, but still, she'd been too easy on him. Discipline, that's what he needs. They should never have done away with the draft. Of course, even the army isn't what it was. Hell, you could probably sue your D.I. for slander. Five guys died when Mead was at Benning. But then they were training to fight Germans and Japs.

Mead got up again and walked over to the mantle and picked up the wood-framed glass case that held his Purple Heart, his silver jump wings, his Bronze Star and his European Campaign Medal. Sophie had purchased the case for him, insisting he display some of his decorations. (She was so proud of them.) He carefully opened the case and pulled them out one at a time, placing them in his palm. On the back of the Purple Heart was the inscription FOR MILITARY MERIT, which always bothered him. Merit my ass, I got in the way of an 88.

He placed the decorations back in the case and closed it. Sophie had always had a certain awe for what he'd done. They all had, his family and friends and neighbors. Even if they couldn't really understand where he'd been and what he'd been asked to do, they honored him for it. But they were mostly gone now. And it wasn't a thing he ever talked about anyway. During all the hoopla for the fiftieth anniversary of D-Day Sophie had tried to get him to go back to France but he wouldn't. He hadn't set foot in Europe since 1945—and he'd be damned if he ever would.

For the first few years after he returned she tried to pry stories out of him, hoping to get her arms around what he'd been through so that she could understand him better. But she couldn't. Nobody could. Sure, he had lots of stories. Just none he wanted to tell. For years he privately slugged it out with the war, jabbing and weaving and bobbing and punching at all the images and sounds and faces that came howling back at unexpected moments. And then in the sheer exhaustion of it he'd found a sort of truce: you leave me be and I'll leave you. That was the deal. He'd kept his side of the bargain ever since, avoiding reunions and politely fending off inquiries. And nothing, absolutely nothing would change him now. He could never understand how other veterans could sit around at cocktail parties retaking every ridge and hedge over and over again. It was dishonest, he thought, reducing it to vignettes, as if combat had a story line. And they never told the whole truth anyway. Not nearly.

He gently rubbed his sleeve over the glass case, then pulled out his book of crossword puzzles, took a pencil from the silver holder he kept on the end table—always stocked with fresh, sharp pencils, tip down—and dropped into his chair, reaching into his breast pocket to pull out his bifocals. The first two words came easily enough, and then on the third he pulled out his crossword puzzle dictionary. But no matter how hard he tried he couldn't stop thinking about the faces at the door.

There was a time right after the war when he wasn't sure he could take it anymore. His mother had been the first to notice.

"I knew you wouldn't be the same," she said softly one evening during dinner a few weeks after he came home. "God knows, your father never was. But I always thought . . ." She struggled to maintain her composure, pushing her shoulders back and sitting up straight in her chair. "I always thought I'd still recognize you."

And then he'd started drinking too much, cutting back only after Sophie poured all the bottles down the drain one night in 1948 and threatened to leave him. "I won't live with a drunk," she'd said in tears. At her coaxing he began meeting with their minister once a week.

"I know exactly what you're feeling," said Reverend Hadding, who had been a chaplain with the Big Red One in Sicily, losing three fingers on his left hand. "I have my days too. We all do. It's a part of our lives. An unforgettable part, no doubt about that, but by golly we've got to keep living."

And that's what Mead had tried to do, aiming only for a simple and honest life; comfortable enough to assure Sophie's happiness. He worked hard at his engineering job—rising slowly up the ranks but never displaying a flair for management, in part because he had no desire to manage people. And he saved and he made sure to help Sophie with the church's annual canned food drive and he gave blood at least twice a year *(There's no more plasma, Captain)* and he always emptied his pockets for the Salvation Army and anyone else who seemed in need. Yet no matter how carefully he tried to walk in the shoes of a decent man, no matter how hard he tried to emulate the other veterans and put the past far behind him *(just let bygones be bygones),* he still caught glimpses of the faces over the years, glimpses that left him silent and shaken for days.

Mead and Sophie had been sitting by the pool of their hotel on their first trip to Hawaii when a group of German tourists came and sat next to them. There were three couples, all of them young and sunburned. Mead tried to ignore them at first, but the guttural sound of their voices soon

made him perspire. And then he looked at the young man closest to him—
maybe twenty, with a high forehead—and he saw the resemblance.

"What's wrong, Sweetie?" asked Sophie, looking over at him.

"I . . . nothing." Mead stared back down at his newspaper, trying to
quell the shaking of his hands. The German youth said something to his
girlfriend and then erupted in laughter.

"Are you feeling okay?"

"I'm fine." By now Mead's whole face was flushed.

Sophie got up from her lounge chair and sat on the edge of his, putting
her hand on his forehead. "Why, you're burning up. Do you think it's
something you ate?"

"Maybe I'll just go up to the room for a minute." He tried to block out
the string of German phrases coming from his left. *Nicht schiessen!*

"Let me help you. Should I get a doctor?"

"I'll be fine."

He'd spent the rest of the day in bed trembling with Sophie there holding him, and no matter how many times she asked he couldn't tell her why.

Mead put down the crossword puzzle and took off his glasses, feeling
unusually tired. He considered taking a nap, yet he always felt guilty
sleeping during the day. Better fire up Mr. Coffee again. Just half a cup.
He'd only closed his eyes for a moment when he felt himself falling. He
reached out to grab hold of something but it was too late.

• • •

Just getting into the plane was difficult, weighed down with more than 120
pounds of gear and already groggy from the airsickness pills. His jump
suit was stiff and itchy from the chemical treatment intended to protect
against poison gas and he kept nervously checking to make sure that his
equipment was properly tied down beneath his parachute harness and the
yellow Mae West life preserver. Unable to sit comfortably in the bucket
seat, he fell down to his knees on the floor and let his gear and chute rest on
the seat behind him, fear coursing through his insides. For the third time
that evening he mentally itemized everything: M1 rifle disassembled and
secured in a padded gun case strapped under his reserve chute; two ban-
doleers; a cartridge belt; a 45-caliber pistol; two cans of machine-gun
ammo; one Hawkins mine; an entrenching tool; a coil of rope, in case he
had to lower himself from a tree; an escape kit containing French francs, a

small hacksaw, a compass and a cloth map of France; a brass cricket; a gas mask strapped to his left leg; four blocks of TNT; two first-aid kits; a French phrase book; a jump knife, buck knife and trench knife; one canteen; two smoke and four fragmentation grenades; a Gammon bomb; clothes; two cartoons of cigarettes; *The GI Prayer Book* bound in imitation brown leather; toiletries and rations; Sophie's letters.

Again he felt the need to relieve himself. Too late now. Must just be nerves. He struggled to pull out and light another cigarette as they circled endlessly above England getting into V formation. Must be a thousand planes. How many would be shot down, maybe twenty, thirty percent? Just get me out of this plane alive—give me a fighting chance.

They'd spent the last days studying maps and aerial photos and three-dimensional models of Normandy, eagerly memorizing every road and gun emplacement. The briefings lasted hours, interrupted by the best meals they'd had in months—even ice cream with seconds—and they had a laugh saluting the men who strolled around the marshalling grounds wearing different German uniforms and carrying various weapons to help familiarize the troops.

Two hours after taking off they finally headed out across the Channel. So this is it. Everything comes down to this night. Mead lit another cigarette, a habit he'd only picked up weeks earlier, and began to itemize his gear again, starting with his rifle.

Once he satisfied himself that everything was secure and in place, he looked across the aisle at Jimmy Smith, but couldn't catch his eye. Known as Jimbo, the lanky Kentuckian came from a proud line of moonshiners and once made a thousand dollars in a single night of poker, which he promptly sent to his mother. He and Mead had become friends immediately when both realized they suffered from an intense fear of heights, which they desperately tried to hide from the others. "It's like I don't trust myself more than ten feet off the ground," Jimbo had whispered in his heavy drawl as they nervously climbed up one of the 250-foot towers at Benning for a practice jump.

Mead tried not to look down. "So why the hell did you volunteer for the airborne?"

"To get girls, why else?"

"Stupid question."

"What about you?"

Mead clung to a railing, hoping his knees wouldn't buckle. "I figured it would cure me of my fear."

"Has it?"

"Not yet."

During a final practice jump in Britain, Jimbo had crashed right through the glass panes of a country manor greenhouse, cutting himself in several places. (Another paratrooper died making a similar landing, the glass shards severing his carotid artery.) Despite stitches in his chin, forehead, hands and shins, he refused to be left behind, saying he'd be laughed right out of Kentucky for such a stunt. "You gotta understand, I *can't* go home without a good story," he explained. "I need a *real good story.*"

Jimbo was frequently teased by the men for his lack of education and extreme superstition—he once feigned sickness to avoid a live fire exercise on account of a warning he'd seen in his scrambled eggs that morning—yet he had more common sense than just about anybody in the company and a sense of intuition that had proven uncanny. Two men died that day. Just before D-Day word spread that Jimbo knew who would and who wouldn't be coming back.

"So what about you and me?" Mead had asked nervously.

"Oh, I could never say a thing like that," Jimbo had responded, avoiding Mead's eyes.

As the plane bounced Mead looked over at Jimbo, who sat in silence, eyes cast down, arms crossed over his reserve chute.

Behind German lines. That's where they'd be soon. Same thing as being surrounded. And those helpless moments floating down, no protection at all. Mead tried to ignore a sharp pain in his bowels. Landing in a lake would be the worst thing. They'd all agreed on that. He looked at his harness and gear and tried to figure how quickly he could get it off if he was sinking. No way. Not in time. Or would he land in a tree or on top of some building or straddling a wrought-iron fence? Jesus, it was just a crap shoot. No saying you weren't going to land right on the turret of a Panther tank.

He looked down the row of sullen faces lit only by the dim glow of a blue light. Mother of God, get me through this night.

Then more turbulence as they descended, everybody wincing at the sound of antiaircraft fire, which grew louder and louder until some men were covering their faces. Jimbo started vomiting all over his gear. "I can handle anything but this fucking bouncing," he moaned.

Looking out the open door near the rear Mead could see the red, green and blue tracers streaking past. The plane heaved as shells burst above, then below, and when flak raked the wings *smack smack smack* like hail against a tin roof they were ordered to stand up. Sixteen snap fasteners clicked as they hooked their static lines to the steel anchor cable running above the aisle, all eyes on the red light near the rear doorway. *Just get me out of the plane.*

"I'm dying," said Jimbo, trying to keep on his feet as he vomited again. The plane rocked hard to the left, slamming Jimbo against Mead, who clung to his static line for balance. "What the fuck are we waiting for?"

Finally green *Go! Go! Go!* and Mead was in the air, smacked by the prop blast *one-one thousand* as the chute crackled open overhead and the suspension lines and connector links hissed past his ears *two-one thousand,* then bracing for the opening shock of the canopy—*POP!* He looked up. *Thank God.* Then falling toward the angry sound of machine-gun and antiaircraft fire, desperately using his risers to steer away from the orange flashes and trying to make himself small and raising his knees up to cover his groin when he thought he was going to get it. *What if I land right on top of them? Oh, Jesus. Stay with me, Lord. Please stay with me.*

He was still trying to make out the ground when he landed, skidding briefly before frantically collapsing his chute. After unsnapping his reserve and harness he quickly rolled his canopy, stashed it in the underbrush and crawled behind a tree, straining to make sense of the shadows as he assembled his rifle. A bush? A cow? And that sound over there? Then more fire, much closer this time. He felt his pockets. Where's the goddamn cricket?

Above, the sky moaned with the low drone of planes. He stared in awe at the colored tracers and flak bursts and burning pieces of planes floating to the ground. He counted two planes with their engines on fire, then watched as another ran right into a flak burst, tearing apart. Jesus, what if the landings are repulsed? What if we're left here?

More small-arms fire on his right. A German burp gun. He recognized the sound from training, just like burping. He squinted and made out a figure sitting on the ground next to his chute and groaning.

"Broke my fucking leg."

Different company. Mead promised to tell a medic, then grabbed his gear, discarding his gas mask, and moved on, crawling through the brush on his knees. Where is everybody?

Across a small clearing he saw a figure hanging from a large tree. He crept closer until a white flash bounced off the clouds and illuminated the expressionless face of Louie Lathrop, a quiet but powerfully built college boy from California. His boots dangled just six feet from the ground.

"Louie, you okay?" Mead shook one leg, causing the body to sway. "Louie?"

And then the sound of German voices—*Amerikanische Fallschirmjäger!*—as Mead quickly crawled back into a thicket. A short burst of machine gun fire slapped across Louie's body, causing it to sway again. *Bastards.* Mead aimed his rifle at one of the dozen figures running past, fingering the trigger. Should I shoot? No way I can get them all. But I could get at least two of them. Two for one. Enough to win a war over time. He'd be expected to shoot. Certain death perhaps, but that's what he trained for, right? *War.* Only, his whole being recoiled. He raised his rifle, trying to blink the sweat from his eyes, then hesitated. Too late. The figures hurried down the road. How many Americans will they kill?

Mead remained hidden in the underbrush for several minutes looking at his compass and trying to figure out how far he was from the assembly point. He tried to recall every feature of the sand table model back in England as he searched the horizon for landmarks but nothing looked familiar. Damn it, where is everybody? Looking up, he saw another paratrooper floating to earth with what looked like coils of rope hanging down below him. Mead watched the American descend. Jesus God, entrails. Once the paratrooper hit the ground Mead ran over to help. The man was dead.

Then he heard cries from across the field. He ran toward the noise, crouching as he went and dropping to his stomach every few minutes to check for enemy movement.

"Help me," cried out a hoarse voice.

Mead ran the last few yards until he came upon an American lying on his back and cradling one arm to his chest. "Is that you, Jimbo?"

"Jesus, Mead. I lost my hand. I can't find my fucking hand!"

"Okay, just take it easy and let's have a look." Mead quickly removed the first-aid kit from his cartridge belt and leaned over Jimbo. Gently lifting Jimbo's good arm he saw that the other arm had been severed just above the wrist, exposing splintered bone as blood streamed out.

"It's gone. My hand is gone."

"You're going to be okay. I'm going to get you some help." Mead looked around but saw no one. Got to think. Okay, first stop the bleeding, then find a medic. Damn it, where is everybody?

"I think I'm dying, Mead. No kidding, I really think I'm dying."

"Hell, it's just a million-dollar wound, ol' buddy." Mead tried to steady his hands as he opened the first-aid kit and pulled out the cloth tourniquet, which he carefully tied two inches above the wound. Was it tight enough? He tried to remember the first-aid lectures but couldn't think clearly. Why hadn't he been given more training? He checked the tourniquet again, then opened a sulfa packet and sprinkled it over the stump, trying not to gag.

"I don't even have a story." Jimbo was crying now.

"Sure you do."

"I do?"

"Darn right, and it's a hell of a story. Now you just rest."

Jimbo looked confused. "I'm thinking so many things. You don't know all the things I'm thinking."

"How about thinking about that warm bed back in England while the rest of us sorry asses are over here."

"I hope my mother's not alone when they tell her. Since my father died she—"

"*Shh.*" Mead took off Jimbo's helmet and then put his hand on his forehead, which was still blackened with linseed oil. "Just think of all those nurses, you lucky bastard." Then he tried to bandage the wound, wincing as he wrapped gauze around the flesh and bone.

"I don't feel so good. I can't even move my legs."

Mead looked down at Jimbo's legs but saw no wounds. "You're just scared." Then he pulled out a morphine syrette, using his knife to cut an opening through Jimbo's clothing before jamming the syrette into his good arm.

Jimbo kept moaning, slowly rocking his head back and forth.

"You'll feel better soon." Mead opened his canteen and held it to Jimbo's lips. "You're going to be just fine, ol' buddy."

Jimbo stared up at him, his eyes still wild with fear. "I'm telling you, I really don't feel so good."

"Just give the morphine a minute. You won't feel a thing." Mead looked around again, suddenly wondering if any Germans were approaching. He reached for his rifle. "You just stay here a minute while I get some help."

Jimbo gripped Mead's arm with his good hand. "Don't go. I don't want to be alone."

"I've got to get help." Mead noticed that Jimbo's face was now draining white. Was the tourniquet tight enough? He undid it and tied it again, making sure the bleeding had slowed.

"I always figured it would be you," Jimbo whispered, now slurring.

"What are you talking about?"

"I always figured you'd get it, not me."

"Thanks a lot."

Jimbo tried to laugh, then started crying again. "I don't feel so good." His eyes rolled up toward the back of his head, then down again, trying to focus on Mead.

"You want some more water before I go?" Jimbo didn't answer. Then Mead saw the blood seeping into the ground beneath his head. *Oh no.* Mead gently rolled Jimbo onto his side and saw the piece of shrapnel protruding from the back of his neck.

"What is it?"

"Nothing, it's nothing," said Mead, trying to stop the quivering in his voice and using Jimbo's gear to prop him up on his side. His hands shook uncontrollably as he tried to think of what to do. Can't compress the wound because of the shrapnel. Should I try to pull it out or just bandage it?

"I can still feel my hand."

"Just be quiet, save your strength." Mead sprinkled sulfa powder on the neck wound, pulled out another syrette of morphine, opened it and shot it into Jimbo's arm.

"I want you to make sure my mother gets the insurance money, you got that? Tell her to pay off the house." Jimbo now struggled for breath. "And don't let Uncle Frankie touch a penny."

"You can tell her yourself."

"I'm thinking so many things, Mead."

"I'm going to get you some help, okay?"

"I've never thought about so many things before in my life."

"You just hold on for a few minutes and I'll be back."

"Ah Jesus, this is just gonna kill my mother."

"*Quiet.*" Mead scanned the horizon for signs of movement.

"It's ten thousand bucks, right? Ain't she gonna get ten thousand bucks? She could sure use the ten thousand, maybe paint the place and fix the roof. Goddamn roof's been leaking for years. . . ."

And then as Mead held Jimbo's face in his hands, he knew he was dead.

• • •

Andrew sat on the bed listening to his headphones and singing, keeping one ear partially uncovered to make sure he wasn't being too loud. Maybe he could save up for a Karaoke machine and make some demos. He imagined top music executives in Hollywood sitting around a large shiny conference table listening to him, their jaws dropping. *Who is this kid?*

He got up on his knees and looked out the window, squinting in the bright sun as he watched a small bird land on the edge of a little gray cement birdbath that stood in the middle of an overgrown vegetable patch, the one part of the narrow side yard that wasn't perfectly tended. The bird turned its head side to side, then looked over at Andrew.

"That you, Matt?"

The bird cocked its head quizzically, hopped a few times along the edge of the bath, then flew away.

Andrew turned the latch and opened the window, examining the screen. It would be easy enough to climb out without being noticed. But where would he go? There seemed to be nothing but old people in the neighborhood. It was like the quietest neighborhood in the world, as though everybody had slipped into a coma and it was just a matter of waiting for the relatives to show up and let out a scream.

He started to pry off the screen when a loud knock startled him.

"Thought we might go for a drive," said his grandfather from the other side of the door. "Maybe hit the beach."

Andrew quickly closed the window and sat at the desk. What would he do with his grandfather at the beach? "I've got a lot of work to do."

"There'll be plenty of time for that."

Of course it *would* be nice to check out the beach. He'd only been to the ocean once, and that was on the East Coast in the winter. (His grandparents had always visited them in Chicago on their annual tour of Midwestern relatives who were scattered across Michigan and Ohio.) A Southern California beach was a different thing entirely. But with his grandfather?

"Yeah, I'll go. Should I put my suit on?"

"You bet. I'll bring the towels."

Towels? Would he swim too? Great, I'm going surfing with gramps.

Mead was standing in the kitchen wearing navy blue trunks, a white button-down short-sleeve shirt, white socks and white leather sneakers like the kind that nurses wear, all shiny and new. On his head he wore a fancy-looking white straw hat with a black band around it and he'd placed large clip-on sunglasses over his gold-rimmed glasses, the shades tilted up. It was, thought Andrew, one of the more pathetic sights he'd ever seen.

They were both quiet on the drive, Andrew staring out the window taking in all the palm trees and cactus plants and trying to memorize how to get to the strip mall with the 7-Eleven they passed. They got to the beach in thirty minutes. Mead paid extra to park close and carried a small canvas tote bag as well as two towels he hung around his neck. Andrew carried the jug of water and two folding chairs they'd placed in the trunk.

As they passed a concession stand Andrew eyed a tanned and disinterested teenager who sat next to a row of boogie boards for rent. Now that's my idea of a job.

"I'm happy to rent you one of those if you like," said Mead.

Andrew shrugged. "Maybe later," he said.

"You *can* swim, can't you?"

"Of course I can swim." Actually, Andrew was only a so-so swimmer. He'd taken a few lessons at the local Y but stopped going after being towel-whipped in the locker room one day by a couple of Hispanic gang-bangers. He'd never swum in the ocean and the waves looked huge.

After they set the two chairs in the sand Andrew stood wondering what to do as he checked out the other teenagers, envying their tans and muscular bodies and sun-streaked hair. He couldn't get over how happy they looked, big, confident smiles on their faces as they ran past with their boards and lunged into the water. And the girls were unbelievable; the prettiest he'd ever seen, so that he knew there'd be no chance of getting through the day without jerking off big-time. He felt stupid and white as a snowman standing there next to his equally white grandfather, suddenly realizing that his bathing suit was way too short. He tried to slide it down lower, then kicked at the sand and took a few more steps toward the water.

"You going in?" asked his grandfather, pulling a book from his bag.

"I might."

"You're mumbling again."

"I said I *might*."

"Water's about sixty-seven degrees. Current's to the south so keep an eye on the lifeguard tower behind us or you're liable to wind up in Mexico."

Andrew looked up at the tower.

"And watch out for riptides. You know what to do in a riptide, don't you?"

"Sure I do."

His grandfather eyed him doubtfully. "You don't fight it, that's what you do. Swim parallel to the shore until you're out of it. And don't panic."

Andrew stripped off his shirt, pushed out his chest and headed toward the water, walking first, then trotting. A real California beach. He couldn't help but smile, feeling the warm sand between his toes. Two girls his age walked past as he reached the water, both ignoring him. They wore skimpy bikinis and laughed and swiveled their heads so that their long perfect hair swayed in the wind. *Shoot me.* He quickly memorized their predominant features, adding them to an extensive collection of mental images that he consulted almost nightly. He'd jerk off to them, too, and to the girls sitting up near his grandfather and the blonde up ahead in the water playing in the waves. All of them. He'd jerk off to every single one of them so they'd wake up in the middle of the night just knowing that someone out there was jerking off to them.

He waded further into the water, letting the waves pound against him and promising himself that one day he would build a house near a California beach.

• • •

Mead watched his grandson enter the water, wondering if he really did know how to swim. That's why he'd parked them right in front of the lifeguard station. He turned and looked up at the tower where two lanky teenage boys in bright red bathing suits reclined in their chairs, their hands clasped contentedly behind their heads. Not exactly vigilant. Both wore mirrored sunglasses and Mead wondered if they were asleep. Probably on drugs. Hell, the whole country was pretty well pickled, as far as he could tell. Dopers and pedophiles. He put his book down, deciding to keep an eye on Andrew himself.

Up until a few years ago, Mead had tried to come to the beach once a month and prided himself on the fact that he could still fend for himself even among the bigger waves. It was the air that he enjoyed the most, the clean dampness filling his chest. And yet he'd always found something a bit melancholy about beaches. Sitting there looking out at the waves, he couldn't help thinking how small and insignificant his life was; the same waves rolling in long before he was born and sure to be pounding the sand long after he was gone, oblivious to his passing. He looked out over the horizon, trying to visualize the curvature of the earth. What impact had he had? Little that you could trace. (He never counted the war.)

Sophie had made an impact. She'd changed people's lives. Two hundred mourners showed up at her funeral, all of them full of stories about the kind and selfless things that Sophie had done for them, things he'd never even heard about before because that was Sophie for you, never boasting. Some of them tried to keep in touch in the months after she died, inviting him to parties and sending him cards now and then. But gradually the phone stopped ringing. He knew it would. There was his friend Marty, who tried to talk him into moving back to Florida to some retirement community, which he refused to do. (He couldn't bear the thought of sitting around listening to people tell their stories over and over—the trip to Kenya and Tuscany and Machu Picchu, and the time that Milly was propositioned by the gondolier, and of course The War, as though it was the greatest damn thing that ever happened.) He still saw Bob and Angela Wright now and then and played an occasional golf game with Harry Braxton, but that was it. The truth was, he'd never been very social. Not like Sophie, who always did most of the gabbing at their dinner parties. (And that girl could gab.) Mead preferred to tend bar and man the grill, offering up a witty remark now and then. Still waters, Sophie would say with her smile.

He watched Andrew wade into the surf, the boy's movements awkward and hesitant. Scrawny little thing.

What went on inside a kid like that? Mead couldn't imagine. Sophie would know how to reach him. She'd know exactly the right approach. But Lord, it would have broken her heart to see what her grandson had become. She wouldn't understand it at all. And neither did Mead.

It was the insanity of the times, all the youth being spoon-fed nothing but garbage and raised in broken homes because marriage wasn't even expected anymore. And the crime! Ought to string up a few in the mall; bring back the road gang. They'd never mess with Mead, though. He still kept his Belgian Browning—lighter and more accurate than the standard issue Colt .45—right there in the drawer by his bed, ready for bear. Harry

Braxton's house had been broken into twice and a neighbor had her bicycle stolen right from her front yard. You couldn't trust anybody anymore. That was the damn sad truth of it. It was dog-eat-dog and let the last man turn out the lights. But they'd never get him. He'd make sure of that.

Andrew was now up to his waist in the water, diving beneath the waves or letting them topple over him.

Perhaps Mead could take him to church, arrange a little chat with the minister. Mead himself had been slacking off a bit since Sophie passed. Every time he went it just reminded him of her funeral until he couldn't stand sitting there listening to the organ and looking at Jesus up on the wall, patiently awaiting the rest of his flock. The truth was, he hadn't set foot in church for over a year now. *I'll keep a foot in the door.* He adjusted his hat and took a drink from the jug of water. Actually, a lot of things had been slipping. He tried to remember the last time he'd played golf or gone bowling. Must be six months. But he just didn't feel like getting out as much as he used to. The place he felt best was sitting in his chair with a good steak and a bourbon and working on his crossword puzzles. It wasn't happiness he sought. No, he'd given up on that the moment Sophie's hand went limp and they'd left him alone with her for another hour before wheeling her away. It was the brief absence of pain that he cherished.

He looked up and watched a seagull swoop down and skim low over the water, rising and falling with the waves.

Sophie loved to walk on the beach. He'd take her to Hernandez's for an early dinner—once a week they'd both get a craving for nachos and chicken tacos—and then they'd drive down to the beach and walk it off, she with her big white hat and scarf that she wrapped around her chin and the oversized sunglasses that she wore like Jackie O. Maybe it was being Midwesterners that made them appreciate the beach so much. Back when they first started dating they talked about how they planned to live within driving distance of the ocean, and that before neither of them had seen anything but the dreary shores of Lake Erie.

"So you see, you have to come back from the war because you've promised to take me to the ocean," she had said on one of their first dates.

Mead smiled to himself, remembering how nervous he'd been sitting across from her at the hamburger joint not far from his father's hardware store where Mead worked after school, and thinking she must have made some sort of mistake agreeing to go out with him.

"I'll do better than that. I'll get us a place near the beach. We'll go every day."

She laughed. "Don't you think we should get to know each other first?"

"I've seen all I need to see," he had joked. And he had. It was written right there in her small, smooth face: her humor, her easy manner, her honesty and through and through goodness. Mead knew right away that he'd found just what he wanted; that he'd do just about anything to wake up next to that smile each day. He just couldn't believe she'd want him.

He was good-enough looking, tall and strong with expressive, if a bit serious, dark blue eyes; but he'd always been reserved, never quite thinking of what he wanted to say until it seemed too late. When he wasn't in school he was usually working in his father's store, so socializing never came easy to him. He wasn't much for drinking or carousing with the guys and he rarely took part in their pranks and posturing, preferring to spend his free time tinkering with one of his three homemade radios.

"The truth of it is, Mead, you're a bit of a square," Sophie had said, leaning toward him with her chin propped up on her hands.

"I'm not so square," he'd said defensively.

"Of course you are. But that's what's so charming about you. You're not the least bit cynical. You're all right there. You're just ..." she held her hands up, *"Mead."*

From the moment he first saw her when they were both in their junior year of high school he'd been acutely aware of her, smitten not just by her emerald-green eyes and oval face and sandy blonde hair but by the effortless way she carried herself, her confidence and poise making him feel clumsy and inadequate. For months he watched her, feeling himself change in her presence like a pointer on a hunt. And then one day she showed up at the hardware store to buy some gardening tools and gave him a smile that seared him like a cattle brand.

He'd never been smiled at in that way before. He never knew that such smiles existed. That night he'd lain awake in bed deciding that he'd never be happy unless he could be around such a smile. And since he figured she'd never want to be around him, he assumed he'd always be unhappy. He'd never felt such sweeping sadness before, finding it almost unbearable to see her at school, like a shipwrecked sailor watching a mast recede on the horizon. He lost interest in everything: food, baseball, his studies. He even stayed for the second sermon one Sunday because he wasn't done asking God if there wasn't some way He could intervene.

And then she'd appeared at the hardware store again, just browsing the aisles and giving him that smile.

"How come you never talk?" she said suddenly, coming up to the counter when no one else was there.

"Talk? I talk. I'm talking." He felt himself blush.

"At school. You never talk in class but I know you're thinking faster than anybody."

"Guess I'm not a big talker."

"I don't like big talkers," she said, toying with a display of work gloves. "But you've got to talk at least a little bit to get to know somebody, don't you think?" She stood there looking at him until he felt the sweat gathering on his brow. Finally she said, "I'm Sophie," and extended her hand.

And right then without thinking he'd asked her out and she'd said yes, which floored him so completely that he did five hundred jumping jacks that night after dinner.

"Did anything unusual happen today, dear?" his mother had asked, watching him from the porch.

Leaving Sophie was the hardest thing about enlisting. He struggled over his letters, never quite capturing what he meant to say and never quite believing that she'd be there when he returned. But she wrote him almost every day; long, tightly-spaced letters that sometimes arrived in packs of six or ten.

I'll always wait for you.

And she had. The greatest miracle of his life came when he stepped off the train and her smile burst from the crowd gathered on the platform. *You waited.*

They married right after the war, skipping their honeymoon to save for a house. Once he'd gotten his degree in engineering at Ohio State—the GI bill was bar none the best damn thing the country ever did—they'd driven down to Florida where he'd found a job with an aerospace firm. But the heat was too much for them and three years later he applied for an opening in San Diego, taking the job sight unseen.

He watched a young couple—mid-forties—walk by holding hands, keeping one eye on his grandson.

Sophie. God, what a girl. Always finding the best in everybody, knowing just when to give him a little room and putting up with his dark moods—happy with the simple things. *Oh Peanut, I had so much more I meant to say.*

Mead stared out at the ocean watching the horizon blur. Then he rose to his feet, took off his hat, shirt and glasses, placing them neatly on his chair, and walked toward the water.

• • •

"How is it?" Mead called out as he waded into the ocean.

Andrew turned and winced at the sight of his grandfather approaching, the skin on his white chest all droopy and covered with a small tuft of even whiter hair, like one of those mummies at The Field Museum. He'd never seen his grandfather shirtless before and it seemed so weird that he felt like he ought to close his eyes. "Great."

"Look at that one coming." Mead pointed to a large wave swelling in the distance.

Andrew looked to his right at the blonde bobbing in the water not far away. *Look at me,* he commanded, only she wouldn't, not once since he'd been out there. He took a few steps away from his grandfather, scooting his feet until he was up to his chest, then turned and looked back toward the beach.

The wave knocked him right under, hitting him so hard in the back that he breathed in before he realized that he shouldn't. Then he was spinning in the dark, knocking hard against the bottom, then rising, then being pulled under again. He struggled for the surface, not knowing which way it was, but the wave kept rolling over him.

He felt a hand grab him under his arm. Finally he burst through the surface and retched and fought for air.

"I've got you."

Andrew felt his grandfather's body pressed against him but he could only cough and heave, then another wave hit him and the grip slipped, then held him again. When he got his feet on the bottom he stood and gasped.

"You never turn your back on the ocean," said his grandfather, pulling him toward shallower water. Andrew kept coughing, feeling an acidic burning in his throat. *"Never."*

Out of the corner of his eye Andrew could see the girl looking at him. Right at him. There was concern on her face, then a hint of amusement before she turned away and slid gracefully under. When Andrew finally caught his breath he turned away from his grandfather and headed quickly to the beach, his limbs filling with anger.

· · ·

He stayed in his room the rest of the afternoon, coming out only for dinner. They ate in silence at the green plastic table in the small backyard. The mosquitoes were bad and Andrew got bitten twice on the leg and once on the cheek.

"I get my hair cut tomorrow," said Mead, finishing his rib eye. "Every other Saturday. Thought maybe they could clean you up a bit, too."

Andrew slapped at a mosquito that landed on the back of his neck, but missed. "I just got mine cut."

Mead looked in disbelief at the boy's tangle of ratty brown, yellow-streaked hair, which had no identifiable part. "Well, I'd say they missed a spot or two, wouldn't you?" He stood and picked up his plate. "We'll leave at nine forty. *Sharp.*" Then he headed inside and finished his potato in his chair in the living room.

· · ·

Andrew lay in bed that night listening to his headphones and wondering what to do. No way he'd get his hair cut, he knew that. If he did, it was only a matter of time before GI Joe had him walking around in a tie saluting and selling bibles. But he had no idea how to refuse him. It was . . . inconceivable. He got up and walked to the window, pulled aside the curtain and examined the screen. He could just pack up and leave, load up at the 7-Eleven with the forty dollars he'd brought and make for the beach. Or he could head down to Mexico and bum around for a couple of years, let the whole thing blow over; maybe even get a job at one of those cool resorts with all the swimming pools and waterfalls and gorgeous girls sprawled out everywhere. He imagined himself driving triumphantly back over the border on his eighteenth birthday in a brand-new, red Dodge Viper with a wad of cash in his pocket. *You should have waited, Matt.*

But then he thought of his grandfather discovering his empty bed and the frantic call to his mother and her crying until her makeup ran down her cheeks. That's what he hated: how every time he tried to free himself a little he had to go face-to-face with other people, like they were surrounding him in a circle and he couldn't break free without knocking somebody over.

Fuck.

He crawled back in bed and pulled the sheets over him.

Then he thought of the girl at the beach and her wet breasts pushing out of her bikini top and the way she looked at him when his grandfather was holding him, like he was just a child. He reached down and took his limp cock, trying to push away all the shame he felt. He thought of the other girls he'd seen that day—their flat stomachs and smooth perfect thighs and especially their delicious round asses churning as they walked. He felt himself harden quickly as he closed his eyes, lining up in his mind every hot girl he had seen that day. Just the word *girls* made him horny.

Girls. The male body was basically disgusting; both he and Matt had agreed on that. But girls?

As he started stroking himself faster the headboard began to knock against the wall and the bed springs squeaked. He slowed down and changed positions until he was lying at an angle on the bed, but that only increased the squeaking. He peeled off his T-shirt and placed it between the headboard and the wall, then tried again. Still the bed squeaked. Finally he lay completely sideways with his legs hanging over the bed, but as soon as he started the bedsprings shrieked. He stopped for a moment, listening for sounds, then got up, put a chair against the door—it wouldn't lock—and lay down on the light green carpet, which itched his back like crazy. Then he took hold of himself and lined up the girls again one right after the other and jerked off faster and faster until he came in a blinding spasm, his back arching up off the carpet. After cleaning himself up with his underwear, which he stuffed under the bed, he crawled back beneath the sheets, rolled to his side and tried not to think about the girl in the water and the look of amusement in her eyes.

· · ·

"I'm not getting a haircut," said Andrew, standing in the hallway the next morning.

Mead was flustered. "Nonsense. Now if we don't get a move on we're going to be late."

"I don't need one. I just *had* one."

Mead thought he saw fear in the boy's face and wasn't sure how to respond. "By God, I told you we're getting haircuts today. You look like a . . ." He couldn't think how to finish.

"Please." The boy said it so softly Mead had to watch his lips. He felt his face redden, not knowing what to do. Sophie would know what to do. And the boy would never challenge her this way, standing there like he was preparing for the gallows. Mead wished he could go and sit in Sophie's room and think it over. He wanted to see and smell her things and pull open the drawers of her dresser and run his hands through her sweaters. *I don't know what to do, Sophie.* In a way she was lucky, not seeing what the boy had become, no longer the shy little child who loved to play checkers and fly kites when they traveled to Chicago to visit, always bringing him an extra suitcase full of presents.

Mead stood looking at Andrew, feeling suddenly lost. "I'll be back in an hour," he stammered, grabbing his car keys off the hall table and heading for the front door. "I want you working on your studies, got that?"

Andrew nodded.

· · ·

After Mead locked the door behind him Andrew stood in the hallway waiting for the sound of the car pulling out of the driveway, then took out his soiled underwear from beneath the bed, gathered up his other dirty clothes and carried them out to the garage and put them in the washer. Then he went into the kitchen, found a medium-sized pot, filled it with water and placed it on the stove, turning the range up to high. After collecting his used batteries and dropping them into the water he took an ice cream bar from the refrigerator, peeled off the wrapper and slowly walked through the house.

He started in the living room, working back toward his grandfather's room as he opened drawers and examined all the things on the shelves—mostly books and photographs, with a couple of figurines and fancy little painted jars and teacups. He opened the dartboard and pulled out one of the darts, surprised by how heavy it felt. He tested the tip with his finger, then ran the feathers of the end along his nose. Serious darts. He backed up a few steps, aimed at the board and threw the dart. *Shit.* The dart buried itself into the wall above the dartboard. He carefully pulled it out and pressed his finger against the small hole, trying to flatten the edges, then put the dart back in the drawer and closed the cabinet. He examined the hole again, wondering if his grandfather would notice. But how well could someone that old really see anyway?

He walked down the hallway, stopping to check out the closet, then continued on to his grandfather's bedroom, hesitating at the doorway. The bear's lair. He felt nervous as he leaned his head in and looked around. The bed, queen-size with a cheesy blue and gold comforter, was perfectly made while the items on the large dresser—a comb, a silver shoehorn, two pairs of glasses—were arranged in tidy little rows. On the walls and matching bed stands he counted nearly a dozen photographs of his mother and grandma along with several of himself as a much younger boy.

The first thing he noticed when he entered was the smell, like cologne and baby powder mixed together. He cracked open the closet and looked at the shoes all lined in a row and the sport coats at one end and slacks hanging at the other. A class-A neat freak. He sat on the bed, testing its softness, then walked back to the dresser and opened the two top drawers. Three old watches, more combs, a little box of gold and silver tie clips, a compass, one of those pocket odometers that count your steps and a neat stack of white handkerchiefs with his grandfather's initials on them. He opened more drawers holding neatly folded shirts and rolled socks and white jockey underwear—Jesus, even the underwear's folded—and then a drawer full of nerdy sweaters. He went back over to the bed and sat down, picking up a gold-framed photograph of his grandparents together on a beach, maybe even the one he'd been to. They certainly looked happy. Were they still like, in love? He tried to imagine what it was like for his grandfather when she died after all those years together. Had to be tough. Was it harder than losing a friend like Matt? But nothing could be worse than that. He looked at another photograph of his grandma on a balcony with the ocean behind her, a huge smile on her face. *Hi, Grandma.* Then he reached down and opened the large bed stand drawer. Pushing aside several bottles of pills and a little packet of tissues he saw the gun.

Bingo.

He sat staring at it awhile, uncertain whether to pick it up. Before finally slipping his fingers around the handle he memorized its placement in the drawer, then gingerly drew it out and held it in front of his face, turning it one way, then another, careful not to finger the trigger. Of course it would be loaded. That's why his grandfather kept it by his bed. The real fucking thing. He felt a tingling sensation as he switched it from one hand to another, mesmerized by its weight and coldness and don't-fuck-with-me authority. Probably from the war. Maybe even used to kill Germans. Man, think of that. He touched his finger to the tip of the barrel, imagining a bullet tearing out and slamming into the chest of a German just about to toss a grenade. *Pow pow pow!* He tossed the gun into his left hand, then back into his right. Then he held his arm out straight and aimed it at the mirror above the dresser, wondering what kind of kick it had, then turned it and touched the tip of the barrel to his right temple. That's all it would take. Bammo. Brains everywhere. He listened to an approaching car and checked the time on his watch. The car continued on. Then he stood and aimed at different objects in the room, pretending to fire. He sat back down and stared at it again, practicing different kinds of grips. The real thing all right. Fuck me. He sat there for a few more minutes holding it, then gently returned it to the drawer, careful to put back the medicine bottles and pack of tissues exactly as they were. Then he got up and went to his room and started on his homework.

. . .

Mead always enjoyed getting his hair cut. He liked the ritual of it and the easy banter with Rick Moreni and the off-color jokes and then the fresh restorative feeling after Rick brushed him off and shook out the apron, spinning him back to face the mirror. "Just right," he'd say, reaching into his shirt pocket for the five-dollar tip he always left on the counter. Rick understood all about what was happening to the country. He'd served in Korea and knew a thing or two about the world. Yes sir, Rick understood. And damn few people did.

But Mead was distracted today, not even following Rick's jokes or his withering analysis of yesterday's game. He'd let the boy stand up to him. Worse, he'd backed down. There'd be a price to pay for that. His hands tightened on the sides of the barber chair. He never should have let it happen. Either he shouldn't have insisted on the haircut, or once he had he should have stuck to his guns. But how? That was what stumped him. How could he *make* the boy obey? He couldn't just seize him by the collar, though it was damn tempting. He could always force the kid to eat a big juicy steak. Grill him some prime rib. (Like to see him live on shit-on-a-shingle for months.) Or maybe demand a few sets of push-ups. Mead must have done a million push-ups in basic. *Drop down and give me thirty, now!*

He thought of his own father. Veteran of the Argonne. Strict as a war-

den. The only time he ever remembered his father touching him—beside
the two occasions when he got himself whopped—was when they shook
hands before Mead boarded the train for Camp Toccoa. "You come back
in one piece," his father had said sternly, as though it was just another one
of his orders. And Mead had. By the time he returned his father was four
months dead, felled by a heart attack in the stockroom of the hardware
store he'd owned for thirty years.

"You feeling all right today?" asked Rick, brushing off Mead as he rose
from the chair.

"Just a little tired, that's all."

"I know that one. Didn't sleep well myself. Rita's veal parmigiana.
Always gives me the worst gas. 'Course, if I don't eat it there's hell to pay.
Can't win, know what I'm saying?"

"I know exactly what you're saying."

Mead placed a five-dollar bill on the counter, then paid for the haircut
up at the cash register.

"Two weeks from today then?" said Rick, as he always did.

"Put me down," said Mead, as he always did. He was walking to the car
when he felt Sophie hovering just above his right shoulder.

You know what day it is tomorrow, don't you, Pooh?

Let me guess.

It's Sunday.

Oh.

You promised, remember?

But—

A foot in the door. That's all I ask.

Chapter 3

       Mead didn't invite Andrew, thinking maybe he'd break the ice by himself and take the boy along the following week. He felt guilty as he parked outside the church and checked his tie once more in the rearview mirror, like a drunk returning to AA after several months' absence. *We were wondering what happened to you,* they'd say, all the widows hovering like buzzards over carrion. *Won't you come for dinner? How handsome you look. Did you hear what happened to poor so-and-so?* And then the look he'd get from the Holy Joe, a comically young minister— what could he possibly know about life?—who seemed to sense that Mead wasn't buying in.

And he wasn't.

Because it wasn't God that Mead sought when he slipped into the very last pew next to the aisle just as the service began. Rather, it was the comfort of seeing hope ritualized; of witnessing how many other people sought God, desperate for something that would right all the wrongs. He liked the hymns too, and the sense of community when they all stood shoulder to shoulder and belted one out. (He remembered a service in the ruins of a church in Belgium just hours after the last German sniper had been killed, and how all the townspeople sang so beautifully that soldiers were in tears.) But he wasn't seeking God. No, he hadn't done that since he saw Jimbo bleed to death in Normandy. *Praise the Lord and pass the ammunition.* He looked down the row at another man about his age. Pacific theater, he guessed. Destroyers. Ordnance. Mead had a sixth sense when it came to that, though others frequently mistook him for a Marine. (There were worse things.) After the service ended he socialized just long enough to be polite and then excused himself and walked quickly to his car, suddenly fearing that when he got home Andrew would be gone.

But he was there all right, standing out front in the driveway shooting baskets. As Mead pulled up to the curb he wondered again how in the world his grandson kept his pants halfway down without them falling completely to his ankles, as though he was just about to relieve himself and suddenly changed his mind. Tape? Some sort of string and hook apparatus? Love to see him run a few laps.

"Game of horse?" asked Mead.

"I'm kind of tired," said Andrew, setting the ball down on the grass.

"Maybe some other time," said Mead, noticing the cookie tin on the front stoop. "I see we've been resupplied."

"Yeah, isn't she great? Ah, I hope you don't mind, but I invited her for dinner. I was telling her about my tofu hot dogs and—"

"You invited her for *dinner?*"

"At seven. I'll cook . . ."

"*Tonight?*" Mead could hardly contain himself.

Andrew fiddled nervously with his earring. "It's just that she seems kind of lonely, you know, and she was interested in trying one of my hot dogs. I didn't think—"

"Jesus, who the hell do you think you are?"

"Sorry."

Mead glanced across the street at Evelyn's house. "From now on, I'll make the social engagements around here, you got that?"

Mead felt unusually tired as he sat in his chair eating a B.L.T. and wading through the Sunday paper, which, it seemed to him, was really nothing but lingerie ads with a murder and a molestation here and there. He put the paper down and tried to imagine the three of them sitting around a dinner table. Good Lord. He felt his pockets for his Tums, popping two in his mouth. And yet he was slightly excited, too, which made him feel guilty. Of course, it hadn't been his idea. He felt his whiskers, wondering if he should shave again, then debated between steaks or pork chops. At least he had plenty of meat. Hell, might as well invite the whole neighborhood over.

He picked up the paper again and read about a mother who drowned her two kids in a bathtub, then about a teenage boy in Los Angeles who shot his driver's-ed instructor twice in the head. He put the paper back down and listened for Andrew, wondering what he was doing. He tried to pretend he wasn't there—oh, for an hour of peace—but he felt bad thinking of the boy holed up in his room like a hermit. The point was to make some impact on him; to spend a little time together. Suppose I could always drive him down to the mall, maybe spring for a real pair of trousers. Mead glanced at his watch. What the heck, the day's shot anyway. He rose from his chair and headed toward Sophie's room.

· · ·

They walked through the mall together at first, but when Mead sensed Andrew's growing discomfort he volunteered to meet up at the food pavilion on the second level in half an hour, figuring he'd let the kid off-leash for a bit. Mead watched him disappear into a music store, then walked slowly to the far end of the mall hoping he wouldn't run into anybody he knew. Some of the wives went to the mall just about every day, using it as an enormous lap pool for their daily exercise, back and forth, back and forth, with a rejuvenating purchase here and there until they were weighed down like pack mules. Mead never cared much for malls himself. Not like Sophie did. She could spend all day in a mall, ohhing and ahhing over things and getting ideas for the dresses she made. Malls felt too lonely to him, a sterile imitation of the bustling street life he remembered growing up, sitting on the bench in front of the variety store after working in his father's stockroom and seeing just about everybody he knew pass by. And then there were the packs of teenagers who prowled the malls like rabid hyenas, once nearly knocking Sophie over as they ran up the escalator.

Mead passed two particularly loathsome-looking specimens strutting and posturing like a bunch of Baby-Faced Nelsons. Ah, to make them drop and give me fifty right on the spot. Bet they couldn't do twenty. So many fat kids these days, atrophying in front of that damned TV. Had German boys gone fat too? The Japs still looked plenty slim and they were the ones who made all the TVs. (Guess who won *that* war.) Mead prided himself on the fact that he'd never gotten fat. He'd slowed down all right, just barely squeaking out ten acceptable push-ups a day (he could do forty up until about five years ago). But he'd never let himself get fat.

He stopped in a bookstore and browsed, repeatedly checking his watch, the Hamilton that Sophie had bought him for their thirtieth. He'd buy Andrew lunch and then take him to Nordstrom, get him something decent to wear, maybe even something he could wear to church. That would be something, telling Sharon that Andrew had come to church with him—voluntarily. He had to make some sort of headway with the boy, enough to give Sharon something to work with. But where to start?

He purchased a cup of coffee and sat at a small table in the corner sipping it and people-watching and checking his watch. He used to sit in that same spot waiting for Sophie to return from one of her shopping expeditions, scanning the passersby until he saw her bright face and the colorful bags in each arm, though she always went for bargains, keeping a file of coupons in the kitchen drawer and waiting months on certain items until it was the right time to strike. *Gotcha!* He finished his coffee quickly, then tossed the cup into the garbage and headed back down the mall thinking he might run into Andrew. As he approached the music store he noticed a group of gawkers gathered around the entrance. Mead slowed as he passed, and then as he looked through the window he saw Andrew by the store counter being held by a large security guard.

No.

He pushed his way through the crowd. "That's my grandson. What the hell's happening here?"

Andrew wouldn't look at him.

"I said, what's going on here?"

"I saw him slip this under his shirt." The security guard kept one hand on Andrew and with the other picked up a CD sitting on the counter. "We're calling the police."

Mead stiffened. "I'm his grandfather."

"Yeah, well you're going to have to deal with the cops on this one. We don't screw around with shoplifters."

"Andrew, did you do this?" Mead's voice was quaking.

"Of course he did it," said the security guard, whose stomach bulged out of his light blue uniform. "I *saw* him."

Andrew still refused to look up.

"Please don't call the police," said Mead. "I'm his grandfather. I'll pay for anything. He's . . . he's had a hard time and I'd like to handle this. *Please.*"

The security guard frowned and looked over at the young woman behind the counter, who held the phone in one hand and shrugged uncertainly.

"We can't just let him go. He was stealing."

"I'll punish him. You can count on that."

"I don't know," said the security guard.

"I'm his *grandfather,*" said Mead, standing as straight as he could.

The guard looked over at the cashier, then turned back to Mead and sighed. "I don't want to see his face in this mall again, you understand?"

"We understand."

The guard let go of Andrew, who remained immobile, shoulders hunched and head bowed down, his hair covering his eyes.

"Come on, son," said Mead, taking him firmly by the shoulder. With one arm on Andrew, Mead made his way through the crowd still gathered in the doorway, then hurried to the nearest exit and across the large parking lot to the car.

"Goddamn you, boy," he said, as he fumbled for his keys and unlocked the door. "Goddamn you."

• • •

Andrew sat in the backseat stunned. He hadn't meant to do it. It wasn't even on his mind. But then, he'd forgotten his wallet and there was the CD he'd been looking for and suddenly without thinking he just sort of slipped it under his shirt. Fuck, he hadn't even noticed the fat-assed security guard.

He looked at his grandfather up in the front seat driving, his silver hair neatly trimmed and the skin on the back of his neck splotched with old-age freckles, or whatever they were called. The car smelled of cologne and baby powder.

This was it. It was all over now. As he sat there feeling the hotness in his face and palms and fighting back tears he knew that it was finally all over. Even after pulling the knife at school he thought that maybe in a few years things would be okay again, that he could eventually recover. But not now. He'd be sent off to some institution somewhere and locked away. He looked out the window at a couple on a motorcycle, the girl hugging her arms around the guy, thighs splayed. *Why not me?*

"Do you want to tell your mother or shall I?" said Mead finally.

"I don't know," said Andrew softly, his fingers digging into the sides of the seat. It was unbearable thinking of his mother finding out what he'd done. And while he was staying with his *grandfather*. She wouldn't be mad, she'd be *crushed*. That was the worst thing, how she'd always start crying when he fucked up, not even yelling at him. If only she'd just yell.

"Stealing," said Mead under his breath. "It wasn't enough pulling a knife on someone at school. Now you're a goddamn thief as well." He glanced at Andrew in the rearview mirror. "My own *grandson*."

.   .   .

Mead had to concentrate on his driving, remembering his turn signals and keeping the car within the lanes. God help me on this one, Sophie. I am out of my league. *Stealing*. At least the police hadn't come; Mead still had control over the situation. But what to do now? And how would he explain it to Sharon?

As soon as they got to the house Andrew peeled off for his room. Mead stopped him. "You sit right here and wait for me," he ordered, gesturing toward the sofa before continuing down the hallway. He stopped in the bathroom to splash cold water on his face, staring in the mirror at the lined grayness of his features, which looked increasingly like someone else's. After wetting his comb and running it through his thinning hair he went into his room and sat on the bed, taking off his glasses and rubbing his temples. Was the boy just plain evil? A born loser? But he didn't look evil. Just shy and miserable. No confidence at all. It saddened Mead to see how little confidence his grandson had. He had hoped to boost him up a bit, find things to compliment him on. But the fact was, he hadn't found a single thing so far. The kid could walk into the room and you'd hardly know he was there except for the sulky face and baggy pants and the dyed yellow hair. He had no presence at all.

Well, the pants would be the first to go. No more of this saggy butt business. And there'd be chores. A whole long list of chores. That's it, Mead would draw up a list of rules and requirements. Start the day off with a few sets of push-ups and jumping jacks, get the blood flowing, then water the lawn, mop the kitchen floor, that kind of thing. He'd make a list that very night. But first it was time for a little talk.

He paused to look at the photograph of Sophie on the bed stand, the one where she was standing on the balcony of their hotel room during their last trip to Hawaii, then rose from his bed, straightened his shirt and walked back to the living room where Andrew sat meekly in the blue overstuffed chair.

"That's *my* chair," said Mead.

Andrew jumped up and moved to the couch.

Mead remained standing. "Well, what have you got to say for yourself?"

Andrew stared down at the carpet. "Nothing, I guess."

"*Nothing?* I'm afraid that doesn't quite cut the mustard."

"It was a dumb thing to do. I wasn't thinking."

"Seems like you haven't been doing much thinking at all lately, wouldn't you say?"

"I'm sorry. Did you call Mom?"

Mead paused briefly before responding. "Not yet."

"What are you going to do? Are you going to have me committed?"

Mead studied the boy, thinking how pathetic he looked sitting there like a condemned man. No starch at all. "It's worse than that."

"*Worse?*" Andrew looked up briefly, as if trying to assess the implications.

"First thing you're going to do is to sit down and write a letter of apology to the manager of that store. Then you're going to work on your studies until you can't see straight and by tomorrow I'll have a list of things for you to do. And rules. I'll be drawing up a list of rules which you will follow to a T."

"Okay," Andrew said quietly. "Can I go now?"

Mead stood looking at him, wondering what else to say. "You can go."

The boy rose to leave.

"And no music. You bring me that music player of yours. Leave it on the kitchen table."

Andrew hesitated, then headed down the hallway. Mead heard him set the music player down on the table, then the click of the bedroom door. He stood in the living room another moment, trying to slow his breath, then went and fixed himself a bourbon. He was just sitting down with pencil and paper to draw up a list of rules when the doorbell rang.

"Am I early?" It was Evelyn. She was wearing a teal blue dress with a white sweater slung around her shoulders and her face was dusted with just enough makeup to sharpen her pretty features.

"No, I . . . come on in." Mead felt his face redden as he gestured for her to enter. *Son of a bitch.*

"Are you okay?"

"Me? Fine." He closed the door behind her, distracted momentarily by the scent of her perfume, which was more subtle and pleasant smelling than the flowery stuff most older women seemed to soak themselves in. "It's just that . . . well," he let out a sigh, "it's been one of those days."

"Andrew did tell you that he invited—"

"Oh, yes."

"Good, I was afraid he might have forgotten." She stood in the center of the living room smiling and looking at Mead expectantly.

He rubbed his hands together nervously. *Stay calm.* "Can I offer you a drink?"

"I suppose one glass of white wine wouldn't hurt."

Hell, he hadn't even gotten to the store. He tried to recall if there was any of Sophie's Pinot Grigio left in the cabinet. "I'll have to chill it a moment," he called from the kitchen. And he hadn't even set the table. *Damn damn damn.*

"No hurry."

He grabbed the last remaining bottle, dusted it off and shoved it in the freezer. Then he knocked on Andrew's door. *"Evelyn's here,"* he growled in a low voice.

"Oh."

"You've got *two* minutes." Mead hurried into the bathroom to fix himself up. How could I have forgotten? He sniffed the armpits of his dark green polo shirt. Should he change? But then she'd know he hadn't been prepared. (And he had laid out his best shirt and slacks on his bed before going to the mall.) He quickly combed his hair and brushed his teeth, then hurried back into the kitchen. Broccoli and steaks, and maybe some cheese and Triscuits to start. He grabbed the matches from the top of the fridge, then dashed out the back door to light the barbecue.

"Are you sure I can't help with anything?"

"It's all under control," said Mead, cutting off the moldy edge of an old square of cheddar he found at the back of the refrigerator. "Just make yourself comfortable." He put down the cheese and ran to Andrew's door. *"Now."*

They ate at the dining room table, Mead and Evelyn at each end and Andrew in the middle. Evelyn loved Andrew's tofu hot dogs, eating two of them and leaving her steak untouched, much to Mead's chagrin and Andrew's unending delight. Despite her good-natured charm and quick humor, the conversation was so strained that Mead's face began to sweat.

"I think it's wonderful that young people are so concerned about the environment," Evelyn said after Andrew finished reciting a grisly series of charges against the cattle and poultry industries. "My husband George was a real meat-and-potatoes man. I sometimes wonder if that wasn't what killed him."

"Don't mind me," said Mead, jabbing his fork into his last piece of steak, which was grilled to perfection.

"You have to admit that Andrew has a point."

"I do?"

"Well, we really don't know what all those growth hormones are doing to us, do we?"

"I for one have no intention of living forever," said Mead.

"If you don't care about yourself maybe you could think of the rest of the planet," said Andrew. "Do you have any idea how much toxic waste a single chicken farm creates? Arkansas is basically a cesspool. And have you seen the machine they use to kill cows?"

"His dinner manners need a little work," said Mead in a steely voice, giving Andrew the eye.

"I don't mind," said Evelyn. "My family never talked about anything interesting. In fact, I'm not sure we talked at all." She smiled at Mead, who smiled politely back, then cleared his throat with a stretching motion of his neck and drummed his fingers on the table. Andrew stared sullenly at his plate.

"So, what did you two gentlemen do today?"

"Well," said Mead, scooting his chair back from the table. "Uh, let's see. I guess we stopped by the mall."

"What fun. Did you buy anything?"

"Not *exactly*." Mead searched the room for an innocuous place to park his eyes while Andrew sank lower in his seat.

"It's none of my business," said Evelyn finally, "but is anything . . . wrong?"

Andrew glanced nervously at his grandfather.

"Wrong?" asked Mead gingerly.

"I just thought that maybe—"

"I guess we're a bit tired," Mead said quickly. "Big day. *Big, big* day."

"I understand." She looked them both over with such a kind and searching expression that Mead suddenly wanted to tell her everything and ask her for advice. *Help!* "You two haven't had a run-in by any chance?"

"No—"

"More like a collision," said Andrew, standing up and taking his plate into the kitchen.

"I see."

"It's nothing really," said Mead. "Teenagers," he whispered with a thin smile. He heard Sophie's door close.

"Are you sure you two are okay?"

"We'll be just fine."

"He's a nice young man."

"One of a kind." They traded awkward smiles.

"I wish my daughter would have kids before it's too late but she doesn't seem the least bit interested."

"They're not for everybody."

"But grandchildren are. All the fun without the responsibility."

"In theory."

Evelyn dabbed her lips with her napkin as Mead ate in silence. "I just want to say that I know how hard it's been for you since Sophie died."

Mead didn't respond.

"After George passed away there were days when I thought that time had come to a complete standstill."

"I've managed."

She leaned over and gave him a quick squeeze of the hand. "It's good to see you looking better. I was worried about you for a while there. You looked so . . ." She didn't finish.

Mead stared down at the table, spotting several smudges and wishing he'd remembered to give it a good polish. And the two silver candlesticks were looking a bit tarnished too. Why hadn't he noticed before?

"I'd drop by more but I know how you like your privacy." She laid her silverware neatly across her plate and then adjusted the embroidered place mat that Sophie had made during her frenzied place-mat phase. "I bring you food because I don't know what else to do for you."

"Nothing you need to do." Mead cleared his throat again, feeling her eyes against the side of his face like the heat from an oven.

She leaned closer. "I'd love to be of help."

"I don't need any help."

"But if you did . . ."

Mead looked at her briefly but couldn't hold her gaze. "I'm just *fine.*"

She sat back. "I didn't mean to put you on the spot. It's just that, well, I wouldn't want you to hesitate to ask, I mean if you did need someone to talk to or if there was anything I could ever do." Mead nodded as she rose and began clearing the table. "Thank you for dinner. I don't get out much."

"My pleasure." He stood and tried to help but she swatted his hands away.

"The least I can do is return the favor," she said.

"There's really no need to trouble yourself."

"But I insist."

Mead followed her into the kitchen, trying not to look at her backside, which held her dress surprisingly well. Exactly how old was she? "Can I get you some coffee?"

She looked at him and smiled. "I think I'd better leave you two to patch things up." After helping him load the dishwasher she took her sweater off the couch and wrapped it around her shoulders.

Mead looked down the hallway, wondering if he should get Andrew to come out and say good-bye. Nah, to hell with him. He turned back to Evelyn, sensing that she was reading his thoughts. "He just gets a little moody. Nothing I can't handle."

"Do you remember being his age?" she asked.

"They didn't have his age when I was growing up."

She laughed. "Well, I remember. I felt so full of life that the world couldn't contain me. I thought I would just *burst* with desire."

"I see," Mead said, avoiding her eyes.

"Of course, I knew I'd never have time for more than a tiny slice of all the life I wanted. Oh, how I used to lie awake at night thinking of all the places I'd never see and all the people I'd never get to meet. It drove me *crazy.*" She paused, a wistful look on her face. "The truth is, it still does. I suppose that's why I garden."

"You're a heck of a gardener, if it's any consolation."

"Why thank you."

He flicked on the front lights, opened the door and walked her to the curb. "Well, good night," he said.

"Good night, General," she said, bunching up her nose and giving him a wink before crossing the street. When she reached her door she turned and waved. He waved back, then waited until she had unlocked her door, closed it and turned off her porch light.

Forgive me, Peanut.

.   .   .

It seemed like the quietest night of his life, lying there in the dark with the silence pressing against him so hard he heard a ringing in his ears. He must have lain there for two hours trying to sleep, and when he finally did he was right back in the forest preserve screaming for Matt to wake up.

At first he thought Matt was just sleeping off the alcohol. But by ten the sun was glaring. Andrew finally pulled himself part way out of his sleeping bag and rolled toward Matt.

"Wake up, buddy."

He shook him once, then twice.

"Come on, we gotta get going."

Matt didn't move.

Finally Andrew got up on his knees and pulled aside the top of Matt's sleeping bag. "Jesus, you don't look so good." He shook him harder. "Wake up."

And then he knew. From the sickly cast of Matt's face and lips and the coldness of his skin he knew. *Wake up!* And then he couldn't stop screaming.

Andrew bolted upright in bed, the sheets wet with sweat. *Damn you, Matt.* He rubbed his face, took a sip of water from the glass he kept by the bed, then lay back down and looked at the light from the street lamp leaking through the edges of the curtain, wondering if Matt could somehow see him. He always thought he'd see some sort of sign. If anybody could come back from the dead it was Matt. Andrew figured he'd raise hell, too. But there was never any sign, nothing that Andrew could be sure of.

"Do you think dead is dead?" Matt had asked as they lay side by side in their sleeping bags drinking from a bottle of Southern Comfort. "Like, that's it?"

"How would I know?"

"Just wondering." Matt was always talking about death and ghosts and suicide, especially when he got drunk. A few months earlier he'd completely redone his room with posters of dead rock stars, and it amused him to no end that his parents didn't get it. "Would you want to come back?"

"Not if I have to wait another sixteen years to get laid."

"More like seventeen or eighteen years." Matt took another swig. "I wouldn't mind being a bird or something; but I'll be seriously pissed if I have to dissect another pig."

"Maybe next time you'll go all the way to the state science fair."

"Very funny." Matt lay back and clasped his hands behind his head. "I've decided I'd rather come back as a ghost than a real person."

"That's just so you can hang out in the girl's locker room."

"We could both be ghosts. Think of the stuff we could do."

"But you couldn't get laid. I don't even think ghosts can jerk off."

Matt frowned. "I hadn't thought of that."

"Anyway, I don't think we're going to get a choice."

Matt didn't respond.

"Okay, tell me what happened." Matt had been acting strange all day and Andrew figured he'd had another fight with his dad.

"Nothing happened."

"Bullshit." Andrew reached for the bottle and took a sip, then stretched out and watched the moon rise through the trees while Matt blew large smoke rings.

"We're never going to have enough money," Matt said finally.

"So that's what's bugging you." For several years they'd talked about going in on a car once they were old enough and then heading down to Mexico to get jobs at one of the fancy resorts. Matt had read *On the Road* twice and figured he might write a book about their experiences, thinking maybe they could get some kind of movie deal.

"I'm just facing facts. There's no way we'll ever have enough money." Matt had worked at Taco Bell over the summer while Andrew bagged groceries, but most of their savings went to buying pot, which they got from Matt's older cousin, and beer, which they bribed panhandlers to buy for them from 7-Eleven.

"Sure we will."

"Not soon enough."

"What's that supposed to mean?"

"That I can't wait any longer." Matt's voice squeaked.

Andrew sat up and looked over at him. "You okay?"

"I'm just su-fucking-perb. Pass the bottle."

Matt sat up and took another drink, then fell back down again and hic cuped. "You're a really great guy, Andy. Did I ever tell you that? I mean it, you're going to do great things. Just don't let the assholes stop you."

"You're drunk."

Matt sighed loudly, then burped. "God, there's a lot of bullshit. Don't you think there's a lot of bullshit?"

"Nothing but."

"Well, I've had it with bullshit. Finito."

"Lucky you."

"I'm serious, Andy. I can't take it anymore."

"Don't start that *I'm going to kill myself* shit again or *I'll* shoot you."

"Would you really shoot me if I asked you to?"

"Don't tempt me."

Matt smiled and looked up at the sky, his face lit by the moon. "You know the funny thing? For the first time I can remember I feel *great*." His words were heavily slurred.

"Boy, are you moody."

"Seriously, I feel fucking *great*."

"Good, then stop complaining. I'm going to sleep." Andrew rolled over and buried his head in his sleeping bag, feeling woozy.

"I hope you make it, Andy, I really do."

"Would you shut up with that?"

"Hey man, you oughta take a look at this moon. I mean, it's *huge*."

"Would you *shut the fuck up?*"

"No kidding, I've never seen the moon so big. I think it's gonna pop."

Andrew buried his head deeper into his sleeping bag, feeling the pot and alcohol take him.

Matt was silent for a minute, then said, "I can see the man in the moon. I've never seen him before but now I can make out his features *perfectly*."

"*Shut up.*"

"Sorry, it's just that . . ."

Andrew let out another groan. "Okay, tell me. I'm dying of curiosity."

"I thought he'd be smiling."

"Who?"

"The man in the moon. I always thought he'd be smiling."

"Oh, *please*."

Another minute passed.

"I'm going to miss you," Matt whispered, sniffling now.

"Would you stop with the weepy stuff?" Hard liquor frequently reduced Matt to unintelligible blubbering.

"I'm serious, Andy."

"Fine, go kill yourself. What the fuck do I care?" Andrew crossed his hands over his head, starting to feel seasick.

And those were the last words that he ever spoke to his best buddy in the whole world.

•   •   •

After finishing up in the kitchen Mead sat in the living room long past his normal bedtime of nine-thirty, a notepad on his lap and the small stereo tuned to a classical station, volume low. One hell of a day. He looked over at the dining room table, wincing as he recalled the long silences. That ought to scare Ms. Raisins away for a while. And yet despite the tension she seemed to enjoy herself, always smiling and trying to draw Andrew out and even getting him to laugh once or twice, which was the closest thing Mead had seen to a miracle in quite some time. He thought of the way she had winked at him and how nice she smelled and the way her dress hung on her hips (and the fact that she had hips at all). Ah hell, I'm too old for such nonsense. Besides, it just didn't seem right.

He stared down at the notepad in his lap, wondering if Andrew was asleep yet. Time to get serious with the little hoodlum. As he started drawing up a list of calisthenics he suddenly thought of Sergeant Fisk at Camp Toccoa screaming at him, his face just inches away. *Give me another forty, now!* As much as he hated the s.o.b., he was always thankful for the training he'd had, first stateside and then in England preparing for the invasion. They'd made a soldier out of him all right, tough enough to take just about anything life could throw at him (except, perhaps, his grandson). But how do you raise a boy nowadays? What's the rite of passage in a world of drugs, sex and violence? He thought of a shooting that occurred a few years back at the high school not three miles away. One kid dead and another paralyzed. American boys, luckiest in the world. And what even made them Americans anymore, except for having the freedom to do just about any goddamn thing they pleased? Hell, in California you had to press "1" to continue in your own language.

He picked up his pencil:

Two sets of twenty push-ups each.

Fifty jumping jacks.

Forty sit-ups.

Could the boy do forty sit-ups? He scratched out the number and wrote down thirty, then rose from his chair and walked over to the stereo, his knees cracking as he squatted down and thumbed through the old records neatly shelved beneath. He hadn't played them in years. Not since Sophie passed. He pulled a few out at random: Harry Belafonte: *Calypso*; Edith Piaf; *Porgy and Bess*; Judy Garland: *Judy at Carnegie Hall* (Sophie wept when Judy died); The Glenn Miller Band. He smiled to himself as he ran his palms over the covers, which were taped in places by Sophie, the tape now yellow and peeling. She always loved her records, forcing him to dance at every opportunity. (That girl could cut a rug.) Finally he settled on Piaf and carefully slid the record from the cover and placed it on the turntable, fiddling with the knobs and levers until he remembered how to work the thing. Then he turned the volume up a notch and sat back down, putting his feet up and listening to the pop-pop-pop of the scratches as the first song began.

· · ·

Roy Rokowski was a Polish meat packer from the South Side of Chicago whose family sent him care packages full of smoked sausages that he proudly shared. Tall and gangly with a pronounced accent, he had fine black hair, extremely pale skin and large brown eyes sunk deep and underlined with permanent dark bags, as though he'd been brooding for years. Though well liked for his simple and uncomplaining nature, he preferred to keep to himself—as much as anyone could in the army—and spent hours whittling animal figurines with his jump knife, especially ducks and fish. His dream was to own a fishing cabin up in Michigan and after a few beers he often got misty-eyed describing his favorite rivers and lakes and explaining exactly where he planned to build his cabin. "What I'd give to be fishing right now," he'd sigh.

Rokowski's reputation grew considerably during the nine months training in England when several of the men began frequenting an ice rink not far from the base. Word had spread that the rink was crawling with lonely English girls and it was only a matter of bumping into them to make an introduction. Unfortunately, Rokowski was the only one who could skate.

"Well, son of a bitch," said Tony Bertucci, clinging to the rail next to Mead as they watched Rokowski glide backward across the ice. Mead couldn't believe how graceful Rokowski looked, nimble and assured as he zigzagged between the other skaters. The English girls were soon lining up for lessons and within days Rokowski and a small brunette with curly hair and a pretty mouth had fallen madly in love, much to the envy of the rest of the company.

"Jesus, the fucking Polack's getting laid," said Bertucci, tossing in his cot one night. Bertucci was a talkative amateur boxer from the Bronx with curly black hair—later shaved into a Mohawk for the invasion—a thick neck and a flat nose, thus earning the nickname Punchy. He was renowned for his acute and nightly bouts of squirrel fever, so that nobody wanted to sleep in the same bunk. "I'm stuck with you bunch of fruitcakes and Rokowski's out on maneuvers."

Rokowski volunteered for the paratroopers because he loved planes but couldn't qualify for flight school. On D-Day he nearly landed on top of the burning wreckage of a C-47, singeing all the hair on the left side of his head and burning the skin on his neck so that it was covered with blisters. Still, he'd been so certain that he'd land in a lake and drown that he was delighted just to be alive. "All this time I'm thinking I'm going to drown and what happens? I just about get my goose cooked," he laughed after he and Mead met up a few hours after the drop, both completely lost and Mead still so shaken by Jimbo's death that he couldn't form the words to tell Rokowski.

"Shh," said Mead, crouching next to a hedgerow and gesturing for Rokowski to get down.

"We must have missed the drop zone," said Rokowski.

"No shit," whispered Mead. "I think we're too far north."

"I was thinking we need to head west."

After some debate they decided to walk west following a narrow road, but soon retreated into the underbrush at the sound of approaching vehicles. They watched in horrified silence as two German trucks filled with soldiers passed by.

"Where the hell is everybody?" said Rokowski.

"I think we have to go south," said Mead, looking at the brass compass strapped to his left wrist.

"What I'd give to be sitting by a river in Michigan fishing right now," said Rokowski. "I know this spot—"

"Would you shut up?"

They waited several minutes, then crawled forward, keeping to the side of the road.

"I gotta take a crap," said Rokowski after they'd only gone a few hundred feet.

"Oh, Christ, make it fast." Rokowski squatted against a tree while Mead kept watch.

"What was that?"

"What?"

Silence, then they both heard a metallic sound coming from a clump of bushes off to their right. Rokowski yanked his pants up and crawled back to Mead. "See anything?"

Mead shook his head and tapped his forefingers together, gesturing for Rokowski to use his cricket.

Click-clack.

No response. They both kept their rifles aimed at the bushes, straining to see.

"I don't wanna kill no Americans," whispered Rokowski.

"Think we should use the challenge?" asked Mead, trying to suck some saliva into his mouth.

"If they're Americans, yes. If they're Germans, definitely not."

They heard a rustling in the bushes.

"Flash?" Mead called out in a loud whisper.

No response. They looked at each other again.

"Flash?"

The first bullet hit just in front of Mead, throwing dirt in his face. The second hit the first-aid pack he kept strapped to the right side of his helmet, jerking his head to the side. They both emptied their clips into the bushes, then slid backward into a shallow ditch and reloaded. "It's too far for grenades," said Rokowski; peering over the edge and firing again before sliding back down.

"Yeah, but what if they're coming closer?"

They both crawled forward and fired off several more rounds, then pressed down into the earth as bullets splattered dirt around them. "We've got to get closer first," said Rokowski, nervously snapping his teeth together. Mead tried to stifle the waves of fear that churned his stomach. "I'll try to crawl through that hedgerow and go around. Count of three, you toss a grenade and cover me."

"You're crazy," said Mead.

"Staying here's crazy. They're probably flanking us right now."

Mead felt a rising sense of terror as he imagined several German soldiers crawling toward them. Or maybe they'd already gotten behind them and were preparing to attack. Mead quickly turned his head and stared into the darkness, trying to make out shapes.

"You ready?" whispered Rokowski, rising to his knees.

Mead reloaded and pulled the pin on a grenade, wondering whether it was common to be feeling as shaky as he did or whether he wasn't going to be able to handle actual combat. Jesus, fighting until someone dies? But he had to handle it. Everything was irrevocable. "Okay, I'm ready."

"One, two, three . . ." Mead hurled the grenade as far as he could, then flopped down on his stomach and squeezed off five rounds as Rokowski scrambled off through the hedgerow. The grenade exploded, then silence, broken only by the sound of distant gunfire.

Mead held his breath, listening. Nothing. A minute passed, then another. Was Rokowski dead? What if they'd knifed him? Then they'd be coming for me. *Just let me go home.* He slid forward again and fired off three more rounds, then pulled out another clip and reloaded as bullets cracked overhead.

So this is it. Only nineteen, just like Thomas. Hardly a life. He remembered the smell of his father's hardware store and the way the worn floor planks creaked and the jingle of the cash register. How will Mother take it? He thought of the day the telegram came informing them that Thomas's ship had gone down, how his parents went silent for weeks. *Gonna miss you, big brother.* Then he thought of Sophie and all the letters she had written him, letters promising more than he ever deserved. Would she really have married me? Would our children have had blue eyes or green eyes? How long before she falls in love with another guy?

Suddenly he heard an explosion followed by rifle fire. He raised his head and saw a figure zigzagging toward him. *My turn.* He aimed and squeezed off a shot but the figure kept coming. He fired another but missed again. After the figure cut right Mead aimed just to the left and began to squeeze the trigger.

"It's me, you stupid son of a bitch!"

Mead lowered his rifle. Jesus, Rokowski.

"Who the fuck are you firing at?"

"I . . . I thought I saw someone behind you. I was covering you."

"Like hell you were." Rokowski collapsed down on the ground next to Mead and gasped for air.

"You all right?"

"I don't know." Rokowski checked his body. "Nothing missing."

"Did you get them?"

"Yeah, I got them."

"How many?"

"Four."

"No shit? That's great."

Rokowski pulled out a cigarette, trying to hide the flame as he lit it. Mead noticed his hands were shaking. "I've never done anything like that before," Rokowski said, rolling over on his back. His blackened face glistened with sweat.

"I didn't think you had." Mead wondered whether he could have done it. No, not a chance.

"Can't believe I really did it, to tell you the truth."

"You're a born killer."

Rokowski looked back where the dead Germans lay. "Wonder how long it will be before their families find out?"

"What the hell are you bringing up a thing like that for?"

"Well, it's strange, don't you think? Four dead Germans and nobody knows yet but us. I'm just wondering how long it will take for the families to find out."

"I could care less."

Rokowski took a long drag of his cigarette. "Guess they'll never know what really happened. Heck, they'll probably be wondering about it for years." Rokowski was like that, always mulling over things other people didn't even pause to think about.

"Just be glad it's not our families."

They lay in silence for several minutes listening to the various gun battles off in the distance and the constant rumble of artillery both in front and behind them, so that it sounded as if they were in a vast echo chamber. Then Rokowski said, "I don't think I could ever kill anybody with my bare hands."

"Hopefully, you won't have to."

"Could you?"

Personally, Mead had strong doubts and desperately hoped he could keep the war at some sort of distance. "If I have to."

They both watched a bright white flare rise in the distance and hover, followed by more small-arms fire. "Crazy world, isn't it?" said Rokowski.

"Crazier every minute," said Mead, getting up and standing cautiously against a nearby tree to piss. "Now let's go find the others."

They wandered in cautious confusion through darkened fields and along hedgerows until daylight, shooting at shadows and hiding from German troop convoys until finally they heard the *click-clack* of a cricket on the far side of a hedgerow. Rokowski answered with his cricket and they slowly raised their heads to see Punchy and Jay Goldberg leading five German soldiers at gunpoint.

"Look what we caught ourselves," said Goldberg, who was from Long Island and once got to throw out the first ball at a Yankees game. Like other Jews, he'd removed his dog tags in case of capture. "Whose brilliant idea was it to put an H on them?" he'd complained repeatedly. "I mean, is that supposed to be for *Hebrew* or *Himmler*?"

"What the hell are we going to do with them?" asked Rokowski, gesturing toward the Germans. They all knew they weren't supposed to take prisoners the first twenty-four hours. It wasn't official policy, but it was understood.

"That's what we've been wondering," said Punchy.

Mead studied the Germans with fascination, feeling slightly self-consciousness when they returned his stare. The enemy. Face to face. Two of them smiled and seemed happy to be finished with the war while the other three looked either frightened or sullen. Behind them the sun was just rising through the trees, stretching shadows across the road.

"Our panzers will be here soon," said one of the Germans, who spoke excellent English and carried himself with enormous dignity. The tallest of the five, he had a long thin scar along his chin and was missing part of an ear. "They will throw you back in the sea."

"Like hell they will," said Rokowski.

Mead studied a short, muscular-looking blonde whose eyes were full of anger. He looked at the insignia on the German's dirty uniform: *SS.* So this is Hitler's finest. Hardly superhuman. Yet the arrogance is still there. All those years the swaggering conqueror. The German caught Mead's eye, his face filled with disgust. Taste of your own medicine, eh? When the German edged closer Mead raised his rifle, motioning for him to back away.

"I've been to Minnesota once," said the oldest German, who looked middle-aged and spoke with a thick accent. "My uncle lives in Minneapolis."

"You should have stayed in Minnesota," said Rokowski.

"We both know that the real enemy are the Russians," said the taller German. "Why fight each other?"

"For starters, because I'm a Jew," said Goldberg. "See, we're basically one big Jewish army. Millions of angry Jews. Isn't that so, guys?"

Mead and the others nodded, trying not to laugh.

"This here is a lead element of the Goldberg Division," he continued. "You have heard of the famous Goldberg Division, haven't you?"

Two of the Germans nodded obediently.

"And off course we got the Schwartz Division on our right and the Cohen Armored on our left, though frankly, neither have quite the reputation of the Glorious Goldberg."

More nods as Punchy, Mead and Rokowski howled with laughter.

Goldberg put his face up to the tall German. "You like matzo ball soup? Good, because our cooks make a fine matzo ball soup. Hell, you probably won't be eating nothing but matzo ball soup from here on in: breakfast, lunch, dinner . . ."

The German took a step back and raised his hands in appeasement.

"That's right, you stupid fucking Nazi," said Goldberg. "We're going to stuff a few matzo balls right up Adolf's big fat ass."

Suddenly the short German lunged at Rokowski, who was standing nearest, and ripped the pin from one of two grenades hanging at chest level from the metal D-rings of his suspenders.

Rokowski stared down at the grenade in disbelief.

One-one thousand . . .

"Throw it!" yelled Mead.

Rokowski dropped his rifle and tried to grab the grenade but the German wrapped his arms around him, locked his wrists behind Rokowski's back and held him in a bear hug, the grenade between them.

Two-one thousand . . .

"Jesus Christ, get him off me!"

Mead grabbed the German by the back of the coat and yanked, then took his rifle butt and struck it against the side of the German's head as hard as he could. The German held on, saliva hissing between his clenched teeth. Mead struck again.

Three-one thousand . . .

Blood poured down the side of the German's head but still he hung on, almost lifting Rokowski into the air.

"Somebody help me!"

Mead hesitated, looking straight at Rokowski. *I can't help you, Roy. Can't you see that there's nothing I can do? I've got to save myself, Roy. You can understand that, can't you?*

Four-one thousand . . .

"For God's sake, Mead, get out of there!" cried Goldberg, who had taken cover along with Punchy. From the corner of his eye Mead saw the remaining four Germans making a dash for the woods.

I'm so sorry, Roy.

Mead turned and started for the ditch along the side of the road just as the grenade went off. He felt it against his back, the concussion lifting him and then a strange sensation of wetness. There was a moment of silence, then Mead heard Goldberg firing at the fleeing Germans. "You bastards!"

"You all right?" said Punchy, crouching beside Mead.

Mead couldn't talk.

Punchy inspected his back, which was covered with blood and bits of flesh. "I don't see any wounds. For a moment I thought it was . . . you."

Mead slowly sat up, resting his head between his knees.

"Crazy fucking Kraut, huh?" said Punchy.

Mead nodded.

"Poor fucking Rokowski. What a way to go. And Christ, you almost got yourself killed too."

Mead started to raise his head.

"I'm telling you, you don't even want to look."

But Mead knew he had to look. He owed it to Rokowski to look. *All I want is a nice little fishing cabin in Michigan.*

Slowly, very slowly, he raised his head.

• • •

Mead remained perfectly still in his chair as the record began to skip, his shirt soaked through. He took another sip of his drink, his eyes fixed on a needlepoint pillow Sophie had made during her furious needlepoint phase, then pulled himself up, walked over to the stereo and turned it off. After closing down the house and checking the doors twice he paused outside Sophie's room, listening for sounds, then cleaned himself up for bed. Before turning off his bedside lamp he went back to the living room, took his list from the notepad, then got a piece of tape and stuck it on the refrigerator.

· · ·

This has got to be a joke. Push-ups? Andrew stood in the kitchen staring at the list. His grandfather was out front weeding the lawn. Jumping jacks? *Fuck me.* The old fart was right, it was worse than being committed. They didn't make you do jumping jacks in the nut house.

No telephone calls.

No music.

Mop kitchen floor each morning.

Prepare room for daily inspection at 8 A.M.

Inspection? Was he out of his mind? Andrew read further down the list.

Homework: three hours a day.

Reading: at least one hour a day. Books to be assigned.

Assigned? GI Joe had cracked. Alzheimer's for sure.

"Good morning," said Mead, entering the kitchen and pouring himself a cup of coffee.

Andrew grunted.

"The mop's in the hall closet. I'll inspect your room in twenty minutes. Then we'll do some calisthenics."

"But I . . ."

"Questions?"

Andrew stood there in his oversized T-shirt and underwear looking up at his grandfather in horror. "I guess not."

"And don't *ever* come out of your room in your underwear."

The obvious thing to do was to get stoned. *Really* stoned. Cleaning could even be fun with the right buzz. Sometimes, after smoking a joint on the way home from school, Andrew would spend the whole afternoon rearranging his room and organizing his CDs and putting his magazines into perfect piles. He went to the closet and searched through his grandma's shoes, trying to remember where he'd hidden his dope. Finally he found the small resealable baggie in the toe of an orange dress shoe. Man she had tiny feet, he thought, sniffing cautiously at the shoe. He pulled out the red

Bic lighter and one of three joints he'd managed to scrounge before the trip and carefully slipped them into his pocket.

"I thought I might warm up with a quick jog around the block," he told his grandfather as he headed for the front door.

Mead looked surprised. "Not a bad idea. Just don't get lost. All the houses around here look the same. Mine's the one with the name plaque."

Andrew walked until he saw a small park with a playground at one end and a small wooded area at the other. He looked around quickly, then crawled into the bushes and lit the joint, deciding to smoke half and save the rest. He preferred drinking to getting stoned because alcohol usually made him feel bigger while pot could make him seriously paranoid if he wasn't careful. But he loved the way weed cranked up his imagination so that he could really appreciate all the poetry in *The Lord of the Rings* and sometimes even feel the deadly pull of the one ring. He took a long hit, keeping the joint cupped in his left hand. He'd gotten stoned before classes a few times but stopped when he realized that it made Kevin Bremer seem even more intimidating than he was, exaggerating all his features until he looked like a huge fucking troll. Besides, pot gave Andrew the giggles, sometimes so bad that he got heartburn. He held in the hit another few seconds, then exhaled loudly, immediately feeling the lightness in his head. Truly, everything was pretty fucking funny when you thought about it. He let out a giggle, then another. Some days sitting in class he felt like his head would burst from trying not to laugh at the hilarity of everything. He giggled again as he thought of how he and Matt used to spend months building model cars, agonizing over every little piece, which they sandpapered down until the fit was just right. And then as soon as the last coat of metallic paint dried, they'd hurry down to the lake, strap firecrackers to the cars, add a sprinkling of gas, then light the fuse and push them down a hill. Now that's funny. He took another hit, then carefully tapped the joint out and slipped it back into his pocket before climbing out of the bushes and brushing himself off.

Hand me the mop and bucket, Sarge, and step aside. I am a cleaning machine!

He sang "Rocky Mountain High" all the way back.

• • •

"Do you have any Cheetos?"

Mead looked up at his grandson, who had just finished sweeping the back patio and still held the broom in one hand, a silly look on his face. "Have a raisin cookie."

"I did."

"Then have some pretzels. There's a bag in the cabinet just to the left of the oven."

"Do you have any Doritos?"

"No, I don't have any Doritos."

Andrew seemed to mull the matter over for a moment. "Guess I'll have pretzels."

Twenty minutes later Mead got up and went to the kitchen to make sure Andrew had resealed the pretzel bag. First he checked the large tin of cookies on the top of the refrigerator. Empty. After searching through the cabinets for the pretzel bag he found it in the garbage pail beneath an empty can of smoked almonds, which Mead had purposely hidden behind the soup bowls. Christ, the boy's going to clean me out. He quickly grabbed a jar of Skippy Super Chunk peanut butter from the shelf along with a box of Melba Toast and took them to his room, hiding them in his closet.

At least the kid could clean. Mead peered into the bathroom where Andrew was furiously scrubbing the toilet while humming loudly to himself, reminding Mead of a smart-mouthed guy from Mississippi who was twice forced to clean an entire latrine with a toothbrush. The odd thing was that his grandson actually seemed to enjoy cleaning. He had the same look on his face that Sophie used to get when she sewed on a button, all radiant and purposeful. Several times Mead even heard laughter coming from the bathroom. Strange kid.

That afternoon Mead went to the library and spent an hour looking through the history collection. He had always shied away from books and movies about the war because he didn't see the sense in going back to a place that he hated the first time. But it would be good for the kid. Give him a little education. And I *am* his grandfather. He should know who he's dealing with.

But what book to start with? *A Bridge Too Far? The Longest Day? The Rise and Fall of the Third Reich?* (That would keep the boy out of the malls for a while.) Then he saw it there on the shelf: *Brave Men,* a collection by Ernie Pyle. Yes, that was the place to start. *Brave Men.* We'll go from there.

• • •

They ate dinner that evening at the kitchen table, both silent. Andrew had some sort of tofu hot dog, piling on the relish, while Mead ate pork chops and baked beans. As Andrew pushed the last piece of hot dog into his mouth Mead got up, retrieved the book from a bag on the counter and slid it across the table.

"I think we'll start with this one."

"Start . . . what?"

"Teaching you a few things."

Andrew glanced down at the book, then back up at Mead. "Did you tell my mom yet? Is she coming to get me?"

Mead paused, taking his time. "No, I haven't told her yet."

"But you're going to?"

"I'm thinking about it."

"You mean you might not?"

"I mean I'm thinking about it."

For the first time Mead saw the hint of a smile flash across Andrew's face.

• • •

Andrew hadn't even considered the possibility that his grandfather wouldn't tell, that she might never have to know. It made him want to laugh and cry at the same time, knowing that she wasn't at that very moment sitting in the living room with her head in her hands weeping and wondering what she was ever going to do with him. Would his grandfather still tell her? But why wouldn't he? He didn't seem like the kind to keep secrets or bend the rules. But maybe he wouldn't. And so Andrew would do everything he could to please his grandfather until the twenty-one days were over. Anything would be worth keeping his mom from finding out.

After taking a long shower he sat on his bed rubbing his sore shoulders—I'm way out of shape—then got into bed with the book. He set the timer on his watch for an hour and began to read.

Chapter 4

The house was looking damn tidy, no doubt about that. Mead even had his grandson hanging the flag each morning—it was a sight to see—and folding the laundry and washing the windows and waxing his old blue Chevrolet Caprice, which guzzled gas like a Sherman but had the heart of a squad car. But the morning exercises were an embarrassment. The boy could hardly do ten push-ups without his back swaying like an old horse. Mead tried to supervise at first, but soon found it unbearable to watch as Andrew gasped and struggled.

"You've got to *push!*"

He still hadn't said anything to Sharon. Part of it was his reluctance to cause her further pain and part was Mead's own embarrassment that Andrew had gotten into further trouble. And then he started thinking that maybe he and Andrew would work it out themselves. And they *would* work it out. Mead was determined now. After three years in the service he ought to know a thing or two about dealing with delinquents.

Mead sat in the kitchen finishing his oatmeal and watching as Andrew bent over to rinse the mop in a bucket. Mead slammed down his spoon. "For God's sake, I can see your undershorts, and even they're falling off."

Andrew stood and tried to hoist his pants up but as soon as he let go they slid down again, exposing exactly four inches of underwear. "Sorry."

"I can still see them."

"That's kind of the way the pants fit."

"But they *don't* fit. I know a good tailor—"

"They're *supposed* to be this way."

"Well you ought to get a good look at yourself from behind. Takes away a person's appetite."

Andrew rinsed the mop and then pushed and pulled it slowly across the floor.

"Listen, I know the budget's kind of tight back home. Heck, I'm happy to buy you some decent clothes. If you hadn't gone shoplifting the other day, I was going to take you to Nordstrom and—"

"I don't need any clothes."

And there Mead was right on the edge again, wanting to say, *To hell you don't, boy. Pull your goddamn trousers up.* It was like keeping your boots shined to a spitting polish as you trained to take on Rommel's panzer divisions. Mead hadn't understood the connection at first. It seemed like more chickenshit to him. But then after a few weeks in Europe he got it. The whole psychological machinery made perfect sense to him. If you let one thing slip then another thing would. You couldn't afford any slips. You needed absolute *perfection.*

He got up and carried his bowl of oatmeal into the living room, vowing to revisit the matter later.

"Looks like we got an invitation," said Andrew excitedly, coming in with the mail and dropping a handwritten note into Mead's lap. Mead cautiously opened the beige unstamped envelope, which was addressed to Andrew and the General.

> Might you two gentlemen do me the pleasure of honoring me with your company for dinner tonight, say around six? I happen to have good intelligence that you are both available so regrets will not be taken kindly!
>
> Evelyn
>
> PS: Vegetarian fare only.

Vegetarian fare? Mead looked at Andrew. "How does she know we're not busy?"

Andrew squirmed. "I might have said something."

Mead gave him the eye.

"So we're going?"

Mead reread the invitation, impressed by the flawless cursive. "I'll think about it."

"Great!" Andrew looked pleased with himself. "Gee, I wonder who the other gentleman is?"

"Very funny."

Mead thought of all sorts of excuses: his back, his sinuses, a fridge full of moldering meat, prior commitments unbeknownst to Andrew, but he knew none would survive Evelyn's look of hurt. So they'd get through the dinner and then they could call it even. Certainly Sophie would understand the logic of that.

Early that evening Mead sent Andrew back to his room three times to find a better shirt until he realized that the boy didn't pack anything appropriate. In the end he grudgingly signed off on a dark blue T-shirt with a picture of a rabid-looking armadillo riding a skateboard off a cliff, which was only slightly less offensive than the alternatives.

"Well, what a treat!" chirped Evelyn as she opened the door. The house smelled of all sorts of delicious spices, reminding Mead of the holidays and how Sophie used to keep a pot of cider mulling on the stove. He followed Andrew in, feeling a twinge of guilt.

"I have a hoop just like that," she said, admiring Andrew's earring. Mead rolled his eyes. "I think it goes great with your highlights."

"Evelyn—"

"Let me guess, the General doesn't exactly approve."

"He hates the way I look."

"He's *sixteen,*" said Mead.

"That's just the point," said Evelyn. "If not now, when? Frankly, I wish I'd taken a million more risks when I was young." She shook her head with a smile. "I was such a prude growing up."

"I really don't think he needs any encouragement."

"I told you she's great," said Andrew, grinning.

Mead rubbed his temple, trying to recall the early warning signs of a stroke. "Would you happen to have a little bourbon around?"

"I've been waiting for someone to help me get through George's stock. God knows, I'll never drink it all." She disappeared into the kitchen.

Mead turned to Andrew. "You watch your manners, you understand?"

"Why are you so uptight?"

"I wouldn't know where to begin."

Evelyn reappeared, handing Mead a bourbon and Andrew a Coke and gesturing for them to take a seat in the living room, which was small but bright and cheery with lots of white and yellow. "So, you must be a junior?"

"Sophomore."

"I hated my sophomore year. In fact, I thought high school was a big waste of time."

"So do I!"

"For Pete's sake, Evelyn." Mead was starting to perspire, wishing he'd worn an undershirt.

"Are we bothering you?"

Mead rubbed his jaw. "Perhaps we could talk about something a bit more . . . *constructive*."

"Fine. I'd *love* to hear about your experiences in the war." She turned to Andrew. "Your grandfather is so modest you'd never know he's highly decorated."

Andrew smiled. "Yeah, I'd love to hear some stories."

"I am not *highly* decorated."

"Don't believe a word he says. You should have heard your grandmother carry on about him." Evelyn and Andrew stared at Mead, waiting.

"Some other time." He took a large slug of bourbon, wondering how he'd ever make it through dinner. "So, are those all annuals out front?" He sighed with relief as Evelyn smacked it right out of the ballpark, talking well into dinner about moisture retention and root systems and soil conditions. As she brought out dessert—pecan and raisin pie topped with whipped cream—he glanced at his watch and figured that another half hour would about do it. And yet he wasn't anxious to leave. Several times he even caught his eyes lingering on her neck, which was surprisingly smooth. He looked down at his bourbon, trying to count how many refills he'd had. Andrew and Evelyn were busy chattering like a bunch of long-lost soul mates.

"When did your husband die?" asked Andrew.

"Ten years ago this Thanksgiving. He fooled all of us right through the holiday, then collapsed just hours after our son and daughter left for the airport."

"What happened?"

"Andrew—"

"Officially it was a heart attack but I know it was stress—and probably his diet, too. He just rusted from the inside out." She folded her napkin in her lap, then spread it out and refolded it again. "George was a world-class worrywart. It wasn't so bad when he was younger; I just thought he was being responsible. But over the years he got worse and worse until he was up half the night running worst-case scenarios." She spread the napkin out again, flattening the creases with her palm. "It seems so silly; all those years wasted worrying about things and now he doesn't have a care in the world."

"So he rusted to death?"

"You'll have to excuse Andrew . . ."

But Evelyn was smiling. "In a manner of speaking."

Andrew seemed to reflect on that for a moment. "What kind of job did he have?"

"He owned a small lighting business. We were never rich but he always made enough to support us."

"So that's why it's so bright in here." Andrew squinted up at the recessed lighting.

"Andrew—"

"Is it bright?"

"I don't mind," said Andrew quickly.

"It's perfect," said Mead. He took another swig of bourbon, feeling a bit like a chaperon.

"I could turn the lights down. Everything's on a dimmer." She smiled. "George loved his dimmers. Frankly, I think he would have put me on one if he could have."

"I'm used to it now," said Andrew.

"I'll turn them down." She got up and lowered the lights. "Better?"

"Way better." Andrew smiled as Mead fired down another belt of bourbon. "So, did you work in the lighting business too?"

"I was too busy being a mother until the children were older, then I got into interior decorating—don't ask me how. My real dream was to go to cooking school and get a job as a pastry chef but George wouldn't hear of it."

"You'd make a great chef," said Andrew, who'd eaten three platefuls of curried vegetables and rice and four homemade dinner rolls.

"Why thank you." She folded her napkin again. "Your grandmother was quite a cook herself." She turned to Mead. "Andrew tells me you've kept all her things?"

Mead put down his fork. "Not all of them."

"I hung on to George's things for years. The truth is, I hadn't given up on the idea that he might come back." She took a sip of her white wine and then cupped the glass with both hands, staring into it. "It wasn't until I got rid of them that I really said good-bye."

Mead felt himself redden.

The scheming little tart.

It's just a dinner, Peanut. I got roped into it.

It's a date.

Mead stood up. "It's time for us to go."

"What?" said Andrew.

"I didn't mean to offend you," said Evelyn.

"It's getting late."

"It's only eight fifteen," said Andrew, looking at his watch.

"I said, it's *time.*"

Mead thanked Evelyn for the dinner, then hurried Andrew out the door and across the street.

"I'm sorry if I said something to upset you," Evelyn called out.

"I'm not *upset.*"

· · ·

Mead was lying on his bed with his clothes on when Sharon called. She talked to Andrew briefly on the kitchen line before Mead picked up again.

"How are you, Sweetheart?"

"My car died," she moaned.

Jesus, thought Mead, what is it with some people? "That old Celica? What's wrong this time?"

"Everything. The guy says it needs a new clutch, for starters."

"How many miles does it have?"

"Just over 180,000."

"I'll buy you a new one."

"Dad, I couldn't ask you to do that."

"You didn't. Now go rent yourself something for a few days and get yourself a *Consumer Reports.* I'll ask around myself."

Long silence.

"You okay?" Mead asked, worried by the frailty in her voice. And yet her mother had had such strength.

"I think I'm going to get fired."

"But you just started."

Another long pause. "I accidentally deleted all of my boss's expense account reports. I don't know how it happened." Her voice sounded so small that Mead wondered if she was having a breakdown.

"Then you'll find another job. Or maybe you could go back to school, get your degree."

Sharon had dropped out of college after falling in love with some slick joker from Los Angeles and never went back after he dumped her, despite her parents' pleas.

"College just isn't my thing, Dad," she'd said.

"College is everybody's thing these days, Sharon. Now would you take our advice just this once?"

But she hadn't. And ever since it had pained him to see how hard she struggled, first as a receptionist, then as some sort of administrative assistant—they didn't seem to have plain old secretaries anymore—then keeping the books for some auto parts shop that promptly went out of business (no surprise there), then for some medical equipment dealer. And on top of it all trying to raise a teenager single-handedly. What sort of life was that? Nothing any girl grows up dreaming about.

The cold truth was, she never should have had the child in the first place. Not Sharon. Parenthood just wasn't for everybody. Or even most people, in Mead's opinion. Hell, nine out of ten parents were over their heads from the get-go and the children themselves rarely seemed worth the trouble, at least once they got past the cute phase, which even Mead enjoyed. (And Andrew had been cute, with big brown eyes and a sprinkling of freckles across a pug nose.)

"I don't even want to show my face tomorrow." She groaned again.

"I'm sure they'll give you another chance."

More silence.

"You still getting child support?"

"When he remembers."

"I could have him killed."

"Dad."

"I'd even do it myself. Pro bono. Think of it as community service."
"Please."

"Then let me pay for a lawyer. We'll get a court order."

"I don't want to talk about it. Listen, I've got to go. I'll let you know what happens."

From her voice Mead knew she was only hanging up to have a good cry. He never knew what to say when she got that way. Was there something I should be doing? Finally he said, "You take care of yourself, Pumpkin, you got that?"

"I'll try, Dad."

"And for crying out loud, don't worry about us."

Shortly after they hung up the phone rang again. Had she been fired already? He snatched the phone off the receiver. "Where you been hiding yourself, you old goat?" Damn. It was Harry Braxton.

"Harry."

"What do you say we play a few rounds Tuesday?"

"I'm a little busy right now."

"You? *Busy?* Who are you fooling?" Harry let out a big chuckle.

Mead ground his teeth. "My grandson's in town."

"Sharon's boy? Great! Taken him to the ballpark yet? I can get you box seats."

"He's not really much of a baseball fan."

"That's too bad. My grandson just got into Harvard Med. Did I mention that?"

"I believe you did."

"Our granddaughter's getting married in July. Great family. Eleanor's beside herself."

"Congratulations."

"Haven't seen much of you lately. You keeping any secrets?"

"I've been tied up with a few projects around the house."

"You must have added on another story by now." Harry chuckled again.

Mead glanced at his watch, then switched the phone to the other ear and stared up at the ceiling, noticing a small water stain in the corner.

Harry drew a breath. "Listen pal, I know how hard it must be for you."

"I'm doing just fine, thanks."

"But you've got to get out now and then. No use sitting around that house all day moping."

"I'm not *moping,* Harry. And like I said, I'm busy with my grandson just now, but thanks for the call."

"Hey, maybe you could bring him over for dinner next week? Eleanor would love it. Give her an excuse to make her meatballs."

Mead winced at the thought of the four of them sitting around Harry's enormous dining room table talking about Eleanor's meatballs. Granted, they were delicious. Even better than Sophie's, truth be told. (And she was always suspicious about that, probing him whenever they drove home from dinner with the Braxtons.) But not with Andrew. Not a chance. He wasn't about to take baggy butt out on the social circuit. "That's kind of you, Harry, but like I said, we're rather booked up at the moment."

"You call if you change your mind."

"Wouldn't hesitate."

After he hung up he noticed Andrew standing in the bedroom door-way. Mead raised his eyebrows.

"I was just wondering . . . when I could have my CD player back?"

"You mean *if.*"

Andrew's face sunk even further. Hard not to pity the kid, mug like that. And yet damn it, he deserved the punishment. Who did he think he was? "You'd better get back to your homework." Andrew turned and shuffled off.

• • •

Mead stood in the hallway outside the bathroom door the next evening waiting to intercept Andrew as he emerged. The streetlights had just come on and the neighbor's Jack Russell was having his nightly attack of hysteria, barking so incessantly that the first time Mead heard him he called the police, fearing some sort of Manson-style mass murder.

"You ever coming out of there?" Mead shouted into the door.

"Almost done."

"Christ, you take longer than your grandma and she took so long I once had to relieve myself behind the garage." Finally the door opened. "What the hell happened to your face?"

"Acne," mumbled Andrew.

"You're better off leaving those things alone." Mead thought of a soldier named Smitty, who had the worst acne in the company, like bee stings all over his face. Every spare moment Smitty would check himself in his trench mirror, groaning at the latest outbreak and blaming the K-rations. And then one day Smitty was shot in the head by a sniper and Mead remembered thinking, well, at least Smitty won't be getting any more zits.

"I was wondering if you're up to a game of backgammon?"

"I was going to read."

"You've read plenty today. Let's have a game." Mead wasn't going to give him any choice.

"I don't know how."

"Then I'll teach you."

Mead opened the hall closet and pulled down his backgammon board from the top shelf and carried it into the living room, thinking of Sophie and the games they used to play, especially double solitaire and Scrabble. He set up the board on the coffee table, then walked Andrew through the rules.

"Ready?"

"I think so."

Andrew won the first game.

"Beginner's luck," said Mead, wondering if he'd been suckered. He tried harder the next game but lost again.

"I like backgammon," said Andrew. "Play again?"

"I'm more of a card man myself," said Mead, quickly closing the board. He plucked a pencil from the holder and picked up a crossword puzzle from the side table. His grandson sat looking at him.

"You must miss Grandma," Andrew said suddenly.

Mead felt himself flush. "Of course I do." He returned to the puzzle.

"I was thinking how hard that must be, losing someone after all those years."

"Yes, it is."

"How long were you guys married?"

Mead put the puzzle down on his lap. "Fifty-one years."

"Wow."

"It's just a matter of sticking with something long enough."

"I miss her. She was really nice to me."

"She adored you." Mead noticed an embarrassed smile spread across Andrew's shiny face.

"How old were you when you first met her?"

"Seventeen. We dated for a few months before I enlisted, and then when I got back she was still waiting for me."

"You didn't think she would be?"

"I had my doubts."

A look of amusement crossed Andrew's face. "How long until you got married?"

"Four months."

"Man, that's fast."

Mead couldn't help but smile. "We just knew. People didn't need to live together for twenty years before making up their minds."

"Do you ever think of marrying again?"

"Of course not."

"How come?"

"I'm too old, for one. And besides . . ." Mead couldn't think how to finish. "Well, it wouldn't be right." He quickly returned to his crossword puzzle, feeling the boy still looking at him. And just what did he see? Mead vaguely remembered his own grandfather, who died when Mead was twelve. He seemed less a person than an institution, as old and venerable as the church. And about as much fun. Mead could see him sitting on the porch after dinner, his worn but still noble features slumped in profound thought. Sometimes he'd sit so motionless that he reminded Mead of a statue, the kind covered with pigeon droppings in the town square. As Mead got older it saddened him that he'd never had the chance to know any of his grandparents, to learn how they'd come to terms with all the losses and disappointments and most of all the horrifying realization that your turn is almost over (and you never even played your best cards when you had them).

"How come you never talk about the war?" Andrew asked suddenly.

"No need to." Mead kept his eyes on his crossword puzzle.

"Mom says it's a shame."

"Oh she does, does she? And why would she say a thing like that?"

"Because we'll never learn about your experiences. It's like, family history."

Mead put the puzzle down in his lap. "Family history?"

"That's what she says. I was going to interview you over the phone for a class project, but Mom said you wouldn't talk about the war."

"She said that?"

Andrew nodded. "Other veterans like to talk about it. You always see them on TV explaining how they attacked and what they were thinking and—"

"Some guys love to talk." Mead tapped the tip of his pencil against the puzzle.

"You took part in D-Day, right? Fighting the Germans?"

"That's right."

"Pretty cool."

"I don't think that's the word I'd use."

"Why did you call them Krauts?"

"You know, sauerkraut."

"*Sauerkraut?* I don't get it."

"Never mind." Mead returned to his puzzle.

"Mom says you were a paratrooper, that you jumped out of a plane at night."

Mead nodded.

"That is like, *intense.*"

"I don't recommend it."

"Do you think about it a lot?"

"Not so much."

"I would." Andrew bobbed his head up and down as if in thought. "What kind of weapons did you use?"

"I don't see any need to—"

"I was, just wondering if you had like, a specialty?"

"I was a rifleman."

"Did you have any grenades?"

"We all had grenades."

"And a knife?"

Mead let out a sigh. "And a knife."

Andrew stood up and walked over to the small glass case on the mantle. "What did you get these for?" He looked closely at the decorations.

"Mostly just for being there." After Sophie died Mead had put the medals in his closet, but every time he went to get a shirt or pair of pants and saw the case sitting on the shelf he heard Sophie tisk-tisking him. Finally he put the display back on the mantle and ever since he'd made a point of keeping the house just the way it was when she was alive.

"What about this purple and gold one? The heart?"

"That's for getting wounded."

"Yeah, I thought you'd been wounded. Where did they get you?" His voice was full of curiosity.

Mead arched his eyebrows. "In the buttocks."

"The butt?" Andrew let out a laugh, which he tried to stifle, causing him to make a snorting sound. "That's *bad*." He studied the decorations some more. "Are any of these for heroism?"

"Not exactly." Mead was lying. He earned the Bronze Star for crawling across a snowy field three times under fire to drag men to safety, though it wasn't courage but a sort of blind fury that guided him. But to tell anything left too much unsaid. He looked back down at his puzzle, trying to concentrate on the next clue.

"Are you going to test me on what I'm reading?"

"Hadn't thought to." Mead looked up at his grandson. "What do you think so far?"

"Some of it's interesting. Parts are actually funny."

"Funny?"

"The way they talk. But there are some sad parts, too." Andrew sat back down on the sofa and browsed through the newspaper, then looked back at Mead. "Were you in a lot of battles?"

"Enough." Mead didn't look up from his puzzle.

"Was it really like they show in *Saving Private Ryan?*"

"Never saw it."

"No kidding? Oh man, you'd go nuts. Hey, maybe we could rent it?"

"I don't think so."

Andrew paused, then said, "Mom was right."

"What's that supposed to mean?"

"That you don't like talking about it."

"Why should I?"

"I dunno."

Mead put down his puzzle. "Okay, exactly what do you want to know?"

Andrew thought for a moment. "Did you see a lot of guys get killed?"

"As a matter of fact I did."

"And was it like . . ." Andrew churned his hands in the air.

"Yes, it was."

"Wow, that's got to be harsh. You probably still hate the Germans, huh?"

"Who said I hated them?"

"I just figured that you did."

"Only some of them."

"Like Hitler?"

"Yes, like Hitler."

"I would have hated him, too."

"He was very hateable," said Mead.

"Is that really a word?"

"I'm making it a word." Sophie was always on him for making up words and cheating at his crossword puzzles but the words he used made perfect sense to him. A language, he told her, must constantly evolve.

"What about the Japs? Did you hate them?"

"I guess I did. Just about everybody did."

"More than the Germans?"

"At first."

"Because they look . . . different?"

"Because they attacked us."

"Did you hate being in the army?"

"Parts of it." Actually, Mead hated a great deal of it. Yet what else in his life had even come close?

"I know I'd hate it."

"It's good for some people. Teach 'em a little discipline."

"I'm not dying just so rich people can have enough oil. *No way.*"

"It's not always so simple."

"At least you had real bad guys to fight. They were like, *evil.*" He toyed with the tiny gold hoop in his left ear, a habit that annoyed Mead immensely. "Doesn't Hitler kind of remind you of Darth Vader?"

"Darth who?"

"Never mind." Andrew tapped his earring with his fingernail. "It must be cool being a hero."

"I never considered myself a hero."

"Really?" Andrew looked genuinely surprised.

Mead felt a rising sense of discomfort. "Look, I just did what I had to and couldn't wait to get home, okay?"

"Mom thinks you're a big hero. Even Evelyn thinks so."

"Evelyn?"

"Oh yeah." Andrew smiled.

"I'd really like to finish this puzzle."

"Sorry." Andrew got up from the couch and started toward the hall-way, then hesitated. "I was just wondering . . ."

"Now what?"

"Well . . ."

"Out with it."

"Did you ever *kill* anybody?"

Mead took off his glasses and rubbed the bridge of his nose. *You killed lots of them didn't you, Father?* His father had stared back wordlessly at him, a look of deep dismay creasing his hard features—before rising from the table. He didn't return that evening. *Wasn't that the whole point, Father? Killing?*

"Good night, Andrew."

The boy stood staring at him for a moment, then turned and retreated quickly to his room.

• • •

It was forty-eight hours after dropping into France before Mead knew for certain he'd killed his first man. He'd thought about what it would be like for months, privately dreading the moment when he'd finally find himself in the front row of the whole war effort, as if perched on the tip of a long sword that would be driven deep into the enemy. So few ever saw the front, which he imagined as a thin and jagged fault line where the conti-nental plates collided. But he was airborne, and that's where the airborne would be. The killing zone. Would he hesitate? Or would it come natu-rally? Some men seemed to have the killer instinct. But not Mead. Instead, he feared he'd have to defy his instincts.

And that's what he'd done.

The Germans were trying to rush in reinforcements to cut off the beachhead and Mead and others were ordered to attack, working their way through the hedgerows and then fighting to take a cluster of heavily defended farmhouses.

"I think we should wait for tanks," said Punchy, lying on the ground next to him and waiting for the order to go forward. While everyone grumbled about army life, few made quite as much noise as Punchy, who howled in protest at every idiotic order and indignity and expended enor-mous energy explaining exactly how he'd do things differently. "Nothing but numbskulls running the show," he'd say. "My life is in the hands of a bunch of numbskulls." And yet despite his constant complaining, Punchy was always the first to volunteer for the most dangerous assignments, if for no other reason than to assure himself that the job would be done right. As the days went on he became almost reckless in his desire to kill as many Germans as possible and get the war over with.

Punchy popped another piece of gum into his mouth and chewed nervously. (He jumped with twenty packs of Wrigley's as well as twelve Clark bars.) "Don't you think we should wait for tanks?"

"No one's asked me."

"I'm telling you, we should wait for tanks." A few minutes later word spread that the Germans had an 88 hidden behind one of the farmhouses. Punchy was apoplectic. "Ain't this just too-fucking much?" he said, chewing loudly.

Mead had heard plenty about the 88s. They all had. But he'd never seen what they could do. The shells from the flat-trajectory gun hit before you heard them fired, and once you became the prey, there was little to do but crawl into the ground or race forward in hopes that a few survivors would get close enough to kill the gun crew.

The first shell landed to their left, nearly vaporizing two men into tiny beads of red and flaying the bodies of a dozen others. Punchy gestured at Mead to plug his ears and open his mouth to lessen the concussion. Immediately another shell struck to their right as men screamed and the air filled with debris.

"Let's go!"

Punchy was the first man up, letting out a war whoop and running madly across the field toward the farmhouses. Mead scrambled to his feet and forced himself to follow, zigzagging back and forth with his gear bouncing all around as he struggled to keep up. Soon he could see the 88 peering out from behind a barn, the barrel pointed straight at them.

Another shell landed behind him, then another as machine gun fire skipped across the ground in front. Mead found himself yelling at the top of his voice as he ran, all the fear and anger tearing at his throat, as if yelling loud enough might keep him alive. They were closer now so that Mead could see the German gunners frantically reloading and firing one last round, then blowing the breech before dashing for cover. Other Germans shot at them from behind stone walls and buildings.

Mead went through two clips, never quite certain if he'd hit anything. As more men fell to the ground writhing or in silent heaps he looked around desperately for some sign of retreat but instead they continued forward, tossing grenades through windows and kicking down doorways. He watched an American get blown backwards by a grenade as another was shot in the head, and right then he knew he'd made a horrible mistake by joining the paratroopers; that he simply didn't possess the courage—the *fight*—that the others seemed to have. But still he kept up, staying close to Punchy as they leapfrogged from building to building, slowly driving the Germans back. Twice Mead saw a German aim directly at him and fire and twice the bullets missed. But usually he had no idea where the shots were coming from. The Germans had smokeless powder, which made it easier for them to hide, while every time Mead fired his rifle let off a telltale puff of smoke. It was, he thought, like being sent into battle with a cowbell around your neck. As the months passed, Mead would seethe at the realization that the Germans had not only the best artillery piece in the war— the 88—but more powerful and heavily armored tanks and a deadlier anti-tank weapon—the *panzerfaust*—and even a better light machine gun.

And then, right up close, he'd killed his first man, or the first one he was certain of. The German was already wounded, slumped against the remains of a half-track as Mead and others rushed by in a confused assault on German reinforcements who were streaming down the road. There were dead and wounded strewn everywhere, but somehow the German on the ground to his left caught his attention.

Mead turned to look just as the German lifted a rifle that lay across his lap. *You or me.* It was that simple. Nothing to think about or consider. No courage or cunning or skill required. Mead aimed from the hip and fired three times. The first round struck the German in the stomach; the second two hit him in the face. And that was it.

"I wasn't sure you had it in you," said Punchy, offering Mead a piece of gum, which Mead declined.

Mead stared at the dead man, feeling his hands suddenly shake. Jesus, I've done it. I've killed a man. And right there by the side of the road he vomited.

"Hey, take it easy," said Punchy, patting Mead on the back. Mead waved him away, then quickly rinsed his face and mouth with water from his canteen before hurrying to catch up with the others. For the rest of the day he struggled to conceal his queasiness, feeling shame and cowardice all over his face. He was *airborne,* for Christ's sake.

He didn't get another chance for two days. Somehow he was always right on the edge of the action, taking fire but never quite getting a clear line of sight at the enemy. He'd been curious to test himself again, eager, yet terrified, too; afraid he might start shaking again or that he couldn't do it. Best to get it over with, he told himself. Just get through it and then somehow get used to it.

And then, as the Germans sent more troops in, part of Mead's platoon set up an ambush, fourteen of them hidden in the undergrowth on the side of the road. Two hours later, in the last hazy light of dusk, a German patrol came walking down the road. Mead counted twelve of them, spaced several feet apart but obviously off guard, unaware of how far the Americans had penetrated. Mead quietly aimed through the brush, first at the lead soldier, then the next, trying to pick his target and awaiting the signal. *You or me.* That's what it always came down to. But still he felt his hands tingle as he aimed at the chest of a round-faced middle-aged German, his moist finger sliding lightly up and down the trigger. What is your name? Are you married? Do you have children and pets and nieces and nephews? Were you a farmer or grocer or clerk? Are you a God-fearing man? But how could you be? He moved his rifle a few inches to the left and trained it on the next German, who was younger with narrow shoulders and a tired face. Or how about you? What are you thinking about? Your family? Some buxom fraulein? Your feet? Has it occurred to you yet that perhaps Herr Hitler has led you astray; that you and all those you love are on the losing side? And what would you think about if you knew they would be your final thoughts?

It was mesmerizing, watching the last seconds of other men's lives, feeling the godlike power to destroy them, to choose the time and place and method of their death. In the heart or the head? The tall one or the short one? Strange, as if their lives had been on a collision course since birth. A boy from Akron. A boy from Hamburg or Stuttgart or perhaps Cologne. And unexpectedly, the moment of contact had arrived.

"Now!"

Thirty seconds later twelve Germans lay dead.

"That was a damn turkey shoot," said Punchy, wolfing down a Clark bar before searching through the pockets of the dead. Mead kept to the side of the road as the others scavenged for souvenirs, trying to hold back the revulsion in his stomach.

"Hey, look at these," said Punchy, gazing through a pair of German binoculars. "I can almost see Berlin."

Mead lit a cigarette, trying not to look at the crumpled body of the young German with the narrow shoulders.

"You okay?" Punchy asked, coming over to show off the binoculars.

"Sure. Just fine."

"How many you figure you got?"

Mead shrugged. "I don't know."

"I figure I got three of them. The three toward the back. See, I was working from back to front."

Mead nodded.

"You must have got at least two of them."

"No telling."

"I'll bet you got two of them." He looked through the binoculars again, then slapped Mead on the back. "We really surprised the fuck out of them, didn't we?"

"We sure did." And despite the weakness in his legs, Mead knew he could do it again.

• • •

The next morning Mead found a small wrapped box on the front porch. Evelyn, he thought, picking it up and carrying it in. He hadn't seen her out gardening lately and wondered if perhaps he'd been a bit rude the other night.

"Open it," said Andrew, sitting on the sofa in the living room with a bowl of cereal in his lap.

"Maybe later." Mead had always hated gifts. The only time he really lost his top with Sophie was when she threw a surprise birthday party for him, all the wrong people jumping out and screaming in his face when he got home from a terrible day at work.

"Then I will." Andrew took the box, tore off the wrapping and opened it, dumping the contents on the coffee table.

Mead tried to make sense of the pile of little white squares with words on them. Some sort of puzzle?

"They're word magnets," said Andrew. "You put them on your refrigerator and you can write things. You know, like poetry and stuff."

"Poetry?"

"Sure. Lots of people have them."

"On the refrigerator?"

"I told you Evelyn was cool." He scooped up the magnets from Mead's lap and took them to the kitchen. When Mead got up to look Andrew had already returned to his room. On the refrigerator he'd written: *Thanks for not telling.*

Mead pulled off the magnets one by one and placed them in a drawer.

Chapter 5

Eleven more days. Mead lay in bed with the lights off, wondering how to make a difference with the boy in the time they had left. There'd be more talks, of course. He still had to get to the bottom of the thing, find the abscess and root it out. He wondered what book to give him next. He'd never read much about the war himself; no need to. But Sophie read a book a week and loved to rattle on about every chapter. And the librarian had been kind enough to write out a list of recommendations, saying it was her favorite era. "But then, you'd know more about it than me," she had gushed, blushing. Yes, perhaps I would. So what next? Fiction? *The Thin Red Line* or *The Winds of War*? Or stick with the facts: something about the Battle of the Bulge or Stalingrad? (It bothered Mead how few Americans understood that it was the Russians who beat the Germans; that more than eighty percent of German military casualties were inflicted on the *Eastern* Front; that Hitler fought the West with one hand tied behind his back.) He rolled over to his side, then onto his back again. Better yet, something about the Holocaust. Give him a glimpse of real horror. He remembered Sophie reading Elie Wiesel's *Night* and how she cried so hard when she finished it that they both got out of bed and went into the living room and watched the late show until she dozed off.

He rolled back onto his side, fearing that sleep would be difficult. He tried to relax himself by thinking of his father's hardware store where he spent much of his childhood, drawing his first salary at the age of fifteen. Of all the places he remembered in his life, the store was the one place he always returned to—a refuge where he could take his thoughts and feel safe. He often wondered whether it would be the last memory he would cling to in the moment of death; whether everything else would fall away and he'd be a boy again among tools and men. Even now he could still recall the pleasant and unmistakable smell: the sawdust on the floor and the hardened wooden handles of shovels and axes and hammers and the metallic scent of piping and fixtures and bolts and nails brimming from large baskets. There'd been four stores in northern Ohio until the Depression, then just the one. But the war would bring prosperity again. His father was certain of that. (And there would be war, he warned his customers.) Only, he didn't live long enough to enjoy the prosperity. Mead wondered what his father would make of Wal-Mart, to say nothing of his great-grandson. No doubt about it, the old man would have blown a gasket.

After several minutes he opened one eye and glanced at the clock, knowing he'd be up like a rooster in three hours to pee, then again three hours later, usually warming himself a cup of milk before retreating to bed. He heard the neighbor's Jack Russell hurl a few last insults at the neighborhood before retiring for the night.

Mead grew up with retrievers but Sophie had been a cat person. And so they had cats, always two of them slinking around conspiratorially and fleeing every time Mead walked into the room.

"I don't think I've even been able to touch Missy since Thanksgiving," Mead complained. "What's the point?"

"You have to be patient," Sophie responded as Missy purred in her lap.

"I'd say eight months is plenty patient. They don't like me and frankly, I don't like them."

"How can you not like Missy?" Sophie scratched Missy's neck, then held her up to her face and rubbed noses.

"It's easy, my dear."

Mead rolled onto his back again, wondering whether to turn the light on and read.

He missed going into Sophie's room. It was almost a physical craving to be among her clothes and shoes and sit in her rocking chair trying to conjure her. And now the room smelled of the boy, a sour sweaty smell that reminded Mead of the army. It would take days to air the place out. Might even have to shampoo the carpet. And then as he lay there in the dark he suddenly had the awful feeling that Sophie's smell would never come back.

· · ·

The next day after doing his chores and calisthenics and homework Andrew got his skateboard from the garage and started playing around on the curb out front. He wasn't very good. The nearest skateboard park at home required a ride from his mom so he didn't get much practice (skateboarding was banned just about everywhere else, which drove him nuts). But he treasured his board—Zero deck, Krux trucks, Pig wheels—and the layers of worn stickers that covered the bottom and the sound it made grinding on a curb.

Evelyn came out of her house and watched him. "Very impressive," she said. Andrew smiled proudly. "Mind if I give it a try?"

Andrew's face dropped.

Evelyn let out a laugh. "That was a joke."

A few minutes later Mead emerged from the front door, a look of agitation on his face.

"Hello, General," said Evelyn.

Mead gave her a quick nod as he headed for Andrew. "Exactly what do you think you're doing?"

"He's having fun," said Evelyn.

"I was skateboarding."

"Never heard such a racket."

"Sorry."

"And what the hell are you doing to the curb?" Mead walked over and inspected it. "Look at these marks."

"It's just a curb," said Andrew.

"It's *my* curb," said Mead, grimacing.

"Don't be such a poop," said Evelyn.

"If you don't mind, I think I know how to handle my own grandson," said Mead. He turned back to Andrew. "I trust you can find a more productive way to spend your time." Then he turned and headed back inside.

"Is there a skateboard park around here?" called out Andrew.

"How should I know?" The screen door slammed.

"He does have a grouchy side," said Evelyn.

"It's the only side he has."

"He's just been living alone too long. Of course, God knows I have, too." She smiled, then pulled a small pair of cutters from her pocket and headed for her flower garden.

Andrew stood holding his skateboard, half tempted to keep grinding away, then went inside and looked through the skateboard magazine he'd packed, which had a directory of parks in the back listed by state. He turned to Southern California. Tons of places.

Summoning his courage he took the magazine into the garage where his grandfather sat at a workbench repairing a small wooden birdfeeder. "I was just wondering, are any of these places nearby?"

* * *

Mead offered to take him to SeaWorld or the zoo instead, but Andrew seemed so eager to go to a skateboard park that Mead finally conceded. Let him have a little fun. The moment they pulled up to the graffiti-covered cement enclosure Mead regretted his decision. In and around the compound—that looked more like a prison yard, only dirtier, with litter piled in the corners—were dozens of baggy butts, each looking ready to jump the nearest bystander. Mead thought of the haunts of his own child-hood: the soupy watering hole where they swam each summer, the ravine where a boy named Joe Figora died of an asthma attack, the woods where he and Tommy Green built a two-story tree house that went up in flames when one of the hobos who passed through left a campfire burning.

Andrew was out of the car before he could stop him, so Mead sat parked next to the cyclone fence with the doors locked and kept watch, try-ing to ignore the glare from a lumpy-looking teenager who leaned against the fence smoking a cigarette with all the attitude he could muster. What a meatball. Has he ever so much as lifted a finger for his country? Does the Bill of Rights mean anything to him? Mead glared back at the boy. Just blind luck he's not freezing in a foxhole with 250,000 Germans on the move, only nobody knows it because Hitler wasn't supposed to have any punches left to throw because the German Army was supposed to be on the verge of collapse. And they just kept coming.

Mead looked over at Andrew, who kept off to one corner by himself kicking his board this way and that as though bent on breaking both ankles. Where was the nearest hospital? Not for miles.

He thought of Evelyn, feeling bad for losing his temper and then guilty for the amount of time he'd spent thinking about her lately. Why had he never really *noticed* her before? Had she had one of those makeovers? He tried to think if there was anything different about her. Did she lose weight? Was it her hair? If only she wouldn't meddle so much. Well, at least he'd put a stop to the little *thing* going on, whatever it was. When Andrew was shipped back to Chicago he wanted nothing but privacy, thank you.

He scrutinized the faces of several teenagers lurking near the entrance to the skate park, trying to gauge which posed the greatest hazard. He couldn't get over how sullen they all looked, many wearing little knit caps on their heads despite the heat, like they were going to rob a bank. No wonder the prisons were bursting. Home of the free and more than a million behind bars, Mead had recently read, which sent him right to the bourbon. And the politicians were all a bunch of blow-dried blockheads.

He decided to give Andrew an hour, but after sitting in the car stewing for thirty minutes he needed a bathroom urgently. That was another reason he didn't like to go out as much, or not without a specific plan of action. He looked over at the small green port-a-potty that sat in the far corner of the park, every inch covered with graffiti. He'd hold it. He waited ten minutes more, then got out of the car and tried to wave down Andrew, but the boy didn't see him.

"Damn," he muttered, locking the car and making his way through a small crowd of baggy butts. They don't even know what tough is, he thought, feeling himself tense as he tried to signal Andrew again.

"Old fart coming through," said a voice.

Mead felt himself blush.

"The wheelchair park's down the road," said another, causing hoots of laughter.

A tall, skinny kid whisked by on his skateboard, nearly knocking Mead over.

"You watch where you're going, young man," said Mead. Oh, to have Punchy and Jimbo with me right now. We could have brought them to their knees just by looking at them.

"Out of the way, gramps."

Would they have been so brave at the sight of a German Tiger rounding a corner, the ground shaking as the huge turret traverses back and forth? Or creeping through the snow on patrol and seeing a concealed German pillbox out of the corner of your eye, knowing they've got you?

Two more teenagers skated past, one of them grazing Mead on the shoulder. Mead held himself perfectly erect as he continued toward

Andrew, the rage making his knees wobbly. People *died* for you, he thought. Maybe even your own grandfather, ground to a pulp beneath the treads of a panzer in Belgium or drowned in the flooded holds of a sinking ship or buried in the malaria swamps of Guadalcanal. Finally Andrew saw him and hurried over. One of the teenagers nearly cut him off, then another clipped him as he passed.

Mead was sweating now, feeling the faint echo of all the power he once had. Could I still take them? Nah, too many. But if I concentrated on that fat one there . . .

"Let's go," said Andrew, a look of panic in his eyes.

"Good idea," said a teenager.

Mead remembered the first time he heard a bullet pass by his ear, how it snapped the air so that he could almost feel it brushing the hairs of his neck, reducing life to a matter of centimeters. Would the next be to the left or to the right? And no matter where they hid, it seemed like the Germans had prepared range cards for every depression in Normandy.

"Come on," said Andrew, pulling at Mead's sleeve.

Mead felt something wet hit his cheek. "Goddamn delinquents," he said, shaking a finger at the growing crowd. "Do you have any idea who you're dealing with?"

"We've *got* to go," pleaded Andrew, standing next to the car and waiting for his grandfather to get in. But Mead took his time, always keeping his eye on the closest teenager. "Your parents would be ashamed of you," he called out the window as he started the engine. An empty soda can hit the back of the car and rolled along the street. Andrew slid low in his seat, quaking.

"You shouldn't have gone in there," he said after several minutes of silence. "I should have warned you."

"I'll go where I damn well please."

"There's always a couple of jerks."

"I've been in worse places."

More silence.

As he drove with his hands gripping the wheel Mead suddenly found himself hoping that Sophie hadn't been watching. He liked to think that she usually was, somehow keeping an eye on him and laughing along at the silliness of things. (And so much of it was silly.) It gave him a secret sense of companionship, helping to make the days endurable. But not today. He had never felt so old before, so frail and humiliated. No, he hoped Sophie hadn't been watching today. Because if she had, it surely would have broken her heart.

. . .

For a brief moment, Andrew had thought his grandfather might take a swing, right there in the skateboard park. It was about the most horrifying thing he could imagine, getting into a rumble with his grandfather. Oh man, they would have been slaughtered. They might even have gotten their pictures in the paper, both lying side by side in some hospital bed, total traction.

Fuck me, that was close.

He couldn't get over the look he'd seen in the old man's eyes, not fear but something scarier. He had always had the feeling that if anybody talked that way to his grandfather they'd die on the spot, that it would not be a survivable encounter. But then, those assholes didn't know what Andrew knew about his grandfather, about the war and the medals and the gun he kept in his bedside drawer. Sarge had stood his ground all right. Still, Andrew couldn't help feeling sorry for him, suddenly seeing how vulnerable he was, being in a place he didn't belong. What the fuck was I thinking?

. . .

"Why did you do it?" Mead asked as they sat in the backyard having dinner that night. They'd hardly spoken since getting home.

"I was going to pay for it. I—"

"I'm talking about the knife. Why did you take a knife to school and pull it on a classmate?"

Andrew stared down at his plate. "I dunno."

"You don't know?"

Andrew shrugged.

"Bullshit."

The word made Andrew wince.

"I'm all ears."

"I guess I was angry."

"And where the hell would we be if we all pulled a knife every time we blew our tops?"

Andrew kept his eyes lowered and rubbed his thighs.

"So this guy picks on you?"

Andrew nodded. "And my friend."

"The one who . . ."

"Matt. He picked on Matt, too."

"I see. So in revenge, you were going to . . . disembowel him?"

Andrew looked up. "I wasn't going to do anything like that."

"Then what the hell were you going to do?"

Andrew hesitated. "I don't know. Show him he couldn't keep picking on me, I guess."

"Because if he did, you'd do what exactly?"

Andrew looked anxiously around the yard. "I didn't think it through like that."

"But you sure as hell should have, don't you think? Because once you start something like that, you better damn well know how it's going to end."

"I guess I figured he'd take me seriously."

"I see." Mead thought for a moment. "You ever seen anybody get cut up?"

"Mostly in the movies. Did you ever see—"

"That's not what I'm talking about."

"I guess I haven't," Andrew mumbled, slapping at a mosquito.

"It's not very pretty."

Andrew flicked the dead mosquito off his arm, then slapped at another one.

"You know what my father would have done if I'd pulled a stunt like that? He would have killed me."

"Really?"

"Really." Actually, Mead had no idea what his father would have done. Such behavior, and the potential consequences, were unimaginable.

"My dad doesn't care what I do."

"Your father is an ass."

Andrew winced again.

"It's bad luck, but that's the truth of it. Nothing you can do but make sure you don't turn out a thing like him."

"I don't think he's an ass."

"Of course you don't. He's your father." Mead considered how to continue. "Look, I know it hasn't been easy for you. The fact is, your grandma and I felt awfully bad about the hand you were dealt. But that's no excuse for this kind of stunt. We all have to take what we're given and make the best out of it. Why, I've known men who've pulled themselves up from circumstances you couldn't even imagine." He could see his grandson's eyes glaze over. If he only understood, Mead thought. By God, just to have both arms and legs and not be shivering and hungry. "You're excused," he said abruptly, feeling his fists tense.

"What?"

"I said, you're excused."

After Andrew went inside Mead slowly finished his steak and potato, then pushed his plate away and sat listening to the rhythmic throb of the crickets.

·   ·   ·

He *was* going to kill Bremer. Another few moments and the big fuckhead would have been dead, slain like the Great Goblin was by Gandalf. *I got him, Matt. You can come back now because I got him.*

Andrew sat cross-legged on the bed looking down at his hands. I would have been a murderer. These would have been the hands of a murderer. He turned his palms back and forth, then imagined them wrapped around the bars of a prison cell, the years crawling by.

He still couldn't believe that he'd done it, or had tried to do it. When he started carrying the knife to school he never thought he'd actually use it; it was just exciting to know that he could, that it was there if he needed it, that he had hidden power. Then one day in the school cafeteria Bremer and several of his football buddies sat down at the corner table where Andrew was eating with Bill Humphrey and Stuart Smith and started making fun of him. He tried to ignore it at first, just letting the heat burn off his face, but then Bremer mentioned Matt. That's when Andrew felt the snapping inside, just like a piece of dry wood breaking in two.

"You really shouldn't cry too much over Shorty. The way I see it, he did everybody a favor." Bremer turned toward his friends. "Little fucker was a stalker. Did you know that? You should read the shit he wrote Megan. Fucking pathetic." Bremer pulled out a crumpled piece of paper from his pocket. "Get a load of this." He put one hand on his heart and began to read in a high-pitched voice.

Dear Megan,
Maybe you're right, maybe I am just a creep. But no matter what you think of me, I'll never regret a single word I've written to you. Sometimes the only thing that gets me through the day is knowing I

might see you (even if you hate me). In fact, I'm starting to think that maybe people like you exist to make up for people like me. Anyway, no matter what happens, at least I'll always know that this stupid world did something right.

Yours forever,
Matt

Bremer slapped his knee and then tore the letter into little pieces, letting them flutter to the ground. "Is that *too fucking much?*"

Andrew looked down at his left hand, watching it slide under the table toward his pants pocket. He didn't even ask it to go. It just went there all by itself.

"It's just a pity you little pussies didn't have some sort of suicide pact."

Andrew watched his other hand slide under the table, then felt the cold metal and heard the click as the blade locked.

"Or maybe you did and you didn't keep your promise? I'll bet that's it. Some friend you are, Sunshine."

Surprise!

Andrew lunged up at Bremer, putting the knife right up under his chin until the tip was pressed against his fleshy skin.

"Jesus Christ!"

"You killed him. You're the one who killed Matt."

"Easy, man. What the fuck are you talking about?" Bremer raised his hands into the air and tried to back off but Andrew followed him in a slow tango across the cafeteria as the crowd of shocked students quickly parted. From the corners of his eyes Andrew saw the gathered faces frozen in disbelief.

"He's got a knife!"

"Oh my God."

"Someone get a teacher."

"Call the police."

"Don't be crazy, Andy."

Crazy? But I am crazy, don't you see? *I'm insane.* He looked again at the faces, faces he'd envied for years, faces of kids who lived in houses and went to parties and dated and had cars and fathers and money. *Why not me?* Tears started rolling down his cheeks as the faces blurred. *Why not me?*

"You killed Matt. You're the one who drove him to it."

"I didn't kill anybody. You're fucking nuts."

"And I'm going to kill you."

"Hey man, calm down. I'm sorry. Let's just talk."

"Someone call the police!"

Andrew stared right into Bremer's eyes, seeing for the first time the look of absolute fear. *How does it feel?*

No matter what else happened, Andrew would always remember the expression on Bremer's face when he realized that Andrew was serious. And no matter what they did to him, he'd always know that he'd finally stood his ground. For once, Andrew was pushing back. He felt the fury building in his chest and shooting out through his arm and fist into the knife until it was shaking. *Watch this, Matt.*

Andrew briefly closed his eyes and gathered everything inside until it was all right there in his arm *push push push* when suddenly Mr. Vickers, the math teacher, grabbed him from behind, knocking the knife from his hand.

"*No!*"

As he was led through the cafeteria in a blur of tears he heard Megan asking Bremer if he was all right and then Bremer saying, "Sunshine just got his ugly ass expelled."

· · ·

Andrew lay awake for an hour, then got up, dressed quickly and placed the fattest joint, his lighter and fifteen dollars in his pockets. Kneeling on the bed he slowly opened the sliding window, then removed the screen and gently lowered it to the ground before crawling out feetfirst and closing the window behind him. Piece of cake. He stopped to listen, hearing only the yap of a neighbor's dog, then quietly made his way through the low hedges to the sidewalk. When he was a block away he reached into his pocket and pulled out the joint, lighting it and inhaling deeply. Precisely what the doctor ordered.

He intended on smoking only half, but he felt so good at the midway mark that he couldn't resist taking his brain cells all the way to town. *Have fun, boys!* He took another deep hit, methodically scanning his central nervous system. *Demons are down 17-0 at the half with no sign of paranoia.* He paused to look into a window where a middle-aged man and woman appeared to be arguing. *She jabs him with a left, then a right . . .* Most of the houses were dark, like little tombs in the Valley of the Nobodies, though occasionally he saw the blue glow of an insomniac who had fallen asleep to the Food Channel.

It took him nearly an hour to walk to the 7-Eleven but only five minutes to convince a Mexican in a rusty pickup sagging with gardening tools to buy him some beer for a five-buck bribe. He downed two Mickey wide-mouths on the spot, then carried the rest in a paper bag, football style. By the time he reached the small park four blocks from his grandfather's house he had already peed twice in the bushes and polished off two more beers.

Cheers, Matt. He opened another beer, raised it in the air and let out a long burp. Then he re-lit the tiny roach and took a deep inhale, determined to obliterate every thought that dared to pop up in his head. *Thought-free at last. Thank God Almighty I'm thought-free at last.* Was there anything good about thinking so much? It seemed like the intelligent thing to do, and he figured he was way ahead of most people when it came to getting the *big picture,* but basically the big picture was depressing as hell. He felt another wave of thoughts approaching. *Take your positions, men. Easy now. Wait until you see the whites of their beady eyes. That's it. A little closer. And a little more. Ready? Fire!* He blasted away with a volley of smoke and beer. Ah, sweet nothingness.

After finishing off the last beer he spent several minutes staring at the street signs wondering why none of the names sounded familiar. Via Flores or Via Fernandez? What the fuck, he'd go by instinct. Once he got close it was just a matter of counting from the corner. Seven houses down on the right—depending on which direction you came from—or was it six? He looked for subtle differences as he passed each house, yet they all seemed exactly the same; white and single-story with a little putting-green of grass on one side of the driveway and maybe a row of flowers and a bush or two on the other. Somebody shoot me if I end up in a dinky little neighborhood like this. He let out another series of burps, then walked into the middle of the street and stood directly beneath the hazy yellow cone of light cast by a street lamp. *How are you all doing out there tonight?* (Deafening roar.) *All right. Got a hell of a show for you.* (Huge waves of applause.) He blew on the mic a few times, then tossed his shoulders back and started singing as he skipped from one yellow stage to the next. *An-drew! An-drew! An-drew!* Just behind the beams of light thousands of Cori

Fletcher clones were dancing and screaming and flailing their arms while panties and bras rained down on the stage. And there right in the front row was Matt sitting with his arm around Megan and giving him the thumbs-up. *This next one's for you, old buddy.* Then the flames of thousands of lighters lit up the night for as far as he could see as he twirled round and round and round from stage to stage.

He was spinning toward the next cone of light when he clipped the fender of a car with his hip, slammed into a telephone pole and flopped face first on the damp grass.

"Whoopsie-daisy."

The street was eerily still as he struggled to his knees, thinking maybe he needed to work on the final number and wondering if he'd passed his grandfather's house yet. But nope, there it was right in front of him. Bingo. Camp Sauerkraut. He tried to stand up but started laughing so hard that he had to sit down again. Jesus, it was all so fucking funny when you thought about it. Sex. Grades. Flossing. Zits. Tits. And people; oh man, people were just *too much.* As far as he could tell, there were basically two types (both miserable): the busy bees—who were terrified of sitting still long enough to give life any serious thought—and the dumb shits, who were incapable of meaningful thought. And Sarge's problemo? Essentially, the old fart was just waiting to die. Come to think of it, a lot of people were like that, killing time in the safest and easiest way possible. Pretty pathetic. He rolled onto his stomach, breathing in the moist green air and thinking that maybe he'd hump Mother Nature if he wasn't so dizzy. Not me, I'm not wasting my life. Noooooo way, José. He rolled to his side and started laughing at the sound of his laughter, which seemed almost girlish. Might just be a teensy-weensy-bit stoned. He gently slapped his cheek a few times, which only made him laugh more. Even Matt's vanishing act was kind of funny in a way because it was just so incredibly unfuckingbelievable.

He sat up and caught his breath, wishing he could pound down a couple of raisin cookies. Then he carefully stood, steadying himself against the telephone pole, and lurched toward the side of the house, plowing through a row of bushes that scratched his face, which was funny too. But fuck it was dark. He tiptoed along a walkway, alternately giggling and then shushing himself, finger to his lips. Now, which window? Eeny, meany, miney moe, my mother told me to count to ten: gotta be that one. He stepped on some plants and nearly tripped over something before reaching the sill. Christ, the window was shut. Had he shut it? Had Sarge busted him? *In the stockade, camper!* He tried to find an edge to get hold of, then pressed his palms against the glass and pushed left, then right. Gradually the window slid open. Hallelujah. First a quick pee, then sleep. He unzipped his pants and leaned against the house, thinking there was no simpler pleasure in the world. When he finished he felt around in the dark with his foot for something to stand on, then tried to peer in the window, feeling a sudden wooziness in his stomach. Uh oh, the spinsies. He grabbed onto the windowsill with both hands. *Just spring up like a panther and in we go.* He reached down and felt his pocket to make sure the roach was still there, then burped one more time before grabbing the sill again and attempting to heave himself up. *Houston, we have a problem.* On his third attempt he managed to get enough of his chest in so that he was one-third inside and two-thirds outside. Half his brain was processing urgent pain signals while the other half couldn't remember the last time anything quite so funny had happened. He tried to suppress a giggle as he kicked his legs. Couple of more inches. He kicked again and felt himself suddenly pitch forward, landing head first on something distinctly harder than a bed.

Luuucccyy? I'm home! (His mom loved Lucy almost as much as John Denver and Andrew had memorized dozens of episodes.)

He tried to lift himself up, straining to see in the dark and trying to ignore an abrupt request from central command for permission to throw up. *Permission denied!* Beneath him the carpet swayed left, then right. Jesus, an earthquake. Or was it the pot? He giggled and burped as he curled up in a fetal position and waited for the movement to stop. Then again, it could be the pot *and* the Big One. *Ride 'em, cowboy!* He drew his knees to his chest and wrapped his hands around them. Let's see now, is it drop, stop and roll; or rock, stop and roll? Or maybe just stop, rock and roll? The carpet swung left, then right. *Surf's up!* He tried to move with it, leaning into the turns. *Whooo . . . weeeee!!!* You watching this, Matt? The carpet bucked a few times as little red phones in his brain rang off the hook. Maybe if I just close my eyes for a moment. He groped around for the bed, then gave up and lay his head down, letting the carpet take him wherever it wanted to go.

Show's over, folks.

• • •

Mead lay awake in bed that night wondering how much time had passed since he last looked at the clock. Unable to fall asleep, he decided he would at least feign sleep, hoping that every two hours of simulated rest might be worth one hour of the real thing. He still kept to the left side of the queen-size mattress as he always had, and ever since Sophie had died he never allowed his feet or arms to stray across the midline into the cool and vast empty space beside him, as if afraid of what he might find.

He talked to himself in his head for a while (the usual chatter, begun with good intentions—no major catastrophes today, health's holding up—but invariably descending into a grim interrogation, like a dental hygienist probing for sensitive spots), then he shot the breeze with Sophie—mostly listening as she critiqued his grandparenting skills and counseled patience—until finally he succumbed to the random images that flashed across the closed lids of his eyes, lulling him into a sort of drunkenness. They were rarely pleasant images. It was enough if they weren't acutely unpleasant. But tonight he knew they would be—that he no longer had the strength to hold the door closed and keep the faces at bay. And he dreaded it.

• • •

German prisoners had begun clearing the dead, using blankets when there was nothing to grab hold of. On the far side of the town shooting could still be heard. "I can't see doing this all the way to Berlin," said Punchy, lighting one cigarette from another and sidestepping around two German corpses as they marched. They were only a few miles inland from the beaches and German resistance was increasing.

Mead considered the prospect but found it incomprehensible. After three nights with little sleep he struggled to keep his eyes open.

"Someone ought to do the math on this thing, figure out just what it's going to cost per mile," said Punchy.

"I don't think anybody wants to know the answer," said Mead, who had found that he couldn't pass a dead body without looking at the face, despite the looseness in his stomach.

As they walked he kept wondering how his father had dealt with it. What did he feel when he saw the faces and how many faces did he see? Did he wonder about the people he killed or the chances of getting through each day? All his silences around the dinner table and on the porch in the evening now came to life. So that's where you were, Mead thought. You were back looking at the faces.

The sound of small-arms fire drew closer. As they passed six freshly killed Germans, Punchy and several other men stopped to quickly search through the dead men's pockets.

"What are you doing?" said Mead.

"Shopping, what else?" said Punchy, sliding his hand deep into the pants pocket of a German sprawled on his back with his mouth open.

"It's not right."

"Fuck off, Mead," said Tom Anson, a tobacco farmer's son from North Carolina who had a big mouth and short temper. "You think these Krauts care?"

Mead watched as Anson pulled off the belt buckle from the pants of one of the bodies and passed it around proudly. "My dad's gonna love this."

"I'm just telling you, it's not right," said Mead, this time just to Punchy, who was now removing a watch from a limp wrist.

"You know your problem, Mead? You're a goddamn choirboy."

Once the bodies had been stripped of all valuables the men moved on. When they reached a Y in the road marked by a large World War One memorial, two squads headed left and two veered right, everybody strung out and fingering their weapons. They passed several dead horses, a smoldering German half-track and a Panther tank, both treads separated. More gunfire, now just blocks away. Mead felt the fear in his intestines, snaking right through them.

"I hate these towns," said Punchy. "Put me in a forest anytime." They slowed their pace, cautiously aiming their rifles down each alleyway as they passed. "Why don't we just go around the towns and surround the bastards?"

"Because nobody asked us."

Punchy spat out the butt of his cigarette as a long burst of machine-gun fire erupted a few blocks ahead. "You know the problem?"

"Which one?" said Mead, aiming his rifle at a doorway, then at a bay window.

"We're completely expendable."

"Thanks for the reassurance."

"It's true. I mean, who really cares? It's not like ol' Ike's gonna run out of fodder."

"You know, Punchy, sometimes you really get on my nerves."

"Hey, I'm just talking. I feel better when I talk."

"I noticed."

Punchy started humming the melody to "Oh, What a Beautiful Mornin'" while Mead looked nervously at the upper windows of the two-story buildings on his left and right, wondering which one a sniper would choose.

It would be suicide. The sniper might get off a few shots before being killed himself. Mead had been taught that snipers generally preferred more favorable rules of engagement, carefully plotting their escape route and shooting only individual soldiers isolated from the rest. But he quickly learned that the German Army possessed a plentiful supply of men willing to face certain death in the interests of the fatherland, even if only to gain the retreating army a few minutes time. As he walked he imagined his head in the cross hairs of a rifle sight. A little to the left, a little to the right. Gently squeezing the trigger. *Now!*

"I'm telling you, Mead, we should go *around* the towns."

Mead's eyes went from window to window as rivulets of sweat ran down his face. I'm going to die, aren't I? He thought of all the bravado he had once felt, secretly assuming he had some sort of immunity. But I'm no different after all. Will he aim for my head or my chest? Soon the fear became so overwhelming that he had to struggle to control his bladder. *Please, not me.*

The first bullet struck Anson in the head, piercing his helmet. Mead dove left for the cover of a doorway when the next shot cracked. He felt it before he heard it; not pain but a smacking sensation against his gear. He crouched down and fired blindly at the windows as more gunfire erupted at the far end of the street.

Then he felt blood seeping through his pants. First a trickle then a flood of it so that he knew he'd pass out within minutes. "I'm hit!" he called to Punchy, who was crouched nearby. He fired off another round before sliding to the bottom of the doorway and curling into a ball, feeling the wetness soak through his undershorts.

Punchy crawled over, grabbed the first-aid kit strapped to his helmet and looked for the wound.

"Gotta stop the bleeding," said Mead, trying not to faint.

"Where is it?"

"Down there. My waist, my crotch. Oh God, I'm not sure." Mead closed his eyes and rocked his head back and forth, knowing he wouldn't have the courage to die well. *Jesus, Sophie, I'm dying. And I knew it too. I knew I'd never make it.* He felt the blood stream down his thighs. *That must have been the deal: I could find you, Sophie, but I couldn't keep you. How could I have expected more?*

"I can't find it," said Punchy.

"What the hell do you mean, I'm soaked through," gasped Mead, desperately feeling his pants with his hand, horrified at what he might find.

Suddenly Punchy let out a burst of laughter. "I'll be damned, Mead, they shot your canteen."

"What?"

"They shot your goddamn canteen. It's water, you stupid son of a bitch! Your canteen just kicked the bucket."

"Water?" Mead sat up and stared down at his crotch in disbelief, as if time had suddenly folded back on itself. And then for the first time since he was a kid he let himself weep.

·　·　·

Andrew woke to the sound of an answering machine. The telltale pause and then the beep made him think he was back home for one brief, sweet moment. Then the voice came on.

"Hi, Mom, it's me. I just got off the phone with Dr. Coleman and he says you haven't been in for *any* chemotherapy treatments. Mom, are you there? I want to know what's going on, Mom. Mom? I'm going to call you right back." Dial tone.

Andrew unglued one eye, revealing a close-up cutaway of a thick white carpet; then the second eye, which gave a slightly elevated perspective and included the animal-like legs of a dresser. Very, very interesting. It wasn't anything like the afterlife he had in mind—silk sheets, Cori at his side, ocean view—but neither was it even remotely familiar. He closed both eyes, then opened them again, hoping another click of the View Master would clear things up.

The phone rang again. "Hello, Mom? It's me again. *Please* pick up." Pause. "I just hope you know how selfish you're being." Sniffle sniffle. "This is really serious, Mom. Mom? Answer me, Mom." Dial tone.

Andrew sat up, panic now shrieking through his central nervous system.

The phone rang again. "Okay, Mom, if you won't talk then I'm going to spell it out and you can just *listen*. Without chemo you have maybe a year to live—*max*. You're only seventy-four, Mom. That's *young*. And why won't you meet with the realtor? You know we agreed that you'd have to sell the house. Did you look at the statements I sent you? You have to face *reality*, Mom. Peter blew *everything*. Those stocks are not coming back." Pause. Sniffle sniffle. "None of this would have happened if you'd listened to me."

Andrew closed his eyes and covered his ears, desperate to block out the mounting evidence suggesting that he'd been reincarnated as someone's disease-ridden mom—he always assumed that reincarnation would be a step up—when the door opened.

"What on earth are you doing here?"

Andrew opened his eyes again and saw Evelyn staring down at him. *Holy shit.* "Evelyn?"

She looked almost as surprised as he was. "Andrew. How did you get in here?"

"Well, I, uh . . . can I get back to you?"

Evelyn looked behind him at the open window, then bent down and touched his forehead. "Your poor face is all scratched and you're a muddy mess."

Andrew looked down and noticed the dirt and grass stains on the white carpet. "Sorry."

She closed the window, then got a tissue and dabbed his face. "I don't suppose you'd care to explain?"

Andrew slowly sat up, trying to ignore the sensation of blood vessels bursting in his head. "Do I have to?"

"Yes. Does your grandfather know where you are?"

"Exactly *where* am I?"

"In my study."

"Oh." Andrew looked around the room, which was so bright and uniformly white—even the wicker chair and desk and dresser were white—that he momentarily reconsidered whether he had in fact died.

"He's going to be worried sick about you."

"He's going to kill me."

"You've been drinking."

Andrew put a hand over his mouth. "What makes you think that?"

She frowned, yet he was encouraged by the persistent kindness in her face. Time for a major charm offensive. Maybe she'd even hide him for a few weeks until things calmed down, then drop him off at the Mexican border. He slowly got up, feeling so lightheaded he thought he might tip over.

"You're going to have to be completely honest with me if you want any help," she said, steering him to a chair. Then she went out, returning with a warm hand towel and a glass of water. "So?"

Andrew guzzled down the water, then glanced over at the window. *You dumb shit.* "Well, see, I thought I'd just stop by to tell you how much my grandfather liked those poetry magnets and . . ." She crossed her arms in front of her chest and shook her head disapprovingly. "I guess I may have had one or two beers on the way."

"Aren't you a little young for that?"

"I didn't make the laws."

She put her hands on her hips and looked him over as if deciding whether or not to toss him back into the water. "You two have been having problems, haven't you?"

"It's like boot camp. The guy's a freak—but he did like the poetry magnets. I think he even wrote a poem about you."

"The General?" She laughed.

"Not a great poem, but there's definite feeling."

"Listen, Andrew, your grandfather is just a lonely old man who doesn't know how to handle a teenager, that's all. He's doing the best he can and you should be proud of him. He's a genuine hero you know."

"Don't remind me."

She kneeled down in front of him and patted his face with the warm towel. "What about you?"

"What about me?"

"I can tell a troubled soul when I see one." She put her hand on his forehead and brushed aside his hair.

"It's just that I . . ." And then without warning Andrew was spilling big hot tears all over the place.

He told her almost everything—except for stealing Matt's ashes, which seemed over the top—then turned bright red and apologized for saying anything at all. *I must be cracking up.* But the hangover had left him feeling so raw and unguarded that he hadn't been able to stop himself. And for the first time in his life he felt that someone actually wanted to listen.

"You're a real piece of work, do you know that?"said Evelyn.

"Thank you."

She sat down on the arm of his chair. "When I was about your age—maybe a few years older—I made a mistake that changed the rest of my life."

"What happened?"

She paused. "The short of it is, I got pregnant."

"Really?"

"Really. George was the father. He was just a kid too—how naïve we were!—but he was decent enough to marry me and help raise our child."

"So it worked out."

She shook her head slowly. "Yes and no."

"What do you mean?"

"I'm afraid we just didn't love each other."

Andrew sat speechless, briefly forgetting the strobe-like pulsing in his head.

"Oh, we got along all right, and I still miss him. He was a good man. But it wasn't love—at least not what I'd always dreamed of."

"You could have divorced him."

She folded her hands in her lap. "No, I couldn't have."

"Why not?"

"Because sometimes we can walk away from our mistakes and sometimes we can't." She stood and went over to the window, her back to Andrew. "Over the years I've come to think of life as this long corridor lined with doors and we only have the time and strength and good fortune to open a few. And the catch is, we never know if we opened the right ones." She turned back toward him, trying to smile. "As for the rest of them, I suppose that's what dreams and books and movies and songs are for."

"I haven't opened a good door yet."

She laughed. "Maybe your luck is about to change."

"Maybe there are no good doors." Andrew tried to ignore a bubbling sensation in his stomach.

"Or maybe there are really no bad doors." She glanced over at the answering machine, which was flashing. "I suppose you heard my darling daughter?"

"I might have heard something."

"She can be a little pushy."

"Who's Peter?"

"My son—the financial wizard." She sighed and Andrew wondered if she was going to cry. *Fuck, what a morning.* "So now we both have secrets." She held his eye a moment, then got him a glass of orange juice and a piece of toast while he went to the bathroom. He peed for several minutes before biting off an inch of Crest toothpaste and working it through his teeth. *I will never ever drink again.*

"The first thing we have to do is get you home."

"You mean you won't tell my grandfather?"

"We have to tell him something."

"He'll kill me."

"Why don't you leave this to me?" She headed him toward the front door.

"Can I have a cookie first?" No point in dying on an empty stomach, he figured, hoping to resolve some serious blood-sugar issues.

She smiled and retrieved two enormous raisin cookies from a tin, then watched with amusement as he wolfed them down. They had just reached the end of her narrow brick walkway when the door across the street opened and Mead ran out.

"Where in God's name—"

"Good morning, General," said Evelyn calmly, firing off an enormous smile that seemed to waft across the street and stop Mead in his tracks. Mead glared at Andrew while Andrew stayed close to Evelyn and averted his eyes. "Andrew was just helping me with my rosebushes out back. Poor thing got all scratched up." She pinched Andrew's cheek.

Mead's large jaw dropped open. That morning he had waited until eight to open Andrew's door, thinking he'd cut the boy a little slack. At first he thought his grandson was buried somewhere beneath the pile of sheets, skinny as he was. Then in a panic he had checked the bathroom and garage twice before charging out the front door. He looked down at his watch. "It's *eight-oh-five* in the morning. . . ."

Evelyn turned to Andrew. "I didn't mean to interrupt your morning run."

"Morning run . . ."

Andrew's sleepy-looking face—the boy looked *awful*—sprung to life. "Oh, gosh, no problem." He looked at his grandfather. "Yeah, see, I couldn't sleep so I was up early. Thought I'd get in a little exercise before breakfast, but then I bumped into Evelyn . . ." The boy smiled hopefully.

"He's quite handy in the garden," said Evelyn. "Must take after his grandfather."

"Morning run . . ."

Andrew beat back several algae-green waves of nausea as Evelyn peppered his grandfather with questions. God, she's brilliant.

"I wonder if it would be too much to ask your help in moving a planter box?"

Mead finally took his eyes off of Andrew. "Of course not."

"I'll just go clean up," said Andrew, flashing his grandfather his toothiest smile before sliding past him and dashing into the house. *Whew.* Once he got to his room he leaned out the window, picked up the screen and secured it back in place. Then he hurried to the bathroom, stripped off his clothes and got into the shower, turning the temperature up as hot as he could stand. When his body was covered with suds he burst into song, feeling giddy despite his pounding head. That was *very, very* close.

Chapter 6

Mead couldn't help notice that the amount of time he spent thinking about Evelyn was encroaching on the amount of time he spent thinking about Sophie. It was like a gala ball going on in his head and he was the only eligible dance partner.

He knew nothing about her except that she had aged remarkably well and baked and gardened with a vengeance and made his grandson laugh hysterically. He'd made a point of never asking many personal questions, not wanting any in return. But he found himself wondering more and more about her. Had she ever gone a whole day without thinking of George? Was she lonely? (But why did she always seem so damn chipper, like she'd just won the Publisher's Clearinghouse Sweepstakes?) What exactly went through her mind when she gardened? (Did she ever think of him?) And yet he resented her too, both because of the way Andrew transformed in her presence, as if she was God's gift to grandchildren, and because he knew that even his thoughts would break Sophie's heart.

Best to leave well enough alone.

And yet he found himself spending more and more time working in his front yard in hopes of seeing her. When he ran out of ways to look busy—the lawn was soon waterlogged as well as dangerously overfertilized—he even started shooting hoops, much to Andrew's horror.

"Morning, General."

"Oh, good morning, Evelyn." He jumped especially high for the next shot, but missed.

"I didn't realize you were such a late bloomer." She was grinning.

Mead blushed. "Just keeping the blood flowing."

She watched him shoot a few more baskets, none of which he made, then Andrew came outside and joined them briefly, wincing every time his grandfather took a shot.

"Why don't you two play?" asked Evelyn. "I'll cheerlead."

"What do you say?" said Mead, holding out the ball.

Andrew shrugged. "I've got a lot of homework." Then he turned and shuffled back inside, the seat of his pants positioned right behind his knees.

"He cuts quite a figure, doesn't he?" said Mead.

"He loves you very much."

"He doesn't have a lot of grandparents to choose from." Mead took another shot, missing again.

"He told me about what happened at school."

Mead picked up the ball and dribbled.

"Don't be too hard on him. He's just a very confused young man. But he's got a big heart. You should be proud of that."

"Like I said, we're doing just fine."

"Of course. Let me guess, he's Costello?"

Mead wanted to tell her to mind her own business, to just leave them be, and yet her face was full of such compassion that he actually thought of kissing it. Was she even seventy? "We may have hit a few bumps . . ."

"You know what I think he needs?"

Mead felt himself tense.

"A big hug. He's a frightened, lonely sixteen-year-old who desperately needs a little TLC right now."

"Is there anything else I should know?" Mead said testily.

Evelyn came closer and looked at him in a way he hadn't been looked at in years. "Just that you seem to need the same thing." Then she smiled and walked away.

. . .

The next morning at nine Mead left for an eye appointment, leaving Andrew alone only after he complained of a stomachache. "If you so much as step off the premises I'll have you locked up." Andrew watched from the living room window as his grandfather's car crawled down the street, then quickly went and pulled out the gun from the bed stand drawer. It seemed even heavier than before and this time Andrew carried it around the house pretending to aim at things. *Freeze!* He fingered the trigger, wondering how hard you had to squeeze and how many rounds it held. What he'd give to fire off a few. *Bam bam bam.* He'd love to see the look on Bremer's face with this jammed up his ugly nose. "What did you call Matt?"

"I was just kidding, Andrew. I promise."

"On your knees, asshole."

Andrew pretended to draw the pistol from a holster on his hip, thinking how awesome it would be to have all that power right there where you could reach it. *Better saddle that horse and ride out of town, cowboy.* Then he sat down in his grandfather's blue, overstuffed chair and held the pistol up to his face like he was about to count off paces in a duel. That's what he could do: challenge Bremer to a duel. Ten paces, then *bang!* He aimed the pistol at the dartboard, then got up and hid behind his grandfather's chair, pretending to ambush an intruder. *Bang bang!* Finally he rolled onto his back on the carpet and held the pistol up to his face, turning it this way and that and laughing to himself. Life and death right in the palm of your hand. He placed his finger gently on the trigger and aimed. *Sweet dreams, sucker.*

After carefully returning the pistol he made himself a tuna sandwich and boiled more batteries, then opened the hallway door leading to the one-car garage. There was a workbench with tools hanging neatly from a rack above it, an old-fashioned stationary bike, the manual lawn mower, a metal stepladder, a row of garden tools, and, on a large storage shelf built high on the back wall, several large, labeled boxes. Andrew took the ladder and leaned it up against the shelf, then carefully climbed until he could read the labels. *Christmas lights. Ornaments. Halloween. Cookbooks. Photographs.* He wondered if his grandfather still decorated the house for Halloween. It was hard to imagine him welcoming trick-or-treaters. *Bug off, you urchins!* Actually, it was hard to imagine any trick-or-treaters in the neighborhood.

Andrew climbed up another rung of the ladder and pushed one of the boxes aside. Behind it was another row of boxes and to the left a dark green wooden trunk. He moved another box aside and saw his grandfather's name stenciled in white on the trunk. Army stuff, he thought. This I gotta see.

He had to carry down two boxes marked *Christmas* to make enough room on the shelf to slide the trunk forward and open it. The first thing he pulled out was a folded cap that lay flat on top of a uniform. He opened the cap and looked closely at the patch sewn on the front depicting an open parachute, then tried the cap on, saluting. *Yes, sir!* Then he removed the top of a uniform, pausing to study the large patch on the left shoulder showing an eagle's head with AIRBORNE written above it in yellow. Pinned just above the left breast pocket were several colored bars and beneath them a silver badge depicting a long rifle against a light blue background. Must have been a big cheese. He unbuttoned the coat and tried it on, putting his nose into the crook of his elbow to smell the musty fabric. It was several sizes too large for him.

Next he pulled out a pair of large brown leather boots. Real combat boots. Probably even stepped in blood. He ran his fingers along the twelve pairs of eyelets and tugged at the ends of the leather thong laces, then turned the boots over and examined the worn soles, pausing to listen to the sound of a passing car. He pressed his thumbs against the reinforced toe before putting his hand inside one of the boots, surprised by how uncomfortable it felt.

After browsing through some sort of army manual, he found a small knife tucked in a white sock and a larger one in a dark green sheath lying next to it. The smaller knife was nearly identical to the one his grandfather had given him. He opened the blade and tested its sharpness. Not bad. Mead's name was engraved on the blade, just like Andrew's. Then he picked up the larger knife and drew it from its sheath, enjoying the feel of the wooden handle. Double-edged, especially for killing. He ran his thumb lightly along both blades, looking for traces of blood, then raised the knife into the air and made several jabbing motions. *Die, Jew killer.*

After placing the knives on the pile next to the trunk he removed two pairs of pants, exposing a wooden cigar box and a larger box made of metal. *This is getting good.* He opened the wooden box first. Inside were various medals and patches as well as his grandfather's dog tags. Very cool. He put the silver dog tags around his neck, then picked up a tarnished-looking badge in the shape of a square cross with three separate metal bars hanging from it. The top one read, "rifle," the middle one, "carbine," and the last one, "pistol." GI Joe must have been a pretty good shot. He looked at some of the other items, placing them in his palm one at a time and wondering what they meant. From the bottom of the cigar box he pulled out a small, blue cardboard box containing a medal wrapped in tissue. On one side was a woman holding a broken sword along with the words, WORLD WAR II. Turning it over he read, FREEDOM FROM FEAR AND WANT, FREEDOM OF SPEECH AND RELIGION. What about freedom from assholes? he thought, chuckling. He tested the medal with his teeth, then put it back in the box, cleared a space and placed the large, black metal box on his knees, excited by its weight.

As he lifted the lid he felt his face flush. Nazi stuff. And a fucking Luger.

Andrew didn't know much about guns but he knew what a Luger looked like. Who wouldn't recognize that distinctive, rounded handle, or whatever they called it, and the narrow barrel? Lugers were like, *the* Nazi pistol. And everybody knew that the German Army had the coolest-looking stuff. Even when he was younger and watching army shows, Andrew saw right away that the Sauerkrauts had better-looking uniforms and helmets and tougher-looking tanks and those wicked hand grenades on a stick and awesome desert cars that Rommel cruised around in. When Andrew and his friends played army with little plastic figures it was always a fight over who got to be the Germans, because even the plastic soldiers and weapons looked better. And here he was holding a fucking Luger. *You talking to me? Bamm!*

After toying with the pistol for several minutes he returned it to the metal box and searched through the other contents, first pulling out three different Nazi medals, surprised by how shiny and new they looked, the red and black colors still full of evil power. Too fucking much, he thought, holding them up to his face. And then there was a silver watch that fit loosely on Andrew's narrow wrist, a small Leica camera and a belt buckle with an eagle standing on a swastika. Next he picked up a small flat object wrapped in green felt, trying to guess what it was. No clue. Carefully unwrapping it he uncovered a piece of a fancy-looking dinner plate with a gold design along the rim. Very weird. Probably one of those decorative plates, he decided, maybe even some sort of award. That's it, and Sarge must have dropped it during the ceremony. Andrew snickered at the thought, then put it back.

At the bottom of the box, wrapped in a handkerchief, Andrew found an oval dog tag, a black leather wallet and a worn booklet of some type. He put the dog tag around his neck, then carefully opened the booklet, tensing at the sight of a face staring back at him from a black-and-white photo attached to the inside left page and partially covered with a Nazi stamp. He thumbed through the pages, which were covered with handwriting. Several came loose as he turned them. Must be some sort of army record. He turned back to the first page. Hans Mueller. Hans the Jew killer. He stared closely at the photo. The first thing that struck him was how young the face looked, practically his age, the dark hair cut extremely short on the sides with a bit more length in the front. Frankly, he didn't really look German, not in the Evil Empire way that Andrew imagined. He was actually kind of sorry-looking, with droopy ears and a large, shiny forehead, so that his eyes didn't start until halfway down his face.

So how did his grandfather get hold of this stuff? Was the guy dead? Captured? He studied the face again and decided the guy was dead; definitely something doomed about the eyes. Maybe his grandfather even killed him with the pistol he kept by his bed. Andrew tried to imagine the encounter, his grandfather sneaking up on the German sentry, then, *bang,* right between the eyes, blood and brains everywhere.

From the wallet Andrew pulled out five worn German banknotes. Nazi money. Must be worth a fortune. He put the bills back and pulled out three photos from a smaller sleeve, their edges frayed. There was mom and dad and a little girl standing in the front yard of a house, none of them smiling. Then another of just mom—a real sourpuss—and then one of a teenage girl, probably a girlfriend. Not bad looking, actually, though the hairstyle was kind of goofy, all wavy and parted way on the side. On the back were several lines of handwriting in German. He tried to imagine what the words might say. *Keep your head down? Kill a few for me? I'll always be waiting for you?* Was she still waiting?

He put the wallet down and picked up a round silver medal that hung from a red ribbon with a single thin black stripe and two white stripes running down the middle. The medal itself depicted an eagle, a swastika, a helmet and a grenade. Was it for killing Americans? Or maybe gassing Jews? *Well done, Hans, you son of a gun.* He held it up to his chest. *Heil, Hitler!* Man, if only Matt could see this stuff. He'd freak.

And then he started thinking: what if I took a few things? It wasn't like his grandfather ever looked in the trunk. Hell, he didn't even like to talk about the war. So basically, there was no way he'd notice if a few things were missing. Or when he did he'd be so old he wouldn't remember what he had in there in the first place. I could even take the medals and Nazi cash and gun to a pawn shop, get some serious money. Then maybe buy a sports car and head for Mexico. Sort of a Nazi scholarship.

He froze as a car passed, then quickly stuffed the three medals and the wallet into his pockets and grabbed the Luger before returning the rest of the stuff to the trunk, careful to fold up the coat he'd been wearing. After putting all the boxes back on the shelf, trying to remember which went where, he removed the ladder, went to his room and hid everything beneath the mattress. He was just getting out his homework when he heard his grandfather pull into the driveway.

.   .   .

"I thought we might go to the beach this morning," said Mead when Andrew finally emerged from the bathroom, which Mead had staked out for ten minutes.

Andrew let out a low grunt.

"Your enthusiasm is infectious." Mead hurried past to relieve himself.

"Sure, I'll go." Andrew hung in the doorway while Mead struggled with his zipper.

"Mind shutting the door?"

"Sorry."

Mead couldn't keep himself from groaning with relief. Hell, any farther than the beach and he'd need a catheter.

"You okay in there?"

"Of course I'm okay." When Mead opened the door Andrew was still standing there. "Yes?"

"Just making sure you're okay."

They were pulling out of the driveway when Andrew suddenly shouted, "Wait!"

The car lurched to a stop. "Jesus, good thing I don't have airbags."

"Sorry."

"Have you got to go again already?"

"No."

"Then what?"

Andrew looked across the street as he fiddled with his earring. "Well, I was just wondering if maybe we could ask Evelyn to come along? I'm sure she's not doing anything and she loves the ocean and— "

"How do you know she loves the ocean?"

"Because she's a nature freak." He opened the car door.

"Stop right there."

Andrew froze.

"It's awfully last-minute."

"It's *spontaneous*." He offered a big cheesy smile. "Please?"

Does the boy have a thing for older women? Granted, she certainly brought out the best in him. And wasn't that exactly what Mead had been trying to do? He looked over at Evelyn's house, thinking of her all alone with her cookies and flowers. Oh, what the hell, if it helps. "Okay, but tell her to make it snappy if she wants to join us." Andrew was already off and running across the street.

"Are you sure you don't mind me tagging along?" Evelyn asked for the second time as Mead drove.

"Of course not." He rolled down his window further, feeling disoriented by her perfume.

"Well, I'm just delighted." She gave him a quick pat on the knee.

Mead was careful to position them right in front of the lifeguard tower and this time Andrew stayed closer to shore, hovering near a cluster of girls bobbing and squealing in the surf.

"I haven't been to the beach in months," said Evelyn, sighing contentedly as she and Mead sat side by side in matching beach chairs. With her oversized sunglasses and widebrimmed straw hat she reminded Mead of Sophie, who'd been buzzing around his head for the last hour like an angry bee.

"You should have brought your suit."

"I did." She smiled as she snapped one of the shoulder straps beneath her billowy white shirt.

"Oh."

A teenage girl in a silver thong bikini paused directly in front of them and began adjusting her suit with a series of tweaks. Mead quickly turned his attention to his canvas beach bag, as if looking for something.

"Maybe I'm old-fashioned, but I always liked the idea of leaving something to the imagination," said Evelyn. "Of course, at my age there's not much left to imagine."

Mead rummaged even deeper into his bag.

"Not that there ever was." She laughed as she worked her bare feet into the sand. Mead noticed that her toes were painted, which surprised him. "What annoys me most about getting older is that I feel entirely misrepresented by my body." She swept her hands from her face down to her torso and legs. "It's like I've got on this wretched costume and the zipper's stuck."

"I hadn't thought of it quite that way." Mead shooed away a seagull that had taken an aggressive interest in his feet.

"My mother used to say that old age was like a hideous masquerade ball."

"What a pleasant thought."

Evelyn laughed, then pointed toward a passing woman who looked to be in her twenties with long shiny hair and shapely hips. "Just wait until she sees her costume."

"I'd have to say that I feel consistently old through and through," said Mead. "I guess you might say I'm evenly cooked."

"Don't you start with your weary-old-soul routine." She waved a finger at him.

"I didn't know I had a routine."

"Oh, you've got it down perfectly. Unfortunately, it's a big waste of time."

Mead felt anger rising to the surface of his skin. Who was she to keep passing judgments?

"I don't mean to be rude, it's just that, well, what's the rush?"

Mead couldn't think of how to respond. Instead he stared out over the water and tried to ignore a slight tug of melancholy. Did the ocean make other people sad?

"There's something I've been meaning to talk to you about," said Evelyn, not looking at him.

Mead tensed. Even Sophie seemed to tense.

"This isn't easy for me."

"We could skip it."

She smiled, though her face was creased with nervousness. Then she took in a loud breath. "I have an apology to make."

"You're forgiven."

She looked perplexed. "What is it you think I'm apologizing for?"

"Let's just say that teenagers are never easy to deal with."

"This has nothing to do with Andrew."

"Oh."

She took another loud breath. "Okay, here goes: I want to apologize for writing those silly poems years ago. I know it wasn't right. I guess I just—"

"What poems?"

She looked at him in surprise, her eyes shifting back and forth between his. "But you must have gotten them. I sent, I don't know, probably three or four to your office years ago. I know it was a stupid thing to do. I didn't mean any harm from it. That's why they were anonymous, though I figured you'd probably guess. I was just so . . ." She suddenly lost her composure.

Mead sank back into his beach chair. "That was you?"

"Who did you think it was?"

"I . . . well, I don't know. I mean I . . ." He felt his face turning such a deep crimson that he wanted to pull his hat down over it.

Evelyn turned back toward the ocean and kneaded her hands together. "But I thought you knew. I thought that's why . . ."

"Why what?"

"Why you've always ignored me."

Mead looked out at Andrew, who was still stalking a group of girls. *I oughta wring his little neck for setting me up like this.* And yet it was so much more pleasant to think that the poems—which had actually been rather good—had come from Evelyn rather than six-foot-three Frances in accounting. He felt a ticklish sensation on the skin of his chest and cursed himself for not saving them, wishing he could remember exactly what she had written.

"I've embarrassed you."

"No, I mean, well, it's a little . . . awkward." Sophie was now buzzing in his ear so loudly that he wondered if Evelyn could hear it.

"I had no right to send them to you."

"There's really no need to go into it."

"I must seem so pathetic to you; a married woman sending poetry to her neighbor." She slowly spun a silver bracelet she wore on her left wrist. "You see, for some reason I got it into my head that I had a talent for poetry—I must have submitted dozens to various magazines, I think I still have the rejection letters—and I just wanted someone to read them; someone who might enjoy them. Someone like . . . you."

Mead cleared his throat and adjusted his hat.

"God knows, George wasn't interested." She sighed. "Anyway, I hope you can forgive me. I was just very confused—or lonely, to tell the truth. I just had so much inside of me and I didn't know what to do with it." Her voice began to crack. "And there you were every day, right across the street. You don't know how many times I watched out the window as you came home from work or washed your car or mowed the lawn. Sometimes it felt like that street was a thousand miles wide."

Mead sat speechless.

"Well, at least I've said it." She tried to smile.

Mead started to say something when suddenly Andrew came bounding up the beach, dripping wet. "Who's going to join me?"

"Not—"

"I will," said Evelyn, standing and taking off her hat.

"If she's going in, you've got to go in," said Andrew to Mead, all smiles.

"I do?"

"If you want to be a gentleman." He winked before sprinting back into the water.

．　．　．

They played in the waves for an hour. Mead could hardly think straight at first, and he felt horribly self-conscious stripping down to his bathing suit in front of Evelyn. (This ought to cure her ardor, he thought, as he looked down at his pale and flaccid abdomen.) Yet soon he was immersed in the simple joy of anticipating each wave, bracing himself or diving into the soft underbelly of the larger ones and enjoying the briny taste on his lips. He made a point of trying not to look too often at Evelyn, though he quickly got the general gist. She was in surprisingly good shape with long legs and a nice little rump—for her age—yet a bit thin. He'd noticed that even her face seemed thinner lately. Not enough meat, he decided.

If only he could remember the poems. And what did she mean about him ignoring her all these years? Maybe he'd kept his distance, but hell, he'd been happily married. And then after Sophie died he was too blinded by grief to notice much of anything. But now seeing her wet and laughing as she greeted each wave like guests to a raucous party was almost more than he could bear.

"Isn't this fun?" she said, standing right next to him and springing up through a wave as it rolled past. Andrew was whooping and splashing next to her.

Mead nodded with a broad smile.

. . .

On the way home they stopped at a surf shop where Mead bought Andrew a couple of T-shirts—"as long as they don't have Satan on them." Andrew spent forty-five minutes trying to whittle down his choices, holding them up one at a time as he posed before the mirror with Evelyn at his side. Mead enjoyed watching the excitement on the boy's face, though frankly it seemed a bit excessive. Did he really think a few overpriced T-shirts would turn the tide? Evelyn seemed to be having a grand old time putting her two cents in and telling Andrew how handsome he looked. She liked one of Andrew's choices so much—it had some sort of psychedelic dancing gecko on the front—that she got one for herself.

"The Bobsey Twins," Mead muttered under his breath.

When they got home Andrew went off with Evelyn for a snack while Mead retired to his chair, thinking he'd need at least a week of uninterrupted silence to make sense of the day. *Christ, I can't take much more.*

He thought of Frances, feeling like a heel for giving her the cold shoulder for two straight years before she finally got fired for filching office supplies. Then he thought of Evelyn's husband, George, wondering if he ever realized just how lonely his wife was. He wasn't a bad man, just dull and self-absorbed without any *umph* at all. "He's a snooze," Sophie said after they had them over for dinner one night. "I always thank my lucky stars that I didn't marry a snooze. And believe me, four out of five men are snoozes."

But why Mead? Did he really mean anything to her—and how could he?—or was it just some passing fancy that had long since faded? He tried to imagine her secretly spying on him out her window, which made him blush again.

And now what? He sat perfectly still except for the bobbing of his left knee. Now what?

When the afternoon light grew dim he got up and pulled off the dustcover from his eight-inch Celestron Schmidt-Cassegrain telescope that stood in the corner of the living room, thinking he'd polish the lens. He hadn't gone stargazing since Sophie had died. He tried once on a moonless evening a few months after the funeral, but staring up at all that cold and infinite space made him feel so horribly lonely that he quickly dismantled the telescope, lifted it back into the trunk and hurried home.

He opened the front door and looked up. Clear skies. And just a crescent moon. He looked back at the telescope, remembering how Sophie would gasp in delight every time she peered into the eyepiece, as though it was magic. Why not?

"Only if we invite Evelyn," said Andrew when he returned, his mouth still full of food.

"Don't you think she's sick of us by now?"

"Nope."

.   .   .

"I hope Andrew didn't put you up to this," Evelyn said as Mead drove east to the county park where he and Sophie always used to go, usually bringing a blanket and a picnic and sometimes even a bottle of wine.

"Not at all." Andrew sat alone in the backseat leaning forward with his head between them, an impish smile saturating his features.

Mead parked in the far corner of the empty gravel lot near the edge of a steep ravine. The hillsides were covered with cactus and chaparral. "Perfect night," he said, slipping the scope into the tripod and tightening a knob.

Two-timer, said Sophie, right into his ear.

"I can't believe the stars," said Andrew, staring straight upward. "We hardly have any in Chicago."

"That's because you've got too much light pollution," said Evelyn, wrapping a scarf around her neck and smiling at Mead.

"There's Ursa Major there—the Big Dipper—and Ursa Minor over there," said Mead, pointing.

Andrew spun slowly on his heels, head tilted back. "There must be thousands of them."

"Try hundreds of billions," said Mead, whose entire sinus cavity was now impregnated with the scent of Evelyn's perfume, producing a tickling sensation.

"You mean millions."

"I mean *billions.*"

"*Billions* of stars?"

"Actually, billions of galaxies, each containing billions of stars."

"Holy shhhhh . . . cow. How could that be?"

"Very good question."

Andrew ducked as something fluttered past. "What was that?"

"A bat," said Evelyn with a laugh.

"What kind of bat?"

"The good kind," said Mead.

"Oh." Andrew searched the air above him, then scanned the nearby brush. "Any wolves around here?"

"Just coyotes," said Mead. "And a few mountain lions."

"Mountain lions?"

"Your grandma and I actually spotted one right over on that ridge there some ten years ago, but it's rare."

"You saw a mountain lion?" Andrew glanced nervously at the darkened ridge line.

"Now don't scare the poor boy," said Evelyn, drawing closer to Andrew.

"Cities are scary," said Mead. "We're in the country." He leaned over the telescope as he tried to remember how to program the computerized motor drive. Finally he gestured toward the eyepiece. "Here, take a look."

Andrew went first. "Wow, what is it?"

"Mercury. It'll drop below the horizon in a few minutes."

"Wicked."

Mead rolled his eyes at Evelyn. A coyote howled in the distance.

"What was that?" asked Andrew.

"A lonely heart," said Evelyn.

"Seriously."

"A coyote," said Mead.

"No kidding? How big are they?"

"About like a medium-size dog," said Mead. "Now relax." He watched as Evelyn peered into the telescope.

"It's just beautiful," she said, her voice suddenly fragile-sounding. She stared into the telescope for so long that Mead coughed a few times, wondering if her back had gone out. Finally she stood up and looked at him. "Thank you," she mouthed, her eyes full of tears.

Oh, Jesus, thought Mead, nearly welling up despite himself. What the hell is it with everybody?

Andrew stepped up to the telescope again. "What does that do?" he asked, pointing to the control pad attached by a cord to the base of the scope.

Mead was glad for the question. "That programs the motor drive so you can track a particular object in the sky. The scope has to keep moving to compensate for the movement of the Earth."

Andrew looked impressed. "I didn't know you were so . . . high-tech."

"Your grandfather is a regular gadgeteer," Evelyn said as Mead let Andrew work the drive.

"I could see getting into astronomy," said Andrew, looking through the eyepiece again.

"You may need to bring up those math grades," said Mead.

"There's a lot of math?"

"It's mostly math." Mead stared skyward with his hands at his waist.

"Ah, man, you serious?"

"Don't discourage him," said Evelyn.

"Just thought a little full disclosure was in order." Mead adjusted the telescope again. "Here, look at this."

Andrew peered into the eyepiece.

"That's Polaris, the North Star. It sits at the end of the handle of the Little Dipper, more than four hundred light years away from the tip of your nose."

"No kiddin'?"

"Pretty wicked, huh?"

Andrew looked up and made a face, then squinted into the eyepiece. "I still don't get how space goes on forever."

"Neither do I," said Mead.

"My daughter's been known to go on forever," said Evelyn.

Andrew looked up at the sky, then back down into the eyepiece. "If you think about it, it doesn't make any sense."

"Most things don't," said Evelyn.

"But *forever*?"

"If it just stopped, that wouldn't make much sense either, would it?" said Mead.

Andrew puzzled for a moment. "Still, it's pretty weird. And what if there's other life out there?"

"Why not? Seems awfully roomy just for us," said Evelyn. "I just hope that whatever's out there has more smarts than we do."

"No shit," said Andrew. He quickly covered his mouth. "Sorry."

"Charming, isn't he?" said Mead.

"As a matter of fact, yes, I think he is," said Evelyn, hooking her arm in Andrew's.

Andrew smiled proudly. "Can we look at the moon?"

"Coming right up," said Mead, trying to ignore the sound of Sophie's voice in his ear. *Who does she think she is?*

"Man, I've never seen it so close up. You can actually see the craters," said Andrew, peering into the telescope. "Those guys who walked on the moon must have freaked. I mean, how do you top that?"

"You don't," said Mead.

Andrew stood up abruptly. "Did you guys hear that?"

"What?" said Mead.

"Don't ask me," said Evelyn. "Either my hearing has gone to hell or the world is a much more peaceful place than it used to be."

"In those bushes over there. That noise."

"It's night," said Mead impatiently. "It's practically rush hour for a lot of creatures."

Andrew edged closer to Evelyn. "There it is again," he said, looking back at a bush.

"I can assure you it's not a mountain lion," said Mead.

"How do you know?"

"For one, they try very hard to avoid humans. Secondly, if we *were* being stalked we wouldn't hear a thing until it was too late."

Andrew's eyes widened. "We done yet?"

"What's the rush?" asked Mead.

"Just getting a little cold."

"You want my scarf?" asked Evelyn.

"No thanks."

Mead took another look through the telescope while Andrew kept glancing nervously around. "There's nothing to be afraid of," said Evelyn.

"Who said anything about being afraid?"

"No one."

"Are you guys scared?"

"Can't say that I am," said Mead.

"Personally, I could stay out here all night," sighed Evelyn as she craned her neck and gazed skyward.

Andrew frowned, then jammed his hands into his pockets and shuffled his feet.

"Look," said Mead, "I hope you don't mind me saying this, but I've found over the years that the trick with fear is to stare it right down. You can't so much as blink."

"Is that what you did during the war?" asked Evelyn.

Mead paused. "It's what I tried to do."

"So you were still scared?" said Andrew.

"Yes, I was."

"What was the scariest part?"

"That's easy: going on patrol."

"Why?"

Mead paused. "You had to leave whatever protection you had—your foxhole, a building, whatever. And you never knew what you might run into."

"Like German machine gunners and booby traps and stuff?"

"Yes, like that."

"That would definitely scare the shit—I mean the . . . that would scare me."

"Yeah, it scared the shit out of me all right," said Mead with a laugh.

Andrew looked surprised, then smiled. "I'm just curious, did they say *shit* back then or was there some other word?"

"You two certainly have a lot to talk about," said Evelyn.

"Some of the guys said *shit* and the f-word about every other sentence."

Andrew looked over anxiously at Evelyn. "Don't worry, I'm not going to faint," she said.

"The f-word too? No kidding? I thought that was kind of a new one."

"There's not much out there that's really new, except maybe the notion that wearing your trousers around your ankles is appealing."

"Don't you start into him," said Evelyn, taking another turn at the telescope. Again she spent several minutes motionless, so that Mead wondered if maybe an eyelash was stuck.

"How come you're crying?" asked Andrew when she finished.

"I don't know," she said, trying to smile as she dabbed her eyes. "Every time I look into that silly telescope I just . . ." She waved one hand helplessly in the air.

"Is it like, an infinity thing?" asked Andrew.

"Andrew—"

"I'm not sure what it is. I guess it's just so . . . lovely."

"If you ask me, there's something kind of creepy about outer space. Everything's basically cold and dead."

"Nobody asked you," said Mead.

"Now, General."

"But I think it's really awesome that stargazing makes you cry," said Andrew.

"Why thank you."

Mead shook his head, then looked into the eyepiece one more time, losing himself briefly to the enormity of space. When he finished he replaced the lens caps and showed Andrew how to remove the telescope from the tripod before they carried it back to the car. Then all three of them leaned against the trunk, Evelyn wedged between Mead and Andrew as they looked at the sky.

"What do you think about when you're stargazing?" Evelyn asked Mead.

"I don't think."

"You must feel something?"

"To tell you the truth, I feel . . . small."

"Me too!" said Andrew.

"See, you two have more in common than you realize," said Evelyn.

"Small is a relative term," said Mead.

"Personally, I think there's something nice about feeling small," said Evelyn. "It means all our problems are small too."

"I don't know about that," said Andrew.

"Except for *your* problems, of course," she said.

"What do you think about?" Mead asked Evelyn.

She paused before answering. "I think about all the wishes people have made."

"So does it make you feel small or what?" asked Andrew.

She took a deep breath. "I guess it makes me feel . . ." But she couldn't answer.

· · ·

They sat in silence for several minutes watching the sky, then Mead stood and stretched. "Think I'll take a quick walk."

"A walk?" said Andrew. "Are you crazy?"

"I believe it's one of those nature walks," whispered Evelyn as Mead disappeared into the darkness.

"Oh," said Andrew. Cupping his hands around his mouth he called out, "I wouldn't go too far."

"I think he can fend for himself," said Evelyn.

"I just feel sort of responsible for him."

"You're a very thoughtful grandson."

"I try."

She leaned back against the trunk of the car and looked upward. "It's a lot to think about, isn't it?"

"What is?"

"The sky."

"I guess it is. It kind of wigs me out a little."

She smiled. "Me too."

"Really?"

"Sure."

Andrew looked at Evelyn, then back up at the sky.

"I want to thank you for inviting me along tonight. I've had a wonderful time."

"No problem. In fact, I was thinking we could all do more together; maybe go back to the beach or take a road trip somewhere."

"I wouldn't want to be a—" then suddenly she let out a small gasp and shuddered, leaning hard against Andrew so that he had to grab her to keep her from falling.

"What is it?"

She clenched her eyes shut and reached out with one hand and grabbed his arm.

"I'll get my grandfather. We'll take you to the hospital. Hey Grand—"

"No no, please." She let out some air, then took another sharp breath. "Just give me a minute."

"But we gotta get help."

"I'll be okay." She took several long breaths as she tried to steady herself, still holding onto Andrew.

"We gotta tell my grandfather." Andrew looked around frantically, wondering how far he'd gone.

"No, you have to promise me you won't say a word to him."

"But why?"

"Because you have no idea what he went through those last months with your grandmother. I won't be a burden to him. Not when he's just coming back to life."

"But—"

She squeezed his arm harder. *"Promise me."*

"Okay okay, but—"

"There you are," said Evelyn, pulling away from Andrew as Mead emerged from the darkness. "We were starting to worry about you."

Mead gave them both a funny look.

"Yeah, we were getting worried," said Andrew, watching Evelyn as she tried to smile.

"Anybody getting tired?" said Mead.

"I'm afraid I am," said Evelyn.

"Yeah, me too," said Andrew, yawning dramatically.

"Let's call it a night," said Mead, walking around to the passenger side and opening the door for Evelyn.

"And a lovely night at that," she said, slipping past him and into her seat. As Mead drove she turned and looked back at Andrew, giving him a wink. All the pain was gone from her face and Andrew thought he'd never seen anyone look happier.

•   •   •

As soon as they pulled into the driveway Andrew jumped out of the car and headed for the house, leaving Mead and Evelyn alone in the front seat.

"I'd say you two are making progress," she said, sitting with her handbag in her lap.

"Only thanks to you. He's crazy about you."

"I'm not related. It's much easier that way."

Mead started to get out, then stopped himself. What's the hurry?

"It must be awfully hard to grow up these days," said Evelyn.

"I would have thought it was rather easy."

"You don't really believe that?"

"What the hell have they got to complain about?"

"For starters, I think the world is coming at them at about a hundred miles an hour."

"You ought to see how fast an artillery shell travels."

"I didn't mean to——"

"I'm sorry. Forget it."

They sat in silence listening to the pings and clicks of the cooling engine.

"Thank you for a wonderful day," said Evelyn, stretching her palms out over her handbag. "I just hope you can forgive me for being so foolish." She shook her head. "All these years I thought you knew . . ."

"There's nothing to forgive."

"I think there is." She laughed to herself. "If nothing else, you could forgive me for writing such lousy poetry."

"You're a fine poet."

"Nonsense."

"No really." Mead felt her looking at him as he stared straight ahead at his living room window, thinking he'd seen something move where the yellow light cut through the seam of the closed curtains.

"I'm making you uncomfortable again."

"It's been a big day."

"You've had a lot of them lately, haven't you?"

Mead sighed. "It's been an interesting week."

"You'd better get some sleep." She reached for the door handle.

"Wait."

She stopped.

"Why did you tell me about the poems?" He ran his hands along the rim of the steering wheel. "I mean, why now?"

She looked down at her hands, lacing and unlacing her fingers. "Because telling the truth seems to be the last freedom that I have." She leaned forward and kissed him on the cheek, then opened her door and headed quickly across the street to her house.

• • •

Is that you, Matt? Andrew was lying in bed, trying to get back to sleep after getting up to pee, when he thought he saw the rocking chair move.

Matt? If that's you man please stop because you're totally freaking me out. He slid down beneath his covers and stared at the chair. Had it really moved? Andrew strained his eyes. Couldn't have. And yet. He scooted down further. Outside the wind was up and he could see the shadow of a large branch swaying through the curtains, backlit by the yellowish glow of the streetlight.

And then he felt Matt. He couldn't say how but he just did. Right there in his grandma's room.

Matt?

How are you doing, Andy?

Jesus, Matt. Is that really you?

Who else?

Ah, Christ, I've missed you, buddy.

Me too.

Why did you have to do it? Why did you leave me?

I couldn't take anymore. I just couldn't stand it, Andy.

I would have helped you. We would have made it.

I'm not like you. I'm not that strong.

I tried to wake you up. I really tried.

Sorry, Andy. I just didn't want to be alone. I couldn't think of any other way.

I didn't mean any of that stuff I said. I didn't think you were serious. I would have stopped you. I—

I know you would have. That's why I didn't tell you.

Damn you, Matt. Andrew started to cry.

Please don't be sad.

Andrew sat up and wiped his eyes. *Did it hurt?*

Not the last part. That was the strange thing. I actually felt great. But those last few days were a killer, knowing that I was doing everything for the last time. That's the weirdest feeling, Andy, knowing you're doing things and seeing things for the last time ever. It was like, totally sad but awesome, too, because for the first time in my life I felt invincible. Nothing could touch me. For the first time absolutely nothing could touch me.

She's just a stupid girl, Matt. You shouldn't have wasted your life for a stupid girl.

She's much more than that, Andy. But it wasn't just her. I didn't want my life. You know that. I hated my life.

I hate my life, too. Andrew started crying again.

But you're different than me. You always have been.

I really miss you.

Yeah, I miss you, too. How are you?

I'm not so good. I tried to kill Bremer. Did you see that?

Yeah, I saw it. You were something, Andy. You were really something.

How did you like the look on his face? Andrew let out a laugh.

You really had him scared.

Andrew stared at the rocking chair, thinking maybe it had moved again. *What's it like being dead?*

Kind of quiet, really.

I'm not sure I'd like it.

It's the easiest thing in the world.

Are you happy? Matt didn't answer. *Come on, tell me. I want to know if you're happy?*

I'm free, Andy. I'm totally absolutely free.

No bullshit?

No bullshit.

Andrew laughed to himself. *I can't wait.*

Don't you hurry.

Why shouldn't I? I'm tired of the bullshit, too.

Because you've got gifts, Andy. You're a fighter.

I don't know if I can make it, Matt. Everything's so fucked up.

You've got to make it, Andy. One of us has got to make it.

I don't know. I feel so . . . And then Andrew felt a coldness on his skin that ran all the way up to his scalp. *Matt, you still here?* He stared at the rocking chair, then pulled aside the curtain and looked out the window, seeing the crescent moon blinking through the clouds just above the trees. *Matt? Don't leave me, Matt. Please don't leave me.*

• • •

"That's it, now one more set." Andrew was lifting barbells in the garage while Mead rode the stationary bike, which he'd oiled and dusted off for the first time in years, figuring he might as well set a good example.

Andrew struggled with the weights. "I can't."

"Sure you can. Soybean power, remember?"

Andrew grunted and wheezed, finally curling the barbells up to his chest three more times before collapsing onto a bench. "I'm wiped."

"They won't recognize you when you get home."

"I'll be dead before then."

"Don't you play any sports?"

"Mom made me do wrestling for a while. I hated it."

"You seem to hate a lot of things."

"I *really* hated wrestling."

"I wouldn't figure you for a wrestler." Mead picked up his pace. "Maybe a swimmer or basketball player." Actually, Mead couldn't see him as any of those things, but he wanted to say something encouraging.

"Am I done?"

"Twenty more sit-ups."

Andrew sighed loudly, then got on his back and started counting off.

"We used to run nine miles in the morning before breakfast at boot camp," said Mead. "And that was just for starters."

"But I'm not in the army," Andrew wheezed.

"Maybe you ought to consider it."

"No way. I'd hate it."

Mead grabbed the hand towel he'd hung on the handlebar and wiped down his face. "Well then, what sort of plans do you have for yourself?"

"Nothing specific."

"You must have some ideas?"

Andrew paused between sit-ups. "I suppose I wouldn't mind having something to do with making music videos, or maybe even being in a band."

"You mean like a rock band?"

Andrew nodded enthusiastically.

"What instrument? Drums? The guitar?"

"I'd sing."

"Sing?"

"It's just an idea." Andrew did one last sit-up, then stretched out on the floor, his hands resting on his stomach. "What about you, what did you want to do when you were younger?"

Mead smiled. "Hell, I just wanted to stay alive."

"Yeah, that's kind of like the way I feel."

"Well now, that shouldn't be so hard. Last I heard we were still at peace." Mead pedaled faster, then gradually slowed, trying to catch his breath.

"You don't know what it's like."

"What, being young? Sure I do. A lot of people think it's the best part."

"If this is the best part I'll . . ." He didn't finish.

"What's so bad about it?"

"Everything."

"For example?"

"Everybody's always telling you what to do."

"You're a kid. What do you expect?"

"That's what I mean."

"What else?"

"School sucks."

"And why is that?"

"It's full of jerks."

"Hell, the world's full of jerks. You've just got to pick out the good ones and ignore the rest."

Andrew sat up and wrapped his arms around his knees.

"Listen, I'm sorry about what happened to your friend," Mead said.

Andrew shrugged.

"It was a stupid thing for him to do. I hope you realize that. There's nothing stupider a person can do."

"Matt wasn't stupid."

"Well, he wasn't too smart, either." Mead hesitated, trying to think of what else to say. "You're not messing with any of those drugs, are you?"

Andrew quickly looked up. "What makes you think that?"

"I read the papers."

"No, I'm not into drugs."

"Good. You need all the brain cells you can muster in this world."

Andrew smiled.

"And I'll tell you something else: I think you boys have filled yourself with so much nonsense from television and movies that you don't know which way is up. That's what I think."

Andrew got up and put the barbells away. "Don't you like watching movies?"

"Not what passes for entertainment these days. Thank you, no."

"So what *do* you like to do?"

Mead looked taken aback.

"I mean, for fun?"

"Why, lots of things. What kind of question is that?"

Andrew shoved his hands into his pockets. "I'm just wondering what kind of stuff you're into."

Mead thought for a moment. "There's my telescope, and of course darts. I got hooked on darts in England during the war. And I play a bit of golf now and then. Hell, lots of things."

"I just thought . . ."

"What?"

"Well I . . ."

"Spit it out."

"I just thought that maybe you've been . . . well, kind of depressed since Grandma died."

"Depressed?"

"Yeah. I thought maybe, you know, that you were down."

Mead glowered. "Do I look depressed to you?"

Andrew looked at him nervously. "Well, sort of. Yeah."

"Sort of? Hell, I'm not depressed." Mead got off the bike and draped the towel around his neck. "Enough of this kind of talk, let's get some lunch."

• • •

Depressed? What the hell kind of thing was that to say to your grandfather? Mead leaned into the bathroom mirror, noticing that his face seemed a little more drawn than he remembered. Depressed?

God knows he missed her. It was like going without water. At first he didn't think he could endure it, seeing nothing but endless days stretching out toward his own death, each echoing hour like a long dark tunnel he had to crawl through. But he'd made it. He'd put one foot forward and then the other until he had some momentum again. The house was in order. He'd kept in shape. Why, he'd even learned to cook a few dishes. He ran his fingertips down the sides of his cheeks. Yes, somehow you made it, old boy. Three years in August. Three years since he'd heard that lilting voice of hers that never seemed to age. And the truth was, there'd even been some relief when she finally died because her agony was over. Seeing her fight for air those last months had about driven him insane, her body shrunken and cool to the touch and her eyes asking him to do something that he couldn't. Dear God, the helplessness of it.

"Tell me another story," she'd say, taking his hand in hers, which was permanently bruised from IVs.

"Which one?"

"Tell me the chocolate bunny story."

And so he told her again about the life-size, solid chocolate bunny displayed on a table in the waiting room where Mead sat anxiously while Sophie was in labor with Sharon on Easter morning. At first Mead nibbled at the tail when no one was looking. Just a discreet little bite. It wasn't so much hunger or a sweet tooth but nerves that drove him to it. Then he ate the little basket the bunny was holding, then the paws, and then a shoulder.

"Look Mom, that man is eating the Easter Bunny," cried a child being dragged down the hallway by his mother.

Mead quickly hid behind a newspaper.

But then he was alone again and took another bite. Then another, always keeping an eye on the big wall clock. Finally he broke off the head and ate it. After that it was a matter of getting rid of the evidence. By the time the nurse came out four hours later to tell Mead it was a girl there was nothing left of the big chocolate bunny but crumbs.

"A . . . girl?" Mead rose unsteadily to his feet, clutching at his stomach. And then right there he had passed out, all that sugar rushing to his head.

"I'll never forget when they told me you'd been admitted as a patient," said Sophie, struggling for air as she laughed. "You just about went into a sugar coma, you silly goose."

Mead blushed.

"Just how big was that bunny, anyway?"

"It was a very big bunny, my dear."

. . .

Andrew had just finished cleaning his room and was heading to the garage for his morning exercises when his grandfather stopped him. "I'm going to visit your grandma's grave. I'd like you to come along."

"Now?" It wasn't quite eight.

"Yes."

Andrew noticed that his grandfather was looking even more spiffy than usual, dressed in shiny brown leather shoes, perfectly pressed khaki pants and a blue sport coat. "Why so early?"

His grandfather paused, tightening his forehead. "It's the best time of day to visit," he stammered. "Nice and quiet."

Quiet? When *isn't* it quiet at a graveyard? But Andrew sensed it was no time to argue.

"And I want you to wear this," said his grandfather, extending his left hand.

Andrew stared down in horror at the shiny brown belt coiled in his grandfather's hand. "But I . . ."

"I'll meet you out front in ten minutes."

Actually, Andrew had always liked graveyards. He and Matt used to hang out in a large cemetery not far from their apartments, weaving among the long, silent rows and making up stories about how each person died. *Coronary while copulating. Cancer. Drug overdose. Asthma attack. Plane crash. Algebra overload. Broken heart.* As they walked they often made a game of competing to see who could calculate the age of the deceased first. *Sixty-two! Eighteen! Eighty-four! Nine! No wait, make that eight.* And of course, there was the inevitable question of foul play.

"Something tells me that ol' Howard C. Walker here was knocked off," said Matt, slapping a large slab of dark granite. *April 3, 1922—May 13, 1977.*

"How would you know a thing like that?"

"I just get a funny feeling."

"You and your funny feelings. So who did it?"

"His wife. Put strychnine in his pudding. She just couldn't take any more of the old gas bag."

One of the coolest things about hanging out in graveyards was that no matter how bummed you were, you always knew you had it better than anybody else in the vicinity. You could be in a cemetery of five hundred people and you were like, the only one who still had anything going for you. And Andrew found it enormously satisfying to think of all the assholes who were dead; rich arrogant assholes now sucking on worms beneath his feet. Even living in an apartment didn't seem so bad when you were walking through a cemetery because hey, at least you were topside. So what if he didn't live in a big fancy house or couldn't afford the right shoes? Everything was basically temporary as all hell. (Of course, that led right back to the essential stupidity of things, which was why it was so hard to take algebra seriously.)

"Your grandma was really something when she was younger," said his grandfather suddenly, a smile seeping through his stern features as he drove.

Andrew wasn't sure what to say. "Yeah, I bet she was."

"What I'm saying is that she wasn't always a grandma. Heck, she was practically your age when we met."

"Cool." Andrew peered over at his grandfather, trying to figure out where the conversation was going. "Was she like, popular?"

"She was no cheerleader. But she was a *doll.*"

Andrew thought of the black-and-white pictures he'd examined. Pretty, maybe, but not a doll. "Were you . . . popular?"

His grandfather let out a laugh. "God, no."

"So what kind of crowd did you like, hang out with?"

"A small one. Your grandma used to tell me that I was a bit of a square." Andrew smiled. "She was just teasing, of course."

"Of course." They continued in silence for several minutes. "Do you visit her grave a lot?"

"Now and then."

"Isn't it kind of . . . depressing?"

His grandfather didn't respond at first and Andrew wondered if he'd said the wrong thing. *Of course it's depressing, you dope. She's dead.* Finally his grandfather looked over and said, "Sometimes it makes me feel better and sometimes it makes me feel worse." Uh-oh, thought Andrew, could be a long day.

They drove through a large stone gate with a towering palm tree on each side and turned left into a newly paved parking lot. The cemetery was huge, sloping slightly uphill with grass as perfect as Astro turf and bouquets of flowers scattered here and there. Definitely upscale, thought Andrew, as he sat waiting for his grandfather to get out of the car. But Mead seemed to be looking for something in the distance, then suddenly smacked the steering wheel with his hand.

"What is it?" asked Andrew, wondering if they'd driven to the wrong cemetery. Or maybe he forgot flowers?

"Nothing." His grandfather sighed. "It's going to be a short visit. Come on."

As they wound their way through the rows of headstones Andrew spotted a large woman in purple perched in a chair and talking loudly to herself. "Who's she talking to?" he asked, but his grandfather didn't answer. As they drew closer Andrew suddenly feared that it was some sort of setup. "She's not a relative, is she?" he whispered.

His grandfather scowled as he continued toward the woman. Somebody's mood has sure soured, thought Andrew. Was it something I said? He looked down at the belt. Should the shiny side go on the inside?

They didn't stop until they were barely three feet from the woman, who looked like an immense plum and was so busy lecturing someone named Henry that she didn't seem to notice them. Andrew briefly considered whether she might be criminally insane, then looked down and saw his grandma's name etched in stone. Wow. He'd never seen the name of someone he actually knew. Kind of creepy, he thought, wanting to touch the letters but stopping himself. He tried to think nice thoughts about Grandma but was distracted by the purple nut case blabbering next to them. This is seriously awkward.

"Who do we have here?" the woman said, turning toward Andrew and smiling like he was a delicious bonbon she was about to pop into her mouth.

"My grandson," mumbled Mead. Andrew had never heard him mumble before.

"What a treat! And where are you from, dear?"

"Chicago."

"*Chicago?*" She sized Andrew up so intently that he feared she might kiss him, then she looked admiringly at Mead. "You must have done something right because Lord knows, none of my grandsons would be caught dead in a belt."

"He's sort of his own man," said Mead, putting his hand on Andrew's shoulder and turning them both away from her.

"Henry, the nicest boy has come to visit," she said, leaning toward the gray headstone in front of her.

Ah, so that's Henry. Andrew tried to stifle a giggle. Good thing I'm not stoned. Or maybe she's stoned? Nah, too old. But this is *weird*.

His grandfather continued to ignore the woman as he knelt down and rested both palms on the top of Sophie's thin white headstone, which came up to Andrew's waist. "I just thought you might want to see it," he said.

"It looks . . . great," said Andrew. "I like the way the letters are. You know, the style."

His grandfather lovingly patted the stone. "She adored you."

Andrew watched him closely, wondering if he was going to cry. No way. Not Sarge. Still, it was definitely intense. His grandfather kept staring silently at the grave. Andrew tried to follow his gaze. What's he looking at?

"I'm sorry you didn't know her better."

Andrew had never heard his grandfather's voice sound so soft before. "I've got really good memories," he said cheerfully.

"Hang on to them."

"Definitely."

His grandfather kept looking at the headstone while the big purple psycho ripped into Henry for failing to file three years' worth of taxes. "Well I . . . I just thought you ought to come here. Pay your respects."

"For sure."

"She would have done anything for you, you understand that?"

"Yeah."

A sad smile came over his grandfather's face. "You see, she had a way with people. Just the right touch."

Andrew nodded.

"And like I said, she adored you. She always—"

"I think it's the nicest spot in the whole place, don't you?" interrupted the woman, reaching over and tugging at Andrew's arm.

Andrew looked around, but the graves all looked pretty much identical. "Not bad," he said with a shrug.

"It's so nice of you to come. I was just telling Henry here that our granddaughter is going to be in the school play. The lead!"

Andrew nodded, then turned back to his grandfather.

"You must have been just heartbroken when she passed," continued the woman.

"Passed?"

"Yes, he was," said Mead curtly as he rose to his feet.

The woman kept staring at Andrew. "Well, don't you have anything to say to her?"

"Huh?"

She cocked her head toward the ground. "You can't come all this way and not say hello."

"We'd just like a little peace and quiet," said Mead.

Jesus, thought Andrew, this is too fucking much.

"You haven't told him, have you?" said the woman.

"Pardon me?" said Mead.

"About the conversations," she whispered, leaning forward.

"What conversations?" asked Andrew.

"Nothing," said Mead. "I think we'd better go."

"But you just got here," said the woman. "And I just happen to have some extra tickets to the theater." She reached into her purse, then waved the tickets in the air, wiggling her immense bottom in unison.

"Can't talk now," called out Mead, already heading toward the parking lot. "Got to run."

Andrew struggled to keep up. "You've really got a way with the ladies," he said when they reached the car.

"Not another word," said his grandfather.

• • •

They both saw the FOR SALE sign in front of Evelyn's house at the same time.

"Oh no," said Andrew.

Mead felt a hollowness in his stomach. Perhaps there'd been some sort of mistake. After all, why hadn't she said anything and where would she go? He vaguely recalled her having a son and daughter somewhere in the east and wondered if she was going to live with one of them. "Looks like I'll be cutting back on my cookie intake," he said as casually as he could manage.

"She doesn't *want* to move," said Andrew, his face verging on panic.

Mead parked the car in the driveway and turned off the ignition. "What makes you say that?"

"Well . . . look how nicely she keeps her garden. I mean, how could she leave that?"

It did seem surprising. "So, it's some sort of mix-up."

"It's not a mix-up. I've got to talk to her." Andrew jumped out of the car.

"Wait . . ." But Andrew was already halfway across the street. Confused and flustered, Mead headed quickly into his house, making a fist at his side to control himself.

• • •

"You can't move," said Andrew when Evelyn opened the door.

"Don't be silly," she said sadly.

"But you can't. Your garden is here, my grandfather is here—"

"Your grandfather?"

"He likes you."

She blushed.

"He really does."

"I don't think he'll even notice when I'm gone."

"Are you kidding? It'll break his heart. He's just shy, that's all. He's, well, he's sort of a nerd when it comes to girls . . . I mean ladies."

"You're very sweet but—"

"And you can't let your daughter push you around."

"I'm afraid she's right. I can't afford to live here all by myself."

"Where will you go?"

"Connecticut. That's where my daughter lives."

"*Connecticut?* But what about your garden?"

"I believe they have flowers in Connecticut."

Andrew thought for a moment. "You could move in with my grandfather. I'll be out of there soon."

Evelyn laughed. "You're quite a little matchmaker."

"You'd be perfect for him. Just look at his garden. It's *dead*. And he needs someone who's . . ."

Evelyn raised her eyebrows.

"Hip."

"Hip? My daughter would have a seizure if she knew I'd been called *hip*."

"I'll talk to him."

"Don't you dare."

Andrew shifted awkwardly in the doorway.

"Can I get you a brownie?"

"I'm not hungry."

"Would you like to come in at least?"

He shook his head. "I just want to know . . . are you doing the chemotherapy?"

"Has anyone ever told you that it's not polite to be nosy?"

"But are you?"

"As a matter of fact, no. You see, my daughter's not getting her way with everything after all."

Andrew frowned. "Maybe you ought to."

"I don't have time for that nonsense." She smiled as she reached out and pressed her palm to Andrew's cheek.

. . .

Mead spent hours circling the matter, trying to find an approach that wasn't upsetting. But no matter how he thought about it, no matter how often he reminded himself of all the little things about her that annoyed him, he couldn't keep from feeling that life was about to close in on him again.

He left his cube steak untouched. Instead he went to his bedroom, closed the door and stretched out on the bed, hands resting on his stomach. Nothing made sense anymore. Not Evelyn, not his grandson, not even his daughter. The world had gotten so confusing that he no longer felt like he knew what to do.

He was still lying in the same position a half hour later when the phone rang.

"Bad news." It was Sharon.

"Did you get fired?"

"It's worse than that." Her voice was flat with despair.

Mead put his hand to his forehead and rubbed it, waiting for her to continue.

"They've decided to hold Andrew back a year. Between his grades and the time he's missed and the incident they won't graduate him."

"They're not pressing charges?"

"Not as long as he does thirty hours of community service and gets more counseling."

"So it's good news."

"Andrew won't think so. He's going to be devastated."

"At least he's not going to jail."

"He won't look at it that way."

"Maybe he'll learn something."

Sharon was quiet for a moment, then asked, "How is he?"

"Just fine."

"Andrew is never *just fine*."

"Then let's just say we're managing."

"He's not giving you a hard time, is he?"

"He wouldn't dare."

"I just don't want him to drive you crazy. I know how you get."

"He's my grandson."

"He's a teenager."

"Granted."

She took a deep breath. "Listen, I'd better tell him. Can you put him on?"

"You sure you're taking care of yourself?"

"I'm fine, Dad."

"You're not smoking again?"

"I *promise*."

"And what about that new car you're going to get?"

"I'm looking."

"Good. I'll go get him."

Mead was out front taking down his flag when he heard a door slam. He started to hurry inside but stopped himself, thinking maybe he'd give the boy a little space for the evening; start fresh in the morning. Everything would look better then. He unhooked the flag and folded it, then walked to the curb and looked at the FOR SALE sign across the street. Evelyn's house was dark except for a single window. He stood watching for several minutes, then headed inside, feeling more tired than he had in years.

· · ·

After slamming down the phone Andrew ran into his room, shut the door and dove onto the bed, pounding it with his fists. A sophomore again, with all his classmates moving up? No way. *No fucking way.*

"You all right in there?"

Andrew didn't answer.

"I said, are you all right?"

"Fine."

"I'll be in the living room if you want to talk."

But Andrew stayed in his room the rest of the evening, the rage bouncing him off the walls and bed so that he finally just stood in the middle of the room with his arms wrapped around his shoulders, wanting to squeeze himself into nothingness.

"You sure you're all right in there?"

"I'm *fine.*"

"You didn't eat anything."

"I'm not hungry."

There was a pause. "Well, I'm heading to bed. I'll expect to see you for breakfast."

"Good night."

"Good night."

Andrew waited for half an hour, sometimes pounding his fists into his pillow when he couldn't contain himself, then quietly opened his door and peered down the hall, making sure his grandfather's bedroom light was out. He waited another ten minutes, then crept into the living room, grabbed the bottle of bourbon from the small bar and quickly carried it back to his room.

He took a big shot at first, then sat on the bed taking small sips and listening to his CD player and tapping his feet.

No fucking way. He'd never last another year. And to be humiliated like that in front of everybody?

No way.

As he sat there drinking he started to feel better, then worse, then so good that none of it seemed to matter. In a way it was a relief, having things framed so clearly. Going back was now out of the question. He thought again of hitchhiking to Mexico, starting a whole new life for himself. That would freak everybody out. And then one day he'd show up and be way ahead of them with a car and good money and a job when they were just graduating. It would be like passing everybody by; beating the game. Maybe he could even bartend at one of those pool bars. He imagined himself tossing bottles and glasses into the air and catching them behind his back as the awestruck customers—all wearing bikinis—broke into applause. Did they have a drinking age? He wasn't sure.

He lifted the mattress and pulled out the medals, wallet and the Luger, laying them neatly on the bed. Wish Matt could see this stuff.

Was the Luger loaded? He fiddled with the handle until he managed to slide out the narrow clip. He counted five bullets. Plenty.

He took another shot of bourbon, then tried to concentrate his gaze on the rocking chair. *Hey Matt, you here? I really need to talk to you, Matt.*

Silence.

They want to keep me back a year. He kept his eyes fixed on the chair, tears coursing down his cheeks. *I won't do it, Matt. There's no way I'm staying back.*

He stood and walked slowly across the room, the gun in his left hand

and the bottle in his right. *You were right, Matt, there's just way too much bullshit.* He sat down in the rocking chair and took a long sip of the bourbon, then another. *I should have gone with you. Why didn't you let me go with you?*

He thought again of trying to run away to Mexico. Could he really do it? No, not alone. He wouldn't know where to start.

He looked down at the gun in his hand. *I can't take it anymore, Matt. I want to go with you, buddy. You hear that? I'm going with you. But Jesus, I'm scared. Weren't you scared?*

He put the bottle down on the floor, then held the pistol up in front of his face and stared at it again, wondering how many others it had killed. Then he stood in the middle of the room, trying not to sway on his feet as he raised the pistol and pointed it at his forehead, putting his thumb to the trigger. But his hand shook so bad he feared he might drop it. He went over and sat on the edge of the bed and put his headphones on, turning the music up full blast and letting the tears wash down his face. After a few minutes he picked up the German soldier's wallet, gently removed the photographs and studied them. *Hello, Hans. You're dead, aren't you? Was it bad? Were you scared? What do you miss the most? Your girlfriend? Your medals? Sex?* He looked at the German handwriting on the back of the photograph of the young woman. *Shouldn't have been a Nazi, Hans. Big mistake.* He slid the photos back into the wallet and placed it on the dresser. After switching CDs he forwarded to the third song and pressed the headphones against his ears, nodding his head up and down as the music began. Then he turned and looked at the gun, which lay next to him on the bed. *I'm coming too, Matt. Wait for me because I'm coming too.*

He started to reach for the gun, then hesitated. After taking another large swig of bourbon, grimacing to keep it down, he took off the headphones, got up and carefully opened the door, checking that his grandfather's light was still off before heading for the kitchen, weaving as he went. Might be just a tiny bit buzzed. After turning on the small light above the table he searched through the drawers until he found the bag of magnets. He emptied the bag on the table and spent several minutes trying to select the right words, then stood and steadied himself before slowly arranging them on the refrigerator, too drunk to tell if the words were straight or not. It'll do. Then he turned off the light and returned to his room, quietly closing the door before putting his headphones back on. After taking another drink from the bottle, almost gagging this time, he screwed the top back on, placed it on the floor and flopped down on the bed.

I'm really coming, Matt.

He picked up the gun.

It made him feel better knowing that he'd be with Matt again; that he wouldn't be alone anymore. And then as he lay there he realized he'd never have to worry about anything ever again. *No bullshit, right Matt?* He smiled, wiping his face with the back of his sleeve as he thought of the power he held in his hand, power to make all the problems instantly go away *forever*; power to free him from homework and tests and acne and putting up with assholes and always needing money and seeing his mom cry and meeting her latest stupid boyfriend and having to stare at Cori Fletcher knowing he'd never get to touch her and most of all just having to face the darkness alone night after night with no way to hide. Already he felt a strange sense of calm, knowing it was all over. Yeah, for the first time in his life he could let go of *everything*. It was just like Matt had said: for once, nobody can touch you.

I'm invincible.

"Jesus fuck, Matt, we'll both be virgins for eternity," he said out loud, laughing to himself as he aimed the gun first at his heart, then at his temple before putting the tip of the nozzle into his mouth, feeling his hand quake again. *Okay, Matt, I'm really coming. Just keep your eye out 'cause Andy's on his way.*

．　．　．

Mead awoke at 1:15 A.M., his bladder so full he wasn't sure he'd make it to the bathroom. After relieving himself, bracing one arm against the wall to support his weight and wincing from the pain, he headed to the kitchen to heat up a cup of milk, which usually eased the transition back to sleep. He looked up at the wall clock. The next call of nature would be between four and five.

As he reached for the refrigerator door he stopped to read the words spelled out in the small black-and-white magnetic letters. He leaned close, squinting, then finally pulled out his glasses from the pocket of his robe.

I'm sorry for everything. Tell Mom I love her.

What? Mead read the words again.

Oh, Jesus.

He ran down the hallway and burst into Andrew's room. The boy was lying on his back on the bed with his headphones on and a pistol pointed into his mouth.

"*Andrew!*" Mead jumped forward and snatched the gun away. "In the name of God."

His grandson looked up at him, his eyes glassy and confused, then burst into tears. Mead stood over him shaking and wondering for a moment if he would awaken from a nightmare. *This cannot be.* Unable to find any words to say, he pulled out the clip from the pistol and placed it in the pocket of his robe before setting the pistol down on the dresser. Then he stood immobile, staring at the wallet and medals, the first time he'd set eyes on them in over fifty years.

Hans Mueller.

"How dare you?" He bent over Andrew, who remained on his back crying with his hands covering his face and his knees drawn up, and took him by the shoulders and shook him. "How *dare* you!"

"I didn't mean to," Andrew cried.

"The hell you didn't." Without thinking Mead slapped the boy hard across his face. "Get up, goddamn you!"

"Please don't hit me."

"I said, *get up!*" Mead yanked Andrew to his feet, smelling the alcohol on his breath. The bottle of bourbon lay on its side on the floor. "You think you can come here and blow your goddamn brains out in your grandmother's room? You think you can just destroy everything?"

"I don't care what you do to me. I don't care what anybody does to me." Andrew swayed on his feet, then reached for the pistol on the dresser. Mead swung and struck him again, sending Andrew reeling back onto the bed. Mead stood above him trembling and watching the blood run from a split in Andrew's lower lip.

"How did you kill him?" asked Andrew. "How did you kill that German soldier?"

"Shut up!"

"Well I don't care if you kill me." Andrew rolled onto his side and curled up, heaving.

Mead stood over him, feeling a burning sensation behind his eyes so that he had to steady himself by holding on to the dresser. Finally he took a few steps backward and slumped down in Sophie's chair, keeping his eyes on his grandson.

"Why?" Mead whispered. "Why?" But the boy wouldn't answer.

Andrew kept weeping for almost half an hour until gradually his shoulders stopped shaking and his thin frame became still. Mead listened to the boy's breathing, hearing him drift slowly and restlessly into sleep. He got up and checked on him, getting a wet washcloth to clean up the boy's lip and face, then returned to the rocking chair where he sat trying to stop the quaking in his hands and asking himself again and again what the right thing was to do.

At first he thought he'd call a doctor; let the professionals take over. Yet as he stared at his grandson's sleeping face it seemed unbearable to just hand him over, not knowing what might become of him. And how would he tell Sharon?

He looked over at the gun on the dresser. Good God, to want to kill yourself at sixteen with all of life ahead of you. How could a life barely begun be worth throwing away? Couldn't he see beyond tomorrow? Was the future really so terrifying and opaque? And yet he'd never gone to bed without a full stomach and a warm place to sleep a night in his life. He was *lucky*.

Mead slowly rocked back and forth, listening to the familiar creaking of the chair and feeling more lost and alone than he ever had in his life.

How do kids so young and pampered feel such despair? Was it the meaninglessness of the world these days, fact and fiction all blended so hopelessly by Hollywood that nobody could see straight anymore? Jane and Max Harquet had a grandson who killed himself, right out of the blue. Found him hanging from a rafter in the attic. Good grades, member of the soccer team, nice kid. No one suspected a thing. And these kids killing their classmates for the fun of it—the luckiest, most spoiled generation ever. No depression. No war. (How many young men never had the chance to grow old?) Mead would never forget reading in the paper one day that suicide rates drop during times of war and how that told him all he needed to know about human nature. My God, is peace and prosperity so tedious that people—even children—will turn on themselves in search of an adversary?

He looked over at the German soldier's belongings sitting on the dresser, beckoning. They'd been calling out to him for years, a cry that over time had gradually become muffled enough for him to ignore until he could pretend that he no longer heard it. *Have you forgotten?* After a few minutes he rose and walked over and picked up the three medals and then the wallet and carried them back to the rocking chair, beads of sweat gathering on his brow and palms. *Hans Mueller.*

He pulled out a photograph from the wallet and looked at it, then quickly put it back. *Forgiveness.* That's what the Holy Joes at church were always talking about. Anything could be forgiven, or so they promised. Absolution. Yet Mead had never felt it. Not for an instant. How could he when he could still see the look in the young German's eyes those last silent seconds, just the two of them, face-to-face, time stretching until finally it *snapped?*

Bitte.

And yet . . .

But he couldn't think of that now. He looked at his grandson still smelling of bourbon and curled up beneath the sheets that Mead had gently tucked in around him. Then he remembered striking him and felt a sense of horror.

Forgive me, Sophie.

But what should I do? Call the police? He got up and walked over to the bed again and leaned over Andrew to check on his breathing. Would they handcuff him or put him in a straitjacket? No, I can't call the police. He gently placed his hand on Andrew's forehead, which was damp. My grandson. Flesh and blood. Unrecognizable, maybe, but still a part of me. And what about Sharon? How will she cope?

He sat back down and wiped the tears from his eyes and for the first time in years he tried to pray. But he couldn't. Each time he tried, the words he flung out echoed mockingly back at him. And then when he closed his eyes tight and clenched his fists and tried to believe, all he could think was, Where were *You?* And he remembered how all those who prayed died just as easily as the rest, sometimes sooner. And Germany was covered with churches.

Then as the sun began to push through the curtains it came to him: I'll take him to Normandy. *Yes, of course.* Family history? I'll give you family history. Mead nodded slowly to himself as the idea sunk in, his fingers tapping nervously on the arms of the chair. Andrew rolled to his side and groaned. *Normandy.* He felt a prickly sensation on the skin of his forearms as he imagined the beaches and cemeteries. He swore he'd never return; not for himself. But for his grandson? He'd do anything for him. He looked over at Andrew's face, so peaceful and childlike in sleep. Would Normandy still have the power to knock sense into the boy? But it must. Even from Southern California, Mead had always felt its power, turning off the TV every time the famous images were broadcast, which seemed more and more often now that everybody was dying off like flies.

Normandy. By God, why not?

We'll stop in London first, see the sights. Mead had wonderful memories of visits to London while on leave from training at a base in Aldbourne before the invasion. As he sat there slowly rocking in Sophie's chair and watching the light gradually run beneath the curtains and pool in the folds of the sheets a smile came over his face. That's what we'll do. Just the two of us. I'll take him to the museums and show him the palace and the Tower of London and tell him about the Blitz. That's what he needs: something to think about besides himself. Does he think he's the first person to feel whipped when the game's just started; to cower with fear and want to toss in the towel? He looked over again at his grandson, watching the boy's narrow chest rise and fall beneath the sheets. Yes, I'll go back for his sake. After all, it is family history.

That afternoon he made an appointment to see a travel agent.

• • •

"You're kidding?" said Sharon when Mead called her, not mentioning what had happened.

"It'll be good for him. And I haven't been back in years."

"Since the war! Mom said you'd never go back. She always wanted to see Europe but she said you'd never go."

"I've changed my mind."

"I can't believe it." There was a pause. "What does Andrew think?"

"I haven't told him yet."

"Oh."

"I wanted to check with you first."

Another pause. "You know, frankly, Dad, it's very generous of you but I'm not sure he'll want to go. He might be a little uncomfortable."

"Traveling with his grandfather?"

"He is a teenager."

"I can be a lot of fun."

"Your doctor didn't put you on one of those mood medications, by any chance?"

"I just want to help him. Broaden his horizons."

"But Europe will cost a fortune."

"It's my treat."

"What about passports?"

"I'll need you to send me his birth certificate. Use one of those overnight services and I'll pay you back."

"I can't believe this."

"I figure we'll be gone about eight days. I'd like to stop in London first—for old time's sake."

"You really want to take Andrew to Europe?"

"Sure. Why not?"

"I can think of a million reasons." She laughed in disbelief. "Mom would roll over in her grave."

"She would, wouldn't she?"

After he hung up Mead checked on Andrew, who was in his room reading, then went into the garage, set the medal ladder against the high shelf he'd built shortly after they moved in, and began slowly climbing. He didn't get to bed until well past midnight.

· · ·

Andrew didn't talk much during the flight. Even thinking was unpleasant. Looking out the window at the clouds, he half wondered whether he wasn't dead after all and in transit to some strange new destiny. Figures I'd get a middle seat in coach.

Everything had happened so quickly. That morning when he woke up—oh fuck did his head hurt—his grandfather was sitting right there in the rocking chair staring at him. "I'm going to give you a choice," he said slowly, "and I want you to listen very carefully." Andrew rolled away from him, groaning at the realization of what he'd done, or tried to do. Would he really have done it? Oh God, his grandfather had seen everything.

"Either you come with me on a little trip and we see if you can't learn something about the value of human life—about what real misery and sacrifice is all about—or we call your mother, tell her what's happened and get you put away in a hospital. Frankly, I'd just as soon put you away myself." His grandfather impatiently drummed his fingers on the wooden armrests.

"A trip?" Andrew moaned. "Where?"

"To Normandy."

Suddenly Andrew's stomach gave way and he leaned over the edge of the bed and vomited all over the green carpet.

Part Two

London

They docked at Liverpool on an overcast afternoon after the eleven-day crossing from New York, the journey spent anxiously waiting for the wolf packs to strike, until the morning when cheers erupted at the sight of the green coast of Ireland. As Mead waited to disembark he thought of the stories he'd heard of his great grandfather, who emigrated from Manchester just before the American Civil War with only the clothes on his back and his carpentry tools. Did he also lie awake at night in fear of the unknown? Which journey required more courage: mine or his?

Mead marveled at the fairy-tale villages they passed during the trip by train and then truck to their base in Aldbourne, eighty miles west of London. The English countryside looked almost medieval and make-believe, rows of identical sheep staring blankly from behind ancient fences and old men in tweedy coats bicycling along the roadside, weaving in and out of the endless convoy.

And then, on his first weekend pass, London.

"I've already fallen completely in love three times," said Punchy as they waded through the crowds of pedestrians, many in uniform.

"We've only gone two blocks," said Mead.

"It's gonna be a long day," sighed Punchy, swiveling his head to follow a passing brunette. "God, I need a drink."

They stopped first at the American Red Cross headquarters and stood in line for an hour before reaching the information desk where they booked cheap accommodations for two nights—barracks style—along with tickets to the Winter Garden Theatre and a discounted taxi tour of the city. Punchy tried valiantly to make headway with the pretty young assistant but she blithely ignored his advances. "I think I'm a little rusty," he said as they walked out.

"Perhaps you should consider a slightly more subtle approach."

"What's wrong with my approach?"

"For starters, you might have been a little hasty when you proposed to her."

"Think so?"

Mead rolled his eyes.

"Okay, maybe I was, but I meant it. Did you see the lips on that girl and the way she tucked the upper one beneath the lower one when she was concentrating? Oh, Jesus . . ."

"You're pathetic."

"I'm Italian." Punchy shook his head. "You wouldn't understand."

"Neither would she."

After the taxi tour they spent hours walking aimlessly, trying to take in as many sights as possible, as though building a store of civilized images to counter what lay ahead. Mead couldn't believe the destruction, the first actual evidence of war that he'd seen. One building was untouched while the next was dissected in half like a playhouse with the bathroom plumbing dangling in midair. And still the city seemed incredibly dignified, Saint Paul's looming defiantly above the ruins.

"It's like the whole town's in heat," said Punchy, looking longingly at a group of nurses who were waiting for a bus. "Must be the war. I'm telling you, we could use an occasional air raid back home."

"Would you shut up?"

"Don't you feel it? I can almost smell it."

"You weren't raised in a kennel, by chance?"

Punchy made a face. "Know something, pal? You've got to start loosening up." He shook out his arms and rolled his shoulders with exaggeration. "And don't think you're fooling anybody with that Mr. Serious shit. I know a horny goat when I see one."

"You done yet?"

"Temporarily." Punchy whistled under his breath at a passing woman. "God, I love them in uniform. It's like gift wrapping."

"Mind if I ask you a personal question?"

"Fire away."

"Have you ever actually had a girlfriend?"

"What, are you kidding?" Punchy laughed out loud.

"How come you never get any mail?"

Punchy hesitated. "I'm not saying they're all college girls."

"So they're illiterate?"

"They ain't librarians."

They ate at a noisy place near Trafalgar Square—restaurants offered American servicemen dinner for a buck—and throughout the meal they both kept enviously eyeing a nearby table of GIs who wore an assortment of badges and campaign ribbons and Purple Hearts. Mead imagined himself walking up to Sophie's house with a chest full of medals and a slight limp, tears springing from her eyes as she opened the door and fell into his arms. *You made it.*

"In a way I'm looking forward to it," said Punchy, still looking over at the other soldiers. "I'm ready, you know? It's like when you're in the ring waiting for the match to start."

"Go get'em, Slugger."

Punchy wolfed down his potato and offered to finish Mead's. "I'll tell you one thing, I'm sure as hell tired of thinking about it."

"So what exactly do you think about when you think about it?"

"Easy. Getting shot in the nuts. Trust me, that's all any Italian thinks about."

"Glad you've got your priorities straight." Mead smiled, sensing from Punchy's expression that he'd already imagined hundreds of ways in which he might be grievously wounded, as though the entire Third Reich had his groin in its crosshairs.

After drinking at several pubs and making little headway with various women—all spoken for—they stumbled out into the darkened street now slick with an evening mist.

"I'm telling you, Mead, if I don't get my hands on a woman soon I'm going to have a heart attack," groaned Punchy as they approached Piccadilly Circus. "I can feel it right here." He thumped his chest. "It's like I'm gonna die."

"You're sick, you know that? You ought to see a doctor."

Just then two women emerged from a doorway. "Hey, fellas."

"Sweet mother of Jesus," gasped Punchy, who sometimes mumbled Hail Mary's in his sleep, a leftover from Catholic School. ("I'm telling you,

Sister Henrietta could whip the entire German Army," he'd say. "Built like a brick shithouse. We ought to drop her on Berlin. She'd have Hitler scrubbing toilets in no time.") "You seeing what I'm seeing?" One of the women caressed Punchy's uniform while the other worked on Mead. "Thank you, Lord!" howled Punchy, putting his arm around the woman, who was a head taller.

"I think there's a small catch," said Mead, trying to ignore the sudden stirrings in his groin. "Come on, let's get out of here."

"You kidding? I'm a pig in shit."

"You're going to be a very poor little piggy if we don't get going." Mead dragged Punchy down the sidewalk while trying to conjure up images of Sophie.

"You can't just walk away from a miracle."

"Think of it as walking away from the clap."

In the next two blocks they were accosted four more times, their first experience with the notoriously aggressive Piccadilly "Commandos" who roved the area and descended on any man in uniform (one pound for a knee-trembler, five for the night).

"I've never felt so popular in my life," said Punchy, waving at a row of women lined along a building. "Look at them. They're practically salivating."

"Must be that Italian charm." Mead struggled to extract himself from the grip of a young-looking brunette while Punchy paused to revel in the attention of two blondes. "No, no ladies, you see, it's *you* who should pay *me,*" he said. "Only seeing as I'm in such good spirits tonight, I may just be willing to offer a volume discount." He put his arms around the two women, who were rapidly losing interest. "Oh, what the hell, my treat tonight—on the house—what do you say?"

"Fuck off."

"Sweethearts, aren't they?" said Punchy as they continued on. "I'm telling you, people have got the Brits all wrong."

They stopped in another pub for a final round, again eyeing men who had fought in Africa and Italy; men in their early twenties with stories that would carry them the rest of their lives.

"Do you know what I could do with a Purple Heart?" said Punchy, shaking his head. "Jesus, the gals back home would be slobbering over me."

"Not if they have to push you around in a wheelchair all day," said Mead.

Punchy sighed as he stared at the legs of the waitress passing by. "I'm going to let you in on a little secret," he said suddenly, leaning forward and lowering his voice. From his eyes Mead could see he was drunk. "I *can't* die."

"Hey, that's great. Congratulations."

"No, what I mean is . . ." he lowered his voice even more, "I haven't had nearly enough sex yet. It would be—" he groped for words "—an *injustice.*"

"You suppose God takes that into account?"

Punchy furrowed his brow in thought. "That's what's got me worried."

Half an hour later they were heading back to their hotel, weaving slightly, when the air-raid sirens sounded, wailing mournfully across the blackened city. They froze and looked up, expecting to see the silhouettes of hundreds of German bombers overhead. Should they run for a shelter? But other pedestrians continued on their way, hardly looking up. Then in the distance they heard the thump-thump of anti-aircraft fire, which lit the sky like heat lightning. After several minutes the flashes stopped.

"Must have scared them off," said Punchy.

"Guess so."

Punchy scanned the sky, struggling to keep his balance. "I was kind of hoping to see more, weren't you?"

"Maybe some other night."

"Yeah, maybe some other night." Punchy searched the sky one more time, then put his arm around Mead as they headed down the street.

• • •

Mead and Andrew took a taxi from Heathrow to their small redbrick hotel in Kensington, arriving just before lunch.

"The trick is to adapt right away to the local time schedule," said Mead, though he hadn't traveled farther than Hawaii since the war. "Don't even think about California time." He glanced at his watch, quickly doing the math. Almost four A.M.

"I'm not tired," said Andrew, eyeing the two narrow beds separated only by a small bed stand. Twin reading lamps hung from the wall, their dirty yellow shades singed by the heat of the bulbs.

"Good. We'll unpack and take a walk. Might even be able to see Westminster, Whitehall and Saint Paul's before the day is done, then maybe Buckingham and the Tower tomorrow and a few museums the day after."

Mead began to unpack, carefully placing his undergarments in the bottom two drawers of the dresser and hanging his shirts and pants. He glanced over at Andrew, who had dropped his black duffel bag in the corner and sat on the bed nearest the window, looking lost.

Should he have booked separate rooms? But he had no intention of letting his grandson out of his sight. Let the little grouch suffer a little. Mead finished unpacking, trying to ignore the weariness in his legs, then went into the cramped bathroom and washed up, pulling out his bottles of pills and trying to decide whether he should double up or skip a dose to adjust to the time change. Cheaper to skip a dose.

As he shaved he thought of Evelyn and how excited she'd been when he'd told her about his plans, slapping her hands together and talking up all the sights they'd see as if she was going herself. "I want to hear everything when you get back," she'd said, cooking up a huge batch of goodies for their flight (by the time they were airborne only a few crumbs remained). She was so happy for the two of them that he knew he couldn't possibly tell her about what had happened, even though he wanted to ask her if he was doing the right thing. And yet when he asked her why she was moving, her face seemed to freeze up. "It's for the best," she said as they sat in her living room drinking iced tea after Mead stopped in to say good-bye.

"Where will you go?"

"My daughter—ace attorney, bills at three hundred fifty an hour!—has a lovely house in Connecticut. She has plenty of room—frankly, I don't know why if she's not going to have kids—and I really don't need much. After all, why should I dust and vacuum three bedrooms?" She gestured around the house.

"I just . . . had no idea."

A sadness passed over her face like a cloud, momentarily obscuring her smile. "To tell you the truth, I didn't either."

"Is something wrong?"

She picked up her iced tea, took a sip and set it down again. "When *isn't* something wrong?" He watched as her smile fell effortlessly back into place. "But we can't let that stop us now, can we?" She got up and walked over to a small china cabinet, opening the glass door and adjusting several teacups. "George never liked this room. He thought it was too feminine." She picked up a saucer and turned it side to side. "He always wanted one of those pine-paneled rec rooms."

"I never knew him very well."

"You two were quite different." She laughed wryly. "So were we. He tried his best. We both did. We were just missing something." She closed the cabinet door. "I'm not even sure what it was, to tell the truth. There was just this big hole right in the middle of everything. Some days I was afraid it would swallow me up."

Mead adjusted himself on the floral-patterned couch, scooting closer to the edge. Again he considered telling her about Andrew. Yet how could he?

Evelyn remained standing. "I don't want you to think I feel unfortunate. I'd be a fool to waste my life thinking about what I didn't have rather than all that I did."

Mead noticed her expression give way just as she turned toward the window. He got up and walked over to her. "What is it?" he asked, putting his arm around her and noticing how thin her shoulders felt beneath her shirt. She didn't respond. "Please, tell me."

"You don't want to know."

"But I do." He held her closer, feeling scared by the sudden pain in her face. She put her head against his chest. "I have been a fool. I've been a fool all my life." Just before he kissed her he closed his eyes and asked Sophie to please forgive him.

• • •

Andrew sat on the bed watching his grandfather unpack and wondering whether he really would have killed himself if he hadn't been stopped. Every time he thought about it he felt his legs go weak. I could be dead right now. (Though he had doubts about whether he really could have pulled the trigger.) The worst part was thinking about what it must have been like for his grandfather to walk in on something like that. *Fuck.* They hadn't talked any more about it since getting on the plane but it was there between them, so that Andrew could hardly look his grandfather in the eye. And now to be sharing a room together? This *sucks.*

He had barely had time to say good-bye to Evelyn. "He wants to take me sight-seeing," he explained, sneaking outside one afternoon when he saw her gardening. (Mead had grounded him, letting him out only to get their passports.)

"So I hear," she said, leaning over a rosebush. "What's come over him?"

"Everything." Andrew looked back at the house nervously.

"I think it sounds wonderful. I always wanted to travel more myself."

"But we won't see you again."

"Of course you will. I'm not moving that fast. I'll cook a special dinner when you get back."

"But what if you need something? What if you . . ."

"I'll be just fine." She clipped off a rose and handed it to him. "For the General," she said.

He'd worried about her the whole flight over, wondering who would take care of her if she got really sick and if he should tell his grandfather and whether she was going to die soon. They never should have left her alone. (And the sparks were just starting to fly.) Yet he had to admit that it was awesome to be in *England*. He couldn't get over the accent of the taxi driver who drove them from the airport—on the wrong side of the road!—and how old the buildings looked and the fact that he was practically on the other side of the planet. If only Matt was with him.

"Aren't you going to unpack?" asked his grandfather. "I left you two drawers." He pointed toward the small dresser.

Andrew looked over at his duffel bag. "I thought I'd just keep it packed," he said. "That way I know where everything is."

"You can't keep it there. We'll be tripping over it."

"I'll put it on the floor of the closet."

"That's for our shoes."

"How about under my bed?" Andrew was already on his knees trying to cram the duffel bag beneath the bed frame.

Mead stood watching with his hands on his hips. "Okay, under the bed." He shook his head as he went back into the bathroom. Andrew listened to the weak and sporadic trickle in the toilet, wondering if his grandfather had a problem peeing, or maybe even penis cancer or whatever it was called. Getting old's gotta be a bitch.

"You ready?" His grandfather now stood by the door holding the room key in one hand and an umbrella in the other.

"Where are we going?"

"Sight-seeing." A rare smile stretched the lines of his grandfather's face.

• • •

As soon as they entered Westminster Abbey—which Andrew recognized from watching Princess Diana's funeral (his mom stayed up all night weeping hysterically)—he decided it was the *perfect* place to scatter Matt's ashes, which were rolled up in a Ziploc in his pants pocket, creating an awkward bulge that caused his pants to sag more than usual. He felt almost giddy at the brilliance of it as his grandfather eagerly pointed out various monuments and read from a guidebook. What could be more perfect? And frankly, all these kings and queens and poets and statesmen could probably use a guy like Matt to mix it up a little. Damn, buddy, who would have believed you'd get a state funeral? He tried to keep from giggling as he considered the logistics. All he'd have to do is stick his hand in his pocket, take one handful of Matt at a time and let the stuff dribble out from his fingers as he walked, maybe humming an appropriate tune. Granted, it might take some time, but he could always come back later.

"Isn't it something?" said his grandfather, pausing to stare up at the ceiling.

"It's pretty harsh."

"What?"

"It's cool."

They headed for the royal tombs. "Are they for real?" asked Andrew, casually reaching into his pocket.

"As opposed to . . ."

"I mean, are they really *in there?*"

"Last I heard." They followed a line through a small entrance into a chapel. Mead gestured toward the large tomb. "Elizabeth the First."

"The one with all the face makeup, right? I saw a movie once—"

"Right."

Andrew tried to visualize how Elizabeth looked now. Probably pretty bad. Was she buried with lots of jewelry? He imagined breaking into the church at night and cracking open her tomb and slipping big fat glittering rings off her bony fingers. Wasn't like Lizzy needed them. Then he wondered if Matt's ghost would meet Lizzy's ghost, which might be kind of a scene. Would Matt remember to bow?

By the time they reached Poet's Corner Andrew had managed to open the Ziploc using one hand. As they stood looking at a memorial to Shakespeare he carefully reached in and took a small handful. Okay, here we go. He pulled out his closed fist and let it hang discreetly at his side, feeling his eyes well up and hoping his grandfather wouldn't notice. *Good-bye, friend.* He was just loosening his fingers when he looked up and saw a janitor sweeping the floor with great big strokes. Oh, shit. The janitor flicked a little pile into a dustpan, then emptied the dustpan into a plastic garbage can and moved on. Andrew carefully put his fist back in his pocket, worked open the Ziploc and emptied the ashes back into the bag. *Whew.*

Big Ben reminded Andrew of *Peter Pan,* which had been his favorite video when he was younger. He must have watched it a hundred times, prancing around on his parents' bed with a plastic sword. *Take that, Hook!* He stared up at the clock, imagining Peter Pan perched on the large hand and waving at him. For just a moment he could almost *feel* being a kid again, diving under the bed covers with a squeal when his dad tried to tickle him. *I'll get you, Pan!*

At Saint Paul's, Andrew again considered scattering Matt's ashes, thinking maybe he'd stuff them into some nook where they'd be safe. He searched for a good hiding place as he and his grandfather toured the tombs and statues but saw none he could reach. He gently tapped his pocket. *Don't worry, Matt, I won't let you end up in the trash.*

When they reached the spiral stairs leading up to the dome Mead suggested that Andrew go up and take a look.

"You're not coming?"

"I think I'll sit awhile. You go on."

Andrew climbed quickly, mesmerized by the churning buns of a teenage girl just ahead of him. He paused at the Whispering Gallery, listening to the echoing voices and remembering just how much he hated heights, which made him feel gooey inside. Then he followed the girl up to the next level, awed by the panoramic view of London below. *What do you say, Matt?* He imagined the ashes whirling through the air and coating the city below in a fine mist. *Hard to beat that, eh buddy?* He felt for the baggie in his pocket, hoping his stomach would hold out. Of course, Matt wasn't much for heights either. He looked over the edge again, then quickly stepped back. Would Matt's ashes float down or would it be more like *plummeting?* He tried to look again but felt so queasy that he had to grab the wall. *No way, buddy, I'm not letting you plummet.* He looked over at the cute girl's butt, trying to ground himself. Much better. Taking deep breaths he slowly followed her around the dome. Much, much better. His stomach had almost recovered when she turned and gave him such a dirty look that he stopped and headed back down the stairs. When he reached the bottom his grandfather was sitting in a pew with a strange expression on his face. Was he praying? Andrew waited nearby, checking out a group of uniformed schoolgirls being lectured by their teacher. Not bad looking. Even a couple of cute ones. He tried to catch one girl's eye but instead she gazed upward as the teacher explained how the cathedral was built. Andrew looked up too, thinking that if there was a God he'd certainly be impressed by a ceiling like that. He watched the girl for a while, then looked back at his grandfather, who hadn't moved. Did he believe in God? Andrew had tried praying a few times, thinking he'd take all the help he could get in his battle against acne. One night as he lay in bed in tears from the loneliness of everything he even tried to be born again, telling Jesus that he believed *totally* and that he'd never ever wank again. But when he looked in the mirror the next morning and saw the huge new eruption centered right between his eyes he decided that either there wasn't a God or, if there was, he was an asshole just like everybody else. After applying a layer of his mother's face makeup he sat on the toilet and quickly jerked off.

He watched as his grandfather rose unsteadily to his feet.

"You okay?"

"Just fine."

Neither of them talked during the taxi ride back to the hotel.

. . .

Mead couldn't get over how different London looked, great big modern buildings—cold and sterile—towering over the old Victorians. For some reason he didn't think of London changing, at least not the architecture. And yet some parts matched his memory so closely that he half expected to see Punchy walking beside him and ogling all the girls. But it wasn't until he and Andrew were walking back to the hotel after having dinner at a nearby Italian restaurant that the biggest change hit him: he'd never seen London lit up at night. Mead paused on the sidewalk and looked at the skyline, surprised by the sudden tearing of his eyes.

"What is it?" asked Andrew.

Mead blinked a couple of times and waited until he had his breath. "I was just thinking, it used to be dark."

"Huh?"

"During the war. Everything was blacked-out. Curtains over every window."

"Really? Wow. I'd love to be in a blacked-out city. Was it spooky?"

"I never thought of it that way." Mead smiled to himself as they walked

on, remembering the furtive couples that would disappear into the darkened parks and how he and Punchy accidentally urinated on a couple
rolling in the bushes. "Sorry about that," said Punchy, trying to stop himself as the woman screamed. "Must have the wrong bush."

· · ·

"Well, what do you think so far?" asked Mead as they lay in their beds
with the lights out.

"It's all right," mumbled Andrew.

"All right?"

"Yeah, I mean it's pretty cool."

Mead smiled in the darkness. "What did you like best?"

"Definitely the tombs of the kings and queens. I've never seen serious
royalty."

"It doesn't get much more serious than that."

Andrew rolled over in his bed. In the hallway two guests giggled as
they passed by. "You ever imagine what they look like now?"

"Sure," said Mead. "Everybody does."

"Really?"

"Of course."

"I never knew that."

They lay in silence, both listening for sounds that the other was asleep.
Then Andrew said, "I'm sorry about what happened."

Mead paused. "So am I."

"I won't do it again."

"Let's hope not."

"And thanks for bringing me here. I've never been anywhere like this."

"You're welcome."

"I know it must be really expensive."

"It's my pleasure."

The couple in the hallway laughed again, then a door opened and
closed.

"Good night."

"Good night, Andrew."

· · ·

After breakfast in the hotel they watched The Changing of the Guard at
Buckingham Palace, which gave Mead goose bumps, particularly the

rhythmic, haunting clatter of the horses' hooves on the pavement—such a majestic yet lonely sound.

"She must be *loaded,*" said Andrew, straining to see over the crowd.

"Old money," said Mead.

"What's that?"

"Something you'll never have."

But Andrew wasn't listening. "Are those guys real soldiers or are they just actors?"

"A little of both."

"That's my idea of the army. I mean, how hard can it be to march around and get photographed all day?"

"Come to think of it, you'd make a hell of a Queen's Life Guard."

Andrew straightened his posture. "You think so?"

"I've never seen you smile, and that's fifty percent of the job right there."

"Very funny."

At the Tower of London Andrew was mesmerized by the Crown Jewels and medieval weaponry and prison cells, thinking how Matt would have gone nuts over some of the stuff. As they stood on Tower Green in front of the spot where Anne Boleyn lost her head he felt the bulge in his pocket. Should I scatter him in the grass? At least he wouldn't be swept up. And not every guy can say his best friend is buried at the Tower of London. Then again it wasn't a particularly cheery place (not that Matt was so cheery himself). And what if he ends up on the rack being tortured? No, better not.

" 'I heard say the executioner was very good, and I have a little neck,' " said Mead, reading from a guidebook.

"Huh?"

"Anne Boleyn's last words—or some of them."

Andrew rubbed his neck while keeping his eye on a big fat raven that seemed to be watching him. "Why'd he kill her?"

"I suppose because she was only his second wife and he had four more to go. Her daughter, by the way, was Elizabeth the First."

"The guy was worse than my dad," said Andrew.

"Oh, I don't think he was quite that bad."

· · ·

After lunch they took a boat tour on the Thames, sitting outside on the upper deck despite the slight drizzle. As Mead looked at the wharves and buildings and passing boats he thought of Evelyn, wondering whether she'd had an offer on the house and bracing himself for her absence. He closed his eyes and remembered how it had felt to hold her—the first time in years he'd held anybody. And then without thinking he'd kissed her.

"Come to Europe with us," he'd said, nearly lifting her up off the ground in his excitement. "You said you always wanted to see more of the world and you know how much Andrew would enjoy having you along."

"I can't," she said, suddenly pulling back from him.

"Sure you can."

Her expression wavered.

"I'll take care of the ticket. You can put your house on the market when you get back. Better yet, take it off the market. You don't really want to live with your daughter, do you? And what about your garden and all the memories you have here? What about . . ." He couldn't think what else to say.

"I can't go with you. Please don't ask me to explain why. I just . . . can't."

He stood looking at her and trying to make sense of things. Had he somehow offended her? Then everything became so clear to him that he wanted to smack his head with his fist: she's not interested in you anymore. Those poems were written *years* ago. He let go of her, feeling embarrassed and confused. "I have to finish packing," he said, heading for the door.

"I'm sorry I can't go with you."

"I had no business asking."

"Actually, I'm thrilled that you asked."

He hesitated. "But why . . ."

"I just can't leave now. There are too many things I need to take care of. Please understand."

"But I—"

"Please."

They stood in her doorway briefly, neither saying anything, then she leaned forward and kissed him quickly. "Have a wonderful trip," she called out as he hurried down the walkway. "And take care of that charming grandson of yours, you hear?"

Mead had gone over the scene endlessly in his head, taking apart all the pieces and carefully reassembling them, yet each time he only felt more foolish than before, then angry at having allowed himself to get so carried away. He pulled his collar up as the drizzle turned to rain. To hell with her. She only would have gotten in the way, telling him what to do and fussing over Andrew.

He looked over at the boy. Charming? No way. But he did seem to be enjoying himself. He didn't sulk once at the Tower of London and even looked downright peppy at the Crown Jewels exhibit. And yet there was so much they needed to talk about. Mead again recalled running into Sophie's room and seeing the boy with the gun in his mouth, which made his insides ache.

"How are you getting along with your mother these days?" he asked, trying to break the ice.

Andrew shrugged. "We don't really talk that much. She's, you know, busy. And she's kind of stressed."

"She's doing her best. You can't blame her for your father leaving."

"It doesn't matter."

"What does matter to you?"

Andrew watched a police boat race past.

"Tell me."

"You really want to know? Nothing matters to me."

Mead searched his grandson's face for some thread he could grab hold of. "Why are you so angry?"

"Who said I'm angry?"

"I did."

Andrew seemed to hesitate. "Everything is just so . . . stupid," he said finally.

"What the hell is that supposed to mean?"

"I can't explain it."

"Is that how your friend felt?"

"Matt?"

"The one who . . ."

"That's Matt." Andrew drained his Coke and fiddled with his earring.

"What was he like?"

A smile came over Andrew's freckled face, which glistened in the mist. "Oh, he was great. Personally, I think he was a genius, only no one knew it. And he was funny, too. He could draw just about anything."

"Did he play any sports?"

Andrew laughed. "Matt? Are you kidding? He *hated* sports."

"Not the athletic type?"

"Not exactly." Andrew laughed again. "He couldn't stand the jocks."

"What's wrong with the jocks?"

Andrew looked at Mead like he'd lost his mind. "*Everything* is wrong with them, at least at my school. They're idiots, only they think they're harsh. The fact is they don't have a clue about what's really going on."

Mead rubbed his chin for a moment as he listened. "What is really going on?"

Andrew shrugged. "You know, *stuff*. See, that was the thing about Matt, he understood exactly what was going on."

"I'm still not sure what it is exactly that's going on."

"You know," Andrew lowered his voice, "bullshit."

"Bullshit?"

"Sure, don't you think so?"

Mead hesitated. "Come to think of it, I guess there is a fair amount of bullshit."

Andrew smiled, as if his grandfather had passed a critical test and their relationship could now proceed to a whole new level. "Only, see, the jocks don't have a clue about all the bullshit that's going on because they're too busy being jocks, which is total bullshit."

"But of course you do?"

"Sure. Don't you ever think about how weird reality is? You know, when you really *think* about it?"

"I guess I'm sort of accustomed to it by now."

Andrew looked disappointed. "Matt figured we're not actually dealing with real reality, which makes a lot of sense. Society is like this PG version of the real thing because people basically can't handle real triple-X reality. It's all about faking it, only, most people don't even remember that they're faking it. And that's what sucks about school."

"Faking what?"

"You know, the stuff we're really thinking about and all the shit that's really going on in the world. Haven't you ever noticed how stupid most conversations are? I don't mean this one, but most of them?"

"You sure you're not taking drugs?"

"I'm *not* on drugs."

Mead shook his head. "You're going to drive yourself crazy with those kinds of thoughts."

"I can't help it."

"Maybe you should consider going to church. Might straighten you out."

"I don't need straightening out."

"You sure need something."

"Tell me the truth. Don't you ever think that life is kind of . . . ridiculous sometimes?"

"Of course I do. That's what laughter is for."

"But people take the stupidest things seriously. It's like what I was saying about the jocks. People are dying by the millions in Africa—have you heard about the AIDS crisis there?—and the forests are all getting chopped down and the ice caps are melting and all anybody at school cares about is what kind of shoes you're wearing and whether we're going to the championships."

Mead smiled. "Well, I suppose you can obsess about shoes and sports or whether the universe will collapse on itself. In the end, it comes down to a matter of temperament."

"Matt could explain it better. He read tons of books about what's really going on."

Mead watched a passing barge. "When I was your age I didn't have the luxury of worrying about such things."

"But you were lucky."

"Lucky?"

"I don't mean about the guys who got killed, I'm just saying that at least you got to deal with stuff that really mattered. Things were totally intense, right?"

Mead paused, not sure how to respond. "I suppose, but—"

"Well, nothing is intense at my school. Trust me."

"You have no idea how fortunate you are, do you?"

Andrew shrugged.

Mead looked out across the river, not knowing where to begin. "Why did he do it?"

Another shrug.

"You must have some idea."

"Sure I do."

"I'd be interested—if you don't mind talking about it."

Andrew looked over at Mead, as if unsure whether he was serious, then rubbed his palms across the tops of his thighs. "Well, there was this girl—I didn't think much of her, but Matt was crazy about her—and she basically told him he was a creep."

"And that's why he killed himself?"

"It wasn't just that. It was everything. See, his dad's a total loser and he got picked on a lot and he was just . . ." Mead watched as Andrew struggled to control his voice. "He was . . . he was real sensitive. He felt *everything*."

"Like you?"

Andrew quickly turned his face away.

"Things are never that bad," said Mead. "They may look that bad, but they're not. And everything passes. Everything."

"You don't understand."

"I'm trying."

"Everybody pushed him too far. They drove him to it."

"What about you?"

Andrew didn't respond.

"Please. I want to understand why you feel so . . . pushed."

"Forget it."

"Not a chance." Mead leaned toward Andrew. "Listen to me, whatever it is that's eating you up inside, it isn't worth throwing your life away for, you got that? Hell, your life will be over soon enough as it is." Mead tried to think of what else to say as the boat passed under Tower Bridge.

"I tried to wake him but I couldn't," Andrew said suddenly, his face contorting. "I really tried."

"I believe you."

"He felt so cold. I never touched anything so cold in my life."

Mead put his arm around Andrew, feeling the boy's narrow shoulders shake. "I'm sorry. I'm truly sorry."

"You don't know what it was like," Andrew whispered.

"Yes, I think maybe I do."

. . .

That Christmas in the Ardenne was the prettiest Mead had ever seen, the fields and trees and houses whitewashed with snow so that even the frozen corpses looked peaceful. It seemed ludicrous to fight a war amid such beauty, which reminded Mead of boyhood, the snowflakes twirling before his face and the tree limbs sagging beneath their crystal white carapace.

"I'm so cold I'm not even horny," said Punchy, pausing to catch his breath as they dug a foxhole in the hardened earth.

"It's not *that* cold."

"Like hell it ain't."

Three hours later they had carved out a space four feet deep, two feet wide and five feet long. After pausing to split a Clark bar and a Lucky Strike they gathered up pine needles and lay them along the bottom. Then they used a hand axe to cut down two nearby trees and section them into logs, which they placed over the top, leaving two small openings. Finally they covered the logs with branches and camouflaged the branches with snow.

"I think my dick's gonna fall off," said Punchy, curling up in a ball on the pine needles and shivering.

"It's your feet I'm worried about." Punchy's toes had begun turning a blackish blue. "Let me massage them."

"You're rather fond of them, aren't you?"

"Hurry up before I change my mind." Punchy extended his left foot and Mead placed the boot between his knees, then struggled with numb fingers to undo the laces.

"Easy," moaned Punchy as Mead pulled off the boot.

"Christ, I've never smelled anything so foul in my life."

"That's my good foot."

"Give me a dry sock." Punchy reached inside his coat and shirt and pulled out the spare pair of socks he kept around his neck. Mead quickly stripped the wet sock off and began massaging the foot, trying to knead some warmth into the cold and unresponsive flesh.

Punchy took the wet sock and placed it inside his shirt to dry, then leaned back and closed his eyes. "I've been doing some thinking," he said. "And I've come up with a lot of questions for Sister Henrietta." Whenever he was miserable, Punchy sought refuge in the Catholic teachings of his childhood, only he could never remember more than bits and pieces, most of which had to do with sitting up straight and cleaning under his fingernails. "For starters, I'd like to know what the hell I ever did to deserve this."

"I could take a wild guess," said Mead, now rubbing the toes gently, afraid the smaller ones might snap off in his hands.

"You should have heard Sister Henrietta. She had all the answers. Fact is, I'm kind of sorry I didn't pay more attention."

"Did she have any advice for frostbite?"

Punchy laughed. "She had advice for *everything.*"

Mead finished with the left foot, then began with the right, pausing briefly to stand up and listen for any movement in the woods in front of their position. As he finished his hands shook so badly that he could barely lace the boot up.

"You're going to make somebody a hell of a wife one day," said Punchy.

"Get some sleep." Mead slid his hands into his armpits trying to warm them.

Punchy was quiet for a few minutes, then said, "You ever worry that you're going to fall asleep and never wake up?"

"We should be so lucky." Mead bent down and tried to gather some of the pine needles around Punchy, making him a nest. "Sweet dreams."

"Nighty-night, darling." Punchy blew Mead a kiss, then groaned a few more times before beginning to snore.

Mead stood and surveyed the snowy woods, trying to memorize the shadows in case they moved. It began snowing again, this time thick wet flakes that stuck to his neck. He strained to hear noises from the other fox-holes to his left and right and the outpost several dozen yards in front but there was only silence. What were the other men thinking of? Food? Girl-friends? God? He tried to wiggle his toes but only the two big ones seemed to move. He thought of the German *SS* prisoners he'd seen the day before, forced to stand barefoot in the snow after being captured wearing American boots. By the time they were sent to the rear they faced certain amputation. News of the massacre of GIs at Malmédy left little compassion. "Please, komerad," one had begged Mead as he passed. And yet he had felt no pity at all.

Ten minutes passed. Then twenty. The wind picked up so that Mead had to blink frequently as blowing snow stung his eyes. He tried to imagine Sophie lying in her bed; how warm and clean and soft and lovely she was. Will I ever touch her again? Such joy seemed incomprehensible. Then he thought of his brother Thomas, wondering what his last minutes were like. Was he dead before the ship went down or did he struggle in the oil-slicked water? Mead had no idea how cold the South Pacific was but figured any ocean had to be pretty damn chilly. He remembered all the warm summer afternoons they spent playing catch in the backyard, the air buggy and moist. Then he thought of the blanket forts they used to make in Thomas's bedroom and how they'd sit in the dark with their flashlights eating candy and telling ghost stories. They shared every secret, at least until Thomas got old enough to start dating, which ruined everything. Thomas was going to be a first baseman for the Red Sox while Mead was going to be an inventor or scientist. Mead smiled to himself, remembering how the future once seemed to stretch out forever like the railroad tracks near their house. Where did you go, big brother? And yet knowing that Thomas was dead somehow made his own death seem less scary, as if his brother would be there waiting for him on the other side. *Whatever you can do I can do. Even that.*

Suddenly Sergeant Fry appeared beside Mead's foxhole. "We're moving out. Orders."

"You're kidding?" They'd only been dug in an hour.

"Some mix-up. We're supposed to be five hundred yards south." Fry disappeared in the darkness.

Mead turned his face up to the snow, wanting to cry but feeling too tired and numb. He crouched down and nudged Punchy. "Wake up." He nudged him again, then finally gave him a gentle kick. "Rise and shine, lover boy."

Punchy moaned. "Ah Christ, three hours already? I was just getting comfortable."

Mead didn't have the heart to correct him. Besides, maybe he'd feel more rested if he didn't know. "We're in the wrong place."

"Huh?"

"Fry says we're supposed to be five hundred yards to the south." Mead began climbing out of the foxhole.

Punchy sat absorbing the implications, then slammed his fist into the side of the foxhole. "Okay, that's *it*. I don't care if they put me up for a court martial. I don't care if they shoot me. I am *not* moving from this goddamn foxhole. Understood?"

"Understood."

"I don't even give a shit if Patton himself orders me. *I am not moving from this foxhole tonight.*"

"Right-o."

"Hell, I don't care if I have to hold off an entire panzer division by myself. I am staying *put*." Punchy curled up again in the pine needles.

"Gotcha."

Two hours later they had scratched out another foxhole five hundred yards to the south, this time only three feet deep and barely big enough for both to crouch in. They set out two land mines in front of their position, then covered the foxhole with branches before crawling in, deciding to wait until daylight to dig deeper and reinforce the roof. Punchy stood watch while Mead slipped almost instantly into a stuporous sleep. As soon as he closed his eyes he found himself crawling on his hands and knees through a warm tunnel.

"Good to see you, little brother," said Thomas, who was sitting cross-legged at the far end of the blanket fort with his face lit by a flashlight. It really was Thomas, and the fort was perfect, with three different chambers and a secret door in the rear. Mead felt so happy his face hurt from smiling. As they sat playing cards and drinking hot chocolate Mead kept looking at his brother's handsome face, wondering how he could know so much about everything and wanting to be exactly like him when he got older. Then it came roaring back at him so that he wanted to scream.

"Don't go, Thomas! If you go you're going to drown in the ocean!"

"What are you talking about, you bonehead?"

"I'm not kidding, Thomas." Mead was crying now. "If you go your ship is gonna sink and you're going to die and I'll never see you again."

"Don't be silly." Thomas flicked off the flashlight, leaving Mead alone in the dark.

"Thomas? Please turn the light on, Thomas. Thomas, *please!*"

Suddenly Mead was jolted awake by an explosion. A mine had detonated in front of their position. He was up instantly, grabbing for his rifle and then firing blindly into the dark alongside Punchy. Shooting erupted from the other foxholes as well and several men tossed grenades. After several minutes the gunfire died down.

"You see anything?" whispered Punchy.

"I can't see a thing." Mead slurred from exhaustion.

Punchy looked side to side. "How do we know our flanks are covered? Hell, I'll bet we're still in the wrong position."

Mead wiped his face and tried to shake his head clear, knowing that sleep was now out of the question. "Tell you what, you scout it out and I'll stay here and keep things warm."

They waited anxiously, but only the wind in the trees broke the silence. Punchy stuffed two pieces of gum into his mouth. "I've never been this cold in my life."

"You said that last night."

"I'm even colder than that." He smacked his gum between his teeth. "How cold do you suppose it is?"

"Let's talk about something else."

"Sure, what do you want to talk about?"

Mead figured that over the months together they'd talked about everything at least once and many subjects dozens of times, so that they could almost mouth each other's responses. He thought for a moment, then asked, "How come you wanted to be a boxer?"

Punchy chewed loudly. "You really want to know?" Mead nodded, expecting Punchy to explain how irresistible he looked in boxing shorts. "Because I had a crooked nose."

"I thought you got that in the ring?"

"That's what you're supposed to think. Truth is, I've always had a crooked nose. Boxing gave me an excuse. You know, boxers are *supposed* to have crooked noses."

"No kidding?" Mead laughed. "But you liked boxing? I mean, you were good?"

Punchy hesitated. "Not really."

"What about all those stories . . . ?"

Punchy made a sheepish expression. "Look, this stuff is just between you and me, okay?"

"Sure thing." Mead wiped the snow from his eyelids. "You know something, you're a lot more complicated than you look."

"Is that a compliment?" Punchy looked doubtful.

"Definitely."

"Thanks." Punchy rubbed his hands together. The snow was now falling so heavily that their helmets had turned white.

"So you were never really much of a boxer?" Mead was still smiling to himself.

"I don't want to talk about it anymore, okay?"

"Fine, your turn."

Punchy worked the gum around his mouth. "Remember that girl at the Red Cross desk in London? The one with the lips?"

"The one you proposed to?" Punchy smiled wistfully. "You still think of her?"

"I think about all of them." He gently knocked the snow off his rifle. "I've got every single one memorized."

"In your case that's no small feat."

"See, it's like I've got these index cards in my head with their photos on them."

"Dare I ask how many cards?"

"I don't know, maybe three hundred. Every night I just start at the top and work my way to the bottom."

"Is that why you make all those funny noises when you sleep?"

Suddenly another mine on their left exploded. Several dozen men immediately opened fire but again there was no return fire and within minutes the shooting stopped.

"You figure they're just probing our lines?" asked Mead, still staring down the barrel of his rifle and feeling dizzy from fatigue.

"Nah, they must be lost," said Punchy. "You couldn't find your own asshole out there."

They struggled to remain alert for the rest of the night, both peering into the snowy darkness and leaning against each other for warmth. The next morning just after sunrise the snow turned to icy rain, exposing the remains of two large deer that had wandered into their position. An hour later they were ordered to pack up and move out.

"All that fresh venison going to waste," grumbled Punchy, who was down to his last Clark bar. "I'm telling you, Mead, we are at the mercy of knuckleheads."

• • •

The next morning Mead supervised exercises in the hotel room before breakfast. "You're up to twenty," he said proudly as Andrew collapsed onto his face. "Keep it up and you might even make varsity next year."

"Are we done yet?"

"One more set of sit-ups."

While Andrew showered—the moment the water came on the boy began singing like a canary—Mead sat at the small corner table and wrote a postcard to Sharon telling her about all the things they'd seen so far and reminding her to buy a new car. When Andrew emerged Mead noticed skin-colored splotches on the boy's face, creating a bizarre two-tone effect. "Are you wearing . . . *makeup?*"

Andrew put his hand over his chin. "It's just cover-up."

"Cover-up?"

"For my acne."

"Oh."

"I got it from Mom."

"She teach you how to put it on?"

"Yeah."

"Figures." Mead got up and grabbed the room key while Andrew hurried back into the bathroom. When he finally came out again his face looked worse than before.

"Where to?"

Mead smiled. "The Imperial War Museum."

As soon as Mead entered the main gallery and saw the German markings on the Jagdpanther tank destroyer he felt an instinctive fear. Silly, he told himself, and yet he couldn't shake it. Andrew walked over and placed his arm through one of the three shell holes that pierced its thick armor. "Check it out," he said. "The Germans inside must have *fried.*"

Mead walked over to look at a Sherman tank while Andrew inspected a German one-man submarine and then a small wooden fishing boat used during the evacuation of Dunkirk. A V-2 rocket towered above them while a Spitfire, a Heinkel and a P-51 Mustang hung from the ceiling. Mead couldn't get over how shiny and new and toy-like everything looked. What would his grandson learn by looking at toys?

After touring the main exhibition gallery they went downstairs and turned left into the First World War exhibit, peering through the glass displays at dozens of weapons and maps and souvenirs. Mead looked at a gas mask and thought of his father, wishing he'd lived long enough to see Germany finally and utterly defeated.

"Hey Grandfather, come see this," said Andrew excitedly when they reached the entrance to a life-size recreation of a trench, complete with wounded men, sound effects and ominous red flashes in the illusionary distance. Mead cautiously followed Andrew in, remembering the foxholes of the Ardenne—always digging—and the constant smell of filth and decay, which clung to him for so many years that he used to keep a box of Altoids in his pocket.

"Was it like this?" asked Andrew, peering over the parapet across the desolation of no-man's land toward the enemy lines.

"We were usually in foxholes," said Mead. "They're much smaller." He looked at the two life-size British soldiers going over the top as voices played over hidden loudspeakers. "But you get the general idea."

"Man, I'd hate it," said Andrew.

"Yes, I bet you would."

Emerging from the trench they passed through an exhibit of Hitler's rise to power, pausing to look at large photos of jeering faces and then endless columns of soldiers and finally a wild-eyed Fuhrer lathering the people into a frenzy like a master of the hounds just before the hunt. Mead remembered sitting around the radio after dinner with his parents and thinking how comical the German language sounded.

"Why must he always shout?" his mother would ask.

"Maybe the Germans are hard of hearing," said Thomas, who'd always been much funnier and smarter than Mead.

"Well, I think it's rude."

"That fella wants war," his father would say, puffing sadly on his pipe.

"We beat them once, we can beat them again," young Mead had boasted, trying to sound tough.

His father looked over at him, taking a long drag from his pipe. "But that's where you're wrong, son." He emptied the pipe into an ashtray and began scraping the bowl with a small silver tool he kept in the pocket of his gray sweater. "You see, we never did beat them." At the time, Mead had no idea what his father meant.

As they continued through the exhibit Mead stopped to stare at a death mask of Himmler, studying the dead man's placid features. Then he paused before a white summer tunic that once belonged to Goering, feeling a sense of repulsion as he thought of the fabric clinging to the sweaty flesh of the Devil's big fat piglet. Had it been dry cleaned? Did it still smell of him? And there was Goebbels, the faithful lap dog. You little shit. Would you have traded it all for a smooth complexion and a few more inches of height? (And how was it to poison your six little children in the end?) He looked at the adoring faces of Germans lining the street as Hitler's motorcade passed. "We never did trust the Nazis," they'd insist when the war was lost and white sheets hung from every house as the American convoys streamed in. "We just want peace." And the damndest thing was, it got harder and harder to hate the German people as they busily cleaned up the rubble and hid colored eggs for the children on Easter and crowded the churches, as though an evil spell had been broken.

He looked again at his grandson, wondering if any of it meant anything to him or whether it was like looking at swords and armor in a medieval exhibit, where the striking thing is the craftsmanship.

"We've got to try this," said Andrew, getting in line for something called The Blitz Experience. After waiting ten minutes with a group of schoolchildren and two old ladies they entered a re-creation of an air-raid shelter. Soon the lights darkened and sirens wailed over the recorded chatter of voices, as if others were with them huddled beneath the city as bombs rained down above. "Just the way I remember it," said one of the ladies. "Gives me chills, it does." After the simulated attack they left the bomb shelter and walked through a life-size diorama of a city street in ruins, bricks piled everywhere and voices calling for help. "Would you look at that," said the other lady, pointing to a smashed storefront. "Dried eggs for sale!"

"That was kind of hokey," said Andrew as they emerged. Mead didn't respond as they headed toward a display for Operation Overlord. "Here's the D-Day stuff," Andrew said excitedly, as if expecting his grandfather to jump for joy.

"So it is." Mead approached slowly.

"I can't believe you were really there. That must have been *wild*."

"Sometimes I can't believe I was there either." They both stood side by side before a large map of the landing beaches.

"What's it like looking at this stuff?"

Mead turned toward a life-size mannequin of a German soldier reaching for his pistol. "A bit difficult, to tell the truth."

"I figured."

They studied the displays in silence for several minutes until Andrew suddenly asked, "Is this where you killed that German?"

"I . . . what makes you think that I killed him?"

"I figured you must have. That's why you have all his stuff. Of course, he could have been dead when you found him. I never really thought of that."

"It happened in Germany," Mead said abruptly, moving quickly to the next exhibit.

Andrew followed closely behind. "*What* happened?"

Mead stopped and turned. "Yes, I killed him. That's what happened."

"Oh."

Mead headed for the exit, pausing before a large chart tallying the death toll of the war.

"Was he coming at you? Was it like a big battle?"

Mead hesitated. "It doesn't matter anymore."

As they headed back to the hotel Mead felt he had made a terrible mistake by coming.

• • •

Andrew tried masturbating in the shower but it was way too weird knowing his grandfather was right outside the door. And fuck me, he never left the room for a minute. I'm gonna go insane, he thought, grabbing a towel. Can you die from horniness?

They were leaving for France early the next morning and he could hear his grandfather packing. He'd been quiet ever since the war museum and Andrew wondered whether he was having some sort of flashback. He'd seen a show once about Vietnam vets who went ape-shit at any loud noise, gunning down entire families. Jesus, what if Sarge wakes up in the middle of the night and thinks I'm a Sauerkraut?

After the lights were out he waited until his grandfather's breathing deepened, then reached down to his crotch and began quietly stroking himself. *C r e a k*. He tried a lighter touch, hoping to find a rhythm that would do the job without alerting the bed springs. But no matter how subtle his movements the bed acted as a highly sensitive motion detector. *Fuck*. Finally he interlaced his hands behind his head and tried to will himself into an orgasm, but that only made him want to jerk off more.

He listened to his grandfather's long, deep breaths, wondering what he was dreaming. Was he fighting Sauerkrauts? Watching a buddy get shot? Taking Grandma on their first date? Then he thought of Evelyn and how much fun she was and how unfair it was that she had to die. Was it cancer? What kind of cancer and how painful was it? He remembered the look on her face when she grabbed onto him, like someone had just punched her. *Hang on, Evelyn. You gotta hang on.* After a few minutes he rolled to his stomach, closed his eyes and tried to count all the different royal jewels and swords he'd seen. When that got boring he tried to create a perfect three-dimensional mental image of Cori Fletcher in the nude, but that left him so agitated that he had to think about staying back a year again. Then he thought of Matt and the bag of his ashes that was stashed beneath the bed in one of the zipper compartments of his luggage. *What am I going to do with you, buddy?*

Stealing Matt's remains had been surprisingly easy. Andrew had a key to Matt's place, which no one knew about, and when he found out that Matt's parents were taking the ashes to Indiana that Saturday to be buried, he figured the ashes must be somewhere in their apartment. (He hadn't been invited to the funeral. Instead, he locked himself in his room and cranked all Matt's favorite songs.)

At lunchtime on Friday he rode his bike over, circling the block to make sure their cars were gone. Then he hurried up to number 3C, put on his mother's lime green Living Hands dishwashing gloves and opened the door, locking it quickly behind him.

Jesus, this is creepy. He stood by the door listening, half expecting to hear Matt's boom box blasting from his room. He fought the desire to turn and flee. *Can't let 'em bury Matt in Indiana.* Besides, Matt's ghost wouldn't hurt him . . . would it?

"Hello?"

Silence. He flicked on a light, then walked quickly down the hall to Matt's door, which was closed. *Why closed? Was it to keep things in or out?* He reached for the knob, then hesitated, placing his ear to the door. *Do spirits hang out in their old bedrooms?* He knocked lightly. "Matt?" He turned the knob and opened the door a crack, wanting suddenly to run from the apartment. "Matt?" He opened the door further. "Don't try to freak me out, okay Matt?"

He stepped inside, surprised by how much the room still smelled like Matt. Only, it was cleaner than he'd ever seen it, the bed made perfectly and not a sock on the floor. He glanced over at the closet, which was closed. "It's me, Andrew. Please don't try to scare me, okay?"

The small white urn sat on the dresser next to Matt's bed. He carefully picked it up, then gave it a gentle shake. He thought it might be sealed but it opened easily. He took the top off and peered inside. "Jesus, what have they done to you?" He took off the Living Hands gloves, reached in and carefully picked up one of the larger chips, holding it up to his face as warm tears ran down his cheeks. *We've got to get out of the Midwest, Andrew. I'm telling you, it's all happening on the coasts.*

"Don't worry, buddy, I won't let them take you to Indiana. No fucking way."

He spent several minutes crying and looking at the ashes, thinking how they weren't really like ashes at all. Then he went into the kitchen and rummaged through the drawers before finding a box of large Ziplocs. Perfect. After transferring the ashes to one bag he sealed it and placed it inside another. Safe and sound. Then he searched through more cupboards before settling on a box of C&H granulated pure cane sugar. Different consistency, but at least it would provide some weight. After filling the urn to the brim he placed it back on the dresser, smiling to himself as he thought of Matt's asshole dad dipping his finger in and tasting it and deciding that maybe his son was a sweet kid after all.

When he finished he went back in the kitchen and liberated a bag of Oreo's, eating half on the spot and stuffing the rest in his pockets. Then he returned to Matt's bedroom and sat on the bed with the Ziploc on his lap, feeling full and depressed. He looked at the posters of Jimi Hendrix and Kurt Cobain and Bob Marley and Sid Vicious, wondering if Matt was partying with them somewhere, which made him feel lonely and left behind. He got up and looked through Matt's desk drawers until he found his drawing tablet, which was filled with sketches of houses. Picking out his favorite he tore off the page, carefully folded it and placed it in his pocket. Then he put on the gloves, grabbed the Ziploc and turned off the light, closing the door quietly behind him.

The call came from Indiana the next day. Andrew knew immediately as he watched his mom on the phone, her jaw dropping slowly to the floor as she violently stamped out a cigarette. Busted. He quickly put on the solemn face he'd been practicing in the mirror and braced himself.

"All right young man, what the hell did you do with . . ." she stood in front of him flailing her hands, "you know . . . *him?*"

"Him?"

"Matt."

"*Matt?* What are you talking about?"

She came closer and stared into his face. Uh oh, mind reading. *All hands below deck. Gamma ray shields, full power. She can't take much more, Scotty.*

"You know *exactly* what I'm talking about."

She searched his room twice, even removing the cover on the heating duct. But Matt was safely hidden in a plastic container in the forest preserve. "Maybe the mortuary screwed up," Andrew suggested after the second search. "You read those kind of stories all the time."

"It was *sugar.*"

"No kidding? You know he always did have a serious sweet tooth."

Matt's parents briefly threatened legal action and the dad even came close to clocking Andrew during one particularly ugly visit. But the whole incident was so awkward that everybody seemed more concerned with avoiding publicity than finding out what happened to Matt.

After Andrew's mom finally gave up her search Andrew dug up the Ziploc baggie from the forest preserve and began carrying it to school each day in his backpack, feeling like he needed all the companionship he could get. And then one afternoon while he was sitting in English class looking at Megan Wynn and wondering what Matt ever saw in her, it came to him. The next morning he arrived in class early and hurried over to the front row left section where Megan always sat in one of two chairs. But which one? He hesitated before selecting the chair on the right. Reaching into his pocket for the small baggie containing a portion of Matt's ashes—which he'd divvied up for this mission—he took a pinch and sprinkled it on the seat, careful to monitor the classroom door. After making sure the ashes weren't too visible he quickly took his spot in the back of the room and waited. *You're gonna love this, Matt.*

Just before the bell rang Megan walked in. She gave the class her customary smile, running one hand through her hair to make sure everyone noticed just how unbelievably perfect it was, then headed for the front left section, hips swiveling. Both seats were still empty. Andrew gritted his teeth as he tried to will her into the chair on the right. *Please please please.* She paused before the chair containing Matt's ashes, then slid into the adjacent seat. *Damn!* The bell rang. At least Matt would be safe. But just as the teacher began the lecture the door opened again and Bill Humphrey lumbered in. *Oh, no.* But Humphrey wouldn't dare sit next to Megan Wynn. It was unthinkable. Humphrey stood scanning the room, a helpless expression flooding his sweaty, red face. *What's he waiting for?* Then

Andrew understood. Humphrey couldn't get to the other two available desks, not without plowing down narrow aisles clogged with legs and book bags. Slowly and sheepishly, he headed for the seat next to Megan, who recoiled in horror. Andrew closed his eyes as Humphrey lowered himself onto Matt's remains.

Courage, Matt.

Andrew made three more attempts, but each time Megan selected the other chair, leaving Matt to suffer a variety of unspeakable fates. Finally on the fourth try Matt got his girl. *We have touchdown.* Andrew could hardly contain himself as he watched Megan settle in right on top of Matt's remains, rubbing her butt left and right as she got comfortable. *Go Matt, go!*

"Is something wrong, Andrew?" asked the teacher as Andrew squirmed in his seat.

"Everything's just great," he said. "Really, really great."

Normandy

They arrived in Caen at dusk after taking the ferry from Portsmouth. Andrew was bored and queasy during the six-hour crossing and spent most of the time listening to his headphones and asking how much longer. Mead sat quietly, walking out on the deck now and then to look out over the rough ocean and then at the Normandy coast coming into view. After disembarking they rented a car—the smallest Andrew had ever seen—and headed for their hotel, stopping to ask three different people for directions, including a cute young French girl who looked at Andrew like he was the biggest tourist nerd in the world.

"I could really go for a bean burrito," said Andrew after they checked in to their narrow room, which was on the third floor overlooking a side street. "Do you suppose they have a Taco Bell around here?"

"Over my dead body," said Mead.

They ended up at a bright and nearly empty café where Mead struggled to translate the menu with a guidebook while the short balding waiter looked on with disdain.

"Sheep brains?" said Andrew.

"I thought that might get a rise out of you." Mead continued down the list. "Perhaps you'd prefer the chicken gizzards?"

"I'm gonna throw up."

"Now, what's the word for frog?"

Andrew looked ill as he sank into his seat. "Is there anything the French *won't* eat?"

"Not if it moves."

Andrew finally settled on a triple order of fries while Mead had a steak.

After they finished Mead pulled out a map, laid it across the table and tried to explain the military situation in Europe just prior to the landings.

"Did guys really piss in their pants from fear?"

"You're not listening."

"I was just wondering. You read about it but I thought maybe it was one of those things like people's hair turning white from fright."

Mead frowned. "As a matter of fact, yes, they did."

"Did—"

"Once."

"Wow. I can't imagine being that scared. Did you ever see anybody's hair—"

"Back to the map." Mead pushed it toward Andrew. "These are the main invasion beaches. The British and Canadian sectors were over here while the Americans landed here and here. The 101st and 82nd Airborne jump zones were in these areas and I landed somewhere around here," he jabbed the map with his finger, "though I couldn't tell you precisely where."

"Why not?"

"It was dark, for one."

Andrew studied the map. "And where were the Germans?"

Mead smiled. "Everywhere."

"No wonder you guys were pissing in your pants."

"So were the Germans. Anyway, I figure we'll start here and drive past Sword, Juno and Gold beaches tomorrow on our way to Omaha Beach. We may even make it to Pointe de Hoc. Then the next day I thought we might drive through Carentan and Ste.-Mère-Église, then tour the jump zones before stopping at Utah Beach."

"Sounds cool."

"I don't suppose you have another way of indicating your enthusiasm?"

"Interesting. It sounds interesting."

Mead sat back in his chair. "How far have you gotten in *The Longest Day?*"

"I've been so tired at night . . ."

"I'd like you to read at least an hour before bed. You'll get a lot more out of this trip if you know a bit about what happened."

Andrew sighed as Mead signaled for the check.

• • •

Mead hardly said a word when they got to the room. Instead he sat in a corner chair and stared out the window before changing into his light blue pajamas and getting into bed.

"Are you mad at me?" asked Andrew.

"What gave you that idea?"

"You just seem kind of upset."

"No, I'm not mad at you." Mead rolled to his side. "Good night."

"Good night."

Andrew stayed awake for another half hour reading and listening to his headphones—it made the battle scenes much more dramatic—then turned off his light, crawled low in the sheets and attempted to masturbate. Creak. Oh God, I can't take it anymore. He put his finger on his pulse, wondering if he was having a nervous breakdown. He'd never last until he got home. It was like walking around with a loaded gun with a hair trigger, safety off; only it was more like a huge naval cannon on one of those destroyers, the kind that can lob a VW Beetle twenty miles. The slightest provocation and *Kaboom!*, he'd swamp all of Normandy with a tidal wave of lust. He forced himself to think of the five most embarrassing moments of his life. The list soon swelled to over twenty as the fever in his groin broke, replaced by a hotness in his cheeks. When he finally fell asleep he dreamed that he and Matt were seagulls flying high above a beautiful white beach, looping through the air and swooping down to shit on the jocks and peer into the bikinis of the girls.

· · ·

Mead lay listening to the creaks in the bed next to him, wondering if his grandson was just restless or upset. Eventually the noises subsided and he heard the telltale rhythmic breaths, which had a childlike tone. And he was still a child; a confused and angry boy. Then he thought of Evelyn, allowing his imagination to briefly roam along the contours of her smile and cheeks and neck before retreating in bitter sadness. What was he thinking, that he could simply start all over again? That Sophie could be replaced? At least Evelyn had had more sense. In a way it was better that she was moving. God knows he needed the chance to clear his head and get back on his feet. It wouldn't be easy at first, not when he'd be reminded of her every time he stepped out his front door, but he'd survive. He always had.

That's what you are, old man: a survivor. He thought of Jimbo and

Rokowski and Punchy, wondering why he'd been allowed to live. Was it just dumb luck? Or was he spared for some purpose he never discovered? Even after so many years he still felt singed by guilt, thinking that any one of them would have made more of their lives. Was it really so long ago? He tried to recall how different his body felt back then, hard and agile, like driving a sports car. What would the boys think if they could see him now? He smiled to himself as he lay in the dark, eyes open and staring at the ceiling. *That you, Mead? Jesus, you look like shit.* He tried to imagine how they would have aged but he couldn't. That was the one thing they had on him: eternal youth, dying at the top of their game. And here he was more than half a century older than they'd ever be, old enough even to be their grandfather. How absurd.

. . .

"We'll begin at Sword Beach and then drive along the coast to Omaha," said Mead as they pulled out of the hotel parking lot the next morning after a quick breakfast, which he left untouched. All morning he'd felt nervous, fearful of what might come howling back at him. Andrew seemed excited, like a kid going to the circus. "If you open the map I'll show you our route."

But Andrew was too busy staring out the window. "Hey, check out the cemetery," he said, pointing to a sign. Mead decided to stop. Best to plunge right in.

After parking they entered the small and neatly tended cemetery and walked slowly among the British, Canadian and German graves. Okay, I can handle this. And yet he couldn't shake the feeling that he was being stalked, that at any moment something—he dared not imagine what— might pounce on him.

"Don't you think it's cool the way the British graves have sayings on them from the families?" said Andrew.

Mead nodded as he stood before the grave of E. G. Winter, killed July 8, 1944, age 21:

OF THE WORLD
HE WAS JUST A PART,
TO HIS MOTHER
HE WAS ALL THE WORLD.

And nearby, J. H. Norman, killed July 22, 1944, age 24:

CAN WE E'ER FORGET
THAT FOOTSTEP
AND THAT SWEET FAMILIAR FACE.

And R. B. Vinall, killed July 22, 1944, age 17:

MANY A SILENT HEARTACHE
OFTEN A SILENT TEAR.
GONE BUT NOT FORGOTTEN
MUM AND DAD

"I wonder if any of these guys killed each other?" said Andrew as he headed over to the German section.

"They seem to be getting along pretty well now," said Mead, who had to stop reading the British headstones in order to maintain his composure. He thought of the simple marker for his brother Thomas that his parents had placed in the small graveyard six blocks from their home. He spent hours sitting on the grass looking at his brother's name and wishing he hadn't been lost at sea, which made him seem even farther away. He made his way to the German graves, which bore only names and dates. Nineteen-twenty-five, what a year to be born. He watched as Andrew hurried from headstone to headstone reading each one, then he stood back and looked up at the trees, which were dense with new leaves. Maybe time alone really is enough, though he had his doubts.

They stopped next at Pegasus Bridge on the Orne Canal. Mead explained how it was captured by British paratroopers but Andrew was more interested in a Cromwell tank on display.

"Did you fight around here?"

"I told you, we're in the British and Canadian sector," Mead said impatiently, already sensing that his grandson wouldn't really understand at all; that he might as well have taken him to Yorktown or the Alamo. Mead decided to skip the small museum and continue on to the coast.

"So these are like, *the beaches?*" Andrew asked as the ocean came in sight.

Mead nodded, surprised by how ordinary everything looked, well-kept but modest houses and apartments strung along the peaceful shoreline. "This is Sword Beach. Next is Juno, then Gold, and beyond that Omaha and Utah, which were the American sectors."

"Where's that Point Huck place?"

"Pointe *du Hoc*. It's near Omaha."

Andrew looked at Mead closely. "Does it creep you out being here?"

Mead thought for a moment, knowing there was no way to describe the sensation. "Let's just say that seeing you here is a little weird," he said, wishing he'd insisted that Andrew wash the yellow dye out of his hair.

They parked near the harbor at Juno Beach and walked down to the shoreline before inspecting a restored Sherman tank that had been salvaged from the sea, then Andrew ran over to a nearby German anti-tank gun, fingering the shrapnel holes in the armor plating. "They must have nailed these dudes," he said.

Mead spent several minutes looking over the gun before hurrying into a nearby gift shop to use the restroom. After buying several postcards they drove further down the coast, stopping to look at the battered remains of German bunkers and a large cross marking the spot where Churchill, Montgomery and de Gaulle came ashore. At the coastal town of Arromanches they examined the remains of the Mulberry harbor before visiting the Musée du Débarquement, where they studied dioramas and working models of the landings.

So far so good, thought Mead as he stared at the black-and-white faces of anxious young soldiers. His stomach felt unsteady and at times he had a slight burning sensation in the back of his throat, yet it was manageable. He had control. He even felt a certain pride in how well he was holding up. He glanced over at Andrew, who was looking closely at a photo of bodies strewn across the sand. The important thing was to make an impression on him; to teach the boy something.

"This may interest you," Mead said as they pulled up at the German battery at Longues-sur-Mer, where four enormous 155-mm cannons sat back from the bluff, each housed in a thick concrete casemate heavily scarred by shelling.

"Awesome." Andrew hopped out of the car and headed for the nearest casemate. "Look, you can tell exactly where the bombs landed." He ran his hands along the battered concrete and the exposed steel reinforcing bars, which were gnarled like bramble bush.

Mead stared at the rusting cannon, surprised by how old it looked, like some relic from the Spanish Armada. He glanced down at his hands. You too, he thought.

"These guns were still working on D-Day despite massive bombardment by our forces," he explained. "It took a few direct hits from the big naval guns to finally silence them."

Andrew stood behind one of the guns, his face taut with concentration. "You've got to admit the Germans were pretty brave."

"I admitted that a long time ago." Mead pulled out a disposable camera from his pocket and took several pictures of Andrew, then asked an elderly British tourist to take their picture together beside the long barrel of one of the guns.

"Mom will never believe it," said Andrew, leaning against Mead and smiling at the camera.

"That's why I'm collecting proof."

After exploring all four guns they walked along a trail to the heavily fortified observation bunker that sat on the edge of the bluff a thousand feet away. Andrew slid down a muddy path and climbed a metal railing to the top, then crawled inside. Mead was out of breath by the time he caught up.

"You gotta check this out," said Andrew, looking through a concrete slit toward the ocean.

"The men stationed here were the eyes for the guns," Mead said, wondering what the German troops would have made of his grandson, yellow hair and all. "They relayed targeting information using communication wires buried underground."

"They must have been kissing their asses good-bye big time when they saw all those ships approaching."

Mead imagined the young men awakening to their certain destruction and felt an unexpected sense of pity. Rotten luck to be born German in the first half of the twentieth century. And it all came down to chance, a roll of the biological dice that made one child a German and the other American; one an Aryan and the next a Jew. Would I have faced the firing squad rather than fight in Hitler's armies? He'd asked himself that question over and over and the answer was always the same: I wouldn't have had the courage not to fight. Not even close. And that's the horror, isn't it; that all over the world people still kill and die for causes they inherit by mere happenstance, accidents of birth that make one a Serb or Croat, Hindu or Muslim, Arab or Jew, Hutu or Tutsi. Why must it be so? *Why?*

As he and Andrew stood staring silently out at the ocean far below Mead resisted a momentary impulse to put his arm around the boy. Instead he took Andrew's picture before they headed back to the car and continued on to Omaha Beach.

• • •

This would be the most difficult part, thought Mead, sitting in the car in the parking lot of the American Military Cemetery after turning off the ignition. How many names would he recognize? Would Jimbo and Rokowski be there? He had no idea if their remains were interred in France or repatriated home. He looked over at Andrew, who seemed uncertain of what to do.

"I want you to take your earring off."

"What?"

"It's not respectful."

"*Respectful?* It's just an earring."

"Just do what I say." Mead was surprised by the force of his own voice.

Andrew hesitated, as if debating his options. Slowly he reached up to his left earlobe and removed the earring, placing it on the dashboard. "Satisfied?"

"No, but it's a start. Now let's go."

As they entered the main gate they paused to take in the long rows of white marble crosses and stars of David. "This place is huge," whispered Andrew. "Did all these guys die on the beach?"

Mead didn't respond.

"Are you okay?"

Mead cleared his throat. "Fine. Why don't we start at the beach first?" Mead hurried across the cemetery toward the bluff.

"Sure thing."

They stopped at the top of the stairs that led down to the beach and examined an orientation table that depicted the landing operations. "Look, you can still see things sunken in the water," said Andrew, pointing to several long shadows offshore. "You suppose there are still bodies trapped inside?"

"Nothing you'd recognize."

Mead was surprised by how clean and desolate the beach looked, thankful that it wasn't developed. He looked over at Andrew, wondering what the boy was thinking. Did he feel anything? Did he have any understanding at all? Fifteen minutes later they reached the water's edge. Mead bent down and picked up a smooth wet stone, placing it in his pocket.

"I wish I had a metal detector," said Andrew, digging into the sand with his foot. "I bet you could find all sorts of cool stuff."

Mead thought of Punchy, his pockets so weighed down with souvenirs that he couldn't carry any more without getting rid of something first. "This is torture," he'd complain, sorting through his collection.

"What you need is a wheelbarrow," said Mead, whose own collection of German pistols, medals, watches and military belt buckles had begun to weigh him down (only to be stolen from him several weeks later).

Mead turned and looked back toward the bluff, pointing out some of the German bunkers and pillboxes. "They could cover every inch of this beach. A lot of guys never even made it to shore." He could see his grandson working to bring the violence to life. "They weren't much older than you."

Andrew squatted down and dug in the sand with his fingers. "Did you ever feel like you were going to die?"

"Lots of times."

"What's that like?"

Mead paused. "I couldn't say."

"Did your life really pass before your eyes?"

Mead smiled. "Just the highlights." He started down the beach.

"It feels kind of lonely here, don't you think?" said Andrew, following close behind.

"It ought to."

"I mean like, haunted."

"I hadn't thought of it."

"Do you believe that places can be haunted; that people—spirits—can come back?"

Mead thought of Sophie and how he often felt her presence in the space just behind his right ear. "It seems rather unlikely."

"I know it doesn't make sense scientifically, but when people have a lot of like, life force, I don't get how it could all just . . . vanish."

"It takes a little getting used to."

They walked on for another ten minutes, then turned and headed back toward the winding path that led up the bluff to the cemetery.

"I feel like my life is boring compared to yours," said Andrew, coming alongside Mead.

"We weren't exactly having a rip-roaring time."

"I know, but still you experienced amazing things. I can't think of anything I've done that's even a little bit amazing."

"You have a whole lifetime to do amazing things."

Andrew made a grunting noise. "I've been thinking about quitting school."

Mead stopped. *"What?"*

Andrew looked at him nervously. "I could get a real job. Make some money."

Mead could feel his face redden with anger. "How could you stand on *this beach* and talk about quitting school?"

"It doesn't have anything to do with this beach."

Mead jabbed a finger toward Andrew. "And you're going to college too, you got that?" A group of passing tourists stared.

"College?"

"You're damn right." Mead started up the path again.

"But I hate school. It's a total waste of time."

"I'm not going to talk about it right now."

"You don't know what it's like."

"I said, I'm not going to talk about it."

When they reached the top of the bluff Mead sat down to catch his breath. How dare he say such a thing. Andrew stood squirming in his baggie pants and black T-shirt, which had some sort of dragon's head on it.

"I'm going to walk around a bit," said Mead. *"Alone.* I'll meet you at the car in half an hour."

"I'm sorry."

"And no funny stuff, got that?"

"Okay."

Mead headed for the large semicircular colonnade inscribed with battle maps, trying to calm himself. He noted the other veterans in the crowd, silently attempting to guess their service and rank and hoping none would approach him. He couldn't believe how old they all looked, even a bit comical in their baseball caps and blue vests covered with pins and patches. After walking through the Garden of the Missing he wandered among the rows of headstones, half fearing he'd recognize a name. Finally he went to the Visitor's Building where a staff member showed him how to search the registers.

Roy Rokowski.

He clenched his fists as he approached the grave, trying to keep the sadness from reaching his face. Left here then eight down. He counted off the crosses as he passed. And there he was: *June 6, 1944.*

Mead crouched down beside the headstone, resting one hand on the smooth white marble. *Hey, Roy, it's me, Mead.*

Well, it's about time. What took you so long?

It's hard to explain. Somehow the years kind of slipped by and, well, the truth is I'm not so good at these kinds of things.

Hell, you've got the easy part.

Mead smiled to himself. *I sure miss you.*

Seems like yesterday, doesn't it? And all the time I was thinking I was going to land in the water and drown.

Mead tightened his jaw. *I tried to get him off of you. I should have shot him but I couldn't think straight and I was worried about hitting you and there was no time.*

Don't worry about it.

I'm so sorry, Roy.

We sure as hell showed them, didn't we?

You're damn right we did. We showed the whole world, Roy. Mead gripped the headstone with both hands.

Ever get up to that little spot I told you about in Michigan? Best fishing you'll ever find.

Not yet. But come to think of it, I just may one of these days.

The fishing's never been better.

You mean you've been . . . fishing?

What else?

I don't know, I just thought . . . Mead looked up and saw Andrew watching from a distance.

Is that your boy?

My grandson.

No kidding? I thought you looked a little gray around the temples.

Oh hell, even my insides are gray.

How come his pants are falling off?

Don't get me started, Roy.

"Did you know him?" Andrew asked softly as he approached. Mead nodded. "Was he like, a friend?"

"As a matter of fact he was."

Andrew stared down at the grave. "How did he die?"

"Grenade."

Mead could see Andrew waiting for further details. "Did you see it?" Mead nodded again. "Wow." Andrew reached out and touched the headstone.

You take care of yourself, Mead.

I'm trying, Roy. I'm really trying.

Mead stood up, hearing his knees crack. "A lot of these guys would have had grandchildren your age by now." Andrew looked around as if doing the math. "What I'm trying to say is that I was lucky, which means that you're lucky. Very lucky."

Andrew nodded, but Mead could see that he didn't really feel it. How foolish I was to think that bringing him here would change anything. "I'd like to be alone for a few minutes," he said.

"Sure," said Andrew, backing off. "I'll meet you at the car."

• • •

It was another hedgerow, identical to the one they'd just taken. Germans dug in across the meadow; a machine gun in one or both corners. No Shermans available to spray down the bushes. And yet when the order came to attack Mead felt his legs go. He tried to shake them but they wouldn't respond.

"Ready, men?"

Helmets nodded. Mead reached down and slapped his thighs but felt nothing. He slapped them again, harder.

"Now."

Mead watched helplessly as Punchy and five others scrambled out of the bushes and charged, tossing grenades as they ran. He struggled twice to lift himself, then tried to claw forward with his hands but his lifeless legs held him back. *Coward.* Punchy turned and waved him forward, then ran back and tried to pull him to his feet. "Come on, you son of a bitch!"

"I can't!"

"Like hell you can't!"

Finally Punchy let go and ran off without him. Mead screamed for his legs to move but still they refused. The others were now halfway across the meadow when the Germans opened up. Mead watched them go down one by one, feeling his mouth move but not making a sound. Punchy was the last to fall, almost reaching the German position and tossing a grenade just before he fell forward on his face, his helmet bouncing off. And then it was quiet.

Mead lay immobile for several minutes. Why weren't the Germans coming for me? Were they dead? Had they retreated? *Please come for me.* He looked at the crumpled figures sprawled across the meadow, then made a fist and began pounding it against his thigh as hard as he could, tears streaming down his face.

"Mead!"

He looked up and saw Punchy struggling to his feet. Quickly grabbing his rifle Mead fired several rounds into the far bushes as Punchy staggered back across the meadow and collapsed on the ground next to him, blood streaming from his forehead. Mead pulled out his first-aid kit and leaned over him. "Looks like just a scratch," he said as he cleaned the wound. "Jesus, I thought you were dead."

"Yeah, me too," said Punchy, still breathing hard. He never said a word about what had happened.

. . .

Andrew was standing by the car waiting as Mead approached. Neither spoke as they got in and buckled their seat belts.

"I brought you here for a reason," said Mead, one hand on the ignition.

"I know," said Andrew quietly.

"But I think I was mistaken."

"Sorry."

"Stop saying you're sorry."

"Okay."

Mead sighed. "I thought maybe this would make a difference to you; that you'd understand how lucky you are not to have to go through what all those boys went through."

"I really appreciate what you and your friends did."

"But it really means nothing to you, does it?"

"Look, I'm sorry for all the guys who died but it doesn't change my life."

"Please tell me what's so goddamn bad about your life? I seem to be missing something."

Andrew sank lower in his seat. "Everything."

"You're an ungrateful little son of a bitch, you know that?" Mead was quaking now.

"You don't have to get so mad."

"Well I am. Don't you think any one of those boys under those head-stones would have given his right arm to switch places with you?"

"I'll switch places. I don't care."

"Goddamn you!" Mead leaned over and slapped Andrew across the face.

"You expect everybody to be like you, don't you?" shouted Andrew. "Well I don't want to be like you!"

"Shut up!"

"Why would anybody want to be like you? You don't have any friends, you don't do anything all day, you don't even have the guts to ask Evelyn out. All you've got are your stupid medals and your stupid secret memories about stuff that happened *decades* ago."

Mead sat frozen in his seat while Andrew continued. "You're just as scared as I am, you know that? Ever since Grandma died you've been scared of even leaving your house. Well, I don't want to turn out like you. I'd rather *die*." He reached for the earring which sat on the dashboard and put it on. "And I'm never taking my earring off again no matter what you say. Ever." He wiped the tears from his cheeks with his sleeve and turned his face toward the window.

Neither moved for several minutes. In the sharp silence Mead felt something give way inside like scaffolding collapsing to the ground. "I'll take you home," he whispered as he started the car. A fine rain blurred the windshield as he drove, hands sticky on the wheel. In the rearview mirror he saw a growing caravan of cars pressing him on.

"I don't want to go home yet," said Andrew softly. "I mean, since we're here we might as well see the rest of it, don't you think?"

Mead drove on another mile, uncertain what to do, then pulled into a driveway, turned around and headed for Ponte du Hoc.

• • •

Andrew was in bed pretending to read while his grandfather sat in the corner writing a postcard. Andrew watched him out of one eye, wondering if it was the dull light from the dinky lampshades that made him look so old. Exactly how old was he anyway? Would he get sick and die in a few years? He tried to imagine his grandfather lying in a coffin or being slid into the furnace at a crematorium. Then he thought of Evelyn, wondering if she was all right and whether she'd sold the house yet. How soon would she die and should he tell his grandfather? He'd been sworn to secrecy, and yet . . .

"I'm sorry about the things I said."

His grandfather didn't look up. "You were right."

Andrew's face widened. "No I wasn't. Well, maybe about Evelyn."

His grandfather put down his pen and pushed aside the faded yellow curtain to look out on the street below. Rain streamed down the window panes. "After your grandma died I figured that was it for me. I didn't want to go on another single hour." He let out a long breath. "We'd spent fifty-one years together."

"I was just angry."

"But somehow I got through that first day, and then the next, and that's what I've been doing ever since." He let go of the curtain. "You see, I thought that was enough. It never occurred to me to try to . . . enjoy them."

"I'm sorry, Grandpa."

"No need to be." His grandfather picked up his pen and held it over the postcard.

"Are you writing Mom?"

His grandfather nodded.

"I bet Evelyn would love a postcard."

His grandfather looked up, raising an eyebrow.

"Grandma's been dead for three years," Andrew said gently.

"What's that got to do with anything?"

"What I'm saying is that she wouldn't be mad at you."

"Andrew—"

"And she wouldn't want you to be lonely. I know she wouldn't."

"Who said I was lonely?"

"I did, and I think it's time you started dating again."

His grandfather shook his head. "I'm a little old for that."

"Bullshit. And Evelyn's definitely got the hots for you."

"That's where you're wrong."

"Give me a break. She's all over you. What does a girl have to do?"

"She's just a friend."

Andrew laughed. "I've heard that one before. Now me personally, I'd date her just for her cookies."

"I don't *like* her cookies."

"Have you tried her pecan brownies?"

"Andrew—"

"Be honest, don't you kind of like her?"

His grandfather hesitated. "She's my *neighbor.*" He looked down at the postcard and tapped his pen against the table.

"So? Your generation didn't date neighbors?"

"What I mean is that . . ." His grandfather raised his hands, then dropped them.

Andrew sat up and pointed a finger at him. "You like her. I can tell."

"I did not say that I like her."

"But you do. And she really is in pretty good shape—for her age. She doesn't even need a walker."

"Andrew."

"So you'll ask her out?"

"No."

"But you'll think about it?"

"You don't understand."

"What's to understand?" Then it dawned on Andrew. "Oh jeez, do you have like, a medical problem? Because there's this new—"

"For Pete's sake . . ."

"Then why won't you ask her out?"

"I'm telling you, she's not interested."

"Well I'm telling you that she is—and there's not much time left."

His grandfather rubbed his forehead, looking confused. "What makes you so sure she's . . . interested?"

"What am I, blind?"

"It's occurred to me. Besides, why would I want to get involved with a woman who's moving to the other side of the country?"

"That's just it. She wouldn't have to move. You guys could . . . consolidate."

"Whoa there."

"One date. That's all I'm asking."

"I told you—"

"*Please.* At least consider it."

His grandfather sighed and rolled his eyes. "I'll consider it."

Andrew clenched his fist victoriously in the air. *"Yes."*

· · ·

Mead hardly slept that night. Instead he tried to keep within the safe perimeter of consciousness like a man by a campfire in a forest full of wolves. And yet as the fire grew dimmer he could hear the rustling in the woods, and then he could see shadows against the trees and he could smell the salty stench of sweat and urine. He drew closer to the fire, bending down to breathe air into the dwindling embers as the sounds in the forest grew closer. But there was no more wood and gradually, very gradually, the last flames died out.

· · ·

Andy?

  Is that you, Matt?

  Who else?

Jesus, you scared me. Andrew sat up in bed and looked around the darkened room. *You gotta be quiet, Matt. My grandfather's sleeping.*

  That's what you think.

Andrew looked over at the adjacent bed, straining to make out the silhouette of his grandfather, who lay with his back to Andrew. *He's awake?*

  Let's just say he's got visitors.

  Visitors? What kind of visitors?

  All kinds.

Andrew slid down beneath his sheets. *You mean like, ghosts?*

  Call them whatever you want.

  You're just joking, right?

  Nope.

Andrew looked again at his grandfather's silhouette. *You're freaking me out, Matt.*

  Sorry.

  Where are you? I mean, how come I can't see you?

  It's just the way it is.

  Are you a . . . ghost?

What do you think?

I don't know. Andrew slid down even further into his bed. *I gotta talk to you about something. Something serious.*

Shoot.

It's about this woman I met.

You got a girlfriend?

Not exactly. She's like, old.

You're dating a senior?

I mean, really old. A senior citizen."

"*Citizen?*"

"*And we're* not *dating. But she's really nice. I never met anybody so nice. And the thing I want to talk about is, she's dying. She's got some sort of a disease and she's gonna die soon.*

I'm sorry.

And I just thought that maybe . . . well I thought maybe you could keep an eye out for her. You know, make her feel welcome. Show her around or whatever.

Matt laughed.

What's so funny?

It doesn't work that way.

How does it work?

I can't say.

Come on, we tell each other everything, remember?

Things have changed.

I don't like the way they've changed. In fact I hate it. Andrew felt his eyes watering.

Then let me go.

What do you mean?

You should let me go, buddy.

Why?

You don't want to end up like him, do you?

Andrew looked over again at his grandfather, who hadn't moved. *What are you talking about, Matt?*

You know what I'm talking about. I can't help you anymore.

Andrew's throat grew so tight it felt like he was hanging from a rope. *But you're my best friend. You're the only one who understands.*

I'm dead, Andy. I didn't wake up.

Don't say that.

You've gotta go on without me. There's no other way.

Andrew buried his face into his pillow and stifled a sob. *I don't want to. I don't want to be alone anymore.*

You're going to make it, Andy. I know you will. Don't let anybody ever tell you that you're not good enough, you got that? You're better than any of them.

I'm too scared.

Good-bye, Andy.

No wait! Andrew sat up. *Matt? Don't go, Matt. Please don't leave me alone. Matt? Matt? Matt?*

· · ·

The next morning Mead and Andrew ate croissants in the car and reached Carentan by ten. Mead was surprised by how familiar the buildings and intersections looked, only cleaner and unmolested. "They called this Purple Heart Lane," he said as they crossed over the long causeway. "The Germans flooded the whole area. It was a big swamp on either side of the road. A lot of men who landed here the night of the jump drowned." Mead could see Andrew straining to find the drama in the passing scenery, which offered no assistance.

They stopped several times to read roadside plaques and memorials and as Mead drove he imagined where the Germans might lay an ambush, half expecting to see flared gray helmets protruding from the bushes. When they reached Ste.-Mère-Église they parked in front of the church where a dummy paratrooper hung from the steeple.

"I read about that guy," said Andrew excitedly.

"He played dead but the Germans eventually cut him down and took him prisoner," explained Mead.

"That definitely would have sucked."

"Worse even than staying back a year?"

"Close."

They stopped briefly in the church, where Mead studied the stained-glass windows commemorating the paratroopers while Andrew pointed out the bullet marks that still scarred the walls, then headed for the Airborne Museum across the street. "You get free admission," Andrew noted proudly, insisting that Mead sign the Book of Honor for veterans. "You're practically a celebrity."

"Enough."

Mead did feel a certain pride. Yet there was so much sadness and shame mixed in that all the pleasure was taken away, leaving him with an acute sense of fatigue. He glanced over at some of the other veterans. What about them? Did they see faces too? And what were their secrets? Certainly they must have secrets. Or had they managed to put their secrets to rest? (And how?)

Together they wandered among the displays and military gear for an hour, Andrew asking lots of questions and Mead fumbling for answers. "Wow, you actually jumped out of one of those?" Andrew asked as they stood looking up at a restored C-47, which loomed above everything else.

"That's it."

Andrew looked at the plane, then back at his grandfather, as if trying to put the two together. "It's kind of hard to imagine you jumping out of a plane."

Mead smiled. "Trust me, it's even harder to imagine *you* jumping out of a plane."

They circled it one more time. "I wouldn't even feel safe flying in something so. . . ."

"Old? Well, it wasn't old when I flew in it."

"Still."

Mead put his hand on Andrew's shoulder. "Sometimes I'd give my right leg to live long enough to see you reach my age—if you ever get there."

Andrew frowned.

They walked around the town reading various plaques posted on walls and trees and browsing in an army surplus store before stopping at a café for lunch. Mead pulled out a map and explained how the 101st was assigned to secure the exits from Utah Beach, knock out German coastal batteries and guard the southern flank before taking Carentan itself and holding off a furious German counterattack by an *SS* panzer division. As he talked he noticed the middle-aged waitress smiling at him. "You should tell her who you are," said Andrew. "I bet she'll give you a free dessert."

"I don't need a free dessert."

"I'd eat it."

Mead rolled his eyes and signaled for the check.

"Where to next?" Andrew's face still showed excitement, which made Mead glad. He'd been worried that his grandson would quickly grow bored.

"I thought we might drive through some of the surrounding countryside a bit, see some of the jump zones, then head to Utah Beach."

"Excellent." Andrew drummed his palms on his thighs like a bongo player. "I still don't get how you jumped out of a plane at night. How could you see the ground coming?"

"You couldn't."

"Weren't you freaking out about whether you'd land on something . . . sharp?"

"As a matter of fact, I was."

"Did you wear a cup?"

Mead smiled, thinking of Punchy. "They weren't offered, but if they were I think every man would have worn one."

When they reached the car Mead studied his map a moment, then put it aside and decided to work from memory.

"Is it like you remember?" asked Andrew as they drove.

"It's a bit more peaceful," said Mead, who was pleasantly surprised by how little the landscape had changed. He looked closely at a meadow as they passed. Could that be where Jimbo bled to death? And what about that old tree there? Could it be where he saw Louie's lifeless body dangling from his parachute? He looked for familiar landmarks but saw none. Yet in a way it was all familiar—the narrow sunken roads and hedgerows and farmhouses and lush pastures, each landscape rekindling a long-suppressed memory until sounds and smells and faces seemed to crowd around him.

"So those are the hedgerows?" asked Andrew as they drove down a road bordered on either side by dense growth.

"That's them." Mead felt a tingling sensation in his legs. "Our intelligence failed to mention anything about them before the attack. Apparently they don't look quite so formidable from the air."

"So maybe you fought right in those bushes?"

"I suppose it's possible."

"That's *intense*."

"The Battle of Normandy was almost a stalemate the first few days. The Germans had all the roads and intersections and hiding places presited by their artillery. It was hell making any progress."

"But then you guys kicked butt."

Mead winced. "After seven weeks of fighting we were no farther than a few dozen miles inland at most—and that's with complete air superiority."

"But I read that we were bombing the shit out of Germany, like, leveling the place."

"We were. I can remember looking up and seeing the sky darken with B-17 heavy bombers flying overhead in formation like a school of silver minnows—and no sight made us happier." Andrew looked up. "But even so, the Germans produced more weapons during the fall of 1944 than at any time during the war." Mead remembered the gaunt faces of slave laborers who begged them for food and kissed their hands.

"You really gotta see *Star Wars*," said Andrew. "It's all about fighting the Dark Side."

"I've seen enough of the dark side."

Andrew began drumming on his thighs again as if fueled by several cups of espresso. "So what's up with the Germans? Are they just like, total assholes?"

"I wouldn't know where to start. And watch your language."

"Sorry."

Mead turned down a small lane and parked.

"What are we doing?" Andrew looked suddenly anxious.

"Time to take some prisoners." Mead got out of the car.

"What?"

"That's a joke. I thought you might like to see a hedgerow up close."

"Oh." Andrew let out a big breath and opened his door.

"How'd you like to try and crawl through that?" Mead asked as they walked along the dense bushes, stopping to peer into the dark entanglements.

"No way."

"Ideal if you're playing defense, not so good for offense."

Andrew reached in with one hand.

"Careful."

"Do you suppose there's still, like, bones and old grenades around?"

"You never know."

"I'd give anything to find a souvenir."

Mead started to say something but stopped himself. "Come on, we've got lots more to see."

By the time they reached Utah Beach Mead was desperate for a restroom. Andrew followed him in, taking the adjacent urinal and glancing over occasionally, so that Mead had to remind himself not to wince. (And it hadn't really occurred to him how much he did wince.)

They started in the museum where they watched old footage and looked at landing craft and artifacts and scale models of the invasion before going outside to examine the memorials and remaining fortifications. Mead felt a sweeping sense of loneliness as he looked out over the beach, which seemed impossibly quiet and barren, as if impervious to even the mightiest human achievements. Looking at the ocean he thought of the men who were dropped prematurely. No fate could be worse.

"You still haven't told me how you got wounded in the butt," said Andrew as they reached the waterline. The surf was rough and the wind stirred small sandstorms at their feet. Mead noticed Andrew struggling not to smile.

"We were in Holland. Fall of '44."

"I didn't know you fought in Holland."

"It was a hell of a mess. Anyway, one day I got hit by a little shrapnel."

"Ouch. How'd it happen?"

"Nothing to tell, really. One minute we were sitting around eating and the next a shell from an 88 landed and my butt started hurting something awful."

"Did you think you were going to die?"

"I wasn't sure I'd ever sit down again."

"Then what?"

"I was bandaged up and eventually evacuated to a hospital in England."

"At least you didn't have to fight anymore."

"What gave you that impression?"

"You mean they sent you back?"

"Damn right." Mead remembered the Purple Heart ceremony on the grounds of the American Hospital in Coventry, then cleaning the Cosmoline off his new rifle as he got refitted. Three weeks later he rejoined the company, overjoyed to see that Punchy was still alive. "Only the dead and disabled went home."

"That doesn't seem fair."

"Nothing was fair. Hell, even after Germany was defeated we figured we'd be sent to fight Japan. We weren't expecting to live until the end of the war."

"I bet you went wild when you got home."

"I ate a lot of ice cream."

Andrew shook his head in disappointment. "I would have gone a lot wilder than that."

"Seems like you already have."

Andrew grew quiet. "I know you think I'm a total loser."

"I certainly do not. But I think you've got some real problems."

Andrew stopped, hands shoved deep into his pockets. "Yeah, well you do, too."

"What?"

Andrew cleared his throat. "I said, you do, too. You're just as messed up as I am."

"Oh really?"

"Sure. You just hide it better. I mean, you still haven't told me basically anything about what happened to you during the war or why you're so secretive about it. Why did we come all this way if you're not even going to tell me anything?"

"Maybe it's none of your goddamn business."

"Why are you so afraid to talk about it? Everybody else talks about it."

Mead watched the whitecaps that stretched toward the horizon, then took out a handkerchief from his pocket and wiped his forehead. "You want a story, is that it?"

"I want to know what you experienced. Like Mom says, it's family history."

Mead carefully refolded the handkerchief, then put it back in his pocket and started walking again. "All right then, I'll give you a little family history."

•   •   •

Punchy's death was the last one that Mead fully felt. After that a heavy sort of numbness descended on him until at times his surroundings seemed almost dreamlike, as if he were a child in bed with a fever, untethered from the passing world. And besides, more and more of the men were replacements, many of whom would soon be replaced themselves. But Punchy's death was different. For years Mead wondered what Punchy's family had been told. Certainly not the truth, because the truth wouldn't do at all.

Eighteen of them had been on patrol in the Ardenne—twelve rifles and two three-man BAR teams—when Bruce McCullum stepped on a Schü mine, blowing off his left foot. Moments later a Bouncing Betty sprang up and exploded at waist height right in front of Mark Foley and Jay Goldberg, filling their groins and abdomens with steel balls. As the rest tried to retrace their steps another mine detonated, then another. The survivors dashed for the woods as a German machine gun opened up.

Mead and Punchy dove behind a tree and lay prone in the snow, firing blindly into the thick forest beyond the clearing. They watched as Foley tried to rise to his knees and was shot dead. Goldberg lay on his back with one arm extended, calling out for help until several more shots silenced him. (Only recently Mead had begun to suspect that Goldberg was one of those soldiers who, despite their bluster, never shoot to kill, hoping to emerge from the war with a clean conscience.) Then mortar rounds began falling, killing a Texan named Walt Slocum. Bark flew into Mead's face as bullets struck the nearby trees.

"Pull back," yelled Tom Duncan, the squad sergeant. Another mortar round landed, killing him instantly. Small-arms fire now came from several directions and Mead could hear German voices approaching.

"Let's get out of here," yelled Punchy, who took off running. Mead followed behind, tripping twice in the heavy snow. They zigzagged through the woods, then dropped down into a ravine, waded through an icy stream and climbed up the other side, grabbing on to branches to pull themselves up the snowy hillside. Mead paused to turn and fire, emptying his clip, then reloaded and took off again after Punchy.

"Which way?" asked Mead, breathing hard as they rested against a tree.

Punchy looked uncertain. "The road we came up on should be this direction," he said.

"You sure?"

"It's more an intuition."

They crossed two more deep ravines, then skirted the edge of a large clearing. As they reached the top of a ridge they finally saw the road down below. It was clogged with German troops heading west.

"Son of a bitch," said Punchy. Crouching in the bushes they watched four Tiger tanks rumble past. They tried to backtrack and loop around to the north, but an hour later they nearly ran into another German force. By nightfall they realized the German lines had swept over them.

"Okay, we know we're fucked," said Punchy, pulling his coat around his neck and stomping his feet. "The question is whether we are permanently fucked."

Mead tried to think but the cold made his head hurt. Hungry and tired, he had an overwhelming urge to sit down and cry.

Punchy lit a cigarette and offered it to him. "Either we can try to reach our lines in the morning or wait until the sons of bitches are pushed back where they came from."

"I say we try to reach our lines," said Mead, taking in a deep drag of the cigarette. "The question is, what do we do now?"

"We find ourselves a warm place to sleep."

"I don't suppose you made reservations anywhere?"

"I'm working on it."

The first farmhouse they approached had two German half-tracks parked out front. The windows were brightly lit and a thin strand of white smoke curled from the chimney, reminding Mead of a Christmas card. "I know what you're thinking and I'm not doing it," he said.

"It would make a hell of a story," said Punchy. "We could each have our own."

"*No.*"

Moments later two German soldiers emerged from the house and leaned against one of the half-tracks, talking and laughing.

"Damn," muttered Punchy.

They quietly retreated, then followed a narrow road until they reached the ruins of another house. Smoke still rose from the ashes and the carcass of a dog lay in the snow nearby. They watched from the nearby woods before cautiously approaching and warming their hands in the embers, which cast an orange glow on their faces. The heat made Mead long for sleep.

Once warm they continued toward the distant lights of another farmhouse across a wide field. As they crept closer, finally dropping to their stomachs and crawling, they could see three German soldiers eating at a table. A lone soldier stood on the front porch with his rifle over his shoulder and his hands stuffed into his armpits.

"We can take them," whispered Punchy, which is exactly what Mead feared he would say. "You get that one and I'll get the three inside."

"There could be more upstairs."

"Then we'll get them, too."

Mead looked around. "I don't like it."

"You want to stay out here all night?"

"Given the choices? Sure."

"Not me. I'm not freezing my balls off. Besides, I'm feeling lucky."

"Well I'm not." Mead watched as the German on the porch lit a cigarette. Four against two. They'd certainly have the opening advantage. And Punchy was a great shot. Mead imagined filling himself with warm food and then crawling into a soft bed. "What about the barn?" He gestured toward the dark structure silhouetted behind the house.

"You stay here, I'll check it out." Before Mead could stop him Punchy had crawled off, working his way around the back of the house. Minutes later he returned.

"It's empty."

"Maybe we could sleep there?"

"When a warm fire and food beckon? Forget it." It occurred to Mead that Punchy was little more than a collection of urges. "So, you with me?"

Mead nodded slowly.

"Let the show begin." They crawled closer until they could hear laughter coming from the house. Punchy glanced over at Mead. "Ready?"

Mead nodded and aimed.

"Now."

Mead hit the German on the porch with the first shot, then fired two more rounds before aiming through the window, where a single remaining soldier staggered from the table. Punchy and Mead both fired simultaneously and the figure dropped from view.

"You got the other two?"

" 'Course I did." Punchy smiled, then pulled out a grenade and ran for the door, stepping over the body of the German. Mead followed close behind, leveling his rifle at the three soldiers sprawled on the floor while Punchy bounded up the stairs.

"Just a couple of warm beds," Punchy said as he came back down.

"These two are alive," said Mead, gesturing with his rifle. One German was groaning softly while the other simply looked at Mead with eyes full of fear. Before Mead could say anything Punchy walked over and shot each one in the head.

"Jesus Christ, what the hell did you have to do that for?"

"They were goners. I was doing them a favor." Punchy bent over one of the bodies and relieved it of a shiny new Schmeisser MP-40 machine pistol. "Hey, look at this beauty," he said, holding it up.

Mead turned away, feeling sick.

"What exactly did you think we were going to do, take them with us? Come on, let's eat." He pulled up a wooden chair and sat down, quickly finishing off the remaining cheese and bread on the half-eaten plates.

Mead walked over to the shattered window and looked out at the pale, snow-covered yard, which glowed from the moonlight. Closing his eyes he filled his lungs with the cool damp air.

"Aren't you gonna eat?" Punchy held out a plate.

"You're a goddamn pig, you know that?"

Punchy smiled, then stuffed another piece of bread into his mouth.

Suddenly there was a light knock on the door. Mead and Punchy grabbed their rifles and dove behind a small sofa.

"Americans?" a voice called out. "You are Americans?" Mead and Punchy kept silent, rifles pointed at the door. "Please don't shoot. We are Belgian." The door slowly opened, revealing an elderly man and his wife, both wrapped in heavy coats and shivering. "Welcome," said the man, extending his hand and smiling.

"This is your home?" asked Mead, rising cautiously to his feet.

The man smiled while the woman stared down silently at the bodies of the Germans. "We were hiding in the barn. My wife is very cold."

"Please, come on in," said Mead. "We were just . . ." He couldn't think how to finish.

The old man gently pushed his wife forward, then quickly closed the door behind him, took off his hat and wiped his brow. "You must be very careful," he said. "The Germans are everywhere."

"We noticed," said Punchy.

"They came in yesterday. All the roads are full." The woman kept staring down at the bodies, her small wrinkled face expressionless.

Punchy looked at Mead and signaled him, then bent down over one of the Germans and took hold of the arms. Mead put down his rifle and took the feet. A few minutes later all four corpses lay side by side in the snow.

"Tonight we will hide them behind the wood pile," said the old man. "Then tomorrow we must bury them in the woods."

When they returned to the house the old woman was on her hands and knees scrubbing the blood from the wooden floor. "Sorry about the mess," said Punchy. The woman didn't respond. Mead wondered if she could be trusted.

"She doesn't speak English," said the old man. "Actually, she doesn't speak much at all. But then, what's to talk about after fifty years, eh?" He laughed to himself as he stoked the fire that still burned in the small hearth. "I would offer you our beds but you wouldn't be safe. Germans have been coming through all day and night."

Punchy frowned. "You got any other ideas?"

The man smiled again, as if enjoying himself, then took a lantern off a hook, lit it and motioned for them to follow. Crossing the hardening snow, which crunched beneath their feet, he led them to the small barn. "They took all my animals," he said as they entered.

"Hell, it's freezing in here," said Punchy, sizing up a mound of straw in one corner.

The old man held up a finger, then handed the lantern to Mead, took a few steps and pointed toward the worn wooden floor, which was made of mismatched boards of varying lengths and widths, like a quilt. "Do you see it?"

Mead guessed he was looking for some sort of trapdoor but saw nothing. Punchy tapped the toe of his boot in different spots, trying to find a hollow sound.

The old man watched with amusement, then dropped to his knees, dug his fingernails into a narrow crack and lifted a small panel, exposing a larger metal handle which he yanked hard, revealing a heavy trapdoor. "Good, eh? My father built it for the last war," he said, showing them how thick the door was. "He was a carpenter."

Punchy and Mead looked at each other, then climbed one at a time down the narrow ladder into a small-but-deep cellar, which had a wood floor, two plank beds and a shelf stocked with candles, a round of cheese, a deck of cards and three jugs of water. A shotgun rested in the corner and there was a large blanket on each bed. The air was damp and fetid. Mead glanced over at a bucket in the corner, which was partially filled with human waste.

"We hid for three nights," said the old man apologetically, taking the bucket. "Please make yourselves comfortable and I'll get you some hot soup."

"You expect us to sleep down here?" asked Punchy.

"Of course!"

After the old man left Mead stretched out on one of the beds, placing his hands behind his head. "Can't beat the privacy," he said.

Punchy stared up at the ceiling, which was supported by four wood beams. "I'm claustrophobic."

"Gee, that's unfortunate."

"You don't understand." Punchy's unshaven face glistened. "See, when I was a kid my older brother locked me in a trunk. Two fucking hours I was in there."

"So this must feel roomy."

Punchy loosened his collar and paced around the cellar. "Don't you think it's kind of hard to breathe in here?"

"Not until you mentioned it."

Punchy's breathing grew louder. "No way, I'm not staying down here."

"You got anything better in mind?"

"The barn," he said, starting for the ladder.

"Wait." Mead sat up.

"What?"

"Listen."

Soon the sound of an approaching tank was unmistakable. German.

Punchy climbed partway up the ladder and stuck his head out the trapdoor. "Must be at least two of them."

"Get back down here."

"Hell no, let's run for it."

Mead grabbed his rifle and followed Punchy up the ladder. After climbing out the trapdoor he hesitated, wondering whether to close it or leave it open for the old couple. Where were they?

"Let's go," said Punchy, standing by the barn door. The tanks were so close now that it was hard to hear anything else. Together they opened the door a crack and peered out. Dozens of approaching German infantrymen were silhouetted by the moonlight.

"We can't make it," said Mead.

"Sure we can."

"Not a chance." Mead ran for the trapdoor and crawled in feetfirst, leaving his head and arms exposed and gesturing frantically to Punchy.

"Come on!" Punchy hesitated as the ground began to vibrate. *"Now!"*

Finally Punchy turned and sprang for the opening, nearly falling on top of Mead. "Close it!" Punchy scrambled back up the ladder and pulled the trapdoor shut. Mead blew out the lantern and they both stood motionless in the pitch blackness.

"I can't breathe," whispered Punchy.

"Shut up."

"I'm gonna make a run for it."

Mead heard Punchy stumble around the cellar searching for the ladder. "You want to get us killed?"

"I can't breathe!"

Bits of earth began falling from the ceiling and Mead could hear the grinding of tank gears.

"It's gonna cave in!" cried Punchy, his voice hysterical.

The tanks suddenly stopped. Mead groped around the room for the ladder, then climbed up halfway and listened. Thank God they'd hidden the bodies. Yet they'd see the blood in the snow and the shattered windows. Where was the old couple? Moments later he heard a woman's screams. Oh, Jesus.

"They're going to tell them about the cellar," said Punchy. "We're going to die down here."

"Quiet."

"I'd rather die fighting."

The screams grew louder. Were they torturing her, or was she watching them torture her husband? Mead clenched his teeth as the screams continued. Surely the old man would tell. Who wouldn't? Punchy had been right, they should have run for it.

He flinched at the report of a single gunshot. A second shot quickly followed. He looked up in the darkness, imagining the door opening and hand grenades dropping down on them. Or would they simply burn the barn down? He heard Germans shouting, then footsteps on the wood planks above him. Mead froze on the ladder, his head just inches beneath the trapdoor. Down below, Punchy's breathing grew shallow and rapid. There was a distant tapping sound above, then another, this time closer. Finally he heard footsteps directly above, then a pause followed by more tapping.

Mead closed his eyes and prayed. There was another tap, then voices. Mead bit into his lip until he felt blood run down his chin. *Good-bye, Sophie.* Another tap, followed by a long silence. Then gradually the tapping grew more distant. Tears filled Mead's eyes. The old man was right to be proud of his father. When the sounds stopped completely Mead quietly climbed down the ladder, then found one of the beds and sat on it. "You okay?" he whispered.

No answer.

"You okay, Punchy?"

"I don't want to die down here."

"You won't. I promise."

An hour passed. Then another. Mead lay on his back listening, unsure whether his eyes were open or closed. He wondered whether Punchy had fallen asleep. Several times he heard footsteps above, but no more tapping.

"We wouldn't have made it," said Punchy suddenly.

"What?"

"If we had tried to run for it we wouldn't have made it."

"I know."

"But we're going to die down here. We're going to run out of air."

Mead had thought of that too. If the cellar was airtight, wouldn't they suffocate? And yet the old man had said they'd hidden for three nights. Mead took another breath, trying to taste the air. Was he getting enough oxygen? He did feel sort of light-headed and the more he thought about it the harder it was to breathe. "For God's sake, don't talk about it."

"It's like being dead," said Punchy. "Just like a coffin."

"Jesus Christ, would you shut up?"

Punchy's raspy breathing filled the silence. "The truth is, I'm scared to death of dying."

"Me too."

"I can't even stand thinking about it."

"Then don't."

"I can't help it."

"Get some sleep."

Mead placed his fingers on his eyelids to make sure they were closed, still concentrating on every breath until he felt dizzy. *Am I dying? Is the air almost gone?* He gulped down several rapid breaths, his chest rising and falling uncontrollably as he fought off the impulse to rush for the trap door. He felt his eyelids again, then thought of Sophie, trying to recall as many of their dates as he could in chronological order. Still struggling for air, he tried to recall the prices of the items in his father's hardware store. He saw the rows of hammers and the bags of nails and the snow shovels in winter and then he heard his father's voice and the chime of the door. He bent down and picked up a handful of sawdust, holding it up to his nose and thinking how good it was to be back. Maybe he and Thomas would even have time for a game of catch after work. He let the sawdust run through his fingers as he gradually made his way to the stockroom, making sure to smile at the customers. Closing the door behind him he poured a glass of lemonade from the pitcher his mother kept on a table next to a bowl of apples, then curled up on an old sofa, thinking he just needed a few minutes rest.

He couldn't figure out why the sofa started shaking but soon everything on the stockroom shelves began falling to the floor. Father? Thomas? He tried to open his eyes but he couldn't. Where's the light? The noise was deafening now. *Father!*

"We're gonna be crushed to death!" cried Punchy as large chunks of earth fell from the cellar roof. Over the roar and screech of a tank Mead heard the splintering of wood. Seconds later the tank was directly overhead, the treads grinding the wood and causing more dirt to fall. Mead crouched against a wall in terror as he waited for the cellar to collapse.

"We're going to die!" screamed Punchy, his voice nearly drowned out by the noise. He's going for the door, thought Mead, jumping up and reaching around in the darkness. Finally he found the ladder and felt Punchy's legs partway up. "We're going to die!"

"No!" Mead grabbed at Punchy's legs and tried to pry him off the ladder until a sharp blow to his face knocked him backwards. Above, the screeching of wood and metal grew louder. "Let me out!" cried Punchy, now banging against the door. Mead crawled around on his knees feeling for his rifle, then rose to his feet and searched for the ladder. When he felt Punchy's feet he aimed high and swung the butt of the rifle.

"We're going to die!"

"Get down!" Mead swung again, harder. He heard Punchy groan, then the sound of his body hitting the floor. Mead froze as the tank passed overhead one more time before slowly driving away. Thank God. He waited until the tank was out of earshot, then felt around until he found Punchy.

"You all right?"

Punchy let out another groan. "I'm dead, aren't I?"

"Not yet." Mead began searching for the ladder. When he found it he climbed to the top and listened.

"What makes you so sure I'm not dead?"

"This." Mead pushed open the trapdoor a crack, letting in a stream of blinding white light. He listened, then opened the door a few more inches and looked out. The roof of the barn was gone and only a portion of one wall remained standing. Across the yard long wind-whipped flames rose from the house.

"Let me out of here," said Punchy, pushing against him from underneath.

As they crawled cautiously out of the cellar they gulped down the crisp cold air, shielding their eyes from the light. Mead dabbed blood from his lip while a thin red trickle ran from Punchy's hairline down his forehead.

"They didn't talk," said Punchy, gesturing toward a large tree in the center of the yard. Mead looked up and saw the old man and his wife, both bleeding from the head and strung by their necks from two short ropes. Nearby four fresh graves were marked by helmets suspended from simple wooden crosses. Mead and Punchy cut the bodies down but were too tired to bury them. Instead they covered the elderly couple with a thin layer of snow, then returned to the cellar and filled up on cheese and water before heading off in search of the American lines.

· · ·

They spent the rest of the day walking and hiding, twice watching German patrols pass close by. By evening Punchy could barely hobble.

"Let me look at them," said Mead as they crouched in a small foxhole they had dug behind a large bush set back from the road.

"You're not taking these boots off."

"Yes I am." Mead struggled with the laces, then finally pulled off the left boot as Punchy let out a cry. Gently peeling off the sock, he held the foot up to the moonlight. The toes were now black while the rest of the foot was bluish white.

"I can't feel your hands," said Punchy.

"Just relax." Mead slowly rubbed the heel and sole but avoided touching the toes.

"I'm going to lose them, aren't I?"

"I don't know."

"I don't care about the little ones. What the hell do they do? But I don't want to lose my big toes. Who wants to marry a guy without big toes?"

Mead cautiously touched the big toe, then began massaging it gently. When he got the sock and boot back on Punchy offered him the other foot. "I'll do that one in the morning," said Mead, whose fingers could no longer move.

They reached an American roadblock the next afternoon, Punchy limping with his arm around Mead. As they approached two sentries leveled their rifles and ordered them to drop their weapons.

"We're Americans, you idiot," said Punchy.

"I said, *drop them.*" Behind the sentries a third GI manned a jeep-mounted machine gun.

Mead placed his rifle on the ground and raised his hands, offering a smile. Punchy hesitated. "I've hardly eaten in two fucking days, I'm tired and my toes are falling off. Now cut the—"

"Now."

"Jesus, a couple of cowboys." Punchy placed his rifle on the ground, keeping the Schmeisser strapped to his back.

"And the other one."

With a curse Punchy took the German machine pistol off and placed it next to his rifle. The two sentries eyed each other. "Don't even *think* of stealing it from me," said Punchy.

"The password?"

"A few days ago it was mayflower or maypole or . . ."

The taller sentry cut Mead off. "Wrong."

"How the fuck are we supposed to know the password?" said Punchy.

"We're with the 101st," Mead explained quickly. "Our patrol was ambushed and we've been trying to get back for two days." He listed the name of every officer he could think of.

The sentries conferred. "I still don't trust'em," said one to the other. "What are they doing with a goddamned Schmeisser and how the hell did they get through the German lines?"

"We went *under* their tanks," said Punchy, starting forward again. "It's a nifty trick. Ever been under a Tiger before?"

"Halt right there!"

"Do what he says," said Mead.

"I'm in no mood for this," said Punchy, stopping.

"Hands up."

"I'm from the *Bronx,* you dumb fuck."

"I said, *hands up!*"

Punchy raised his hands.

"It could be an ambush," said the shorter sentry, looking nervously down the road behind Mead and Punchy.

"An ambush?" said Mead with a laugh. "Listen guys, I'm from—"

"We got orders to shoot anybody who doesn't know the password."

"Akron, Ohio. I went to Millfield High and my father owns a hardware store and I went to basic at Camp Toccoa and jumped in Normandy and Holland and if you'd like I can probably recite some of the Pledge of Allegiance."

The taller sentry aimed his rifle at Punchy. "How many home runs did Gehrig hit with bases loaded?"

"Hell, I don't even know the answer to that one," said the shorter sentry.

The taller sentry furrowed his brow. "Okay then, how many career runs did Cobb get? Ballpark figure."

"Frankly, I don't give a fuck," said Punchy.

"Can't say I know that one either," said the shorter sentry.

"Fine. You try," said the taller sentry, tilting his head and spitting angrily to the side.

The shorter sentry thought for a moment. "Got it. Name the seven dwarves."

"The seven dwarves?" asked Punchy in disgust.

"Go ahead," said Mead.

"I'm looking at two of them right now," said Punchy.

Mead jumped in. "There's Doc and Sleepy and—"

"I think they're Krauts," said the taller sentry.

"Look, fellows, we've had a long couple of days," said Mead.

"They caught three Krauts yesterday wearing our uniforms and driving a stolen jeep. Spoke perfect English. Besides, I don't like the looks of this one." The sentry gestured toward Punchy with his rifle.

"You wise-ass son of a bitch," said Punchy, stepping forward and reaching out to swat the sentry's rifle out of the way.

"*No!*" cried Mead.

The soldier fired, hitting Punchy in the chest. Punchy took another step, then collapsed to the ground. Mead crouched over him. "Get a medic!"

"You are Krauts, aren't you?"

Mead pulled out his medical kit, removed a morphine syrette and jabbed it into Punchy's arm. Then he ripped open Punchy's coat and shirt and undershirt, took out a compress and gently held it against the wound, which made a gurgling sound.

"You can't tell 'em I died like this," cried Punchy, his lips quivering.

"You're staying right with me. Right here with Mead."

"I don't think he's a Kraut," said the shorter sentry nervously.

"Then why'd he rush me like that?"

"Get a goddamn medic!" screamed Mead.

The shorter sentry turned and ran back toward the jeep while the taller one stood staring down at Punchy, a look of fear in his eyes.

Suddenly Punchy reached up and grabbed Mead by the collars. "Don't tell anybody I died like this, you understand me?"

"Shhh," said Mead, placing the palm of his hand against Punchy's cheek.

"I didn't mean to shoot him. Honest to God I didn't."

"Shut up!" said Mead.

Punchy's lips were moving but Mead couldn't hear him. He leaned closer, straining to make out the words. "I was right," whispered Punchy. Mead waited for him to continue. "I knew I was dead. You said I wasn't but I knew I was."

"You're going to be okay."

Spasms shook Punchy's body. "You tell them the truth: you tell them how Punchy died under that Tiger tank."

"I'll tell them."

"I can't breathe down here."

"The sun's out, ol' buddy. Take a look."

But Punchy didn't seem to hear him. "Sweet Mother of Jesus, don't leave me down here. Please, anywhere but down here . . ."

When the medic arrived Punchy was dead.

• • •

Andrew was silent when his grandfather finished, trying to pretend he didn't notice the tears in the old man's eyes or the way his voice changed pitch near the end. Something about seeing his grandfather—*Sarge*—get choked up made Andrew feel prickly inside, like nothing in the world was really solid. He focused his attention on a seagull that had been circling above their heads. It landed and took a few steps toward him, turning its head to one side as if waiting for him to say something. *Is that you, Matt?* The seagull came closer, sinking its head low in its feathers, which were remarkably white. *Matt?* It would make perfect sense. What better way to hang out on the beach? And in a way it kind of looked like Matt, a bit cocky around the eyes. As Andrew knelt in the sand the seagull flapped its wings and rose high in the air, then swooped down and skimmed low over the waves. Andrew watched it until it disappeared against the gray horizon. *Come back, Matt.*

"I have his ashes."

"What?"

"Matt's ashes. They were going to bury him in Indiana and so I stole them, or him."

"You're pulling my leg?" Mead looked at Andrew hopefully.

"Nope." Andrew braced himself. "Please don't get mad."

"Jesus Christ."

"Sorry."

"You *stole* them?"

Andrew nodded slowly, watching the skin on his grandfather's face start to twitch in anger.

"What the hell did you bring them *here* for?"

"I've been trying to figure out where to bury him." He swallowed, then continued quickly. "At first I figured I'd bury him in California, like at the beach, because Matt always wanted to live on a beach in a place like California, but then when you said we were going to Europe I thought he might like that better. He'd never been to Europe."

"Are you out of your mind?"

"I couldn't let them take him to Indiana."

His grandfather slapped his palm against his forehead. "For God's sake, you even took them through customs."

"I was a little nervous about that." He tapped the large bulge in his pants pocket.

Mead looked down at Andrew's pants in disbelief. "He's in your *pocket?*"

"Most of him. I spilled some in this forest preserve back in Chicago when I was—"

"I cannot believe this."

"Sorry."

"Give them to me." Mead held out his hand.

Andrew's face reddened. "No, please."

"We are *not* carrying . . . *ashes* . . . around Europe."

"You can't just throw them out." Andrew's voice was breaking now as he covered his pocket with both hands.

Mead started toward him, then hesitated, muttering to himself. "Exactly what did you have in mind?"

"I dunno. I was gonna scatter them in Westminster Abbey. It seemed like, *perfect*. But then I saw this guy sweeping the floor and that totally freaked me out. Then I thought maybe I'd sprinkle them around the Tower of London— you've got to admit it beats Indiana—but then I started worrying that maybe the place was haunted by all those people who got their heads chopped off."

"I see." The skin on Mead's face began twitching again.

"And yesterday I was going to scatter them at Omaha Beach—it seemed pretty intense, and Matt was a totally intense guy—but then it just seemed too depressing. So actually, I was thinking of taking them back to California and sprinkling them on that beach you took me to. He would have loved that beach."

His grandfather stood rubbing his forehead.

"Please don't take them."

"Let's go to the car."

. . .

As Mead stormed down the beach with his arms stiff at his sides he imagined the search in customs, then trying to explain why his grandson was returning to the States with the stolen ashes of a friend who killed himself in Illinois and should have been buried in Indiana. Of course, the story was so implausible that it just might stand.

Jesus.

He thought of his big blue chair back home, wishing he could sit for a minute and work on a crossword puzzle. Yes, everything would be better when he got home. He imagined a nice, thick porterhouse on the grill, then his evening walk just as the light softened, the air quickly cooling. What the hell was he thinking coming here? Did he really believe that his own past—that the sheer unspeakable enormity of what he'd witnessed— somehow held the key to his grandson's salvation? What an old fool I am. And what had he achieved but to stir up memories that now threatened to engulf him; dozens of soiled young faces drawing closer and closer, their sad, imploring eyes filled with questions he could not answer; and sounds too, sounds of shouting and gunfire and explosions and the animal-like shriek of the wounded and always the angry staccato of German phrases, which still produced a dense fear low in his gut. He looked over at his grandson, hating his sullen arrogance and his yellow-streaked hair and his earring and the mousy way that he carried himself, like some sort of underfed stray. It's all his damn fault. But soon he'd be back in Chicago and Mead would have his house all to himself again. (And Sophie's room.) What would he tell Sharon? He had no idea. Perhaps he could pay for a shrink or get the boy into the army. He pulled out his handkerchief again and wiped down his face, walking faster despite a weakness in his legs. If only I could sit for a minute.

But he couldn't go home. Not yet; not when the thing he dreaded most was so close he could feel its moist breath on his neck. *You wouldn't, would you?* Somehow he always knew that it would come to this, that eventually he would no longer have the strength to keep it at bay. *(All those years.)* It wasn't enough that he'd been a decent man; that he'd been faithful to his wife and honest at work and generous with the church. Because no matter what he did or how many years he safely tucked away, the accusation stood, the charges ringing louder and louder in his ears until it had become hard to hear anything else. *Murderer.* And now there was nothing left to do but to stop running and hold his ground and try to stare right into the face of his accuser—to confront the very thing that had ruined him—and say, *I'm sorry. Now please leave an old man be.*

There was no other choice.

"Are we going back to the hotel?" Andrew asked nervously when they reached the car.

Mead opened his map and studied it before starting the engine. "Not yet."

. . .

"What's this?" asked Andrew, looking at the sign. *Cimetière Militaire Allemand.*

"A German cemetery."

"No kidding?" Andrew looked at his grandfather, who seemed distracted. "Are we going in?"

"Yep."

After stopping in the modern visitor's center they walked through the stone archway and entered the burial grounds, which didn't look like any cemetery Andrew had ever seen. Clusters of small decorative crosses, each roughly chiseled from dark stone, were scattered at regular intervals while the graves themselves were identified only by small flat markers. In the center, atop a large earthen mound surrounded by flowers, stood a tall stone cross and the sculptured figures of a man and a woman, heads bowed in grief. Parents.

"The American cemetery is much prettier," said Andrew.

"This is all the sorrow without the pride," said Mead.

"I think it's kind of creepy." Andrew looked down at the names on the markers as they walked, trying to pronounce them. "How come they have more than one name on them?"

"Comradeship in death."

"What?"

"It's a nice way of saying they had to economize."

"Oh." He followed behind Mead, reading more names and wondering how each died. "There's really 21,000 Germans buried here?"

"Just a drop in the bucket."

Andrew tried to visualize the entire student body at Montrose, then multiplied it by seven. Holy shit. And the weird thing was thinking they'd all been killed; 21,000 *violent* deaths. He tried to imagine the worst pain he'd ever felt—the time he cracked a tooth trying to pry open a beer bottle with his teeth—then having it get worse and worse until you die. Fuck me. And then to die for the losing side. Hard to put a good spin on that. He looked down at the grass, wondering if some of the skeletons were wearing medals like the ones his grandfather had. Be amazing to dig the place up.

He heard people speaking German on his left and turned and watched as a small group slowly walked down several rows, turned right, then left, then stopped at a small marker, gathering around it. Wow, the family. He stared at a teenager his age, looking away quickly when the boy caught his eye. So that would have been the enemy. Him or me. *Bang!*

He watched the family a few more minutes, feeling unexpectedly sad and thinking how glad he was that he wasn't a Sauerkraut, then looked around for his grandfather. He finally found him standing off by himself on the far side of the large grassy mound. Andrew approached slowly from behind, thinking he shouldn't disturb him. Maybe he killed some of these guys with his bare hands; maybe even the German whose family was visiting.

Suddenly his grandfather reached into his shoulder bag and pulled out several objects, laying them one at a time on a stone ledge. Andrew squinted, then took a few steps closer. Jesus, he brought the dead German's stuff. I can't believe this. He watched as his grandfather dropped down on his knees. Is he having some sort of heart attack? Andrew started to approach, then decided to wait. His grandfather's lips seemed to be moving but from the distance Andrew couldn't hear anything. God, I hope he's not freaking out. Andrew looked around to see if anyone else was watching but the cemetery was now deserted. He looked back at his grandfather, who was now staring up at the two large stone sculptures. Please don't let him have a heart attack. Finally his grandfather rose to his feet and straightened himself. So he's gonna leave the stuff. Andrew debated trying to grab the things without being noticed. But then, just as his grandfather seemed about to walk away he hesitated, knelt down and gathered up the belongings, placing them back in his shoulder bag.

"How would you like to go to Germany?" he said as he walked quickly past.

Andrew followed behind. "Germany? Why Germany?"

"Because there's something I have to do."

This is getting too weird. "When?"

"Tomorrow."

"*Tomorrow?* You're kidding, aren't you?"

"Not at all." His grandfather continued toward the parking lot.

"Why? Are you going to return his things?"

His grandfather slowed. "I'm going to try."

"To . . . who?"

"I don't know yet. There's an address among his papers. We'll start there and see where it leads us." He turned to Andrew as if gauging his reaction. "You didn't have any other plans this summer, did you?"

"Not exactly, but—"

"Good." His grandfather hurried on to the car.

Germany

They caught a train to Paris early the next morning, then took a taxi from Gare St-Lazare to Gare de l'Est, where they loaded up on food and sodas at a concession stand before boarding a train to Germany.

"So he's from Stuttgart?" asked Andrew, finishing his second croissant as the train pulled out of the station.

"According to my map he's from a little town nearby. We'll transfer to a local line when we get there."

"Maybe the town was bombed to smithereens during the war and never rebuilt."

"Maybe."

"Maybe everyone in his family died or moved away years ago."

"Maybe."

Andrew leaned left, then right in his seat. "My butt's already killing me. How come we didn't fly?"

"Because I wanted to take the train. Good enough?"

"Just asking."

They sat across from each other, both next to the window. Andrew patted the large lump in his pants pocket, where Matt's ashes were stuffed in the Ziploc. Would they be searched at the German border? He imagined snarling German shepherds and Dobermans sniffing at his pants. *Maybe I should hide Matt under the seat or in my bag. What if they confiscate him?*

He looked over again at his grandfather, who stared out the window, his leather bag on the floor between his feet. *So basically, we're both carrying the remains of dead people: a murdered Nazi Sauerkraut and a short,* green-haired teenager from Chicago who killed himself. What a family. Are other people's families this weird?

"How long do you think we'll be in Germany?" he asked.

"As long as it takes."

"Does that mean like, days or months?"

"I'm paying the bills, aren't I?"

"This could get expensive."

"I'll manage."

Andrew listened to his headphones for a while, wishing he'd bought more batteries, then ate another croissant. His grandfather remained almost motionless, face turned toward the window. Andrew couldn't believe how bad the old man looked, like he'd gotten hammered and slept on his face all night. Must be some serious shit going on in his head. "Are you nervous?" he asked, regretting the question immediately. His grandfather glanced over at him without responding, then returned his gaze to the window. "I'm just saying that I'd be nervous, that's all."

"Yes, as a matter of fact I am a little nervous."

Andrew pulled out his notebook, thinking maybe he'd write some lyrics. He jotted down a few lines but kept returning to the story his grandfather had told him about how Punchy had died. Was that worse than waking up next to your best friend's dead body in the forest preserve? Tough call. He looked at his grandfather again, trying to imagine how he killed the German and why it was such a big deal—it *was* war—but too afraid to ask. He wrote a few more lyrics, tinkering with a long song he was writing for Matt, then closed the notebook and lay his head back, quickly lulled into a deep sleep by the gentle motion of the train. Within minutes he was dreaming that drooling Dobermans were snapping at his pants. When he awoke his grandfather was staring at him, looking even worse than before. "Welcome to Germany."

• • •

The first thing Mead noticed as U.S. troops entered the concentration camp at Landsberg in Bavaria at the foot of the Alps was the smell, a smell he could recall for years after. Once inside they stared in stupefaction at the bodies, stacked row upon row, barely human. And then Mead struggled with a sense of repulsion as dozens of inmates surrounded him and kissed and hugged him, their bodies filthy and lice-ridden.

So the stories were true.

Mead couldn't stop himself from retching, and then later that day behind a barn he and another GI watched in horrified fascination as a pack of prisoners cornered a guard, spitting and kicking at him, then tearing him apart like piranhas. Neither of them dared intervene. It seemed like such a *private* matter.

And then, in a barrack filled with those who could not move, they passed out candy and rations, trying again to ignore the suffocating smell. Mead knelt next to a young boy with huge dark eyes. "What's your name?" he asked, placing his hand gently on the boy's forehead. The boy said something in a language Mead didn't recognize. An older prisoner on the wooden bed just above translated.

"His name is Grzegorz. Gregory. Polish. He says he wants to go with you to America; that he's a good worker."

"He can go home. He's free."

The inmate translated again. "He says he doesn't have a home."

"How long has he been here?"

The translator and the boy talked back and forth for some time. "Two months. He was working for a wealthy German family—a household slave —before they were forced to flee the approaching front. He says that he knows where they buried their silver. Very expensive things, he says. He will take you there if you promise to teach him English and take him to America."

Mead smiled. "First we have to fatten him up." He pulled out a bar of chocolate and broke off a piece, placing it in the boy's mouth. Suddenly the boy lifted his hand and snatched the rest of the bar from Mead, stuffing it into his mouth and chewing greedily. Mead laughed. "Easy there."

"Jesus, don't feed them any solid food," said a medic, entering the barrack. But it was too late. Within minutes the boy went into convulsions. Mead stood by helplessly as the frail body rocked and heaved, the face turning beet red and the big brown eyes bulging. Five minutes later the boy was dead. As Mead left the barrack two other prisoners had begun convulsing.

•   •   •

They checked into a hotel near the train station, eating dinner in the small dining room off the lobby, which smelled to Andrew like a butcher shop. He couldn't look at anybody in the face without thinking of Nazis, especially the creep in *Saving Private Ryan* who knifed the Jewish guy. He nibbled at his bread while eyeing the other diners warily. It's like being on the Death Star. Definitely should have packed a knife.

When they got up to the room Mead polished his shoes and ironed his slacks, then changed into his pajamas, brushed his teeth and climbed into bed.

"You going to sleep already?" Andrew didn't feel like being alone.

"I'm tired."

Andrew wondered if his grandfather was having flashbacks. And what would happen tomorrow? Just thinking about it made him jumpy. "Mind if I stay up a bit?"

"Not as long as you get some reading in."

Andrew forced himself through ten pages but couldn't concentrate. He got up and peed, then tried to finish the chapter but kept losing his place. He looked over at his grandfather, who had his back to him. Was he dreaming of the war? Was he killing that German right at that very moment?

He put down *The Longest Day* and began browsing through the photographs in one of the guidebooks they'd purchased in Normandy: first three dead bodies by a burning tank; then a wounded German with his hands up, eyes round with fear; then more bodies, some in strange, inexplicable positions; then two muddy-faced GIs carrying ammo and wincing from exhaustion. He tried to imagine his grandfather being so dirty but it was incomprehensible. Mr. Tidy must have gone nuts. Finally he reached for the small bedside lamp and flicked off the light. Immediately he felt the silence closing in on him until his ears ached like he was at the bottom of a deep pool. Was there enough air in the room for two people or was he just breathing in his grandfather's exhales? He rolled to one side, then the other. What I'd give for a big fat joint and a couple of beers. He tried to visualize Cori taking a bubble bath, thinking he'd rather be horny than paranoid. Yet no matter how hard he tried he couldn't assemble her in his mind. Bad sign.

He was sweating now, wanting to kick off the last sheet but afraid to be naked. In the darkness his thoughts began swooping down and clawing at him like hundreds of bats, wings flapping in his face. He thought of the day his father left home and how for weeks he ran to the front door every time he heard a car door slam, certain that Dad had come back. He thought of the color of Matt's cold lips and how peaceful he looked and then of his mother's endless tears and all the faces at school jeering at him. He thought of his grandfather and the awful things he'd been through; the killing and destruction and seeing his buddies die and then losing his wife and having nothing left but his ghosts. He thought of Evelyn dying in some house in Connecticut without even her flowers to keep her company and how all she wanted was a chance to love a grumpy old man without hurting him. And then he thought that maybe everybody was lonely; that perhaps loneliness was the unspoken reason for everything else: for music and sex and getting high and gardening and his mother's tears and Matt's suicide and even God. So they were all lost: his mother and father and grandfather and Evelyn and even his teachers and Cori Fletcher and assholes like Kevin Bremer. Every single one of them was lost and alone and yet nobody had the courage to admit it; loneliness was the dirty little secret that nobody dared talk about. And that, he realized, was what he hated above all else. It wasn't the loneliness, it was the silence. The infinite unbreakable silence. He ran his hands through his scalp and pulled at his hair, feeling so much fury for the way things were that he wanted to smash something. *It was the silence that killed you, wasn't it, Matt?*

When he opened his eyes he saw a pale moon peeking through the curtain. *I always thought the man in the moon would be smiling.* Andrew pulled the sheet aside, got up and tiptoed to the window, his thin frame shaking with fear. He glanced at his grandfather, then quietly pulled the curtain aside a few inches and looked up, squinting.

Jesus, Matt was right. The man in the moon wasn't smiling. Not if you looked hard enough. Andrew pressed his face against the pane. He even looked like Matt, cold and pale and so far away. Anger swelled in Andrew's throat. Why did people say he was smiling? Couldn't they even be honest about that? He clenched his fists in rage as he stood in the darkness looking up at the saddest face he'd ever seen; a face that stared down at the Earth night after night and couldn't bear what it saw; a face that understood the awful, cold, lonely truth of everything. When he got back into bed he wrapped himself around his pillow and rocked slowly back and forth. God, what was the point of even being born?

"Evelyn's dying," he blurted out.

His grandfather's breathing stopped.

"I'm not supposed to say anything but it's true. She's *dying*." He let out a sob. "I overheard her daughter. She won't do chemotherapy and she's broke and that's why she has to sell the house and she's going to die soon."

The room was so silent that Andrew thought he could hear the moon inching across the sky. Then he heard the adjacent bed creak and felt his grandfather's large warm hand on top of his.

"It's true. I swear it's true. She made me promise not to tell you because she doesn't want to hurt you. You gotta believe me."

"I believe you, Andrew."

"I just hate it. I hate everything." He couldn't control himself now. All the anger and pain rushed out of his eyes and nose and dribbled down his chin as he cried.

"Sometimes, so do I." Andrew felt the roughness of his grandfather's cheek press briefly against his. The hand remained until the last terrifying thought flew away in the night.

•   •   •

His grandfather said nothing the next morning over breakfast. Instead they ate in silence and then Andrew sat in the lobby while his grandfather talked to a middle-aged man who worked at the front desk. After a few minutes the German, who had a round red face and wore small wire-framed glasses, invited Mead and Andrew into a back room. "There wasn't much damage to our town during the war, thank God. Nothing worth bombing." He pulled out a telephone directory. "Now, what did you say the name was?"

"Mueller," said Mead.

"Do you have an address?"

"It's here." Mead pulled out the wallet from his shoulder bag. Andrew watched as the German's eyes widened.

"Are you an . . . investigator?" the man asked warily. Andrew tried to imagine him doing the *Heil Hitler* thing. And yet he seemed friendly enough.

"Oh, no," said Mead. "I just . . . I have some things. I'd like to find the family. It's personal."

"I see." The German studied the wallet for a moment, then looked carefully at Mead again. When he seemed satisfied he opened the directory and began slowly turning the pages, making little noises as he carefully traced his thick forefinger along the columns. Then he picked up the phone and dialed.

Oh great, thought Andrew, he's alerting his neo-Sauerkraut skinhead buddies.

But after the third call the German hung up and smiled, looking pleased with himself. "We have three Muellers listed—it's a common name—and I'm afraid none are at the address you have. I managed to reach one of them and the man doesn't know a Hans from the war. That leaves two, and neither seem to be home at the moment."

"Well, thank you for your help," said Mead.

Phew, thought Andrew, wishing he could put his headphones on, close his eyes and leave Hitlerland far behind.

"Ah, but the good news is that one of our Muellers lives very close to the address you have. Maybe three, four blocks away. Same neighborhood. The other Mueller lives in a new development across town. Ugly buildings, if I may say."

Mead stiffened.

"Perhaps I could try later?"

Mead was silent for so long that Andrew gave him a little nudge. Finally he said, "May I have that address—the one in the same neighborhood?"

"Of course." The German jotted it down on a piece of paper and handed it to Mead.

"Is there somewhere around here I can rent a car?"

"Three blocks down, right across from the train station. Come to the front desk and I'll get you a map."

Andrew was desperate to ask questions as they walked to the rental car agency but his grandfather was so tense that he didn't dare. This has got to be the vacation from hell. Once they got in the car—a Mercedes with leather seats, which was the most promising development in days—he couldn't stand it any longer. "So we're just going to knock on the door?" he asked, working the powered seat back and forth.

"Actually, I thought I'd have you knock."

Andrew's face whitened. "You're kidding?"

"Yes." His grandfather glanced over at him and smiled, though his face was colorless. He drove so slowly that Andrew could see a convoy of impatient drivers in the side-view mirror, which made him cringe.

"I like the car," he said. "Nice and roomy. Probably goes real fast too—if you give her a little gas."

"It's a bit fancy for my tastes, but it's all they had."

Andrew looked into the side-view mirror again, wondering if they were being followed. "Maybe they save it for veterans. Kind of a courtesy car. It's the least they could do." He powered his seat forward again.

"I rather doubt it." For the second time his grandfather pulled over to study the map, then finally turned down a small residential street lined with drab brick row houses, each with a small patch of green out front.

"This is it?"

His grandfather looked down at the piece of paper given him by the hotel clerk, then rolled down his window and slowed the car. "We're looking for number twenty-two."

Andrew counted down the houses. "It should be that one." He pointed to a plain two-story house, the upper-floor curtains closed and the brick darkened with age. Red and yellow flowers filled two small flower boxes on each side of the front door.

His grandfather continued on to the end of the street before parking. "Well, here we are," he said, unbuckling his seat belt and reaching into the backseat for his leather bag.

The dead German's stuff, thought Andrew anxiously. "They probably won't even know who we're talking about, right? I mean, it was so long ago?"

"Only one way to find out."

"But then again, the whole block could be filled with relatives. Are you sure they won't be . . . mad?"

"I'm not sure of anything."

Andrew watched a tall, heavyset German teenager walk past, hair cropped close and feet embedded in big, black shit-kickers. Definitely a storm trooper. "Maybe we should call first, or we could e-mail them? I know all about computers."

His grandfather took a deep breath and opened his door. "Come on." He walked quickly down the sidewalk and through the little gate to number twenty-two, hesitating briefly at the door before ringing the bell. Andrew stood back a few feet, ready to bolt. Good, nobody home. But then the door opened a crack and an elderly woman peered out. Oh, shit.

"Do you speak English?" asked Mead.

"Nein."

"I'm American."

She opened the door a few more inches, looking puzzled, then shook her head and began to close the door.

"No English?"

"Nein."

"Wait." Mead pulled the German military ID from his bag and held it up. "Do you know him? Hans Mueller?"

The woman's eyes widened. Uh oh, thought Andrew, taking another step back and scanning the street. Slowly she opened the door all the way and reached for the ID, her gnarled hand visibly shaking. Andrew braced himself for screams as she stared at the photograph, holding it close to her face. But instead she just let out a small cry as she pressed it to her chest. Andrew looked at his grandfather, who stood frozen, a look of anguish on his face. Jesus, this is too fucking much.

"I have more," his grandfather said, reaching into his bag and pulling out the wallet and then the medals.

With both hands the woman grabbed at her wiry gray hair, her eyes fixed on the objects. Then she lowered her hands and carefully took the wallet and ran her crooked fingers over the smooth black leather before opening it, slowly shaking her head back and forth.

A young man emerged from a house two doors down and looked curiously at them. Uh oh, backup. He said something in German to the woman, who answered him back, pointing at Andrew's grandfather. Andrew tensed. If only I had a light sword.

"You're American?" asked the young German, staring at the medals.

"Yes, you speak English?" The man nodded. "Wonderful. I . . ." Mead gestured toward the wallet but seemed at a loss for words. "I . . ."

The woman interrupted, saying something to her neighbor.

"She wants you to come in. She asks please. I will translate."

Mead turned and looked briefly back at Andrew before following the old woman into the house. Andrew held back a moment, then quickly followed. Can't leave Sarge alone in a house full of Sauerkrauts.

The woman led them into a small living room with two low chairs and a sofa covered with a frayed vanilla-colored cloth. Andrew figured he'd just stand but the woman caught his eye and gestured toward one of the chairs. His grandfather sat in the other. A series of small landscapes—

mostly of mountain lakes—hung on the walls and a small dusty cupboard was filled with glasses and china. Andrew wondered if all German homes were so dark and depressing.

"She would like to know what she can bring you to drink?"

"I'm fine, thanks," said Mead.

"I'm fine too," said Andrew, half-tempted to ask for a big shot of Southern Comfort.

The woman frowned, then disappeared down the hallway.

"She hasn't been well lately," said the neighbor, watching her walk away. "I try to check in on her." Mead nodded. "She was a tailor until a few years ago. She has trouble with her—how do you say?—balance."

Mead nodded again, rubbing his palms along the arms of his chair.

"You knew her husband?"

"Not exactly."

Andrew squirmed in his seat.

"I always feel sorry for all the women who lost their husbands. There were millions of them, including my own grandmother. There were no men to marry after the war."

No men? Andrew tried to imagine an entire generation of men being killed. Then he thought of the huge German cemetery in Normandy. How many others were there?

"So what brings you to Germany?"

Mead reached into his leather bag and pulled out the German dog tags and wristwatch, adding them to the medals, wallet and pay book that lay on the coffee table. "These," he said.

"You came all this way just to . . . return them?"

Mead nodded.

The German looked at Mead appreciatively, as if letting it sink in. Andrew guessed he was in his mid-twenties. "And this is your grandson?"

"Yes, I'm sorry. This is Andrew."

The German leaned forward and shook Andrew's hand. "You are very lucky. I always wished I had known my grandfathers. They were both killed on the Eastern Front."

Jesus, thought Andrew, the whole country's a fricking morgue.

When the elderly woman returned she offered milk to Andrew and coffee to Mead, then placed a plate of sliced cheeses and meats and cookies on the table. After easing herself onto the sofa she stared at

Mead for several moments, then leaned toward her neighbor and said something.

"She says she remembers many young American soldiers. She says that you were very kind and she thanks you." He paused as the woman continued, then translated again. "Not like the Russians, she says."

Andrew watched as his grandfather picked up his coffee cup, spilling several times as he tried to bring it to his lips.

"She asks if you are long in Germany?"

"Just a few days," said Mead, putting the cup down with a loud clatter.

"She says you have a very handsome grandson; that you are lucky."

"Thank you."

The woman continued to stare at Mead, her creased features now alert and animated. "She would like to know if you have a large family?"

"Rather small, actually."

"Very small," added Andrew meekly, holding his thumb and forefinger a few inches apart. He reached for a cookie and popped it into his mouth, hoping it might ease his anxiety.

The neighbor continued to translate as the woman talked. "She says you must have been very young in the war. She thinks you have lived a good and healthy life."

"He's in great shape," said Andrew proudly. "He's kind of an exercise freak."

The woman pointed to her knees and then tapped her chest as she spoke. "She says that she has many problems; that old age is, how should I say . . . ridiculous." The woman interrupted. "But she thinks that maybe there is something worse than growing old."

"Tell her I think she is right," said Mead.

Andrew popped another cookie into his mouth, then tried to catch his grandfather's eye, thinking it might be a good time to go. But no one moved. Then the woman began talking again as her neighbor tried to keep up. "She says her husband was a very good man but a terrible soldier." The old woman laughed and Andrew saw that she was missing two teeth. "She says he was in trouble many times for being, what is the word? A funny man. Too many jokes."

Andrew thought of the black-and-white photograph of Hans, trying to imagine the droopy young face cracking a joke. What could possibly be funny about being a Nazi?

"He planned to be a schoolteacher like his father. English and geography, that's what he wanted to teach. She says he was very smart, but she warned him that his students would never learn anything because they'd always be laughing. She thinks he would have gotten into trouble, just like in the army." The neighbor couldn't keep from smiling as he translated.

"I'm starting to like this guy," said Andrew, thinking he'd chip in now and then. He kept his eye on his grandfather, who listened without looking directly at the woman.

"She says she last heard from her husband in a letter two weeks before the war ended. He said he was coming home." Now the old woman's features constricted into a large knot. "She says she waited and waited . . . but he never came." The neighbor put a hand on the woman's thigh as she rubbed her lower lip with her fingers and blinked rapidly.

"Does she know what happened?" asked Andrew without thinking. Mead's eyes flashed at him.

The German man translated. "She thinks maybe he died in prison. He was sick many times in the army. Bad lungs." The neighbor added, "We had many many missing in action, especially on the Eastern Front."

Mead started to say something when suddenly the old woman rose and gestured for them to wait.

"She wants to show you something."

Andrew polished off three more cookies before the woman returned. She held a small, dark green photo album, which she placed gently in Mead's lap. Then she stood beside him and opened it to the first page, pointing. Andrew leaned over to look.

Holy shit, it's the Sauerkraut. The woman turned to a wedding photograph. Hans Mueller stood proudly in a Nazi uniform with a pretty young woman in a simple white dress at his side. Andrew looked at the young woman's face, then at the old woman. Unbelievable. The woman was now full of excitement as she turned the pages and tapped her crooked finger on the photographs. Andrew looked over at his grandfather, whose face was gray and sweaty, like he was going to get sick. What if he had a heart attack or stroke? Oh man, don't croak on me now, Sarge.

"I killed him," Mead said suddenly, pushing the book away.

The woman looked confused while the neighbor stared at Mead, his expression uncertain.

"Tell her I killed him."

"Maybe it's better—"

"Tell her."

The woman said something to her neighbor, apparently asking what was being said. The man hesitated, then spoke several sentences in German. Andrew sat gripping his chair, his eyes darting back and forth between the woman and his grandfather. A look of confusion crossed the woman's face, then she walked over to the sofa and sat down, her hands folded in her lap. Finally she spoke again in German, her voice small and dry.

"She says it was war. You are not to be blamed."

Mead sat trembling. "No, you don't understand. You see..." He stopped and wiped his forehead with his sleeve. "You see, I ... I murdered him."

"But—"

"He was unarmed." Mead turned to the woman. "Your husband was unarmed."

The young German waited a moment before translating. The woman sat stunned, staring at Mead. Finally she turned and whispered something to her neighbor.

"She doesn't understand why you are telling her this?"

Andrew sat on the edge of his seat, wide-eyed. His grandfather raised his hands slowly in the air and then dropped them, a look of helplessness on his face. "I don't understand either." He wiped his face again with the back of his hand, then leaned toward the coffee table, gently picked up one of the medals and placed it in his palm. "Maybe it's because I have to." He glanced briefly at Andrew, his eyes red and unfocused, then looked back down at the medal and slowly closed his fist as he began to talk.

•   •   •

In the final weeks of the war Allied intelligence feared that Hitler would create a last redoubt in the rugged Alpine mountains of Bavaria and Austria, using the radio to rally resistance from his heavily fortified mountaintop retreat above Berchtesgaden. Though the German Army was in a state of collapse, remnants of the *Waffen SS* and the *Hitler Jugend* were expected to put up a costly fight while small bands of commandos called Werewolves had been instructed to retreat into the countryside and begin guerrilla warfare.

Allied forces moved quickly to seize potential Alpine strongholds. The 101st was transported in open rail cars and then trucks from the Ruhr pocket to Bavaria, the men marveling at the destruction caused by years of Allied bombing. On May 5th, American troops drove unopposed into Berchtesgaden, once the luxurious retreat of the Nazi elite, and quickly made their way up to Hitler's beloved Berghof, perched at three thousand feet with sweeping views of the snow-capped Alps. Though largely destroyed by British bombers, Hitler's home and compound were a souvenir hunter's dream. Soon drunken GIs were taking joyrides in the Fuhrer's long black Mercedes staff cars, testing the bulletproof windows with point-blank shots from their rifles. Others fanned out to search the remains of nearby villas owned by Martin Bormann and Hermann Goering as well as officers' quarters, SS barracks, warehouses and a series of underground bunkers. At Goering's Officers' Quarters and Club, troops discovered a huge wine cellar stuffed with thousands of bottles of Europe's finest vintages. For men who had lived for months in foxholes eating K-rations, the opulence was stupefying.

While some high-ranking German officers sought to disguise themselves and others headed for the hills, most Germans quickly laid down their arms, relieved that for them the war was finally over. The Third Reich would survive only two more days until delegates signed the unconditional surrender at Allied headquarters in Reims. Yet for some combatants, the transition from war to peace would prove simply too difficult, causing unnecessary tragedies on both sides.

Mead wandered the streets in a sort of exhausted stupor, stunned into silence by the beauty of the surrounding Alps, which seemed almost incomprehensible after months of warfare. And yet he remained haunted by what he'd seen at Landsberg; by the pleading eyes and weakened cries of starved prisoners and the stench of rotting corpses, which not even the crisp mountain air could flush from his nostrils. As he looked at the well-fed German civilians and the large gingerbread houses and the fancy cars and stocks of goods he felt a building fury inside until he could just barely contain himself. *How dare they.*

He took some satisfaction from the pained look on the faces of German soldiers and citizens as American troops swiftly stripped them of their valuables. Serves them right, he thought, wishing that the inmates he'd seen at Landsberg could take part in the looting. Eager for a few souvenirs of his own, he tried several houses but found them empty. He watched with envy as GIs loaded down with fur coats, Nazi flags, cameras, watches, artwork and liquor caroused through the town in liberated Schwimmwagens and half-tracks and motorcycles and luxury cars, as if Berchtesgaden was a giant piñata that had been busted open. Gradually, as the looting continued, he felt almost a sense of panic, like a child during musical chairs when the music stops and all the seats are taken. What about me?

"Look what I got for my girl," said a short GI from New Jersey named Joey Ovito, holding up a set of silverware with Hitler's initials on them. "And Phil got himself a couple of the Fuhrer's personal photo albums!"

Prevented from reaching the Berghof by MPs, Mead hitched a ride back down into town, where he searched through several more houses but found nothing except a pair of lace curtains, which he soon tired of carrying. Weary and frustrated, he headed toward a brown and white chalet nestled into the hillside, hoping at least to find a comfortable bed and thinking that maybe after some rest he'd have better luck.

The door was unlocked. He entered warily, rifle at waist height. Months of battle had worn down all the elasticity of his nerves so that he was perpetually on edge. He closed the door behind him and locked it, desperate for a few hours of privacy and maybe even a bath. After crossing a short hallway he entered a large living room with polished hardwood floors. Two couches and several chairs were covered in rich brown leather and several large landscapes and two pairs of snowshoes hung from the walls. Pairs of skis and poles were stacked in a corner. He paused to take in the panoramic mountain views out the floor-to-ceiling window. So this is how they lived. Is evil easier from such a distance?

On a long dining room table he noticed two silver candelabra, making a note to take them if they weren't too heavy. He stopped to listen for sounds, then walked over to the large fireplace, blackened with soot. The ornate, mahogany-colored mantle was covered with silver picture frames. He picked one up and stared into the fleshy face of a beaming German officer who stood with his arm around a tall and attractive woman. In another photo the same officer—now in battle gear—stood proudly in front of a tank while in another he shook hands with Himmler. Old chums. He put the photograph back, then rested his rifle against the side of the fireplace and drew his pistol before heading down another hallway into a dark, wood-paneled den. He gazed at the leather-bound books that lined the recessed shelves before pulling out several at random, trying to guess at the titles. He thought of his mother, who was on the library committee and always said that books were the foundations of civilization.

He was heading down the hallway toward the stairs when he heard a creak in the floorboards above him. Then another. He quickly stepped back around the corner, pistol ready. Soon he heard hobnailed boots— German—on the stairs. He pressed against a wall and waited as the sound drew closer. There was a pause at the bottom of the stairs, then the footsteps started slowly down the hallway, pausing again, then coming closer until Mead could hear shallow breathing. He waited another second, then swiveled around the corner with his pistol leveled at chest height.

"Don't shoot!" cried a boyish-looking German soldier, who stood holding a suitcase in one hand while clutching a small bundle in the other.

"*Hände hoch!*" shouted Mead.

The German dropped the suitcase, then squatted and carefully placed the bundle on the floor by his feet before standing and raising his hands into the air. "Welcome, komerad," he said in good English, offering a nervous smile. Several inches shorter than Mead, he had narrow shoulders, a soft face, a large forehead and a slight droop about his brown eyes, which made him look permanently sad. His uniform was dirty and frayed and his brown hair was matted on the top of his head. Only the dregs are still alive, Mead thought.

"Step back."

The German retreated two paces. "I was just leaving," he said.

"Where did you learn to speak English?"

"My grandmother was British."

Mead looked for a weapon but saw none. "I don't suppose this is your house?"

The German laughed. "Do I look like a general?"

"What does the German Army do to soldiers who steal from officers' homes?"

"There is no more German Army."

Mead looked down at the suitcase, which was expensive-looking. "What's in there?"

"My things."

"I didn't realize the Wehrmacht traveled so well."

The German shrugged. "I will leave you alone." He started to reach for the suitcase and bundle.

"Hands up."

"But—"

"Now."

"Okay, *komerad*."

They stood staring at each other.

"Open it," Mead said, gesturing toward the suitcase.

"The house is all yours. These are just my things."

"I said, *open it.*"

The German hesitated, then bent over the suitcase, placed it flat on the floor and clicked open the two latches. The he stood and stepped back.

Mead crouched down, keeping his pistol pointed at the German, and lifted the lid. Pushing aside a fur shawl he saw silverware, two ceremonial knives with *SS* markings, a new pair of men's leather boots, three pairs of women's dress shoes, a Luger, two clips of ammunition and several dresses.

"You travel well."

The German didn't respond.

"What's in there?" Mead pointed toward the towel-wrapped bundle on the floor beside the suitcase.

The German's face tensed. "It's nothing. Just a . . . plate."

"A plate?" Mead carefully picked it up and unwrapped it, pulling out a gold-rimmed china dinner plate with an eagle and swastika emblazoned on the top and the initials A.H. on the bottom. As he stared at it he felt a sudden giddy sense of excitement like a child discovering hidden treasure. Pay dirt.

"A.H., huh?" Mead smiled as he held the plate up to the light, the pistol still in his other hand. "Rings a bell."

"I had five others, but the rest were taken from me."

"The Fuhrer wouldn't be too happy with you now, would he?"

"The Fuhrer is dead."

Mead ran his fingers along the rim. "Come to think of it, I could use a plate like this. Great conversation piece at Thanksgiving. Probably worth something too, wouldn't you say?" Mead could already see all the neighbors back home gathered around and then the front page photo in the local paper. *Hometown boy cleans Hitler's plate.*

"I'll sell it to you," said the German.

"Sell it?" Mead laughed. "You greedy son of a bitch."

"I have a wife and—"

"You don't seem to understand. You lost."

"The war's over," said the German, trying to smile. "We can all go home."

Mead felt a rush of anger as he thought of the German machine gunners who would wait until they ran out of ammunition before offering to surrender, emerging from their pillboxes with friendly smiles for their American *komerads* and explaining that they had relatives in Milwaukee. "You think it's that easy?"

The German shrugged his shoulders again. "I didn't start the war."

"But you fought it, didn't you?"

"I had no choice. I'm just a common soldier."

Mead took a step closer. "I've seen what you common soldiers can do."

"I'm not a Nazi."

"Suddenly no one's a Nazi." Mead looked down at the plate in his hand, trying to imagine Hitler feeding from it, his appetite fueled by his latest conquest. Then he remembered the souvenirs from the Great War that his father kept in his closet: a German Iron Cross 1st Class, a helmet, a watch and a knife, but nothing like this. Not even close.

"Have you been to a place called Landsberg, by any chance? Near Munich?"

"I don't know what you're talking about."

"Bullshit."

"You can have everything in the suitcase. Take it."

"But you want the plate?"

"I found it."

"Where?"

"At the Berghof."

Mead studied the German's face closely, trying to see beyond the uniform. "You weren't at Normandy, by any chance? Or Bastogne?"

"I was on the Eastern Front."

Mead looked down at the plate again, feeling suddenly overwhelmed by the thought that the war really was over. Why did he survive? Was it a certain calculated cowardice that improved his odds? Had he really done his part? And yet, wasn't he secretly relieved—glad, even—every time it was somebody else's turn to die, as though the gods would be appeased until their next feeding?

"I had a friend named Rokowski," Mead said slowly. "Meat packer from Chicago. Shy kid, but a hell of a skater. You should have seen him on the ice." Mead smiled to himself. "Drove the English girls crazy, and I'm telling you, Roy was no ladies' man." He paused. "A German prisoner blew him up with a grenade. Damndest thing."

"I too lost many friends."

"Ol' Jimbo never even saw the sun come up in France." Mead shook his head. "Poor son of a bitch died right after he landed. Bled to death. And Punchy, well, there wasn't anyone quite like Punchy."

"Perhaps we could find some Schnapps in the kitchen." The German gestured down the hallway.

"Schnapps?" Mead laughed out loud.

"I find it helps." The German began to move.

"Don't you dare."

They remained motionless, each staring warily at the other. Mead held up the plate. "What exactly would a *common* German soldier do with a plate from Hitler's dining room?"

"Sell it."

"Of course."

"Please, my family has no—"

"Do you expect my pity?"

"I expect nothing."

"But you expected to win. That was the idea, wasn't it?"

"I was never asked what I expected."

Mead nodded slowly, feeling his palms sweat. "It's not so much fun when the tables are turned, is it?"

"Come, let's have some Schnapps. We are both tired of this war."

"To hell with you," said Mead, feeling the anger building in his temples so that he wanted to close his eyes and rub them. He blinked a few times, fighting the exhaustion in his limbs and a sense of awful sadness that swept over him. Ah, to sleep for a month and never dream. That's all he needed. Yet—to have a plate from the Berghof. He felt the adrenaline rolling back into his veins. He could just see the look on his father's face. And Sophie, what would she think? But if only Punchy were here.

Mead caught himself lowering his pistol and raised it again. The German's eyes darted toward it.

"My father fought in the Great War," Mead said.

"And mine, too," said the German, smiling hopefully. "You see, we are not so different. Are you married?"

"My father was right: we should have finished you off when we had you." The German waited nervously.

"What's wrong with you people?" Mead felt his arms quaking.

"I don't know what—"

"There was a bully on my street when I was growing up. Picked on everybody smaller than him. Used to beat the bejesus out of me."

"I don't understand."

"And then one day this kid named Scotty—used to be a scrawny little thing, always getting whopped—well, one day he realized that he'd grown taller than the bully only no one had noticed because bullies always look bigger than everybody else. So you know what he does? He waits until the next time the bully starts teasing him at the bus stop and then he just hauls off and pops him in the face, breaking his nose." Mead laughed while the German's expression grew more anxious.

"Go ahead, take the suitcase," said the German. "It's yours."

"So how did he do it?"

"Who?"

"Hitler. How did a madman get so far?"

"I'm only a soldier."

"Or maybe you're all mad. Yes, that must be it." Mead wiped the sweat from his brow, wondering if he had a fever. "A whole goddamn country full of bullies."

"The war is finished, we can go home now." The German's voice was almost childlike now, which annoyed Mead. What did he sound like when he was winning? And how would this meeting end if *he* held the cards? Mead remembered seeing a Belgian family shot with their hands tied behind their backs and left in a frozen heap in front of their ruined home, the children on top. The German started to move again but Mead waved his pistol.

"There was this Polish boy at Landsberg. Gregory. Just a skeleton. Sweetest eyes. I tried to feed him some chocolate . . ." Mead couldn't continue.

"You don't look well. Would you like some food? I have—"

"I'm perfectly well, goddamn it. We won, didn't we?"

"So I'll go."

"Tell me, how does it feel to lose?" The German glanced down again at Mead's pistol. "Please, I want to know."

"Why so many questions?"

"Because I need some goddamn answers." Mead wiped his face again. "Ever since I set foot on German soil I've been wondering how it feels to lose a war."

The German didn't respond.

"Then I'll tell you what I think. I think it feels like shit. I mean, you stupid Krauts really bet the bank." Mead laughed out loud, a cold, mocking laugh.

"Are you going to kill me?" The German's voice was soft and reedy.

Mead smiled, thinking how pleasant it was to see fear, even submission, on a German soldier's face. No, he wouldn't kill him. But in a way it was tempting. After all, why should he get to go home to his family when so many others never would? What justice was there in that?

"It would be murder."

"Murder?" Mead spit out the word. "You've got a lot of goddamn nerve."

"May I show you a picture of my wife? We only got married a few—"

"Shut up!" Mead tightened his grip on the pistol.

"What are you going to do?" The German's smooth young face—was he even eighteen?—looked pathetic now, like one of the raccoons Mead used to catch in a trap by the chicken house, guilty as could be.

Mead looked back at the plate in his left hand when suddenly the German reached out and snatched it from him.

"You son of a bitch."

The German held the plate out to one side, arm extended. "If you shoot me, I'll drop it."

Mead raised his pistol, straightening his arm. "Give it to me. *Now.*"

The German's large brown eyes swelled with fear. "You can't shoot an unarmed man."

"Like hell I can't." Mead's limbs shook with anger. "What about the Americans at Malmédy? Or the slaves you starved to death at Landsberg? How many of them had a fighting chance?"

"I don't know what you're talking about."

"Oh, I think you do."

"I told you, I'm a simple soldier. You can't blame me."

"Then who can I blame?" screamed Mead. "Tell me, *who?*"

"Please, you must calm down."

"Give me the goddamn plate."

"But if I do you'll shoot me."

"I'll shoot you if you don't."

"I will trade. You turn me over to an American officer and I will give you the plate."

Mead saw the sudden defiance in the German's eyes, which infuriated him. And yet he felt confused too, not knowing quite how he had suddenly found himself on the brink, face to face with the enemy yet wavering between war and the vague expectation of peace. Sweat from his palm gathered on the pistol grip and his mouth felt so dry that he had trouble swallowing. He looked longingly at the shiny gold rim of the plate clutched in the German's small hand, suddenly wanting it more than anything, as if it were the prize he'd been fighting for all these months, a trophy that would pass down through generations of his family with stories of his deeds. And it was for Punchy too, and Jimbo and Rokowski. All of them. They'd paid for it with their *blood*.

"A deal?" Mead lunged for the plate with his free hand but the German was quick and managed to sidestep him. Mead lunged again and this time managed to get a grasp of the plate. They struggled briefly before it slipped from their hands and fell to the floor, shattering.

They both froze, staring down mutely at the pieces.

"There, now neither of us can have it," said the German, a smile spreading across his long and dirty face. The smile quickly vanished as Mead raised his pistol.

You wouldn't, would you?

Oh yes, but I would.

But it's cold-blooded murder.

No, you see, it's only war.

Mead pulled the trigger.

The first shot hit the German in the upper chest just as his face sank in disbelief. As he fell backward the second shot struck him in the shoulder and the third ripped open his cheek.

Then silence.

Mead stood over the body for a moment, pistol still in hand, then put the gun back into its holster and quickly rifled through the German's pockets, pulling out a wallet, a military pay book and three medals before removing the dead man's dog tags and wristwatch. Then he reached into the suitcase and grabbed the Luger.

He was rising to his feet when two GIs burst through a side door, rifles at the ready. "What happened?"

"He . . . he tried to take my gun away," said Mead, stepping back.

"You all right?"

Mead nodded slowly.

"Hey, look at this stuff," said one of the soldiers, crouching by the open suitcase. The other soldier headed for the candelabra while Mead bent down and picked up the largest piece of the plate.

"Mind if we help ourselves?"

"Be my guest," said Mead, trying to avoid the face of the dead German, who looked like a mere boy with his eyes closed. He slipped the piece of plate into his pocket, then turned and headed for the door.

·   ·   ·

When Mead finished he sat in silence, eyes unfocused and face stricken so that just looking at him made Andrew want to cry. No one spoke.

"I came to say I'm sorry," Mead said finally, looking up at the German widow, who was wiping tears from her eyes. "And I wanted you to have his things. They never belonged to me." He rose unsteadily to his feet and walked over to the woman. She took his hand and patted it but stayed seated. Mead looked as if he might say something else, then abruptly turned and headed for the door, shoulders slightly stooped. Andrew followed quickly behind.

"She says she's sorry, too," said the young German, standing by the woman with his hand on her shoulder. "It was a terrible time."

Mead paused, then bowed his head slightly before continuing out the door and down the sidewalk. Andrew stayed right behind him, not daring to look back.

After Mead slid the key into the ignition he seemed to hesitate.

Andrew glanced over at him, surprised by how different he looked, smaller and more fragile, which made Andrew feel that maybe he wasn't really so alone after all. "What are we going to do now?" he asked gently as he buckled his seat belt.

"We're going to give your friend a proper burial." Mead started the engine.

"We're going to Indiana?"

"We're going to California."

Andrew felt a spreading sensation of warmth in his chest as his grandfather drove in silence, both hands high on the wheel. After several blocks he suddenly pulled over to the side of the road, turned off the ignition and sat back in his seat.

"I've been doing some thinking," he said, letting out a long breath and keeping his gaze fixed straight ahead.

Andrew waited nervously for him to continue.

"Well, I thought perhaps that maybe—with the way things are going with your mother lately—well, I thought . . ."

"What?"

Mead turned and looked at Andrew, then stared straight ahead again. "I thought perhaps you might consider staying in California for a year. You could enroll in the local high school; see how it goes. It's a good one, I hear. Anyway, you can't beat the weather. Maybe you could even learn to surf. And then there's Evelyn, who's going to be needing our help. You could visit your mother anytime—heck, maybe we could even get her to move out, too. Of course, if you'd rather not . . ."

"Really?"

"Really."

Andrew could only smile before quickly turning his face away and concentrating his watery gaze on a small German boy peddling by, wondering if by any chance it was Matt.

Home

They took turns sleeping on the couch in the living room to keep Evelyn company at the end. Some nights, as Mead stared wearily through the darkness at the green glow of the monitors, he was almost convinced it was Sophie's shallow breaths he heard coming from the bed beside him. In a way it no longer mattered, not so long as one breath followed the other until the sun crept beneath the curtains and he could search Evelyn's face for the defiant smile he'd grown to love. He preferred to lie on his back so that he could easily reach through the metal railing to take her hand, always shocked that even those who give off the most warmth can turn so cold. When they tired of talking he would patiently await the responsive squeeze of her fingers until finally sleep eased her pain. Then he would follow along with each tentative breath, gently coaxing them on one after the other until morning. If the silence became unbearable he would get up and lean over her bed and put his ear to her mouth, reminding himself of his promise that this time there would be no ambulance.

She had just finished transplanting the last of her flowers into Sophie's old garden when Mead and Andrew returned from the airport. Mead was so startled by the sight that he drove right on down the street, thinking he must have made a wrong turn. When he finally pulled into his driveway he sat staring out the window as Andrew jumped out and pounced on Evelyn, nearly lifting her off the ground as he hugged her.

"Well, what do you think?" she said, taking off her leather work gloves and gesturing toward the flower bed when Mead finally emerged from the car.

He could only nod.

That evening she cooked up a huge vegetarian feast in their honor and peppered them with questions until well past midnight. "Don't leave out *anything,*" she said, sitting between them at Mead's dining room table and ladling food onto their plates. To her delight, Andrew set a new record by consuming seven macadamia nut and raisin rolls while even Mead admitted that it was the best meal he'd had in days.

"I don't think I've ever had such so much fun," she said as Mead walked her home. "And I didn't even go anywhere."

"I wish you'd come," said Mead, stopping as they reached her walkway.

"So do I," she said softly. "But Andrew needed time with you. And anyway, I've been so busy since the offer on the house and—"

Before she could finish Mead took her by the shoulders and kissed her firmly on the lips.

"We need to talk," he said, still holding her.

"Actually, I'm happy to talk later," she said with a smile as she kissed him again. "Any chance you want to come in?"

"You mean . . . now?"

"I mean right now."

Mead called Sharon the next morning.

"I've been worried sick about you two," she said just before she accidentally dropped the phone, causing Mead to wince as the receiver bounced across a hard surface. "Sorry. So don't tell me, it was a disaster."

"Not at all."

"What happened?"

"We got along just fine."

"And?"

"And it was . . . very educational."

"Educational? For you or for him?"

"For both of us. He's a great traveler. I'd take him anywhere."

"I want whatever your doctor's got you on."

Mead heard a telltale inhalation on the other end. "Are you smoking a cigarette?"

There was a pause. "Jesus, Dad, how do you do that?"

"I'm a parent."

"You ought to work for one of those psychic networks. But don't worry,

I'm stopping tomorrow. Promise. I've even got a patch ready. It's just been crazy lately."

"Were you fired?"

"Well, actually, things have taken a rather interesting twist."

Mead cradled the receiver with his shoulder and lay back on his bed rubbing his forehead. "What happened?"

"I'm not sure you want to know."

"Of course I do."

"He asked me to dinner."

"Who did?"

"My boss."

"The one whose expense accounts you deleted?"

"That one."

"You said no."

Another pause. "Actually, we've had a couple of dates."

"Sharon."

"I know, I know. But it turns out he's really a nice guy."

"He's not a guy, he's a boss."

"I'm a big girl, Dad."

Mead looked over at the photograph of Sophie taken on the balcony of their hotel in Hawaii. "There's something I want to talk about."

"You're going to lecture me."

"Tempting, but no, it's about Andrew."

"I can come get—"

"I want him to live with me."

"What?"

"Just for a semester. See how it goes. It's a good high school and he could use a change, and besides, I could use a hand around here now and then—and I thought you could use a break or maybe you could even join us."

"You're kidding?"

"Of course not."

There was a long silence before she started crying. "You're really serious?"

"He needs a fresh start, Pumpkin. Frankly, I think you do, too, but if you won't join us you can always visit. We could just try one semester and see how it goes."

More sniffling. "What does Andrew think?"

"He's game. I think he's sort of taken to Southern California. You know, the beaches and all."

"I can't believe this." Mead heard a quick inhale, followed by a long exhale. "I want to talk to him."

"Of course. And then why don't you think it over and we'll talk again tomorrow, okay, Sweetheart? Just consider it."

"Mom wouldn't believe this."

"There are a few things she wouldn't believe."

Another big exhale. "I don't know what to say. I mean, you've thought this through?"

"Yep."

"But aren't you a little old to be raising a teenager?"

"Oh hell, I'm just hitting my stride."

Once Andrew was on the line Mead headed out front, turned on the hose and began watering the flowers.

• • •

The following Sunday Andrew, Mead and Evelyn drove to the beach and held a small sunset service for Matt, the three of them standing in a small circle around the Ziploc bag at their feet. Mead had argued for a more dignified means of transport but Andrew wouldn't hear of it, saying that Matt didn't give a hoot about appearances, and besides, the Ziploc had seen more of the world than most people. Even so, Mead insisted on wearing a suit and tie while Evelyn wore an elegant black dress that completely undermined Mead's efforts to think morbid thoughts. After several aborted attempts Andrew managed to get through a song he'd written for the occasion, which made Evelyn cry so hard that the service had to be stopped twice so that she could collect herself. "Sorry," she squeaked, dabbing her eyes. They finished with a moment of silence, which was actually quite noisy, and then Andrew reached into the bag and took out a small handful of Matt's remains, hesitating briefly before sweeping his arm through the air and tossing them to the wind. Then he took another handful and let the ashes gradually slip between his fingers as he headed down the beach and along the water's edge, first walking and then running as fast as he could while his best friend trailed out behind him.

Evelyn declined quickly after that. As soon as her house sold Mead and Andrew moved her in with them, first into Mead's bedroom—which gave Andrew the heebie-jeebies, even though he approved in principle—and then onto a hospital bed they set up in the living room. "It doesn't get any better than this," she liked to say as she worked the automatic bed recliner and gazed out the window at her flowers, the bedsheets littered with recipe clippings that she was determined to finish pasting into one of three enormous books.

"You're kidding, aren't you?" Andrew finally said one afternoon when he got home from school.

"Actually, not at all."

"But how can you say that? I mean, we both know it gets *a lot* better." His chin was trembling.

"Only if you imagine yourself in someone else's shoes."

Mead wanted to sleep on the couch every night but Andrew insisted on taking turns, sometimes finishing his homework by flashlight. He had promised his grandfather to wake him if anything happened and not to call 911 under any circumstances. But secretly Andrew still hoped that nothing would happen, not so long as he remained awake to watch over her.

"Tell me again about the look on your grandfather's face when he saw the beaches at Normandy," she said one night as they lay talking in the dark.

"Oh man, I thought he was going to freak. I was like, *tiptoeing.*"

"I can't imagine what he felt."

"How do you think *I* felt? I already had Matt's ashes to worry about, and now it's looking like the General's about to stroke out on some beach in *France.* Jeeze, I could have been stranded."

Evelyn let out a laugh. "Now that would have made a story."

"But the scariest part was being around all those Sauerkrauts."

"I believe the correct word was *Kraut,* and it's just a bit outdated."

"No, you see Kraut is just short for Sauerkraut. They're Sauerkrauts."

"Never mind."

"Anyway, when we got to the widow's house I figured we were goners. To tell you the truth, I was prepared to fight my way out."

"All the way to the border?"

"At least to the train station."

"That would have been some fight."

"No kidding. The place is crawling with storm troopers."

"But not in uniform?"

"No, that's the thing. The whole country's gone undercover. But you can just feel it."

"I see."

"You should have been there when he started telling the woman about how he killed her husband. I could almost hear him sweat."

"I'm surprised *you* didn't have a stroke."

"Yeah, me too, but I figured at least one of us needed to be in control."

"Good thinking."

. . .

Andrew talked about the trip almost every time it was his turn to sleep on the couch, telling Evelyn all about the Crown Jewels and Elizabeth's tomb and the fortifications at Normandy and the rows of white crosses and how there's hardly a thing worth eating in all of France. Sometimes he kept talking even after he knew she was asleep because at least that way he figured he could keep himself awake. And when he did finally drift off he would wake with a start, afraid of what he would see when he opened his eyes.

It was his turn the night Evelyn died.

"I'd like you to sing at my funeral," she said after he turned out the lights.

"I couldn't do that," Andrew said nervously.

"Of course you can. And you have a wonderful voice. Anyway, you have no choice. It's a dying woman's request."

"Don't talk like that."

"I'm done."

He looked over at her, trying to make out her silhouette in the darkness and wondering if maybe there were things she needed to talk about. Finally he asked, "Are you afraid?"

"I have my moments." She let out a hoarse sigh. "I just keep telling myself that a path this well traveled has got to lead somewhere interesting."

"You really think so?"

"The truth is, I'm not entirely convinced." She coughed several times, then made a soft moaning sound that Andrew had come to dread.

"Are you okay?"

"No . . . but it'll have to do."

"You want me to get another one of those blue pills?"

"If I get any more schnockered I'm liable to start dancing on the tables."

"I'll get you some more water." He quickly got up, turned on his flashlight and refilled her glass, holding it to her lips.

"At least I'm flying first-class," she whispered, resting her head back on her pillow.

When Andrew returned to the couch he pulled the blankets up to his chin, keeping his eyes wide open as he waited for her to fall asleep. But every time her breathing seemed to ease into a pattern she would let out a sudden gasp and her breaths would quicken again.

"I hate this," he said, clenching his fists at his side.

"Me too," she whispered.

"What can I *do?*"

"Just keep your head up and promise me you'll look after the General. He's had about enough of this nonsense."

"He's a lot tougher than he looks."

"No one's that tough."

"I'll keep him out of trouble. Promise."

"And make sure he gets plenty of air. After your grandmother died he sat in that chair of his so long I was afraid he'd turn to stone."

In the silence Andrew wondered whether maybe stones didn't have it easier. "Want to talk some more?" he asked.

"I'd rather have you rest up for school."

"I don't need much sleep. Really. Let's talk."

"Okay then, what shall we talk about?"

"I don't know. I've been wondering what kind of stuff you think about. I mean, is it mostly old stuff or new stuff?"

She tried to laugh but her voice was dry and thin. "A bit of both. That's one of the few pleasures of old age. You have an enormous catalog to choose from." Her bed creaked as she turned to her side. "The real truth is, I'm bursting with advice but I don't think you really need any of it."

"Advice about what?"

"Oh goodness, all sorts of things. Dating, work, gardening, the best way to remove red wine stains from fabric. That's the silly thing about getting old: you start feeling like a how-to manual that nobody's going to bother to read." She coughed again. "But I promised myself that I wouldn't start telling you how to run your life."

"It probably wouldn't make any difference. Matt used to say that everyone has to . . . screw up their lives in their own special way."

"Oh really? Well, he just may have been on to something."

"He was basically a genius, only no one listened to him."

"You must miss him terribly."

"I wish you could have met him."

"So do I."

Andrew felt his throat closing. "See, he believed that everybody has to put up with some major bullshit—sorry—sooner or later, and that it's just a question of when. So he figured that we were just getting it out of the way early, and then we'd be in good shape."

"Sort of like clearing the decks; work before play."

"*Exactly.* Only . . ." Andrew couldn't finish.

"I'm sorry."

They were both silent until Evelyn spoke again. "You know what I think the real trick is?—and I've only just figured this out."

"What?"

"You have to have some momentum in life. That's what gets you through the tough times." Andrew listened as she tried to catch her breath. "Come to think of it, that's what this feels like."

"What what feels like?"

"Dying."

"Don't say that."

"But it's true. After years of rolling along I'm afraid I'm finally running out of momentum."

"Maybe I could give you a push."

He heard a rustling of sheets and then felt her hand sliding across his cheek. "But don't you see? You already did."

Epilogue

Evelyn was cremated according to her wishes and her two children agreed to hold a small service in California before taking her remains to Connecticut for interment. Mead spent hours working on a eulogy, sitting up late in his blue chair with a cup full of sharpened pencils and pausing now and then to run his hands over Evelyn's old gardening gloves, which he kept on the table next to him. But once he reached the lectern and looked down at his grandson and daughter watching him he knew he'd never be able to say what he wanted to say, not with all the voices filling his head. He tried once more to speak, then stared down helplessly at his notes, feeling the full weight of his life pressing down on him. He was just about to return to his seat when his grandson stood up.

Andrew looked at his grandfather, then nervously surveyed the other mourners. "Hang on to your hats, folks, because there's something I have to do." He coughed, then took a deep breath. "I wrote it myself." Then he clutched the pew in front of him with both hands and began to sing.

He started softly at first, his cheeks flushed red and his voice quivering. When it looked like he wouldn't be able to continue Mead figured they'd both be booed right out of the church. *Sorry, Evelyn.* But gradually the boy's voice grew in volume until finally at the end he was singing with his fists clenched and his eyes squeezed shut. When he finished there was a moment of stunned silence before the church filled with applause.

"I have nothing to add," said Mead proudly as he stepped from the lectern.

It wasn't until the following week that Evelyn's children discovered that their mother's ashes were missing, replaced by a substance that tasted remarkably like sugar. (Her son did the tasting, using his moistened pinkie when nobody was looking.) Despite investigations by both the police and the funeral parlor, the remains were never found and no charges were filed.

That spring, Sophie's garden had never looked quite so good.

F
HULL

Hull, Jonathan.

The distance from
Normandy.

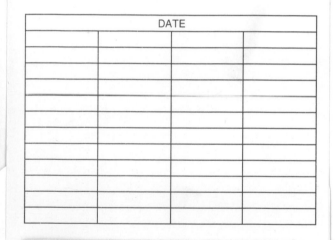

DATE			

BAKER & TAYLOR